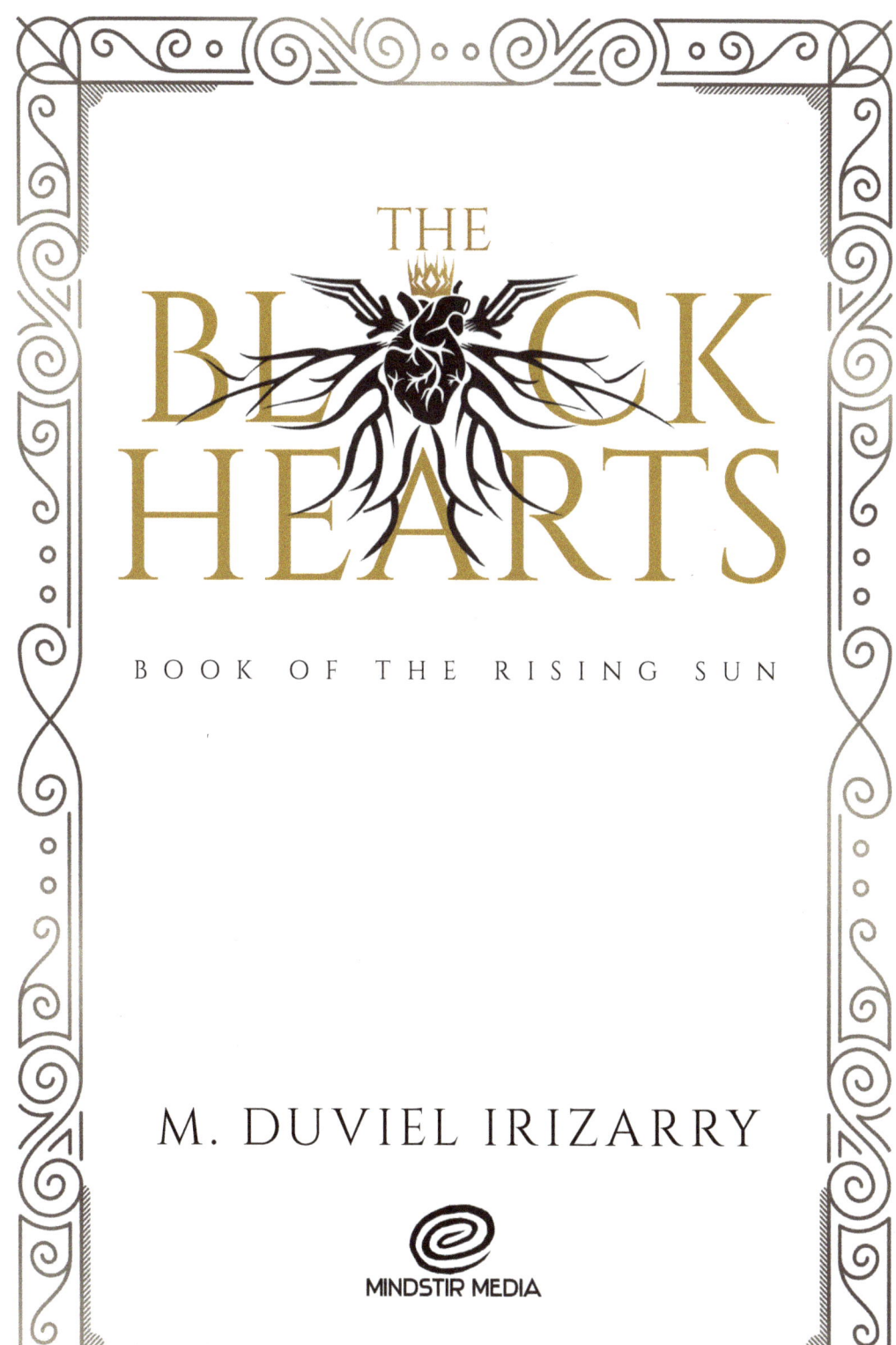

THE
BLACK
HEARTS

BOOK OF THE RISING SUN

M. DUVIEL IRIZARRY

MINDSTIR MEDIA

Published by Mindstir Media, LLC
45 Lafayette Rd | Suite 181| North Hampton, NH 03862 | USA
1.800.767.0531 | www.mindstirmedia.com

Printed in the United States of America

ISBN: 978-1-958729-36-6 (paperback)
ISBN: 978-1-958729-37-3 (hardback)

I can only start by humbly saying THANK YOU.

I have been blessed, but more than blessed, I am thankful for every single person who has crossed my path, those who have done so to bless it, and also those who have done so to do harm.

I want to thank God/god/gawd/you name it.

I want to thank my family:

My parents, Sara and Jaime, for giving me the best life possible while denying the same for themselves.

Jaime who helped me realize reading and writing were my passion (after having done my and his homework for many years).

Cynthia, for being a supporter and cheerleader in life, in front and behind the scenes.

Ian and Stella, for blessing my life with your very existence.

Omar, for composing music that inspired me (where's the rest? Grrr!)

Luis, for being a most reliable sounding board.

Toby, for having always looked at me with eyes of love. Lacey, for being the most beautiful little girl in the whole wide world. I miss you both every day.

All those patients of mine who have heard or been a part of my stories throughout the years.

My friends: Diego, Patty, Mike, Gladys, Alena, Perry, you guys are too many to number.

The artists: Wen Li, Melissa Filar, Jaycee Sandvig, Aleksandra Erkayeva, Zhitov, Azgaar's Fantasy Map Generator.

To all the hopeful souls who joined the "Kingdom of Blackheart/The Black Hearts" on the Discord channel and who have supported me, stuck around through thick and thin, and who always trusted the Crown. Your names are way too many to mention, but your deeds are celebrated and remembered.

To the very active members of House Darkholm and its allies:

Tenslea Darkholm - Jessica Johnson
Alex Darkholm - Christian McLlelan
Aiden Sanglune/Atelas Darkholm - Nathan Keffer
Tora/Toradmus Darkholm - Connor Shaw
Gustavus Darkholm - Fredrik Thorsteinson
Elleonora Darkholm - Ariel Thorsteinson
Ilhar Kal'Daka - Jason Clark
Fengo Darkholm - Jeffery Corbin
Isolde Darkholm - Rachel Sears
Arcanmene Raganark - Nicholas Harris
Sylen Darkholm - Mitchell Struck
Azareth Darkholm - Luis Camacho
Lady Charon - Sage Dennis
Serverus Ecru - Moses Clark
Azareth Darkholm - Luis Camacho
Lady Charon - Sage Dennis
Serverus Ecru - Moses Clark
Lady Narkari - Gabrielle Brooks
And all those who made our RP sessions exciting and fun.
To everyone, thank you from the bottom of this black heart.

Life is full of small, fantastic moments so intricately intertwined they are not often perceived, while fantasy is tinged with innumerable tiny specks of real life.

The Black Hearts is a collection of stories that are both fantastic and inspired by real-life events, by the imagination, words, and actions of real people.

It is my biggest wish that you can find yourself within these pages, that you may find as much happiness as brokenness. I hope that the person who starts reading this book is not the same one who finishes it.

This is a story not of heroes, of their great deeds, or of slaying dragons for glory. This is the story of those we call villains, the stories that make us hate them, and the unsung tales that, if known, would make us fall in love with every one of them.

We are all villains to someone else . . .

The Savage Expanse

Quintarchy of Tardus

Heplit

Logkili

Gretneau

Termestski

Japho

Hfet

Arcantaerea

VITCHENYA

Jonnus

Kerkrangi

Laiqva

Gratdon

Afehvorca

Exgnee

Maceta

Nicia

Kingdom of Eileos

Cosconia

Stelnia

Lembalnia

Palheiros

Swadinia

Rockshall

OHNEOS

Domagne

Criatus

Ritanlus

Bradenton

Alerose

Bro

The Inoxa

Heglis

Taccarino

Asettia

Carintesia

Imperium Rovelsi

Oppenandara

Philocomasitum

Seiras

Sphaero

Scomallatla

Rignalia

RIGNALIA

Clyteus

St Sobritus

Oponnes

Tivestac

Kingdom of

Alcemon

Paraoulos

Crithia

Blithesda

Geyunne

ALASTEN

The Dire Sea

Mdin

Laenicus

Eshoren

Sundstoune

Erones

Brondown

MESH

Elas

Seafare

panse

Hoel
Ohor

Suhne Empyre

Uhn

Kaleq

Shimmering Gulf

The Barren Sea

Sel-li

City of Suhne
CITY OF SUHNE

Alm

Oh-qaamar   Ahni

Naa-tele

Shalrech

Chestnouque   Witburd

r of Taerea

Arakzabofald Whiterose

Najju

ran

The Horne

Skyreach Valador/Volanar
Omikholm

Dusktorge

Haemonor

Kingdom of Blackheart

Gloomrise
Featherfeil

Bulwharf

Sildrane

Brumovel
Misthaven

Darkholm

Galdust
Alcyn

Abindire

Aligrand
Cetris

COLDFORGE

Kingdom of Ardenay

Whisperwind

Ultberagh

Himelane
HIMLEN

The Grave Expanse

Plener

Zagos

Ashvail

Walcrast

Seloren

Olath Valm

The Blood Sea

Ravencrest

Bloodgate

Mycernase
Seaspire

O nce upon a time . . .

   Funny, I always hated children's tales, and yet I know no better way to tell a story before going to bed, resting, or sinking into oblivion.

Just now, my thoughts traveled as fast as this arrow embedded itself in my chest, through fleeting memories of what I was, who I am, and who I could have been. One of those memories was of the time I thought, 'the day I tell a child's tale will be my last.'

Boy, I was right.

These rivers of blood pooling around my now-numb legs remind me of the story of a land most dark, of a queen of blood.

Blood that would drown the whole world as we know it.

Kingdom of Ardenay, Beacon of the Light (King Esdrah Heikken)

-Royal Duchy of Himeland (Duke Aorius Heikken)
-Grand Duchy of Alcyn (Duke Orionne Eomener)
-Grand Duchy of Ashvail (Duke Anderei Magenan)
-Grand Duchy of Bulwharf (Duke Varen Bulwharf)
-Grand Duchy of Walcrast (Duke Yel Ileva)

Kingdom of Blackheart, Land of Blood (King Septem Darkholm)

-Royal Duchy of Darkholm (Duke Davidov Darkholm)
-Duchy of Aligrand (Duke Primon Ferertr)
-Duchy of Duskforge (Duke Arcanmene Raganark)
-Duchy of Featherfell (Duke Brandobuh Driscoll)
-Duchy of Haemonor (Duke Eadric Carondoin)
-Duchy of Misthaven (Duke Hecator Laecanius)
-Duchy of Mycernase (Duke Tavadon Everitas)
-Duchy of Olath Valm (Duchess Ilhar Kal'Daka)
-Duchy of Ravencrest (Dukes Myr and Shira von Corvus)
-Duchy of Valador (Duke Crannon Coronn)
-Duchy of Volanar (Duke Dokkon Gillspiel)
-Duchy of Whisperwind (Duke Fayt Kenbu)

Empyre of Suhne, Land of the Sun (The Almighty Sun)

-Basqh of Ahni (Lorq'a Saasa)
-Basqh of Alm (Lorq'a Yada)
-Basqh of Htet (Adabah Tah)
-Basqh of Lmet (Lorq'a Neeraj)
-Basqh of Ohor (Lorq'a Rafat)
-Basqh of Uhn (Lorq'a Aakar)

CONTENTS

ARDENAY

Location: Kingdom of Ardenay, Duchy of Himeland,
Capital City of Himlen, Royal Palace

"Thank you, my lord, for the chance I had to serve you," the woman muttered, her lips caressing the nobleman's hands.

The rampant lion on the signet ring, proud as he who wore it, seemed to come to life for just an instant, if only to surpass the beauty of the other rings on his fingers. Soft was his skin, quite different from the leathery surface of her own.

She looked at her own fingers, devoid of any jewelry but still shiny from the swollen joints, the reward given for work unending.

"Thank you, my lord, for the chance I had to serve you." Those same dry hands caressed his silken vest, its hypnotizing deep blue, trimmed with gold embroideries of arrowheads. It had been tailored by the best, for her lord would have had it no other way, from the finest silk brought from across the continent. Its softness almost melted in her calloused hands. But her body wore a sack, black as the darkest void. It was the only thing she was allowed to wear, and she had to sew it herself.

The woman kissed his medallion, a circular piece of gold mounted with lapis lazuli and rusted metal. Her lord had always loved the contrast between his nobility and the rust that represented the rest of the world. She would have probably already lost count of the many times she had gazed at this medallion as she rose from her prostration. Seeing her reflection, her hands inadvertently moved toward her aged neck to find the only thing that hung from it, a cold manacle and a chain.

"Thank you, my lord, for the chance to have served you." Almost ritually, she kissed his forehead and caressed his gray, well-kept hair. Each strand was as carefully placed as soldier units in a mighty military plan. It looked so perfect that whoever saw it would have never guessed this man had been a great warrior in his youth. Only strands of straw-like hair adorned her head which made her look like a witch.

From the nobleman's lips, not a word was heard.

"Thank you, my lord, for the chance I had to serve you," she said as she knelt to kiss his boots. And for once, she did not flinch. Perhaps because she had already lost all her teeth from the many times he had kicked her, or perhaps because she had already abandoned all sense of worth and pride.

Walking backward, her calloused, bare feet took her toward the door, and her lips, for the last time, repeated the words, "Thank you, my lord, for the chance to have served you."

But despite all the honor shown, he did not move; he did not respond, perhaps because this man had truly been as arrogant as history has defined him, or perhaps, because while she stood by the doorway, he still lay inside his casket.

———————— ✛✛✛✛✛✛ ————————

So large was the Great Hall in the capital city of Himlen it could have housed a small army with its mounts, supplies, and all.

To Ealas Heikken, it felt strange to have everyone's eyes on him. All the nobles who would value themselves enough to vie for even the briefest of attention were present and, just as present, of course, were the most influential priests.

All present drowned in the noise of their own voices, knowing every word uttered could grant them the advantage each one sought in this fragile balance of wealth and power.

Noble banners of all sizes and colors were displayed by their bearers as if to attest all were witness to the presence of their respective retinues, for the day would come when fingers would be pointed to question loyalties, and it was ever important to say, "We were always there."

The silver wheel of the Eomener, the great traders, on a background of royal blue present and allowed only in the banners used by the founders of Ardenay, was held high on the leftmost side of the room. Closer to the center, the four wings of House Ileva stood. The impeccable formation of its men spoke of the discipline of its forces. Among them, young Siul, his confidant and childhood friend. The visor, with the knight's help, opened to reveal his playful eyes of blue, which met Ealas's in a friendly tease.

To the right, the banner of the majestic ox of Bulwharf, Ileva's great rivals, was present. The Thunders of Bulwharf, imposing in strength and numbers, filled a large part of the chamber despite the rest of those present. Many other banners stood, but all of them faced the royal blue standard, with a golden rampant lion bearing a crown over its head.

Closest to Ealas, his uncle, Duke Aorius Heikken, and his cousins, Langel and Vallein, stood. The eldest of the two was much like his father—tall, regal, gazing at the horizon with the eyes of an eagle, while the younger brother's eyes darted around the room before gifting his cousin with a congratulatory smile.

From behind, the voice of the Archbishop rose. "With this Crown, blessed by our Lord of Light, we name you, Ealas Heikken, King of Ardenay: he who is good, Bearer of the Light, and Blessed of the Heavens."

The elderly hands of the priest placed the crown upon his head, its golden surface studded with the bluest of sapphires.

Upon contact, the glorious moment was followed by one of silence, sending all but the head of the Church and the statues adorning the room kneeling.

"Blessed be your glorious majesty, and may the Light shine in every corner of the world," the holy man's voice exclaimed what the witnesses shouted in unison, the chant of Ardenay, the Beacon of the Light.

So many times had the words been rehearsed, Ealas's nervousness did not show. "May our light shine true, and may we fight our enemies in the name of our God, in the name of our kingdom, and for the glory of our crown." It was now his responsibility to ensure the kingdom remained strong, for the world was vile, and many kingdoms sought any opportunity to decimate their neighbors.

Ealas, proud as the lion on his banner, looked at all the men who pledged their hearts to him. The mighty, the proud, the wise, the learned, and even the most powerful in Ardenay recognized him as their leader. All of them knelt to show their sworn loyalty.

Even the Thunders of Bulwharf, known to be the fiercest commanders of the land, took a knee, but not before lifting their right fists as was their custom.

Ealas Heikken

Again Ealas's lips parted as he was ready to announce the beginning of the festivity, but no words left his mouth when he saw that one other figure who had not knelt.

She was there, at the end of the room, hiding by the doorway.

The young monarch's smile disappeared. Raising a hand, he summoned silence while he beckoned with his fingers and pointed toward the floor, a clear order for her to approach.

Hobbling slowly, the old woman, used to obeying without question, walked inside. She followed his signal until she reached the center of the aristocrat-filled room. Her name mattered not. It never did, for Ardenay's slaves, the nameless, lost all identifiers upon being acquired by their respective masters.

With much difficulty, and yet without hesitation, she prostrated herself, waiting for the king's signal to stand.

And his signal came.

'My first words will define my reign throughout history,' he thought.

"My first decree . . .," King Ealas savored the words, "will be . . . to free *her*." The entire chamber stood still for a moment before whispers were heard. The reigning expression, including the one on the slave's face, was one of disbelief.

"For she was like the mother I never had for the last twenty-five years. And I will have my masons," Ealas commanded, "build her a cabin along the stream where she washed my clothes every morning." Even if any disagreed, no one would dare question the Crown, at least not openly. In his uncle's eyes, there was nothing but discontent. In his friend Siul, he saw the approval he did not need but still welcomed.

"My lord," the woman's voice trembled, "if I may ask for just one thing?"

"Ask," King Ealas's grey eyes met those of the old slave.

"Please, do not spend your resources on me." Her tongue moistened her dry lips before she spoke again. "All I ever wanted . . . is to go back home."

A wave of murmurs washed over the room. Freedom had not been granted to a slave in the entirety of Ardenay's history.

"But you have nothing," the monarch said. "If you go back, you'll have nothing. When my father defeated Blackheart three decades ago, he left but a shell of what was once a great kingdom. You would go back to nothing to become a beggar in your own land."

Looking down at the marble floor, she found the courage to speak, "Yes, my lord, but I was born of the Blood, I am of the Blood, and I will die of the Blood, and the way of the Blood is such that being in my land, having nothing, I would still have everything, for my Blood will never let me die hungry."

Once again, the eyes of those gathered centered on the monarch. Showing weakness at this time would cost him for the duration of his reign, and he would go down in history as Ealas the Weak.

"I will answer you on the morrow." His words were firm, yet he hoped she felt the gentleness hidden in them. If the woman did, she did not show it, for she simply nodded in acceptance of his will.

With a slight signal, the servants quietly approached, their heads bowed as they curtsied, showing deference to the king. They helped the woman off the ground and took her away to her quarters.

"Your Majesty." The voice of the herald, strong even as he whispered, broke the silence that had captured King Ealas's attention. How much time had transpired, he asked himself. Everyone was still kneeling, waiting for the words that never escaped his mouth.

"Forgive me, friends. Please, rise!" Ealas exclaimed.

The herald intervened, raising his voice over those of the crowd. "Let us all celebrate with a banquet such as only Ardenay can muster!"

<hr />

The splendor of the banquet hall was dwarfed by the jewels in the king's crown. Lapis lazuli, sapphire, and aquamarine all had a place near each of its peaks.

"I believe it would look much better resting on my head," Siul chuckled, lightly pretending to touch the golden circlet. "Don't you agree, Ealas?"

"'Your Majesty,'" Varen corrected. The Bull[1] was as serious as he was militant. Despite not having reached his third decade, Varen Bulwharf was a natural leader, highly respected among his own. He had fought fiercely for his position as head of his people against many much older and more experienced than himself[2]. While his responsibility had kept him largely away from Ealas the last few years, there was still a closeness among the trio that no one could deny.

"Ealas," the king interrupted. "To you both, I will always be Ealas, and I will have it no other way," he smiled.

"If that is your wish, man must only obey his king," Siul jested with an exaggerated bow.

"Siul, Your Majesty . . . our friendship might never change, but we do, we will, we must. The whole fate of a nation, of the world, will depend on Your Highness."

"The time of children is passed," the king's uncle interrupted. "From now on, you will face a new danger every day. A leader must always see beyond what the world sees and must play the part of prophet, commander, and king."

"Cousin, if I may ask." Langel's soft speech ended the silence that followed his father's words.

"Ask, cousin. I hide nothing from you all," Ealas responded.

"Do you feel prepared for the burden you will carry from now on? Have the years of preparation done anything to ease the tension you must feel today?"

At his words, Ealas stood silent for an instant, seeking proper words that would show him as assertive and honest at the same time. "I have been preparing for many a year now, that is true, but no amount of preparation will ease the burden on my shoulders. The only thing that can do that is your support and that of those here present. Every House, every nation, and clan that comprises Ardenay will help carry that burden and will make it bearable so that even in my time of weakness, we can be strong."

"Why do you ask, Langel?" his older brother, the more militant of the pair, questioned, seeking to ridicule his brother. "Do you have anyone in mind who could make a better leader?" Laughter followed.

"If you would all excuse me," the monarch said as he left the group to their musings. He walked toward the balcony, from where the captivating gray eyes of Ileina, eldest daughter of the Silver Lord[3] of Eomener, summoned him.

The maiden's raven black hair cascaded to her exposed right shoulder. A plain, silver pin kept the left sleeve in place, allowing the evening breeze to dance playfully with her coral silk gown.

"Your Majesty" Ileina curtsied. "You honor me with your attention." Her parents had raised her well. The Silver Lord was one of the wealthiest men in the known world, but still raised her with a great humility Ealas found irresistible.

"How could I not?" he responded. "You honor me with your presence almost as much as with your beauty. It makes a man understand why the Light blesses us. There is no other way we could see, understand, and enjoy what's in front of us."

Lowering her head as she blushed, Ileina bit her lower lip. She turned to face the gardens below and, drawing a deep breath, she looked up at the quarter moon above. "It would have been perfect to have Kaeris, the eye of the night, fully open, witnessing your celebration."

"It's just an orb in the sky," he interjected.

"It's a goddess," she said.

"It's a moon."

"It's shying."

"It's revolving."

"Watching all of us."

"Maybe just the two of us," Ealas added as his hand met her cheek and caressed it softly. Ileina's eyelids closed, her hand now resting over his own.

"Your Highness," the terse voice of Creod of the Royal Guard called their attention. "Your presence is needed."

As the man she loved half turned and walked back inside the banquet hall, Ileina simply watched.

He was received by the words of Duke Aorius, as those present raised their cups "To our king. We pledge our loyalty, our hearts, and souls. The throne and the crown are big for any man but small for the Crown of Ardenay. Blessed be our glorious majesty, and may the Light shine in every corner of the world."

In unison, those gathered repeated the words while Ealas's own thoughts drowned in the cheering.

———— ++++++ ————

Past midnight, Ealas's guards opened the doors to the royal chamber, where he would spend his first night. It was twenty-five summers ago when he was born in this same chamber and nearly as many years since he last slept in it. Yet, the smell of it was strangely familiar.

That morning, this room had been filled with laughter, family members, and advisers who waited behind a white curtain while the queen brought her firstborn into the world. The midwives were singing, as was customary, to fill the newborn soul with joy. But the midwives gasped as they saw the queen's bleeding would not stop. The visitors heard the songs change to wailing as the royal mother convulsed and died in her husband's arms.

The king's pride was wounded, but he would move on, never taking another wife, so as to avoid any conflict in his succession.

"Do you mind if I peek inside?" Siul's words brought Ealas back to the present moment. "I have never seen the royal chamber, and I'm quite curious."

Ealas's father had not allowed anyone but himself or the maids inside the bedroom since his mother's death just after childbirth.

"I will think about it," Ealas jested, following with heartfelt laughter. "Of course, you are welcome to come anytime. For now, that is."

"Ah, that's right. How soon before you have to choose a wife, we all wonder. That's what would change the rules of the game. The days when brothers are friends, and friends become, well, acquaintances. A king cannot rest until his dynasty's creation is set in motion."

"You are somewhat right."

"Who will it be, then? Do you have someone in mind? Or will you allow the Church to choose her for you?" Siul's eyes rested upon the steeple, seen from every point of the capital, its fine point an arrow that reminded all they served their God above. His hand moved toward a perfect apple on a tray by the king's bed. He took a bite, waiting for an answer.

"I do not have anyone in mind, not right now. First, I want to get acquainted with my full responsibilities. It is certain there will be no lack of candidates."

Leaning on the windowsill, Siul slowly turned his body toward Ealas. While usually talkative, he could only exhale deeply.

"Say it," Ealas said to his childhood friend.

"What?" Siul's eyes now looked at his king. In an instant, he had stopped being the friend who he used to hurl mud at, the one who helped him escape his duties, that brother he never had but whom he loved dearly. Now Ealas was his lord, and, as a son of House Ileva, he understood and respected his station.

"You want to say something." The king placed his hand on Siul's shoulder. While his frame was lithe, it hid his prowess in battle. "You, of all people, should never fear speaking to me. Never. Do you understand that?"

"I do, Your Majesty."

"Your Majesty?" Ealas feigned surprise.

"I have been at your side for so long. You are perhaps who I, aside from my family, love the most."

"And you too. I love you too," Ealas interrupted softly.

Love . . . there it was. That word that, to Siul, meant everything but that he only professed to Ealas in such ways he could only hope Ealas could truly read between his lines. But while Ealas did love him back, his love was not the same.

"Regardless of how much you change in the performance of your duties—"

"I will not change, brother. I will change the world instead." Ealas's ungloved hand lightly touched his friend's cheek.

Siul shook as he had never done before. Not even the busiest battlefield had made his skin tremble. He wanted to say so much in this perhaps most perfect of moments, and yet he couldn't.

"As you well know, you have been the closest friend I've had. It would bring me the most honor..." Siul held his heart in hand, "if you would choose my sister Aelle as your wife."

The words felt heavy on Siul's own lips. Did he truly want Aelle to be Ealas's wife? He surely did not. In fact, he wanted no one to be his wife. As powerful as he was, he felt powerless at the thought of losing Ealas to someone else.

At least by his sister's side, he could still have him close, even if he could never touch him.

"Your Highness!" The alarmed voice of one of his servants interrupted the pair. She stood by the doorway, her trembling hands clasped, a pair of royal guards stepped aside at the monarch's signal.

"What is it, woman?" Ealas words came forth, unable to hide his discontent at the interruption. Embarrassment filling his heart, Siul took a step back.

"The woman you freed today . . ." The maid's voice, perhaps used to the verbal abuse of the nobles, was barely audible. "She's dead."

His eyes opened wide as the irritation disappeared, to be replaced with an unexpected chill that caught him in place. Time seemed to slow down as Ealas Heikken ran through the hallways. Siul, his guards, and servants hurried to follow his steps. The slaves scurried, rats in Ardenay that felt safer when they were out of a noble's way.

Quite swiftly, the retinue reached the tower where she had been given a chamber. Immediately upon entering the room, Ealas froze in place.

For the first time in the last twenty years, her body lay on a bed instead of a straw mattress across the floor. Looking down at her frail body, dressed in the same sack garment the color of coal, he turned to his servants, questioning.

"My lord," a woman started, "we offered her other attire, but she would only wear black. She said she didn't know if she was going to be let go."

Where a proud nobleman had stood, a vulnerable child now seemed to have taken his place, looking at her inert body.

The noble took a deep breath, and with his own hands, he tore his royal vestments as he screamed to the top of his lungs, "I was going to let you go!"

Visibly intimidated, the servants stepped back toward the walls of the small, circular chamber.

"I could have done it." An ocean of tears rolled down his features. "I could have freed you sooner had I been man enough to stand up to my father. I could have done it . . ." He looked to the horizon as if he could see her soul departing. "Had I abandoned pride, I could have told you what you mean to me."

Siul placed his hand on his beloved friend's shoulder. His eyes watered, but despite any effort, he would never feel the pain Ealas was enduring at this very moment. He caressed his king's hair, holding back any tears from escaping as a shepherd gathered his sheep. "Your Majesty, Ealas," he whispered, "what would you have us do with the woman's body?"

"Astas," the broken word escaped Ealas's lips, "her name was Astas." Rarely in the history of Ardenay had a nobleman uttered the name of a slave. Once their servitude began, slaves became hands, feet, and nothing else. This division and distinction between castes in the Kingdom of Light was such an integral part of their society that this was never questioned.

Unconcerned with their customs, the king lay his body close to hers and placed his head on her now-cold bosom.

Siul signaled to those present, and each quietly yet promptly left the room under the command of the nobleman. He then looked at his devastated friend, knowing there was perhaps nothing he could say or do to ease the pain. Lowering his own gaze, he walked backward toward the room's entrance. The pair of eyes the color of the sky could hold back the sheep no longer. Their gates opened before they disappeared behind the closing door.

Exhausted from all the agony, the King of Ardenay's eyelids became as heavy as a barricade falling to guard a besieged door.

"I could have done it," As all his strength left him, he whispered, "but I didn't."

* * *

The morning sun's rays broke as they touched the stained glass panes of the tall windows on both sides of the hallway, filling it with a playful, rainbow appearance.

Siul would have marveled at these, even stopped to enjoy them, but his mind was captive by concern.

He had opened the door to Astas's room to find the bed empty. 'What did Ealas do with the body?' he wondered, his footsteps taking him to King Ealas's chamber.

The Ileva noble was stopped by the guards guarding the door.

"My lord, His Highness does not want to be bothered," one of the guards explained.

"I understand, but I must speak to His Majesty. It is an important, personal matter," Siul's words showed his determination.

"We understand, my lord, but the king said no exception."

Now, that was not the Ealas he had grown up knowing, admiring, some might even say loving. It was the Ileva's own insistence that would create any separation between the two. In regard to his friend, young Ealas has always ignored formality and etiquette and always brought Siul closer.

Siul turned and left the guardsmen's presence.

* * *

Fooling the guards on the parapets would not have been easy for any man, but Siul Ileva was not just any man. Over the years, he had been known for his discipline, charm, and archery skills but also for his agility and climbing skills.

From where he stood, over the main keep, he walked along the edge of the roof, as surefooted as a cat. He easily avoided being seen by the guards on the towers and the people below.

Finding the open window to the king's chamber, he tumbled in through the opening, landing with a casual thud.

"We will need to keep a better watch. This was far too . . . Ealas?"

Fine, royal garments hung by the large, circular mirror in the room. On its reflection, Siul observed, on one side of the room, the royal bed, its scented bedding perfectly in place. On the other side, the banner of the rampant lion hung over the desk. On it, the crown of Ardenay rested over a piece of rolled yet unsealed parchment.

As if having a life of their own, his fingers slid over the scroll, his eyes of the firmament consuming every word.

'I, Ealas Heikken, King of Ardenay, Bearer of the Light, and Blessed of the Heavens, have found that my thoughts are not my own anymore. Lately, my heart has been drifting away from everything I have always thought I had known. While hardships might come from my decisions, hardships of the soul will undoubtedly befall me if I were not to make these. In order to avoid dishonoring my own, I forsake all my titles, I forsake my name, and I do so gladly, proudly, knowing Ardenay will not have a lack of great leaders who will stand up to the task. Hereby, thus, I abdicate the throne. I have decided to leave, to find my way, to become a beggar in the land of Blood, for one thing I have learned, that in that land, having nothing, I will have more than here having everything.'

Siul's eyes rained as he clenched his fists around the parchment. The wet, sky blue of his eyes sought refuge in the horizon as he murmured through gritted teeth, "Ealas, what have you done?"

(1) The citizens of Bulwharf were known as 'bulls' due to the bull in their banner, representative of their prowess in battle and steadfast demeanor

(2) Bulwharf respects prowess overall. No political or military positions were inherited in their lands. They were all earned by surpassing other challengers in a series of physical feats and confrontations.

(3) The mercantile duchy of Alcyn's ruling caste is made up of powerful merchant lords. Minting the coin and owning the banks being more important in their eyes, the Lord of Silver is recognized as the ruling head among them.

SUHNE

Location: Empyre of Suhne, City of Suhne, Palace of the Sun

One day the Sun will be no more . . .

The nightmare echoed so vividly that it woke her up, leaving her naked, tanned body drenched with sweat. Her hands had gone numb from the intensity with which she had clutched at sheets the color of bleached bone.

Vamya panted like a beast under the desert heat until she finally let go, her hand moving to shield her emerald eyes from the rays of the sun above.

It took a few moments before she could overcome this sensation that had taken over her, this *fear.*

Is this recurring nightmare a sign of sorts? Vamya thought.

Just on the previous day, the Sun had departed this world. The god made man, and the man made god, had left his children to fight for the ashes he left behind.

Three were the heirs of this generation, three roads, three possibilities . . . but ultimately only one future.

The three had grown up studying the many customs, rituals, enemies, and most importantly, at least Vamya so believed, the prophecies of their people.

Prophecies formed the unbreakable backbone of Suhne, but the Sun was still its head.

Vamya wondered if she believed, or perhaps *feared,* prophecies more than either of her older brothers, for although they shared the same blood, their hearts were quite different from each other's.

As a potential Sun, however, there was no time for fear. She needed to prepare herself for the ceremonies this day would bring.

Vamya saw the familiar servants lighting the morning incense that, to her, was even more familiar. She closed her eyes, taking several deep breaths as if seeking to renew her energy before rising from the wooden bed covered in flowing, white silk drapes that stood barely a foot off the ground.

A crone's lips filled the air with a chant in the ancient language of Suhne.

From the eastern portion of the faceted, crystal-domed ceiling[1] of her room, the Sun's light bathed her bed, lightly kissing her nipples and almost every inch of her exposed flesh with its warmth.

Thick drops of sweat trickled down her skin and toward her womanhood to become one with the pool her feet entered.

From the crone's ebon hands, dried herbs fell onto the water. Upon contact with it, they released the fragrance of the earth, of rosemary and red thyme.

'I must dismiss what troubles me,' the heir thought.

Vamya breathed in deeply once again before submerging herself in both shallow water and deep meditation.

Her 'being' floated high above the mountains at the end of the world, far northwest of the city of Suhne.

High up it wandered, flying over the Windless Mountain and around where the Silver Peaks touched the heavens. It passed over Daygamanu, the angry desert of Suhne, and over the capital city, where countless worshippers from all over the land mourned the loss of her father.

Like a moth to a flame, her 'being' was drawn to the center of the capital, where the main temple was located. It slowly floated toward the entrance of the Grand Temple and into the polished crystal dome of the main chamber, where she found the Rays of the Sun. All of them were standing, but not one of them was facing her direction.

They seemed to be frozen in place, in time.

Vamya's 'being' made its way around them, curious as to what captured the holy men's undivided attention. Each of the eleven Rays appeared to be in a state of shock. Their eyes were fixed on the chunks of broken crystal that lay on the floor around the main altar, its own structure collapsed under the weight of an enormous black rock.

The boulder's uneven surface was laden with runes written in a tongue she did not know but somehow could comprehend. 'One day, the Sun will be no more.'

A sudden chill ran down her spine. Her cough gave birth to innumerable bubbles that escaped her lips to die at the water's surface. For a moment, Vamya thought about opening her eyes, jumping out, and catching a breath to start again. But she was stronger than that, she knew.

I must dismiss what troubles me.

The heir sank again into her underwater meditative trance and sought to calm down. Like many times before, she looked to dismiss every thought, every scene, every name until her mind would go completely blank.

It made her feel stronger, strong enough to dismiss the thoughts, clearing her mind of doubts and fears.

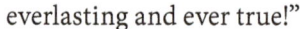

"People of the Sun!" The voice of an aging, bald man shouted from the elevated entrance of the Grand Temple to the thousands gathered below, "Our Almighty Sun has set. His spirit returns to the Windless Mountain to renew itself. Our Sun god must regain its strength. But fear not. The Sun still shines through his Rays. Today marks the start of a new era, and soon he will rise once again, everlasting and ever true!"

Malek of Suhue

The black-clad multitude[2] cheered at the words of Exis, the man in the bright yellow robe, whose head was shaved, his face unadorned except for the yellow tattoo of the Sun that crowned his head. Exis's medallion of the Sun, like the adornments on his fingers, hands, and feet, were of gold so lustrous it reflected the light of the sun itself.

But they also cheered at the other twelve men behind him, the ones wearing copper and who wore the same yellow garments, whose heads had been marked the same way.

Exis stood by the enormous, sacred, coal-black brazier where public sacrifices were burned as a dedication to the Sun himself. It was surrounded by smaller ones that were already lit. While he could easily fit in the brazier more than ten times, the old man's presence dwarfed that of the metallic structure.

As the Speaker, Exis commanded the attention of his colleagues. As a Ray, however, he held no political power aside from the selection and worship of the new Sun. Still, the respect their position held in Suhnite culture was unquestionable, for these men had the power to find and elevate a god from among mankind.

"Now, people of the Sun," Exis spoke again amid the clamor. "In his glorious mercy, the Sun wants us to remember he will always be with us, and thus, the Sun has left us his progeny.

"This time, he has left us three heirs, and while all three are blessed, it is only through the Tests that one and ONLY ONE," he raised his voice to an almost insane scream, "will shine through and Ascend with the spirit of the Almighty Sun!" At his crescendo, the ecstatic multitude joined in and roared in unison.

"Sons of the Sun, come forth!" he commanded, "and present the color of your lineage." He signaled the three who stood on the dais behind him, garbed in tunics of the tan color that represented the previous Sun.

Standing in place, each one was given their turn to speak.

The first to address the crowd was a broad-chested man, his muscled body chiseled like that of the most perfect statue. Black hair curled softly toward and below his shoulders.

While his blood was noble, his appearance was like that of a beast. His forehead was firm, adorned with strong, bushy eyebrows that accentuated his intimidating masculinity. A golden bar ran through his nasal septum above the alae of his nose, each side ending in rings from which dangled a gold chain that connected the bar to each earlobe. Midway, another ring connected the chain to piercings on either side of his lower lip.

"I am Malek, Son of the Sun," his voice boomed like rumbling thunder. "I am the first-born, he who will rule the world. I have chosen the color gold as my line. I will add a golden era to our history." Malek pointed at the banner of Suhne, its sand background depicting the tan sun, along its bottom, fringes of the different colors chosen by the Sun of each generation since the beginning of Suhne.

He then raised both arms and shouted at the top of his lungs, "I will expand our borders as never before, to the ends of the earth, for I am the Conquering Sun!"

Maylen of Suhne

The multitude acclaimed him, proud of the warrior of renown, much like his father had been.

The secondborn was lithe yet well-built. What could be seen of his covered body showed his skin was lighter than his brother's, for the outside world had hardly seen his presence. While his hair was straight and just as black, his eyes were smaller and more slanted, his eyelids colored so as to accentuate their hazel intensity. His nose was pierced on the left, where a small golden chain dangled to be connected to his earlobe. On his right ear, the chain left a ring and toward his right eyebrow. His voice was soft and yet, firm. "I am Kaylen, Son of the Sun, he who will be the scourge of mankind, the one who will make the world our slaves. I choose red, the color of burning passion, of the blood spilled from every man I will break." Kaylen's hand swayed, "I will break the knees of the world so that they have no option but to worship the only, the true god, the Searing Sun!"

His words, too, were acclaimed.

Vamya then took a step forward, her brown hair flowing and arranged in multiple braids that danced on her shoulders and mid-back. Her full-bodied lips were colored the same tan as the tunic. From her left earlobe, a single golden chain dangled toward her nose.

Before speaking, Vamya hesitated for a moment. She knew her words had to be chosen carefully. There was no pride in calling herself a son when she was a daughter. The Rays watched her, asps testing the air for any sign of weakness.

"I am Vamya . . . Child of the Sun." The majority of the Rays did not seem to disapprove. "The Sun who will evolve this world to bring an era, unlike anything the world has witnessed. As we know, in nearly fifteen centuries, every time the Sun has had a daughter, he has killed both her and her mother to marry again and start anew. So if my father did not do so, it is because he must have wanted something to be different. I thus choose the color green, the color of that which has a hard time growing in the desert, of that which we long for, that which we need." Vamya opened her arms for everyone to see, "I am the Sun of Change!"

Again the voices rose, although her ears briefly captured some jeering from the crowd.

Her emerald eyes darted in an attempt to detect where it came from, but the deafening shouts drowned any other noise as Exis took center stage, walking toward the crowd.

"The time has come to allow our Sun to rest," Exis announced, directing his attention to the other Rays.

The Flame Guard walked into view, and the roaring went silent at the sight of the inert body they carried on their shoulders. Even in death, the Almighty

Sun's presence was more commanding than the imposing, muscular bodies of those who had protected him in life. The ceremonial walk brought them toward the brazier, where his body was carefully placed.

The Sun's skin glistened from having been bathed time and again since the morning with sacred, scented oils that would make the burning easier. Now that time they had waited for had come. Each Ray grabbed a brazier and set it alight. Each mumbled a small prayer to the Almighty Sun as they set the giant brazier ablaze.

The three siblings watched quietly, in reverence. Their god was their father, and their father was their god. There was no love nor admiration for that being who was no more. At this moment in time, only one thing surely crossed their mind: this was the beginning of the end of their lifelong training.

The flame grew, feeding the hysteria of the crowd. Many among the thrall shouted, others screamed, and yet many stretched their hands toward the brazier in desperation, their eyes wide open and filled with tears, for the loss of the Sun was the loss of the man they had lived to worship.

————————— ·+♦♦+· —————————

When the fire finally died, it was close to the end of the day. Still, despite the long hours, the crowd remained.

None in the multitude had left their place, not even the elderly. The sanctity of this day had required that they fast. Many had even voided where they stood to avoid losing sight of even the last wisp of smoke. With as much fervor as reverence, the weaker among the many leaned on the stronger ones for support to ease the cramping of their legs.

In silence, nine of the Rays placed their hands on the ashen remains of what was once the incarnate body of the Almighty Sun, while Exis and the remaining three brought forth a golden urn, which they filled with the ashes using their

Vamya of Suhue

own hands. The nine walked toward the sons, three to each, so as to avoid showing any sign of preference.

After the urn was filled, servants brought a small, golden water basin to wash Exis's hands. He did so meticulously. The once clean fluid now turned a dark gray.

Exis took the basin in his hands and lifted it up above his head "People of the Sun, behold the Sons. They will be tested, and after seven trials, a new Sun will rise, a Sun like no other. A Sun so mighty, the whole world will know its name!" The Speaker looked at the three siblings, studying each one ever so carefully. He shouted to the Sons, "Come to us, Sun of Suhne! Reveal your power so that we and your people can bask in your almighty glory!"

At his signal, each trio placed their ashen hands on the bodies of Malek, Kaylen, and Vamya. Their hands caressed them, painting every inch of their youthful bodies with the ashes of their god as the crowd roared once more.

Exis took three small, golden chalices, the sun engraved on each. He filled each with the gray water from the basin. Then he handed one to each one of the trios around the siblings. A Ray among each three placed the chalice on each one of the siblings' lips to have them consume.

"Now drink, and feel the power of the Sun!" the Speaker raised his voice.

As the liquid touched her tongue, Vamya closed her eyes.

The ashes, it was said, would give her a taste of the heavens.

She heard the crowd, but this time they screamed in agony. Their cries were muffled by the burning conflagration she felt. Hideous laughter echoed as the distant gallop of heavy warhorses approached. The clanking of metal kissing metal was heard everywhere as women, the elderly, and children screamed, begging for mercy that would abandon them.

Vamya wondered if somehow her tongue had missed the taste of the heavens, of that, she was not certain. But one thing she was sure of—if there was ever a hell, she had just tasted it.

Startled, she opened her eyes at the words of the Speaker. "Glory be to the Sun, and may it rise again, stronger and more powerful than ever!

"After this day," Exis continued shouting at the multitude, "as the Sun rises in the sky, so will begin the lengthy preparation of the flesh to receive the mark of the Sun. May the glory of the Sun burn forever!"

And the crowd echoed his praise endlessly.

Finally, the Speaker took the three chalices and hurled them toward the crowd. Immediately, the many swarmed around each, fighting, clawing, and even biting one another in desperation to lay their hands not only in a piece of history but also in a piece of that which Suhne held most sacred.

The crowd's communal suffering rose as the terrible cacophony of an insane choir. Through the chaos of it all, Exis smiled; for as long as there was confusion and discord in the believers, the spiritual leaders at the top would always retain control.

(1) The Domes: Suhne's palace consists of several towers topped with crystal domes, each resembling gigantic crystal scutes placed around a circular lens. The central lens is lined by a single circular ring of stone. Runes on the ring read, "Almighty Sun, God, Father, Ruler of All, Blessed of the Heavens and Only One." It also depicts symbols that allow the Suhnite to use the ring as a compass that helps determine direction, date, and time. Suhnites believe the first Sun placed those himself.

(2) Color choice was limited for the people of Suhne. The Rays could only wear yellow robes. For the populace, the colors allowed were white, black, gray, or brown. Unmarried women could wear any color so as to be spotted more easily by the Sun in his search for a wife, who would then be known as a vessel. Her direct family would be burned in order to sever any ties existing between the vessel and the world of mortals, erasing any potential claim to the throne. To the Suhne, this was a great honor every family looked forward to.

THE DARKHOLM

Location: Kingdom of Blackheart, Royal Duchy of
Darkholm, County of Coldforge, the cliffs of Darkholde

T he wind moaned, its haunted howl dancing along the stone cliffs that
sprouted from the frenzied waters far below.

Along that same massive, natural wall, a jagged peak protruded. It angled and twisted in various places, giving the appearance of a lightning bolt that had once turned to stone.

A tower, its own surface black as coal, almost lay hidden by the night sky in its backdrop. Its builders had raised its base barely a few feet from the stone peak. Such was their proximity that they appeared to merge in several places near its base, but several stories high, only the tower rose triumphantly. Both the one created by nature, and the one made by the hands of men, held the same name: the Spire.

Toward it, nearly three dozen figures walked quietly. The heavy crimson cloaks they wore covered their features perfectly, exposing little more than the lower portion of their pale faces. They followed a single female who carried a small fabric bundle in her arms.

Every few steps, she swayed briefly as she tried hard to regain her strength, her balance. A single, intricate silver clasp hung loosely by her ear, fastening what it could of her now disheveled, black hair. On her body, not a crimson cloak, but a peacock blue gown, now tattered, stained with fresh blood oozing from the gashes covering her back from every opening where a scourge had caressed her.

They trailed her like a flock of carrion birds waiting for the inevitable. Such was the strange sense of patience about the group, which halted their progression every time she stumbled, and only moved again when she was able to resume her step.

Once, her legs faltered. The woman's knees clumsily hit the ground, yet her arms held fast to the velvet bundle. The sudden motion brought the fabric covering it to life. As it moved, the cries of a newborn no more than a day old could be heard from within. On the surface of her knee, a small rivulet of bright, fresh blood appeared, but her attention was so centered on the newborn, the pain did not seem to bother the woman much.

Her eyes, goldenrod in color, were filled with concern as she contemplated the small creature in her arms before she resumed her advance toward the Spire's natural stone steps. She still needed to climb many to reach the structure's oaken door. Determination filled every muscle in her body, giving her the strength to stand.

The wooden door stood in her way, its surface polished to perfection, nearly hiding carvings that formed words understood only by the learned of ancient lore. *Struvak leimen isn*. Duty above all.

One female among the cloaked followers stepped forth to approach her. Both their eyes, goldenrod and bright yellow as the sun, met.

The cloaked female reached for an iron key hanging from her own neck. The sliding of her sleeve revealed an arm ridden with tattoos connected by a swirling vine that disappeared under the fabric. Her hands freed the key, and offering it to the woman in front of her, she spoke, "As it is written, so it shall be done. You opened the door that led us here. Now it shall be you who leads the way." The tattooed woman handed over the key that would allow them entrance to the building ahead.

With the bundle in her arms, the woman in blue struggled to keep her balance while she fumbled with the key. The door gave way, allowing the entrance of the woman and the quiet procession that followed.

Another step, another ounce of strength left her, yet the blood did not. It clung to her back as it dried on her skin and rags.

From atop the structure, their fiery yellow eyes could see the horizon, the night sky with but a few solitary clouds. Countless stars filled the firmament, the witnessing eyes of the gods from beyond, and below their divine eyes, dozens of vultures[1] glided down as black, silent tears to wet the parapets they perched themselves upon.

Every silent pair of eyes now stared at the woman.

Almost involuntarily, as if commanded by an invisible force greater than her, her steps took her toward the edge of the tower. Briefly, she contemplated the distance to the bottom of the cliff while short gusts of wind played with the few strands of hair that had escaped the complex bun she wore.

For a moment, she knew every orb in the sky, every eye, and perhaps even every god observed her every move. Even the gibbous heavenly orb with its porcelain face had come to bear witness to the event that was about to transpire.

'Is this what it feels like to be center stage?' she wondered.

But her thoughts disappeared, as did her sad smile. It mattered not. She had to go on.

The woman's heart beat rapidly against the soft skin of the newborn her breasts were feeding. She could only wonder if he could feel the same love for her she felt despite him having been present on this earth for such a short time. Slowly, she turned toward the group as her lips parted, but nothing would come out of them, not even the pure smoke of her breath on this cold evening.

The tattooed woman stepped forward, the images in her left arm seeming to come alive as she held her cape fast against the wind's fury.

"Sasha," the tattooed woman said firmly, "you have failed everyone. You have learned the Traditions. You have been given everything, and yet, you have betrayed that which is most sacred . . . your Blood. Some of your own blood has been spilled to cleanse your transgression, but some is not enough.

"Before proceeding," she then spoke to the spectators, "if there are any objections, speak now."

A strange silence took command of the scene. There were no words, no hissing of the vultures. Even the wind had stopped as if joining the ceremony it witnessed.

"With no objections," the tattooed female proceeded, "I must now ask, do you have any last words?"

Sasha's moist eyes looked at the newborn and then at the intense yellow eyes that were like her own but stared back coldly.

"I . . . am sorry. I am so sorry. I have always known the way. I saw the danger, and still, I strayed. My Blood, I ask for your forgiveness."

"Today," the judge interrupted, "for you have strayed away from the path, you stand alone. Today we come not as your Blood but rather as executioners." She opened a small book, its leather bindings carefully unfastened so as to preserve the dark sanctity of that moment.

"And with the Founder's children as witnesses," she read out for all to hear, "Sorja Darkholm pronounced the words: *We do what must be done* . . . and the House was forever cleansed.

"Now, Sasha, I, Ira Darkholm of the Vine, ask you: Will you do what must be done to remove your transgression from our House?"

Upon the words, Sasha's body trembled. Behind her, the void seemed to whisper hungry words into her ears.

Turning toward the emptiness, she held her child close. Her arms moved him away from her, lifting him up so that she could see him against the moon's surface. His skin was as pale as her own, yet his opening eyes were the color of chestnut wood.

"We do what must be done ..." After the words escaped Sasha's mouth, none of the witnesses moved, and neither did the moon or her arms. High above the Spire, a small, crying figure could be observed falling, a star headed toward the hungry reefs below.

As if summoned by a divine wind, the vultures took to the air once again.

"Cousin ..." Sasha looked at Ira, waiting for some words of comfort. But the judge stood still, her eyes only slightly nodding in approval before she turned to leave.

After Ira, most of the witnesses followed suit, except for several females who walked toward the condemned.

Among them, a young maiden carefully fastened one of the red cloaks around Sasha's shoulders. "Mother," the young woman whispered, "come now, let us tend to your wounds."

Black as the darkest night was the war horse he rode through the gates of Darkholde Keep, a striking contrast with the pale color of his robes. Even the snowiest of winters would envy the pure fabrics he always wore, the ones that gave him the name Septem the White. As intense as the blazing sun in the deserts of Suhne were his eyes, and yet, just like the coldest winter was his face, unmoving, as if frozen in time.

Despite having reigned close to six decades, it would be hard to believe the Darkholm patriarch was a day past fifty.

Septem's face barely showed a wrinkle. His long, straight hair that flowed down to his lower back barely saw gray.

On his head rested the crown of Blackheart, a white gold circlet of intricate depictions. On the front, a faceless crowned man embraced himself, arms bound with chains. The same traveled toward each of the spikes of the crown where, on each, another man knelt in reverence to the first. Each kneeler held the chain in his hands, pulling and trapping the monarch they adored before allowing the chain to continue to the next. Over each, perfect white pearls were mounted, as beautiful and round as a full moon in the sky.

Undoubtedly this, like many other things, was part of Septem's grand design. He had forged the Blackheart from the crumbling kingdom of Celeas when everyone foretold its demise and had turned it into a powerful land and prosperous kingdom.

In everything he had created, he sent a message to his people, the ones who called themselves the Blood.

Trailing him on horseback, a female in her early sixties, taller than many other women, always armored, and always ready. Her marigold eyes were ever watchful, an eagle ready to strike. Eriadna Darkholm was the head of his guard and, for nearly half a century, had been his Shield. Wherever the monarch went, Eriadna followed.

By the doors of the main keep, his House awaited. All of them as pale as the king, with eyes flaxen like his own, watching his arrival, their hair as black as the clothes most of them wore, as black as the armor of the knights who surrounded them.

It was with good reason the world viewed House Darkholm as an eternal funeral procession.

The moment he dismounted, two younger men approached to assist their lord. One, a tall, two-decades-young version of himself. While his hair was half the length, his presence was just as commanding. Erdrick Darkholm, son of Septem, bore the seals and cape of the Commander of the Black Knights. He was, without a doubt, a knight in every action and every word.

By his side was the taller man on his right hand, who had been his squire and was also his most trusted friend. Gustavus Darkholm's figure was large, but despite his muscular frame, he was quick and able. He followed the king's son as if the nobleman had cast the largest of shadows. The two men were as different as they were alike, and yet they acted as if they had been close siblings.

"Your Majesty," Erdrick bowed as he spoke first, his salutation echoed by the rest.

"Commander," Septem's gilded gaze of fiery ice met that of his son's, "the Great Council will convene in a few days. Important matters will be discussed. Your presence is expected there."

"I can make the arrangements for the Commander to meet privately with you, Your Highness," Gustavus suggested, "so that you can discuss in private prior to the meeting."

"No," Septem killed the idea at its inception. "The Commander, like the rest of the Council, must wait until the meeting for the details."

Gustavus nodded. "I apologize, Your Highness."

"There is no need." The king walked toward the rest. "Your idea is not without merit. Know that I founded the Great Council with the idea that all dukes were equal. And so none of its members should have an advantage over another, be it political or knowledge, for it would tip the delicate balance of power and destroy everything we have created. Being my son should give the Commander no special advantage. It would make him weak and incapable and would give me reason to doubt his ability."

At the bottom of the staircase, the king turned toward Gustavus. "You might one day have a seat in that Council, so it will be important for you to remember those words."

"Thank you, Your Highness, your words do me honor." The large figure knelt in reverence while Erdrick's stern face showed approval.

Before beginning his climb, a retinue of women appeared before Septem. All but the first one curtsied, her eyes a bright yellow hue. Despite the many embroideries in her dress, she wore a plain headpiece, which turned into a cloak before melding with the many folds in her flowing skirt. Raja Darkholm was known for her striking beauty and her graceful steps, but more than that, for her quiet presence and support of her lord, her king, and her husband. Any time she spoke, she rarely did in more than a whisper. She was known as the Blood Rose for her love of crimsons[2], but sometimes among her own also as the Ghost for even if present, she would many times go unnoticed.

"My lord," Raja's lips parted in a whisper, "your daughter's name day was today."

Septem's gaze rested upon the eyes of his wife, the Princess[3]. "It still is."

"We dined in her honor."

Septem walked past his wife as he responded, "I am glad you did."

Raja turned to face his back as her hand lightly touched him. "We all did, all but you."

The Crowned King halted his climb. He half turned his body to speak, his voice showing no emotion. "Since when has celebration been important to House Darkholm?"

"You speak truly, my lord husband, but you are her father."

At those words, the king turned toward his wife. "Indeed, I am her father . . . I have been her father from the moment of her conception. I was her father yesterday, I am today, and until death and even beyond, I will still be her father. No amount of disagreement between us will ever change that, for a father could choose to renounce his child all he wants, but he can never renounce reality. Nothing, no one, can change that, and Rowena surely knows it."

"But . . . she could have felt your presence at her side."

"I am certain she has felt me at her side, every day, every moment, even if my presence is not. The Blood[4], however, must always feel and see their monarch among them. In a way, I am also their father, and they must be reminded of this every day. I spent all day in the city for the Blood, and now for them, I will spend all night."

Raja's hands lifted her husband's, which she used to caress her own porcelain face. Her soft lips kissed the palm of his hands as a small sign of affection. And yet, as he contemplated the small figure of the woman who had given birth to his children, Septem's statuesque expression remained unchanged.

As the White King climbed the stairs to ready himself, the black retinue followed.

(1) The Lords of Darkness see themselves in these birds, as they are often misunderstood. While vultures are many times associated with death, they actually represent respect for the dead. Nothing should ever go to waste. Vulture venues typically fly during the day, but the Darkholm vultures have been specially bred to fly at night.

(2) Crimsons: Blood-red roses that grow solely around the duchy of Darkholm. Upon being cut, the sap produced is similar to blood in color. Their color is a sharp contrast to the drab darkness that reigns over the walls and streets of Darkholm. Despite the many attempts, crossbreeding crimsons with any other flower has proven fruitless.

(3) In Blackheart, Septem's statutes dictated only one monarch would be known as the Crowned One. His partner would not have the power of the Crown but rather became a symbolic presence. This would reduce the chance of conflicting orders or tardiness in agreements between parties.

(4) The people of Blackheart are known as the Blood of the Black Heart, a name given since Septem founded the kingdom.

THE GARDEN

Location: Kingdom of Blackheart, Duchy of Darkholm,
County of Coldforge, Darkholde Keep

E very morning his feet traversed the same path, each firm step the rhythmic beat of an earthen drum. The unfailing discipline was evident in his every move.

Like the perfectly synchronized plates in a scarab's carapace, his armor moved, barely hampering the surprisingly agile knight within.

The amount of engraving on the armor and the details in the demonic-looking helmet he carried at his side evidenced this was not just a knight, but a high-ranking Black Knight of Darkholm.

Black as the void was the steel covering his body, adding to the contrast between the ebon of his skin and the striking ecru eyes of Serverus.

After the winding stone stairsteps, his legs took him to a most wondrous garden, one where visitors would perhaps question why there was no gate to welcome the spectator. But there was no need for such here, as the labyrinthine walls of the garden were off-limits to anyone but the closest to the royal family of Blackheart.

Not only did his status as a Black Knight allow him access, but Serverus had a claim unlike anyone else's in the kingdom.

While he did not share Blood with the ever-loyal House Grey, the zealot Sanglune, or the stealthy Devereau, he reminded himself each day of the chance he had been given to live close to the royals.

On both sides, tall walls of rose bushes, so perfect they appeared an illusion, grew from the ground. They were rarely maintained, as the botanical skills of the Darkholm gardeners were such that they were renowned throughout the realm and beyond. With ease, they trimmed the roses so that they would hide their ever-present thorns. Each time the roses were coupled, as a pair of bloody eyes, always silently watching the visitor.

If Serverus had wanted it, the knight could have numbered the steps that would take him to his destination, but his mind was not on his journey but rather on what lay at its end.

The knight's steps halted the moment he entered the clearing at the labyrinth's center. Herein, the true garden opened itself before him.

Resting over the carefully kept grass, dozens of statues found a home, each one of a martyr in their moment. They were colloquially known as 'the nameless' precisely because none of them were ever named.

The very existence of these sculpted beings spoke of the philosophy of the royal family.

To the Darkholm, sacrifice was ever present and important. The Darkholm House preached heroic deeds should always be performed because of man's belief in them, not because of the search for glory. As heroes sacrificed their lives and became martyrs, it was their deed, and not their name, that became immortalized.

On one side, close to the entrance, stood the statue of a young man, an axe splitting his stomach, his face eternally frozen in agony.

Somewhere else, a woman crawled, her mouth open in a silent scream, her back ridden with arrows sculpted from the same stone.

And yet the knight's ecru eyes gravitated toward the statue of a bald man lying on the ground, his breastplate pierced by a broken lance. Despite the grievous wound, the empty pupils of his stony eyes were filled with emotion as he seemed to look up to the heavens, his expression one of serenity.

And every time Serverus's eyes set upon the frozen image, it brought back the memory of that time, twenty-five years before.

―――――――•••♦♦♦•••―――――――

The battle had roared as the two forces tore at one another. The blue banner of the raging lion fluttered furiously as the red banner of the black heart defended its territory, like a legendary drake fighting to defend its hoard.

After days of fighting, the lion had retreated, for they would not suffer another great loss against the granite-like morale of the Blood.

Lord Selleran Ecru was strong, the strongest man the child had ever known.

His father, the child thought, was brave beyond compare and even more loyal than he was brave. Serverus's father stood tall, so much his heart swelled as he would always look up to meet his progenitor's eyes. But today, his eyes looked down as his heart broke.

Selleran lay on the ground, the knight's breastplate pierced by the broken lance of the opponent whose life he had taken. Around the fallen knight, the scattered bodies of both enemies and kin.

The son had been brought by servants, upon his father's request, so that he could see the battle from the distant campground.

Young Serverus held his father's hand fast, his tears wetting his face. The man with the deep voice now wheezed as his chest rose and fell under his broken plate.

"Father, don't go," he cried.

Behind them, two figures appeared. The first one, the messenger Selleran had sent to summon the one who followed.

Behind the messenger stood the towering presence of the man clad in white, whose armor was perfectly engraved, the nobleman who bore the crown.

"Lord Ecru," the messenger said, "the king has come."

Serverus's small, trained knees touched the ground. The king's eyes, however, remained on his father.

"Your Highness," Selleran wheezed, "pardon me for not being able to kneel."

Septem Darkholm's hand extended, perhaps to mollify Selleran's angst.

"Your Majesty," the grounded knight coughed, "if I may, I would like to ask something of you if you would grant it."

"Ask," the monarch's words were usually brief, but this time they were unusually so. Perhaps there was much to do, and there was little time to waste, or perhaps he was aware of the inevitable moment that swiftly approached.

The White King did not shower his knight with praise. He simply watched his man speak.

"Your Highness . . . It is my hope that you have found my House to be loyal to you. I have lived my life for you, and now I am dying . . . for you."

A brief moment of spasms, accompanied by a pulsating stream of blood, interrupted his words.

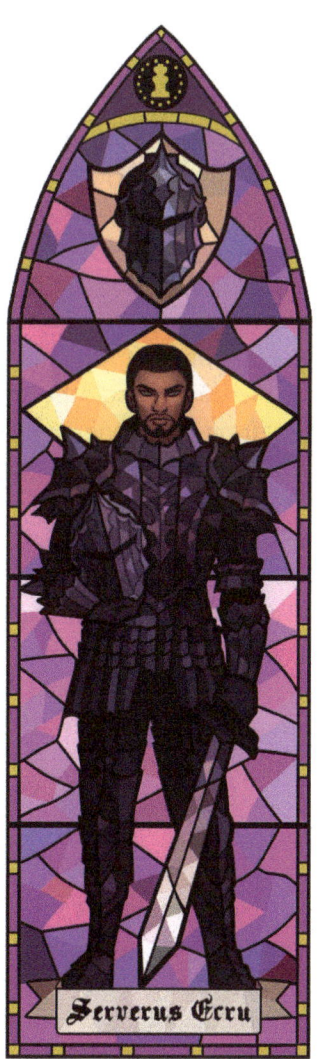

Serverus Ecru

"My kin and men died today. We have given it all. All I have left . . . is my son." The knight's eyes momentarily rested upon his child.

"My lord," he continued, "if my words and deeds have honored you, I ask you, please, do not allow my name to die in vain."

King Septem's eyes, gold as the sun, met his dying knight's and then those of Serverus. While his expression did not move, he ungloved his hand and took the child's hand. "I will raise him as one of my own."

A brief silence followed before the ecru eyes of Selleran moistened before his lips struggled to express, "I could not . . . ask . . . for a greater . . . honor."

He had asked the king to take him away so that he didn't have to see his father die, but the king did not grant this.

For what seemed like an eternity, Septem held Serverus's hand in his. Despite the cold demeanor, the child felt the monarch's palm to be quite warm.

He would never forget that moment.

The royal lips parted briefly. "We are Darkholm. We remember."

He would never forget those words.

Each statue represented a great dichotomy, a most horrifying yet heroic deed. And of dichotomy, Serverus Ecru knew quite a lot. He had grown up among the royal family, closer than even their greatest allies.

To him, they were the family he had lost at an early age.

To them, he was the closest tie to the world of men they had remained distant from for so long, an incomparable ally, the most trusted friend, and a close relative . . . or at least that's how his heart wished they felt.

The knight fixed his eyes on the center of the clearing where a tall fountain stood. On it, the statue of a long-haired man, cleaving his chest with his own claymore. His head bowed in what could either be a sign of pain and suffering or of reverence and commitment. From his wound, precious water sprouted, feeding the basin to give life to the fountain and the scene that was frozen in time.

While it was also nameless, the words around its base, *My life for your eternity . . .* would always tell this man could be none other than Valdemar Darkholm, the founder and first of the Darkholm name and household.

For a moment, his heart seemed to beat at a different rhythm when he saw *her.*

She knelt in the same spot he saw her every morning.

He could always see the porcelain skin of the back of her neck and the raven-black hair that was, at times, skillfully arranged in intricate styles. The glint of amethysts in her earrings was reflected in the ecru of his eyes.

The maiden's soft hands gently took a mortar and pestle from her right, feeding it dried herbs and seeds from her left.

Serverus observed a crimson resting by her side; the fine, black dress lined with black feathers which seemed to caress her skin that, despite its exquisiteness, only served to accentuate her unearthly beauty. The Black Knight saw it all, but the one thing he could never see in this place was her face.

Somehow, he always felt relief knowing she could not see him either.

Serverus had grown close enough to her and would even eat dinner at the same table. She was like a sister, but in his heart, she felt like more. He was fully trusted among the royals as a noble knight, but she was the Master of Life, and while his duty was to protect them, to keep them and their kingdom safe at all times, hers was to be the king's physician, head of the healers, and, together with the Master of Death, one of the main alchemists in charge of helping the Darkholm achieve their goal.

While they were both guardians in their own way, their duties kept them at a distance, and so these daily visitations were the only moments when, despite the distance between them, he felt he could be alone with her.

"Are you there, Rowena?" he almost cursed under his breath. The knight would have rather preferred to spend hours watching her work without uttering a word than interrupt her.

"I am, Serverus," Rowena's voice was was a most perfect melody pronounced as she lifted her head. Her meticulous hands never stopped mixing the herbs, slowly grinding them with utmost precision and care.

"You are early this morning," the knight said.

"Or perhaps late last night," she replied. If he knew her as well as he thought, he could picture her smiling.

The knight wanted to smile, too but held back. Despite his standing at the edge of the clearing, he always felt somehow, she could read him.

Silence followed the brief exchange, interrupted only by the scraping of the pestle that efficiently pulverized the dried leaves.

What could he possibly speak about to engage her in conversation, he wondered.

That was his greatest ordeal on most mornings. The knight was a master of the sword, he was rarely bested, but a master of spoken words he was not, a skill Septem's daughter had excelled at since childhood. Almost every morning, he felt the woman he admired pulverized his words as easily as she did the dried herbs.

"I am not certain if you were made aware of an outbreak at the sanitarium." He hoped for an ace.

"Outbreak?" There was concern in her voice.

"I am not certain of the details, but I heard one of the healers has fallen ill, boils appearing on her feet."

"Did they appear on both soles?" The one thing Rowena Darkholm had always been was curious, more so regarding matters involving her responsibilities as Master of Life, the royal healer of Darkholm. Despite her curiosity, however, she spoke with a calmness one could only find in the most still of waters.

"Both, I believe."

"On the heel, arch, or forefoot?" she continued.

"All of them."

"Did it start on all locations simultaneously, or on one and spread to the rest?"

Rowena Darkholm

"Of that, I am unaware," the knight responded.

'I have her attention,' he thought, imagining a dueling sword striking fast as he held back another smile. "If you would like, I can accompany you to the monastery."

"That is not necessary," she responded, filling the vials before her with newly ground dust.

He imagined a shield blocking his strike. 'Why did I give her the option?' the knight cursed at himself. He needed to strike again before it was too late. He felt her engaged, "It is important to ascertain you are protected."

"Serverus." For a moment, he saw the side of her porcelain face. "Only you, of all knights, would seek to protect me in the one place I need no protection." It was her strike that took him by surprise.

"You always need protection."

"Is it not what everyone needs?"

"We all do, yes, but know that I will always protect you."

Like the last sliver of the moon disappearing on the horizon, Rowena's face returned to her work, "Will you, then, never sleep as you stand by my bed every night?"

While Septem's daughter was the Master of Life, to Serverus, she would be the Master of

Words if there was ever a need for one. The young knight felt he was almost at a loss for words. Truly, this was her battlefield.

"Rowena," he said again, after a brief silence, "if these end up in an outbreak beyond our control, what would the Master of Life do, and what would she have us Black Knights do?"

"The Master of Life position behooves me to study, to take samples, to try my best so that we can find a cure."

"Even if that means exposing yourself to contagion?"

"Even if it does. There are parts of our duties that one cannot simply shy away from." He felt amusement in her voice. "Now, to answer your question. Let us suppose a treatment failed. It would do no good to allow it to spread in our kingdom. I would offer the afflicted the option to either lose the legs, to become a study subject, to die in peace and isolation, or, if the king thought it wise, to visit a foreign land."

"A foreign land?" It was now he who was curious.

"Indeed, dear," her warm word was a kiss on the imaginary wound to his pride, "they could very well spend their last days enjoying the beauty of the world . . . while also spreading a message on enemy lands."

This time the silence was his. Her words were as enrapturing as they were sinister. What else could he expect, if not the beautiful dichotomy of one who shared the Blood of the Darkholm?

"You would make a great queen one day." This time his words were not a sword but an arrow that stopped her movement, striking at its mark.

"Queen?" Her words were just as soft, but there was no amusement in them, "I would never wish to have the weight upon my head. There are other Darkholm, more fitting than I. There is nothing that makes me feel I deserve those chains.

"If I believed in the gods," she continued, "I would pray day and night that they would deliver away that cup from me, but I believe not, so my days and nights are only filled with dread."

At this, Serverus quiesced. What could he possibly say to make her feel differently? Every sentence that started forming in his mind was immediately dissolved before conception.

Thankfully, it was she who raised her palm to the side and broke the silence. "Is it raining?"

Serverus's eyes looked up to capture the sun as it disappeared behind dark clouds. "Yes, it is. Come."

"It is just rain."

"Let us go now before it is too late."

"I cannot," Rowena responded. "You go on ahead. I need to stay. There is much I still need to do."

Reluctantly, Serverus closed his eyes and bowed before stepping back the same way he had at first come. Behind him, she was left alone as the rain fell, and while he didn't want to leave, he had to.

Once again, the Master had won, at the duel of words, at a battle of wills, and the price had been yet another small piece of his heart.

THE ESCAPE

Location: Kingdom of Ardenay, Capital City of Himlen

I t was still dark when he left, diving into a mound of clothes in the back of a merchant's cart to hide until the morning.

Over his shoulders, an ill-fitting black sac tunic. At least it felt that way, for he had never before worn one.

'Hopefully, this will take me far,' the man thought, trying to ignore the smell of dried, accumulated sweat in the linens and wool that provided the needed cover. His eyes remained closed while he lay motionless, his left hand keeping the coins on his belt pockets from clinking, his right hand wrapped around a small leather pouch that hung around his neck. Other than that, a sheathed, fine, yet plain short sword hung at his side.

Even with his eyes closed, he could trace the steps and guess the time it would take to exit the castle grounds.

Bartholomew.

He told himself as he recognized the voice of the veteran guard standing by the gate, the one who coughed between sentences as he had done for years now. The guard saluted the wagon drivers.

It must mean we're at the north gate.

The thoughts were followed by the sound of the massive gate as it readied itself to let the moving cart free from its grasp.

The bridge.

A hopeful smile appeared on his face when the iron wheels contacted the shaking wood underneath before the cart made a turn and then another.

After a few minutes that seemed to last days, the fugitive had lost his way. He could no longer tell where he was.

If they stop at the market, I'm doomed.

But there were no loud noises of busy streets, heralds, and town criers. There were no whores, no vendors announcing their wares. All he heard was the loud noise of the cart wheels as they hit the uneven rocks, telling him they were off the main road.

Soon, the burbling and bubbling sound of a stream flowing over the pebbles in its body was heard, its song interrupted by the voice of half a dozen washer-women, singing and gossiping as they approached the cart.

Ealas's eyes opened in alarm upon hearing their voices closing in.

They're approaching from the left.

With some difficulty, he dragged his body from under the heavy load of clothes. The nobleman fell to the right of the cart, cringing, praying to the Lord of Light he wasn't heard.

"I never trusted the man. He seemed married," a middle-aged woman spoke to the rest.

"Oh yeh, married he is. Married twice, actually," another one responded.

"Twice? What happened to his first wife?" a third one immediately joined in the conversation.

"His first wife, you say? Oh, she's alive," the second one responded. "He's married twice within a year. Neither woman knew of the other!" All three giggled like a flock of birds that had found a tasty worm to devour.

There was movement in the front of the cart.

Think quick.

Trees . . . but they're too far for a sprint. I won't even be able to make it past the bushes without being seen.

In a flash, rolling along the ground, Ealas hid under the body of the wooden cart.

Now the other women approached, too, to carry a load of clothes to the nearby stream.

The drivers on the other side spoke some nonsense to one another before hitting on the women across the cart.

The horses took a few steps before being reined in by a driver. Ealas crawled as fast as he could, staying under the cart's cover.

One of the drivers went back to his seat, as the other voided by Ealas's feet, whistling a tune that told the nobleman they had not noticed anything amiss . . . until the cart moved.

The wagon driver laughed heartily as he left his friend behind.

He pulled his pants up as he screamed, "Hey, you loiter-sack! Wait for me, now!"

The driver took off, laughing.

The chaser, however, stopped at the visage of the crawling black sack.

"Heeeeey, you slave, what do you think you're doing here?" he spat.

Thinking quickly, the nobleman lifted himself off the ground and went for a run.

A sudden, blunt hit on his thigh made him stumble as the driver kicked him solidly.

"Fuck off, now! Be gone!"

The man grabbed a few pebbles from the road and hurled them toward Ealas to the laughter of the washerwomen.

"You throw like a li'l girl, you," one of the washerwomen mocked.

"Oh, c'mon now, maybe if you throw them all at the same time, one of them might hit!" another one laughed.

Ealas ran as fast as he could, diving toward the bushes when something hard struck his temple. He fell flat on the ground, the hit setting off a ringing cacophony inside his head that would last beyond the celebratory laughter of the peasants.

The nobleman felt a warm liquid running down his temple.

Just what I needed, he told himself at the sight of blood on his hand.

Just in case they were following, he darted off and immediately south, where he waded across the stream, diluting his bloody trail.

++++++

Hungry patrons sat at only a few of the tables of the Holy Mackerel, which was once called the Holy Goats, and before that, the De'Vine Fury, a bar that had rebranded itself several times in the last twenty years. Its original location in Zagos had been quite successful and profitable, but after the Church ruled taverns unholy and illegal in the capital of Ashvail Duchy, it had to move underground before finally relocating to Himlen, and in the church district, of all places.

A jug crashed on the floor, the ale wetting its thirsty surface all the way to the entrance, where the cloaked figure of Ealas stood.

Having already heard some street rumors of his disappearance, aside from hearing he had died in his sleep, that he was really a female, and that the Light had smitten him down during the Crowning, he felt paranoid at the prospect of being searched for. His eyes scouted the room for potential acquaintances or anyone who would or could possibly recognize him.

Nearly every patron was drunk, wasted, or well on his way there, except for an Illustrean man who brooded in a corner seemingly speaking to himself, a middle-aged woman by the bar garbed in traveling attire, her graying hair picked up in a long braid as improvised as the bandage over his own head, the tavern master and his somewhat clumsy daughter who seemed pretty only in the eyes of the drunks present.

While perhaps it was safer to sit among the drunken customers, it could also be most unpredictable, especially if a fight erupted. Ealas walked toward the bar.

What should I order? he thought.

"Yeah, you look like you could use a drink this evening," the tavern master pointed out, leaning back toward his station.

"Ehm, yeah, what wine do you have?" Ealas asked, seeking to deepen his voice.

"Oh, sure," the man responded. "We have all sorts of wine. From the best imported Rovetsean grapes to the fruity Tardese sweetwater."

"I'll have a cup of Red Dream if you have some. And some food, venison roast, duck, pork, whatever you have."

"We have all of them. Which one would you prefer, kind sir?"

"Venison, then."

"Oh, most certainly!" the man replied with a mocking, exaggerated smile.

"Tonna!" he signaled at the serving girl. "Cup coming, just for you!" the tavern master added.

Ealas felt the woman at his side studying him. Strangely, she was quiet, too quiet for comfort.

His thoughts were interrupted by the slamming of the tankard in front of him.

"How much is it? And this doesn't look like—"

"Listen," the serving man now leaned his elbows on the bar's surface toward Ealas, "for over twenty years, all we have served is rum and ale, *cheap* rum and cheaper ale. For food, all we got is chicken and boiled potatoes with butter and sage. You take it for three copper, or you leave it, aye?"

Ealas was taken by surprise by the man's apparent aggression. Instinctively, he placed a hand over his sword sheath. If they knew who he was, they would never raise their voice at him, but they did not know, and it was best they never knew.

The woman at his side spat her drink as she laughed.

Fighting to contain his irritation, the nobleman faced her.

"Before you say something, she's mute," the server added.

"Oh, I am sorry," Ealas took a sip of the terrible-tasting drink and swallowed, pretending it was very palatable. The barkeep shook his head, chortling.

"Don't apologize, nobleman. I am not mute."

Her words made Ealas feel he was about to regurgitate his drink. "You're not mute!"

"No kidding! Surprised, are you?" she chuckled. "Name's Alasa," she added in a soft, Solorean accent that reminded him of his friend Siul and contrasted with her somewhat unkempt look. "They call me 'the bear.' People believe I fight like one, but the reality is I just love those creatures. I think the bear is my spirit animal."

"It should've been a parrot," the server interrupted.

"I'm . . . eh . . ."

"Hey, it's okay. You can use 'slave' if you want. Makes your introduction easier, actually, although you either need to lose it soon or get a manacle around your neck," Alasa winked.

"How did you know?"

"You just don't fit. Your accent, your poise. To someone like me, it's quite clear you don't belong here."

The woman's tone changed to one of mockery. "Add to that the fact that you ordered classy stuff in this not-so-classy place."

Alasa

Another crash, but this time the broken vessel was in the hands of an angry patron. "Oh sh . . .shuddup!"

Right in front of him, the victim lay on the ground, his mouth bleeding as his intoxicated screams resonated through the tavern.

"Whadda PHAKK!" Another man jumped on the first, arguing in unintelligible speech as both lost their balance.

Within a second, others around them joined the fight.

Ealas cringed and watched the tavern master's anger fume as he charged to break up the fight, followed by the Solorean woman.

Attracted by the commotion, a group of guards stormed in through the door.

Seeing Ealas place the sack hood over his head, Alasa came to his side.

"Pretend that you're kissing me."

Upon his hesitation, the woman discarded the idea. "Hey, forget it. Come with me," she nearly whispered, grabbing the back of his neck.

They escaped through the window, the woman leading the way toward a nearby two-story building.

"You can stay here if you want," Alasa said. "The Silent Stairs is an affordable inn. I stay there for months at a time. There's nothing special about it other than no one will look for you there. In that, I guess it's quite special."

Walking in, she reached for his pockets.

Swiftly, the nobleman caught her forearm.

"I'm *not* going to rob you!" Alasa scolded as their eyes met. There was a strange beauty in her mature eyes. "But I'm also *not* going to pay for your stay, you know."

He handed her the money requested by the innkeeper. "I'm sorry, it's just . . . I just feel like I know this city, and yet I feel lost."

"It's ok, I understand."

Alasa handed his change back. "Give me a few more coins if *you wish*. I'll break them for you and bring you some clothes. In this part of town, it is unusual to pay with gold unless you're desperate to attract the attention you surely don't want."

Handing her a few coins, Ealas nodded, rubbing his temples. For a learned man, he felt so ignorant. There was so much he needed to absorb and assimilate, and so fast.

"You look tired. Go rest. I'll meet you at the break of dawn here. We can break fast, and I'll have your coin. Perhaps then we can talk."

"Thanks, but I'm not sure I want to talk. I want to keep certain things to myself."

"What's up with you people always thinking the world revolves around yourself? It's like when one invites you out, you think it's a date. No! Sometimes people just want to go out with you! I said 'talk,' which means we can speak about anything, really. I never said, 'let's talk about you'!"

"Oh, I apologize."

"Stop it, really," she placed her palm over his mouth and a finger over her lips as a sign of silence.

"Don't ever apologize. You don't have to be sorry. Be sorry to yourself, and then, only about your situation."

Flipping one of his coins, and with a wink, she left, her braid awkwardly dancing behind.

THE KNIGHT OF LIGHT

Location: Kingdom of Ardenay,
Duchy of Himeland, Capital City of Himlen

Sometimes there's no better move than to stand still . . .

His knees, seasoned despite his young age, had never faltered.

Today, however, they felt as if they would give way at any moment under the weight of the news he carried.

The morning had gifted him with the most painful event, the surprise like an arrow through the heart of an indomitable warrior, one who had never been seen as a vulnerable man.

Siul Ileva now perhaps felt as the many men the young veteran had taken down in battle from a distance.

No . . .

This was worse, for at least they died from the wounds. He was very much alive, while with each beat, his heart wished he weren't.

Despite all the warring emotions inside, he had to act. There was a choice he had to make.

Choosing the right person to inform first about Ealas's abdication would avoid disrupting the delicate balance of power in Ardenay and, likely, all of Caelris.

Who to inform first when the head was gone, and the two remaining forces were opposed and equally powerful?

Siul walked the busy streets where greedy merchants attempted to shout over one another in search of those who would purchase their wares.

"Sir," a middle-aged man called, "would you bless me with a moment of your time?"

"I'm sorry," he raised his palm, "I don't have the time."

"You seem like something is not quite right." The merchant's words drew his attention.

"Alright," a feigned smile appeared on the Solorean knight's lips, "You called?"

"Yes, thank you, sir knight. You seemed pensive."

"Hmm, did I, now?"

"Oh yes, sir, and I may just be able to help you."

Help. . . that was the exact same word his lungs wanted to scream for the world to hear.

"How so?" the knight shifted his stance.

"Here, take a look at this!" The merchant drew a fine piece of fabric from a mound resting on a crate behind him. "This gray tunic will accentuate your handsome young eyes!"

Of course, Siul thought, *what else would he refer to if not to his trade?* Siul raised his hand to stop the merchant from insisting and began to turn away.

"No? Wait," the merchant's eyes opened wide as if he had just remembered a great discovery. "What about *this one*? I can promise you, sir knight, that all the maidens will be hypnotized, not able to think of anything other than you! They'll be obsessed!"

Obsessed is how he felt, not being able to dispel the thoughts running around his head like animals escaping a burning forest. A warrior could easily and quickly adapt on the battlefield, but this battlefield of emotions was an entirely different one.

Navigating the courts was something he understood quite well but as a knight of the Wing Army of Ileva. Siul was a warrior more than a courtesan, and politics were still something he didn't excel at, mostly because he had never truly been interested in more than being close to his friend. Still, he understood one thing well, both on the political and physical battlefields, every second was precious.

Snapping out of it, he looked at the man again.

"Look, sir knight," the man said, "I can promise you, you will never forget this!"

In his hands, the merchant now waved a plain royal blue fabric.

The same blue that was the backdrop of Ardenay's banner that, just as this piece of fabric, missed the lion at its center.

-------- ++++++ --------

He had prayed to the Lord of Light to direct him . . . and perhaps the god did, for either by his own will, by the guiding hand of the divine, or simply by an unconscious response to the religious influence that permeated his upbringing, he now stood at the end of the main hallway of the Grand Illuminated Cathedral, watching the eminent visage of Archbishop Angevin Arene, Patriarch of the Light, approach.

While Siul wasn't completely certain coming here first was the right move, at least he believed it would surely be judged as such by the eyes of the Omniscient Lord of Light.

The archbishop approached slowly, his face as immutable as it was heavily wrinkled. His ice-blue eyes were as firm as the jewel-mounted stand he carried as a sign indicating his status as an undisputed leader of the Church, were fixed on the young, handsome knight.

Siul Yleva

Around the pious man, seven altar boys stood ready to attend his every need, garbed in white as pure as his own robes, their garments embroidered, each in the sigil of one of the seven dioceses they had been chosen from within the religious duchy of Ashvail.[1]

Something about the older man's presence brought him to his knees.

"Holy Father," Siul said reverently.

"Blessed be the Light and those who carry it to enlighten the world," the old man responded.

"Bless my soul, Holy Father," Siul bowed.

"Your soul is blessed, my son," the holy man pointed his open palm at the knight as a sign of his benediction.

"I pray I have not disturbed you with my message," Siul looked up.

"The Light sees all, captain," the Archbishop smiled warmly. If one thing Angevin Arene had learned in so many years as the head of the Church in Ardenay was that sometimes just a gesture could ease the most troubled of souls. "It has seen the past, it sees the present, and foresees the future.

"As followers," he continued, "we must walk the way it sets for us. Nothing should ever disturb us enough to make us lose our peace.

"Please, stand, captain," he instructed, his voice calm and humble, "You have my ear and the eyes of the Light."

The knight produced the parchment left by Ealas. "Holy Father, here is the reason why I'm here."

One of the children took the document and unrolled the parchment, holding it up so that the Archbishop's aged eyes could read its contents with minimal effort.

Whispering what he read, the holy man took his time to carefully read every word before speaking again. "I see. Walk with me so that the Lord can illuminate us and so that we may determine the best direction we shall move toward."

He did not have to ask twice. Both men, trailed by the altar boys, moved along the long hallway, the sun's rays blessing them with their warmth as their luminescence descended through countless windows.

"Holy Father," the captain spoke. "I am somewhat troubled."

"Troubled?" The priest continued his slow walk. "Tell me what troubles you so that the Light can hear the confession of your lips and may put you at ease."

"Ealas has always been a friend."

"Every friend is also an enemy," the priest interrupted. "We only have enemies who act and enemies who don't. It is why the Lord says we must always keep our eyes open and walk in the path of the Light, where every evil of man will eventually be revealed."

"Yes, but I know his heart."

"No one truly knows a man's heart," the priest interjected, "not even himself."

"We grew up together!" The Solorean knight's retort came as an uncontrolled reflex. But he was quick enough to catch himself, and ashamed of his outburst, he approached the holy man to bend a knee and ask for forgiveness. But Archbishop Angevin Arene just shook his head slightly while his hand signaled that, for forgiveness, there was no need.

"You grew up *together*." As they neared the garden, the priest continued, "A cobra does not dance for a mouse to make him a friend. Its dance hypnotizes the rodent so that it is never ready for the strike."

"Pardon me, Your Holiness, but he has shown me what a true friend is."

"A *true friend* that did not tell you what was hidden in his heart. One that lets you find out *like the rest of us*."

The archbishop's soft words dug into the fresh wound. He was right. The priest spoke words of wisdom that the faithful would never dare question, and if one thing Siul certainly was, it was a man of faith.

Moments felt like minutes as they walked along the garden without the exchange of words.

"Holy Father," Siul broke the uncomfortable silence, "I think . . . perhaps the burden of the Crown was too much to bear. With loyal advisers at his side he—"

"What we think does not matter in the eyes of the Almighty," the priest's eyes looked into Siul's intently, "for he knows all."

"Blessed be the Almighty," the young knight lowered his head in reverence. "I do feel, however, that—"

Archbishop
Augevin Arene

"What he *feels* is the principle that should guide us always, for it comes from what he *knows*." The priest did not even allow him a moment of respite before his words, again, silenced him.

The precepts of the Church, at times, seemed strange, at times conflicting. Siul remembered discussing these with Ealas on occasion. In the end, they always concluded, even if they didn't agree with them, who would challenge a god, especially one that had blessed and protected their kingdom for centuries?

"Holy Father," the young knight asked again, "we don't have a precedent for this event. What will happen now? What will happen to Ealas's kingdom?"

At the honorific, the holy man suddenly halted his advance. "A man who has abdicated his throne is not a king, my child . . . As to what will happen, the Council must meet and decide under the ever-watchful eyes of the Lord."

"We must move with haste then and inform the dukes."

"Haste is a great friend and an unforgiving enemy, Siul Ileva. Yes, we must move, we must act, but more than that, we must pray faithfully and think carefully." The archbishop interrupted. "The dukes are departing to their own lands. There is no telling who will be informed in time before they take their leave. It is important no duke feels slighted by having others informed before they themselves are. I am sure you understand the feeling ... I can only imagine how you must have felt by not hearing the news from Ealas himself."

Siul felt a pressure building inside his chest, one that did not let him pronounce a word for fear of showing the weakness his heart felt.

As a veteran preacher, Archbishop Angevin knew quite well when to change his tone to lighten someone's mood. "Have you informed Duke Yel Ileva?"

"No, Your Holiness."

The Holy Father was perhaps taken by surprise. That the knight had not even informed his own father spoke volumes of the trust he had for the Church. "Doesn't that *trouble* you?"

"It does feel *strange*, I must say. My lord father would want to be informed, but he is also a man of God, and he will surely understand why I did not inform him first."

The archbishop resumed his walk while still addressing the young man. "The Lord is Father, and the only father mankind will ever need. We must be grateful children and honor him with every action, with every word. Have you informed House Heikken yet?"

"No," Siul lowered his head again.

"They might already know by now."

If at *these* words or at the prospect of having the upper hand over the royals, Siul couldn't tell, but the archbishop seemed to be smiling.

"Perhaps not. I brought the letter." His eyes brightened.

"But not the Crown." The archbishop's smile now did not seem as warm.

"Aorius Heikken is not a man to miss details. Because of this, we must then move with haste."

(1) The Duchy of Ashvail was the religious center of Ardenay. The Grand Illuminated Cathedral in Himlen was only rivaled in size by the majesty of the Cathedral in Zagos, Ashvail's capital. Ashvail itself was divided into seven dioceses, each presided over by a bishop. The Archbishop title was always reserved for a bishop from Ashvail, who would be served by seven altar boys, each one hailing from each diocese.

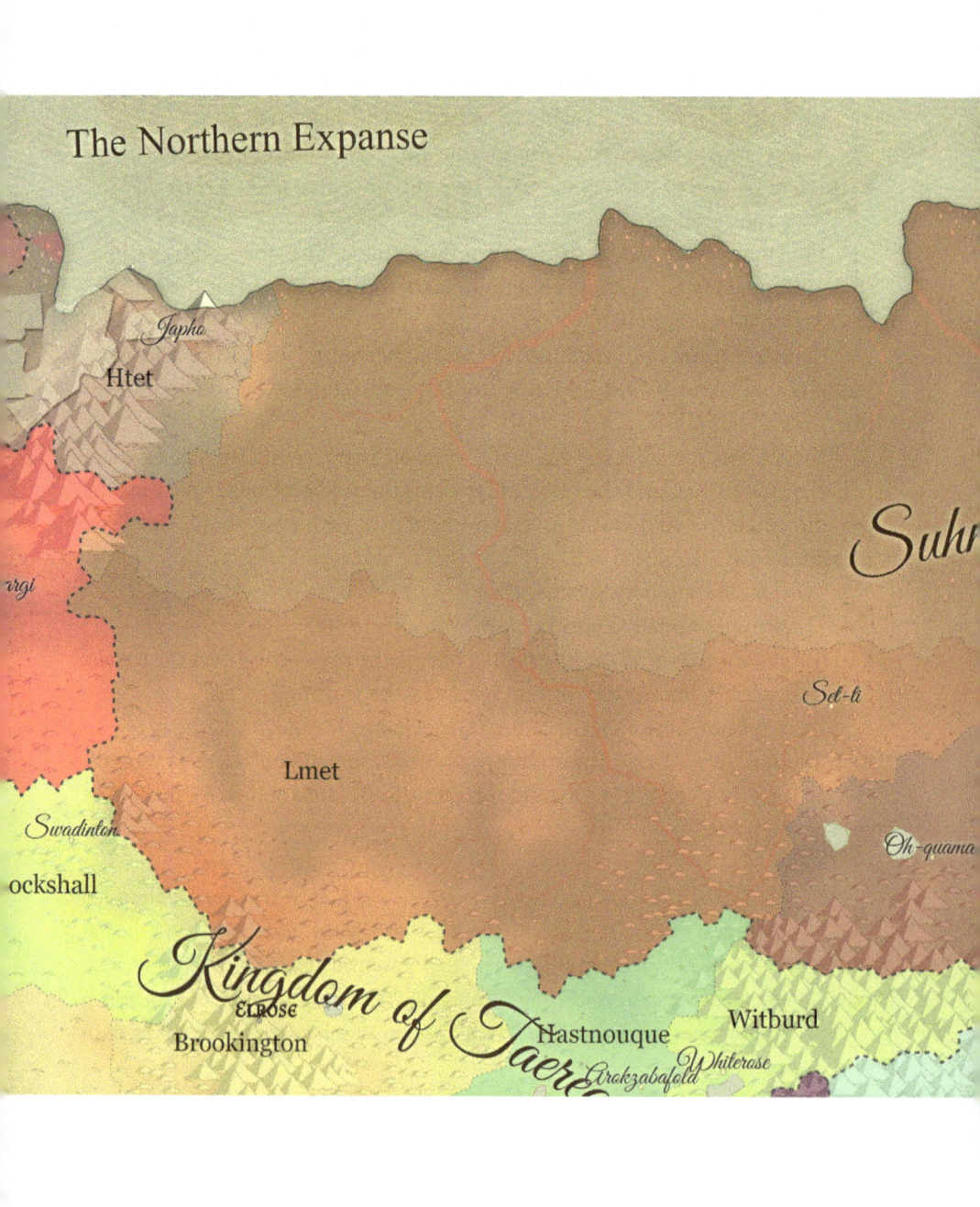

The Northern Expanse

Japho

Htet

rgi

Suhr

Set-ti

Lmet

Swadinton

Oh-quama

ockshall

Kingdom of Jaere

ELROSE

Witburd

Brookington

Hastnouque

Arokzabafold Whiterose

ror
nor

Empyre

City of Suhne
CITY OF SUHNE

Elbu

Kliba

Uhn

Kuloq

Shimmering Gulf

The Barren Sea

Alm

Nag-lelo

ii

Skyreach
Omikholm

Valador/Volanar

Duskforge

Shalrech

THE MARKING

Location: Empyre of Suhne,
Capital City of Suhne, Palace of the Sun

The time approaches...

*T*he whisper reverberated through the blackness that surrounded her.
Her eyes opened wide, but she could still only see impenetrable darkness, nothing more than the emptiness of the void.

'Where is this?' Vamya thought she asked, but no answer came, for she was alone in this place, if 'this' was even a place.

'Am I alone?' she asked herself, moving her hands to her face. Yet, no matter how close she got them, she still couldn't see.

And just as she couldn't see, or say, or hear anything, she believed she heard a rustle somewhere ahead.

'I am not alone.' How far, she couldn't tell, but she did notice that the rustling didn't leave an echo. Her eyes were as good as blind but somehow captured movement in the blackness that surrounded her.

'The time is nearing.' Once again, nothing more than a whisper.

'Who are you?' she asked, yet no response came.

She didn't know what or who it was or even if it was anything other than her mind playing tricks on her.

But one thing she knew, it felt different.

While it was not seen, she was certain it was there.

"The time has come." It was close to the break of dawn when the woman's hand touched her shoulder, rousing Vamya from her deep slumber.

Her eyes adjusted quickly, aided by the oil lamps in the hands of the other women who had come to her chamber to assist in her preparation.

Vamya sat on her bed to collect herself and think of what that dream could mean if dreams *did* mean anything.

'Should people conduct their lives according to what transpires in their dreams?' she pondered. 'If not, then why should people aspire to even achieve their dream.'

"Allow us to help you, Blessed One." The leading woman held her arm, signaling to the others to assist.

One week had transpired since the ceremonial burning of the Sun—one week of prayer, meditation, and for Vamya and her siblings, of fasting in preparation for the mark of the Sun.

"Here," the woman held a cup for her, "have some sweet water. The Sun knows you'll need it. This will be a long day."

The heir imbibed. Each step she took toward the pool in her chamber made her legs twitch. Even the aroma of the dried herbs floating on its surface that would normally lift her up did nothing but confuse her.

She submerged herself in the warm water, that realm where she could distance herself from the world. Vamya brought her hands together and closed her eyes so that she could travel from that realm and into her own.

⁙⁘

The procession that escorted her left by the same entrance they had come through moments before, as waves leaving a shore they had just touched.

She found herself wearing nothing but a green tunic inside the dome of one of the tallest palace buildings, in one of the sacred chambers that was used only on special events such as today's.

At its center, an elderly pair, a man and a woman, sat cross-legged, their heads bowed as they recognized her. "Good rising, Blessed Vamya of Suhne."

Between the two rested a small bed, barely a foot off the floor, and a small mirror. To each of their sides, a series of vials, mortars, and other instruments their aged hands surely knew well.

"Son of the Sun," the man said, "this is a crucial moment of the journey you must go through in preparation for your Ascendancy. We bless you so that you might bless us when your time comes."

"How holy can our actions be," the woman continued, "if our appearance is not that of the divine? Through our body's semblance, our spirit is judged. Can you please say the words?"

Vamya nodded slightly before reciting the words they awaited, the ones they had learned, those she needed not only to know but had been taught to profess and believe. "While our actions are ever important. Our body's appearance is a sign of our spirituality. It shows our holiness."

"Blessed One," the woman then said, "our greatest honor is to mark your body."

She then pointed at the bed. "Let us start. The Sun is about to rise."

Vamya removed her clothes and placed her body on the surface of the hard bed. High above her eyes, she could see the glass dome and beyond, the night receding before the bronze power of the Eye of the Sun.

The moment the Sun's disk first broke the heavens saw the pair lift their hands in a sign of praise, elated.

"Blessed be the Sun, He who shines forever. Blessed are we, for we live to serve."

Wetting a piece of cloth, she commenced wiping Vamya's body as she began her chant with a low hum that later switched into syllabic intonations of the old language of Suhne and other words Vamya could not understand. Her counterpart, in turn, lit sandalwood incense. He then lifted his tools, one by one, for the Sun to bless.

Anxiety crept in. Despite her lifelong preparation, nothing could possibly feel like the moment itself one had prepared for.

Her musings were interrupted by the man's ceremonial taking of a thin brush, and, closing his eyes, he inhaled the aroma of sandalwood that permeated the room. Delicately, he placed the tip of the brush against Vamya and proceeded to glide it softly against her skin.

The dry brush traveled through each arm, each leg, even through her chest and abdomen, always leaving an invisible path that repeated itself as he came back to the same area as if the man knew and saw exactly what to draw.

After long and slow repetitions, he took the brush in one hand and a small spoon with ground emerald dust in the other. Meanwhile, the woman continued her chant, pausing only for breath, holding a round, convex crystal in her hands.

Once again, he led the pattern, drawing invisibly on her skin. This time, however, it was trailed by the hands of his companion as she held the round crystal a few inches off Vamya's skin. It captured what it could of sunlight, concentrating it so that every ray would coalesce in one particular spot of the heir's skin.

A terrible burn . . .

Every inch of her body through which the path was being drawn was exposed to a sharp pain that felt as if someone was skinning Vamya alive. She wanted to scream, droplets of sweat forming on her forehead and ignored by the couple.

Fortunately, the light just touched the skin for mere seconds at a time, causing enough damage to burn some of it off but not enough to cause disfiguration.

Still, it would be hours of torture under the merciless job of the markers before she could simply have some respite.

Yet, there was no other option. Not tolerating the pain would simply show an heir to be *unworthy*, remaining then, forever, *unascended*.

It was only after the pass was done Vamya realized another one would follow, one that would feel worse, if it were even possible, for it would burn the same areas that were already injured.

Blood started dripping from Vamya's skin, blood that was quickly cauterized by the burning and by the left hand of the marker, who covered each wound in emerald dust.

The Blessed One turned her head, grinding her teeth in desperation. Despite what felt like endless torture, despite the dehydration and discomfort, even despite the flames in the oil lamps, which danced mockingly at her suffering, her emerald eyes did not cry.

'Where can I find strength?'

Vamya closed her eyes and sought to remove herself.

Her eyes looked up to the domed ceiling, to the Eye of the Sun above shining down furiously at noon, and she asked herself, *'Where is my refuge? Where can I find help when my god and everything I believe in is gone?'*

But, like many times before, she shook her head. *'I must dismiss what troubles me.'*

Her chest rose with a deep breath and fell. It was hard to disconnect herself without silence, without calm and peace . . . and yet she needed to, for it would otherwise be impossible to withstand the agony for much longer without giving up.

'I must dismiss what troubles me.'

She found herself sitting on the bed of the quiet chamber where the woman's lips moved silently, and the man drew on her skin . . . or at least on the skin of the chest her being had just separated from, for although she couldn't feel anything, her body still lay there, twitching and wincing.

She clearly saw the woman's hand collecting the bright beams of light into the round crystal she used to mark her body. The Blessed eyes saw the Eye of the Sun above, staring at her through the dome, looking magnificent and ever-powerful while protecting itself from her reach.

Pushing herself off the bed surface, the heir levitated upward toward the dome's center when a sudden wave of pain coursed through her, stopping her in midair. *She looked down to see her body, trembling, sweating profusely, her blood staining the bed, and yet none of these stopped her. She fought on.*

'Strange,' Vamya thought for a second. She had never felt anything physical while present in this realm. Just as it appeared, however, the sensation was gone.

Time was of the essence.

Resuming her climb, the great domes of the city started appearing through the glass dome. Even the expanse of the lands around its vicinity could easily be appreciated. Halfway, her ascension suddenly stopped by a searing pain that struck both her wrists and ankles simultaneously.

Looking down, she could see each limb attached to a chain link that went through her own skin and bone, and on the other side, the chains fastened the same way to her inert body's palms and soles.

And just as fast, the pain disappeared once more.

Gazing above, Vamya wondered how much longer it would be before she got to the top of the dome when a third time, the searing pain castigated her. This time, however, it was followed by a jerking motion from below.

Bothered, the Blessed One looked down for the culprit, but the flickering oil lamps allowed her to appreciate only that the shadows in the room appeared to have deepened as they toyed with the minuscule flames while the chain between her and her body had become shorter.

Right before her eyes, she saw the chain starting to sink through her body's hands and feet as if the skin itself was devouring them.

It dragged her being once more, and the pain felt increasingly worse and lasted a few moments longer each time.

'No!' Vamya thought, reaching up to the heavens with arms that were stopped midway by the tugging chains that now felt heavy.

It was then Vamya felt something beneath, a force bigger than she was, something she could not allow to swallow her being. She fought fiercely, with all the strength she could muster, against this ravenous gravity that wanted her.

I might be able to break these chains. Her thoughts disappeared upon the gut-wrenching scream that accompanied the forceful extension of her limbs, the clenching of her fists, and the writhing of her torso from the indescribable pain.

If the markers had paid attention, perhaps they would have seen her eyes wide open, fixed on the Sun above her head, her irises having turned the color of the purest peridot refracting sunbeams through its center before returning to her deep emerald green.

But they did not. Their work continued mercilessly and yet patiently while Vamya's emeralds hid behind her eyelids, and she lost herself.

Once again, the scent of sandalwood.

Vamya's eyes once again opened to see the Sun above had long passed the afternoon.

Dizzy and confused, she looked around for the markers she couldn't, at first, find, for they were prostrated by the side of her bed, repeating time and again, "Blessed be the Eternal Sun, and blessed are we, who live to worship."

What was left of her strength she used to lift herself off the bed, grasping the sheets which had contained her blood that now cracked and fell in pieces, as the dried leaves of a bloody fall.

She walked toward the mirror to see her exhausted face that, while clean, contrasted the body below her neck. It was still naked but ridden with mystic, swirling patterns burned into her skin and cured with the emerald dust that now left its color in her marks.

'Who would go through something like this and live, or worse, remain sane?' Vamya asked herself, taking the only water cup by the reflective surface.

But she dismissed the question. There were things one had no business questioning. All that mattered was her brothers were somewhere, in two other chambers in the palace, living through the same ordeal.

And even that did not matter.

All she could think of at this moment was she had never appreciated water as much.

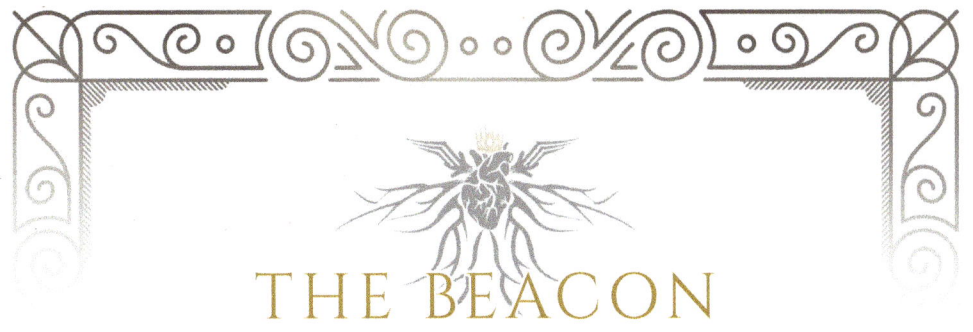

THE BEACON

Location: Kingdom of Ardenay, Royal Duchy of Himeland,
Capital City of Himlen, Palace of the Beacon

"It is never to show respect that hyenas approach a carcass..."

*G*randiose.

The mere word would be considered an understatement, perhaps even an insult in the eyes of any member of the Royal House of Heikken if it were ever used to describe the Royal Council Chamber of Himlen, capital of Ardenay.

The majestic beauty of the capital itself was said to surpass that of its sister city in the neighboring kingdom of Daneran to the west, for while Daneran had once been the eye-capturing center of the Church of Light, its more militaristic focus had allowed the church architects to thrive without limitation among the people of Ardenay.

The architectural design of all royal structures had been said to have been inspired by the God of Light himself and, as it was said of every work of the Holy God, no word of mortal tongue would ever do its grandeur justice.

White were the walls that lined floor-to-ceiling with a highly detailed yet perfectly etched symmetrical design that seduced the eyes, guiding them toward one side of the circular chamber where the throne of the monarch rested.

And the throne itself was a sight to behold.

Its dais rose nearly ten feet, elevated by an array of columns and stairsteps sculpted from white marble depicting angelic beings that carried lanterns in a humble offering.

The seat itself was polished smooth, with swirling, engraved detailing that served to ensure all attention was always centered on the monarch as the blessed representative of the Light.

Lining the wall of the chamber, four other seats stood, also raised and sculpted from beautiful, plain marble. Each one was identical, adorned only by the presence of the dukes who sat on them during their meetings.

While prominently elevated, these fixed seats stood nearly half the distance from the ground, and just two feet below them, each was surrounded by the only distinguishing feature—heavy, white cedar chairs that varied in number according to the regions comprising each grand duchy.

To the right of the throne sat the Dukes of Bulwharf and Alcyn, the one with two seats and the latter with a quintet.

To its left, the Duke of Walcrast, with its four regional seats, followed by the seat of Duke of Ashvail, the Holy Duchy and most important arm of the Church, with a seat for each of its seven principalities.

Varen Bulwharf's brow had furrowed the moment he received the news of Ealas's disappearance a few days ago. Since then, he had spoken little, waiting for details from the Council itself before he would comment or make a move regarding him, who had been his closest friend.

The Bulwharf's eyes looked at the seats under him. They were empty, as he would expect, for each of the two representatives of his duchy stood, disciplined and proud, while most of those from the other duchies, just as their own dukes, sat calmly.

Having ruled for nearly five years, Varen had been the newest member of the Council. Perhaps the others were already comfortable in their positions, but one thing he had promised himself, for as long as he was the Lord Bull, for his nation and his king, he would always proudly stand.

The distant melody of the pipe ranks interrupted his thoughts, the same that announced the assembly of these most powerful lords in Ardenay. The head organist's hands would play each key and his feet each pedal with such grace, his essence and that of the instrument nearly merged into one.

Outside the royal palace, the organ's echo would command a moment of reverence from nearby believers, sending some to their knees to pray the Light would bless their leaders so that their meetings would bear good fruit.

"Lord Aorius Heikken," the herald raised his voice inside the chamber, immediately prompting everyone to stand, "of the Royal House of Heikken, Duke of the Royal Duchy of Himeland, Count of Himlen Vale, and ruling Baron of Himlen."

Duke Aorius Heikken walked in as a renowned veteran would march toward the approving eyes of his general. His stature was dominant, his chest broad, his face and body stern and well-built. Six decades had not made him any weaker of a man. Quite the contrary, they had made him a most fearsome lion. The deep blue of his clothes only served to accentuate the cold steel in his gaze. His short, dull gray cape trailed behind as he took his place on the dais from where he now faced the rest.

His counterparts nodded quietly as he did, albeit slightly, in turn.

"Our Most Holy Father," the herald announced next, "the Archbishop Angevin Arene, Chosen of God, Patriarch of the Light, He Who Keeps the Darkness at Bay."

The archbishop entered with a steady pace, carrying the sacred staff, its jeweled head that represented the Light captured everyone's eyes. Despite being shorter and less imposing and over a decade older than Aorius, he walked fast, dragging his grand blue-and-gold-trimmed robes behind as if his own holiness could not be contained by mere mortal vestments.

Taking his place to the left of the throne, the Holy Father smiled as he saw everyone present lowering their head, waiting for his benediction.

Varen, too, lowered his head, but not after having seen everyone else do the same, everyone but Duke Aorius, who nodded slightly and kept his eyes open, and the archbishop himself, who seemed to hesitate before speaking as if wanting to enjoy the reverence given a moment longer.

"Blessed be the Light and those who carry it to enlighten the world. May the Darkness always recede in your presence."

"The Crown of Ardenay," the herald raised his voice, allowing the last entrance before the double doors to the chamber were closed.

All attention was on the entrance where, for the first time in over nine centuries, the crown was no longer resting on the head of a Heikken, of any man even. This time it rested on a deep-blue cushion carried in the hands of a young page, a young boy who walked solemnly toward the throne, where he laid it to rest.

Filled with uneasiness, those present stirred.

Varen Bulwharf shut his eyes firmly. How could a material crown have so much power over men? he thought. It was not simply a crown, he realized, but instead everything it represented: the wars, the laws, the lives, and the history of the most powerful men of the most powerful kingdom in Caelris that commanded all attention.

And that attention which brought a great sense of security and stability, now brought great strain, for the crown that had been taken just a few days ago now lay abandoned, like a virgin who had been displayed just for show before the man who had used her left her. Worse than that, the perpetrator had been someone he had called a friend and not just a friend, but the best among them.

An uncomfortable silence ensued. Without a king to begin the meeting, there was no obvious way to start, but that silence did not last long.

"Uplifted Dukes of Ardenay," Duke Aorius began, "thank you for returning with such short notice, but we face a pressing matter, surely you must have heard by now, that which has required us to reconvene—"

"There is no reason to be alarmed," the archbishop interrupted, making Aorius clench his jaw. "The Light knows all, and the Church is promptly working to ensure stability."

"The royal crown provides stability," Duke Aorius spoke, more to Angevin than the rest.

"And yet here it rests on a cushion," Angevin smiled, "idly."

"But please, don't misunderstand me," the priest continued, "our God wants nothing more than stability and prosperity for Ardenay and his people."

"Then we should all be glad the Light's interests are aligned with our own," Aorius's sarcasm was not lost on the priest.

"My lords," he addressed the rest, "as Duke of the Royal Duchy and representative of the Royal House of Heikken, it falls to me to inform you that my nephew, King Ealas Heikken, has disappeared from our midst."

His words provoked a wave of murmurs around the room.

"His whereabouts are unknown," he continued, raising his hand in an attempt to silence the room. "Our search in and around the palace grounds have so far proven fruitless."

"Lord Aorius," Anderei Magenan, Paladin Lord of Ashvail, interrupted, "with all due respect, how certain are we of this disappearance?" Several of the principals under him nodded in agreement with their middle-aged lord.

"We are," Aorius responded. "It is clear my nephew has not been attending to his duties, just as you do not see him here today. The details of his disappearance, however, are in the hands of the archbishop."

Angevin's countenance did not change, not even the slightest, but Varen Bulwharf observed how his fingers clutched the body of his staff while the Paladin Lord lent his ear to several of his principals' whispers.

"Is this true, Holy Father?" Varen asked. "Could you please explain what Lord Aorius is referring to?"

"We believe his disappearance to be true, my lords," Angevin's voice was as calm as a lake's surface. "We are awaiting further news. In the meantime, we are praying and working hard to first confirm what has come to our attention." Varen saw a glint in the eyes of the Lion, a smile short of a smirk that had found a moment to pounce.

"Can the rest of us see *the letter*?" Aorius asked, his words coursing like swift and effective venom.

"Letter?" Varen immediately questioned.

"What *letter*?" Lord Orionne Eomener's chin-below-his-chin trembled when he spoke at last. The merchant Lord of Silver had always been as practical as he was large, weighing in mostly to make final decisions, but the insinuation of something hidden moved him to intervene immediately, "And if there is a letter, why do we have to ask about it?"

Without hesitating, the Holy Father produced the scroll from under his sleeve before anyone could inquire further, "This scroll still holds pieces of the royal seal. It was entrusted to me as a neutral arbiter."

"By whom?" Varen Bulwharf's suspicion was raised.

"By someone whose identity I must protect, in the confidence of our Lord Savior of the Light.

"Please," the holy man continued, "allow me to read it fully before we can discuss it."

> 'I, Ealas Heikken, King of Ardenay, Bearer of the Light, and Blessed of the Heavens, have found that my thoughts are not my own anymore. Lately, my heart has been drifting away from everything I have always thought I had known. While hardships might come from my decisions, hardships of the soul will undoubtedly befall me if I were not to make them. In order to avoid dishonoring my own, I forsake all my titles, I forsake my name, and I do so gladly, proudly, knowing Ardenay will not have a lack of great leaders who will stand up to the task. Hereby, thus, I abdicate the throne. I have decided to leave, to find my way, to become a beggar in the land of Blood, for one thing I have learned, that in that land, having nothing, I will have more than here having everything.'
>
> —*Ealas Heikken the First, King of Ardenay,*
> *Bearer of the Light and Blessed of the Heavens*

"Why do I have to hear about this with everyone else?" Aorius demanded.

"My Lord Heikken," the archbishop smiled, "you may be the Duke of the Royal Duchy, but still a duke and the will of the Crown of Ardenay has always been that every lord in this Council is treated the same."

"Why are we finding out about this *now*?" Varen argued, his brow furrowed as the furious bulls that represented his people.

"For safety reasons, my lord," Angevin responded calmly.

"Safety?" the Duke of Ashvail questioned. "Your Eminence, you are talking about our head of state moving into the lands of Darkness, which places the world in danger. I would expect the heads of the Church to be more concerned."

"Holy Champion," the priest spoke calmly. "We are concerned, no doubt about it, but we also know the Darkness is dangerously shrewd. King Ealas may very well still be within the royal duchy, while his mind might well be under the control of the deceiver."

"If he passed through our lands, we should have known," the Bulwharf frowned. "I have no doubts our forces would have searched and intercepted him. There is no way they could have slipped through."

"*They?*" Duke Aorius questioned.

"It is no secret I have been close to Ealas for most of my life," Varen responded, secretly lamenting the growing distance between them as of late, "but these do not sound like words from the Ealas I know. The Ealas Heikken I grew up around wanted nothing more than to become our king. He must have been influenced, even captured. It is unlikely he is traveling alone."

"I agree with Lord Varen Bulwharf," Duke Yel Ileva of Walcrast added. "Something doesn't feel right. Walcrast's forces are the best trained and most powerful in the kingdom, and they know the layout of our lands quite well. Had we been informed appropriately and in a timely manner, we could have been meeting today with King Ealas himself to discuss other matters."

"Regarding the 'best trained' or 'most powerful', Lord Ileva, the entirety of my great duchy will disagree with you, Lord Ileva. But aside from that. I agree with your sentiment," Varen affirmed, "as ruling lords of this Council, this delay in informing us is a grave matter."

"There is definitely an explanation," the archbishop said.

"Holy Father," Yel Ileva spoke from under his pronounced mustache, "pardon me, but there's no need to explain. Discussing that now will change nothing."

"It does nothing but erode our trust," Lord Eomener half smiled.

"Let us not judge precipitously," Duke Magenan lifted a hand. "Certainly, our Holy Father must have had a good reason."

All eyes were on the archbishop, all ears ready for his response. "Surely, and the erosion of the foundation of our trust is what the Darkness would attack first. The Codex of Radiance, Book of Innocent, chapter two, verse nine reads, 'My heart never faltered, it strayed not, for I understood in the wisdom provided by the Light that affirmation is cemented by confirmation and not by doubt.' Blessed be the Light."

Immediately, Yel Ileva's blue shoulder cape moved as he nodded in agreement with the words of the religious leader, echoing the words of others in the room.

"It is in this spirit of the search for the truth that the Church has launched an investigation into the true whereabouts of King Ealas Heikken," the archbishop explained, "so that we can contribute information and not confusion."

"Please," Varen stood in place and spoke in earnest, "do not take me wrong in any way, Holy Father, but isn't it the duty of the Crown, and upon its absence, the Uplifted Council to investigate? To ensure we keep our kingdom safe?"

The archbishop still smiled, although, to Varen, it seemed as if that smile was struggling to survive. His gaze drifted toward Duke Aorius Heikken, who didn't smile but also didn't have to. His leonine eyes told, without a doubt, he was pleased.

"Indeed, we are thankful for the interest and intervention," Aorius raised his voice, "but it is not necessary for the Church to take that role. It is the duty of the Royal Crown."

"My lords," the Paladin of Ashvail stood, as did the principals who had just whispered to him, "the throne sits empty. The Crown is restless. In order to prevent unrest in our people, the Church can provide the advice and guidance we require."

"We don't *require* guidance, my lord Anderei," Aorius took a step forward, suddenly appearing taller than he was. "Uplifted Lords of Ardenay," he said, "the world cannot suffer the throne of Ardenay remaining empty. While we spend time investigating, our enemies will claw at our borders. They will grow in power and influence while our throne will grow weaker as it sits unfilled for an unknown amount of time."

"Without a doubt, it seems you want to ensure the crown returns to the hands of House Heikken," Sir Anderei's many medals sang as he refuted.

"Lord Magenan," the lion furrowed his brow. "I can tell you without a doubt it never left them."

A few moments passed before the archbishop spoke again. "The Lord of Light wants nothing more than peace and prosperity in our land and beyond its borders. To do so, the Church has stepped up to become a neutral, unbiased arbiter in these most important and stressful of times."

"Except for the fact that said unbiased arbiter controls an entire duchy." With a few words, Duke Aorius had slapped everyone's faces. While there was a balance of power among the duchies in Ardenay, it was a known fact that Duke Anderei Magenan, the Paladin Lord, was, despite all his titles, nothing more than the representative of the actual rulers of Ashvail, the seven principals of the Church.

"My lords," Orionne Eomener of Alcyn spoke next, "the stability of the kingdom is of utmost importance, as it affects us all. Any disturbance of that stability alerts the eye of our greedy neighbors. What best options do we have to avoid stalling in these discussions, to ascertain we remain strong?"

"I agree there has been enough of this discussion. There is no time to be wasted," with a quick stride, Aorius reached for the throne, his hands close to touching the reflective golden circlet of the crown. "As the highest-ranking representative of the Royal House of Heikken, I will take the crown."

"That's preposterous!" Sir Anderei Magenan's protests were echoed by his men.

"Our priority must be to remain in a position of strength in the eyes of our enemies," Aorius claimed, his eyes fixed on the sapphire blue mounted on the circlet.

"Yes," the archbishop responded, "but things are not as simple. The God of Light wants the Church to ensure Ardenay doesn't just remain strong, but actually *becomes* stronger."

"And what better to tell our God we will ensure the kingdom's legacy continues?" Aorius's fingers wrapped around the cold metal of the crown.

An uncomfortable silence followed before the archbishop spoke once more, "Man can never order our God. One must always humbly submit to his will."

"Oh, I'm certain you can convince him." While Aorius's brother had not been the most pious of men, at least he had reserved respect for the Church and its leadership. Aorius's insolence, however, had only grown over the years.

"My lord," the archbishop stood face to face with him, "for all we know, King Ealas may or may not have written that letter. We must first be certain."

Aorius smirked, "And what of the stability of the kingdom the Light *wants?*"

The reflection of Angevin Arene's smile could almost be seen in the mounted crystal of his staff. "For that, we must pray. Moving fast toward a second coronation after just one would be most chaotic, something hard for the masses to grasp and understand."

"They *will* have to understand. Today, tomorrow, whenever, they will understand," Aorius responded. "Better to understand now during the time of peace than to be forced to accept it during the struggle of an invasion wrought by our enemies. In the meantime," he smiled slyly back at Angevin, "you can take your time *praying* with the Holy Mother, whose support you'll need to deny me the crown."

Angevin's smile became less sincere. Aorius had just reminded him, and everyone else, that since its foundation, the Church had not one, but two heads and that every major decision had to be agreed to by both.

Upon his hesitation, Aorius raised the crown over his head, "I, Aorius of House Heikken, rightful heir to the throne, will take the crown that, through the power of my lineage, through the purity of my blood, belongs to me.

"As the rightful heir, you will all now bend your knee."

Varen Bulwharf's knee was the first one to touch the ground, followed by the fanatical Orionne from Alcyn, who struggled with his weight. Lord Yel of Walcrast hesitated briefly but nonetheless bent his knee.

Only the Paladin Lord remained standing, as did the archbishop. He was militarily powerful and loyal, but he had the interest of the Church at heart.

"It is now or never," Aorius warned Lord Magenan. The Paladin hesitated for a moment, his eyes meeting those of the archbishop briefly.

In a sudden, unexpected move, his knee kissed the ground.

"Now *crown* me, priest," he commanded the holy man who remained standing, "or I will crown myself."

Those present waited expectantly as Angevin moved slowly and placed the crown on Aorius's head.

Aorius stood firm, his chest prominent, planting his foot on the land he would call his. While any man would have shirked away, intimidated by the presence of the royal lord, the archbishop did not, for while Aorius was the proud lion, Angevin was the quiet hunter.

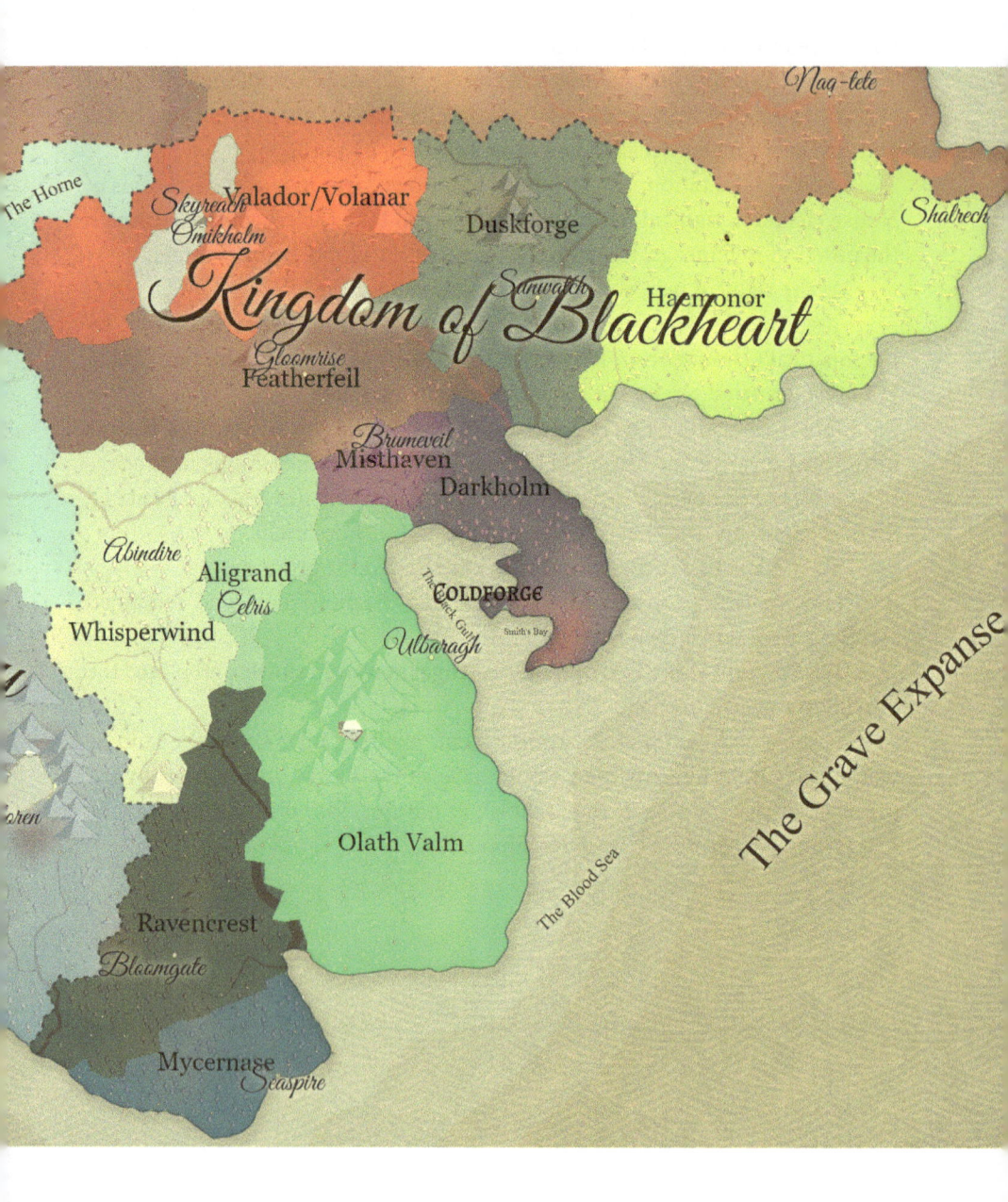

The Horne

Skyreach
Omikholm

Valador/Volanar

Duskforge

Naq-tete

Shatrech

Kingdom of Blackheart

Sanwatch

Haemonor

Gloomrise
Featherfeil

Brumeveil
Misthaven

Darkholm

Abindire

Aligrand
Celris

Whisperwind

COLDFORGE

The Crack Gulf

Ulbaragh

Smith's Bay

The Grave Expanse

oren

Olath Valm

The Blood Sea

Ravencrest

Bloomgate

Mycernase
Seaspire

THE GREAT COUNCIL

Location: Kingdom of Blackheart,
Royal Duchy of Darkholm, Darkholde Keep

D arkholde Keep rested upon the cliffs at the end of the world, on a rocky peninsula that seemed small thanks to the sheer vastness of the architectural wonder.

Despite its spacious corridors and many hallways that could accommodate numerous people, its lords had preferred to remain largely detached from the world of men.

Therefore, upon its construction, the Darkholm had built a smaller castle that would serve to house the Black Knights while keeping their lords protected. This castle was Ironholde, and all interactions with the outside world were conducted within its dark, granite walls.

Inside its main building, known as the Tower, meeting rooms, where both the ducal and royal courts were held, were located, with the sinister presence of Darkholde appearing to be keeping a distant, perennial watch through its many tall windows.

It was here where the ruling class of Blackheart held its most important of meetings, the Great Council of Dukes.

Twelve chairs stood along the curved side of the large, semicircular table at the center of the Council chamber. Each piece had been carefully carved, as ordered since the time of the former kingdom of Celeas, from the most abundant wood in the land each ducal seat represented. Despite their slight differences in polish or density of their material, to an untrained eye, they seemed to be copies of each other.

Erdrick Darkholm's cape trailed behind as he entered the chamber. He was followed by the larger figure of his cousin, Gustavus, who studied everyone present before setting his bright yellow eyes upon the perfectly carved black heart of the kingdom that served as the centerpiece of the table.

Upon their entrance, not one of the dukes moved. At the announcement and entrance of the one who followed, however, all the noblemen moved. They rose from their seats and took a knee to the side, allowing each backrest to show the carved sigil of their respective duchy. From the turquoise moon of Duskforge to the ship of Mycernase and even the pampas white around the windmills of Whisperwind, all sigils had been masterfully represented by the greatest royal artisans as a way to honor each land. Gustavus noted that the dukes' heads bowed in no way to salute the son but instead to the man in white, he who wore the crown of Blackheart.

King Septem nodded to the Council, his striking, golden eyes meeting those of each one present, before taking his place at the long side of the table.

After the monarch, the dukes took their places, followed by the Council advisers sitting on either side of the monarch.

"Lord Dukes of Blackheart. I salute you all," the king spoke through lips that barely moved. "Baron Evarde Bishop," Septem directed his attention toward a middle-aged adviser, "what has been discussed?"

"Your Majesty," the man stood from his seat and began his report, "Duskforge Duchy has established a new mining region. Its production of ore should increase noticeably within the next season. Duke Arcanmene has offered to pay some of the kingdom taxes in brute ore to reduce the financial burden on his people."

"Was it granted?"

"It was unnecessary, my Lord King. The duchies of Haemonor, Valador, and Volanar have offered to increase their purchase of ore, providing Duskforge with the coin it needs.

"Secondly," he continued, "some of Ravencrest's larger crops, mostly vineyards, have been infected with grubs and lost. Duke and Duchess von Corvus have requested either a delay in payment or a small, temporary reduction in taxes until they can settle this. They are offering to pay back whatever the amount is reduced by now at a later time. This has been granted. Lord Aubin Raine of Whisperwind has offered assistance. He is sending agricultural sages to study and combat the infection before the damage becomes irreparable.

"Other than that," Baron Bishop added before returning to his seat and annotations, "we were waiting for Your Majesty to move on to the next, and most important matter, brought up by Duke Crannon Coronn of Valador."

"Duke Crannon Coronn, you may address the Council," the king directed. For the patriarch of a House of traditions, one known for its numerous and complex rituals, even in the Council, Septem had always been quite pragmatic.

A man rose from his seat, his serious demeanor as gray as his eyes and the clothes he wore. "Your Highness," he said, "given the recent events in Suhne, our scouts have reported a notable withdrawal of its people from the border. As we know, it is likely the Suhne Empyre in the north will lay dormant for most of a year, maybe much longer. In addition, we have received news that Esdrah Heikken, Crowned King of Ardenay, has just passed. The news couldn't have come at a better time. This can be a most fruitful time for our kingdom."

"Fruitful?" Meener Torenus, the representative of Duke Hecator Laecanius of Misthaven, asked with an almost comedic amusement. "Would you care to explain, friend?"

"Yes, fruitful. This could be a time for our kingdom to go on the offensive," Coronn added, his eyes moving to each of his counterparts, "for our forces to conquer, at the very least, some of both lands."

"But it is not our way, Duke Coronn." The voice of Shira von Corvus, duchess and wife of the Duke of Ravencrest, was as melodious as it was firm. Neither she nor her husband had accepted the position of representative of their duchy. Their connection was such that the Council members felt they were one and the same, and so their joint presence in the Council was an acceptable exception to the rule.

The molten sunlight of her hair parted to reveal multiple large onyxes hanging from her earlobes. Each gem, like the her black eyes, reflected the light of the torches while enhancing the dark gown that accentuated her curves. It would have been hard for any man to ignore her presence in a room.

Shira stood behind her husband, placing her hands on his shoulders.

"Indeed, my lord," Myr von Corvus added almost casually. "We are a land of patience. It would do us no good to invade, at least without a perfect plan, and risk suffering a defeat such as the one in the Battle of Dragon Tears."[1]

Primon Ferertr's young eyes seemed to have been set ablaze when he rose from his seat to speak. "While the dragon of Aligrand suffered a major defeat, that was three decades ago. We have proudly recovered. As its duke, I can ascertain our numbers are ready."

"As we have recovered, the strength of our enemies has grown," the fiery Ilhar Kal'Daka, ruler of the forested Olath Valm, replied. Her red hair was as wild as an untamed mare. Some scholars had theorized Ilhar's yellow eyes spoke of a distant relation to the Darkholm House. While this might have been nothing more than a theory, one thing was certain: both duchies' borders touched, and just as close was the relationship between the two.

"And that is why the timing is perfect, my lords. I agree we must not only strike, but we must do it soon, before our enemies are taken advantage of by another enemy," Sir Dokkon Gillspiel, duke of the underground duchy of Volanar, was a tall man of heavy musculature, true to the war elephants his people raised. It was quite formidable to see the man speak with such grace and eloquence. "Our enemy may have grown, but so have we in might, wisdom, and power. They will never expect an attack from us."

"Let me ask you this." Leaning forward, Ilhar's nails scratched the table surface playfully, as she gazed at the Duke of Volanar. "If we were to attack, my lords, the conquering of these lands would expand Blackheart's borders by expanding Valador and Volanar—"

"And thus, expanding Blackheart's influence." Sir Dokkon sought to finish her thought, but he was not as successful as he expected.

"By expanding your two duchies," she slightly raised her voice, "while we would continue to provide for you." Ilhar Kal'Daka seemed to have ignored his words, her eyes on the Duke of Whisperwind, who nodded. "So, would you accept, then, to give part of your duchy to your neighboring ones as you expand so that when you spread outward, we all grow?" The duchess's question forced everyone's attention to the pair.

"What more do you want, Ilhar?" Duke Primon Ferertr questioned, exasperated. "Doesn't Olath Valm already have enough land?"

"Bah, I don't know what you're talking about," Ilhar dismissed his questioning, "I think it's still a fair question."

"Ilhar," Primon insisted, "you took a third of my land."

The duchess's head turned slowly toward him, her eyes almost piercing Duke Ferertr's. "I did not, at least not yours. You speak of the land that was rightfully mine."

"Ask the people of the Arande who have migrated to Aligrand because they lost all their land."

"You mean, the same people who once invaded it and took all that same land from us?" she rose from her seat, "The same people whose previous invasion forced the migration of mine?"

King Septem's raised hand stopped their argument as effectively as he had stopped the battle between Olath Valm and Aligrand for the contested lands decades before, which had ended with the transferring of lands back to the first. Even though neither Ilhar nor Primon had been at the head of their respective duchies back then, the animosity of their people toward each other was still fresh.

With another simple gesture, he gave the floor back to Duke Dokkon.

"Thank you, Your Majesty," Dokkon responded. "Now, to answer your question, My Lady Ilhar, I don't see why we would have to—"

"Ilhar," Coronn interrupted the words of the larger man, "quite frankly, I fail to see why giving a portion of our own land would be necessary. We would be working to grow the kingdom. We would sacrifice men and lives for the kingdom, for we are one with the kingdom. That alone should be enough."

Making no effort to hide her disgust, Ilhar raised an eyebrow, turned to face the guests, then the other members of the Council, and lastly, King Septem. A smirk was drawn on her face as her arms crossed and her mouth opened, "Enough said."

The king spoke again, "Whisperwind would sacrifice resources to feed your armies, Featherfell would sacrifice their rangers to scout for you, Ravencrest would sacrifice reinforcements, Duskforge would sacrifice their ore, and Olath Valm wood in the creation of your weapons. Which is the greater sacrifice?"

Duke Crannon nodded. "I understand, Your Majesty."

His counterpart in Volanar took the reins of the conversation. "My lords, in order to consider this further, I would like to hear the opinions of each as representative of your duchy. It is clear Valador and Volanar are in favor. It is also clear Olath Valm is against, and Ravencrest is undecided. There are eight more of us. Would you each offer your opinion?"

"I'm neutral." Duke Taevaon of the maritime Duchy of Mycernase was typically a man of few words, and this time was no exception. His land was far from the borders contended, just along the southern coast of Blackheart, but he would provide all assistance needed if it came to that, even navigating upriver toward the lands inside the kingdom.

Duke Myr von Corvus slightly raised his palm. "Perhaps I was misunderstood, and if I did not speak clearly, I apologize. For clarity's sake, the Blood of Ravencrest is ready to go to war, if need be, as we will always be, but we wholeheartedly oppose the idea."

The young Duke of Haemonor, whose lands were on the coastal desert border, spoke next "Tactically, I do not think it is smart to go against both forces, even if they are leaderless, but I am in favor of going at least against one of them." He smiled with the charm of that guest who sits at your table but whose feet play with your daughter's while you dine. "Going against Suhne, of course, is more convenient to me, but I will favor whatever is most convenient to all."

"Aligrand seconds you, Lord Eadric. But we favor moving against Ardenay. I have to admit our defeat left a thirst for vengeance that will not be easily satiated," Duke Primon mused.

Meener Torenus smiled. The same, usual soft smile parted as he said, "If your forces need to traverse Misthaven to expedite the campaign, we will always be there to guide you. If there is no war to be had in the lands of my lord duke, then even better."

The orange brocaded fabric of Aubin Raine, Duke of Whisperwind, opened to show his fingers crossed. "If we are to do this, I would have to leave immediately to start preparations. There will be much produce and food needed for such a large force. If we decide not to, as with Misthaven, then my land will be more prosperous."

"A senseless battle is a lost battle," From behind the strange, avian mask that hid his features came the muffled voice of Duke Arcanmene Raganark of Duskforge. "Nothing tells us these two kingdoms can't fend off our forces simply because their leaders are gone. We would need time. We would need to study the situation and then consider options if any. With that said, I oppose this venture."

Duke Driscoll of the griffons of Featherfell directed his words to Arcanmene. "I agree with your statement, friend. Wise words, but I would not totally oppose the idea. I would contemplate it while sending our scouts to gather information before we reconvene and decide. Therefore I abstain from deciding at this point."

Then there was silence.

Duke Crannon's eyes moved to the quiet corner of the table where a frail-looking man sat. He wore heavy robes as black as the eyes of darkness itself, while his gaunt, heavily wrinkled skin was as white as the purest soul. Over his shoulders, a feathered cloak of black, gray, and white that, together with his balding head, gave him the appearance of a vulture.

The depth of his sunken eyes could not hide his golden, menacing gaze.

Davidov Darkholm was known for being as insensitive as he was old. Even the oldest people in his duchy remember him as a mature adult back when they themselves were children. Even the least attentive nobles would remember him walking with his men along the battlefield after all was done, scavenging for trinkets and prisoners, one of his responsibilities as Master of Death.

So stubborn was he that, despite his weakness and his age, despite the swollen joints and limping gait, he would never use a cane.

Even in the present day, the Master of Death was said to be respected and feared by Death itself so much that Death wouldn't dare touch him.

"My lord," Crannon continued, addressing the oldest, longest-serving member of the Council, "Darkholm once took the crown and founded Blackheart, and thus it grew in strength, riches, and power. This is yet another chance for Darkholm to grow, much more as it weakens our neighboring kingdoms."

"There is a great difference between greed and necessity," the Master of Death's voice was dry and full of scorn, his intense gaze burning Crannon's soul.

He then slowly looked at every other duke as he continued, "Darkholm was never interested in meddling in the affairs of the kingdom; we did it out of necessity, and now we hold the crown. We have much less interest in meddling in the affairs of the world and neighboring kingdoms."

No words would come out of the Duke of Valador's mouth.

The king spoke once again, "I have heard what Valador, Volanar, Aligrand, and Haemonor desire. This, however, will not be."

"But, my king," Duke Coronn of Valador interrupted, "Four are in favor, four are against, and four are undecided. Each side could present arguments and persuade the neutral voters to—"

"Blackheart is not a democracy, Lord Coronn. There are no votes to be tallied." Septem's golden eyes quickly moved toward the duke of Valador. As intense as the gaze of the king was, it would have frozen even the bowels of a fiery fiend. "This is an assembly gathered to discuss ideas, to hear one another. The desires of a majority will not weigh more than the prosperity and safety of the whole."

Duke Coronn stepped out of his seat and walked toward Septem Darkholm, kneeling before the crowned monarch, "Your Majesty, I mean no disrespect, but at this time, we must be wiser than this."

"You mean no disrespect, but yet you disrespect your king." Duchess Ilhar's words interrupted the man's speech, "Are you calling yourself wisest among us all? Wiser than the king?"

"The Crown has spoken, Lord Coronn," his Volanar counterpart added, "leave the matter alone. There is immeasurable wisdom in our king's words, and our desire will yield to his vision.

"Your Majesty," he then added, "we will continue to train our forces and gather our resources in case the Crown changes its mind. We want to be ready."

The Darkholm king rose from his seat. "Blackheart would only expect us all to always be at the ready. This, however, will not be our battle. A wounded lion fights the fiercest. A dying sun burns the brightest. One should never dive for prey that lies out in the open. While it might seem a blessing, a way to gain sustenance while conserving energy, it might cost much more to fall for a ruse."

The monarch looked each one of the dukes in the eye. While his features showed no hint of emotion, his eyes showed the utmost respect before adjourning the meeting with the salute of the Blood, "For your candor and time, Blackheart thanks you all, my lords. *In Tenebris nos.*"

Without another word or ever looking back, Septem walked out of the chamber, a white specter flanked by obsidian knights.

Behind him, the dukes and advisers saluted one another and prepared to depart.

"My lords," the Knight Commander said to those present, "preparations have been made for you to stay at the Tower[(2)] if any of you desire to stay the night."

"I'd rather save travel time," Duchess Ilhar responded, her lips meeting each of Erdrick's cheeks in Darkholm tradition, "besides, I would rather travel at night when I can." Olath Valm was close enough to the Royal Duchy, but the distance from each one's capitals across the bay was significant. Aside from that, the noblewoman had no need or desire for comfort. In her mind, this was a sign of strength. To her left and right, a pair of wolves had been silent all along. She caressed their heads, speaking in a much softer tone to them, "Let us go, my children."

Following suit, Duke Arcanmene Raganark of Duskforge also left.

Shira von Corvus took hold of her husband's hand. "We will gladly accept your invitation, Lord Commander."

"We thank Darkholm for its hospitality, as usual," her husband added.

Gustavus and Erdrick stood by the doorway, watching the Council members who left for the Tower.

"My lord," Gustavus murmured in protest, "this is crass disrespect. Upon your entrance, no one even acknowledged you, and now many still do not before they depart."

"I do not need acknowledgment, cousin," Erdrick's tone was firm.

"You are the heir."

"I am a knight."

"The Commander of the Black Knights."

"And the Commander just happens to lead, but he is still a knight, nothing more, nothing less. Respect is not required or needed, cousin. It changes not who I am."

The large man uttered nothing, knowing quite well he lost the debate the moment he started it.

"Wise words," the silence that had remained between the two men broke. They turned to see Lord Davidov hadn't left the room. The duke emerged from the shadows of the chamber, his eyes fixed on the knight.

"I have been trained well," Erdrick replied.

"Nonsense," the impossibly old man spat, "Even the best training means nothing if one does not learn from it. One can learn a great deal from the most meager of masters."

Each slow step brought the Master of Death closer to both men. Despite their being two heads taller than he, despite his swaying gait, he commanded the respect of both and that of much taller men.

"You were a natural in the Council chamber, Commander."

"Not once did I speak, my lord," Erdrick responded.

"Alas, but your eyes moved in the right direction, capturing details that needed to be. Words expressed are ever important, Commander, but one should never underestimate the power of the words left unsaid." Davidov walked past both younger men and toward the entrance.

"I thank you for your words," Erdrick bowed slightly, but the only response he received was the soft scrape of the feathers on the floor, and the echo of the slow steps of the Master of Death as the aged man continued down the hallway.

(1) The Battle of Dragon Tears occurred thirty years before the present date. Ardenay invaded Blackheart, destroying a large portion of the Duchies of Whisperwind and most of Aligrand (the Dragon). So significant were Blackheart's losses the duke took to the streets to cry with his people. In the end, what stopped the campaign's progress was the swamps of the neighboring lands, which bought time for Blackheart to organize itself and repel the invasion.

(2) The Tower is a large, round building in Ironholde. It is Darkholde's closest section to the marketplace in the main plaza. From its top balcony, Septem would speak to his people. It held many chambers for visitors. Meetings with foreigners would be held in the Tower and not in Darkholde itself.

DEPARTURE

Location: Kingdom of Ardenay, Capital City of Himlen

The glare woke Ealas up. The blinding sun showing up among the cathedral towers reflected in the broken mirror that hung from a rag nailed to the wooden wall of that musty room.

So sound was his sleep, Ealas just now noticed the noisy street outside.

Stomach grumbling, the nobleman remembered he had not eaten since lunch the day before.

Ugh, the bath had been a stranger.

Quickly, he searched the room to ascertain all his belongings were there and then headed down to the main chamber, the creaking of old wood under his feet reminding him of the irony of the inn's name.

"G'morning." Alasa sat by a small table near the entrance, the light of the sun shining down through the window blessing her with its warmth. She smiled at him as she broke a large chunk of bread and nearly forced it inside her mouth in a most ungracious way.

She was wearing the same clothes, and her braid looked the same, except that it hung lower and, if possible, was more unkempt.

'I guess she won't notice I haven't bathed either,' he laughed inside.

"Good morning."

"I got you some vinegar, potatoes, butter, and pork bacon. There's also a piece of bread, although it's all gone cold by now." Her buttered fork pointed at his plate, breadcrumbs shooting out of her mouth as she spoke.

"Thanks." Closing his eyes momentarily, Ealas silently also thanked the God of Light for his blessing and for the food provided.

"The beds are not as comfortable, you'll find, I'm sure, but you'll get used to them in time."

"Actually, mine wasn't terrible. Well, at least they're comparable to the barracks."

"Ah," the woman spoke through a mouthful, "so you are a soldier . . . Figures, from the posture."

"We can say so." He cursed himself, 'I must bite my own tongue.' "So, how can I thank you for last night?"

"*Thank me*," the woman laughed and drank. "You don't *have* to thank me. There's just *something* about you that, I don't know, that told me you could use some help."

"How so?"

"I have dealt with many a noble over the years. No matter what problems one solves for them, they seem to believe they're made from a different material than any one of us. They're never happy or satisfied." Without grace, she placed her cup on the table. "You just seem, like you said the other night, *lost.*"

Without uttering a word, Ealas started eating.

"Plus, as much as I love their money, if there's a chance I can stick a finger up the aristocracy's ass, count on me!" Alasa laughed again. "Now, here's your change before I forget it. I don't require coin, but if you want to say *thanks,* some coin will do," she winked.

Consumed in thought, Ealas did not catch her insinuation. The man was too distracted, wondering how he could ask for more help or if he should just go his own way before the whole kingdom was alerted.

"I have something to ask of you."

"Sure," she leaned forward.

"What exactly do you do that you say you get paid by the nobles?"

"Ah, not just the nobles, don't get me wrong. I make *ends meet*, you know. When you're born like me, you do what you have to do to survive. I purchase things for them, things they don't want anyone to know they purchased. I help them hide their mistresses and smuggle them into festivities, or out of them, among other, *shadier* things," Alasa smiled.

Smuggle.

"Could you help me *leave* the city?"

"One can easily leave Himlen, and yet you can't. This is interesting." The woman leaned closer.

"Well, leave Ardenay, then?" Ealas's eyes met her own.

Her brown eyes glinted. "Now *that's* even more interesting! You must have done something really, really bad to need help leaving the kingdom, or you must be really important."

"Please," he implored, hoping she wouldn't ask more.

"Which one is it?" Alasa squinted, grinning.

"Please, I will pay you well."

"*Now* we're talking." She crossed her arms and rested her back on the chair.

"Ok, then, how much will it be? When do we do this?"

"Wait, wait. It's not just like that, you know. I need to contact the right people, make sure they're available, and ask for their fee."

"How long does that typically take? One day, two?"

"Oh no," she laughed hard, "that can take a day, a week or two. It's unpredictable."

A week or two. By then, it would be obvious to the world who he was and where.

"Alasa, what if I pay extra?"

"No, it's not that. Well, *extra* is always *extra* welcome, but these things can't be done at the flick of a nobleman's fingers. Finish your food. I'll let you know once everything is ready."

"Thanks."

"No, no thanks, you're paying for it."

"Still, thanks."

"You *must* be ready at all times."

"That won't be a problem."

"That's good. In the meantime, lay low." Rising from her seat, Alasa walked toward the stairs in the direction of her room.

"Alasa?"

"Yes?"

"Is there a place you recommend for a bath around here?"

The woman rolled her eyes. "Lay low!"

"Hey, have you decided on getting rid of that cloak or finding a manacle? I have a blacksmith friend."

"I'll discard it." A manacle around his neck would not be the best disguise, Ealas thought. It would look too new, or he would look too clean, for one thing. Plus, what if he didn't find a way to remove it? It was not worth the risk. The sack cloak he had obtained from another slave as he left the castle meant nothing to him.

"Then you'll need to think of a name," Alasa smiled, waiting for a response, one that didn't come. What was an aristocrat without his birthright? What was a noble without his name?

In the end, all he had to do was remain quiet, to keep who he was safe, and the best way to do that was, as Alasa had said, laying low.

Another morning and he filled his plate with boiled potatoes, sage, and chicken legs. Ealas had convinced a serving boy to bring some eggs to accompany his breakfast, which he gladly did . . . for a few coppers.

While he knew he shouldn't have been making any moves that could attract attention, Ealas thought it wouldn't be noticed.

"What do you think you're doing?" Alasa's abruptness startled him.

"I'm about to break fast, that's all."

"I told you not to call attention to yourself."

"What are you talking about?" he questioned.

She pulled the boy by the ear from behind her, the same boy who held three eggs in his hands. "You offer this child copper for eggs."

"And what's so wrong about that?"

"He has been desperately asking around for eggs for this man who gives him money."

"How is that so strange? It's just one copper. Besides, it makes my meals less boring."

"Eggs are a commodity in this shady part of the city. This is all people have to eat here, besides a few vegetables. You are sending a signal that you don't belong here." She was bothered and did not make an effort to hide the fact.

"Oh, I wasn't aware," Ealas responded.

"It doesn't matter now, thankfully."

"Why not?"

"Because it's time if you have a few hundred gold."

"Wait, a few *hundred* gold?" Ealas could not hide his shock.

It has been nearly a month since she started contacting her people. During those days, although they had barely exchanged words, there was not much about her that had changed.

Somehow, though, her demeanor felt different today.

Alarm.

Irritated, she pressured, "What are you waiting for? Go get your things, and I'll meet you outside. We only have a small window of time."

Ealas returned to his room to gather his things. His short sword, his belt, the small pouch, a change of clothes, everything was there.

Then again, it was easy to keep track of so little in such a plain room.

Before leaving, he caught a glimpse of his reflection in the mirror.

He was growing a beard. While he had never done so before, it would make him look less like himself but more like his father.

In either case, it wouldn't help. He would still be somewhat recognizable, but time was not a luxury he had right now.

He met Alasa at the entrance. Her two companions were on the alert but spoke little.

"Let's go," one of them instructed.

They moved fast.

They had to, for there was an unusually high number of guards in the marketplace, among them, some of the Paladins of the Light.

Fortunately, none of the Royal Guard.

If their presence tempted Alasa to find out more and tempted her even more to betray him, he didn't know. Thankfully, he wouldn't have to know, for while people were being stopped, questioned, and searched by the guards, Alasa and her companions moved swiftly.

A guard captain on horseback caught a glimpse of them fleeing the market and ordered, "You, stop!"

"Now we run." Alasa pulled Ealas's sleeve and darted forward. "Buy us time, friends, and I'll buy you some ale!"

"Run!" one of her companions screamed, calling the attention of the guards as he placed his hood over his head and ran in a different direction.

"Yeh, I'll meet you there!" the other man shouted. His vault over a vegetable stand sent a group of guards behind him while instigating a flocking group of angry merchants that inadvertently blocked the way.

Alasa and Ealas moved on, the man gasping for air as he tried to keep pace with his more athletic companion. He knew he couldn't afford to stop. There were times a man had to continue the path he started, and this, he believed in his heart, was his path now.

After a few dodges and turns, they finally came upon a small, nondescript cart flanked by two men armed with maces.

The driver, middle-aged, somewhat gaunt and white-haired in a magenta cloak and reddish-brown robes, didn't even acknowledge him but immediately held his palm up in expectation of payment.

"Wait." Alasa held Ealas's arm before he produced the payment, placing her hand on the hilt of her sword. "Who are you?"

"If you don't know, why are you here?" The driver was curt.

"Are you Demos?"

"Daemos," the driver corrected, his palm still waiting, "the gold?"

"Go," Alasa ordered.

"How much exactly?" Ealas opened his pouch and started counting.

"One hundred, now," Daemos responded.

"Go," exasperated, Alasa jerked the pouch from Ealas's hand and handed it to the driver. "Don't ever count gold in front of the poor and hungry. Just go!"

Looking around, Ealas saw people with ill-fitting, dirty clothing who had noticed the scene. Some walked toward the cart to ask for alms. But that was not as worrisome as a few shadier-looking people who took note and also approached.

From the left, searching guards came to view. Alasa ran away, chased by the guards who had recognized her. Afraid he would be found, Ealas was forced to lie down in the back of the cart. "Can we just go?"

"Counting here," Daemos replied.

"How do I know I didn't pay too much?"

"Counting here," Daemos repeated.

"It is urgent," the nobleman pleaded, only able to see the blue sky and the back of the driver's head.

"Sixteen coins," a small pouch with coins fell at Ealas feet.

"Thank you for your honesty," the nobleman thanked, to which Daemos asked only, "Where to?"

"Didn't you know? Blackheart."

"Where in Blackheart?"

"Whatever's left of it," Ealas responded gravely.

Daemos did not seem, for a single moment, concerned. He turned his head and glared at Ealas from the corner of his eye before looking at his bodyguards, one of whom chuckled.

With a quick flick of his wrist and his instruction, the horses started their gallop. "To whatever's left of Blackheart."

A HEAVY SHIELD

Location: Kingdom of Blackheart, Royal Duchy of Darkholm, Darkholde Keep, Ironholde, training courtyard of the Black Knights.

"What do you see?" Erdrick asked the men at his side. To his right, the hulking presence of Gustavus, proudly encased in his heavy armor, the skull-shaped helmet over his head. To his left stood the Darkholm man known as the Twins. He was much older than the Knight Commander, perhaps around nine decades, but his appearance was of a man not a day over sixty.

While Erdrick was the Commander, the Twins had, for nearly seventy years, been more than the man-at-arms. This man had dedicated almost his entire life to combat, to sharpening the martial skills of every single Darkholm in the House. Thus, no one better than he knew the strengths and weaknesses of each Darkholm, at least in regard to combat.

It had been the Twins who had created both the Darkholm fighting style and the true Darkholm fighting style the family kept wrapped in secrecy.

He would speak words of reassurance and pat the younger ones on the back. While he had lived through perhaps the greatest tragedy any member of the House could speak of, the Twins often smiled, often for a Darkholm, that is.

"One man's folly is another man's wisdom, Commander. Perhaps you wish to ask me something more specific?" the Twins asked as both men observed the dueling training of the dozens of knights in the ward.

"Do you see any gaps?"

"I see gaps everywhere, Commander. It is what my style focuses on."

"Indeed," Erdrick addressed him formally, "I wish to eliminate those."

"Gaps cannot always be eliminated, Commander," the older man spoke. " Hidden, perhaps."

"Oftentimes, a weakness is not seen. It is present in the mind of the man. A good opponent will always find it, even create one where there seems to be none."

"As a knight, which one of our styles do you find to be better," Erdrick asked, "the Black Knights' or the Darkholms'?"

"You are asking the creator of the Darkholm style himself as if he would show no bias," the aged master trainer chuckled. "It is the man behind the blade that makes a style better, would you not agree?"

Erdrick appeared to grin. "To a certain degree." He walked toward the training knights. "Malacar, Serverus," he commanded the men who saluted their leader.

"Malacar, you will fight in the Darkholm style. Serverus, you will fight in the style of the knights."

Malacar Darkholm nodded. He had almost lost his right eye in battle, evidenced by a scar that crossed his face. During that battle, he used the spurting blood from his face to blind the lion that was his opponent, using his own hands to claw at the beast's eyes. Since then, he had been known as the Black Lion of Darkholm.

The Black Lion removed his armor so that he could move with ease and armed himself with a long sword made for training.

Facing him, Serverus Ecru, the man of the ebon skin who had been raised among the royals. He saluted with his claymore in front of his face, in the custom of the knights.

Upon Erdrick's signal, the men initiated the duel, Malacar taking a step back, grabbing his cape in his off hand. Serverus, in turn, took a step forward toward the Black Lion.

"Serverus is too close," Gustavus pointed out.

The Twins squinted, studying the scene.

Erdrick's eyes were fixed on each man's stance.

Malacar twirled the fabric of his cape to reduce the visibility of his opponent, although he knew that, having been trained in the Darkholm style, Serverus would likely see through the ruse. What he would not know, however, was *when* the strike would come. 'One, two, three,' Malacar counted silently the times he twirled the fabric.

He lunged forward, not waiting for a complete spin so that there would be less of a chance of his move being expected. But Serverus was swift on his feet, as dangerously quick as a panther, even in armor. He spun his body, elbowing Malacar's back and pushing him away, keeping the distance between the two men.

The Black Lion laughed, turning again to face his opponent. He needed to be like the beast he was named after. '*Patience*,' he thought, '*wait for his opening or make one.'* Both men swung time and again, blocking and dodging one another with ease.

"He needs to widen the distance," Gustavus spoke his mind again.

"I believe he is getting his opponent comfortable," the Twins replied. "He is good. Unusually so."

The Knight Commander smiled. Erdrick was proud of Serverus. While he was not of their Blood, over the years, they have learned to trust the man as one of their household. Serverus was firm, honorable, reliable, and loyal. *'Then again,'* Erdrick thought, *'what else can he be? He has everything to lose.'*

Gustavus Darkholm

His thoughts were interrupted by cheers when Malacar wrapped his cape around the knight's claymore. Serverus let it go. He closed the distance and kneed the Lion's stomach, stunning him.

Regaining his composure, Serverus took two steps back and, wrapping his hand around the hilt of his claymore, he yanked it from the cloth the same way a most seasoned warrior would unsheathe a blade. With the third step back, he swung the sword sideways, striking Malacar's temple with the flat of the wooden blade.

Malacar stumbled.

Upon seeing the fresh blood, Serverus closed in and held him up. "Are you alright, brother?"

"My lord," Serverus asked Erdrick, "with your permission, I will take my brother knight to the healer's quarters."

"Go," Erdrick responded, "you represented us well, brother."

The leader of the knights turned toward the Twins, a proud smile on his face.

"As stated before, it is the man behind the blade that makes the style *better*," the Twins smiled.

"My lord!" Gustavus turned to face both men, his eyes fixed on Erdrick. "I have always admired your work. I have been trained by the best in the capital, but yet I have never chosen an order to join. Will you offer to provide me with the greatest of honors, that of accepting me among the ranks of the Black Knights?" His large body started to bend a knee when a familiar female voice froze him in place.

"Gustavus!" Eriadna Darkholm, the Shield of the King, vaulted over the wooden fence of the ward. "You will *not* become a knight!"

Gustavus rose again, displeased. In his close to three decades, he had faced many perils and made many an enemy. He had learned to dislike many a thing. The one thing he hated the most, however, was to be embarrassed in the presence of others.

"This is my choice," his voice boomed.

"It will not be." The strong woman neared him, carrying the confidence of a mountain.

"I have decided," Gustavus said through gritted teeth.

"You fool," Eriadna spat, "this is *not* your decision. Pick a weapon," she added. "Strike me once, and you will have it your way."

Erdrick signaled the knights, and together with the Twins, they watched from the northern side of the courtyard.

Gustavus's eyes filled with anger. Quickly, he walked toward the weapons rack and picked up an oaken two-handed sword. He breathed in deeply and ran toward the woman.

The man swung his sword horizontally. Eriadna knelt, feeling the wooden surface too close to her braid for comfort. She rose again, uppercutting his jaw. He took a step back as he heard her say, "You will *never* be a knight!"

Again he swung, once, twice, toward her head and then her legs. Both times she dodged, always keeping her eyes on his.

"I will! It is my will!" His scream was heard in all the nearby courts.

The young man was surprisingly fast for someone of his size, but even with her armor, the Shield matched his speed. He grabbed her cape and pulled her closer to find her unfastening it with a quick jerking motion.

His anger grew, more so when he saw some of the servants spectating. Again he dashed toward her, swinging time and again. But not once could he strike true.

"You do not have what it takes to be a knight" Eriadna didn't have to dance around the ward. She just measured every move, studied every muscle, and conserved her energy to respond at the last second.

Gustavus stopped himself. He needed to calm down. She was reading him like a children's book. By lowering his great weapon and holding it with one hand, she would not expect the move.

When she noticed his breathing, Eriadna lowered her guard and walked toward her opponent. As soon as he saw her blink, Gustavus swung his weapon again toward her torso with all his might. Right before contact, Eriadna spread her legs and let herself fall backward.

"You FOOL!" she screamed.

With the same momentum, he saw an opportunity. Seeing her grounded, he swung his weapon in a large arc downwards, eyes wide open.

Eriadna spun both her legs quickly and rose, inches from the weapon that struck the ground. She planted her right foot on the middle forcefully, breaking the oaken surface in two.

Eriadna Darkholm

Immediately after, she dashed toward him. "Listen! You will . . . never . . . be . . ." She punched his stomach once, twice, thrice, dizzying him.

"A knight!" she kicked his torso, sending his large body flying toward the now broken weapon rack.

"Eriadna," the king called.

She turned to see him standing by the fence. "My king," she responded.

From where Gustavus lay on the ground, he saw her about to leave and with her, left his pride. He would surely become a mockery in every man's thoughts.

Instinctively, he reached out for a handle as he rose again. Without even knowing his weapon, he swung both arms forward and hurled it, a wooden headsman's axe that spun and struck Eriadna's back.

Some among those present cheered.

The woman turned to face him, clearly displeased. With three quick strides, she unsheathed her sword. She headbutted him and tripped him, his back hitting the ground with a solid *thud*.

"What will get you killed one day is not a lack of skill. Of that, I have no doubt," she spoke. "What will get you killed is your own stubbornness," were the last words he heard her speak, before the kick, before his world turned to blackness.

The king's steady steps took him along the perimeter of the training hall, forming an orchestral performance with the rustling of the cape around his shoulders.

Behind him, Eriadna, his bodyguard, the only shield Septem had ever needed since having taken the crown.

They prepared to head back into Darkholde Keep. It wasn't until they were out of the knight's hearing range that he spoke to her. "Have you ever wondered if perhaps you are too harsh on your children?" the monarch asked, watching the knights returning to their training.

"My lord," she responded, "I have three sons. One of them is broken, and another one is weak. All I have left . . . is Gustavus. I need him to be strong so that he can follow in my footsteps. The life of a knight is a cage. It will place a burden on the man and perhaps stop him from doing what must be done when the time comes."

Eriadna's eyes met Septem's. "Now," she added, "if it is your will, just say it, and I will raise them differently."

Silence followed her words, a lasting silence that was broken only by the king's footsteps as he walked past her toward his destination.

THE BEAUTY OF
THE BEAST

Location: Kingdom of Blackheart,
Duchy of Darkholm, Darkholde Keep

The waves pummeled the jagged cliffs where Darkholde rested as a black stone vulture, ready to dive into the sea.

Over centuries, the salt water eroded the coast presently known as Smith's Bay, devouring it unmercifully, one little bit at a time. Hundreds of feet below the keep's walls, reefs valiantly attempted to break the sea's advance.

Closer to the coastline, as man-made reefs themselves, ruined forges still protruded where smithies had once stood.

Despite having been licked by the sea for so long, the surface of the many anvils seemed quite intact. Rumors would believe the ancient runes on their surface had kept them protected from being weathered all this time.

Most of the forges, more so those furthest from the new coast, had fallen in disuse. The remaining ones would rarely feel the hands of a master smith, sacrificing might and strength with each strike, giving shape to the metal on its surface in the creation of exceptional work. But a careful eye would notice there was no heat source to work with. These forges had actually never felt the intense heat of smith's flame. The smithing technique had required great strength and even greater skill, but most of all, almost indescribably endless patience.

After every few strikes from a hammer, the artisan would drench the metal in seawater so that no warmth would take part in the process, tempering its surface and reducing its shine while increasing its density. It was this same hidden technique they used that had given the capital of Darkholm its name—the city of Coldforge.

A lone smith worked this stormy night against the waves that unleashed their fury, testing his endurance, bathing him with their relentless arms.

High above, a cloaked figure walked along the stone walkway the color of the night, like heavy charms in a stone necklace of the gods. Despite the angry wind's attempt to unravel the mystery within its attire, the figure advanced with unfaltering determination.

It moved in the direction of a lone tower that protruded where the cliff would disappear in a corner, closer to the water, nearly one hundred feet up from the wave breakers below.

Before reaching the last tower, the walkway ended in a heavy, black stone door. Its large, iron hinges and frame were sculpted to resemble hundreds of human bones. It was this that gave the door its name: the Bone Gate.

At the entrance of this last tower, another heavy, plain, and nondescript surface of a black stone door brought all visitors to a halt. It had been in this tower where a man named Idian the Second, also known as the Black Gate, and Deana, the Angel, had sired their children, still within Darkholde but as far away from the world as possible, in an attempt to curb the prophecy of the Master of Cosmos.[1]

On the present day, however, it was not Idian II or Deana who lived in this tower. Neither did Eriadna the Shield nor even their own son, the storm incarnate, the one who bore the name Raganor. These chambers lay now largely empty, filled only by the nightmarish howl of one tormented man, their descendant, Aram Darkholm.

The visitor walked into the tower, her cloak drenched by the merciless weather. Her hands unfastened the golden brooch, and the cloak receded to reveal eyes of the same color and lips the color of fresh, pulsating blood.

Carefully placing the falling cloak on a table, the visitor's hands pulled the carrying case from under the wet fabric. It was laden with vials and herbs, instruments and pestles to ground and mix the concoctions that only the Master of Life was adept at preparing.

She quickly studied the vials to ascertain none of them were broken. She then looked up and climbed the spiraling stairs toward the upper chamber.

A spectator's eye would judge her as careful, perhaps somewhat intimidated. The reality was that despite her regular visits, her every move was always ceremonious, almost planned.

Rowena opened the door to walk inside the room.

Not once did she knock. Not once did she announce her presence, nor did she ever need to, for, as usual, at this time of the day, he was quietly waiting.

The Master approached the table at one end where what little light there was this rainy morning entered through arched windows. Her hands removed different vials from the case, replacing them with empty ones that rested on the table.

The room was cold, the fireplace dead. Setting her work aside for a moment, she took time to start the fire. As if conjured by a spell, once the flames came to life, the slow clinking of metal was heard behind her.

"Aram," she greeted.

"Rowena." A large man lay huddled on the floor by a makeshift bed, its frame broken for wood that would feed the fireplace. The man's skin was the same color as her own, but while some light jewelry adorned hers, his was rich with heavy scars, some attained in battle, others self-inflicted.

Fine, black lace adorned her skirt in perfect patterns resembling roses.

While his clothes were as black and fine, they were torn in many places, some of them nearly impossible for his own hands to reach.

She walked back toward the vials on the table. He crawled toward the middle of the room on all fours, each limb dragging a chain that was fastened to the wall. A near admiration of her showed in his intense yellow eyes.

In this chamber, the Master of Life wasted no time in pleasantries. She skillfully mixed vials and powders, bringing them close to the fire to warm the liquid inside. She worked quietly and delicately while his breathing was hoarse and heavy.

"I have not seen you in more than a week," she spoke.

"I have not been . . . well," he responded.

"Tell me, how so, dear cousin?" the Master asked.

"Nothing has changed, Rowena. My condition is worse."

"Then *it has* changed, dearest."

"What difference does it make?" he snapped.

Seemingly unaffected, she added, "Aram, I need to know this. These details are important. There is only so much one can do without information."

Aram turned his head angrily, looking out the window to the clouds that started to part.

After a long pause, his cousin spoke, "It would do you good to join us for dinner tonight. Being close to us—"

"I . . . just, I just do not know, Rowena," he interrupted.

"I understand, Aram. Then know that it would do us all good to see you join us for dinner tonight," her serenity unchanged.

She glanced at the swirling substance inside the vial in her hand.

"Rowena," the large man eased his tone, "I am losing control."

"Aram," the woman approached and knelt so that both their eyes could meet. "You cannot. You *will* not." She placed the vial on his palms and closed his fingers around it, almost as if in prayer to gods of mercy that would never listen.

Rowena observed Aram holding the vial in his hands and studying it for a moment.

"I am tired of drinking these!" The vial immediately shattered upon contact with the stone wall, its precious concoction traveling down toward the slabs that lined the floor.

In an instant, the chained man had laid waste too-long hours of work and research.

If the Master of Life was bothered, her expression did not betray her. Her hands remained calm, carefully picking up the pieces of broken glass from the stone floor.

"I am tired . . . Rowena," his tense muscles eased for a moment, echoing the fatigue his eyes reflected. "Why was I born like this?" a glint of the sun reflected in the water that now appeared in his yellow eyes.

"Shh . . ." she whispered; her index finger moved toward his lips. "There is nothing wrong with you."

"Nothing, you say. I am nothing but a monster."

"And so are we all," she added softly.

"You will never understand."

"We do not need to understand each other in order to accept one another." Her lips kissed his forehead, frustration evident on the scarred face.

Rowena stood up and headed toward the entrance. "I must go now."

"No! Please, stay!" Aram pleaded.

"I have to. There is so much I need to attend to."

"Please, no!" Aram crawled toward her feet, dragging his chains like a beast begging for its master's caress. "They are coming for me!"

"Aram," Rowena said, "they can come for you all they want, but they cannot take you. We will not allow it."

"How can you leave me like this? PLEASE!"

"One does not always want to do things one simply must do."

"THE ROAD IS MUCH EASIER FOR YOU!" he snarled, his tears wetting the corner of his frothing mouth.

"Is it?" Rowena's golden eyes met the intense goldenrod of his own. "Perhaps I carry a much heavier burden, but I choose not to falter under its weight. I choose to carry it differently."

Aram saw the wooden door close behind the Master of Life.

Rowena's presence was the only thing that brought him peace when he was unwell.

He turned his head to hear the main door to the tower shut, and immediately after, his muscled body started to sweat.

(1) Idian II was known as 'the Black Gate.' The Master of Cosmos had predicted that from his seed, a great darkness would come to the world. Of his wife, Deana, known as 'the Angel,' the Master has predicted that a lineage of heroes would come forth. They chose to marry to mitigate the curse of one with the blessing of the other.

FIRST TEST

Location: Empyre of Suhne, City of Suhne,
deep within the Palace of the Sun

Sometimes man must descend into the bowels of the earth to find the sun . . .

It took thirty stairsteps to reach the bottom, thirty steps that allowed the brown-robed man an escape, a respite from the outside, where the sunlit structure was beaten by the unmerciful heat of the desert, and into its underground, where the hot steam blessed the walls with its watery touch.

Itosh had been raised to be a servant and nothing more, but his position today had allowed him to gladly leave the unforgiving heat of the desert, although only to arrive at the just-as-unforgiving presence of the Searing Sun.

"Blessed One," the servant bowed as he entered the room where Kaylen's bath was located.

So dense was the steam the silhouette of the Son's head could barely be perceived above the water's surface.

"What?" The Searing Sun seemed indifferent, recognizing the familiar voice.

"I have contacted everyone, all but two."

"Explain yourself."

"Kazaa died several weeks ago," Itosh replied. "You now have only five Chosen. Forgive my questioning, but I received six names when you need seven. Am I missing something?"

"You are the last one, the sixth one now," the Son stated coldly. "I have named you my confidant."

"Your confidant! Leader among your Chosen?" At the revelation, Itosh could not hide his surprise.

Suhnite tradition required seven Chosen to be selected by each contesting Son so that they could be used as either consultants or substitutes whenever they were needed in one of the Tests. While each of the Chosen could assist only once, the great honor and responsibility this brought were indescribable.

They would each be remembered for generations to come, and their families provided for at least if they brought victory to their respective Son. The Chosen of those who lost would be publicly burned for having supported a false god.

"I am blessed," Itosh bowed deeply, his shapely chest swelling with pride, "I am honored." This is something the Suhnite youth could only ever dream of, the greatest achievement a mortal man could have.

Itosh stood quietly, listening to the slow agitation in the water as Kaylen moved. Then, feeling somewhat above the rest, the servant took a step toward the pool and asked, "Can I join you in the pool, Blessed One?"

"*No one* touches the water while I am in it." The response was immediate, stopping him as a whip would stop a trained wildcat.

It was then that Itosh noticed Kaylen's maidens standing by the edges of the pool, waiting for any instruction from him, but stepping away from the hot water that licked the floor.

"I apologize if it offended you, Blessed One," the man bowed.

Through the steam, he saw the Searing Sun's silhouette as he exited the pool, the only response given by the drops of water dying on the tile floor's surface.

Kaylen's handmaidens closed in quickly to dry his body, carefully ensuring that only the towel, and not their hands, touched his skin.

"What should we do about the seventh?" Itosh returned to the pending subject.

"Find someone old," Kaylen responded.

"An old person?"

"I see I do not have to repeat myself."

"Which old person? Is there a name I should ask for?"

"Any old person. The older, the better."

"Blessed One, forgive my question, but how will we . . . how will *you* know if this one old person is the right person to assist you in the challenges?"

"I don't want an elder's help. I have no use for them. The old can't adapt," the Son spoke derisively. "What I need is their presence, for it will give the impression of diversity in the eyes of the onlookers, allowing everyone to believe they're represented. I want that person to simply fill a slot."

"Blessed One, they have knowledge."

"And I have my own."

"Yes, of course, but their diverse knowledge and experiences can give us an extra edge that can more easily lead to victory in the end."

"Diversity does not equate to effectiveness," Kaylen snapped before he began climbing the steps leading to his chambers.

"Diversity can help a man adapt."

"Then tell that to a man," Kaylen stopped one last time before resuming his climb. "I . . . am a god."

———————— ·•••••· ————————

The morning sun rose, its light bathing the vastness of the valley where a limestone dome stood. It was perfectly located at its center, connected to eight smaller ones that radiated from the central one. It was a testament to the masterful skill of the ancient architects of Suhne to see the sheer weight of the heavy structure supported by columns of the same stone.

Inside the central dome, the Rays were seated, waiting around the platform where the Sons of the Sun would stand. Outside and around it, like ants ready to enter their nest, the worshippers, having traveled from across the Empyre to bear witness to at least one of these historic events, watched anxiously.

Three retinues approached from the east, each led by one of the heirs, each seven strong, clad in the respective color chosen by each of the Sons.

The three Sons led their Chosen close to the platform where they would wait. There was no need for instruction. Suhnites knew etiquette very well. It was ingrained in them, and in a society where the individual rarely, if ever, saw even a minimal change in their social status, these norms were the air they breathed.

Malek approached, his swift steps shortening the distance to his place as the firstborn on the platform. He wore little more than short brown breeches with gold accents, allowing much of his muscular body to be seen. His frame was clearly much larger than that of his younger siblings. The combination of the time he spent training under the sun and his countenance made him appear much older than either.

Kaylen's steps were slower. The secondborn appeared less imposing than Malek, but there was an air of superiority about him that made him just as intimidating. Most of his body was covered in flowing robes, while some parts were tight-fitting, in an arrangement that seemed confusing to any spectator. What was clear, however, is that all of it accentuated his striking, hazel eyes. Unlike the firstborn, whose emotions were always visible, Kaylen's eyes spoke for him and even appeared to smile when his lips rarely did.

It was Vamya's turn to make her entrance. The green retinue walked in, led by her. The thirdborn, and only daughter, understood the importance of this moment. Sometimes the entrance alone would be enough to sway a good observer.

Vamya's brown hair was arranged in an intricate, waterfall-twist braid adorned with green silk attached to yellow bands. Her body was covered by a long, dark green robe. After a few steps, she parted it to reveal light green silk covering little, while most of her body was adorned with jewels. She was tempted to look at the reaction of the men around her, but the sheer silence alone spoke volumes of how she had captured the moment.

Today, three determined Sons faced the people of Suhne. In the next seven days, one exalted being would rise to rule them all.

Exis, Speaker of the Rays

"People of the Sun," Exis announced, "As the scriptures read, 'There is no intuition like the Sun's. His words are a honeyed sword that cuts deep into the hearts of men.' On this sacred day, the new Sun will begin his path toward his ascension and transcendence. Today, we test the Sun's insight!"

For the masses, it was the second day of fasting, a second day many would stand under the sun but a day no one would want to miss.

Exis signaled one of the Rays, who spoke first, "Blessed Sons, we are blessed to stand in your presence. To you, here is my question: a man owns a beast that cannot nourish its offspring. What should this man do?"

Malek signaled to a wizened man from among his group. The man walked to his side and engaged in a discussion with the Conquering Sun.

'Strike first, strike last,' Vamya thought as she raised her voice. "First, the man should be asked how many offspring. Perhaps the burden imposed on the beast is too heavy, or too much is expected of it."

"Let us say it has only one offspring," Kaylen interjected.

"That offspring could very well be consuming too much, as it is thus not properly fed," Vamya answered as her eyes met Kaylen's, "or perhaps the teats have dried up."

"Perhaps the beast's teats were never wet, to begin with," Kaylen smiled wryly. "It could very well be male. It is not its responsibility to feed the offspring. Where is the mother, I would ask."

"First," the baritone voice of Malek silenced the other two, "I would ask, is this a beast of burden, a house pet, or a beast of war? Is this a beast who has already sired and fed enough and is now too old to feed one more who can feed himself? For then, it would not reflect negatively on the beast but rather on its offspring. Fair judgment would depend on these many variables."

"The beast and its offspring could very well be in different locations, or perhaps either the beast or the offspring has passed," the Searing Sun added. Throughout his life, Kaylen delighted himself in finding holes in every theory and even more in making his findings evident. This time was no exception.

"But it is even more complicated than just that," Vamya's voice broke the silence after Kaylen's words. "Nourishment does not come from feeding alone, but also from nurturing the spirit and soul. Could a beast feed the soul of its offspring when the offspring are unwilling or faithless? There is nothing, then, a parent could do but grieve. In that case, it should stop grieving and focus on nourishing itself and others."

After her words, no other response came. Kaylen quiesced. It was hard to read his expression. Malek was not pleased.

'Strike last,' she smiled.

The Ray bowed and returned to his seat while Zurek, oldest of the Rays, rose. He looked at the siblings with his tired black eyes before he raised his eyes to the orb in the sky, squinting, perhaps even frowning. For a minute, he did not speak. More than once, he had seen this same scene before.

Exis signaled the old man, "Zurek!"

As if waking up from a trance, the ancient Ray spoke to the three, "Honored are we to have you bless us with your insight. Here is my question: A tree cannot bear fruit. Is it the tree or the earth who is at fault?"

Once again, Malek spoke to his adviser. He spoke briefly, his impatience getting to him. The voice of the firstborn was heard first. "Is this tree supposed to bear fruit? If not, that alone would make the question moot, but let us suppose fruit is expected. Then it could be the tree's fault for not giving what is expected. It could otherwise be the earth itself for not providing for the tree. Ultimately, both could share the blame, for it is the combination of their communal work that would bring forth fruit."

Kaylen's lips drew a smile. He knew he needed to stop finding holes and focus on answering the question, or he would be outperformed. For someone as knowledgeable as he was, that would be unacceptable, at the very least. Did he have good advisers at his disposal? Absolutely, but his pride would not allow him to use such. He would shine through alone.

"We cannot simply blame one or the other, brother," Kaylen added. "Is there any access to water? If not, it is neither one's fault. What is the ground this tree was planted in? Was it planted in mud, swamp, sand, or rock? Then it is not the earth's fault, but the fault of the hands that planted the the tree."

Vamya spoke next. "As you say, brother. But there are illnesses of the plants or the earth that can make them unproductive. Is either of them, then, to blame? It is the same in mankind. A man and a woman may not bear the fruit of children because either could be barren. Is this their fault? While they may not bear children, they may bear the fruit of their love. That love would lead to understanding and compassion. The same compassion that would lead to loving children who have lost their forebears. In the tree's case, even the water could be poisoned. The Sun itself could be searing them and, thus, at fault."

Kaylen caught the jab and promptly addressed her response, irritated, "The Sun is what it is. It is all-powerful, the eternal judge, and no one, nothing can change that. Blame the sky instead, blame the clouds for blocking the Sun or for bringing too much rain, but it is just short of blasphemous to even consider blaming the Sun."

Vamya's words were expressed with calmness to assure the Rays saw she had not for a moment lost control of herself. "We should not focus on assigning blame, but rather on seeing what fruits we expect, and what fruits we do not see, but are, nevertheless, there."

Zurek of the Rays bowed, accepting their answers with a furrowed brow.

Malek was irritated. Kaylen's eyes rested on Vamya. He studied her body language, her demeanor. Her pace was easy for him to follow. Vamya was pleased with her performance so far.

Exis then stood. He bowed briefly as he prepared to ask, "Blessed Ones, this is the last question. To you, I ask: A man broke fast on a sacred day so that he could travel in a caravan with his family: is this a sin?"

"It is a sin, an offense to that which is most sacred. This man should die a terrible death. If his family participated, so would they perish too!" the Conquering Sun blazed.

"But they could very well be nonbelievers," Kaylen interjected.

"We will address nonbelievers after they convert or perish," Malek responded impulsively, without consulting his adviser, without a moment's hesitation.

"This would not be a sin," Vamya made sure to allow a dramatic pause. "It is more of a custom rather than a sacred ordinance. As such, the man should be given a chance to rectify his actions before being so severely punished. Besides, the man could very well not be a part of our society, in which case he is not required to fast."

"And that would bring great stability to the Empyre of the Sun, I suppose?" Kaylen did little to hide his sarcasm. "It is a custom, yes, but customs make our society, and our customs and beliefs are intertwined. Most of the time, they simply cannot be separated, and doing so could bring peril and times of trouble. As such, it is also a sin, for it is ingrained in us and our belief system. In this case, was his caravan headed toward, let's say, the marketplace? This man had no good reason to break fast. His punishment would be severe. If, however, his reason was his caravan was headed to bring supplies to our soldiers, and the travel would be long, then I see it as less of a sin but more of a necessity. He would be admonished and receive a less harsh punishment."

While he was weaker and perhaps less charismatic than his siblings, Kaylen was inarguably sharp of mind. Vamya's emerald eyes studied him carefully. Where had they distanced themselves, she asked herself. They were full-blooded siblings, of that there was no question, but throughout their lives, there was little they shared with one another aside from blood. Such was the way of those who lived their lives in perpetual preparation for Ascendancy.

The Rays stood from the seating to allow the Sons to leave. Today had been brief but would surely be no less intense.

Malek's golden retinue departed, leaving the other two behind.

Kaylen appeared unassuming as he left, but his hypnotic gaze disturbed her. 'I wonder what they see in me,' Vamya thought. What she saw in Kaylen, without a doubt, was a snake in the grass.

A DARKHOLM DINNER

Location: Kingdom of Blackheart,
Duchy of Darkholm, Darkholde Keep

One person's bitterest fruit is another's sweetest morsel . . .

"I CURSE YOU!" a male voice screamed. The same voice then became an almost solemn whisper as it continued, "with my last ounce of strength, I CURSE YOU ALL!"

His bony fingers lightly patted a page of the libram that rested atop the granite podium in the center of the room, the same sacred *Liber de Finis* he had read from before every dinner for most of his long life.

After having read the words, Davidov Darkholm's squinting eyes moved toward the listeners as if taking note of the reaction of all present. Tonight, as dictated by one of their many traditions, all of those present were of the House of Darkholm, all but Serverus Ecru, who, since the moment he was taken under their wing, had dined with them.

"These were the last words of Annil Heresen," the aged man continued reverently, "soldier of Walcrast."

"And with this, I now become one with you," his ancient lips pronounced, "*In Sanguine nos.*"

"*In Sanguine nos,*" all present responded in unison.

From where he stood, Davidov saw Septem at the center of the grand table that curved ever so slightly, allowing everyone seated to see the monarch's expression at all times. At the king's left, Raja, his wife, her face nearly covered behind a veil, as usual. She was always quiet yet invariably present. Raja was followed by Eriadna, Shield of the King.

To Septem's right, an empty seat, immediately followed by the commander of the knights, his son Erdrick.

That one empty seat was Davidov's, as it had been for many years since the moment Septem became the Patriarch of the House. While the monarch had great vision and far more charisma, had the old man wanted it, he could have kept his place as the Head of the House.

As he slowly walked toward his place at the table, he remembered a time very long ago.

"Father," a young, expressionless boy asked the man who sat at the center of the great table in that same dining chamber of Darkholde.

"Yes?" the grim old man who could have very well been his grandfather responded.

"I am ten today," the boy affirmed, "may I sit by your side during dinner?"

"No," was his immediate, cold response.

"Then, where may I sit?" the child asked.

Davidov had stood, irritated. He had walked toward the end of the table, where he stopped.

He grabbed the very last chair and pulled it back. "Here. Sit."

"But Father, it is farther from where I normally sit."

"It is good that you noticed."

"Why, Father?" Young Septem sat on the chair, and his father pushed it toward the table, "I wanted to be closer to you."

"If you have to ask for a place," he knelt to see his child eye to eye as he hissed, "then you do not know your place. And if you do not know your place, you must stay far away so that you do not become an obstacle to those who do know their place.

"That one," from where they spoke, he pointed at his own seat, "is my place. You will have to make your way over there all by yourself. In the meantime, this is your place."

He remembered walking along the table, just as he did now, but this time, to sit by the seat his own son had earned.

Septem Darkholm's life had truly been one of sacrifice. His work had been rewarded with

Davidov Darkholm

harder work and even greater responsibility. Yet, despite it all, the weight of the crown on his head did not seem to affect him, at least in no way that was evident, not even to those closest to him.

His youth had not been one filled with extensive travel, revelries, or dances but rather with battles, research, strategic planning, and the political maneuvering that helped him succeed with his subjects in many ways Davidov couldn't have dreamed of, for while the Blood of Darkholm was committed to following Davidov out of tradition and fear, Septem was followed out of admiration and respect.

Throughout his lifetime, Davidov had never enjoyed his time as a duke. It was quite the irony that he would rule and mediate important social issues so that people could live better, while in the deepest dungeons of Darkholde, he would bring death to the condemned without hesitation.

Between being the Duke of Darkholm and the Master of Death, he actually enjoyed the latter. As the many years had passed, he had learned to enjoy it much more.

"Esteemed body of the House of Darkholm," his thoughts were interrupted by the voice of Rowena, the Master of Life, who now stood by the same podium. "Blood of Valdemar and Sorja, Guardians of the Kingdom," while she spoke softly, something in her voice, in her inflections, in the beauty of her face accentuated by the amethysts hanging from her earlobes, commanded their attention. "As per *Caena Sanguis,* the Second Tradition, we adjourn tonight, as we do every year, to remember our pact, to remember our duty, to continue our road toward life unending."

Her hands held a silver jug, its surface engraved with the wolfen skull of the Darkholm sigil, while the rest of its surface was covered in mysterious symbols that only a master of the truly occult could, perhaps, decipher. She stepped in front of her father and said, "Patriarch and Head of the House, I serve you so that you may serve us all." She poured the opaque garnet-colored fluid into his goblet.

After her, Septem followed suit. He served Davidov, his own father, to his right and pronounced the same words. Davidov, and the rest of the House, followed suit, serving whoever was on the right. In the end, everyone was served except for Serverus, who, while present, had never partaken in the rite.

Rowena took note of those who were not present but whose dose would be saved and provided. She seemed to smile as she looked at the yellow eyes of her kin in what was, to her House, a nearly sacred moment. She lifted her goblet as her voice rose. "With this chalice of True Blood Tea, we reaffirm the pact of our founder, 'so that we may fulfill our duty in this world, let our temporary vessel become eternal, may we never be visited by Death . . . *In Sanguine nos.*'"

"*In Sanguine nos,*" the House echoed as one, lifting their goblets and quietly partaking in the entirety of the precious fluid.

The chamber was filled with deep breathing and the closing of eyes, with some palms grasping the edges of the table and the closing of eyes, with the lowering of heads in what outsiders would perhaps interpret as a mockery of prayer, for most Darkholm believed in many things, but not the gods.

Silence filled the room.

For a few moments, there were no movements other than the twitching of Seria's left hand, which she quickly pressed against the dinner table's surface. A sudden gasp came from the larger figure of Gustavus that disappeared as quickly as it came.

The servants remained outside, some of them believing the shadow of death was cast over the dining chamber during the ceremony, passing judgment over the lords of the House.

While none of them was certain this was the case, it helped them explain why, in the distant past, more than one Darkholm had died immediately upon participating in *Caena Sanguis.*

As if of one mind, almost simultaneously, the Darkholm opened their eyes and looked upon one another. Davidov stood up, his eyes traveling along the room. Rowena's gilded gaze met with each member present, who, in turn, nodded slightly to the silent question in her eyes.

The eyes of the Masters of Life and Death then met with Septem, each one nodding in approval to the patriarch.

"May we be served," Septem's voice broke the silence, followed by the servants coming through the doorway to promptly bring food to the table.

An array of morsels quickly appeared everywhere, from mint-glazed lamb and duck cooked in honey to wisp muffins, peppercorn cocoa potatoes, and even an arrangement of fresh fruits and desserts. Bottles of Blood Tea of the kind Serverus and the kingdom could drink were opened.

One thing any guest could always note, every member of the House always waited 'til the last one was done before they all moved to the next dish.

In the eyes of many, the Darkholm were as vultures. If that was the case, this was their wake.

Unlike the Darkholm hallways and homes, which were always dark and mostly silent, family dinners, while largely solemn, were somewhat different. As a norm, they mostly wore black and purple, except for young Ignatius of the flaming tongue, who raised a few eyebrows with his occasional green, laced vestments.

While seeming boorish, their words were far from it. They spoke little, but their conversations were laden with information. Despite trusting their servants, however, the royal family knew not to share anything but the most closely guarded secrets when not in complete privacy.

"Before his death, Annil possessed such anger inside," Branden Darkholm spoke. The man known as 'the gallant' rubbed his chin, submerged in thought, while initiating the conversation among his kin.

"Anger?" the serene voice of Ryssa Darkholm questioned, delicately placing both hands around the base of her cup. Her clothes were as dark and rich as the rest of the House, but unlike most, even what little jewelry she wore was the color of coal.

"If I recall correctly, the man had already lost his two children. He probably joined the battle hoping that, if victorious, he could get to see them again."

"And hope was his folly," Ira of the Vine whispered, lifting the cup, her sleeve sliding as if seeking to show the tattoos on her arm before bringing it to her lips. She then placed it on the table and lightly wetted the tip of her fingers on its contents before pressing each against the tip of her tongue with all the grace of a master seductress.

"Man should never dream and wish for things to happen unless he keeps those dreams and wishes to himself," she continued, turning to face a younger, nearly identical version of herself. "Every other man is a potential enemy, therefore, sharing one's dreams risks arming one's enemies against oneself."

Nodding in agreement, her daughter, Xenovive, lifted her own cup and imbibed.

"Can anger be of such strength it can fuel one enough to extend one's life?" Ryssa Darkholm curiously asked.

"For sure," Brenis 'the blunt' replied, the deep voice of the large warrior reverberating, "an angry man fights harder, and defeating his opponents simply allows him to live to see another day. His life is then extended."

"Very *enlightening*, coming from you." There was always a sharp edge among the silken, soft words of Elleonora's mother, Rydia Darkholm. "We all know of my twin's endless anger and how that ended for him. Anger may fuel the journey," looking at Brenis's eyes, she smirked, "but if the misdirected fuel consumes the life and soul, it leads to ruination."

"Uncontained anger can drain a man's health," Charon tossed her pampas-white hair back playfully as if seeking to shine in the dark sea around her. The young woman continued to smile, proud of her contribution.

"It can drain a man of everything, actually." Branden placed a hand on Charon's shoulder, patting it lightly to show his support. He had always enjoyed discussions, especially so with his kin, "Even his coffers may suffer as a consequence." Having said these words, he smiled at Sellayne.

The flower of Darkholm, the woman with the will of iron, responded with a smile of her own, "If the enemy's coffers suffer much more, then I, for one, would gladly bear the burden and sacrifice."

"It is not like you have much choice, sister," Ignatius smiled slyly, "your two moods are anger and brooding anger."

"Oh, stop it!" She quickly stood from her seat, ready to slam her hand against the table.

"And instead of brooding in a tower like a coward, I would bear that anger with you, Sell," Brenis followed Sellayne's words, his support calming her outburst.

"Brooding in a tower does not make anyone a coward, Brenis," Rydia's words quieted the table, "while you may continue undefeated on the battlefield, there are some of us who have *something* inside our skulls and choose to use it to benefit and assist you from inside our towers.

"So, can anger serve as fuel to extend someone's life?" Ryssa wondered again, her eyes on the swirling reddish fluid in her cup.

"I think it can," Brenis replied.

"I think it *cannot*," Rydia smirked.

"In time, we will find out," the commanding voice of Septem silenced them all. "*In Sanguine nos*," he added, ending the discussion.

"*In Sanguine nos*," the House responded.

On the other side of the table, Gustavus was the first one to reach for his plate. The hulking man was known for his voracious appetite, eating as if he knew food would be scarce the next day.

"Here, I will save my duck for you. I can trade it for an apple," a woman placed poultry serving by Gustavus's dish.

"Thanks, Tens." So focused he was on eating, he didn't even look at her while he replied. Nor did he need to, for he knew quite well only Tenslea's hands couldn't move without the echoing melody of their bejeweled prisons.

"Here," his large hand reached and placed an apple on Tenslea's plate.

Tenslea Darkholm placed the now-paired fruit on the plate while she looked at the eyes of those closest to her. "I heard in Coldforge about this eating method, they call it 'dietary plan'," she seemed to gossip. "Apparently, it helps people lose weight."

"And?" Elzabeth Darkholm asked, exaggerated indifference in her voice.

"Well, you know, I want to watch my figure." Throughout generations, the members of their House had learned not to worry about the trends of the populace. Tenslea's forays, however, brought her to the city almost daily, where she found fascination with the ways of the townsfolk.

"Ah, I see," Elzabeth leaned forward, her massive body pushing the chair back as she stood up. The sizable woman placed another apple on Tenslea's plate, "Here, sweetie, so that you can watch your figure more! I will trade it for your dessert. Yes? Well, thank you," Elzabeth continued, the woman's head bobbing as she spoke, her surprisingly deft hands grabbing Tenslea's dessert and bringing it with her back to her seat.

"You do not have to thank me," Elzabeth added with a wink, "I know you need it. Besides, I am not a big fan of apples myself."

Fixing her sleeves, the large woman then happily wrapped her fingers around the last leg of ham in the middle of the dinner table, but the leg wouldn't give. She tugged, at first slightly, then somewhat more forcefully, and still, the leg wouldn't budge.

Gustavus's hand was clasped around the other end of the leg,

Elzabeth's eyes met his, and she yanked the leg, but the hulk held fast and yanked it back.

The menacing tone of his voice and his furrowed brow gave him the appearance of a starved dog protecting his food, "Leave it. I am hungry."

"Oh well, so am I," Elzabeth warned him.

"I have been training all day," his face moved close to hers.

"I have been training *all my life,*" she grinned.

Letting the leg go, Gustavus crossed his arms. "Really? What is all that, then?" he pointed at her voluminous body, "Are you going to now say you are big-boned?"

"Ah!" Elzabeth covered her mouth, pretending to feel offended, before she leaned forward and smiled coyly, fingers playfully wrapping around the ham. She responded, "As a matter of fact, my bones are huuuge."

Gustavus laughed heartily, joined by his brother Fengo, Brenis, and the others.

"You all can laugh as much as you want, but you will never understand that, in every imaginable way, as I say," Elzabeth lifted her chin almost arrogantly, but the sweet smile she did not hide, "my weight has always been an asset."

The dinner was interrupted by the entrance of a man in a red surcoat, his chest emblazoned with the crowned heart of the kingdom, the sigil of House Darkholm on the shoulder, and the horn hanging on his side made him a herald of Darkholm.

All but the king stood from their seats. In a flash, Ryssa draped the veil she wore over her face and walked behind her family, promptly leaving the room through a hidden back door.

"Your Majesty, my lords," the herald lowered his head, waiting for the chance to address the House.

"You may speak," King Septem instructed.

"Pardon for my intrusion, Your Highness, but there's an important kingdom matter that requires Your Highness's and the general's attention."

"If the matter is of the kingdom, then it is a matter of our House."

"*In Tenebris nos,*" the House's murmur followed as an unearthly choir of whispering shadows.

"Speak so that we may all listen." The monarch's voice was calm but just as effective.

"Your Majesty, great general, my lords and ladies of the House of Darkholm, a messenger from the Royal Army has come to Darkholde bringing alarming news."

The members of the House barely blinked. They only listened; their eyes attentive to the herald as a wolf pack readying for the kill.

"My king, we have received news that the duchies of Valador and Volanar have initiated an armed incursion against the border region of Bulwharf, bringing us to war with the kingdom of Ardenay."

Upon the news, Septem rose, his brow furrowed. The silent attention of all the members of his household was now on their patriarch.

Where another monarch would have perhaps raised his voice to shout in anger at the disobedience, Septem's stony demeanor changed not.

"I will take it from here," Erdrick instructed the herald, "thank you. My king," he addressed his father, "If it is your will, I will take the Black Knights and take care of this matter."

With no second wasted, Septem left his place on the table and strode toward the entrance of the room, his Shield, Eriadna, a shadow by his side.

"Commander," the king spoke to his son, "bring your knights, but I will deal with this *myself.*"

At his order, Erdrick signaled and promptly left the room, followed by Serverus, Gustavus, and the knights who stood by the doorway. The rest of the House remained still, awaiting instructions.

"General," Septem called first.

"Your Highness," Idian Darkholm lowered his head before him, his hair as white as Septem's cloak.

"Alert the other dukes," Septem ordered.

"As you wish. I will inform the border dukes immediately," Idian spoke, "and prepare them for potential retaliation from our neighbors."

"Send alerts to all of the rest too. To avoid chaos, it is best we are all informed so that we can best support one another."

"Azareth," to Septem's voice, the Master of Lore bowed, "where is Ashildr?"

"My Lord King, she is still . . . away," he responded, "would you like me to summon her?"

"No," Septem answered coldly. With nothing more than a nod, the king continued, ready to exit the dining hall.

"My King," Idian questioned, "how many battalions would you like me to have follow your march."

"None," the king stopped by the doorway, "It would take us too long to recruit large forces. Alert our forces, but have them await further instructions. As many as you can muster in what little time you have. We know not what to expect if both duchies were to offer resistance. While we do not know to what extent their people are involved, it would be too burdensome and unwise to attempt to mobilize fully without knowing if it is even truly needed.

"The rest," Septem looked back at his House before he left, "carry on."

ASHILDR

Location: Kingdom of Taerea, Duchy of Witburd, City of Linrith

There's no mightier weapon than fear . . .

"They are on the move. Ready yourself," Ashildr Darkholm got off the bed and sipped a cup of leftover wine from the previous night. She looked outside the window at the busy street below of this small city of Witburd, the easternmost duchy in Taerea, the kingdom wedged between the south of Suhne and north of Ardenay, called by some the bellybutton of the known world.

"Atelas," the warrior woman called, placing her forefoot over the chair to facilitate sliding a boot in place. As soon as she fastened it, she stomped her foot on the ground, twisting the high heel to ensure it fit snugly. Before putting the other one on, even before putting anything around her bare, toned body, she took another sip of wine.

"Atelas!" she called again, pulling the sheet away from the bed and casting it over the lone chair in the room.

The man she uncovered was older than she was, with sharp features and broad shoulders that made him both strong and proportionate. His hands rested behind his head, playing with the short, black hair their cousin Brenis best described as "the spiky head of a morning star."

Although less pale, the skin on his scantily-haired chest was unmistakable evidence that he was also a Darkholm.

"Hmmmm," he sighed deeply, his deep yellow eyes on her nude body, "I could do last night all over again . . . and then every dawn wake up by your side."

"I could not," she cut him off as she clad herself.

As if struck on the face, he sat up. "Why do you say that?"

"I could not be with a man I would have to defend."

"Given your skill, Ashildr, a cold, empty bed would be your only companion, then. Is that what you want?" he asked.

"Then let that be my curse," she shrugged.

While he was half a foot taller than she was, the Darkholm man had found that, despite rarely having spent time alone with her, she commanded his heart much more than he cared to openly admit. "You would not have to defend me," he got off the bed and walked toward her, "I, for one, would be glad to have my face bloodied and broken a thousand times if it meant I could be by your side and watch you fight."

Ashildr turned to face him with a smile, but her bright, slanted eyes were serious when she said, "Hmm, no."

Atelas Darkholm

Having left the inn, Ashildr walked down the middle of the street, her steps long strides that, while not as mesmerizing as Charon's deer-like prance, were surely steady and graceful like a hunting cat's.

She was clad not in steel but in tight-fitting leather, exposed in every place she needed not less protection but rather more freedom of movement. Her straight hair was loose, reaching her mid-back, so beautiful one would think she groomed it often.

The Darkholm woman walked along the middle of the small streets as if to ensure everyone, from the stable hands helping the few visitors to the simple merchants by the fruit stands, could see her.

Her hips swayed, and her eyes smiled with a confidence that would inspire those who accompanied her, her cousin Atelas of the Darkholm, Kasabaru Crosse, and four of her men.

But men she didn't need. It wasn't because of need that they accompanied her.

Atelas's artistry and cartography skills were exquisite, and he hadn't visited the region Kasabaru knew quite well in a while. Each of her men excelled at his own skill, but while she enjoyed their company and loved a good camaraderie, well . . . they also came because someone had to carry her things.

Aside from that, she also brought her men along for support, but not support like one would think, as there was none needed for the most fiercely independent woman of Darkholm, of course. While Ashildr's bounty hunters could very well fight, trained in part by Ashildr herself, her men either shouted their support, placed bets on her opponents—on whom she would bring down first and how—or simply provided her with information while taking turns to spread the word that Ashildr Darkholm had come.

And it was this news that made the six armed men walking toward her find her so easily.

"Ashildr Darkholm," the first one called, "what's your business with us?"

"You have something I want," she offered a sly smile, "that is all."

"Not if we stop you," the man spat.

"Hmm," she took a step toward them, "I would love for you to try."

"Marekys," the man instructed, "you duel her. The rest of you, one on each of her men."

"Oh no," she waved a finger, "you men are all mine."

"I'll duel you first, wench!" the duelist drew his sword.

Ashildr looked back at him, her penetrating eyes piercing his gaze, "Think of a weapon. You will be the fifth one I kill."

"Atelas!" she instructed, "do not let the big-mouthed one escape. Huntsman, you men just sit back."

The commotion sent some bystanders away, windows closing. A few curious, however, approached instead, perhaps finding some entertainment in the otherwise quiet city.

Her eyes were on each of her opponents who wielded short swords and were clad in light metal. 'Huntsman is right,' she noted, 'there is money here.'

Ashildr Darkholm

The first man lunged at her. With a simple move, she dodged his strike and dashed past him toward the second, who, caught by surprise, ended up on the receiving end of a kick to the legs that swept him off his feet. Before he fell, she grabbed his cloak, and, twisting it rapidly around his neck, Ashildr placed him in a chokehold while she unsheathed his sword to deflect an incoming blow.

With almost supernatural precision, she circled around the choking man, tightening the hold while deftly deflecting each attack of the three men who attempted to surround her.

"Ok, let's see who's next," Huntsman said to Cerian, his companion, one who polished the surface of his crossbow.

"Two bronze droplets that she kills the fat one next," the crossbowman responded.

"Nay," Huntsman differed, "my two bronze go to the short one, the one with the newest armor. It's clear he has never used it."

"Can I play?" Kasabaru asked, "I bet two bronze that she kills the duelist next."

"If you say that you don't know Ashildr," Huntsman told him, "When that woman says she'll kill him fifth, believe her, he *will* be fifth. Choose another one."

"Then I choose . . . the bald one."

Ashildr wedged the sword on the heavier man's knee guard and, kicking it forcefully, she dislodged it, exposing his knee and snapping the blade that clattered on the street. She then rolled along to grab the broken blade and stood up in a single move, slicing upwards, cutting the man's patella off his knee, and sending him to the ground.

"Fat man's it!" the man with the crossbow celebrated.

"No, he's still alive," Huntsman responded.

The man with the newest armor lifted his arm to strike, but her kick on his chest sent him against the wall right behind him while her deft arms caught his sword in midair and plunged it right above the manubrium of the bald man.

Using her elbow, she broke the blade, and, smiling, she spun around and kicked the man's chest, sending him against the wall to be bounced from and kicked again before nausea made him double over. Before he realized it, he felt the weight of her thigh against the back of his neck, bringing him down and snapping it in place.

"Now, as for the duel." She threw the broken hilt over one of the four dead bodies. Placing her hands on her hips, she spoke to the man who had challenged her, "What is your weapon? And you can choose mine too."

"I can choose . . . anything?"

"Anything," she crossed her arms.

"Then I'll wield my blade!" the man shouted. "You . . ." he looked around in every direction until he found something of his liking, "will use an apple."

"An apple?" Kasabaru thought he had asked inside his head.

"Oh, wow," Huntsman exclaimed, "a silver that she picks a red apple."

"A silver to yellow," the crossbowman bid.

On the other side of the street, Atelas held the leading man who had tried to escape at sword point.

"Just look at her," the Darkholm man sighed, "is she not the marbled muse that inspires any man's dream?"

It all sounded like a bad joke, even a mockery to the pinned man. Still, he wouldn't say a thing lest he arouse Atelas's ire. But he didn't have to say a word. No matter what he could have expressed, what Atelas saw in her was something he would put in writing only in the poems inside his head.

He saw her dancing around the man, the night silk that was her soft hair, weightless, suspended in time. Her faerie hands wrapped around an apple the color of basil.

The ripe fruit, its shell unmarred, flew from her hand to be seen up close by the man's left eye before echoing that aerial dance back to her hand and toward the right.

With his eyes covered, a fountain of nectar appeared between his fingers, his mouth open, singing a song in a single, loud note.

Then the apple flew from her hand and met its twin under the skin on the man's neck, and like a sudden blizzard, the song froze.

Slowly, the man arched his back toward the ground, where his legs danced in every direction they celebrated.

And then the muse, sad her dance was over, flew up in the air and spun around, like a whirlwind playing with a dandelion's seed, until she rested her body on top of his and placed the apple inside his mouth, the same one she shyly bit, as her spirit grieved, for his time was up.

"Beautiful, isn't it?" Atelas smiled, looking back at the man who had run away from him. "Cursed be!" he muttered under his breath as he prepared for a scolding.

Moments later, Ashildr rebuked Atelas not with embarrassing words, especially in front of her men, but with her cold eyes that said nothing other than, 'You had one thing to do.'

"Lady Ashildr," Kasabaru addressed.

"I will have none of that, Kasabaru," she responded. "My name alone will do."

"As you wish, Ashildr then," the young man nodded, "it's best we make haste. We are not far from the capital city of Whiterose, where we could lose track. From there to Hastnouque is an easy march."

"And once in Hastnouque," she pondered out loud, "the division and animosity among its many clans will make it nearly impossible not to lose them."

"I see your knowledge rivals your prowess," Kasabaru smiled, "you're well informed of the happenings in these parts."

The warrior woman resumed her pace with a wink, "One cannot spend so much time around the Master of Lore without having some rub off on oneself."

———————— ++++++ ————————

Ashildr would find that man, she knew, for while great at it herself, Huntsman would track him in the fields, and Cerian's eyes would trail him in the cities. It also helped that while Atelas was mesmerized at her performance, Cerian's quarrel had struck the man's back as he escaped.

Thus, like hungry land sharks, they followed the trail of blood.

"Kasabaru," Ashildr instructed, "stay behind. Ensure the city guard does not intervene. No harm from us shall befall the citizenry."

"My lords of Darkholm," Kasabaru bowed and stepped away.

Soon after, they entered a side street where a man sat over one of many crates, a sheathed sword on his side and a lit pipe in hand. He wore a chain shirt, and his bushy, prematurely gray eyebrows met the moment he saw them walk into view.

He placed his foot over a chest on the floor.

"I hear you took care of my men, Ashildr," he said mockingly, blowing smoke.

"And now I will take care of you," Ashildr said confidently, reaching to the side and grabbing the wounded assailant who tried to sneak up an attack on her.

"We have a job to do," the man argued, "and we mean to complete it."

"And so do I," she responded, slicing his throat before she turned her attention to the remaining leader of the men she had killed.

"State your name!" Ashildr demanded.

"What matters to you when I'll kill you right here."

"My name is Ashildr Darkholm," she smiled, "the name you will curse and remember in your last moments, the one you take to the beyond . . . if there is one."

The man cleared his throat and spat all the way toward her, his phlegm landing right on her shin guard.

"I will kill you where you are before you take a single step." Her menacing, eagle eyes looked around swiftly. "I will vault over that wall, grab that cup sitting by the second story's windowsill, from where I will swing across the street to open that cask and pour myself a drink, and then, I . . . will . . . kill you."

She had been offered many blades, from those she had obtained for the Master of Lore's collection to one masterfully forged from Darkholde ore, but she had refused all of those. She had given every excuse, from "it is too heavy" to "I am allergic," nonsense that last one, for the mask she wore in battle, that avian raptor's face, was itself forged from Darkholde steel.

She even said once she was worried she could lose the weapon when she had never lost a thing.

Wield a sword that would take credit for her kill? "Hah!"

She unsheathed her blade, the weight of which was on her hands as easy as breathing itself.

Ashildr just preferred her very common, very ordinary sword. What was truly uncanny was her skill.

The moment the leader touched the hilt of his sword, Ashildr reached for her own and, swinging it with all her might, she flung it in the air and through the man's abdomen, impaling him in place to keep him seated, blood gushing as his shocked hands struggled to keep his entrails inside.

Then, she calmly walked toward the wall she vaulted over to climb to the second story, where she took the cup from the windowsill. Ashildr then cut a rope and swung toward the other side of the street, and, kicking the cask open, she served herself some ale.

Taking all the time in the world, she slid toward the man, taking a gulp, and smiling, she sat beside him before she wrapped her fingers around the hilt of her blade to twist it enough to end his life.

"That is the chest, I suppose?" Atelas questioned.

"It fits the description," Ashildr answered.

"What lies inside?" He passed his fingers over the smooth metallic surface laden with protective symbols.

"I do not know," she responded, taking another gulp, "and Azareth said not to pry. In any case, is it ever wise to open anything destined for the Master of Lore's hands?"

While some in her position would've been curious, she was different. If she had not been told by Azareth, it was because it didn't concern her, and so she wouldn't waste time or energy digging a hole she would then need to climb out of.

Even if she had been curious, she was committed to obey, for she knew that whatever the Master of Lore wanted was surely important if he had sent *her*.

Atelas wanted to find out. He felt the urge to see what mysterious artistry was so well-protected, why he felt so strangely drawn to it. He wanted to find out, he needed to, and his only chance was on the way back, whenever her eagle eyes were distracted.

SERA

Location: Empyre of Suhne, Basqh of Uhn,
deep within the Elhu mines

Sera's pupils widened, hungrily seeking to adjust themselves to the dying illumination that would allow the man to garner his bearings at the end of the long tunnel.

It is nearly time, he thought, watching the most distant rock walls disappear before his eyes, each one slowly swallowed by the shadows that were kept at bay only by the dimming, pink glow of the rose quartz-like stone resting by his side. It was their ability to produce light, which would persist for as long as it had basked under the sun, which gave them the name sunstones[1].

Sera looked ahead at the picks he had laid aside and then at the wooden copies he would soon use, for somehow, he *felt* he was close. But, despite the echo of the picks behind him, he contemplated the blackness creeping in silently.

'It never does good for a man to walk in the darkness,' his silent lips whispered the prayer verse.

The miner's calloused hands wrapped around the colored crystal, lifting it off the ground to light his way past the other workers and their respective stones of various sizes. Each miner was focused on the job, striking the earth time and again, like worker ants, for such was the labor they had been *chosen* for.

Sera's hands were deft, yet he lacked the precision and talent that would have allowed him to obtain the job he had most longed for, that of a crystalsmith. With little other option, he accepted the fate of a miner, a job he had performed for the last ten years deep within the Basq of Uhn, a mining region with little else to offer. It had been either that or allow himself to become a *saqit*[2], one whose job was considered impure for not directly honoring their god.

Once back at the entrance, he placed the stone among many others like it to bask under the light of the orb in the sky so that, once again, the crystal could emit its glow as a preacher would speak of the glory he had witnessed.

"Ready another one," Sera signaled a pair of young boys, who scurried to bring one of the other sunstones that was ready, having basked under the sun long enough.

"You," he then spoke to a group of women who waited patiently, "gather the dry cloth. We are close."

"Sera!" the voice of Debem, his longtime friend, stopped him.

"Friend," Sera smiled broadly. The men approached one another, resting a hand over each other's head before their foreheads met briefly, in Suhnite custom. "Blessed be the Almighty Sun, and may your life find grace in his Eye."

"Blessed be," Debem kept it short. He smiled gleefully and nodded.

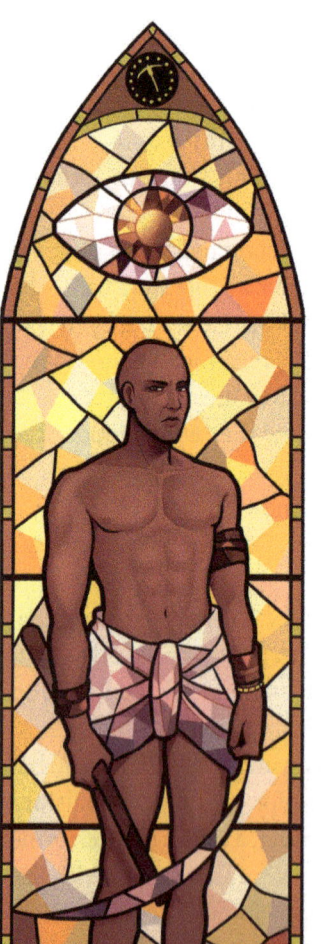

Sera of Suhne

"When did you return from your *malaha*[(3)]?"

"A day ago, but I had not come across you. My heart is full of joy. We visited Gada," Debem continued, tapping the chain around his friend's wrist that indicated he was also married, "She is beautiful as always, running behind your children while she still can. She sends her love."

Sera's chest swelled upon the mention of his wife. "How is your wife?" he asked.

Debem grinned. "She's . . . good."

"And your child? What name—"

"There's no child," Debem interrupted.

"No child?" Sera appeared confused. "But, what about—"

"Died at childbirth," Debem interrupted again, "so *malaka* will be my curse forever, it seems." The familiar voice had an unfamiliar tone.

Debem was smaller in frame, also in his twenties, and not as talented. It was short of a miracle he had become a miner. He had attained his position by Sera's insistence and intervention but also because the man had a sunspot, a pale mark on his dark skin that began near the left side of his lower lip and had slowly grown, creeping over time toward his neck. It was never known if they were the mark of a blessing or a curse, so sunspots always made the Suhnite wary.

"Debem, is everything alright?" Sera asked.

"It is," the smaller man responded.

"You would not lie to me, friend," the larger man smiled, "tell me."

Debem's eyes betrayed him. "You're right. I am concerned about many things."

"If it is about your wife . . ." Sera said.

"No, not at all. My wife might be barren," Debem interrupted, "or I might be. Hey, I am cursed! It wouldn't surprise me if it was both of us!"

"Don't say that. You need to have faith."

"Sera, friend, I've had all the faith in the world," Debem responded, "I ran out of faith long ago. I've accepted that my line ends with me, and so it's something I don't want to discuss anymore. What I'm mainly concerned about is the situation here."

"Situation?"

"Things are not looking good for us, Sera. This mine is drying up."

"We have nothing to worry about, friend. We will be fine."

"Fine? It certainly doesn't seem like it."

"It will. I am certain of that."

"How can you be certain when the mine is drying before our very own eyes? It is as if the mine itself is giving up on us. I heard we are producing much less than what we produced just three weeks ago."

Sera rested his hands upon his friend's shoulders so that Debem could see him smile, "I can feel it, Debem. We are getting close. Something special is about to happen."

"Something special, you say? You can feel it? I really wish you could transmit that same hope to me, to the rest of the miners who spoke all night about what's really happening," Debem continued. "The mine is drying up, Sera. Some say the earth itself is jealous of our taking its fruit and giving it to the Sun."

"That's blasphemous, Debem," Sera warned. "The earth might not be producing right now, but the earth is just the earth. The Sun is the only god, and the earth, and everything over it and below it belongs to him."

"So you're a priest now?" Debem jested but did not get a response back. Sera had always been much more of a believer than Debem could have ever been, but then again, how could he not be? While their lives had not been easy, it had been, in every way, certainly less difficult for Sera than for himself.

"A man must never lose hope," Sera spoke.

'Hope,' Debem grinned, 'can man hope for change in a changeless world? That is not hope. It is nothing more than foolishness.' But he knew better than to speak of his doubt, even around his best friend. Both men had seen even close relatives report nonbelievers to the temples, as required by the Sun, and the punishment had always been severe.

"Friend," Debem spoke again, "you can muster all the faith you want, but you cannot deny what our eyes are seeing. Production is decreasing. The mine is almost dead." He pointed at the distant, scattered, vertical surfaces of the other rocky desert mountains being mined. "I wonder how many of them will give up before the new Sun rises."

For many years, the miners had performed the same duty, walking in and out of the mines nearly every day for months at a time. As arduous as the labor was, however, the Suhnite were taught to believe that every drop of sweat they spilled was done for the glory of the Almighty Sun.

But the Sun had set, and here they were, still working endlessly, and for what? In a few months, the Sun would rise once again, and his labor would continue, as always, until he couldn't perform it anymore, and nothing he or any man could do would change that . . . *or would it?*

'What does it matter,' Sera thought, squashing any minuscule possibility of doubt. He was just one man in the grand scheme of things in this world the Sun had created. Nothing anyone ever did could change the great plans a powerful god had for mankind.

Besides, his thoughts wandered, his wife would soon give birth to their fourth son. With this low productivity came low income and, with it, certainly a scarcity of food.

Scarce food would bring deep hunger, and hunger would breed desperate measures, and what would a desperate man be willing to do for the sake of his children?

'This will not come to be,' Sera thought, 'I will never allow us to get there.'

"Blessed be the Sun," he whispered. His eyes wandered toward the rocky desert mountains scattered along the Basqh. They were as anthills where miners would incessantly search for the fruit of the earth. "Blessed is his Eye, which sees even that which is hidden," with these words, Sera kissed his left palm ritually, extending it toward the fiery orb in the sky, "and blessed are we, who live to worship."

Debem mirrored the larger man's movements. His lips repeated the words though, in his heart, his circumstances had brought him to doubt every one of them.

"So, Sera, what is this 'feel' you speak of, the one you have?"

"I never wanted to share this with anyone before, Debem. But I believe I have a gift."

"A gift?" the sun-touched man chuckled, "like the ones stories say these so-called sorcerers of the dark one are supposed to have?" Once again, Sera did not smile.

"Yes, friend, like the gifts the Sun sometimes bestows on his most faithful. Have you noticed how I have always guided us to find the sky crystals?"

"Well, yes, you have been good, I admit."

"It's because of this gift of mine. It's like some sort of guide."

After a brief pause, Debem asked, "So, this *gift* . . . you just rise up in the morning knowing where the crystals are?"

"No, not like that. I just walk along the mine, and something drives me to move in a certain direction. It's like some tingling sensation that tells me something big is going to happen, like there is a greater purpose in me moving a certain direction."

"You should listen to yourself talk, friend. Special gifts are tales told for children to remain faithful."

"I know it sounds absurd, but I can assure you, it has been there for many years, and every time I have trusted this gift, I have been right." His words made Debem turn to face him.

"I know what you're thinking," the larger man said, "that I am making this up to bring you hope in these hard times." This time it was Debem who didn't smile.

Both miners stood in silence, their dusky skin glistening under the Sun's intense blessing.

A few feet away, both men saw a pair of soldiers approaching, their eyes set on Sera, "Fore-walker Sera," one of the pair raised his voice, "you are wanted in the mine master's tent."

"Friend," Debem patted the larger man's chest, "gift or not, make no mention of it again." He signaled a pair of approaching soldiers, "For the love of your wife, Gada, keep it to yourself."

Shortly after, Sera found himself inside the largest tent of the encampment.

"Salmaanu," Sera greeted as he entered. The mine master sat at the center of the tent, garbed in brown robes, usually fat and sweaty but always made comfortable by the constant fanning provided by two young girls. This time, however, Salmaanu appeared drenched and worried despite the best efforts of the children.

Standing by his side, the middle-aged bald man clad in white robes with yellow trim could be none other than Vaqqaru, Shimmer of Uhn. Between the two, a wooden table laden with parchments where the master kept inventory of the crystals found by number, size, and weight.

"Sera, friend, please meet—"

"I know, Shimmer Vaqqaru, chosen of the Rays," Sera bowed.

The priest's lips smiled slightly at the words of the miner. If one thing the Shimmers fought among themselves for was recognition, and any bit of it filled them with pride.

"Sera, I won't waste any time. I'll break it to you as it is." The master's eyes did not move away from his quill, "things are no good, Sera."

"If you speak of the mines—"

"Of course, I speak of the mines. What else are we here for, Sera?" The master interrupted impatiently. "Shimmer Vaqqaru, this is Sera. He's our best fore-walker. All three of them have been working the mines hard. As you can see, the production of earth stones is still significant."

"I would not call it significant, but rather, somewhat adequate," Vaqqaru responded. "Still, even your earth stones have seen a noticeable decrease in both number and quality."

"Pardon me, Shimmer, but is the loss of a fifth of any significance in the grand scheme of things? Our numbers are still good," Salmaanu questioned.

"Would it be just as insignificant if you lost a fifth of your body?" The holy man's soft threat silenced the mine master. "Earth stones are of the least use to me, Salmaanu, and even those you are losing. Sunstone you have found, but you're at nearly a fourth of where you were just two months ago. Skystone you have produced, what, nothing in the same amount of time?"

"But, Shimmer Vaqqaru, in the past, we have been one of the top producers of sky stones. That should surely count for something." Salmaanu shoved one of the girls and fanned his drenched robe.

Vaqqaru wrapped his hand around the master's forearm and dug his nails into the fat man's skin. "Therein lies the problem. When you bask in the glory where everyone can see you, all eyes will be upon you when you fall."

The mine master was afraid but knew better than to show weakness around his own subjects. Sera had been a friend, but there was an image Salmaanu had to maintain. Knowing he needed to hide it did not make him any good at it, however. "We will find them soon. Just give us time. In the meantime, we can double the efforts and produce enough earthstones to make up for the lacking ones."

The holy man's face twisted in anger as he vented his frustration on the scrolls he threw off the desk. "Earthstones are NOTHING! They will get us nowhere! DO YOU NOT UNDERSTAND?"

It was a matter of time before one among the Rays passed. The eldest among them was almost a century old. If Vaqqaru was to be considered from among the Shimmers for the position, he had to stand out, and what better way to do so than by producing skystones?

Staying the rest of his life in Uhn was not an idea he would consider, but his advantage was gone. The productivity of Shimmers Ala'qo and Q'halla were noticeable, making him third among the four Shimmers, and that was something he could not tolerate.

"I will take half of your men and transfer them to work the mines in Klihq," Vaqqaru stated.

Salmaanu pleaded to the holy man, "You can't just take them. I need all the able hands I can get!"

"Since when do I have to ask you?" Vaqqaru sneered.

"I apologize, Shimmer Vaqqaru," the master pleaded. "Please, I need every man I have. We will double our efforts."

"You already did and produced nothing."

"Then we will *triple* it, I promise you. I will not disappoint you."

"It's too late. I'll take half your men now. I want your best. Starting with *this one*." The Shimmer pointed his finger at Sera, who stood motionless all this time, simply watching and listening to the exchange of words of the other two.

"I cannot go," Sera interjected.

Vaqqaru clenched his jaw, exasperated at the disrespect. He turned his head so swiftly that a drop of sweat flew toward the miner's face. And yet, Sera let the drop fall without a single sign of discomfort or unease. "I am sorry, Shimmer Vaqqaru, but I cannot go, and neither should anyone, for something big is about to happen."

The Shimmer's temples tensed, "Something big, you say."

"Yes, Shimmer, I know it."

"Tell me, miner, how do you know this?"

"I have a gift."

"A *gift*?" The Shimmer's blood simmered.

"Yes, Shimmer Vaqqaru. I have a gift, and I believe it is a gift given to me by God."

Upon his words, Salmaanu's face was a mix of confusion and hope. Vaqqaru's was one of suspicion and wonder. "A gift . . . from God? Tell me about it."

"I can't really explain, but I get some sort of feeling, some urge that drives me to search in particular areas for the skystones."

"You swear under the Eye of the Almighty Sun you speak truly?"

"I do. I swear my life and that of my family under the Eye of the Almighty."

"How accurate is this?" Vaqqaru's stern face was now but an inch from Sera's.

"I will say that not once have I been wrong."

"Is that so?" The priest was incredulous at first. "Since when have you had this gift?"

"Since I can remember, Shimmer, since the moment I started working on the mines."

"And why had I not been told about this?"

"I . . . I'm sorry, Shimmer Vaqqaru," the mine master interrupted nervously "this is the first time I heard of this." To his words, the priest raised his eyebrows at the miner, expecting an answer.

"The mine master speaks truly. I have never spoken of this to anyone, Shimmer Vaqqaru. I have never heard of anything like it, so I never knew who to consult. But I also know the Sun works in mysterious ways that only the Rays can understand."

Again, the Rays, that dream Vaqqaru hoped for, that seemingly unreachable blessing that he dedicated every waking hour to obtain. "How close are we to this big happening?" the priest asked.

"Very, very close. I cannot say exactly, but I'll know for certain when we are closer."

The priest's expression softened. His eyes stared at the infinite possibilities, drawing what appeared to be a smile on his face. "Salmaanu, buy me some time. I'll be back in a tenday." The man walked out of the tent hurriedly, followed by both Sera and Salmaanu. They trailed him to his soldiers as the priest readied to leave immediately, signaling to the servants to ready his palanquin.

Once lifted, he slid the curtain to speak to both men, "Salmaanu, allow your men a few days of rest. They are exhausted, and I want them to look their best when the other Shimmers of Uhn come with me to witness this grand event." Cold sweat and chilling fear ran down Salmaanu's spine when he heard of their coming.

"And ready yourself, Salmaanu. This can be the end of both your lives in the mines!" Vaqqaru smiled. Sera just nodded. Salmaanu smiled nervously. He only wished Sera was right.

"Blessed be the Sun," Vaqqaru recited.

"Blessed be the Almighty Sun," both men responded.

The Shimmer's retinue had begun their march toward the Uhn capital when his hands parted the veil once more. "Wait, one more thing before I go." Vaqqaru rubbed his chin and then pointed his finger casually at Sera. "Why haven't you found anything for the last month? Where has this so-called gift been?"

"I do not choose when to use it. It just comes to me, I suppose. Every time it comes, I listen. Besides, it has never mattered much to me, for I am a man; I don't question the will of the Sun."

Curious, the Shimmer asked Sera, "What do you think you are here for?"

"To worship the Sun with our lives," the miner responded.

A gleeful smile adorned the face of the Shimmer. "Blessed be your life, for you understand your place under the Sun."

(1) Sunstones: The rose crystals, known as 'sunstones,' were large pieces of rose quartz-like crystal that would emit a soft, pink glow after having basked in the sun for several hours. Each Suhne miner takes one with him inside the tunnels. Their light illuminates the deepest portion of the mines where torches are be too dangerous to be taken to; there had been accidents in the past, from volatile gas vents to the more dangerous sky crystal, the blue quartz only the ablest men worked and obtained, to quickly send to the crystalsmiths.

(2) Saqit: The lowest caste of Suhne citizenry, superior only to slaves themselves.

(3) *malaha*: In Suhnite tradition, this is a month off given after three months of arduous labor to those men who have families and children. The unwed or barren would instead get *malaka* (every five months), as not reproducing was seen as not honoring the Sun by multiplying his worshippers.

(4) During this month, the man would visit his family, bring his saved income home, spend time with his wife/wives and children, and attend religious ceremonies

THE MINER

Location: Empyre of Suhne, Basqh of Uhn, the Elhu mines

"Blessed be the Sun," Shimmer Vaqqaru directed his words at both the rows of miners and the three groups of soldiers that had escorted Shimmers Ala'qo, Q'halla, and Mahall.

"Blessed be the Sun," everyone repeated, bringing a satisfactory smile to his face. Vaqqaru cared not for the large drops of sweat on his head that made him seem like one of the miners. This time, the miners would be the center of attention, the workers that would propel him toward his ultimate goal.

"Blessed be the Almighty Sun," he added, so enraptured by his own dreams that he ignored their response to his blessing. "It has been the will of the Sun Almighty to have us gathered today to witness his power and his mercy." His dark eyes studied the reactions of his counterparts. Mahall was much older than the other two. The old Shimmer was dark-skinned and lithe. If it weren't for his robes and his advanced age, he would be easily confused with the rest of the miners. Mahall was so simple, he seemed content enough with just being present.

Ala'qo stood one head taller than Vaqqaru himself, with his bushy, dark eyebrows and beard. Q'halla was slightly shorter and of dark complexion, whose weight would surpass that of the other two combined, putting even Salmaanu's girth to shame. Q'halla's body mass alone spoke volumes of the productivity of his mines.

He could see them where they stood under the tarp, all clad in robes of the same white color in the traditional attire of the Shimmers.

While Mahall stood quietly, the other two men smiled at one another as they whispered what Vaqqaru would think could be nothing more than slander directed at him. Vaqqaru deeply loathed the two men as much as they loathed one another, but today the two appeared like members of the same choir.

Shimmer Vaqqaru took note of their moves before continuing, "Today is a blessed day of the Sun, for we are going to witness something big."

To Debem, Vaqqaru's words were lost in the background. He was much too concerned, and while pretending to stay attentive, he addressed Sera, "Friend, don't you think for at least a moment that this is maybe going too far?"

"I don't, friend. What is too far for God?" Sera responded.

"Sera, the Shimmers themselves may not even believe in this god."

"They do."

"What do you know, Sera?" Debem was nervous.

"I do know."

"Really? You know this?" Debem met his friend's gaze.

"I do."

"And how are you so certain?"

"Because I *feel* it."

At the words, Debem's eyes widened in disbelief.

"Sera, what do you *feel* that I believe?"

Sera paused briefly and looked above before taking a deep breath. He then smiled. "I feel you have gone through a lot, friend, but I feel that you believe me. More than that, despite your troubles, you still believe in the power of the Almighty."

"Sera!" Debem desperately took his friend's face in his hands and brought their foreheads together. "I don't . . . I don't believe in any of this!"

"You are wrong," Sera spoke softly in an attempt to calm his friend.

"No, *you* are dead wrong, friend! I have never believed. I'm worried for you, for if you were so wrong, you might be just as wrong with these stones."

"I know I'm not wrong, Debem, friend. You don't want to accept that I'm right. It doesn't bother me. It's your choice. We live to serve the Almighty Sun, and—"

"We are slaves, Sera!" Debem interjected. "They got us good for generations and generations. We are the worst type of slaves, for we are slaves of the body, the spirit, and of the mind."

The fore-walker contemplated his friend with eyes of pity at his friend's lack of vision. Despite his blasphemy, Sera's love for his friend was such that his pity would quickly turn into compassion.

"Just wait and see, friend. If you say you don't believe after today, I know you will."

"Before us stand the men of this sixth mine of Elhu," Vaqqaru's voice rose, pausing every so often to sound important, "following the divine command, working for the glory of the Almighty." To his words, each of the miners lifted his left hand to kiss the palm before lifting it toward the fiery orb in the sky in reverence.

"The Sun himself has always provided us with guidance, and today is no exception. Our God has, once again, provided for us by blessing a man with a gift." Vaqqaru raised his voice. "Sera, of Elhu, of Uhn, of the Sun!" the Shimmer's hands beckoned.

Everyone's attention was now on the miner. Ala'qo and Q'halla were filled with suspicion. Mahall, on the contrary, appeared curious.

"Sera," Salmaanu grabbed the miner's arm and warned in a whisper audible only to those adjacent, "you better be right about this."

The miner's calloused hands, in turn, grabbed Salmaanu's wrist and eased the mine lord's grasp. "Maybe you should just have more faith in the Sun, Salmaanu."

Vaqqaru stood by Sera's side, his hands clenching the miner's trapezius. If it was out of nervousness or excitement, Sera could only guess.

The Shimmer thought about having the miner explain what was about to transpire. But could he allow anyone other than himself in the spotlight?

At first hesitating, he then signaled for the fore-walker to speak. "Tell us, Sera of Elhu, what are we about to see?"

Sera's hands felt clammy. He has never pictured himself standing in front of such a large audience. Everywhere he looked, he saw others looking back at him intently. Nearly choking, he thought of Gada and his children. He thought of his friends. The miner then thought of the Sun himself, and the mere thought of the divine being smiling back at him was calming.

"Blessed be the Sun," he saluted the spectators, who echoed his words in response to his salutation. "We are close."

Seeing the worker was not great with words, Shimmer Vaqqaru stepped in. "What he means to say is that the Sun has blessed us with something that can only increase our faith. While many thought the mines of Elhu were drying up," he looked at the eyes of his counterparts, a mocking smile on his face, "the Sun himself has guided us to where we are today. But let us not waste any time on this. Let us witness his glory!"

Thankful for not having to address the multitude any longer, Sera proceeded to do what he did best, taking a sunstone and walking inside the mine.

Behind him, Salmaanu fidgeted with the hem of his robes. Shimmers Vaqqaru, Ala'qo, Q'halla, and Mahall followed, trailed by some of their guards and two dozen workers also carrying sunstones, Debem among them.

"Wait here," Sera asked the rest as they neared the end of the tunnel. The fore-walker walked slowly, his sunstone the only companion by his side.

He traded the glowing crystal for the tools he had left resting on the stony surface.

The fore-walker signaled to the miners behind the group to help brush smooth dirt aside as his metal tools met the wall briefly and meticulously.

Inside the tunnel, any man would lose track of time, any man but the miners who guided themselves by a combination of the strength left in their limbs, the repetitive sound of their picks, and the duration of the glow each sunstone emitted. But Salmaanu and the Shimmers were unlike the rest. Hard labor was not something they had known, and the heat inside the tunnels was becoming unbearable.

"Bring some water," Q'halla ordered impatiently. A pair of men scurried back toward the entrance.

"No water," Sera's voice traveled. "If you cannot resist, Shimmer, then please return to the entrance, but no water must be allowed."

"How much longer do we have to wait?" Q'halla asked.

"What is this big thing you have summoned us for, Vaqqaru?" Ala'qo's eyebrows rose like a puff of slow, dark smoke.

"Just wait and see, brothers," Vaqqaru smiled.

"So we are brothers now?" Ala'qo sarcasm was not lost to the man.

Having his opponents on his turf, Vaqqaru was filled with confidence. "Patience, fellow Shimmers. Patience is a great virtue one must learn to cultivate."

"Don't give me any of that nonsense, Vaqqaru. We know what you really want," Shimmer Q'halla snapped. "It will be nearly impossible to surpass my production. We know of Klihq, and even if it gave you nothing more than sky crystal, you would have to surpass Alo'qo first, and I more than double his numbers."

The men's chatter was interrupted by the nearly silent crumbling of rocks accompanied by a small gust of wind coming from the miners' location. Salmaanu darted ahead, nearly shoving the holy men aside. All three trailed the large man.

Where a wall had been, the stones had given way to a large cavern. Sera walked slowly inside, his face confused, indicating for the rest to remain still at the entrance of the chamber with a single gesture. Even all their sunstones could not illuminate the entirety of the natural chamber. But their light was enough to show nothing other than natural stone, the same stone they had worked for so long.

Shimmer Vaqqaru strode to the side of the fore-walker and whispered his demand, "Why are we halting, miner?"

"I lost it."

"What do you mean you *lost it*?" The echo of Vaqqaru's voice was heard by his counterparts.

"We might as well abandon this foolishness. A gust of wind indicates we are close to the surface," Ala'qo commented.

"Search for other tunnels," Q'halla ordered the miners.

Upon seeing not a single man moving, but confusion appearing in the faces of the miners, Q'halla's exasperation became evident. "What are you waiting for? Do you want to be lashed? I ordered you to search!"

"I am sorry, Shimmers," Salmaanu said to the two men. "My men mean no offense. They are not used to following orders from anyone but myself."

Q'halla's larger body stood before the mine lord's, his brow furrowing.

"It's here," Sera interrupted, standing between the two men to separate them. "It is inside this chamber, right under our feet."

The fore-walker knelt near the center of the chamber and placed his hands on the stony floor. With eyes closed, he waited as if listening for an inaudible signal from the earth. His calloused hands brushed the dusty surface lightly before his index fingers drew intersecting lines and sound surfaces on the floor.

Debem observed the scene, wondering what was going on inside his friend's head.

"Bring me my wooden tools," Sera asked of his friend, who immediately fetched them for the fore-walker. He placed a towel over his shoulders as he began to slowly erode the stone with his sharp, wooden tools.

Sera removed some of the rubble with his hands, his fingers carefully wrapping around a small object resting at the bottom of the hole he had just dug. Turning, he walked toward the rest. "I knew something big was going to happen."

The fore-walker's hand opened to reveal a piece of nearly perfect blue sky-stone, the size of a finger, caught between his index and thumb.

"You fool! You did it!" Debem smiled widely, placing his forehead against Sera's, the miners raising their voices joyfully, their echoes reaching the mine's entrance.

Vaqqaru's chest was inflated with pride, but not even half as much as Salmaanu's. The Shimmer's eyes grinned at Ala'qo's scowl and Q'halla's concern.

"Today we celebrate! This mountain production will be large enough to perhaps allow even *you* to stand in my shadow, Q'halla," Vaqqaru mocked his counterparts. "Please, make sure you don't leave quickly, scrambling back to your mines after we get out. I want you three to enjoy this precious time with me, for when the time comes, I will never forget what you always did for me."

Wait . . . something's wrong.

"Sera!" the familiar voice of his sun-touched friend startled him. "Why are you so dour?" Debem took the skystone from Sera's hands, his eyes hypnotized by the stone's beauty.

"Something is not right, Debem," the fore-walker responded.

"Of course it's not! Everyone but you is celebrating. This is *your doing* and nobody else's. You were right, friend. You were right all along!"

"No, friend, it's more than that." Sera's eyes closed again for a few seconds. He searched within himself for that *feeling* but felt nothing. He didn't feel a rush, a tingle . . . nothing. For just a single instant, something caught his attention.

He walked around the large chamber, searching, ignoring the celebrating men, the Shimmer's discussion, and Vaqqaru's mockery of the rest. He even missed Salmaanu's tears of joy as he praised the Sun for having given him a chance to redeem himself.

The man's knees kissed the stone floor, his hands touching the cold surface, seeking again for that strange sensation that, despite the years, was still never too familiar.

There . . . Sera thought.

He felt something.

Wait . . . It was a small twinge, an almost imperceptible spark underneath his fingertips that disappeared before he could fully capture it.

This time, it was unlike anything he had ever felt before.

The miner placed his forehead against the stone surface and tried to clear his mind, to listen to the minerals of the earth speak to him.

But he felt nothing.

Wait . . . there it is!

Sera's hands felt a small vibration in the stone, but his mind was confused. His heart, his being, felt nothing. And not just *nothing*, for nothing would at least be something. It was simply strange, for while he sought to identify it, to describe it to himself, all he could *feel* was . . . a void.

In a flash, his eyes opened. He lifted his head off the floor, where large drops of sweat marked where skin and rock had met.

What does it mean?

Placing both hands on the floor to help himself up, the miner noticed a single, small pebble rolling against his fingers. He felt the slight vibration under his hands as several other pebbles followed suit.

No!

His eyes opened wide, but not wider than his mouth to scream, "Get out!"

The celebration was prematurely ended by the falling stones, by the ground caving in, by the bloodcurdling screams of men falling, their bodies smashed between rocks hundreds of feet below, one after the other crushed, like the stomped grapes of the Darkholm.

STOMPED GRAPES

Location: Kingdom of Blackheart, Royal Duchy
of Darkholm, County of Coldforge

A sudden spurt of dark fluid escaped the wooden canal.

It was quickly followed by a small, pulsating stream that wet the surface of the stained wood. Like rivulets feeding a river, multiple streams of that precious liquid converged along the way before traveling toward a nearby collection barrel.

At its origin, a dozen workers danced to the tune of a *dorole*[1], treading carpets of grapes covering the floor of the wooden vats that basked under the morning sun.

They danced for minutes at a time, frolicking for hours each day of their long lives dedicated to the vineyards.

During their breaks, the workers composed improvised songs. Sometimes they even pretended to be actors, reciting exaggerated verses as they balanced themselves on the pallets their feet stained.

It was clear to anyone that the vineyard workers were a joyous lot.

It was just as clear that their lords were not.

Upon her arrival, the revelry abruptly stopped.

As the workers' dance ended, they quickly resumed the maceration, now simply walking in circles with their heads down in silence, as if seeking to avoid her gaze out of utmost respect or perhaps great fear.

If she noticed the change, none could say, for her perfect features did not move, her blood-red lips did not part. She stood calmly on the low balcony, a bleached statue garbed in charcoal, her head slowly turning, searching for someone with her gilded gaze.

"Master of Life, the morning graces us with your presence," an older man quickly approached, bowing.

"Winemaker," she nodded in response.

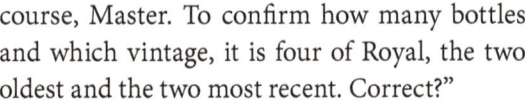

"My apologies, Master, but if it is the ceremonial one you come for, I have not readied it yet," the man added, lowering his voice, not because there was ever any need to hide the discussion with the rest of the servitude the Darkholm so trusted, but mostly out of humility and respect. "I was not made aware Your Honor would come a day early."

"Understandable," Rowena responded. "Can the bottling be expedited in any way? The Master of Death was quite busy this morning."

Contrary to her chilling words, a smile, warm as the summer, appeared on her lips, a smile he had seen a few times in his long years of service. The old winemaker could have stood in place for a whole day contemplating it. "Of course, Master. To confirm how many bottles and which vintage, it is four of Royal, the two oldest and the two most recent. Correct?"

Rowena gracefully nodded.

"I will work on them immediately. I will have them ready by the end of the hour and can bring them to your laboratory myself if you so wish."

"That would be greatly appreciated."

The old wine master bowed deeply and left for the cellars below while her gaze returned to the silent laborers and the fields beyond, adorned with acres of vineyards, all belonging to the House of Darkholm.

Tenslea Darkholm

She closed her eyes and took a deep breath to enjoy the aroma of the relatively early morning, where the steady, seemingly endless march of the workers wrote a song to which the agony of the grapes was the choir.

"Rowena," a familiar voice interrupted her musings.

"Tenslea," she turned toward the speaker with a smile, "it always pleases me to see you."

"My heart fills with joy at your words, cousin."

"So does my own. I did not hear you arrive."

"You could not possibly have. I was already here. It was I who saw your arrival," Tenslea said proudly, pouring over some notes she had written minutes before.

She did not lie. Of all members of House Darkholm, only Tenslea was known to adorn her arms with extensive jewelry, something that added an almost magical sound to every action she took. It would have been practically impossible for her to arrive without being noticed.

"You were here so early? Doing what?" Rowena asked.

"Inventory, you know," she answered casually. Tenslea turned a few pages in her notes before she addressed her cousin again. "Out of all the Blood Tea[2], we are quite low in Twin's Delight. I am not certain if you are aware, but the last crop of it was completely lost."

"Indeed, I am quite aware. However, I am unaware of the specific number. How many do we have left at this location?"

"Nine bottles."

"Nine?" The number was much lower than the Master of Life would have guessed.

"Alarming, is it not? Last year's crops were below every expected quantity. We are hoping for better production this time around, lest we end up having that imported Rovetsean garbage in our tables."

"The last report I received," Rowena began, "was that we should be catching up, at least with most of our crops this year around. Regarding the nine bottles, let us set those aside and ready them to be sent to the Darkholde cellar."

"But, Rowena," Tenslea Darkholm asked, "is that not for the Head of the House to decide?"

"It is, dear cousin," Rowena's eyes met Tenslea's, "but should men ask a herder if they can protect a lone calf to then find it eaten by predators? There are times we must act first in order to keep something of value safe."

"Yes, cousin," Tenslea responded, "but what if it was the herder's intent to use that calf as bait? The men could get scolded and punished."

"In that instance, one must gladly receive the chastisement, knowing that not having acted could have risked everything one has worked to protect."

Their eyes looked into one another's for a few breaths before any words were uttered.

It was Tenslea's jewelry-laden arms moving toward Rowena's hand that broke the silence before she spoke again, "I have missed you so."

"I have always been here," the Master of Life responded.

"Yes, you are, and yet I have felt you . . . *distant*."

"Our time is caught in the web of responsibilities that grow by the day. And yet, we are still here."

Tenslea caught Rowena's hands in her own. "We are, but I wish we could spend time as we used to, just being close to one another."

"We still can." Rowena's hands softly clasped her cousin's.

A wide, mischievous smile appeared on Tenslea Darkholm's otherwise delicate features. Immediately, she let Rowena's hands go. Tenslea walked toward the vats where the workers tread. She removed her shoes. "Then come, join me!"

Rowena's eyes saw her cousin climb the ladder and into one of the vats, where she held her black skirt up and began stomping grapes among the workers.

"Come, Rowena, do not be a cowardly statue. Join me!"

Perhaps for just a minute, Rowena thought.

The Master of Life walked toward the vat and, first checking for the winemaker, who was far from returning, she followed suit.

Directing a mocking grin toward her cousin, she cast her shoes aside. She grabbed the hem of her skirt in her delicate hands, and she walked toward Tenslea with exaggerated steps like a pugilist.

Tenslea giggled, circling her cousin as she screamed in jest.

"Music!" Tenslea directed. After a moment's hesitation, the worker's *dorole* began its tune, followed by other workers, who resumed their dancing in the surrounding vats.

"Let us see if you can stomp more than I, like in the old times!" Tenslea danced and spun, her clinking bracelets and charms accompanying the glide of the musician's bow over the strings.

"How can we tell?" Septem's daughter laughed. "We are stomping the same grapes and collecting the same wine, silly you."

"Then we count the steps!"

"Faster," she directed the musician, who gladly followed her order.

Both girls kept the pace, barely missing a step, stomping around as some of the laborers clapped.

Their skin glistened. They danced and laughed until their hair became undone and fatigue approached, but yet they giggled and smiled as they ran after one another.

"You are *it*! You are the bog hag now!" Tenslea lightly touched her cousin's back when Rowena stopped to catch her breath.

Waving her hand, she laughed, "I cannot do this anymore. That was good enough for today, Tens. I am exhausted."

Hastily pulling her own hair back, Tenslea's hips swayed as she approached. "Yeah. I think I won anyway."

"You won?"

"Yes. I win most of the time at nearly everything, you know."

"When did I ever agree to a competition?" Rowena laughed.

"What a terrible loser!" Tenslea laughed.

"But I did not lose," Rowena smiled.

"Ah, that is correct, because you were what, second place?"

"Well, now that you say it."

"Hahaha, you are terrible!" Tenslea shouted in disbelief. "Rowena, you lost. I won. Admit you lost. I already admitted I won."

"If that is what competition is to you."

"What do you mean? What else is it?"

"Tenslea," Rowena faced her cousin. "Competitions are not about winning or losing, but rather about spending our time enjoying the things and people that are important to us."

"Well," Tenslea bit her own lip, "what comeback can I say to *that*?"

"None. I guess I won," Rowena winked as she readied to leave the vat.

"Aaaargh, Shut up!" Tenslea jested.

"How can I? You just make it so easy!"

With clearly feigned, dramatic anger, Tenslea closed in. Once mere inches away from her cousin, she slowed down her pace and proceeded to fix Rowena's hair. "I am so glad we were able to spend a little time together. Can you promise me something, cousin?"

"What do you want me to promise?" The question escaped through a warm smile.

"Promise me you will never change."

The Master of Life remained silent, thoughtful.

"Promise me you will be the same Rowena no matter what."

"I cannot promise you that," Rowena said in earnest.

This time it was Tenslea who became silent, for the words were not the answer she expected to hear. Seemingly confused, she looked into the eyes of her beloved cousin.

"Everything changes," Rowena continued, "even the most stalwart of mountains changes, for as time passes, the mountain might look the same, but it is an older mountain, now sustaining different creatures. Since change is thus ultimately inevitable, what we should always seek is to change for the better, while that essence of who we are remains the same."

Tenslea remained pensive for a moment, looking unsuccessfully for something to respond that she felt was good enough.

"Ugh!" As quick as a hummingbird, she reached down for a ball of pomace and flung it, having it land on Rowena's chest. Seeing the astonishment on her cousin's face, Tenslea laughed hard.

"Oh," Rowena joined in the laughter, "come here for one second." She darted toward Tenslea, who reached down and flung another piece, and another after that.

Both girls ran, continuing their pomace fight. Their skin was not like delicate porcelain anymore but looked more like that of a bloodied newborn. Grabbing each other's hands, they wrestled one another.

After a few moments, both girls lay face up over the carpet of crushed grapes, looking at one another, smiling fully while holding each other's hand as they sought to catch their breath. Their eyes looked to the sky above, simply enjoying that moment that reminded them of so many others growing up.

"I still won," Tenslea jested.

Rowena nodded quickly, rolling her eyes in disbelief at her cousin's persistence.

"Tenslea, before I go . . ."

"Yes, cousin?"

"I almost forgot one thing."

"What is it, Row?" Tenslea squeezed her cousin's hand tenderly.

And in the blink of an eye, Rowena's graceful hand splattered Tenslea's face with a large pile of pomace.

(1) The dorole is a six-stringed, violin-like instrument played with a bow. Another version is the taurean, a large instrument commonly made from a pair of large horns connected at the tips by eight strings. It is played with a bow while the base rests on the ground. The ditriean is similar to the taurean, but the horns are hollow and have smaller holes the musician can cover to emit sounds like a flute.

(2) Blood Tea: The principal business of House Darkholm is a wine they call Blood Tea, of which there are many varieties. Due to its name and the common belief it is actual blood, it is rarely distributed outside of Blackheart. Some varieties are exclusively available to the royal family.

CHARON

Location: Kingdom of Blackheart,
Royal Duchy of Darkholm, Darkholde Keep

Nothing adds to a story like its backstory . . .

"N o, no, no!" The male voice rose as the books slipped from his grip, sending his walking cane rattling against the floor to roll out of arm's reach.

Despite his elegant clothing, Count Azareth Darkholm took a knee to pick them up immediately, protecting them as a hen would care for her chicks.

"See?" It was the first time she had held his cane. She admired its smooth surface, light weight, detailed carvings, and the symbols etched along its silver head. It was much like her brother, detailed, not ostentatious, but exquisite in every way, even proper. And just like her brother, Charon thought, while it wasn't old, something about it made it appear so.

Of course, in the case of Azareth, while he smiled often and teased more, it wasn't the pipe he had between his lips but the crow's feet and premature gray on his temples that perhaps told the story of the weight he carried, of the suffering he had endured.

The very first time she had seen him, only a few years ago, she had noticed the grays. She had even pointed at them before saying anything else, giggling, exclaiming, "I thought I was the only one!" while playing with her lengthy hair that, like her eyebrows, was of the purest white.

She tilted her head, looking at him with a smile as pure as the hair on her head.

"What is it?" he asked.

"Nothing!" She rustled his hair before twirling around to make her own dance in the air. "Well," she added, "you should have let me help you."

"You can assist me by doing something else, Charon," Azareth teased, "maybe just hold my pipe, will you? It is expensive, unique. I even had to special order the herbs from Daneran's Duchy of Severenda."

"Argh, why don't you ever let me help you?" She took a book and placed it on top of another and then a third one over the tower her brother already carried. The lithe young woman then spread her arms wide. "See? Look at that! Perfect balance!"

Again the books fell. "Perfect what?" Her older brother laughed.

"I saw you! You did it on purpose!" Charon exclaimed.

"I did not!"

Charon Darkholm

"Oh, that's right, I forgot you can never lose, and you can never be wrong. Oh no! Well, I insist, like it or not, I will help."

Even after her Return[1], Charon had not found a suitable position to fill within Darkholm. It was not because of a lack of skill, however. Charon had quickly learned the ways of the House, but it had been through great effort, for she had struggled with her distractibility.

She had preferred to spend most of her time around Rowena or wandering around the Darkholm Library, dancing, whistling, or even singing out loud while her brother Azareth studied and worked on his countless archives.

While his sister was highly distracting, her presence and antics never bothered him. He had lived nearly a decade without her, not knowing if his eyes would ever see her again. Therefore, every second she was around, at least to him, was most valuable.

Once again, Charon helped him pick up the books. This time, she read each title. "Can I guess who was reading what book?"

"There is no time for that," the Master of Lore answered.

"C'mon!" she begged.

"Charon . . ."

"I promise you, just a few of them!" Her charming eyes pleaded behind the pale hair that started to fall on her face.

"Well, but let us get moving."

"Yay!" She celebrated with a twirl, lifting both her arms like a small child while her brother wondered if she had also been like this in the childhood years he had missed.

"*Lenses, Light, and Divine Refraction*," she interrupted his thoughts. "That sounds like . . . Anivar?"

"Is that your guess? Because all I hear is a question." Azareth's lifted eyebrow appeared from within a puff of smoke.

"He's the religious one among us all. So, yes! That's my guess. Anivar Darkholm!"

"Hmmm . . . you are right!" Her brother smiled at her celebration of something as simple as a guess.

"Uf, well, one point for me."

"There are no points, sis."

"To me there are, and I have one!"

"Well, I guess you have one point then," Azareth smiled.

"Second one . . . *Grains and Productivity, Granaries and Production*," Charon stopped for a second before drawing an exaggerated smile on her face, raising her eyebrows excitedly. "Toradmus Darkholm!"

"You are . . . right! But you know you do not have to say 'Darkholm' every time. They are all Darkholm."

"But what if it was another person with the same name?"

"True, but no one else has access to our library," Azareth replied.

"What if it was Serverus?" she quickly added.

"Hmmm . . . yes, I guess. But Serverus is not Darkholm, so there would be no confusion there. Just use the names, please."

"Look at you, always right!" She pinched his cheeks. "Next one . . . *H'din River Sediment*. Now, what in the name of the gods is that?"

"You will never guess that one. It came from the Headmistress of Fennec. Lady Narkari recently had notes organized into this book. We have some time before I have to send it back after copying it into our library."

"I see." Charon was surprised by how thick the book was. "Aza, do we copy every book in the world?"

"I wish! We copy every book in Fennec Academy's libraries. My scriveners copy every book we get our hands on, at least those who will go to the Darkholm Library. Those destined for the occult library I copy myself. You should know this by now."

"I know, brother, I just sometimes forget, or maybe I just like to hear you say it because you sound so . . . masterful!" she shuddered mockingly, expressing the words in an exaggerated tone.

"Last one! *Writing, Grammar Exercises for Correct Writing*?" Charon's hands pushed the book away in disbelief, furrowing her brow, but then she brightened up. "Ianne, of course! He's the youngest."

"Hmmm, you are . . . wrong," her brother replied.

"Ah, wait! I got it. I got it! Yraias!"

"Wrong again." He took the book from her, "Enough now, let us go."

"Tell me then, who?" Charon insisted.

"Forget it. The game is over," her brother replied.

"But you have to tell me! Who needs to improve their grammar?"

"I do not have to tell you," he said softly but firmly.

"W—. Yes, you do have to tell me. You can't just leave me like that!"

"Charon," her brother stopped her, "sometimes people are embarrassed by things they see as faults in themselves. While we might find it curious or even humorous, making it known may only serve to embarrass the person further. We need to respect that, even if it does not bother us to have others know about our own faults. We must understand not everyone feels the same way."

"I understand, Aza," Charon lowered her head slightly.

"Good."

"Aza?" she asked again.

"Yes?"

"Can you at least tell me this one time?" A mischievous smile appeared on her face.

"Stop it," his tone was firm. "This person opened up to me only because I was the only one who could help. That was hard enough as it was. I am certain this same person might be afraid at times that I would share the secret I promised to keep. I can be many things, but a promise-breaker I am not."

"I understand." She bit her lower lip.

"Is it you?" she promptly asked shyly.

"No, know that it is not me," he responded. "Now, drop it and let us go."

"Okay, well, I'm sorry for insisting."

"Do not worry, now let us hurry to the library before it rains."

Charon looked up at the sky she had learned to read so well during the time she had been raised among fishermen. She saw a clear sky and the distant night approaching.

"Rain? There's not a single cloud. It's not going to rain."

"It will if you start singing," her brother laughed and sprinted, carrying the books while she followed, swinging the cane playfully at her brother.

The run along the incline, although short, left them winded. The siblings stopped and sat close to one another, as they often did, this time to catch their breath before resuming the climb.

"Can we go slow now, at least for a little bit?" Charon asked. "The sun will set, and I would very much like to see it today."

"We are almost there, but yes, we can."

"Thank you," she whispered. The maiden kissed her brother's cheek and took her shoes off. Almost as easily as a cat, she climbed up on top of the wall.

As if summoned by her presence, the wind immediately played with her hair, moving its long, silky strands of white in every direction in a hypnotizing and chaotic performance.

"Come back down," Azareth said.

Her brother knew Charon possessed a fantastic sense of balance, praised even by the Twins himself during her training. Despite that, Azareth was always wary of the cliffs and the reefs below, the accursed rocks that took his mother, the same ones that had almost claimed her life too.

"I'm fine, Aza, look!" She twirled, and she danced, briefly closing her eyes, her feet full of grace, touching the worked stone steadily as if becoming one with the stone wall itself.

Deep inside, Azareth felt nervous, but true to what was expected of his Darkholm heritage, it was never evident. "Charon," he wanted to ask but commanded instead, "let us go."

"Just one more minute." She stopped her dance and just walked slowly, shoes in hand, the tips of her bare feet teasing the parapets with their brief touch. "Brother," Charon asked, "can I ask you something?"

"Of course. You can always ask me," he said, "you can ask me *anything*."

While he was always ready, her question was something he did not expect. "Is there ever something deep within your heart that you regret or that you wonder about?"

Regret . . .

Azareth regretted not having clasped his mother's skirt on that fateful day to try and stop her from throwing his newborn sister off the cliffs.

He regretted not having spent more time with his mother when he could.

He regretted not having been with her, to talk to her before she jumped.

"Not really," he responded instead, shaking his thoughts.

"Really? Like *nothing*? Like nothing about the past?" she insisted.

"Really, nothing," his voice was warm, warmer than the sun that had just disappeared over the horizon. "I only worry about the present, about the future, things I can perhaps modify. But, since you are asking me, there must be something that troubles you. What do *you* wonder about?"

"You are so smart," she looked back at him, "that's why you're the Master of Lore! I wonder about many things," she added. "I sometimes wonder what it would feel to be like you."

"Like me?" The Master could not contain his surprise.

"Yes," Charon responded.

"You do not need to be like me. You are a smart girl."

"It's not that." Her hand inadvertently caressed her pale skin, along the almost visible veins, traveling to the scars that covered her neck and shoulder then resting over the eyebrows the color of snow. "I wonder what and how I would feel today if I had been born like the rest."

Count Azareth steadied his books, treading carefully as he spoke, "Every person is born different from the rest, Charon."

"And while we are all different, there are many who still like to single us out," she added.

"Some people just like to single out someone else," Azareth spoke, "because they themselves are weak, so profoundly weak they can only find strength in numbers while isolating others who simply do not deserve such treatment.

"Besides, in the case of our House, it is because you were born different that you experienced things none of the rest of us ever did," he added.

"Many of which were painful," Charon said.

"Of that, I have little doubt," he replied. "You did not have these obligations we are bound to. You had a choice. You chose to return. As hard as it made it for both of us, your journey has ultimately brought you here and has made you special."

"Yes, while I made my choice to be here, I made my choice because I wanted to feel that I belonged somewhere. Still, even here, I am nothing but a stain," she continued. "I can't help but ask myself who I would be if I had been born like the rest. What and how would I feel today if I had not gone through my journey? I wonder *who* I would have been if I had just been born different?"

"You are not a stain, Charon," Azareth slowed his pace. "You are of a different color, another pigment in the grand painting of this life. Like you, everyone wonders at times who they would have been if they were different, but instead of spending the time wondering who we could have been, we should all wonder how to grow each moment and become better people instead."

This time it was she who walked quietly, submerged in thought, tapping the wall lightly with her brother's cane.

After a few moments, she spoke again, "I . . . wonder why mother jumped."

Azareth hesitated for a moment, finding himself unable to speak.

"While I was gone, she still had you." Her words hurt, not because she sought to, but because of how true they were and because for so long he had wondered the same. "She even had Isolde later on."

"Let us not speak of this." He wasn't ready, "At least not right now. We have other things to worry about, other things to do."

"Ok, Aza," she replied, "but I think about it often. I could never do that to my children." Every phrase was soft to his ears, but to his heart, they were as sharp as daggers.

Charon only took two more steps before she broke the silence again, "I wonder if Mother ever loved me." Her eyes revealed a profound sadness Azareth had never glimpsed in them. Before, they hid behind the curtain of pure white hair.

"You know . . ." His sharp mind sought for the proper words to say as he gave it his best to try to smile. "I have no doubt she did."

Azareth told her about that time when, long ago, his mother entered the dining room she had recently left, closing the doors behind her.

"My daughter is alive." She had looked at all their faces, announcing it with a voice that seemed to break. "I have named her Charon, so in the event she ever returns and I am not here, you all know what you need to do."

Azareth's sister did not smile back, perhaps she didn't try to, or perhaps she simply couldn't. "That sounds beautiful if it only were true. But the truth is we don't know, and no matter what, we will never truly know, for she is not here."

The words were a stake driven fast through the Master's soul, words that cut so deep it left him at a loss for words. And yet, he sought to recover. "You are right. That much is true. Our mother is not with us any longer, but, having known her as I did, I can certainly tell you that she loved you deeply. But, even if she did not, today it matters not, for today I am here with you, and I love you."

Charon bit her lower lip and turned to face her brother. His words were beautiful, words unlike most of what she had heard in a life full of rejection.

"You know," Azareth mused out loud, "I believe I had forgotten to give you some good news."

"News? What news?" As always, she was easily distracted.

"Our sister, Isolde, wrote a letter."

"What?" Charon asked incredulously, "she wrote *to us*?"

Azareth smiled, "You know she has been away studying."

"Yes, 'til next year, I know," Charon replied.

"Well, it seems she is done early," Azareth seemed pleased, "and she is coming to meet you."

"What? Whaaat?" Charon shook excitedly. "I can't believe it! Finally! This is the best news ever!"

"Well," Charon caught her brother's eyes, studying her reaction, "don't get me wrong, Rowena and Elle are good to me. I love them. But to have a sister to call my own!"

A gust of wind blew Charon's hair in the direction of her brother, who could see the glistening in her eyes of marigold.

He read her lips, and in Azareth's head, he could hear his sister whispering, 'Thank you,' before she jumped off the wall to embrace him for what seemed to be a timeless moment.

(1)   The Return: As per the Traditions, upon being cast out at birth without ever being approached, a surviving Darkholm would have a single chance to willingly return to the House. They would be accepted as a full member of the House, but with strict limitations imposed upon them.

SECOND TEST

Location: Empyre of Suhne, City of Suhne, Palace of the Sun

Worse than the absence of courage is the presence of fear . . .

Again she rose, drenched, heart pounding inside her chest. Vamya looked down to see her breasts firm. *There is nothing wrong,* she thought. The scent of incense permeated her chamber. It was early enough, so she would have time to read before she headed out to the Test.

She stood up from her bed and approached a pile of scrolls resting over a small reading table identical to the ones found at the sacred temple.

"What will you tell me today?" she asked herself. The tips of her fingers barely touched each scroll until she grabbed one and opened it.

"Here," she spoke as if anyone was listening. The servants had already prepared her bath. The scent of dried herbs on the water mixed with the incense was calming.

The god of ruin will be birthed from the death of the dark god, and as he feasts on his corpse, his reign will prosper.

'What does it mean?' she wondered. There were very few things Vamya had grown up fearing. Among these were words that could in no way be interpreted to bring a message of optimism. It was a bad omen. Her hands set that scroll aside. The Daughter of the Sun refused to dwell on negativism.

Searching for a better message, she deftly opened a second scroll.

A sword of truth will emerge from the mouth of the false oracle. It will cleave the unseen wall and bring ruin to immortal putrescence.

The Blessed One leaned back, pushing the scroll away. Today she would face her siblings in a challenge of prophecy interpretation. While it was undoubtedly one of her strengths, she realized that perhaps it had been a bad idea to try it before the moment when she had no choice but to do it.

Prophecy interpretation was stressful in itself, as one misplaced word would change the meaning of a message that in itself was obscure enough.

Vamya saw her hands shake and cursed under her breath.

'This was just a terrible idea,' she told herself, wondering if her nerves would betray her and place what would have otherwise been an easy victory for her in the hand of one of her brothers.

'I must dismiss the thought,' she told herself. 'I cannot allow fear to feed on my thoughts. The Sun is with me.'

'The Sun is within me.'

'I am the Sun.'

———————— ·•++++•· ————————

The second day of Tests brought the three to the main chamber of the temple. On its circular, stony walls, paintings of the great deeds of the Sun reminded everyone of their ancient history. These were surrounded by images of calendars, sacred weapons, and other esoteric designs.

At the center of the chamber, the most sacred of altars rested, and on it, a golden statue of their late father stood erect. Both of its arms were raised to make it the recipient of the light from above, as if over the sculpted image of the Sun, there was a roof, but there would never be, for the Suhnites believed the highest being in this world and beyond was the Sun himself, and nothing could and would ever be above Him. From its eyes, the blazing rays of judgment[1] of the three who entered wearing no more than a light tan tunic, the same color the previous Sun had added to their line, bathed the three who walked in.

Vamya entered the chamber behind the other two. Each of them wore minimal fabric to cover only their genitalia, all of the fabric the color of gold, in the representation of the former Sun's eyes on them. They entered quietly, toward the three benches basked by the reflected light.

In that silence, the Sons took their place, each of the three kneeling toward the altar.

The Rays followed, each one carrying three scrolls, their wooden cases sealed with wax. The thirteen Rays placed their scrolls on the ground, side by side, three in front of the Ray that had carried them.

Along the walls of the chamber, waiting to assist when needed, the retinues stood, six for Malek, seven each for Kaylen and Vamya.

Outside, near the entrance to the temple, a large group of barefoot people watched silently. It was not often they could stand so close to such a holy place, and they would not allow themselves to mar such a sacrosanct ceremony with their words.

"Blessed Sons of the Sun," Exis began, "the scriptures say, 'Prophecies are the will of the Sun, and only He can truly understand the meaning of His words.' Even the Holiest of Holies was once kneeling where your knees rest, undergoing his own trials so that his spirit would evolve into the almighty majesty of the Sun. Today you will seek to understand and interpret prophecies. Sons of the Sun, today we test your wisdom!"

Without hesitation, Malek signaled an ancient woman, Ehta, his confidant and eldest of his golden group. The elderly woman walked to his side and knelt with him.

Kaylen did not do the same.

'It is *my* interpretation and no one else's. As such, I don't need anyone,' Vamya thought as she looked at her band and then back at the scrolls the Rays had laid on the floor.

"You may each walk forward and pick a scroll to read and give us your interpretation of the prophecy within," Exis instructed.

Malek wasted no time. He stood up and went for the first scroll that had touched the floor. The first scroll to his right, the first one before the first of the Rays.

He handed his scroll to his adviser, who held it almost protectively with her ancient hands.

Kaylen's steps were slow and steady, almost seducing the floor's surface with their caress. Despite his chosen title, Vamya could see that, now that he was uncovered, her brother looked innocent. The Searing Sun's skin was almost perfect and well-groomed. His long, black hair rested on his upper back. The well-spoken lips appeared as soft as the hands of a newborn. His body was lithe yet somewhat muscular, even for his small frame. If it weren't for his being her brother, she would find him attractive, especially with his charming eyes. But no, for his eyes, while appearing as beautiful and sweet as the purest honey, their expression was one of dangerous determination.

He looked straight at those of the Ray he walked toward a young man close to their age.

'What does he see?' she wondered, for, as much as she tried, she could not perceive a change in expression on the face of the priest.

The Searing Sun casually took the third scroll the young priest had laid on the stony surface.

Vamya then walked along the priests, her hand extended toward the scrolls on the floor. She sought to perceive something, anything, that would help direct her hand. A sudden warmth made her stop. She looked with emerald eyes at the aged priest in front of her. Seiris was his name. His beard could not hide the warm smile his parched lips reflected.

Looking down at her hand, she saw the reflected rays of the sun. Vamya looked toward the statue at the altar. Its eyes blazed with the light of the sun, appearing to be looking in her direction.

'Is this a sign?' she questioned herself. 'Is this what the will of the Almighty is guiding me toward?' The Child bent her knee and picked up the second scroll, the one where the light shone the brightest.

As his second choice, Malek took the last scroll laid on the ground by the last priest. "I am the first, and I will also be the last," he said before heading toward his place of reading.

Kaylen walked toward another priest, the second youngest of all. From him, he also took the third scroll before stepping back to his reading table. In his mind, he knew that, given a choice, the priests would first choose their preferred prophecy, perhaps a second one they liked too.

There was less of a chance they had a third preferred one. If that were the case, the third scroll was one less studied, and so, it would be easier to impress them with an interpretation of that which was less known, especially if chosen by the younger, less experienced Rays.

It was Vamya's turn to take the second of her two scrolls. She proceeded to stretch her hand to feel for anything, searching for a sign. Her eyes closed to allow her more profound concentration as she continued to walk around.

Suddenly, she felt a shiver in her spine.

One day, the Sun will be no more.

Upon hearing the feared words inside her head, her eyes immediately opened to find Exis himself standing in front of her, a smirk drawn on his face.

Vamya looked down at her own hand. There was no reflection of the sun's rays. Yet, she felt the warmth on her back. As she turned to meet the eyes of the statue, she saw it reflected the light ever so brightly. It was her own body that blocked the light. Vamya took half a step aside, and the light bathed the scrolls at Exis's feet. Not a single beam touched his hem, she noted.

'It might not mean anything,' Vamya thought. Despite the thought, the Daughter moved as far as possible. Smiling to herself, she chose the scroll diametrically opposed to Exis's and followed her siblings.

The three heirs knelt just a few steps from one another, facing the Rays, who sat down to scribe their interpretations. Exis spoke so that the challenge would begin.

The Speaker called the first. "Malek, Son of the Sun."

The firstborn broke the seal, letting the red wax fall on the table. With a single swipe, he sent the pieces away, flying to the floor for everyone to see. Malek spread the scroll to read, holding its parchment open with his own hands, as the crone's eyes feasted on the writings. "The sky will move, bringing with it great terror, and under it, the land will fail. Famine will crown itself, and its unjust children will bring justice to the righteous." Malek leaned to hear the old woman's whisper in his ear. The hard expression of the firstborn softened as he nodded.

"The Almighty Sun is the ruler of the sky," Malek explained. "His forces will crush the earth, bringing hunger to every land. It is then when the lost will see the falseness of the beliefs they have grown up with, and they will rebel against their leaders and bring those leaders as an offering to our feet."

A scratching sound followed his words as the quills of the Rays danced across their parchments. Some of the priests nodded in approval; others were careful not to even hint at their thoughts.

"Kaylen, Son of the Sun."

Kaylen broke the seal with a *snap* that echoed in the silent chamber. The pieces of dried wax touched the reading table's surface, where they were ignored as if they had lost all value after having been of use. Unlike his brother, he held each end of the parchment in one hand, unrolling with one and rolling it back with the other, as he read its contents out loud. "The smiling night will betray the hearts of men, its clouds will rain death upon the crown of justice.

"There is only one thing Suhne can trust, and that is the will and the presence of the Sun. The world schemes by night so that it can cloud our minds with doubt. If we let the faithless corrupt our beliefs, only death will follow, death most vile at their impious hands."

The quills followed, annotating their thoughts on Kaylen's interpretation.

"Vamya, Son of the Sun."

She carefully broke the seal on her scroll. The Daughter graciously caught every waxen piece before they struck the table. She then kept them as she rolled the scroll open over the reading surface as if the fragile wax would have a better fate under her care.

"After the Sun's final slumber, the earth will cry out in agony."

"It is the greatest of responsibilities," Vamya began, "to gather the citizens of the world under the guidance and protection of the Sun. As such, it is of utmost importance we uphold the values and the laws of our society. If the Sun's legacy were to end, men would fight each other, taking each other's lives so that they can get their hands on just a sliver of power. If the Sun were to die without an heir, this world would plunge into disarray, and the earth would consume itself in the flames of chaos."

The first round concluded with Vamya's words. Each of the Rays took note of what they thought was most important, words that would become part of the sacred collection of knowledge of Suhne.

From the expressions of those gathered, she couldn't tell if there was a favorite in this event yet.

"Malek, Son of the Sun."

The warrior broke the second seal and read, "The life of the king who is will be ended by the death of the king who is not."

Malek lent his ear to the ancient lips. He then stood to speak, "The world will seek to stand together one day under a single king to resist us. We will stand against them and smite them, for we do not follow a king. We follow God, the one Almighty Sun who will send death to every man who dares call himself king."

He sat back, satisfied with his answer, a swift motion of his hand sending the wise woman back to her place.

"Kaylen, Son of the Sun"

"The great warrior will not Ascend; his name will be forgotten. In silence, it will erode the great columns that hold the sky in place. And the sky itself will plummet, turning the temple to dust."

The Searing Sun rose from his seat. His careful steps took him to the center of the room, close to the golden statue. He looked up as a loving child would look to meet his father's eyes. Though not a sound was heard, the moment drew everyone's undivided attention.

That flair for the dramatic, Vamya thought, but her deep thoughts were interrupted by his soft words.

"The Sun, in His wisdom and power, has given His people many blessings. Among these, the birth of His first son, a warrior of undeniable and incomparable skills." His words would have filled Malek with pride, but instead, his expression was one of wariness.

From the center of the chamber, Kaylen quickly turned his gaze toward his older brother as he pointed a finger at him. "Such is his prowess that a prophecy was spoken with him as its center."

"The Sun knew Malek would be less than worthy, and thus, it predicted his loss." Kaylen smirked as he saw Malek tense uncontrollably, his anger obvious to all.

"Yes, there, we see. The ire at even the thought of himself losing shows there is little, if anything, in him worthy of rising. He will never be able to handle the

Empyre and much less Caerea. But his loss will not be his end. He will seek to whisper corrupt words that will destroy everything we believe in."

All eyes were on his older brother. Malek's blood nearly boiled inside his body. Both of his hands clutched the reading surface's edge as he breathed deep and hard in order to contain himself. Kaylen's smirk, which only Vamya saw, turned into the smile of a twisted mind who would find joy in seeing the harm he had just caused another.

"Vamya, Son of the Sun," the Speaker made his last call.

This is my moment, she thought. Kaylen had just masterfully pinned Malek against a wall. Even if any of the Rays thought his interpretation was fraught, Kaylen had ensured to negate any value in his brother's own performance.

Kaylen's had been a dirty move, but she had to admit she wasn't completely displeased. While the two brothers were at each other's throats, the stage was set for her to shine.

Vamya looked into the eyes of the statue and felt the warm gaze of her father upon her. She broke the last seal and hoped no one could see her almost smiling.

A smile that disappeared instantly upon reading the contents.

"One day, the Sun will be no more."

Vamya's mind went blank. Her eyes looked around to see all eyes upon her.

Was Exis smiling? She couldn't tell among the deepening shadows of the room. Her hands trembled. The Sun of Change felt her soul shake as much as Malek's body had done.

Dismiss the thought, she told herself, but yet she couldn't. She had to continue reading.

"One day, the Sun will be no more. Rivers of blood will flow backward and soak the altars of the temple."

She looked down to see her palms had soaked the rest of the words, ruining the writings that followed.

She felt lightheaded, but she had to perform, even through her now tingling lips. "One day . . . the Son will be no more . . . perhaps it will be a Daughter."

The Sun of Change smiled nervously as her own world plunged into darkness.

(1) Unknown to the general population was that the top of the Sun's statue was open, its golden head hollow. Its eye sockets were also just as empty. As the day progressed, the rising sun would shine its rays down and through the statue's eyes. The gold inside the head would reflect the light, which would be seen inside the statue's eyes. When it rained, water would fall from the statue's eyes, thus giving the impression it wept.

A DEMON'S JOURNEY

Location: Kingdom of Ardenay,
Duchy of Walcrast, Wing of Evemere

This one morning he felt as if his head would explode . . .

Having slept in the back of the cart, often shifting to better accommo-date himself among the crates and jars that clattered every time the cart ran over a rock, Ealas got little rest.

What made the journey particularly bothersome was the last few hours. The driver had apparently left the main roads and was now driving the cart over trails that a driver would only traverse if he sought to destroy the cart's wheels.

"Good morning," Ealas came from under the fabric he had been given for cover.

The only response he received was an acknowledgment from just one of the strongmen, which at this point didn't surprise Ealas in the least.

After a few weeks of travel, there was much he had learned from his com-panions. Not really from them, for they only acknowledged him when it was a safe time to relieve himself or when it was time for a meal, and even each meal Ealas was charged for.

Everything he had learned from the trio was from their behavior and demeanor, something he had been taught to do among Ardenay's aristocracy where words were many times little more than an adornment for the vicious intentions of men.

One thing he had noted, he hadn't ever heard their names. Each spoke to the others as if they always knew who they were referring to. The dynamic of their relationship was as if they were connected in thought and deed.

Then again, there was little more exchange among them than 'hey, your food' or 'let's stop here' to begin with.

Trying to make light of an otherwise tedious journey, Ealas just chose a name for each of the strongmen.

The one always rode to the left of the cart was slightly heavier and appeared to be older. He was middle-aged, with what seemed like three tattooed bracelets of different patterns on his distal forearm and a long, distinct mustache and beard the color of chestnut. It was he who, at times, would have minimal communication with Ealas and who often appeared to be talking to himself. Ealas baptized him as 'Beard.'

The other one, 'No-beard,' rode behind or to the right. He was tall, with legs that appeared unusually long for his torso. Although he seemed younger, No-beard was balding prematurely. That one always seemed wary and would communicate with the driver with a signal or two.

And well, there was also Xarnata Daemos. The best word Ealas could use to describe him was 'strange'.

"It's been almost a week, and you still won't talk to me?" Ealas jested, rubbing his stiff neck. "If we keep this up, we will never be friends."

"You're not my friend," the driver said dryly. "You're cargo."

"Ouch, well, thanks for that, I guess. At least I am not bat guano. Do you mind if I sit with you in the front? At least for a time?" he continued.

"No." The response received was curt.

Ealas looked at each of the two horsemen, both galloping just a few feet behind, their eyes staring back from time to time but not reacting in any way.

Giving up on the small talk, the nobleman observed the land around. The sun shone brightly among the sea of clouds floating over the ocean of green they traversed.

To the right rose the distant peaks of the Duchy of Walcrast, land of the Wing Lords. Its vastness made the duchy the size of multiple ones in neighboring kingdoms, its strength a testament to House Ileva's power.

To his left, the rolling hills and valleys defined the landscape of the mighty Bulwharf, which bordered three kingdoms, the honorable lords of battle.

Daemos guided them westward through the countryside toward the kingdom border, close enough to the line between both duchies but still within the confines of Walcrast itself. While in the eyes of men, it would appear to have more breathtaking views, it was also a more dangerous region.

Though both lands were bound to the Crown of Ardenay, Walcrast's fanaticism always seemed to outdo Bulwharf's, for while the bulls were known for their fierce loyalty to the Crown, over time, the Wings of Walcrast had become closer to the Church of Light and, as if competing for its benediction, they swiftly exacted punishment upon brigands and others the Church deemed criminals.

But one thing Ealas didn't have to worry about was punishment. At least, he thought he didn't.

Far ahead, a glint called their attention. Daemos drove the horses farther away from the trail they traversed.

From the new route, Ealas could see it had come from the helmet of one of six men. Clad in mismatched armor and hiding behind some trees along the road, their group was evidently suspicious, even more so when one of the men pointed at them.

Xaruata Daemos

"Don't get seen or captured. I got only the first half in advance," Daemos stated.

"First half?"

"First half," Daemos responded.

"Wait, but I thought you said one hundred," Ealas questioned.

"One hundred, now."

"Exactly."

"There's also one hundred later. At arrival," Beard interjected.

Feeling tricked, Ealas did not hold back. "This is a travesty."

"Do you not have the money?" Beard asked.

"What does it matter? What you're asking for is a robbery. This is just short of a crime."

"Criminals hide. Who's the one hiding now?" Beard asked, to which Ealas couldn't say anything back.

"Now, do you have the coin? Because if not, you can stay here," the bearded companion continued, his tone stating clearly he wasn't saying it in jest.

"I don't seem to have an option."

"Well," Beard replied, "you can say you won't pay and stay here."

"No, of course, I'll complete payment. I just wanted you to realize the price is, quite honestly, ridiculous."

Daemos looked back at Ealas. "I know."

To the highborn, the audacity of the man was as unbelievable as it was bothersome. How many people were taken advantage of by this group? But he also wondered how many people took advantage the same way in this world full of the maliciousness of men.

This was certainly commonplace in Blackheart, he thought, for the further men lived from the beacon, the less Light they could see, and their morals would always reflect that.

In any case, staying behind was not really an option, especially not in the middle of nowhere in Evemere, where he could potentially be recognized.

They stopped to camp near a large outcropping of rock, one of the many in this region.

No-beard pulled dried seeds out of his bag and threw them inside his mouth unceremoniously.

Behind No-beard, on a distant hill to one side, Ealas observed a strange scene: two columns of eight figures walking at a slow, almost rhythmic pace.

Their cloaks, too heavy for the spring, covered most of their body, except for where the hands of half carried either large weapons or oversized staves.

From within the folds in their fabrics, pairs of large horns, some curved, others branching, protruded in all but two of the travelers.

His attention was so fixed on the columns that only late did he realize, upon setting his eyes on the cart behind them, the humanoid figures were larger than the horses that pulled it.

"Never have I imagined I would get to witness such a scene." Beard appeared by his side, his deep voice dispelling his musing. "Do you believe in luck?"

"Luck?" Ealas shrugged, "Sure! I mean, why not? Why do you ask?"

"Because your eyes are lucky if you ever see them in your lifetime."

"You mean the caravan? How so?"

"That's the M'din right there," Beard pointed at the cloaked figures before bringing his hands to his belt.

"The M'din?"

"Yah, they're the monks of the isle of M'din on their pilgrimage. It is said the mere sight of them brings great luck. Who knows, maybe it's those who are blessed by the greatest luck ever who get to see them."

"I thought the stories of the M'din were more tales of fantastic, foreign giants. Where are they headed?"

"Yah, well, as for fantastic, I don't know. Where are they going? Well, I don't know that either. But you can go ask them if you want and then tell us, if you're lucky enough to escape with your life, that is!"

"Has anyone ever trailed them?"

"Boy, where do you get your education anyways? They're the most dangerous people in this world! You know what, I don't know, and I rather mind my own business anyways," Beard spat before returning to the bags.

'Where have I gotten my education,' Ealas told himself, 'well, perhaps in a very limited and biased place.' He continued contemplating the caravan that moved at a steady snail's pace over the back of the hill until they disappeared behind the tall vegetation.

———— ++++++ ————

Once back, Daemos appeared to be searching for a place, reading from a piece of paper he kept close to his chest before charting his course in a hand-drawn map of the region.

Curious, Ealas approached him. "Can I take a look?"

"No," Daemos's response was immediate.

"Do you mind if I ask you a question, then?" Ealas asked.

"Yes."

And there it was, once again, an abrupt answer that would stop the conversation as a wall would stop a feather blown by the wind . . . or *would it?*

"Well, allow me to ask you anyway. What are you looking for? I see you reading from that note."

"Some rocks," Daemos responded.

"Some rocks? There are rocks everywhere in this region." For a moment, Ealas wished he could squeeze his neck and get a complete answer.

"Sralfalle," Daemos replied.

"Sralfalle . . . huh." The sole name of the rare flower made him curious, so he inquired, "What for?"

"Because I want it."

"Can I ask you what you want it for?"

"No."

"Well, I'll tell you this, you are looking in the wrong place. While I do not know much about herbalism, I do know sralfalle. It grows in a very particular way, in a specific region of Evemere." He was expecting Daemos to inquire further, but quite quickly Ealas learned he was perhaps expecting too much.

"We are . . ." he looked around at the mountains and villages he had visited before whenever he had visited the lords of House Ileva, "about two to three hours away from where we could find it."

"Then let's go," said Daemos.

"Shhhh," No-beard interrupted, "We're not alone." He reached for his mace and armed himself. At his signaling, his companion's hands were on his own weapon.

Xarnata Daemos moved fast toward the cart, leaving Ealas behind, still sitting on a rock.

The sudden hooves of horses galloping from different directions alerted the strongmen.

"Move, now!" No-beard shouted, sending Ealas dashing toward the cart as each of the strongmen flanked it, and the horsemen started appearing in sight, three to each side.

'Who should I assist?' Ealas thought. He knew it would be best to wait at least until the initial attack was over so that he could better assess his opponents. The wait, however, could cost the life of one of the men on his side. There was risk involved with moving first, but there was also just as much in moving last.

"Outnumbered," the helmeted man spat, "lay down your arms, and we take the cart, and you live."

Xarnata raised his hand, momentarily calling everyone's attention.

"Yes?" the man in the helmet asked.

"Kill them," Xarnata's order followed. Immediately after, the whinnying of a horse whose skull had been struck by Beard's mace. The beast reared its legs, forcefully dismounting its rider.

No-beard ducked a highwayman's axe and struck another equid, its knee buckling under the strength of the impact.

The helmeted man charged toward Daemos, swinging widely to behead the man. Ealas's sword swiftly interrupted the attack, deflecting the blade of the bandit leader. The nobleman then jumped and dragged the attacker by his vest to the ground. Losing his helmet, the man kicked Ealas and crawled quickly toward his men.

Beard and No-beard's every move were uncoordinated but surprisingly effective. In a matter of seconds, they downed two of the attackers and two beasts without receiving a scratch. Ealas's blade, in contrast, slashed only at men but showed respect for the beasts they rode.

In the meantime, Xarnata sat on the cart calmly. The driver reached under his seat, from where he pulled a long, thin, hollow wooden cylinder and cleaned its inside with a long stick that had a piece of cloth attached to it.

Ealas dodged the helmeted man's clumsy strike, not realizing he exposed No-beard's thigh instead, allowing the blade to slice through flesh and muscle, stopping short of hitting bone. No-beard cursed, swinging back at the bandit leader and barely missing his face.

Beard's mace smashed against an opponent's haft, sending the head of his axe flying toward the cart.

It fell near the feet of Xarnata, who now peered through the tube with squinting eyes before he began stuffing it.

Despite being off balance due to his new limp, No-beard kept fighting. He clasped his wounded thigh to try and stop the rapid spurting of blood he couldn't contain. His assailant rapidly approached. Extending his hand, No-beard blinded him with a splash of fresh blood.

The surprise ended quickly, with a half spin and deft swing of Ealas's sword finishing the blinded man.

"RETREAT!" The bandit leader ordered his men, mounting his beast.

One of the remaining bandits galloped away quickly.

Darting like a striking snake, Ealas promptly chased after the last man before he could take his mount and escape. The bandit reached his horse and hurriedly jumped on the saddle, leaving his axe on the ground and breaking free from Ealas's grasp.

The nobleman swiftly picked up the weapon and, just as in the old axe-throwing competitions held in Ardenay's fairs, he swung hard and fast.

'Lord of Light, guide my hand.' While the hand axe was not well balanced, Ealas's skill would have it fly like a smith's masterpiece. As if guided by the deity himself, it hit the arm of the bandit.

But it was the heel and not the head which made contact.

And so, the man galloped away, scared and unwounded, for Ealas's attack had both hit and missed its mark.

"Twisted fate," he smiled, embarrassed. Suddenly, he felt a sharp sting on the back of his neck and a quick trail of blood traveling down. He reached back and pulled out a sharp needle the length of a dagger, red feathers on its other end.

Confused, he looked back at his traveling companions. No-beard was being aided by Beard, while Xarnata, yes, Xarnata stood in his seat, removing the long tube from his lips, on his face a smile as twisted as fate.

———— ·•◆◆◆•· ————

Again the terrible headache.

This time, however, it was accompanied by a stiff neck.

Ealas woke up in the back of the moving cart once more. As to how he got here, he didn't remember, and no matter how hard he tried, he simply couldn't.

Without wasting a second, he sat up straight.

Beard was on horseback, mumbling to himself, as always. No-beard rode his horse, his leg bandaged, and not just with any bandage but with a clean, apparently professionally placed bandage that wrapped both his thigh and shin in a flexed position. He was wearing clean, better clothes.

Driving the carriage was Daemos, Xarnata Daemos, quiet and absorbed in his own world.

His stomach groaned. He was hungry, nauseated even, and the sun's bright light made his headaches worse.

The sun . . . wait, the sun is just rising?

"Beard," he called the only man he expected an answer from.

"You're finally awake," he responded.

"How long has it been?"

"Just one day."

"*Just* one day?" the nobleman asked.

"Yes, only one."

Looking at the back of the cart that had by now become too familiar, he saw new bottles and small crates in the places of some that were missing.

"Did we stop somewhere?"

"Bellmorell."

"Bellmorell?"

"Yes, to treat his wounds and trade what we got from the assaulters."

Ealas climbed up to the front and sat by Xarnata's side, who just kept driving.

"What happened back there? Did you just drug me?"

"Yes," Daemos responded casually.

"With what?"

"Don't bother asking. It's none of your concern," Beard responded.

"Torment," Daemos interjected.

"Torment? What is *torment*?" Ealas asked.

"It's to put large beasts to sleep," Daemos responded.

"Oh, I see, and I suppose you were attempting to save my life with it from bandits that were running away?" the nobleman interrupted.

"No."

Ealas made no attempt to hide his exasperation. "Then WHY? I had just saved your life and helped you fight!"

"You owe me half the payment. You also have to take me to the sralfalle."

"And *why* should I take you to the srallfalle now?" Ealas almost shouted, "Give me a good reason, just *one*!"

"You said you'd show me."

"Yes, I did, and what if I change my mind?" Ealas quickly noted No-beard looking at him from the corner of his eye.

"It also gives you muscle spasms and the runs," Xarnata spoke again.

"What?" his words had befuddled Ealas.

"Severe, sometimes, after the first day," Daemos mumbled.

Frustrated, he just sighed. He thought about simply going on his own toward the accursed kingdom. It would not be safe, but maybe he would be safe from this insane group. Not knowing what was coursing through his body, however, gave him much less of a reason to abandon them. Besides, what if he was shot with a second dose of this *torment*? He didn't even want to think about it.

Ealas just accepted the fact that he was in this predicament, traveling with two unfriendly men led by some weird bastard.

There were times when one simply had to continue the road one took in the first place, no matter what happened, for a man could jump off a cliff, but regardless of what he saw at the bottom, he could never undo the jump. He just had to close his eyes and fall.

Ealas sighed, taking note of Beard reaching slowly for his mace, riding closer to the cart. Ealas said, "No need, man, really. Just at least give me something to eat."

He then lifted a finger and pointed in the direction of the srallfalle.

⸻ ⊹⊹✦⊹⊹ ⸻

It was close to noon when they arrived outside the town of Norcrag, a rocky region laden with unpredictable outcroppings.

Northeast of the town, where few plants would grow and no cart would travel through, thousands of irregularly shaped rocks adorned the landscape, ranging in size from that of a horse to that of a small fort. Even the road seemed to shy away, for it found only one way into the town, which was the same way out, and it lay at the opposite side of the rocky region.

In the past, Walcrast engineers had attempted to use the abundant rock in this area to build forts, but they had found it to be too porous and brittle and had thus been deemed essentially useless.

Upon their arrival, they had bumped into a group of young adolescents carrying bunches of the flowers.

Ealas had suggested they buy some from them. They had likely picked them to sell them in the marketplaces of nearby towns anyway.

"No," had been Xarnata's abrupt response, "I need to gather them myself."

"What do you mean?"

"I was told 'bring me srallfalle flowers'."

Ealas waited for a moment for more details that, of course, would not come. "And how do you get from that to you having to pick the flowers yourself?"

'Wait, why am I even asking this?' In the end, he just shook his head and, knowing there would likely be no use in disputing, Ealas had him stop the cart near the base of the stony hillside.

They would continue on foot over the trails he knew.

He thought about offering to pick the best flowers and bringing them, but knowing Xarnata would nevertheless insist on gathering the flowers himself, he instead recommended both bodyguards stay behind, watching the cart while he accompanied Xarnata to the flowerbed.

For most of an hour, the men walked the uneven ground uphill. Even this low, close to the ground, they could note a few rocks crumbling under their feet. He damned himself for having forgotten to drink some water before the climb. Despite the sweat and the cumbersome robes the merchant wore, Xarnata seemed unfazed.

They reached a craggy area surrounded by shriveling, dried bushes. From their location, they could look down and see the cart below and the town of Norcrag farther away.

Ealas recalled the times he had come here with Siul and Varen during their travels, hiding from Creod of the Royal Guard accompanying them.

The memory of his cousin Vallein, shouting protests from below while Vallein's younger brother, Langel, braved his own fear of heights and climbed Ealas's back, brought a smile to his face.

"Look, Xarnata. Isn't it curious?" he pointed at the strongmen. "We are not that far from them, and yet they look like ants."

"I need to gather srallfalle," was the response he received.

Shaking his head and laughing under his breath, Ealas let the memories go.

"You must come closer to the edge," Ealas said, "but be careful where you step. These rocks are—CAREFUL!" He grabbed Xarnata's sleeve and pulled him as pieces of the crag broke off under the man's feet, sending millions of pieces tumbling below.

"For the love of God! What's in your mind?" he exclaimed, alarmed. "The ground is too brittle. We will have to crawl from here on to better distribute our weight."

After having agreed, both men then moved on all fours, separated from each other by only a few feet.

They reached the craggy edge, where Ealas waited for his companion to join him.

Below them, the rocky wall waited, the occasional rock reaching out from its uneven surface.

"It is under these ledges that the srallfalle grows. Our weight will make it difficult for us to grab them without falling," Ealas cautioned. In response, Xarnata raised an eyebrow and pursed his lips but said nothing.

Ealas remained pensive.

One of them would have to stay up, holding the other one by the legs, while the second would have to reach for the flowers. Who would do what was the dilemma. The decision wasn't easy. Ealas would have to place his life in the hands of this untrustworthy man and have faith he would have the strength and stamina to keep the nobleman from falling. Otherwise, he would have to hold the man and wait for him for God-knows-how-long to choose the flowers. While he knew his strength, Xarnata was heavier than he was.

"Well, this is a real test for us. We must trust each other if you are going to get those flowers."

Daemos looked at him, but somehow it felt as if through him. Ealas continued, "I need you to trust that I will get the best flowers for you. Since you are heavier than I am, you will need to lean back and grab my legs and not let go. Can I trust you to do that?"

The merchant's mouth moved. He flicked his tongue and smacked his lips but said nothing.

'God of Light, while we know we shall never tempt and test you, I will need to test both your love for me and my faith in you.' He held his hand to his heart.

"Trust me. I promise you I will get you the best flowers I can put my hands on. How many flowers do you need, Daemos?"

"Six," the man responded.

The nobleman crawled to the ledge, Xarnata's hands clutching his ankles. "I will need you to move just a little. I can't reach just yet."

In an instant, small pieces of rock fell rapidly to his immediate left and right, followed by a slip from Xarnata's grasp.

Ealas closed his eyes, his forehead was quickly drenched. He prayed hard and fast when a brusque pull stopped his fall, a jerking motion pulling the legs of his pants, tugging time and again until he finally felt stable.

Opening his eyes, Ealas saw a beauty he thought he had forgotten.

Before him, a bed of small flowers that hung like a chandelier, held in place by the roots attached to the stone roof, feeding from its minerals and yet, keeping it from crumbling. Their tiny blue petals curved outward. They were blue, like the sky above, like the bright eyes of his best friend, the one he had to leave behind, for such was his love, he couldn't drag Siul into this perilous trip, on a journey that would make him a pariah, but that he simply *had to* undertake.

The honeyed pistils danced in the wind bending the flowers' stems before they quickly returned to their original shape, that of a perfectly straight line reaching toward the ground far below as if escaping the midday sky from which they had stolen the color. Their fragrance brought memories of his childhood, of the times Astas had placed these favorites of his mother's by his mother's urn.

"I am here," he shouted. "I can see the srallfalle!"

Suddenly, movement above, the return of the dust, the small rocks, and now larger ones fell past Ealas and broke upon contact with the wall before ending far below.

More rocks fell to the right, where Xarnata's head and cloakless torso appeared, carelessly reaching down, pulling himself with the rocks, each pull producing a tug on Ealas's pants.

'I should have known better,' Ealas gulped. He looked back at Daemos, but what he saw was something he never expected: Xarnata's hands reached out and delicately touched the flowers' petals. His long hair, covered in dust, now pulled away from him and toward the distant ground. His eyes of amber were fixed on the flowers, quickly moving from one to another and then swiftly to the next. But what really caught Ealas's attention was the pleasant smile on the man's face.

Both men hung like bats in the same circumstances but in different worlds of their own. The one praying he wouldn't fall to his doom, wondering if that fate would be better than the dark journey that awaited him. The other one seemed unaware of his surroundings and lived this moment, happily picking his flowers.

++++++

Both men sat atop the crag, having crawled over the crumbling ground, their blood finally leaving their heavily blushed faces.

It had taken them many tries, most of them accompanied by scares, to climb back up.

Ealas's face paled when he saw they had been held in place by Daemos's tearing cloak ledged on a sharp piece of rock that broke off immediately upon their final pull. While he would have probably tried that years ago with his friends, he was sure he wouldn't do the same again now that he was older and wiser.

He proceeded to dust himself while Xarnata remained largely covered, in his grasp, the six srallfalle he had chosen.

"This was really crazy, friend," Ealas puffed.

"I have no friends," Daemos responded.

Ealas knew not how to respond. His own noble life, he had learned, had been filled with people he knew but that he couldn't really call friends.

"Well, there is this *one* friend I have," the merchant added, "*these* are for her."

The nobleman turned toward him, smiling quietly, but Xarnata's attention was just on the flowers.

"I wonder if your friend will ever find out everything you would put yourself through to bring her these flowers."

He then placed his hands around Xarnata's, their eyes meeting. "Tell your friend," he continued, "she's lucky to have you in this friendless world."

The merchant's eyes went back to the flowers.

Ealas again looked at their bounty that grew in the most impossible of places, in the strangest and direst of circumstances. These were flowers that, as far as the world knew, had no medicinal properties, bore no fruit, and brought no nourishment. They could not even grow anywhere else and would quickly shrivel and die when planted around others.

'To the world,' he thought, 'they are nothing more than useless, and yet, in their own special way, they are beautiful.'

This morning the headaches were different.

After having woken up on the back of the cart for over a tenday, Ealas believed he had finally gotten used to the neck stiffness and the headaches that accompanied them. He had used what fabric he could put his hands on as a headrest, but even on the main roads, the travel had been far from smooth. Thus, every night he ended up going to sleep sore and tired, and he woke up every day unrested and in pain.

This morning, however, he woke up alarmed and alert as he felt his body jerk when the cart suddenly stopped moving.

He waited for the voice of one of his companions to announce the reason for the stop, but all he could catch was the protest of the horses and an unintelligible conversation ahead.

'A quick glance,' he thought, popping his head out from under the fabric, hoping to remain unseen before the conversations ended; his eyes caught the small, red box where Xarnata had placed the flowers, the same that rested by his side and never left it.

Beyond the box, he saw a backdrop of gray. He moved back to adjust his eyes, and yet for a moment, he perhaps felt what it would feel to be Xarnata, for his amazement wouldn't let him react upon seeing that wall.

That massive structure of nearly thirty feet of stony height, with a winding body that extended beyond his sight. Its ashen surface was weathered and dark in places that had seen war many times before. In other parts, it was quite light, where it had been rebuilt after the destruction it faced decades ago.

'The wall stands again,' Ealas marveled.

A structure this large would have taken a whole army and much longer than twenty summers to be rebuilt. 'Then again,' he posited, 'if the tales of its obliteration had been true.'

As if attempting to force its entry, the wind blew in the direction of the wall, lifting a cloud of dust in its wake that quickly settled, as if even nature gave it a second thought before proceeding.

'Who in their right mind would seek to destroy this wall' Ealas wondered. 'Its impregnable body would certainly keep the people inside protected from the world, but more than that, it would most certainly keep the world protected from the evil inside Blackheart.'

He was just a crewman on this ship he had taken. The ship had sailed. He just hoped it took him to the destination he had envisioned. Every event was part of the journey. He had to survive them, for there was no jumping off the ship of life.

THE FIGHTER

Location: Empyre of Suhne, Basqh of Uhn, Aqaba village

Few things are deadlier than a man's desperation . . .

Sara . . .

The world spun rapidly. A choir of unintelligible shouts echoed around him like a sandstorm.

Every thought, every memory he sought coalesced into a disorienting flash before becoming complete darkness.

Sara . . .

'My daughter?' Parental suspicion raised, he lifted his forearm instinctively, effectively blocking the impact that brought him back to his senses.

"Sera!" Spectators celebrated upon seeing his muscles tense. "Sera!" Sera ducked under his opponent's fist to knee his stomach, driving nearly all the air out of his lungs before the man fell to the ground face-first, bringing the fight to a screeching halt.

Immediately, he raised his open palm toward the stone ceiling and lowered his head, mumbling a short prayer through lips of silence. He then left the sandy pit, leaving behind both those who celebrated his victory and those who were made poorer for having bet on his loss.

"What is wrong with you?" The exasperated presence of Bahul appeared by his side. The elderly man's strike barely moved him, "You scared me back there!"

"I won, didn't I?" Sera half-smiled.

"Yes, you did, after getting your face pummeled like an idiot!" the collector responded. "You have gotten credit for one-twentieth *mahk*[1]."

"One-twentieth?" Sera halted, "I have a family to feed."

"You're not the only one who does," Bahul smiled through stained teeth.

"You agreed to one-tenth."

"I did not," Bahul began packing his earnings, "I said I would consider it."

"Bahul," Sera grasped his hand, "you are making a lot from our fights."

"Yes," the collector responded, "and we have a deal. I am following our agreement." He looked at the younger man, "Now let me go, will ya?"

Sera did as instructed, as he had done for the last few months since he had come to Aqaba. "Bahul," he asked, "then I want to fight for three-tenths from now on."

The old man sighed. "Let me tell you something, Sera," He stopped stuffing his bag, "there's something about you that I like. You're unlike any man I have collected wagers for. But no matter how much I like you, I have to run a business. You can't expect to make that much fighting the small fights you do."

"Then I won't fight," Sera threatened. "I won't stain my soul."

"Then don't," the collector shrugged his shoulders. "There's plenty of men who would do it without hesitation and for much less than you're getting. I'm sorry, but you're not indispensable."

Sera knew the man spoke truthfully. After the blunder of the mine's collapse, most of the men had scurried like rats to the four winds, some finding work in other mines, others broken and handicapped, most of them becoming little more than lowly servants to the *iqit*. But Sera hadn't been as lucky. He had been blamed for the collapse, and his infamy had spread as fast as the wind, often by those whom he had believed to be as close as family.

He had been fortunate, if he could call it that, to have given the news to Gada himself. Her lips had trembled as they had kissed. That alone had broken him. He could only think of his wife's undeniable love, despite her fearful expression at the prospect of a bleak and unpredictable future.

Wherever he had gone, Sera had found nothing but scorn. There was no work for him. There was no help, no charity. And so, despite Gada's protests, he had decided he had found no other option to feed his family than to fight at the pits.

While he had wrestled his colleagues for sport in his free time working the mines, he didn't have the spirit to threaten anyone, so he would fight unarmed, only to subdue.

This, however, was a different fight he had to win, a struggle to stay afloat, to survive so that he could send provisions to the family he had dishonored. He had to learn as fast as he sharpened his combat skills.

It would take time, and both Sera and Bahul knew it.

"Hey, look at me," Bahul studied his face, "it's one-tenth, and your cheek is swelling. Go see a healer."

"But that will cost me what, half of what I just earned."

"Maybe more," Bahul responded, "so next time, stay on your toes."

Weeks later, Sera stood ready to fight once more, to fight not for glory for himself but for the fate of those he cared for the most, for his loving wife, for his innocent children whom he sought to shield from what one day would be his shameful past.

The miner looked down at the curved, sharp knife in his hand. He then looked up at the stands above and felt he found himself, as in life, once again at the bottom of the same smelly pit.

There were a lot of patrons today, but Sera didn't fool himself. They weren't here to see him. In this noisy arena, his fight was nothing but the first of several passing spectacles preceding the main fight, simple entertainment that would allow gamblers to arrive and find their respective places on the stands.

Sera looked down at the knife in his hand, its blade as twisted as the smiles of those who mocked him from their seats, as twisted as the fate he had been handed.

This was his first armed fight, a fight to three cuts. A less dangerous one wouldn't have allowed him to participate today of all days, where more spectators and risk meant more provision for his own. Today's participation alone would earn fighters one-eighth *mahk*, enough to feed his family for a few weeks, an amount that would be doubled to the victorious fighter.

In front of him, one named Hal-ahl. Hal-ahl was somewhat younger but more experienced, bald, dark-skinned, and scarred in the many places he had been cut before. The blade danced deftly in the young fighter's hand. Despite his larger frame, it was clear to Sera that every moment he had spent working the earth, his opponent had spent fighting.

The announcer's shouts had been swallowed by the chaotic din of the uninterested who either chatted with one another, argued in the stands, or were already drunk. No one seemed to care who either of them were or how they ended up here.

"Blessed are you, Almighty Sun," Sera whispered, honoring the faith with his open palm, "forgive my sins and help me provide for my children."

Sera stepped in, slashing at empty air upon Hal-ahl's step back. Quickly, the younger man responded with a slash of his own, his blade opening a gash on Sera's forearm. He knew he had been too quick to act, a mistake he couldn't afford to make.

He studied his opponent, his every move, how he almost danced around the pit looking for an opening to wound the miner once again.

But Sera was quick to adapt. His own moves, while slower, allowed him to find a pattern to his opponent's attacks that allowed him to deflect them. It was during one of those deflections that Sera kicked Hal-ahl's thigh, making the younger fighter stumble momentarily. Before he realized the gravity of his mistake, Hal-ahl slashed in response back at Sera's leg, opening up yet another wound on his calf.

This time, however, Sera didn't waste a breath. His hands reached out and grabbed Hal-ahl's armed wrist. The younger man sought to stab him, but Sera used his lunge to drag his opponent down and slam him against the ground. In a flash, Sera slashed the man's forehead not once but twice.

It was then that Sera realized their fight had garnered attention. This last, quick move had drawn the applause and cheers of more than a few who now spectated. Even Bahul was shocked.

That brief moment was what Hal-ahl needed to escape from under Sera.

Muttering under his breath, the miner moved back to examine his wound. Now on the opposite side from him, the young man was visibly frustrated. Not only had Sera marked his face, but he had done so in an unexpected, single move.

"Sera," Hal-ahl called, "you might not know me, but I know you."

The miner ignored the young man's taunt.

"Well," he continued, "I don't really know you, but rather, I know of you from your wife."

At her mention, Sera quickly responded, "You can't possibly know my wife."

"Gada," the young man taunted.

"All of Bahul's men have heard my wife's name. I will not fall for those mind tricks. Do not stain her honor by mentioning her name. Let us just fight and be over with it."

"She's mother to your four children," Hal-ahl smiled, "or well, your child, Sara. The other three are mine." His words made Sera's brow furrow, his muscles tense. "Halla, Aht, and Saris. Who do you think named them?"

'It can't be true,' Sera questioned. But his forced, long absences from home while at the mine cast an unshakable spell of doubt. He recalled how he had chosen the name of his firstborn. Somehow less clearly, he seemed to recall how his wife had come up with the names of the other three.

Anger bred under Sera's shoulders, trembling like the sudden birth of an earthquake.

"There's nothing to worry about. She'll still get food from whoever is victorious. But I'll shut up now, cursed miner, so I don't stain her honor as much as she stains the sheets every time I'm done with her."

M . D U V I E L I R I Z A R R Y

In the blink of an eye, Sera had closed the gap between them. Slashing with one hand and reaching out with the other. Hal-ahl dodged, drawing a line of red where his blade had traveled along a third of Sera's back. He seemed to smile at his own performance until he felt Sera's grip on his forearm, followed by a sharp pain on his flank . . . that was followed by another one on his back, and then another one.

The stands were filled with shouts both of those enjoying the thrill of what they expected to be an uneventful fight and those unaware of the conditions of the same. Bahul himself shouted, horrified, watching Sera stab time and time again as if digging for red, liquid gold within the body of his grounded opponent.

•••••••

"You fucking idiot," Bahul scoffed, his face just a mere inch from Sera's. "Your first real fight, and you fuck it up like this."

The miner was seated, flanked by arena guards, his hands tied up with a rope. The collector stood by another, taller man, one dressed in a fine, sand-colored *kandora* and brown *shemagh*.

"I'm sorry," Sera lowered his head some, "for a moment, I don't know what overtook me."

"Well," Bahul clasped his own hands, "you just ruined your future!"

"What's the plan for someone like him?" the visitor asked.

"Oh, well," Bahul's eyebrows frowned before they almost rose to the heavens, "since he broke the rules, no one will trust him in a fight. He's better off just finding something else to do."

"Good," the visitor added, "then I would like a moment to speak to him alone."

His suspicion piqued, Bahul rubbed his chin. "That's not possible," the collector's body swayed, "not without me in the room."

"Is he your slave?" the taller man asked.

"Ehem," Bahul cleared his throat, "no, but I'm his collector, and thus he fights for me, so if this is regarding—"

"Then he can speak privately," the man interrupted. "Here, for your trouble," he dropped a bag of coins on the table. Bahul's curious, starving hands weighed its contents.

"I guess I'll be back in a few moments," the collector dropped a few of the coins on the guards' hands, ensuring they would follow him out of the room.

The visitor crossed his arms before addressing Sera, "I have a proposition for you."

"It's hard for me to trust a man whose face I can't see, whose name I don't know."

"For now, it will remain that way," the man responded, "my mission is very important."

Nodding, Sera remained attentive, "I am dishonored. What can I offer you that you cannot find somewhere else?"

"Much," the man responded. "If you were given a chance to visit the capital city, would you take it?"

"The Holy City of Suhne, the Grand Temple of the Sun, they're monuments to the sanctity, to the power of the Almighty," Sera responded. "I pray that someday the Almighty blesses me with the chance to see his creation firsthand."

"I see you're a true believer in the power of the Sun."

"I am. How could I not be?"

"True," the visitor responded casually.

"If you were given a chance to kneel before the Almighty Sun, would you take it?"

"Absolutely, but as it stands, I am unclean," Sera responded immediately.

"I could bring you to the capital on an important mission." The visitor watched his reaction intently, "One that would allow you to do so."

Sera lowered his head humbly, "What have I done to earn the greatest privilege a man like me could only dream of?"

"It's not about what you've done," the visitor responded, "but about what you will do."

"And what exactly will I do?" the miner questioned.

The visitor's *shemagh* moved, hiding what could only be a smile, "Let's say you'll play an important part in the Ascendancy of the new Sun." His words seemed incredible. A mere mortal from Uhn, a poor, dishonored miner among the *saqit,* right at the very bottom of the Suhne food chain. What role could he potentially have in the rising of an all-powerful god?

"What part would I play?" Sera asked curiously.

"You will murder one of the Sons of the Sun."

His words sent a shiver down Sera's spine.

It was a preposterous proposition, an utter blasphemy, to move against the holiest and mightiest. What could one ever hope to achieve other than eternal damnation? What could make a man curse himself and the family he was trying to keep safe?

"Maybe I didn't understand exactly," he said.

"It is quite simple," the man closed in, "you will be trained, you will be armed, and when the time comes, you will take the life of one of the Sons."

"I . . . I can't do that," Sera shirked away, "an attempt against the Almighty is the gravest sin."

"You're right," the man responded, "but you're not moving against the Sun, but rather against one of his children, a false god. Your actions, while damnable, will allow the rising of the true new Sun. Do you think a grateful, Almighty God will not reward you?"

Sera couldn't do this. While the words of this strange man sounded right in many ways, Sera's actions would be completely wrong if he were to go through with them. He would be cursed, and even if he survived, his family would be spurned. Besides, could he even trust this mysterious man he didn't know?

"I can't," Sera responded.

"You have a wife," the visitor pointed at Sera's bond chain[2].

"A wife and four children, all blessings from the Almighty, a family I must feed. Providing for them is my only priority."

"Something difficult to do right now," the man tapped the rope around Sera's wrists. "But a risen Sun will hear your plight, will bless you and every generation of your family. He might even marry your children into the *Zetq'a* or even make you one!"

"That sounds great," Sera responded, "but I don't seek any status. All I want is for my family to be fed and for my children to have a chance in life. I can't risk their lives in the hopes I can make it better."

"Ah, but you have to," the visitor's voice lowered to a sinister whisper, "you have no choice. You're guilty of murder and will be put to death soon enough. Your children will be sold as slaves, while your wife will be stoned to death for being a whore."

"She's not a whore!" Sera yelled, not knowing if he was trying to convince the man or himself.

"But she will be, I promise you that," the visitor answered. "I'll make sure she's so ruined she will have no option but to sell her body for sustenance. And after she's done it long enough, I'll personally ensure her actions are known, and she will be stoned per the law."

"You wouldn't do that!" Sera's voice trembled, "She's an innocent, faithful woman."

"I'm asking you to murder one of the Sons, and you say I wouldn't do that?" The visitor laughed. "Now show me, Sera, how much does your family really mean to you?"

Sera lowered his head again. His heart pumped hard; its rapid beating felt all the way up to his choking throat. "I need to think about it," Sera stated, "but first, how do I know I can trust you when I don't know your name, when I haven't even seen your face?"

"Ez-srah," the visitor revealed his half-smile from under his *shemagh*, "my name is Ez-srah."

(1) *Mahk*: Silver coin, the main currency of Suhne. It depicts the current Sun on one side and the city of Suhne on the other. It is valued at half Ardenay's 'state' and Blackheart's 'droplet.'

(2) *Bond chain*: Marriage is very particular in Suhnite culture. Each man is able to take two wives, while each woman can only take a single man as husband. To represent this, a man wraps a bracelet around his wrist for each wife, of the same type the wife will have on both wrist and ankles. The more conservative families bind the chains on the wrists and ankles together to represent complete submission to her husband.

ILEINA'S WAY

Location: Kingdom of Ardenay, Duchy of Alcyn,
County of Galdust, Capital City of Riverbed, House of Silver

There was one name that was known by every shrewd maiden and aspiring young lord in the courts of Himlen, and that was Ileina of House Eomener's name.

She was beautiful, warm, and quick of mind, her clothes as soft as the colors they were dyed with as if to enhance her already irresistible charm. Not only was she born beautiful, a shining star, and a prodigious writer, but part of her success, her opponents claimed, came from being the oldest daughter of the ruler of the richest duchy in Ardenay, the mercantile duchy of Alcyn.

Ileina's father, Duke Orionne Eomener, was, without a doubt, one of the most powerful men in the kingdom. For over three decades, he had held the position of Lord of Silver, head banker, and undisputed leader of the ruling Court of Lords in the duchy.

In only a few years, the lord would turn sixty, and while his hairline receded like the shore following an earthquake, his mind was as sharp as his ever-present smile.

If Lord Eomener's prosperity had been measured by the size of his abdomen, then it could be said he was very, very prosperous.

Orionne sat in his study, looking out the window toward the capital's main plaza, accompanied by Lady Astrice, his wife, Ileina herself, and their nun, deaconess Seana, on one of those days when they discussed books and exchanged stories.

"As much as I have no admiration of men dressing in scanty clothing," he signaled a servant to pour some tea on his cup, "there is something we can appreciate from the bird people of Avenanti."

"They're not really bird people, Father," Ileina smiled. "It is nothing more than children's tales." Her gray eyes and black hair she had gotten from him, but the dimples, grace, and delicate beauty she had clearly gotten from her brown-haired mother.

"Some of it is, yes," he sipped. "While they are entirely human, of course, their society imitates the behavior of birds. Men are the ones who wear seductive attire in hopes they're noticed by the women so that she can select who will have a lineage."

"I believe many of those are tales told to manipulate us into behaving a certain way," Ileina interrupted.

"It could very well be," Orionne shrugged, "but we should always keep the message in mind."

"But also the intention of the messenger," Ileina added. At nineteen, she was well-versed in the ways of the courts, having attended the university of Himeland, her fascination with literature and poetry sharpening the talent she had already excelled in, something that had drawn the attention of Ealas's father, the late king, and even of Ealas himself.

"Well spoken, my daughter," he said from the other side of the room, lifting his cup, drawing a chuckle from Ileina and smiles from his wife, who read, and a smiling nod from the nun, who spent her leisure time knitting.

"Father," Ileina asked, "I need to ask something of you."

"What is it, pearl of my eyes?"

"I wanted to talk about Ealas."

"What about him?" He sipped, picking up a pastry from the tray in front of him.

"Do you truly know what happened to him?" she asked.

"I don't, at least not with certainty." He looked at his daughter when he spoke in earnest, "From the letter he left, he was weak, unprepared. Unfortunate, really. I, for one, believed he had potential."

"Have you considered maybe he didn't leave the letter?" she questioned. "What if it was someone else?"

Orionne Eomener

"You know, everything is possible," Orionne responded, "although less likely than what I just said. Once the responsibilities of rulership materialize, sometimes the men who are now responsible shake and change their minds."

"Do you not wonder where he is now?" Ileina questioned.

"I did at first," he responded casually, "not anymore."

"Why not?"

"Because there are more important things," Ileina's father said. "There's a nation we have to run."

"I have heard he crossed the border into Blackheart."

Ileina's words made him pause for a moment. He then looked down at his plate before he looked at his daughter's inquiring eyes once more. "That's unfortunate."

"What are we going to do about it?"

"We?" Lord Eomener chuckled, his abdomen moving like a wall of gelatin. "Ileina, we can't leave what we are doing to pursue a single man."

"*I* can," she interjected.

"Oh no," raising an eyebrow, her father stopped her idea.

"What do you mean, oh no?" she asked. "Father, I don't have your responsibilities."

"But you will have them someday!" Orionne placed his cup on the saucer, clearly planting his foot on the ground to show he was ready to face Ileina's strong will. "What is the motto of our House?" His thick fingers pointed at the banner over his desk, with its blue background over which a silver wagon wheel rested.

"Moving onward," she responded, furrowing her brow.

"And that's what you have to do. Those are the words you need to live by—you leave the past in the past, and you move on!"

"Father," Ileina begged, "all I'm asking for is for a chance to travel to Blackheart as an ambassador, to meet with those in power and—"

"Ileina." He placed both palms on the table, the tension in his fingers evident. "Are you listening to yourself?"

"But Father," she argued, "you always wanted us to be close!"

"You're right," He leaned back, "but he's not in line for the throne anymore."

"Father!" She raised her voice.

"Oh, Ileina," he signaled for more tea, "All I'm doing is ensuring a prosperous future for you, my beloved daughter."

"But what if I don't want that future?"

"You will not understand it today, but you will someday," Orionne added. "You will now set your eyes on Vallein, son of King Aorius."

"That's ridiculous!" she argued.

"He's courageous," Lord Eomener stated, "well-respected and proud. He's a Heikken through and through, and the royal lineage is strong in him. Besides, he's the firstborn."

"But how do you know what I want?"

"It doesn't matter, my pearl," he looked at her with decisive eyes, "it's what *I* want."

It was she who looked down this time. She loved her father, and the words he spoke had, until today, been true. Everything he did, Orionne did thinking of the prosperity of his duchy, but his family was above even all that. He was powerful, one of the richest men in the world, but despite having grown around those riches, Ileina Eomener had come to understand her happiness did not lie in a life of material comfort.

"Father," her gray eyes challenged him, "I love Ealas."

"What do you know about love, child," Lady Astrice Eomener approached her daughter.

"I know it's the powerful emotion toward that person I feel the strongest for," Ileina responded. "Everything I feel inside has Ealas's name written on it."

"Love is not like that, my child," Lady Astrice said. "That's merely a blinding emotion, butterflies we feel that many times lead us to decisions we quietly regret for the rest of our lives."

"Is that what happened to you two?" Ileina challenged.

"Ileina!" Lady Astrice blazed.

"She's right, dear wife," Orionne walked toward them, his eyes softening on his daughter, "Yes, Ileina, it's what happened between your mother and me."

"We barely knew each other's names when our marriage was arranged. Through a hundred agreements and a thousand disagreements, we've made it work. Our opinions have clashed many times, but one thing we have always done,

Ileina Eomener

we have always agreed to do what's best for our House so that you and your sisters can have the most fruitful of futures."

"So now," he continued, placing the cup on the desk, "it's settled. I don't want to hear more about this Ealas nonsense. I have matters to attend to!"

Without another word, Lord Orionne left the room to resume his ducal duties.

Ileina stood there, her will keeping her from feeling defeated, even when she saw the nun pausing her work and beginning to put her tools away.

"Mother," Ileina asked, "what should I do?"

"Ileina," Lady Astrice responded, "love is always beautiful in the beginning, but it often becomes a desert one needs to learn to traverse in order to survive. Your father is right in many ways. You need to move on."

"Yes, but it breaks my heart not to see him, not to be with him! What do *you* say, Mother?" Ileina questioned. "What does your heart say?"

Lady Astrice grasped her daughter's hand, and she whispered in her ear, "If your heart beats that strongly, you are right to love Ealas. Go find him!"

Before she left, the aging nun who had seen Ileina's entire life responded, "My lady child, don't forget to ask yourself, 'As my heart breaks for him, does his heart break for me too?'"

After a few minutes, when she couldn't help but stand speechless, Ileina Eomener was the last one to leave the study. But she didn't go to the dining room, as her mother and nun did. She didn't go to the court where her father spent most of the day and where she had sharpened her smarts and wit.

She walked toward her room to pack, to contact those who would join her, for she would make her choices from the heart, which told her to stand firm and, although in a different direction, to be strong and continue "Moving onward."

THE LIBRARY

Location: Kingdom of Blackheart,
Duchy of Darkholm, Darkholde Keep

Life teaches important lessons we often don't care to learn . . .

A single droplet escaped the heavens as if relieved after freeing itself from the tumultuous weather or perhaps cast down as punishment for its failure.

It fell thousands of feet from the night sky toward the blackness of the rocks on the cliff below. But its journey was cut short as it died in the blink of an eye, breaking into minuscule pieces upon contact with the pale surface of Charon's forehead, that moment when her yellow eyes contemplated the gray clouds above.

Both of her usual companions stood by her side, each long haired, one's strands white as bone and the other one dark as the void. All three women looking up at the approaching clouds that heralded the worsening weather.

"More rain," she giggled, wiping her forehead, "if it keeps raining like this, we will drown."

"All the way up here?" Elleonora asked flatly.

"Oh, you don't want to question the power of water, Lora," Charon smiled playfully.

"Very well," Rowena added, placing her hands on each of her cousin's shoulders, "let us move on before our clothes are drenched. There is much we have to cover."

"Do we have to?" Charon pleaded playfully, "I'm not in the mood today."

"Are you ever in the mood, Charon?" Elleonora smirked.

"Come," Rowena responded, "knowledge awaits." She pointed softly, almost teasing the air, toward the large building ahead, and she smiled, more so when she saw Charon cringe at the mere thought of studying.

The three women hurried toward one of Darkholde's most sacred chambers, the grand repository of knowledge, the Darkholm Library.

The building was located high and on one side of Darkholde's main building. While not as tall as the Spire of the Eye, its long windows captured the attention of any onlooker, making it quite a sight to behold from a distance. Its outside had the appearance of a cathedral, as if the Darkholm, known for their agnosticism, had decided to build a church to knowledge itself.

The building appeared much larger on the outside than it was on the inside. Rumor had it this was due to the presence of a second, secret library that was hidden from plain sight, but few believed the rumors when it was also said that non-Darkholm were not allowed this far into the keep.

The three maidens were caught in the falling rain.

They laughed, remembering those times when, as children, even Charon who had grown up away from them, they would each play and dance in the rain.

As they hurried toward the library's entrance, something caught Rowena's eye near the main doors.

"Rowena, come!" Elleonora, now ahead, signaled.

"You're getting wet. You know that, right?" Charon asked when she saw Rowena stop.

"Wait," Rowena raised her hand, kneeling close to the ground.

Her porcelain skin contrasted the dark surface of the pavement where rivulets of water formed. And yet, trying to escape those small currents, a small scarab walked awkwardly, seemingly distressed or perhaps confused.

"What are you doing all the way up here, little one?" Rowena's hands cupped the scarab tenderly, bringing it closer to her, her companions returning to her side.

"Rowena, just drop it there. We have to go," Elleonora insisted.

"I cannot simply let it die, Lora," Rowena protected it from the rain as it inspected its elytra, the pattern resembling a hollow-eyed face that, through one's use of imagination, appeared to show a twisted grin. "Is it not beautiful?" she asked.

"It is dying, Rowena, and we are getting drenched," Elleonora sighed.

"It's a paradox bug!" Charon smiled. "Don't people say the color of their wings represents a portent?"

"Yes," Elleonora responded flatly, "the single color in their wings is supposed to."

"Yay!"

"But those are just superstitions, Charon." She closed in and lightly grabbed Rowena's arm. "Come now, let it be. Look at it. It is already dying."

"I am still going to save it," the Master of Life responded.

Both women's eyes met in silence for just a moment before Elleonora spoke again, "Cousin, saving that insect now will save it from its doom, but perhaps will send it to a worse doom in the future, a life of suffering. Just look at it. It can barely walk straight. It is dying."

The Master of Life's eyes gravitated toward the creature before meeting Elleonora's again.

"Perhaps you are right. Perhaps saving it now will have it meet a greater doom later on. But, you see, perhaps it will not, and we cannot make a decision based on either. I am choosing to save it because, at this moment in time, it is simply the right thing to do."

"It does not change that it is dying, Rowena," Elleonora replied.

"Yes, it is dying, but it is dying because it is still alive, and every second of life is precious."

"I disagree," Elleonora spoke.

"And I accept that," Rowena responded. "While each one of us has an opinion, only one of us is making the decision." She then placed the scarab in Charon's hands, who shook with excitement.

"We can go now. Will you cover me?" Taking Elleonora's hand, she then placed it jokingly over her own wet head, drawing a smile on her cousin's face.

Behind them, Charon caressed the scarab and smiled happily. Her blood-red lips parted in a whisper. "Hello, little one. What are you doing in Darkholde? Are you here to visit someone?"

Walking slowly toward the entrance, she continued her one-sided conversation. "You who represent both the great blessings and unending maledictions, show me your wings."

She then blew its back lightly. "Show me a color. What do you have for me?"

Upon the caress of Charon's breath, the scarab lifted its head up and spread its elytra, from under which a pair of hypnotizing, iridescent wings appeared that left Charon mesmerized, unable to move.

"Charon!" Elleonora's shout brought her back to her senses. "Come on!"

<hr />

"I was beginning to think you would skip today's studies," Count Azareth blew a puff of smoke toward the doorway, seeing the girls enter. "It almost broke my heart."

"I cannot seem to recall where and when I misplaced it," he smiled, tapping a cigar against the reptilian-shaped ashtray that rested on the table between the large figure of Gustavus and himself.

The library was large, with shelves upon shelves filled with tomes of all kinds, so many the Master of Lore could run an entire university from up here. And if he so wished he could, for House Darkholm did not only find knowledge to be a precious commodity, but long ago, they had established a pact with the headmistress of the largest university in Blackheart, the Fennec Academy, allowing them to copy every single book Fennec had access to.

Back then, the most vocal professors had argued against allowing the Darkholm to take the material, warning, 'What if the books are altered while in their possession?' or 'What if they never returned them?' but so far, the scriveners, now under Azareth, always returned every book, carefully copying every tome in case a replacement was ever needed.

"There is only one of us who seems to be haunted by books," Rowena quipped, drying her face and hands with the towels Azareth's attendants promptly brought. Elleonora followed suit, her eyes on her husband, who, with a stern face, exchanged words with the Master of Lore at the library's main counter.

"Thank you," Azareth spoke to Gustavus, "I will take care of this myself." The count placed his hands over a storage box he wrapped in leather before sliding it toward himself. Gustavus turned, marching toward the doorway. He looked down upon Rowena with indifference before he met the eyes of his wife, whom he greeted with but a nod.

Behind the girls, Charon walked in. So fixed was her attention on the scarab, she almost bumped into her cousins. "You are so beautiful, little one," she smiled broadly. "Would you like to be my pet?

"But first, we'll have to find you a name," she said when the scarab spread its wet wings open to fly off her hand and onto the floor, where it was caught by Gustavus's approaching figure and frowning eyes.

"Wait, come back!" Charon giggled, kneeling to scoop the scarab into the palm of her hands, but her thoughts were interrupted by a sudden stomp, squish, and crunch that left her startled.

"NOOOOooooo!" she screamed, seeing Gustavus twisting his boot to ensure the bug was dead. "How could you!" Her eyes watered, looking down at the stained floor where her new pet had been flattened.

But Gustavus didn't seem to care. He continued on his way back into Darkholde, ignoring Charon's cries.

———— ·•••••· ————

Elleonora sat down close to Rowena at a table to one side of the room near one of the library's large windows. One hand held the book she had just started reading, *Mushrooms of Varnje: A Guide to Olath Valm's Hidden Treasure,* while her right hand drew and made notes. Rare was the time she would leave a book unfinished. So single-minded was she, other than her notebook, there was no other book in front of her.

On the empty seat across from Elleonora, several books on different subjects lay open to what appeared to be random pages. Only one didn't have a marker near the beginning or end, but only because the marker destined for its pages rested over its cover.

"Charon," Azareth leaned against the table, "come, sit. You are behind in your studies."

"Aza," his sister twirled and pranced around the room, "can't you see I'm sad? I need some distraction."

"You need no distraction," Elleonora said. "Come sit and study."

"Easy for you to say," Charon's hands moved to the rhythm of an unknown tune like snakes in a desert dance. "You're trying to make me forget Gus is a murderer." But her weak jab didn't seem to bother Elleonora, who just rolled her eyes and returned to her reading.

"Ignore her," Azareth whispered to his cousins. "She will come read, at some point, hopefully. Did you know that, of all mushrooms—"

"Thank you, Azareth," Elleonora looked into his eyes, "but I would rather read it myself."

"What I was about to say is not in that book," the Master of Lore interjected.

"Then I will read it whenever I get to that book," she replied. "For now, I would rather focus on my reading, yes?"

"Indeed," Count Azareth grabbed Charon's unopened book. "Charon, I will take this one back. I do not think you should be starting yet another one until you have finished at least one of these."

"No, wait, Aza," Charon darted back, "that one called my attention!"

"*Small Mammals: Memorable Encounters,*" he read, picking up another one of her books. "What does that have to do with *"Boiling Point . . . Ritual Ensembles and . . . Cooking with Fish Eggs*?"

"It has drawings!" Charon bit her lower lip.

"No, Charon," he brought the book to his chest, "Finish at least one of them, and I will let you read another one."

"You say knowledge is chaos!" Charon smiled.

"Yes, but we must organize that knowledge and its acquisition," Azareth replied. Moving away from the table, he caught a glimpse of what Rowena was reading.

"You asked me for an herbalism book," he pointed at the book he had given her, "and yet you are reading the biography of a Rovetsean sailor. Why is that?"

Septem's daughter smiled back at him. "When my eyes get tired, and my mind is fatigued, I seek something different to learn to allow me some rest."

"Reasonable thought," the librarian puffed, "but while one part of your brain is resting, another is working."

"Rowena," he turned to face her, leaning against the table, "In the decade I have been in this position, I have seen the Masters of the Grey Circle often come to either share knowledge or study. And yet, I have come to notice that, of all the masters, you are the only one who, instead of focusing your studies on your area of expertise, on herbalism, medicine, on life itself, you study everything else. Do you think you have acquired all knowledge there is regarding those subjects?"

"It would be unwise for anyone to think so, dear cousin," Rowena responded.

"Then why?"

She calmly closed her book before she produced a response. "When the day comes that the crown rests over my brother's head," she said, "he will need a loyal, most rounded adviser to help him navigate the wills and thoughts of men to support his rule. Otherwise, he would depend on multiple people, each one with his own agenda, ready to pull the entire kingdom in his own direction. I must learn what lies within our borders, the lands, and people we have never seen, what their beliefs are, what they fear, what they long for."

"And what do *you* long for?" Azareth asked.

Thankfully for her, he didn't let her answer. "Wait, you have never been to Himlen, right?"

"I have never been beyond Blackheart's border wall," Rowena said.

"Then I have something you will *want* to read," he stated and dashed to a distant shelf from where he produced a beautifully bound tome, *Stairway to Heaven.*

"Here," he flipped the pages and pointed a finger halfway, "this is an important piece I have never seen you read, one that will give you a glimpse of what lies beyond our borders."

Rowena's eyes devoured the pages. While she had studied the way of life of their neighbors, what she had studied was not as deep as this book Azareth had presented her with. She read about Ardenay's people's beliefs, about its grand cathedral with its marbled walls and domes and tall spires, about how its grandiosity almost dwarfed that of the royal palace itself. She read about how, for centuries, a choir of a hundred stood by the cathedral's steps, singing holy hymns every hour of every day, groups of singers taking turns so that the beautiful song to the Light would never cease.

And while Elleonora didn't care, Charon read over Rowena's shoulders, her eyes wide open in amazement at what she had just read.

"Wow!" the white-haired girl exclaimed, lifting her arms and dancing across the room, "what would I give to be able to visit there and hear the melody of those angels!"

Rowena said nothing. She didn't smile. Her mind silently echoed Charon's words. She looked outside the window at the infinite possibilities beyond what any eye could see, or any mind could comprehend.

One day she would stand by her crowned brother's side, supporting him, hoping he would overlook her, as many times he seemingly did.

But what if when the time came, he didn't overlook her? What if he *chose* her?

Erdrick was sharp, she knew. Maybe he would one day see value in not picking her as their father had picked their mother. But in the event he did, in fact, choose her to share his burden, could she resist?

She could, perhaps, say 'no,' but *would* she? Above everything and anything, she was Darkholm, and duty was more important than the anathema freedom represented to their Blood.

Since the beginning of their name, even when one of their line had taken a sibling as his most trusted adviser, she would be in the best position to persuade him to choose someone else . . . perhaps one of her cousins . . . she thought, but which one of them would deserve being chained, being so close to the unending prison that was the throne?

Rowena didn't want to dwell on it, she wanted to exorcise the thought, but she wouldn't. She simply couldn't because deep inside, she knew it made no difference, or perhaps it actually did.

Ignoring those thoughts would only make her unprepared for when the day came with all of the ramifications that would stem from it.

What if he chose her? She looked at the chaotic uncertainty of the endless ocean.

What if Life chose her?

HUSBAND

Location: Empyre of Suhne, Basqh of Uhn, Aqaba village

Trust is the strongest weapon and the one most easily broken . . .

*C*ould he bring himself to forgive her? Sera wondered, sitting alone by the small table in his home, the same one where he would often sit by Gada, watching their children play and fight.

She would spend the time talking about what had transpired while he had been out at work, all idle gossip, while he really didn't have much to offer in regard to conversation.

Is that why she betrayed me? Because she was bored of me?

But what stories could he tell when all he did was work, and the last thing he wanted was to remind himself of the hard labor that was his daily life, of the worsening struggle to bring sustenance? He had preferred to kiss his wife, to take her clothes off amid her protests asking him to be careful because she had not much to wear.

Was that true, or was it an excuse because she had been hiding something from him? Perhaps the bruises from the men she slept with while he enslaved himself, coming every three months and missing most of his own children's milestones, sacrificing his life for what?

So that she could sacrifice her body on the altar of other men's hands?

No, that wasn't like Gada. That wasn't the woman he had loved.

Or, was she . . .

Sera's fingers felt the metal around his right wrist, the same pattern around his wife's wrist and ankles. He could have worn another woman's on his left, as was allowed and even expected of him, but he hadn't. His entire dedication and loyalty had been to Gada. His fingers began pulling the chain softly, but he stopped himself.

Sera was a man of faith, and the sacred vow of marriage was something he couldn't or simply wouldn't break.

But he could, had she been unfaithful.

But had she been?

His same faith had taught him to believe without a doubt in things he hadn't seen. It was that same belief in the unseen that told him his wife had been unfaithful. Something inside him told him time and again that it had happened.

'I will ask her,' he told himself. But deep inside, he knew he couldn't. If she had lied all this time, why wouldn't she just lie once more?

He was furious, tormented by the conflicting thoughts, by the doubt. He clenched his fists. As irate as he was, he couldn't be violent, or could he? He wouldn't. He couldn't behead her or punish her as per the laws of the land, not because of her actions, but because of himself, because of the kind man he had always been, and because of the love he had for her, and for his children . . . that perhaps weren't even his.

His muscles tensed the moment he heard Gada's voice as she approached, accompanied by the laughter of his children.

'Can I forgive her?' he asked himself before clenching his fist, 'How can I forgive her when I can't even face her?'

'Damned be all evil,' he slammed his hand on the table, looking out the window to see both the Sun and the moon in the sky. "Damn the accursed eye of the moon, which has come to mock me in my misery, to witness how I murdered the woman I have given all my love to."

Sera looked up at the fiery Eye of the Sun, his anger at the all-seeing Eye of God.

"How can you allow her to see us, to come and laugh at us in our time of tribulation?" His eyes trembled.

'How can the Sun Almighty allow this,' he thought. But a thought came as words whispered into his ear. 'Who or what is watching us from up there? Whose eye is that when . . . there is no Sun?'

There is no Sun.

'Someone must make the new Sun rise!'

Gada opened the door to her home. It was empty, as it had been for a few weeks now since the last time she saw her husband. Her children ran in and played, filling the house with the laughter of the innocent. She closed her eyes, her heart beating fast and strong. Somehow, briefly, she could feel the faint scent of her husband that disappeared with the wind coming to the window she had perhaps left open.

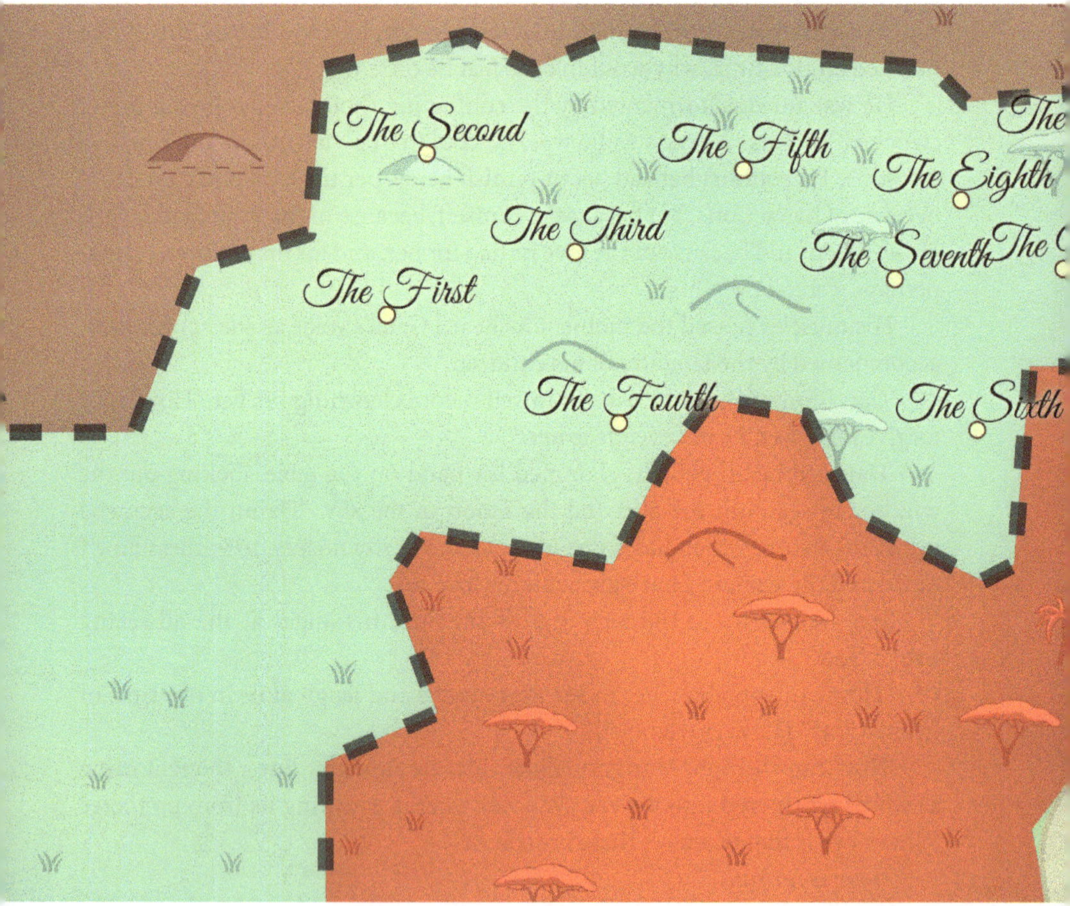

The Second

The Fifth

The Eighth

The

The Third

The Seventh The

The First

The Fourth

The Sixth

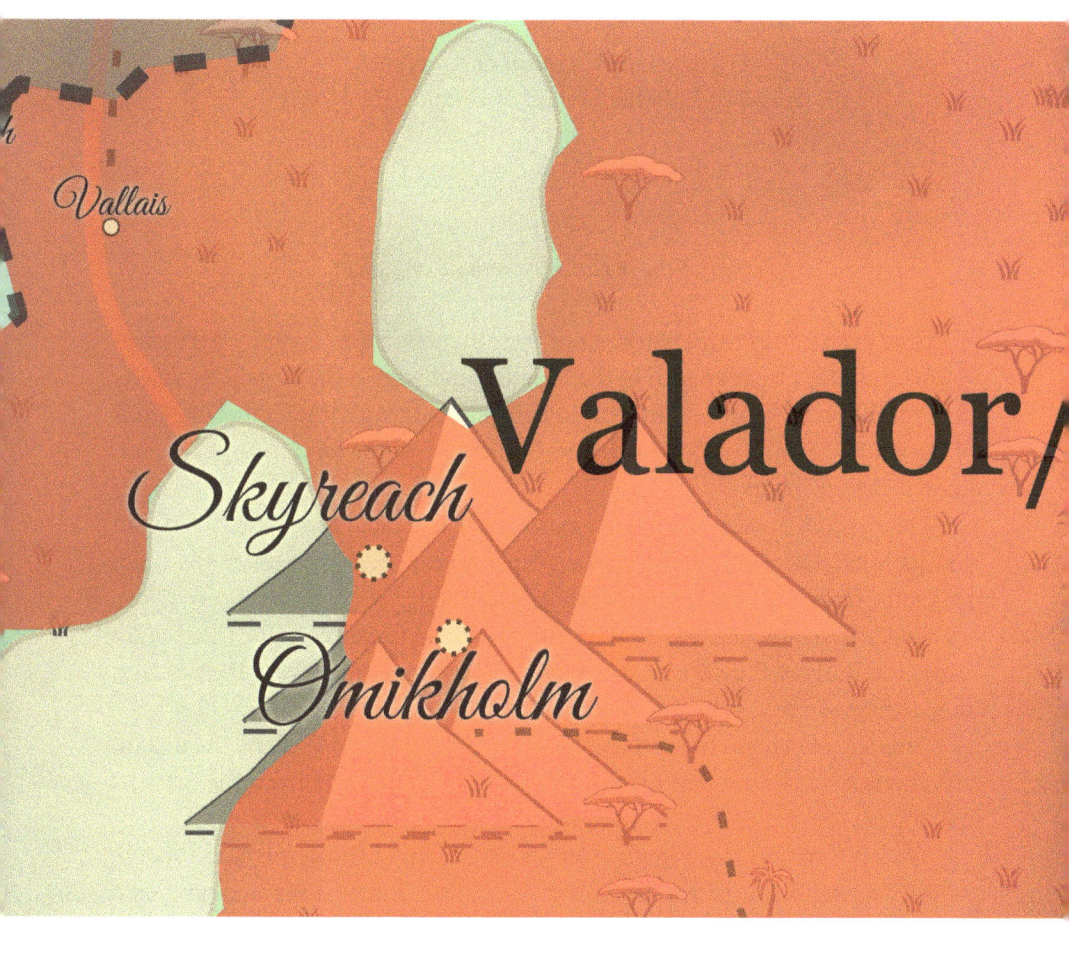

INITIATIVE

Location: Kingdom of Ardenay,
Duchy of Bulwharf, State of Darane, the Horne

Every first move can very well be one's last . . .

It had been nearly three weeks since their incursion into the hilly northeast-ernmost tip of Ardenay, into the coveted land within the largely flat duchy of Bulwharf that stood like a middle finger insulting the neighboring lands of Taerea and Suhne to the north and Blackheart to the west, into the region known as the Horne.

No one could really say if the region's name had been given after the pagan god its inhabitants once followed or after the large men who defended these lands, the ones who called themselves bulls.

Regardless of which was true, like their ancient, forgotten deity, they fought hard. The Bulls of Bulwharf did not back down, drenching every inch of land they either won or lost in the blood of war.

This late afternoon the sun's figure started disappearing behind the distant elevations, as a child, upon his parents' arrival, would hide from the mess he had made.

On a hill within that region, a large fort known as the Tenth stood watch, its walls rising from the ground as a crown of stone firmly planted on a bald king's head. The fort's crenellations were lined with tall men who lit torches each night to guide their trebuchets and the ballistae that would mount a most destructive defense.

Below, the detachments of the allied forces of Blackheart's duchies of Valador and Volanar moved uphill under the command of infuriated lieuten-ants, their towering shields slowing their pace but allowing them to advance, at least for as long as the halting message of the defender's artillery wasn't delivered.

A few yards away, the remnants of two detachments retreated, a single man from the first and a quartet carrying a bloodied fifth from the second, to lick their wounds back at the main camp under the shadow of the banners of Valador, Volanar, and Blackheart.

Their captain walked toward the commander's tent to deliver news of the decimating of his troops, of yet another impending failure.

"Damn them!" a flustered Crannon Coronn hurled a cup of Blood Tea to the floor, spilling its contents inside the command tent, "Our forces are more than twice the size of theirs!" He brought his hands to his shaved temples, slowly but impatiently grabbing the loose hair on top of his head.

Around his desk, his commander's eyes and hands studied the map of the region, their fingers pointing at the landscape they felt lost in.

From Blackheart's border wall into the enemy territory, they had advanced quickly, taking the first five miles with minimal effort, but it had taken their forces nearly twenty days to advance the next two.

While the skill of Valador's scouts was unquestioned, the layout of the hilly Horne made it hard for any large force to maneuver effectively. So even without a regional wall of its own, the region of scattered forts was hard to tame, and the bulls' forces had resisted with no significant losses.

This, Duke Coronn knew, and he hated the thought not just of a failed campaign but one in which he was defeated, having barely moved from its starting point.

As if that fact alone hadn't been bad enough, he and the Duke of Volanar had taken it upon themselves to march forth without the support of the other duchies, and the bulls waited inside their forts for reinforcements under the legendary command of the Thunders that would turn the invader's advance into nothing more than an impossible feat.

Valador and Volanar's little time was dwindling, and they had much to achieve and too much to prove.

Duke Crannon had started a meeting with his own men just minutes before the general meeting's scheduled time. He fully trusted Duke Dokkon. How could he not when they shared the largest peak at the center of their combined duchy? But even in this relationship, a man could not show his weaknesses, his doubt. If Dokkon ever realized that even with smaller forces, he was in a stronger position inside the mountain than Crannon at the top, their relationship, Duke Crannon feared, would perhaps have been very different.

"Lord duke," the arriving captain said, "we are having a hard time maneuvering the region. The ten forts are at the top of the hills. One of our advance units was nearly decimated by the enemy's ballistae upon its climb."

"What do you suggest we do?" Duke Crannon asked.

"Our combined forces' role in the kingdom has been largely defensive, Lord Coronn," another captain responded.

"Tell me something I don't know," the nobleman mumbled.

"Ignoring the forts and passing through is plausible, but it will spread our forces thin and exhaust them. They would have to keep watch on multiple fronts."

"How long do you think the bulls can withstand a siege?" Coronn asked.

"That is the problem, my lord," a captain responded, "for them to withstand a siege, we would need to be in place, and the hills make it difficult, if not impossible."

Crannon Coronn

Duke Crannon's inquisitive eyes of gray scanned the room as he asked his men, "What do you suggest then?"

For a moment, they remained mostly quiet, studying the map, mumbling to themselves.

"As our enemy has," a relatively young captain spoke up, "we should entrench ourselves and stop their advance."

"And allow all of Bulwharf to mobilize against us?" Crannon complained. "As we speak, Lord Usman Velias has been mobilizing Darane's forces to fully support the Horne. It will not be long before we feel the brunt of it."

"Less than a day, as a matter of fact," the deep voice of Duke Dokkon Gillspiel corrected. Larger than his counterpart, albeit of a calmer demeanor, the Lord of Volanar's bald head barely scraped the top of the tent's entrance. He was flanked by four of his captains. "We have just received news they are marching through the night. Unless they are stopped, they will get here within just a few hours."

"When did you hear this?" Crannon sounded alarmed.

"Just now," his ally responded, "while you were busy starting without me."

"I did no such thing, my friend."

"Then what is that?" Dokkon pointed at the map on the table.

Crannon wrested for a moment inside his head before responding, "I apologize if it seems that's the case. I was discussing with my men to come up with a plan we can bring to fruition *together*."

Lord Dokkon lowered his head somewhat, his eyes on his ally. He cleared his throat and continued, "I would appreciate those discussions of our work together being held by us together. In any case, here we are. Darane is marching toward the Horne."

"What do you believe is our chance of standing against Lord Usman Velias?"

"As it stands, our chances are small," the larger man responded, "and he is Bull Usman Velias."

"He can call himself what he will. His equivalent title is lord."

"I'm not quite certain lord has the same weight," Dokkon corrected.

"Does it matter, friend, when we will erase his name off the face of Caerea?" Crannon asked.

"Unless you plan to kill every single one of his people, it matters." Duke Dokkon approached the table, his fingers on the map, pointing at the Horne and traveling toward the edges. "Bulwharf is divided into three regions, each one ruled by a Bull."

"Yes, of course, this is known," Crannon stood from his seat and rested his arms upon the table, "and each of the Bulls has the right to challenge the Lord Bull to a duel for his ducal seat in Sildrane."

"Yes," Duke Dokkon added, "but upon the challenge, the challenging Bull must first complete a mission assigned by the Lord Bull in order to have the right to duel."

"Well, he must first defeat us to even think of challenging Varen Bulwharf."

"Oh, he has issued his challenge, and his mission, my friend," Dokkon smiled, "is to kill you."

"I . . .," Duke Crannon sought for the best words to respond, "will order our heaviest units to mobilize."

"You?" Dokkon leaned on the desk and eyed the smaller man. "Would you care to explain?"

"I am referring to the elephant units," Crannon responded, "and, of course, the volaphanes[(1)]." He looked at the captains in search of support. Upon mention of the larger, more powerful proboscideans, all of them nodded.

"I believe there is a misunderstanding, my friend," moving away from the desk, Dokkon crossed his arms. "They are among our most reliable units; they are solely under my command. Our alliance contemplates us as equals, so please understand you cannot *order* my units without my consent."

Crannon's blood boiled, but he could not hurl a cup, much less an insult, at his friend. Everything they had planned depended on the delicate balance of power between both men. In time, if he wanted, he could assert himself as the superior of the two, as he knew how his ally preferred to avoid unnecessary politics. He couldn't afford to lose him, even if their victory together was far from certain.

"Duke Dokkon, friend," he tried to contain himself as best as he could, "you must bring your elephants."

"A unit is here, at the ready," Dokkon responded.

"I am afraid that is not enough," Crannon added, "I need more."

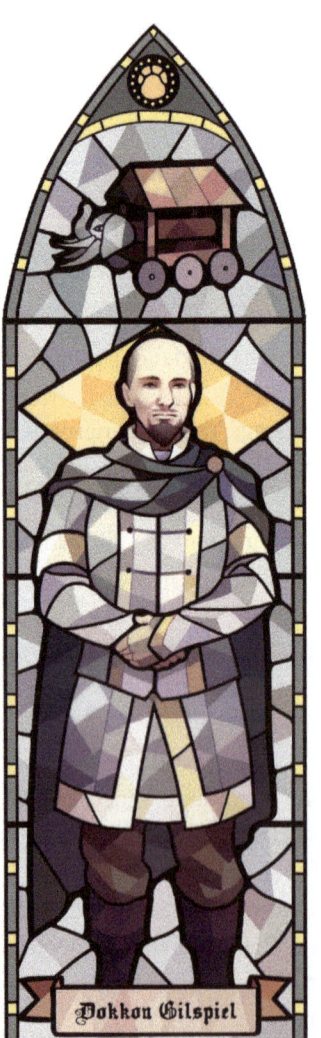

Dokkon Gilspiel

"I have summoned two more units; they will get here within two days."

"As you mentioned before, Usman Velias will arrive before they do. In this campaign, I feel Volanar's forces are hesitating. Where is the problem? Is something troubling you?"

Duke Dokkon puffed. He half-turned toward the entrance, seemingly bothered by the veiled insult. "We are treading carefully. Elephants take long to raise and just as long to train. We cannot afford to throw them into battle the same way we throw humans. Volaphanes are even harder to train."

"If you had this hesitation, why did you not say it before we marched?" Crannon sneered. "One cannot redo a battle. We either go all out, or we lose everything. I need you to bring your volaphanes."

"That I cannot do. They are watching our backs."

"From what?"

"From Blackheart," Duke Dokkon responded.

"Do you think they would betray us like that?"

"Duke Coronn," Dokkon smiled incredulously, "it was you and I who moved against the will of Blackheart. Regardless of our intentions, the Council will not take our advance lightly and will likely see us as traitors, which is why we have, unsurprisingly, not found support."

"My lords," a messenger rushed in, "a missive." Dokkon took the sealed parchment and eyed the signet in the wax. Breaking it under his fingers, he unrolled the parchment, and his lips moved as he read its contents.

"What is it?" frustrated, Crannon asked from his seat.

"Good news," Dokkon smiled broadly, "at least one of the duchies has offered support, but—"

"All hail King Septem Darkholm!" Dokken's words were cut short by the thunderous shout and sudden entrance of Eriadna's armored figure, anger across her brow, the trailing braid of graying hair swinging at the speed with which she strode, "King of Blackheart, Duke of Darkholm, Count of Coldforge, Baron of Ironheart, Lord of Darkholde and Father of the Blood!" She squinted, quickly assessing for danger before stepping aside to make way for the king.

Behind her, the towering presence of Septem made his entrance, the white of his attire alone sending a shiver down everyone's spine, a chill dwarfed by his icy stare that froze every man inside the tent.

Erdrick followed the monarch, accompanied by Gustavus, Erdrick's knights flanking the Crown, the terrifying visage of their armor contrasting with the magnificence of the man they protected.

"Your Majesty," Duke Dokkon turned toward the newcomers and took a step forward toward Septem.

But Erdrick's eagle eyes caught the move, and swifter than a flash of lightning, the Knight Commander took a step forward to intercept the move.

He blinked just once, and in that split second, time itself appeared to bow down to the Black Knight.

His left hand left his side to wrap around the exposed hilt, not of his sword, but of the venerable one resting in the king's ivory sheath.

Effortlessly, with a single move, he plunged its pommel into the center of Dokkon's abdomen, doubling the man over in both pain and breathlessness. Duke Dokkon fell on one knee, his hand outstretched toward the king, his eyes wide open as he gasped for air. Legs shaking, Dokkon attempted to stand once more.

Erdrick stood by the doubled man, his face proud, illuminated only by the golden fire of his eyes, the reflections of which he saw in the scarlet surface of *Sanguinus's* blade. Perhaps he heard the song of the agony of its many victims seducing him, for the knight stopped for a moment before time resumed from under its trance. His gauntleted hands lifted the sword he both admired and coveted for all to see as if he had intended for everyone to witness how the light touching its blade broke into a vermilion scatter.

But the knight turned the blade toward the ground, his eyes widening furiously.

"Bow before your king!" Erdrick spat, plunging the hungry blade on the ground, but not before it passed barely an inch from the duke's neck, between his ribcage and his clavicle with surgical precision, through his clothes and into the center of his hand, leaving the man impaled, like a bloody, broken and devout puppet before the presence of its unmerciful, white creator.

The move was followed by the clinking plates of the knights, each advancing half a step, placing the hands on the hilt of their swords. One by one, the captains inside the tent took a knee and bowed their heads to the ruler of Blackheart.

But Septem's eyes moved toward Duke Coronn, who sat behind his desk, his hands tense over its wooden surface, his jaw clenched as if seeking to break his own molars under the pressure. Upon seeing the heavy boot of the king moving one step closer toward the desk, Duke Coronn broke down. Hurriedly, clumsily, he let his seat fall backward as he ran around the desk and prostrated himself on the ground before Septem.

"Your Highness—"

"Crannon Coronn," Septem's words were as cold as they were firm, "Dokkon Gillspiel, you have both acted against the will of the Crown."

"But, Your Highness, while my actions can be misinterpreted, I will be able to prove in court they were for the good of the kingdom."

"You will not be judged by your peers in the Council. You have been judged by the Crown, and you have both been found to have acted only in your best interests and to the detriment of the kingdom. You are thus both stripped of your titles and branded traitors to Blackheart."

"But my lord," Coronn shouted, "please, have mercy!"

"You are now the property of House Darkholm," Septem continued, "and are hereby condemned to spend the rest of your days in Darkholde's prison."

Upon hearing the words, Coronn's shouts turned into desperate shrills, "Your Highness, please! I beg you, my good king!"

"Your words cannot honor what your actions have betrayed," Septem turned toward the impaled body of Dokkon, to the sword that gorged on what blood did not cover the floor of the tent. His hand wrapped around the hilt of his sword, freeing it from both the ground and the nobleman's wounded body.

"Stabilize him," he instructed the knights to have the healers among them take care of Dokkon, "so that he will survive the journey back."

Before leaving the chamber, the king then stood in front of Erdrick, their aurean eyes locked on each other. "Commander," Septem said, "until the time comes for you to wield it, *do not* lay hands on *Sanguinus* again."

Erdrick lowered his head in response, his brow furrowing, "As you command, my king."

"And Commander," Septem stopped, looking at his son from the corner of his eye, "well done."

(1) Volaphanes: The volaphane is a distant, larger (1,300 stone) relative of the elephant (430-930 stone). It is raised underground in Volanar. It is exclusively albino, with large ears, pale white and gray mottled skin, and large red eyes. It has four tusks and six powerful legs. They are nearly blind above ground during the daytime and depend on their riders for guidance.

DRAGON BLOOD

Location: Kingdom of Ardenay,
Duchy of Bulwharf, State of Darane, the Horne

The one thing that can be truly predicted is unpredictability...

Erdrick waited.

Something he had gotten accustomed to doing his entire life, although with great difficulty. Despite having initiated the military training he excelled at early on, he had waited to be called a warrior, much more to be called a Black Knight.

As a knight, he had waited as a subordinate to 'the Tower,' Eleanor Darkholm, until that first female commander of the knights had died in battle before he was unanimously chosen from among his peers to follow in the footsteps of the tall and stern woman.

He had waited many years for the time to become the Head of the House or the Duke of Darkholm, things that were as likely as not, for Septem held the seat of the patriarch and switched the ducal seat back and forth with Davidov who, despite seeming frail, simply did not die.

What deal does he have with Death itself that he keeps it at bay, that makes him its Master? Erdrick asked himself.

Achieving immortality was the noblest goal House Darkholm sought, and while it would be a resounding victory to one day find it, it would be a heavy blow to all his personal goals, to all his dreams.

Are Darkholm even allowed to dream? Erdrick wondered, his long strands of hair blown by the wind.

Immortality, if achieved, would keep him in place as commander of the knights, nothing more.

He would not sit on the throne of Blackheart. The crown would continue to be displayed on his war mask alone, as he had chosen it to be upon his mask's design, but would otherwise never rest upon his head.

Only one thing ever troubled Septem's firstborn son. His father had prepared the Darkholm House, informing them that while he preferred for the crown to go to one of his children, in the end, he would pass it to whomever he thought would make the best monarch.

Those words had fueled Erdrick's desire. He had studied harder than ever and trained even harder than that. He had followed every order and commanded his men in a most fair and disciplined way, managing to expand their numbers and boost their morale at every opportunity. He had even delved into some of the darkest secrets carefully hidden by the House.

But what if everything was simply not enough?

I was not born to stay in the shadows.

"Brother," Serverus's hand on his shoulder brought him back, "Idian's forces have sent notice. They will be here within two hours."

It had already been most of a week since Septem had left for Darkholde with his prisoners, and the presence of the monarch had been noted by Usman Velias's scouts. The Bull, upon hearing his main target was being taken away, launched a furious attack intending to get his hands on Duke Coronn while hopefully capturing Septem in the same swipe. But the attack of the larger men in his army had been thwarted by the organized forces of Valador and Volanar under the command of Erdrick and his Black Knights.

Usman was forced to retreat back to the Tenth, where the only thing that stopped him from launching again was the imminent arrival of the larger forces of Lord Bull, Varen Bulwharf.

"Very well," Erdrick's eyes studied the landscape, the enemy forts that had prevailed against Blackheart's forces. He thought of many things he would have done differently had he been leading the assault.

"The battlefield would have been yours," Gustavus stood by his side, contemplating the hills of the Horne, "if you had led the attack."

"I have no doubt that would have been the case," Erdrick responded without looking at his cousin who, despite not being knighted, always accompanied him, "but those were not the orders we were given. We are here to keep order and defend."

"It is wrong," Gustavus complained. "You have the skill and the charisma to lead us to victory. The king knows it, and yet he does not use it to his advantage. He does not use the sword where the sword is needed."

"Are you questioning the wisdom of our king?"

"He is wise, Erdrick. But wisdom does not make him infallible."

"It does not. That much is true. But wisdom allows us to learn so that mistakes are not repeated. Do you not remember the Council's meeting?" Erdrick asked. "This is a battle the king did not want in the first place."

"But it has already started," Gustavus argued, "and upon the inevitable, we should have gone on the offensive to guarantee victory."

Erdrick quiesced. While his heart agreed with Gustavus, he remembered his position and the orders he had been given. "What do you think, Serverus?"

"I agree with Gustavus." He saw the larger Darkholm close his eyes and nod in agreement, "but I also differ." As if he had just been insulted, Gustavus's eyes opened again. "The king's orders were to avoid war and, if attacked, to stall the enemy until the arrival of the general. As knights, we must obey the orders of our monarch. A king sees from the throne what we do not see from the battlefield."

"Well said, wise words," Erdrick agreed.

"I wish your sword arm was as clever."

"What do you mean, brother?" Serverus asked.

"Do not think I have not observed your moves during our drills," the Knight Commander responded, "Even without sparring with you, I can tell something is amiss. Something troubles you."

"I am sorry if my skills have disappointed you, Commander," Serverus spoke.

"Do you take me for a fool? Do you seek to insult me, brother?"

Despite his cold demeanor, this time it was Erdrick who placed an arm on Serverus's shoulder, his eyes squinting, "is there something I should know?"

Could Erdrick have somehow known? Could he have figured out how Serverus felt about his younger sister?

Impossible. Serverus had never shared those thoughts, those feelings with anyone, not even with his closest friend, who now questioned him.

"Everything is fine, brother," Serverus touched his hand, "I promise you."

"Do you, now?" Letting his shoulder go, Erdrick left his side.

"Let us go." At his signal, Gustavus immediately followed.

"Serverus," Erdrick said as he left, "know that there are many things of which I am aware, many of which I really do not even care to know, but also many of which others would never want me to have knowledge."

It was near the end of the day when Idian Darkholm arrived atop one of the thoroughbreds of his House, its hide as black as if the beast and its rider's armor had been sculpted from burnished coal to purposely clash with Idian's gray facial hair.

The black heart of the kingdom seemed to come to life from its engraving on the center of his plate. His crimson cape trailed behind, hiding the armed forces that followed the head of Blackheart's army.

He was accompanied by a battalion, the standard of Blackheart among nearly five hundred soldiers of the Royal Army, the scarlet chest plates of the captains noticeable from afar. Smaller contingents set up camp behind and around them, and now devoid of their leaders, Valador and Volanar's forces rallied.

The general's mount snorted, echoing Idian's disapproval upon seeing Blackheart's banner fluttering between those of Valador and Volanar.

"Take that flag down," Idian instructed his men, his tone terse, and he dismounted. He then raised his voice for all to hear, "The use of the kingdom's banner without the king's approval is an insult to Blackheart that will not be tolerated."

"General," Erdrick saluted.

"Commander," Idian greeted before addressing Erdrick's men. "Always knight." The general placed a fist over his chest, "I salute my knight brothers."

"Always brothers," they responded in unison.

Both leaders proceeded toward the command tent, Erdrick accompanied by Gustavus, Serverus, and high-ranked captains, and Idian flanked by his grandson Maxius Darkholm, also known as "the spear of darkness," and Maxius's eldest son, Aeron of the Black Knights, also known as "the horse."

The aged general walked inside, his attention fixed on the regional map resting on the desk. "What is the current status, Commander?"

"Usman Velias has launched a downhill attack from the Tenth," Erdrick pointed at the map. "He split into two waves, which we have been able to repel with some losses of our own. He was emboldened by the king's presence and possibly the only chance to gain ground before your arrival."

"I see."

"Valador was able to maneuver around it, and we almost took the Eighth," a captain from Valador added, but his words were cut short by the penetrating yellow of the general's eyes.

"A soldier that almost lived is a dead soldier, captain," Idian spoke. "You may continue, Commander."

"The Eighth's main fort has been besieged and badly damaged here in the northernmost border with Suhne's region of Ahni. It has changed hands several times. Currently, some of our forces control most of its main fort while they still control its main tower.

"Valador and Volanar's forces attempted to isolate the Tenth, but reinforcements are still coming from the Seventh, which serves as the triangulating lifeline for the Sixth, far south, and the Eighth and Ninth, both of which feed the Tenth. It has been impossible to cut the Seventh off, given the arrival and support of the duke, the Lord Bull, who's now stationed at the Ninth, southwest of where we stand."

Rubbing his chin, Idian nodded as a sign of understanding. "Bulwharf's weakness is the Horne. While not small, the region is the thinnest where it starts. Their general seems to realize we know this as well as they do."

"Of note," Erdrick added, "Usman Velias is the younger brother of the Lord Bull's future wife."

"Hmmm," Idian lifted his gaze to address all present. "We must tread carefully. What are our losses?"

"Aside from military losses, Usman Velias's forces have razed to the ground Blackheart's two scouting outposts, of which not a single ranger remains alive."

"From now on, nobody marches without my knowledge and consent. Thank you, Commander. You and your men are relieved of your responsibilities here. You may return to your duties elsewhere."

"Aeron," he instructed his great-grandchild, "send a messenger to stage a meeting between the Lord Bull and myself."

"Lord General," Erdrick said, "my men and I will stay. We march with you."

"Commander," Idian's voice was little more than a rumble, "other than by a Royal Order until you become the Patriarch of Darkholm, or the crown rests atop your head, I will not bow to you. Your job here is done. The battlefield is mine now. Take your leave, I will take it from here."

There was a legend among men that spoke of the celestials, the Lord of Light and the Knight of Darkness, facing each other in the heavens while their sister, Penumbra, watched. Their eternal clash produced the stars, and their stumbles formed the mountains as they fought in a deadly and perfect dance that would find no end.

One day, the sweat from the celestials' brows fell on Caerea, giving life to mankind.

So amazed were the gods, their hesitation broke the rhythm of their dance, and in the flurry that followed, Penumbra was mortally wounded. The sky turned deep *red, the stars bled, and the gods' grief for their lost sister turned into oceans that created the continents. The Lord and the Knight's furious clash that followed cleaved each other's blades, and the blinding light gave shape to the new constellations.*

But even the gods could not escape fate, and still, to this day, the brothers fight not from hatred but from guilt.

Both men stood before each other; Idian Darkholm, the Black General, and his counterpart, Varen Bulwharf, Lord Bull and Commander General of the Kingdom of Ardenay. The one with his great armor, his receding grays, and bushy eyebrows as soft as the man had perhaps never been. His right hand calmly rested upon the sheath of the sword his cousin had gifted him with,

the one named Fraenum[1]. The other one with his heavy plate, the rearing bull of his station engraved in its metallic surface. Varen's heavily bronzed skin was a testament to the time the Duke of Bulwharf spent training under the sun.

Each man of noble blood eyed the others. Never had they stood so close, close enough to end the life of the other, if they wanted, with a single swing of their swords. But that was not the way of Varen Bulwharf or of Idian Darkholm. It wasn't the way anymore.

The ken of their meeting while the sun readied to disappear on the horizon between them was something not even the most talented painter could ever truly capture.

It was Idian who commenced,

"Lord Bull, I am not a man of words, so I beg your forgiveness if I did not address you properly."

"That is my title," Varen responded, "it is enough. It is I who should apologize for not knowing how to address you most properly. I believe you are also knighted?"

"Lord General will do. Men like us typically address one another with a blade."

"And tomorrow might still be the day we do."

"Indeed," Idian agreed, "which brings me to the subject at hand. How do we resolve this conflict?"

Idian Darkholm

"An invasion requires retaliation."

"Lord Bull," the general allowed a moment before speaking again, "it is not always necessary."

"Isn't it?" Varen questioned.

"Allow me to ask you something," Idian said, "Are you not a religious man?"

"I am," Varen responded warily, "I follow the tenets of the Lord of Light."

"Is this what your religion preaches, what your god teaches you?"

Having fallen into the trap, Varen sought to avoid sinking into it. "It is what's required of men in my position. You invaded my lands and must now face war as a consequence of your provocation."

Varen Bulwharf

"War?" Idian casually spread his hands. "This is not war. This is not even a battle. It is only the skirmish of foolish men who advanced without being sanctioned by the Crown. They will be punished for their actions, and the conflict will end."

"Do you speak for your Crown?"

"I do not, Lord Bull, but all my actions seek to protect my Crown. Am I the only one of us who seeks to protect yours?"

"I will not fall for your Darkholm manipulations," Varen fumed. For someone who claimed to not be a man of words, Idian certainly spoke like one of the courtiers in Himlen he avoided dealing with as much as he could. "We are here to settle this conflict. Neither of us speaks on behalf of his superiors."

"Must not having the voice of their leaders make men unreasonable?"

The Lord Bull wouldn't fall for this. This wasn't one of those pranks Ealas and Siul played on him to see him lose his temper. His decisions today, while not those of the Crown, would likely be backed by King Aorius . . . if they were the right decisions, that is.

"The Bulls of Bulwharf will not simply retreat. It is not in our blood."

"It is not in my blood either," Idian added. "I, therefore, suggest a duel. Let us be represented by the best among our warriors."

"What would Ardenay obtain if we were the victor?" Varen questioned.

"The same as if Blackheart is," Idian responded, "we each retreat with the glory but without a single additional loss of life."

"What about the Horne?"

"It was not our intention to take the region, but here we are. If we were the victor, we would take the tower you call the Eighth and rebuild—"

"A stronghold you claim you took from us without wanting to."

"As the outposts and the lives you took from us."

"Fair enough. But you must realize you'd have a station surrounded by enemies," Varen was quick to point out.

Idian paused for a moment before he spoke again, "We live surrounded by enemies every day.

"If you were the victor," he continued, "we would abandon all of the Horne and return to our lands behind the wall."

The Bulwharf questioned Idian's true intentions. Like Varen himself, he was a knight, a man bound by the honor of his words and actions. But he was also a Darkholm, and the annals of history had always signaled them for the lack of honor in their actions and words.

Could he trust Idian?

Varen's scarred forehead furrowed. While he could ask himself these things, it would be most dishonorable for him to openly question the honor of another knighted man, especially one who had, at least until this moment, behaved in a chivalrous manner.

What would he get from questioning, anyway, other than a stain on his own name? Idian's notoriety preceded him. He was known to be a terrible man, a ruthless opponent, but here Varen had come face-to-face with someone who, if it hadn't been for his representing an opposing side of a battlefield, could have perhaps been a great friend.

"I accept," he stretched his open hand toward Blackheart's general, "The Bulwharf himself is the greatest warrior of these lands. I will thus be our champion."

Idian closed in fast but did not stretch Varen's hand. Instead, he lowered his voice, either to avoid the possibility of their distant forces overhearing or to avoid showing a slight irritation. "This is beneath us generals. Are we not seeking to end a conflict instead of adding chaos and disarray? Do not be foolish, friend. Do not throw away your life like that."

There was a certainty in Idian's voice that could have made a lesser man tremble. But Varen Bulwharf was no ordinary man. He was the Lord Bull of Bulwharf, the most militant duchy in Ardenay. Much like his father, he had obtained the position through combat and, like his father and every other Bulwharf who had held the position, he would keep it until his death. He had no doubt he could best any man, but in the eventuality that he did, in fact, fall in a duel, all of Bulwharf would be placed in a precarious position before the border enemies of Blackheart and, if Bulwharf fell, Ardenay could consider itself lost.

"You speak wisely," now closer, Varen offered his hand again to seal their agreement.

"It is the experience of having fought too many battles, my friend," the general stretched his hand in response, "Wisdom is what tells men what battles are not worth fighting."

⸻ ✦✦✦✦✦ ⸻

His name was Dragan Darkholm, and every time he was called onto the battlefield, someone had to die.

To his own, he was known as 'the Dragon.'

His pace was steady, his stride long, not because he was taller than the rest, although tall he was, but because of the spirit of confidence that drove him.

Just a year over two decades, he was one of the youngest Darkholm, but while his skin was perfect—unmarred by blemishes of the sun or untouched by a single scar, scratched only lightly by the slight curves of hair that reached only his neck—it showed the premature appearance of crow's feet that didn't come from his slanted, piercing eyes, but from the constant grim expression on his chiseled face.

His clothes were fine, quite tight-fitting, and, as expected of a Darkholm, as black as the deep of night. A purple lace kept his vest closed, hiding most of the shirt underneath. The lace was the same tone as the embroideries at the hem of the half-cape that rested upon his left shoulder that had been specially commissioned for him.

Dragan was not known for his social graces. As a matter of fact, he was known for their absence, for his social ineptitude. While gallant, able to speak beautifully and write enthralling poetry if he so desired, there was an emptiness to his words that was evident to those who knew him, and he had no interest in changing that. Even if he had wanted to, it would have been next to impossible, for the disdain in his eyes reflected only the bursting top of the volcano of hatred within one of such a young age.

With those outside the actual members of his House, the Dragon found it difficult to connect, barely exchanging words with the servants, limiting his interactions with even the most trusted vassals of the Darkholm to the bare minimum.

It was why, upon becoming of age, despite his talents gifting him with the option to an apprenticeship with any of the vassal Houses, Dragan had chosen to stay apprenticed to House Darkholm alone.

Anyone outside his small circle within small circles was just someone he looked down upon.

Where all this came from, no one in his House perhaps knew, or at least they didn't really care as, for all his arrogance, the Dragon channeled his emotions through either fine writing or the art of the dueling blade.

Dragan Darkholm's steps brought him toward the center of the circle where he studied the man he would soon duel, the same he cared not for, other than for knowledge of his name and status.

That man was Usman Velias, the mighty Bull of Darane.

Usman was one of the three presiding Bulls of Bulwharf, lords of the regions who would only bow to the one who had surpassed his challengers in ritual combat. He had led the Darane region for less than two years, having obtained his position after his victory over the previous Bull of Darane.

His hair was braided, reaching the upper back of his heavily built body that was barely able to be contained within his studded leather shirt. His skin was dark, close to that of Serverus Ecru of the Black Knights. One could easily tell he had not wasted a single training moment. For all the time he spent in combat, he was also charismatic and persistent.

But Lord Usman Velias was, above all, ambitious, and he had found his spirit was not satiated even after having attained that which he had sought.

No sooner had he become the head of Darane that he had started eyeing the seat of Bulwharf in the capital of Sildrane. Usman Velias had then challenged Lord Varen Bulwharf for his own position at the head of the duchy.

Dragan Darkholm

Surely many across the continent would have frowned upon the affront, especially one coming from the younger brother of Varen's own betrothed, a man who has been supported by Varen himself in every move.

As long as it was for the betterment of all Bulwharf, the bulls saw this challenge as a warrior's right, and so the custom was followed.

To prove he was worthy, following tradition, Varen had sent him on a mission—to end the life of Duke Crannon Coronn of Valador, but Erdrick Darkholm's men thwarted Usman's desperate ploy when they intervened to reinforce King Septem's retreat.

His prey had been taken far away inside the kingdom of Blackheart, and so the Bull of Darane had missed his chance, at least for now.

'The greatest warrior takes the greatest risk,' Lord Varen mumbled the words of one of the seven philosophies.

He could have called the mission a failure, ending any chance his subject had to challenge him, but he trusted his instincts, his strength, and he looked forward to once again proving in combat why he was the Bulwharf, so he would allow Usman to pursue Crannon into Blackheart.

But to Lord Usman, that chance was not enough. He needed to show his worth. While he had stopped Blackheart's advance, he had not been able to do so before Blackheart gained ground, and while Blackheart had been unable to advance further, neither had Darane's forces under his command. What Bulwharf could he be with that record?

In order to prove himself, he had asked to be the one to fight Dragan, something Varen conceded. After defeating Blackheart's representative, he would resume his quest, even if it took him to the very bowels of Blackheart's deepest hell.

"My name," he slammed his fist on his chest, "is Usman Velias, Bull of Darane, Ruler of the Towersend, and general of the northeast banner. My father was none other than Alkegan Velias of Darane. I am the chosen champion of Ardenay!"

His boastful claim was followed by a loud cheer, but he received no response other than a frigid stare from Dragan.

Usman seethed inside, but he could not lose his cool, not now, not when everyone's eyes were on him. "Who are you?" he called for all to hear, awaiting his opponent's introduction.

But Dragan's lips moved only to form a sneer.

The Dragon reached in his pocket, drawing a single golden droplet[2]. Flipping it, his dexterous fingers hurled the coin at his opponent in the way an indifferent nobleman would toss meager change to a vagrant.

"The black heart," Dragan spoke, "or the blood, take your pick."

Usman's blood simmered at the insult, but his veteran mind quickly reminded him he needed to remain in control. Smaller opponents like the one he faced this day needed every advantage they could have to best a warrior of his caliber.

His large hand studied the coin's weight. It seemed well-balanced, with the crowned heart on its face and twelve drops of blood forming a circle on its back.

"I choose the heart," Usman tossed the coin back.

In a flash, Dragan took a step back. All Usman heard was the sudden slice in the air, followed by a barely perceptible clinking sound. Before him, Dragan stood alert, legs together, standing sideways, his cloaked arm behind him. In his right hand, his unsheathed sword, pointing at Usman as it slowly returned to its resting place.

The coin fell on the ground, revealing what Fate had perhaps decided. The twelve drops of blood lay there for all to see on the surface, now scratched by the tip of Dragan's steel.

"By the rules, then," Usman spoke, "you choose the—"

"I choose sabers," Dragan stated, walking back toward Idian and ignoring his opponent.

"Then, as for me," Usman added, "I choose first blood."

Those words were something Dragan could not ignore. Those on his side saw rage fill his eyes. He always humiliated his opponents before finishing whoever stood in front of him in every duel he was a part of.

He had not come all this way to play, and the mere thought of being limited in his performance was making him the one to lose control.

———— ‡‡‡‡‡ ————

The duel took place at the height of noon, Dragan having chosen the location, right at the center of the contested field, and Usman having chosen the time.

The bull wanted to ensure the duel did not last long and that neither representative would be handicapped. Facing the sun was a disadvantage any seasoned warrior such as himself would seek to avoid, and having studied Dragan's movements and mannerisms, Usman suspected the smaller man could turn a disadvantage into an advantage as quickly as the blink of an eye.

The leaders of both forces stood around the improvised arena, Lord Varen and his betrothed, Eraysa Velias, flanked by captains and high-ranked soldiers to one side, and Lord Idian, accompanied by Maxius, Aeron, and their men.

The hands of each of the two generals held the gray banner.

"Blackheart's invasion of Ardenay's lands had brought us here," Lord Varen Bulwharf proclaimed.

"The Bulls of Bulwharf have risen to fight for the Light, to defend the honor of our kingdom. As leaders, we have agreed to resolve this conflict with a duel, and as long as the rules are observed, we will all accept its outcome."

Varen waited for Idian's intervention, but the general only nodded in agreement and signaled for him to go on.

"This challenge," Varen continued, "will be held with dueling blades and on the condition of first blood. As such, upon the appearance of the first drop of blood, the duel must end, and the victor declared."

The Bulwharf then signaled at Idian, and both men lifted their banners. They let go simultaneously, in a second that felt like minutes before the second banner touched the ground, indicating the beginning of the duel.

"I can defeat any man!" Usman was quick to draw his blade in a wide arc that added power to his momentum as he dashed forward toward Dragan.

Before even drawing his saber or even taking a breath, the Darkholm shifted his stance, placing his right foot forward and the left to the side, each knee slightly flexed to maximize mobility.

Half a second later, he stepped aside, using his cape to deflect Usman's attack.

But his dodge, while masterful, wasn't enough to make the larger warrior lose a single ounce of balance. The Bull, Dragan found, was quicker than he appeared, something he promptly took note of.

Usman attacked again and then some more, forcing the Darkholm to bare his blade to deflect his assault. He sought to keep Dragan on the defensive, attempting to overpower the Darkholm with his relentless moves. Those attacks Dragan did not use his sword against, he deftly misdirected with the twirling of his cape.

While Usman was a stormy sea, Dragan was the fish that found his way amidst his furious waves.

The Bull swung wide and missed. 'By the Light, I hate these swords.'

With a heavier weapon, he could have cleaved Dragan's sword in two, but these were just too flexible. Much of the might he placed behind each attack was lost as the blade bounced off Dragan's on each strike that connected.

'Is he enjoying this?' He looked at the eyes of his opponent, but Dragan did not look back. The smaller duelist's gaze was on Usman's shoulders, reading the contraction and reaction of his muscles.

As much as his eyes were on Usman's moves, his mind was elsewhere.

'What is Sellayne doing at this very moment?' he wondered, thinking about his beloved. 'Knowing her, perhaps she is getting fucked by Atelas.

'That is fine, I do not mind,' he continued, 'as soon as I am done here, I will go back and pin her against the wall and make her mine time and time again.'

The loud whistling from Usman's sudden flurry of attacks, barely missing Dragan's chest brought the Darkholm back to the matter before him.

Dragan noticed a change in his opponent's tempo. Usman's strikes were starting to become somewhat slower. As he continued his assault, the Dragon saw several openings, yet he hadn't gone on the offensive a single time.

Was the opening a feint? They could have easily been. Unlike his cousin, Ashildr, he wouldn't go for it, even if it ended up being a ploy from Usman, from which he had no doubt he could easily recover.

'Why give him the satisfaction that he almost had me?' Dragan smiled inside. 'Why give him any hope?'

Once again, his thoughts were interrupted, this time by an extended lunge that narrowly missed the forearm and instead slashed Dragan's breeches. Had the Darkholm duelist not reflexively moved a half-inch back, it would have opened a gash in Dragan's thigh.

In that same step, the Darkholm's body turned, and, twirling the cape, he entangled Usman's saber within the fabric.

Before he had fully realized it, Usman saw his blade leave his hand to be sent flying, landing nearly ten feet away.

But the Bull wasted no time. While Dragan's cape was still moving, Usman dashed and, sliding along the ground, managed to wrap his hand around his weapon's hilt.

He breathed heavily, thick droplets falling from his forehead toward his grounded hand. While he had not been able to effectively penetrate Dragan's defense, at least he had ensured that the Darkholm did not get a chance to attack, or so he wanted to believe.

What is his weakness? Every man had a vulnerability, one that could give a great advantage to his opponent if it were known.

Briefly, he set eyes on the proud figure of Varen, who was both his respected leader and now political opponent. Even through his chest plate, he could almost feel the duke's heart beating, giving life to the rearing bull engraved in its steel.

By Varen's side, his older sister Eraysa, whose proud eyes of amber were carefully studying the exchange.

After he was done, she would scold him, as she often did, pointing out every error he had committed, every lesson she had taught him growing up that he hadn't followed.

He could hear himself laughing at her, while he could almost hear her say, "Every opponent has a weakness, one many times fed by a flaw."

'A flaw!' Usman snapped back. Instead of going on the offensive, he took a second to study Dragan, his steady form, his confident poise, how he closed in in a way only the most watchful eyes would perceive. Everything about Dragan not just reflected but reeked of his arrogance.

Having observed Dragan's reflexes before the start of the duel, Usman had not given him an opportunity to attack, and while giving it was many times unwise, it was the riskiest and perhaps only way he could understand the combat language his opponent spoke.

Much like Dragan with his cape, Usman needed to create his own diversion, an opening of sorts. While he had tested the Dragon's defenses, he had not witnessed him attack, and while Dragan had survived his attacks, he had not seen Usman's defense.

'I have to create an opening,' Usman thought, 'one not too obvious, or he won't fall for it.'

Usman stood once again, sword ready. He saw the sun past the zenith, favoring Dragan. Behind his opponent, the presence of the Bulwharf and his forces only meant it was the untrustworthy Darkholm who were behind him.

'If he thinks he's a bullfighter and my stamina is drained, he will be surprised to find I can fight for hours with minimal rest.'

In a flash, he dashed toward the right, shifted his weight toward the left, and poked forward, swinging his saber wide and running past the twirling figure of his opponent before he fell on his knees.

The rising, celebratory voices of his men alerted him. Had he struck true?

He turned to see, through eyes stinging from the dripping sweat, Dragan finishing his move.

The Darkholm duelist raised both hands to show a large gash on his cape, but his skin was still intact.

Usman studied the opportunity he had created, waiting to see if his counterpart had taken the bait. As if fueled by anger at his opponent's premature celebration, Dragan changed his stance, approaching Usman with more certainty and less precaution. He saw the cape twirling ahead of Dragan as a spinning whirlwind in a black ocean seen from the heavens.

'This is it,' Usman Velias thought, 'it is now or never. For the Light, for my ancestors, I cannot let them down!'

Amidst the waves of black fabric, Usman saw Dragan take a leap and, for the first time, the Dragon's mocking smile and twin eyes of bright yellow looking back at his.' His feet then pushed the ground, in a way history will

always remember that moment, his prowess, driving his arm forward with all his might.

The deafening clamor from both sides that followed echoed for miles. It swallowed the clatter of a single sword on the ground but not the harrowing screams of Eraysa Velias, who was only stopped by Varen and his men.

Just a few feet away, her younger brother's body knelt on the ground, held up only by Dragan's saber that had pierced his left eye, from where a waterfall of red sprouted all the way toward the back of his skull from where its tip still protruded. It was as if Dragan had decided he wanted his opponent to pay him homage.

He heard her agonizing screams clearly. He could have looked at her. Dragan's menacing eyes of yellow could have burned a memory in Eraysa's mind of what it felt like to face a dragon.

But he didn't. He wouldn't give her that sense of importance. Instead, as if he had enough, he rapidly removed his blade from the sheath Usman's skull had become.

Usman's dead body slumped forward, promptly caught by his sister before his face hit the ground.

Half-turning casually, Dragan flicked his weapon to clean its blade.

"There. First blood," he stated coldly before he walked away.

The Darkholm's fingers lightly patted the minuscule, amethyst dragon head that hung from the base of his blade. It was a gift from his only sibling, his half-sister, Tenslea, one with whom he played as he had played with the life of his opponent.

Eraysa's face wet, she stretched out her hands as if wishing she could strangle Dragan where he stood.

"Look at me!" Her heart was torn into infinite pieces, not as much for the defeat of her brother, but for the humiliation he was put through, at the derision shown by Dragan. "Look at me, you fuck, incestuous freak!"

Dragan ignored her plea. He walked away, leaving her behind with the lifeless body of the warrior who had said he could defeat any man.

But he wasn't a man. Dragan . . . was a Darkholm, and this was the ballad he wrote, the way he preferred to speak. It was beautiful. It was sharp. It was, in many ways, perfect.

"Branden and Eleanor's son," Idian prepared to depart, "he never disappoints."

Blackheart's general climbed upon his horse, his crimson cape flowing as the sea of blood that represented his kingdom.

Behind him, the only thing bloodier than the cape on his shoulders was the ground Dragan walked away from.

(1) Fraenum: 'Rein' Idian's sword was forged for him by the Master of Steel and given to him by Septem as a reminder that not every time there's conflict a blade must be drawn.

(2) Droplet: The currency of Blackheart. On its face, the coin depicts the crowned heart, its back, twelve drops of blood. It is minted in gold, silver, bronze and copper. Its value is comparable to Ardenay and Daneran's state, and double the value of the Suhne mahk.

THIRD TEST

Location: Empyre of Suhne, City of Suhne, Palace of the Sun

The morning sun stood firm in the sky, as firm as the stance of the soldier in his room, almost as firm as Malek's phallus under the hand of one of his golden maidens. His eyes opened to find her caressing every inch of his body with one hand while she stroked every inch of his shaft with the other.

Malek's muscles tensed. A rush of blood surged, energizing him with an addicting, ecstatic sensation that announced the coming climax.

"Stop." His hand clutched her forearm firmly. Hastily, the Son swung the woman onto the bed and jumped on top of her perfect body. His arms separated the legs easily, as easily as his mouth opened to bite her womanhood, making the golden maiden moan in a combination of pleasure and pain.

The Son of the Sun's eyes saw her body twitch and tremble as he drank her.

The woman's skin glistened under the dripping sweat of the near-divine torso as the firstborn stood. He grabbed both her legs in his muscular arms and looked into the woman's eyes as his pelvis slammed itself against her own.

Again she moaned; again, he was delighted. Both of his hands wrapped around her neck, almost choking her against the sheets, as his manhood explored her vault, a savage beast seeking to devour whatever it found in the lair it invaded.

A sudden rush drove him to stop right before his emission exploded.

Malek stood, breathing heavily, watching her almost-unconscious body draped over the now wet sheets.

He breathed in deeply and breathed out before jumping again on top of her, driving his fingers into her vault as he held her shoulder with his other hand, pulling her in so that his hand could be driven more forcefully and deeply inside her.

Again, the rush.

Again, he stopped.

Bringing his right hand to his face, he sniffed it. Loving the scent of sweat, pain, and pleasure, the Son licked his own fingers.

But it was not enough. It was never enough.

As if possessed by some inner demon, Malek's eyes locked on the soldier.

With two strides, he stood by the military man's side. His strong arms doubled the soldier over the bed and started ripping his clothes off, tearing pieces of armor from their places.

The man-beast pushed the soldier against the woman and watched the man enter the golden maiden's vault uninvited.

Again, the golden maiden moaned, her nipples hard, now being bitten by the soldier, sending spasms through Malek's muscles.

Malek, Ascended

A sinister, almost insane grin appeared on his lips.

Immediately, his large hand pulled the soldier's hair back as the Son entered him forcefully from behind. The military man would feel pleasure, but his pleasure would be paired with pain.

It was now the man who moaned as the Son conquered his inside, pinning his almost naked body against the bed as the maiden almost drifted to unconsciousness.

The pain was great, even for a veteran of the armed forces of Suhne, but it came with a great sense of pleasure, and there was no greater pleasure for anyone in Suhne than to please or give pleasure to the deities, even at the cost of unendurable pain.

Malek's hand wrapped around the soldier's cock, clutching it to stop it from exploding until the Son himself allowed it. He bit the man's trapezius, his eyes rolling up as he felt the man convulse from pleasure.

Finally, he let go of the soldier's phallus, the military man's voice rising as his manhood spilled over the bed and maiden's abdomen.

And yet, right before his own emission, the Son stopped himself.

Malek stood by the bed in all his naked glory, looking down at both exhausted bodies, a near-divine being having conquered everything he had willed.

He was still hard, his precum dripping toward the floor, but quickly rescued by Malek's hand, soaking his fingers.

Without a second thought, he brought them to his own mouth, where his own tongue had a taste of his divinity, the divinity that he would not allow to touch the ground.

"Get out!" the Son commanded.

The soldier knew better than to prolong his stay, than to anger the Son of the Sun. Barely clutching what he could, he knelt to pick up the cloth and armor plates on the floor, the same ones Malek kicked toward the hallway. "GET OUT!"

Enraged, he grabbed the unconscious woman by the hair and dragged her along the floor and toward the entrance to his chambers, where her head clattered hitting the hallway floor as he let go.

The Son turned and closed the door behind him as he went deeper into his lair.

After he had conquered their bodies, he was ready to conquer the day.

The arena was packed with thousands of followers clamoring for the banner of Suhne. While the games were held biannually for the glory of the Sun, this time, the participants would be the Sons themselves.

The crowd roared, their clamor rising as an offering to the heaven above upon instruction from Exis.

The Speaker was pleased. He smiled, witnessing the crowd that had gathered, at the control they kept, having averted a mutiny when the Suhnites filled the arena seats to the point of almost bursting.

Many had chosen to stand, for there was no place among the seated, and they would not want to miss the Test this day would bring.

On the east end, the Flame Guard stood around the stone seats where the Rays and the Blessed Ones rested, what was unused of their Chosen retinue stood behind each of the Sons, five of Malek's and seven each of Kaylen and Vamya's.

"People of the Sun," Exis raised his hand, silencing the anxious crowd. "Today, we face the first physical Test of the Sun. The Blessed Sons will each choose their champion from among their retinue. With the blessing given, their respective champions will fight to the death, the surviving champion bringing victory to the Son and thus bringing us one step closer to revealing his divinity. Today we test the Sun's foresight!"

A young Ray showed three tokens, each etched with a sun colored in gold, red and green, respectively. He placed the three facedown inside a circle on the ground, all the same distance from the center and one another.

Exis stood a spear in the center, its tip pointing toward the heavens. The tension broke when he released it to see where it would fall. It clattered as it touched the ground close to one of the stone tokens.

He lifted the token for the crowd to see a green Sun. "Vamya, Son of the Sun," Exis directed his attention toward her while keeping his voice raised so that the multitude could hear. "Who will champion you?"

"Speaker." Vamya wore a simple, green silken robe. Her hair was tied up in three buns, one to each side and to the back of her head, each wrapped around in golden, handmade leaves. "I have chosen two champions to represent me, one male, one female. Each has what the other lacks, and in perfect balance, they will bring us all victory."

The crowd roared at her words. Women among the populace, especially, were most raucous.

A man and a woman from Vamya's retinue climbed down into the arena, both clad in green-tinted leather armor, the man holding the traditional shield and spear. His companion, a short spear and whip.

Once again, the spear stood, to be released by the hand of the Speaker. This time, a red Sun was revealed. "Kaylen, Son of the Sun, who will champion you?"

The Searing Sun's lips were the only thing that could be seen from under the maroon and red cloak and robes he wore. Even his eyes were covered with a red silken fabric from which pearls dangled. Behind, a cream quartz ring rose like a halo, wrapped in places by some of Kaylen's own hair.

All present waited for him to speak, yet not a word came forth.

With a slow wave of his hand, Kaylen sent the unspoken message to his Chosen.

Three lithe yet muscular men jumped down to the arena, all clad in red leather.

The first with a spear and shield, another with sword and shield, and the third with a scimitar in each hand, a spiked buckler attached to each of his forearms.

"I find it irritating that you can't even address the Speaker when he asks," Vamya turned her head to speak to Kaylen, who faced her in turn.

While she could not see his eyes, she knew they were fixed on her, and she could feel his disdain.

"Do you try hard to be so bitter, or does it come naturally?" the Sun of Change asked.

Her brother remained silent.

"Answer me! Show some respect and say something!" Vamya's exasperation was notable.

Kaylen's lips parted briefly . . .

But only to imbibe from a cup he had been served.

After an uncomfortable silence, he turned from Vamya to face the arena.

Again, the crowd chanted, stomping on the ground as their anxiety grew.

"Malek, Son of the Sun," Exis added last, lifting his token to reveal the golden symbol "choose who will champion you."

The eldest of the three stood in place to address the crowd.

"Great wisdom is shown when choosing our champions, but choosing our champion shows even greater cowardice. I choose myself!"

At these words, the spectators roared, their exhilarating clamor like that of thunder in a stormy summer.

"It is a fight to the death," Seiris of the Rays almost whispered through a heavily grayed beard, his face unable to hide his concern. "There will be nothing we can do to protect you if you were to fall," Exis added.

Malek's menacing eyes captured the warriors below as he adjusted his golden tunic and bracers. "And *nothing* is what you should do to protect me. If I were to fall, then I was never worthy of becoming the Sun."

The Son armed himself with a spear, and, together with his shield, he jumped down to the arena grounds.

The drums rumbled, each pounding heavier than the last, ending with a sudden double beat that sent the warriors against one other, their fury fueled by the bloodthirsty crowd.

Malek sprinted between both groups. Surprised at his risky move, both opposing him remained where they stood, all but Vamya's girl, who cracked her whip swiftly.

The Son dove and rolled along the ground when he felt a stinging sensation biting his ankle. Grimacing, he looked back.

While anyone would have seen his move as foolish, Malek's seasoned instincts knew better. Having tested his opponents, he now knew whose reflexes he had to keep in mind at all times when fighting.

One of Kaylen's men dashed toward Malek, both his scimitars spinning wildly as he neared the larger man. Dancing as waves in the ocean, both scimitars moved with perfect synchrony.

The Son lunged with his spear, but the swordsman spun around leftward, both swords following a move that could have beheaded his opponent if not for his quick thinking and the deflection of his shield.

Malek recovered, staying low.

The deadly dance of swords continued, and Malek thrust again, the spear's tip deflected by one of the incoming bucklers.

Dancing to a perfect tune that balanced offense and defense was throwing Malek off. He needed to find the rhythm. He needed to disrupt the harmony.

"Hurgh!" he shouted upon finding a window of opportunity, thrusting the spear toward the swordsman's chest.

Switching his steps, his opponent danced still, increasing the speed of the swings, the sharp edges of his blades cutting the spear one-third of the way. Again the endless waves came, but this time from the right.

One thing the Conqueror was known for, however, was his adaptability on the battlefield. Just in time, he pivoted to have the blades scratch his shield's surface. With the same momentum, he spun further, bludgeoning his opponent's leg with the metallic disk's surface before kicking his leg with his own muscular one, sending his body to the ground.

With a loud scream, Malek plunged the broken haft on the man's neck, the blood splashing on his chest an indication of the effectiveness of his attack.

At the same time, Vamya's pair stayed close to one another while fending off the charge of the remaining pair. Cracking the whip, the female kept them both at bay to allow her companion to find an opening.

Knowing his companion's reach, he sprinted toward his opponents, shield first, and spear held fast as the lance of a western mounted knight.

Both his opponents targeted him.

Vamya's spearman's thrust met the shield of his opponent. His opponent's spearhead did the same, but the move opened a single moment Kaylen's swordsman would use to slash his arm off if it weren't for the sharp stinging on his face, followed by the echo of the cracking whip.

The green spearman then blocked his opponent's weapon while using his own to thrust twice at the stunned swordsman, once on his lower abdomen and once inside his armpit, incapacitating him.

"One, one, and two," Vamya spoke with a smile of approval. She briefly looked at her seated brother.

'How can he remain so calm when his men are falling for him?' she wondered. 'If I were him, I would—" Her thoughts were interrupted by the crowd's cheer.

The whipmaster focused her attention on assisting her companion. He was too close to his opponent, their moves too fast for her to strike and know she would hit the right one. At this point, the only thing she could do was focus her attention on Malek, who was rapidly approaching.

Twirling out of the way, her whip lashing around her like a lightning cage, she earned a moment of respite. All he earned was a blood streak across his back, sending searing pain that would have doubled over any man.

But Malek was not just a man, he was the Son of the Sun, the Blessed One, and he would spill his last ounce of blood to become the Sun of Suhne.

Using that same momentum, he punched Vamya's spearman's back, the crunching sound of several ribs releasing an agonizing scream as the Son continued his sprint past the spearman.

The whipmaster closed in on her companion, the cracking sound and the snap in the air close to Kaylen's man's face stopping him in his tracks.

And that was exactly what Malek was waiting for. Pushing off the ground with all his might, he ran toward the back of the red spearman.

"Chaaarge," the whipmaster announced, allowing Kaylen's man to turn in time and brace with his shield, the same one Malek stepped on as he vaulted over them, a giant feline pouncing on its prey.

But again, the woman's lightning reflexes were his match. Cracking her whip to catch him in the air, she tried to duck, but Malek caught the leather weapon in his now-burning hand. His eyes filled with an almost demonic fury, his other hand caught the woman's hair, and as he touched the ground, her back slammed onto the ground.

The Son's hand made contact with the ground. Grabbing sand, he threw it in his opponent's face as he punched her.

Blinded by it, the woman screamed, thrusting with her spear several times, fighting like a wasp. Her desperate attack produced a warm gush of blood as it wounded Malek's right shoulder.

Infuriated at the sight of his own blood, the Firstborn rose. With all the strength he could muster, he stomped on the woman's ribs, sternum, and neck time and again, snapping bones, her piercing cry ending as her floored body continued to writhe.

Insanity took over the crowd. They shouted the Son's name.

On the platform, Vamya stood in place, her hands to her chest, as she watched in disbelief.

The Son charged toward the back of Vamya's other man, plunging the short spear he now held, its tip coming through the other side of the man's torso.

Kaylen's spearman lunged and scratched his skin as the Son spun, but a javelin hit his side.

Dazed, Malek looked up to the platform, where he saw his sister standing.

His brother, however, owned a sinister smile, his hand up, having signaled to another of his men to join the fray, the one who had hurled the javelin and now was ready to jump down to the arena.

Fury took hold of the Son. The world turned red, and all he could and would see was uncontrollable fury. Grabbing a spear from the ground, he hurled it as the reinforcement jumped. It went through the man's mouth and against the wall, where he now dangled like a used, forgotten rag doll soaking in its own blood, his legs contorting as life escaped him.

Again the crowd howled, they chanted his name, but it didn't excite him anymore. Rage had taken over every fiber of his body.

The last spearman attacked.

Malek blocked with his shield, and in a flash, he wrapped the whip around the man's neck.

The Son tightened his grip as he kicked the man's abdomen furiously. His opponent's eyes rolled up, begging the Sun for mercy. But the Sun would not listen, for he was standing right in front of him, and the Sun wanted nothing more than to see his lifeless corpse on the blistering sand.

Having finished, Malek lifted both arms, the crowd incessantly praising him. After the battle, he was now feeling exhausted.

But destiny was not done with him.

A sharp sensation on his thigh woke him from his trance.

The Blessed One turned to face the platform and felt a sharp pain on his flank. Where the pain started, an arrow was stuck.

Raising his eyes, they caught a glimpse of a bowman standing on the platform, his tunic red . . . red as the world turned when he saw Kaylen, with that ominous smile, and his hands ending the signal that had sent yet another champion.

Malek sprinted toward the platform, deaf to the roaring crowd, ignoring all pain in his body.

He climbed up fast as an ape escaping grave danger.

He stood by the bowman, who cocked yet another arrow.

But Malek's prowess was legendary, at the very least. The Firstborn took the man by the shoulders and lifted him in the air, screaming wildly as he slammed the archer against the stone platform's floor.

The bowman's crawl was interrupted by the Son grabbing him again, this time slamming his body against the floor near his siblings' chairs.

The large hands then caught the man's head and banged it against the stone handrest of Kaylen's seat, once, twice, and many more times until his skull was crushed, sending brain fluid flying toward his brother's maroon cloak.

Both brothers' eyes locked—the pair that blazed with fury and the hidden ones separated only by a few inches and a silken curtain.

Before anything else could happen, the Flame Guard stood by Kaylen's side.

On one side, Vamya was startled, and somehow, she was certain her brother was too.

Despite both having lost this event.

Despite his discomforting serenity.

Despite that smirk she would someday make sure to have erased from his face.

ILEINA'S HEART

Location: Kingdom of Blackheart, Duchy of Darkholm,
Barony of Ironheart, Ironholde Keep

*One's willpower can, at times, be one's best weapon,
or the best weapon of our enemies . . .*

"The king will receive you," the servant bowed, signaling for Ileina Eomener to follow his steps toward the audience chamber of Ironholde.

The double doors were ornate, with symbols of gargoyles, scavenging birds, and others that were hard to name either because they had been depicted to be less identifiable or simply too grotesque.

A great chamber with enough space to accommodate a small army opened before her. It was remarkably beautiful, she thought, with its few tall, arched windows and black armored men seen only thanks to the candelabra breaking the stranglehold the darkness seemed to have over the dark stone that comprised the entirety of the building.

Strangely, Ileina noted, she could almost hear the echo of her footsteps and those of her bodyguards, as if the chamber had been empty when it obviously wasn't.

"Lady Ileina Eomener," a man bowed lightly. His hair was short, slick, and as dark as his skin was pale. He looked at her with bright, yellow eyes unlike any she had ever seen before. He was garbed in elegant black attire, with silver medals and a pin in the shape of a herald's trumpet.

"Welcome to Ironholde, home to the throne of Blackheart," the man greeted. "My name is Vhimir Darkholm, Royal Herald of House Darkholm."

Ileina nodded, offering the hand he kissed, showing her he had knowledge of the customs of others.

"Please allow me to introduce you, my lady," Vhimir walked toward the center of the large room.

"Lady Ileina of House Eomener," his voice rose before stepping aside, "ambassador of Ardenay, heir to the ducal throne of Alcyn and Baroness of Riverbed, has requested an audience with His Majesty, our Lord King, Septem Darkholm the White, Crowned King of Blackheart, Duke of Darkholm, Count of Coldforge, Baron of Ironheart, Lord of Ironholde, Father of the Blood."

Ileina curtsied deeply, rising to see the monarch about whom she had heard so much. He didn't seem demonic, irate, or insane. There was no blood coming out of his mouth, trickling down bloodshot eyes. There were no large fangs or sharp talons on his hands. This man was regal, dressed in the purest white that seemed to have a shine of its own, like that of the moon she loved to write poems about. His long cape draped toward the right, allowing her to see the fine clothes of the same color underneath. On his head, the crown of Blackheart, beautifully detailed and yet hard to describe from a distance, in what appeared to be white gold.

He sat on a large, ornate throne that was slightly raised but not elevated as if to make the monarch almost seem he had come down from the heavens, as was Ardenay's.

But it was his face that called most of her attention. He had a serious, calm demeanor as if the monarch had been chiseled from white marble, his intense gaze mounted with the most refined gold.

By his side stood an armored woman, tall and firm as the granite the walls were made of.

"Your Majesty," Vhimir announced, "Lady Eomener has requested an audience to seek information regarding a missing person."

Following the herald's words, the monarch's eyes set on her. His deep, penetrating gaze made her feel he was seeing not just her but beyond her.

Could he read her thoughts?

Could he see that she was not truly an ambassador, that she had taken her father's seal without his knowledge and written the travel papers herself?

"You may speak," King Septem instructed.

"Your Highness, I am honored to be in your presence," she curtsied again, noting the monarch would only nod briefly but say nothing.

He didn't welcome her, Ileina noted. Was it because his customs were different or because she simply wasn't welcome?

It wouldn't matter. It just couldn't. She was here on a most important mission, and while not a seasoned diplomat, she knew enough to maintain composure. "I have traveled from the capital of Riverbed in Alcyn to seek information regarding the whereabouts of one of our people."

"One you believe is in our midst," Septem responded.

"Yes, Your Highness," Ileina's determined eyes looked straight into the monarch's. "I have obtained word from trusted sources that he is somewhere in your land."

"Your Majesty," Vhimir spoke next, "here is a detailed physical description, with an artist's depiction of this man Lady Eomener describes."

In a few moments, silence filled the room as the aurean eyes of the monarch consumed what was before them.

"Of high importance, must he be, that you have journeyed long and sought an audience . . . for one person," Septem stated.

"He is, as a matter of fact," Ileina looked up at the throned man, "very much so."

"You have come to the land of those your Crown regards as *enemies*," Septem said.

"Your Highness, in this we don't have to be," Ileina added, hoping to move the monarch with the words she had practiced in her head for over a tenday. She allowed a pause, but she saw the White King unmoved, his expression as serious and determined as when she had first walked into the chamber.

"Much depends on me finding this man," she continued, to not lose her momentum. "He is a most valuable asset to our kingdom. His kind heart, his stable mind, those things, and much more are needed in our land. I believe only he can achieve the great things that are needed for our kingdom to prosper and have peace . . . *with its neighbors*."

Ileina expected the words to have an effect on Septem, any effect actually, but yet once again, his immutable expression did not betray his thoughts.

"Your Highness," Eriadna, the Shield of the King, spoke, her suspicious eyes on Ileina, "If this man's importance were so great, would they not have sent a bigger escort or more important ambassadors?"

"Unless he is an enemy of the state," Septem responded. "Deluded is your hope," he said to Ileina, "for it depends on finding one among countless."

Ileina Eomener took half a step forward, a move that immediately alerted the knights, who shifted their positions. "Your Highness," she lifted her hands to show she meant no harm, "I am a woman of faith, and I have faith these things are possible if he returned."

"Faith equates blindness," he continued, "if it is placed in the changing heart of a single man. What is this man's name?" Septem asked.

She heard what seemed like the rustling of fabrics in the darkness of the room, beyond the reaches of the candle's light. She looked out the windows, where the Darkholde appeared as a shadowy giant that was as close as it was distant. Somehow, Ileina felt she was being watched, *perhaps from that last window of the keep, or that other one closer to the top, or even from that one on the nearby tower . . . or maybe from all of them.*

To add to that, inside this chamber, she felt oppressed, the echoing whispers of its dark corners from where others resembling the king appeared.

She was in the center, like a colorful butterfly in the midst of it all, while they were quiet, patient, as ravenous spiders waiting for her to fall into their web.

"His name is Ealas." Ileina stopped herself before speaking further.

"And who is this Ealas?" Septem inquired.

Would she share more? Could she state his position? It would likely be unwise, but what if it made it easier to find him? Should she tell these people, the same who were her kingdom's sworn enemies?

"He is . . . my betrothed." Another lie had been easily born from her lips.

It was not uncommon to stretch the truth or even lie among the nobles. Despite it being deemed sinful by the church, even those claiming to be most pious were known to say things that were not exactly true or were simply not true at all, but it was often a justifiable means to an end, she had learned.

In that moment, she wondered how many of the nobles in court and the holy men of the church spoke only half-truths, and so the entirety of their meetings and agreements were based on a perception of honesty that was, in the end, just a bed of lies.

Still, while Ealas had not truly been her betrothed, they had grown to be close, and in that closeness, Ealas had played with her hair, caressed her skin, and even written her beautiful poems describing the beauty of nature, the flowering mountains and the adventures of men. She thought, no, she was sure those poems were really talking about her, even though Ealas never told her so. Ileina loved him, and, she was certain, he loved her just as much.

"The Blood of Blackheart are numerous, as grains of salt in the ocean," Septem stated. "With the small amount of information you have provided, it would be hard to identify this Ealas you speak of. We will not offer any assistance."

"But, Your Highness, Ealas—" Ileina blurted out in frustration but then recalled it was best to keep the information to herself. If they had found Ealas, they would have surely said something, or would they?

A simple signal from Septem sent Vhimir in her direction. He stretched a face-up palm toward the door to direct her toward the entrance. As politely as he had welcomed her, he dismissed her, almost rudely, "Your lady's business here has ended."

"I would like to ask one more thing," Ileina said to Vhimir.

"My lady must take her leave; the audience is finished. There are other matters the Crown must attend to." With his own signal to the knights, she was escorted out of the chamber.

Ileina Eomener walked along the long, dark hallway leading to Ironhold's entrance. She was angry at herself, at having come all this way and gone to great lengths to choke at the last second. But it was best she had done so. Providing the enemies of her land with such valuable information could very well be arming Blackheart against them. She could then lose both Ealas and the safety of her homeland.

To her right, the rustling of fabric and clinking of trinkets were heard among the shadows. This time, it was more obvious, more pressured. She turned her head to the side in an attempt to adjust her pupils. "Is someone there?"

At her question, a pair of maidens walked out of the shadows, the one with amber eyes, all her jewelry relegated to her arms, laden with bracelets and dangling charms, the second one wearing a most exquisite black dress and earrings that ran along the back of her auricles. "It is a pleasure to become your acquaintance and see you up close," the first one said. "My name is Tenslea, and this is my cousin, Sellayne Darkholm."

Sellayne curtsied and smiled, as she looked up and down at the entirety of Ileina's attire.

"You look like sisters," Ileina noted.

"We do," Tenslea responded.

"But we are not," Sellayne added, "I can assure you."

"Your skin is beautiful," Tenslea walked up to better see Ileina, "almost radiant."

"Thank you," Ileina responded.

"Your dress is so pretty, the color of salmon in spring," Sellayne's marigold eyes refused to blink. "Would you mind if I touched the fabric?"

"Go ahead," Ileina offered one arm for her to touch, smiling.

"It is softer than it looks," Sellayne's eyes twinkled with fascination, "silk, but somehow finer."

"Yes, it is Taerean silk."

"Taerean silk? May I?" Tenslea's hands also touched the fabric delicately. "I would have expected it to be Tardese."

While the maidens' attention was on her dress, Ileina contemplated their faces, with their perfect, pale skin and hair as dark as the shadows they had emerged from. "There's only a single family in Taerea that cultivates it."

Their conversation was interrupted by a few rapid footsteps and by the appearance of the slender figure of Lady Charon, who spun around and smiled, her snowy hair trailing behind as she pranced.

"Girls," she tapped their shoulders playfully before grabbing their hands, "we need to go."

Charon then turned back to look at Ileina, placing a finger in front of her own lips to say 'shh,' and pointing it toward Ileina's back before taking her cousins with her, leaving as gracefully fast as she had come.

The moment she left, Ileina turned back and was surprised to see the cloaked figure of Rowena, only a few steps away, walking slowly toward her, with eyes as commanding of respect as those of the monarch himself while also filled with shrewdness.

"There is a passion in your words." Rowena's lips appeared as the ripe cherries Ileina had loved so much, her eyes gold as the richest pieces her mother wore.

"Thank you," Ileina responded, "passion is the wind that fuels the journey of the greatest ships."

"And also capsizes them." Rowena smiled slyly. "I like you," she continued, "your beauty . . . your freedom . . . your strength . . ." Septem's daughter then closed in, almost cheek to cheek, her perfume of blossoming crimsons. Her touch was like that of the softest fabrics. But her voice was even softer, and yet she whispered powerful words, "Please, heed my warning. For your sake, at least to oppose us, never cross our paths again."

There are many things Ileina regretted on her journey back to Alcyn. *She could have revealed the truth about Ealas. She could have convinced his father to send a real diplomat. She should have never taken his seal.*

But none of those thoughts troubled her as much as that mysterious woman's veiled threat.

Would she listen? Why would she heed the word of an enemy?

She would be back.

"Onward." One way or another, she would find Ealas before he fell into their hands.

ISOLDE

Location: Kingdom of Blackheart, Royal Duchy of
Darkholm, Capital City of Coldforge, Darkholde Keep

The harder you punch, the more you hurt your hand . . .

The echo of her footsteps brought back memories, memories of the times when she ran along the long, shadowy hallways of Darkholde Keep.

She was young, thirteen to be exact, and not shapely like some of her cousins. In fact, she was quite lithe, her breasts still buds under her clothes. The massive expanse of the royal stronghold was a world in itself, and it had been the only world she knew until her eleventh year.

The last few years she had spent away from home traveling, learning all she could so that one day she could become an assistant to the Master of Life.

In her pursuit of knowledge, she had been forced to leave, and in her departure from Darkholde, she had left her childhood behind.

Strangely, though, Isolde felt that child crawl back under her skin, perhaps a little angry at her abandonment.

Nonsense, she thought. She was someone else now, a grown, more mature version of herself.

Her steps were steady and strong, secure even. Young Isolde had grown not only in knowledge but just as much in confidence. With each step, she approached the dining hall, consumed in thought, ignoring the knights who escorted her.

As if seeking reassurance, her right hand fidgeted with the golden brooch that held her oversized cloak in place, the same one that covered the drab clothing that made her look like a boy.

Everything will be fine.

It had been seven years since the last time she cried.

She had sat on the stone-cold floor at the top of the Spire, her eyes raining at the news of her mother having jumped, her body now broken by the reefs below. Isolde had not dared look, nor did she need to. She trusted the young man standing by her side, her beloved brother, who had shared the same mother. His eyes had been closed as he trembled slightly, but cry he did not.

Not only was he nearly a decade older, but growing up, Azareth had always intellectualized every event, removing any emotion from it.

That, in Isolde's mind, made him a pillar of strength.

"Brother," Isolde wept, her tears wetting her own kneecaps as she hugged them firmly. "How are we going to live without her?"

One thing Azareth wasn't was silent. Through his apparent calmness, Isolde perceived his voice almost breaking.

"We will, little sister. You and I are still here."

"I cannot, brother. It hurts. I . . . I always thought Mother loved us so much that she would never leave us alone like this. I hate her for this."

"Sis," Azareth had knelt and softly kissed his half-sister's head. "Do not hate her. Our mother's life was not easy. She never forgave herself for having hurled Charon off the Spire. While I must not approve of her actions, I must simply accept what has transpired."

"Brother . . . I do not think I can live without her . . ." Isolde had sobbed.

"You must, you will, beloved sister." He unfastened his favorite cloak and wrapped it around his sister's shoulders. The Master of Lore then used his brooch to fasten it around her neck.

"You are my favorite, and I need you by my side so that I can remain strong. Know that, as this cloak, I will always be there for you. I will always be at your side. Against anything and everything, I will always protect you . . . and everything will be all right."

Nearly two years before, she had received notice of her return. Charon had come back to Darkholde Keep months after Isolde had left to study.

It had bothered Isolde so much that she sought to study as fast as she could so that she could return to her brother's side, having achieved four years in three.

Everything will be all right, she told herself as the dining chamber's doors opened before her, the knights announcing her arrival to all.

"Isolde Darkholm."

Those present stopped. Every member who was not away stood from their seats. Rowena, Vhimir, the Twins, and even Davidov himself, near the head of the table, stood to honor the arrival of one of his own House.

But she did not seem to notice.

All Isolde focused on was her brother Azareth, with his elegant clothes, his prematurely graying temples, and his warm smile accentuated by his full goatee, tilting his head to the side as he opened his arms for her.

Even this meant nothing, for there lay an empty seat on his left, the only empty seat on this side of the table, and where Isolde would have to sit. On his right side, right where Isolde's place used to be, there she was—the tall, beautiful woman with long white hair, sticking out like a sore thumb she couldn't ignore.

That was surely Charon, his brother's right hand now. The realization filled Isolde with an anger she tried to contain.

Everything is not going to be all right.

Trying to hide her irritation, the young woman walked toward her seat.

"Stop," Davidov's terse words were strong, despite being no more than a raspy whisper. "What-do-you-*think*-you-are-doing?" He stressed every word.

Snap out of it, Isolde told herself. One thing the Darkholm House was known for was tradition, and any member knew that after a long absence, they were expected to join the House for dinner before resuming their duties in the expanse of the Keep. It was the way they would keep accounts of who was where, and more than that, it was simply *the way*.

"Isolde Darkholm," Davidov's voice broke the silence.

"Yes, my lord?"

"I, Davidov Darkholm, Master of Death, Archduke of Darkholm, Count of Coldforge, Baron of Ironheart, former Head of the House and Head of the House upon the absence of our Lord King and Patriarch, welcome you back to Darkholde Keep. State who you are and what you are here for."

"It is I, Isolde Darkholm, student of botany and hopeful apprentice to the Master of—"

He raised his hand to halt her words while the Master's eyes pierced her soul. "Did you gain any noble titles while away?"

"I did not, my lord," Isolde responded.

"One does not introduce oneself with words of hope, of dreams, and such," he waved. "They are nothing. When a man brags about the things he does not possess, he brags about his emptiness. If one does not have the title, then one speaks not of it."

"Like saying the *former* Head of the House . . . my lord?" Isolde's pupils met the Master's own as she curtsied ever so slightly.

The House stood quietly, the uncomfortable moment opening a space for one of the infamous ripostes from the man known as the Undying . . . but the riposte didn't come.

"Clever," his pupils appeared to smile that dangerous smile of a predator that had found a victim to toy with before the kill. "Very clever, but, you see, the title, in this case, is just a reminder for you hopeful apprentice of whoever as to *whom* you respond. Now," he continued. "I suppose you seek to join us for supper?"

"If we do this quickly, we can partake before it gets cold," the young girl replied.

"Life will not always treat you like royalty, young one. There will be wars, and even if not, get used to having dishes served cold. Some are even better that way." Davidov's eyes showed amusement.

His hands rested atop the table. "Now, let us leave your impertinence aside and listen to you speak like a proper Darkholm."

What can I say, she thought. Not having the last word was something Isolde disliked, for it made her feel *weak*. Still, in this, the Master was right. There was a respect and etiquette all Darkholm would show, and she was not the one to go against them . . . at least not today.

"I . . . am Isolde Darkholm," she spoke. "I am untitled. For the last two years, I have traveled around Darkholm and Blackheart proper, studying every plant and herb I could get my hands on. After my studies, I have returned home, and I ask you, Patriarch, my lord, to allow me to join my House at this dinner as the symbol of my return."

"*Somewhat* better," he retorted. "Isolde Darkholm, hereby you rejoin *my House* to become one with us. Now, take your seat and join us at the dining table."

Walking toward her seat, she realized that she had been so excited and focused on returning that, unlike everyone else at the table, she was still wearing her traveling clothes.

Too late, she realized. She wouldn't have time to change and dress appropriately.

Those closest greeted her warmly.

"Look at you now. You look great," Tenslea smiled, holding her hands together.

"Well, yes, and you will look even better when we reinvent you," Sellayne waved her hand as if dispelling her attire. The girl with impeccable taste kissed each of her cheeks, careful to move in her expensive garb to avoid ruining it.

Charon bit her lip as she sought an opportunity to say hello, but her cousins were all over the newcomer.

"Isolde," Tenslea said, "meet Charon!"

"Wow," Azareth interrupted. "Way to steal my thunder, Tens! By the gods." He shook his head in disbelief.

"I am sorry, Azareth, I was too excited!" she apologized.

"Isolde, sister. This is Charon." He stepped aside to give way to Charon, who smiled shyly.

"I know," Isolde tried to feign a smile, failing miserably and perhaps being caught by Charon, who was immediately embarrassed.

Serving started with servants walking in and out of the banquet room with multiple yet simple dishes.

The aroma of potato and crimson petal soup with fresh green peppercorns permeated the chamber. It was accompanied by freshly baked cranberry bread, roasted chicken with mushroom cream, and fire eggplants.

Azareth held her hand, squeezing it playfully. It made her smile, remembering how he used to tickle her under the table to make her laugh when silence was sought in the room.

A repetitive clink sound interrupted the dinner. Charon stood from her chair, hiding something behind her back.

"Please, everyone. I would like a moment of your attention. I have something I want to say," the white-haired woman walked around the table and stood where Isolde could see her best.

"I have been here for a time much shorter than most, but I have been well received, and I am grateful today for the chance given. I wanted to address Isolde."

The young girl felt a chill down her spine when she heard her name.

"Isolde . . ." Charon smiled, "*sister.*"

"Half," Isolde flatly clarified.

"Isolde!" Azareth interjected in disbelief, squeezing her hand forcefully under the table before letting it go.

"Azareth," Charon sought to calm him, clearly shaken, her voice nervous, "it's ok. What she says is not untrue. I am her half-sister. But, to me, she will still be my full sister, for she is the only one I've got."

Lady Charon ran her fingers through her head, the screen of her pampas-white hair covering most of her eyes so that perhaps no one could see her sadness. In doing so, Isolde could now see most of the long, red scars on her neck and shoulder where the reefs had touched her skin soon after she was born.

Immediately embarrassed, the young girl's eyes darted and met Charon's.

"It's ok," the white-haired woman tossed her hair "you can look. This is me. I want you to see me as I am.

"Isolde," she added after a pause, "I have a small gift for you. It's something simple, of course, but I wanted to welcome you with something special."

Charon revealed what she was hiding, a ceramic vase in the shape of two female hands holding one another, the opening between them filled with different flowers, all of them tied together by a purple ribbon. All but one, a white lily, was placed in the center of them all.

"This vase I made with my own hands. It depicts a pair of female hands, each different, to represent you as the sister I never had but always and still long for.

"These," she added, "are all your favorite flowers from among those you studied. They're from every region you visited during your studies. Rowena has been helping me during my alchemical studies identify and choose them." Charon tried to smile, trying to cause the same reaction in her half-sister. "I have also included this one," her fingers lightly touched the lily, "as a representation of myself, for, while I have not belonged, I wish to be among the things you love."

Charon stretched her hands, offering the vase. Isolde's hands stayed put.

"Isolde!" Azareth's brow furrowed. "Do you not have something to say?"

"Yes," she responded. "Indeed . . ."

She looked at Charon's hopeful eyes and then at the rest of the House. "When do we start eating? I am starving. This has been quite the long journey."

As if having just been slapped across the face, speechless, Charon wanted the floor to swallow her body and soul so that she could disappear in this most embarrassing moment. Her hands placed the vase on the surface of the table, right in front of Isolde, and she lowered her head to avoid meeting anyone's gaze and walked toward her seat.

Charon's tears started rolling down her quiet face, which she covered with her hands. The moment he noticed, Azareth sought to console her, but Elzabeth came to her rescue, whispering to the Master of Lore she would take care of her.

The large woman grabbed Charon's hands and, excusing herself from the dinner, took her aside to the hallway.

"I feel terrible," Charon's tears rained.

"I am sure you do, muffin," Elzabeth responded, touching her face tenderly, "but you need to calm down some. This is not the time."

"I can't," Charon bawled, "I'm trying, but I can't stop. I'm not strong like that."

"Look at me," Elzabeth grabbed her chin tenderly. "When you feel weak, sometimes you want to just suck your own thumb and fall asleep. Sometimes one simply must, and that is okay. Just make sure to do it while no one is watching."

Charon nodded and wiped her tears with the handkerchief Elzabeth provided. "I'm ready to go back," she said.

"Are you certain?" Elzabeth asked.

"Yes," Charon offered a sad smile.

"Good, then let us get back before Gus eats it all!"

For most of the rest of the dinner, the only sound was that of the cutlery and of the servants' footsteps.

Silence had taken hold of the room like a curse in an abandoned tomb.

Everyone's eyes remained on their plates—everyone's but Elzabeth's, who would look at Isolde, making no effort to hide her disappointment, and Davidov, who, from his seat, stared coldly in Isolde's direction.

· ·+·+·+· ·

It was late. The family dinner had been prolonged but quite uneventful.

Azareth and Isolde traversed along the deep coal stone bridges, from the main Darkholde building all the way to Isolde's room in one of the towers touching the cliffs.

She walked by his side, just one step ahead, carrying a satchel in her hands, for it was on its own where the ceramic vase was carried.

"Isolde," he spoke softly.

"Yes, brother?"

"Something feels *wrong*," he replied.

"I am fine, Aza. Thanks for the concern."

"No, you are not fine, little sis. Tell me, speak to me. What is wrong?"

"Nothing!" Her voice showed her irritation, "Leave me be!"

"It is Charon, is it not?"

"Stop it, Aza," she stood by the door so that her brother could hand her the key.

"It is, it must be, for your letters changed after I told you she had returned. You asked so much about her, and then you asked nothing else, not once, other than if she was still here when you were planning your return."

Suddenly, a realization dawned on him. The Master of Lore smiled mischievously. "Wait . . . you are jealous. You must be! Sis, you *are* jealous! Hah!"

Isolde stretched her hand to reach for the key. "That is stupid. Why would I be jealous of that freak?"

"Hey, that is not nice, sis." His laughter stopped, for somehow he felt Isolde meant her words. "That was mean, Isolde."

He walked toward her desk and placed the vase by the window. Azareth rested his body against the surface of the writing desk. His right hand caressed his sister's cheek. "She went above and beyond, even urging Rowena to help her."

Bothered, Isolde turned her face. "Stop it! I do not care! It is just a vase, okay?"

His mustard-colored eyes held her chin fast and made her face him once more.

"Isolde! She poured her heart in hand, and you stepped on it in front of the House."

The girl grabbed her brother's forearm and removed it from her face. "I do not care."

As if lashed by a whip, Azareth took a step back. "What is *wrong* with you? I barely recognize you."

"Really? Then perhaps you should spend more time with her so that you can find me unrecognizable!" Irritated, she looked out the window.

"I do not understand why you dislike her so much?" Azareth asked.

"Nobody dislikes her. I can tell she is quite lovely." She made no effort to hide the sarcasm in her voice.

"No one but you. And you have no reason to be jealous. Isolde."

"No reason! You say I have no reason? I have studied *for years* outside my home, alone, so that I could at least be considered Rowena's apprentice. Now this, this harlot—"

"Isolde! Stop it!"

"She gets to study with Rowena, and what did it take? Nothing? She is tall, she is beautiful, and everyone thinks she is sooo charming!" Her eyes watered profusely "She even gets a second chance to have a mother!"

Moved by the pain he saw in his sister's eyes, Azareth calmed down some and only half turned. "Isolde, little sister, she will never take your place."

Isolde Darkholm

"She even sits by your side! Where I used to sit! I was hoping she would not be here when I came back!"

"Isolde! Why do you hate her so much?" he asked.

"I do not hate her," she responded, "I hate the fact that she is alive."

Moments felt like hours as Azareth, who was never at a loss for words, suddenly knew not what to say.

The Master of Lore's voice darkened as he moved toward the door.

"You know, Isolde . . . perhaps you need an extra year outside of Darkholde. That way, you can bring back my little sister and leave behind this person you have brought instead."

"No, Aza, please. Do not do that to me!"

"I will make the arrangements."

"But I am supposed to start my apprenticeship with House Devereau soon!" She raised her voice.

"It will have to wait," Azareth responded calmly.

"It cannot wait, Aza! All the other Darkholm have done it at thirteen! I am almost late!"

"That is because of you going to college, Isolde. Besides, not all of us at the age of thirteen."

"Yes, Aza, everyone!"

"Not everyone, Isolde," he started to explain. "Yraias, for example—"

"YRAIAS IS A RETARD!" the girl screamed.

The Master of Lore's mood darkened. He spoke softly but firmly, "The fact that Yraias cannot communicate with us does not mean there is less intelligence in him. Maybe *we* are the ones who cannot understand him. It is my decision, Isolde, and you will abide by it."

"YOU CANNOT DO THIS TO ME!"

"I can, and I will!" Azareth grabbed the door's handle and readied to speak when a sudden crash by the wall at his side startled him.

He froze in place and looked to see countless white shards on the floor, among them, dozens of misshapen flowers, among them, a white lily

Azareth struggled to contain himself and, through gritted teeth, he hissed before he left, "Do not . . . unpack . . . your things."

OUR PRAYER

Location: Kingdom of Ardenay, Duchy of Bulwharf,
State of Sildrane, Bulwharf Stronghold

*Perhaps the greatest gift a god can give mankind
is to have its prayers unanswered . . .*

T he high towers of Sildrane's main stronghold rose from the ground, granite cylinders and tall walls that seemed to have naturally grown to protect the people of the bulls from their arid environment, from their neighbors, and at times even from themselves.

Its location in the northernmost part of Ardenay made Bulwharf quite unique. It shared the border with not three, but four neighboring kingdoms, and while Daneran's crown in the west was mostly amicable, Taerea in the north was, at best, neutral.

That left as enemies the pagan Empyre of Suhne and the heretic kingdom of Blackheart looming closely. That same location had prevented Bulwharf from ever becoming the trade center it could have been, but while some in the Church of Light claimed this was because of 'the sinful practices of their neighbors,' it was just as likely due to the difficulty caravans would have traversing their dry land, especially when they had a much easier, and safer, route traveling through Walcrast in the south.

But the church preached that Bulwharf would one day become one of the most, if not the most, important beacons, and its horn would pierce through and defeat the pagan forces of their evil neighbors, all with the blessing of the Lord of Light.

Smithies were commonplace, rangers and merchants traded wares, while children ran along the streets playfully, fighting each other with mock weapons. Even here in the capital city of Sildrane, far from the border, the life of the bulls was one mostly militant, revolving around the possibility of war, and the preparedness of the castles and forts scattered along the land.

While Bulwharf Stronghold itself could not compare to the exuberance of the Palace of the Waterfalls in Walcrast, the clean lines of the Lighthouse in Ashvail, and was even outshined by the simple dullness of Anvelum, Duskforge's ducal fortress in Blackheart, its position atop a hill, the symmetry of its towers and watchposts, and the conglomerating, busy city around it made it beautiful in its own way.

"I'll get ready to leave *your* room," Eraysa Velias looked out at the many towers of the stronghold from one of the windows of that chamber she would also perhaps call her own someday, once she and Lord Varen Bulwharf exchanged vows.

"You mean 'our'?" Varen's large figure still lay in bed, watching her nakedness slowly disappear, swallowed by the clothes that climbed up her perfect skin of dusk.

"It will be ours when we are finally married," she teased, "for now it is just yours, Lord Bull. I am nothing but a girl invading your chamber so that you can invade mine."

Sitting upon the bed, he beckoned, "C'mere."

"What for?" She smiled, biting her lip mischievously, "are you going to show me I'm more than that?"

"Not really," he grinned. "Our vows will be exchanged . . ."

"I know, a year after the promise, so as not to offend Tradition," she scratched the tip of his nose lightly before she drove her fingers through the back of his head and pulled his hair back.

"For now, since fucking your woman before your marriage offends the 'sensitive' feelings of the Light, I guess I'm not your woman," Eraysa's tongue wetted his neck and quickly climbed up toward his chin, "I'm just some random whore . . ."

"Come here!" He reached out, but her body escaped his grasp.

"Wait, aren't you supposed to have your morning prayer?"

"Come . . ." he grabbed her arm and pulled her in, meeting her full lips with his, almost fusing their bodies in their embrace.

Lord Varen's hands unclad her firmly, yet delicately, to avoid ruining her attire, and he pinned her against the bed, and she smiled, as she spread her legs to capture him, to trap his body and flip the roles, riding him slowly and yet powerfully, dragging him into her chamber from where he would escape only whenever she wanted.

Lord Bulwharf lay in bed once more, the sweat over his skin almost dry when Eraysa's voice woke him. She lay naked by his side, softly scratching his back "I can't stop thinking . . ."

"What?" His eyes half-opened.

"Of my brother . . . today is the anniversary of the day he chose Courage as his Principle.[1]"

Varen hesitated briefly before he moved her aside, leaving her in bed as he sat once more, "It is time for my morning prayer."

"Oh, is it now?" Her voice was not as soft this time, "It wasn't when you were aroused, when you needed, or simply wanted something from me."

"That is nonsense. Your brother's spirit is in the Light realm."

"Then why do you have to go all of a sudden? Am I to you just a whore, a woman to deposit your wishes on but not your trust? Someone to carry your milk and not your burden?"

"Stop that."

"Then why don't you listen to what I think, what I feel?"

"I apologize if I have made you feel that way," Varen sought to clad himself, "we don't have a lot of time. But tell me, I will listen."

Sitting at the edge of the bed, Eraysa's frowning eyes eased some. "I am thinking of what happened to my brother," the fresh wound was still evident in the trembling of her voice, "how he was *murdered* . . ."

"Your brother was not murdered, Eraysa," Varen interrupted, "he was defeated in a duel."

"Was it a fair duel, then?"

"I believe it was."

"Do you truly believe so?" she asked, as if a sudden spark on a dry branch had given way to a forest fire. "Were you not there to see what happened?"

"If I have not said it enough, I say it now, I am truly sorry for the loss of your brother."

"How can you just say that? Did you not see how the Darkholm cheated?" She pushed her body off the bed.

"Eraysa, I do not like what happened at all. But we cannot accuse an opponent of cheating because they were victorious, even if we strongly believe the victory was rightfully ours."

"Then why is my only brother dead, eh?" Eraysa fumed. "His opponent was Dragan Darkholm. If he were half the duelist he is portrayed as he would have known to follow the rules of the duel, to attack without killing, as was supposed."

"There is the problem," he frowned, "maybe that's exactly what he wanted."

"We should retaliate. They have been holding the Eighth for most of the summer in their clutches."

"As was part of our deal. It is over Eraysa."

"To you it might be," she challenged him, "to me it is not. I want to bring my forces to retake the Eighth and ultimately confront that 'Dragan' to avenge Usman's death!"

"That is not for you to decide," Varen responded.

"They're my men," she furrowed her brow.

"You don't have the power to do that against my will, I am the Bulwharf," he stated firmly.

"That's right," she lowered her voice some, "and I'm nothing more than your whore—"

"Stop that, now, we have got to go" he stopped her.

"Why now, because you don't want to face the truth?"

"Because we both know we are late for prayer."

••••••••

The altar room was circular, its walls uninterrupted except for its single entrance and seven round windows above recessed alcoves of the same number. On each rested a replica of the symbols of the philosophical pinnacles of their society—the helm of truth, the cane of tradition, the spear of courage, the breastplate of vigor, the shield of protection, the horn of war, and the banner of honor—where once there were an eye, a tail, a hoof, a heart, the hide, the horn, and the tongue.

The Church of Light, in its eagerness to spread their word and convert the Bulwharf, had found a need to modify these symbols to better relate to the tenets of the Light, in a way some of the most faithful bulls, especially those adhered to the Pinnacle of Tradition, had considered perversion. Surprisingly, for such a powerful people, the bulls' protests did not last long. Some say they found common ground with the Church of Light, others quietly state the influence of the Church was far too great, and the dissent that had arisen had quickly been yoked.

Today, in a matter of only a few decades, most of what remained of their belief system was the memory of what it once was, of the glory of the past, and even that memory couldn't be fully believed, for fear that perhaps much of it had been altered too by the constant, aggressive preaching at the hands of the church's zealots.

Eraysa thought of this when she entered through the only, westward door of the shrine, walking toward the golden altar that now existed in its center. Its majestic crystal would capture the light of the circular windows high above at noon, but was now only absorbing the morning light of those to the east.

Behind her, as in every shrine of their former gods, was the opening that would see the light shine through only near the end of the day, after the dust had settled, the window of Truth.

Walking ahead of her, Varen moved toward the altar.

"Lord of Light, Oh Radiant One who sees and reveals all." His calloused hand traveled across his face. "Remove all darkness from before me." He turned toward her, offering his hand so that she could join him in prayer.

Eraysa lowered her head momentarily and, taking his hand, she knelt by his side.

"Lord of Light," the Bulwharf spread his arms and looked up to the crystal, "shine your merciful light upon us humble servants." He then closed his eyes and, lowering his voice to a murmur, began his prayer.

Each time Eraysa followed, her silent lips moving after his own, but the words they were expressing were not the same.

Opening her eyes, she looked at her betrothed. His eyes remained closed, his neck bent, the most powerful man in all of Bulwharf in deep submission to a god unseen. Above them she saw the crystal, without a doubt a beautiful piece of glass that was deemed sacred by the church.

"When we pray . . ." her words interrupted Varen, "do you ever wonder what I pray for? Or who do I pray to?"

"I don't." His response was curt, as if her interruption were unwelcome.

"Why?" she continued.

"Because it should be nobody's business."

"Or because you're afraid of the answer." The defiance in her words forced him to open his eyes, his gaze still on the altar.

"Well, I do wonder," she continued upon his silence, "who do *you* pray to?"

"I pray to Light, our unquestionable god."

"Do you?" she challenged him.

"I do," Varen turned to face her, the creases on his forehead deepening, "as should we all."

"Well, I pray to our ancestors," Eraysa looked into his eyes, "as I always have."

"While I give thanks for my ancestors in my prayers, I only pray to God."

"What 'god'?"

"The One True God, Eraysa."

"Oh, you mean the one you're taught to believe. You know you're wrong," Eraysa spoke assuredly.

"You know *you* are, Eraysa. Ancestor worship is a condemnable sin."

"And yet," she stated, "it has always been part of our culture."

"Was," Varen corrected.

"What happens to all of us when we die?" Eraysa questioned.

"It depends. Those who follow the tenets of the Light, to the Light they go. Those who do not—"

"No one really knows, Varen," Eraysa placed a finger over his mouth. "Therefore, we must honor the memory of those who came before us. We are bound to honor their dreams, their commitment, their love. We must show respect, because it is the very least we can do for them."

"Things have changed, Eraysa, we have a new faith."

"Our ancestors worshipped theirs. It kept their spirits alive. It is in the foundation of who we are."

"The foundation is our past," Varen corrected, "and the past is no more."

"You're right, and yet deny it or not," she grabbed his wrist, "it is still part of us."

"Well, I do not sin anymore," his hand moved away from her, "and nor should you."

Not knowing if to be offended more, at his words, or his recoil, she snapped back. "What are you going to do about it? Accuse me?"

"My love—"

"Is the love you profess less powerful than your new-found religion?" she raised her voice. "Tell me, are you going to stop me from worshipping those who loved us so that they don't go into oblivion? Are you going to have me burned for being truthful to my own heart?"

"Speak no more," he thundered.

"I may not," she challenged, "and yet I will stand here, always by your side, praying with you . . . perhaps joining you in your prayers, or perhaps not. You, in turn, will have to choose what you truly love, for your accusation will be complicit in silencing my truth, and yet your silence will be complicit with my sin."

An uncomfortable moment of silence followed. Eraysa stood before the man she so much loved, the one she had always supported, the only one in the entire duchy with the power to alter the direction the bulls were headed toward.

"Varen," her voice softened some, "it is not too late for our people. There are many who still believe in the old ways. We can still change."

"You will need to change," he stated firmly, "the course is set. We will not denounce our God. We cannot move against the current."

"Someone has to save our people," she spat, "I thought that person could've been you."

"Our beliefs are different here and now."

"Then I will pack my belongings and head out back home."

"Stop this," he protested, "you're being irrational."

"My ancestors stir my spirit," she spoke through clenched teeth. "My brother was cheated of his victory. His restless spirit needs vengeance."

"Eraysa," he sought to calm her, "hard as it might be, you have to accept his defeat. While the Darkholm undoubtedly manipulated and bent the rules, they did follow them. More than angering us, it should teach us a lesson."

"So noble of you," the sarcasm in her voice felt like a whip. "I want the position of Lord Bull of Darane."

"I can't simply grant that to you, you know that."

"Why not?"

"It's not the way, ritual combat is required."

"And yet," she squinted, "it has been done before in cases of great need."

"This is not one of those cases, Eraysa."

"You are all powerful in Bulwharf. You can fill the position if you so wished."

"No," he interjected.

"You're the ultimate power in Bulwharf."

"That is not our way."

"Oh, so you can change the way you worship, but for the benefit of someone other than yourself the way things are done cannot be changed," she said with contempt. "You religious folk are all the same, worse manipulators than that Dragan.

"I'll head out to Darane and challenge the bulls in ritual combat for the position of Lord Bull of Darane."

"Will you throw out years of love and courtship just like that?" he questioned.

"Will *you*?" She stood, offended at his hesitation, "Fine then. I'll take my leave immediately."

"You won't do that," he ordered.

"Other than by force, you, the most powerful man, don't have the power to stop me," Eraysa said just inches from his face, "by all my ancestors and the ones you deny, it is my right."

---

(1) Before the ascension of the Light, the bulls revered the Seven Pinnacles: the spirit-gods of Courage, Protection, Vigor, War, Honor, Tradition, and Truth. Although all were equally important, upon feeling 'the calling,' each believer would make a pact with one of the seven, choosing it as his Principle, as the tenet he would live and die to follow, to later join that god in its realm.

HEAVEN

Location: Empyre of Suhne, City of Suhne, Palace of the Sun

Only too late will one realize if one is truly bound for heaven . . .

It was early morning when the aroma of herb incense and saffron tea being served permeated the domed room where Vamya meditated.

Around the Daughter of the Sun, servants moved busily, one making her bed, another warming her bath, while a pair prepared her attire, each a daily dancer in the most perfect of well-rehearsed performances.

From behind her moving eyelids, Vamya's twin emeralds appeared.

In front of her was a plate of marinated cactus strips, camel cheese, and small brightly colored fruits. Taking a deep breath, she placed a piece of fruit inside her mouth.

This morning she felt rested and renewed. Even her dreams had added to the sensation of ease. She felt everything was aligned to provide her with a most perfect day in a most blessed life . . . but then she saw Aaghari.

Her confidant stood close but kept enough distance, leaving Vamya as much space as possible, as if he had been truly afraid of breathing the air Vamya was supposed to take. But her confidant's lips were attempting to draw a smile. His hands still carried the vase with which he had just served Vamya's tea. His eyes, Vamya saw, appeared humble.

The Blessed Child looked down at her tray, contemplating every bit before she spoke to Aaghari.

"Have you broken fast?" Vamya asked.

"I have, Blessed One," the man responded, "the Sun has made provision."

"Then blessed are you," Vamya smiled. "What is planned for today?"

"Today," Aaghari responded, "you have morning study at the library. After the Eye's Zenith at noon, you will be joined by Aldah of the Rays for mentored study."

"Cancel those," Vamya ordered, "I want to do something else."

"Something else?" her confidant questioned. While Aldah of the Rays was amicable and would surely not mind the last-minute cancellation of an unofficial appointment, Vamya, he had learned, was not one to follow momentary, random impulses.

"Yes, today," Vamya smiled at his words, and bringing the cup to her lips, she responded, "I would like to see my people."

Nodding in agreement, without hesitation, Aaghari walked toward one of the glass walls near Vamya's bed. "Here you can see them, down below, Blessed One, as always." He pointed down with his free hand. "Each one living every day for the Sun and by the Sun's mercy. Their hearts long for your Ascension."

Vamya stood up and moved toward her confidant. "You speak with such certainty."

"I do, Blessed One." He looked into Vamya's eyes, "Every breath they take speaks your name. Every beat of every heart is a drum that plays for you."

"Your words are beautiful, Aaghari," Vamya replied, "but they're not real. While many follow me, at least as many follow my siblings and want nothing more than for either of them to be victorious."

"Blessed One," Aaghari lowered his head, "every voice that speaks your name has recognized your essence. It is true that some men blindly follow your siblings, but that's because they haven't realized that, while their hearts faithfully wait for a Sun, their spirits are truly already aware of who their creator is. Even if they are blind today, upon your Ascension, they will all recognize it and kneel before you."

Vamya's gaze traveled over the rooftops of the capital city, where none of the countless adobe buildings could reach either the magnificence or height of the palace or its temples. Below, numerous people walked, most in the traditional, conservative attire that would keep them protected from the celestial body they worshipped. They

Vamya, Ascended

walked and stopped at times to speak to each other or perhaps to argue. Who could really know from up here?

Were Aaghari's words true?

While Vamya didn't doubt the certainty of her words, how much did he truly know about the hearts and intentions of men? He was just a mortal man, and as such, he could easily be mistaken.

'But what if he's not?' Vamya mused. 'There is only one way to truly know.'

"I don't want to see them from here anymore," Vamya said, "I know every corner of this palace. But how much do I know of the current affairs of my people?"

"You are informed daily of your people's affairs, Blessed One," Aaghari responded.

"Yes, I have no doubt I am well informed. But I have rarely left this palace. If not for the challenges, I would have likely never left the palace's vicinity. I want to walk among my people. I want to be among them. I want to see how they live, where they walk, what they talk about."

"But, Blessed One," Aaghari warned, "that's impossible."

"While many things can prove difficult," Vamya turned to face him, "nothing is impossible for the Sun of Change."

・◆◆◆◆・

"This will not do," Aaju, the officer of almost three decades and second only to the captain of the Flame Guard, stated firmly to both women. Upon hearing their request, he had sent those under him away, perhaps to handle this himself or to be candid in his conversation.

His dusky features were not smiling under his glass-adorned beard. While Aaju wasn't as large of frame as Malek or even as his own superior, Usat of the Flame Guard, his presence and charisma commanded respect among everyone in the palace.

But Vamya wasn't just anyone. She wouldn't simply accept a 'no' for an answer. "It is the Flame Guard's duty to provide protection," she demanded.

"Blessed One, the Flame Guard's sworn duty is to protect the Sun," Aaju corrected, "and provide security within the palace."

"And it is my duty to understand the people of Suhne," she retorted. "So now our duties place us at odds—Do I follow your rules and stay inside the palace, ignoring the people that are the backbone and lifeline of our empyre, those who have for so long lived under a yoke? Or do you send guards to protect us outside the palace so that we can ensure a better future for our people? Which one is it, Aaju?" she asked.

But the guard only offered her a quiet response. She remained firm on her conviction. "So much depends on this, Aaju. The history of the entire world depends on this."

"That might be the case, Blessed One," Aaju responded respectfully, "but I would fail in my duties. I would also fail the world, and even my God, if I allowed any men to abandon the palace to follow you around. Besides," he continued, "the touch of the *saqit* might contaminate you."

At his words, Vamya nearly scowled. "Do you think my holiness will be diminished by the touch of a mortal, especially one who needs it most? Do you believe the power of the Sun to be that weak?"

"Of course not, Blessed One. I have no doubt of the immense power of their Sun, but the *saqit* response can be unpredictable upon seeing you."

"So, as you know, leaving for the city without protection might place my life at risk," Vamya insisted.

"Blessed One," Aaju took a step toward her, "then don't place yourself at risk."

Frustrated at not having won the argument, Vamya looked for what she could add, what she could use to sway him. "Should I ask Usat then?"

At the mention of his superior, Aaju could not hide his frustration. "Blessed One, why get Usat involved? If he agrees with me, he and the Speaker might stop you from leaving the palace with or without guards. If he disagreed with me, you would chip away at my authority. If that's what you wanted, I would accept it, but I believe I don't deserve it. Why ask me, then, in the first place? Why ask, when if you get the answer you don't want, you'll ask someone else?"

Aaju was right, Vamya thought.

Her entire life, she had been surrounded by guards, servants, and priests, people who were never really personally connected to her. During the last ten years, Aaju had become a constant around the palace halls. She had found herself exchanging words with him, although only occasionally, and even then, just briefly. Was Aaju truly bound so firmly by his sworn duties, or was he concerned because perhaps he considered her a friend?

But that last one couldn't be, or could it? Vamya couldn't call him a friend. Then again, she didn't truly feel she had a friend. She had wondered, however, if one day she would ever feel that connection with someone.

In other circumstances, even against the Speaker of the Rays himself, Vamya would have spoken up. She would have barreled through with the impetuosity of a great desert rhino. But his words had moved her. She didn't have to consider his position; she didn't have to care. But she did.

"I accept your position," Vamya responded, "but I will inform you that I will be leaving for the city within the hour."

"Blessed One, please," Aaju asked, "by leaving, you're placing yourself in great danger."

"No," she responded before she walked out, "I would be placing myself in greater future danger by staying here."

———————— ••••••• ————————

After leaving the palace, Vamya's steps first took her around its immediate vicinity, where the prosperous markets sold their wares under the shade of the great domes.

Her body was garbed in a single, long piece of green silk that wrapped around her upper thighs and pelvis before it continued its climb to cover her breasts and shoulders, over which it finally draped down toward the back. A long braid fell from the back of her head, connected to smaller, parallel braids by golden rings that ran through the main braid's segments. Her body was so exposed she would have been stoned to death for her indecency if her tattoos hadn't made obvious who she was, that the laws men would use to accuse her did not apply the same way to her. Instead, those who saw Vamya moved out of her way, lowering their heads to show respect.

To her right, Aaghari stood with his green robe and turban over his balding head. He was accompanied by a young woman among her Chosen, one named Adulla, whose body was mostly covered in green fabrics that showed only her hands and face. She carried a small bag with provisions. To Vamya's left, in a dark green *kaftan*, young Zofer walked.

Zofer was a dark-skinned camel shepherd of unassuming features and average height. At just fourteen, he was also the youngest of Vamya's Chosen. Anywhere Zofer went, he would have been easily overlooked for his simple, lanky demeanor, for his slouching shoulders, but the blue tattoo running from his nose toward his forehead and the same shade along the border of his lower lip made it obvious he originated from one of the nomad tribes of the Basqh of Ohor in the northwest.

The boy was gifted with a voice that was as soft and crisp as a spring flower. What moved Vamya to bring him all the way from the harsh life in his home-land, however, was having heard he would sing to the animals he cared for and cared deeply for the beasts that were old or wounded.

She looked at the young boy walking by her side, at his calm demeanor, and she wondered for how long it would have remained so had he stayed living in Basqh Ohor, where each man had to follow those water-seekers who lead each tribe in search of sustenance while keeping an eye out to avoid becoming the sustenance of those tribes that hunted them.

As terrible as it sounded, that had been the way of life in Basqh Ohor for millennia, and its citizens had come to accept it. While right now, she couldn't just change their entire way of life, it helped fuel her determination. It helped her convince herself of why she needed to triumph over her siblings so that she could lead her people down a different path.

Vamya had plans for Zofer's gift, for his enthralling voice. The Rays had been asking for details of her participation in the Sixth Test for the performance challenge, and so far, she hadn't given them any details. While it helped her avoid any potential information falling into the ears of either her siblings or those who supported them, the reality was she hadn't decided what to do.

She had considered using Zofer either as her substitute or perhaps as an actual part of her demonstration. She did not have a lot of time to decide what she would do with him, and that troubled her, but every time she had set aside those thoughts, knowing in her heart that, even if she didn't end up using him at all, having chosen him had changed Zofer's fate.

At the thought, her lips drew a smile, one as natural as the one Zofer was reflecting back at her.

While there was surely much the city had to offer, Vamya turned away from it. Instead, she ordered Aaghari to be their guide, to take her to the district where the numerous *iqit*[^1] lived.

Her confidant guided them around the marketplace and into the streets away from it, where shortly after, the tall houses of the *Zetq'a* nobility appeared before the group.

Each building in the *Zetq'a* district was adorned with beautiful, tradi- tionally shaped windows and fasciae sculpted to depict significant events in the history of Suhne. Each home was spacious and seemed busy. The families within were, at times, so large it was hard to distinguish them from their own numerous servants.

Vamya admired the captivating structural composition, but she continued past them, past the smaller buildings and every block where the lower nobility lived, not letting anything deter her from reaching her destination.

Once they passed the last *Zetq'a* house, they came upon a small guard garrison that was stationed, like in many other parts of the city, where it could face the poorer districts. While the guards did not seek to intimidate the less fortunate citizens, they kept watch and ensured order, although mainly to bring safety to those living in the more affluent portions of the capital.

As they passed the garrison and walked into the district, Vamya observed around her the numerous, weathered structures that appeared, at times, almost impossibly run down, like broken teeth in a desert hag's jaw. The streets were filled with people and poorly kept, with the smell of urine and feces permeating the area where the local inhabitants both walked and also relieved themselves. Children ran and played around excitedly, largely unaware of the dire circumstances surrounding them, while emaciated dogs searched for a chance to get something more than fleas.

"Is this where the poor live?" she asked.

"This, Blessed One," Adulla signaled across the street from the garrison, "is where we, the vast majority of your people, live. This is the home of the *iqit* and *saqit*, the poor and the poorest."

Vamya's eyes went to the structures that, although small, seemed to pile up on each other "There are so many."

"Yes, Blessed One," Aaghari smiled, "your followers are like the grains of sand in the desert, impossible to count. And you only see the number of buildings without taking into account the number of people within."

Vamya's eyes moved from one building to the next, having just realized most of them consisted of little more than a single room. "How many people live within each?"

"Many, Blessed One," Aaghari responded, "anywhere from four to as many as the walls can hold inside."

"So many in a single home," Vamya struggled to contain her disbelief.

"Yes, Blessed One," her confidant answered, "often in a single room."

"Blessed One," Zofer interrupted, "it is not always like that. Back home in Ohor, when my oldest brother got married, he was given a marriage tent to sleep with his wife for three nights."

"What happens after that?" Adulla asked.

"After the three days, the married have to share the same tent as the rest of the family. If the woman is fertile and brings fruit, after the child is born, they are rewarded with three more nights spent in the marriage tent."

"What kind of *reward* is that," Vamya questioned.

"It is a great blessing to be able to produce more worshippers for the Sun, Blessed One," Aaghari lowered his head slightly.

"It is a blessing to be fertile, yes," Vamya looked back at both of her Chosen, "but to award one's followers with scraps so they can proudly add a burden to their backs when they are lacking the means to carry it, for struggling more. It is not right. It is not just. It must be changed."

'Where did we go wrong?' she asked herself as they walked deeper into the district.

The eyes of many had been on them since the very moment they had left the now-distant palace, but so far, wherever they had walked, onlookers had kept their distance, at times bowing their heads but mostly going on with their business. Somehow, the Child of the Sun felt that, since they had entered the district, all eyes were on her, but these were different. Each pair was set on a body that was dressed in simple fabrics that were often dirty, smelly, and unkempt.

Still, these simple people looked at her, some who seemed filled with amazement, others with longing, still keeping a respectful distance, but some slowly approaching, following their every step.

Wherever they walked, people hurled blessings, at times raising their open palms as a prayer sign.

It was one such woman who, after exchanging a few words with Aaghari and finding resistance in the confidant, planted herself in front of Vamya. She appeared to be over three decades old, but with a face heavily wrinkled from both prolonged restlessness and grief that appeared from within her simple, black *hijab.* Her wrists and ankles were adorned with a simple *bond chain* indicating she was bound to a man in marriage.

The woman prostrated herself in the middle of the street. "Blessed are my eyes that have seen the coming Sun." She raised her nervous voice, her fingers just inches away from Vamya's feet. "Blessed be, oh holy Child of the Sun."

"I apologize, Blessed One," Aaghari grabbed the woman by the hands, signaling the others to help remove the woman from Vamya's presence.

"Wait," Vamya ordered softly, "let her be."

"She cleans the stables, Blessed One," Aaghari explained. "This woman is thus of the impure *saqit*—"

"And there's nothing that I consider impure in that," Vamya interrupted. "Blessed are you." The Child stretched her hand toward the woman. "What is your name, and what do you want?"

"Hagdah, Blessed One," the woman continued. "I want to beg you to please save my child."

"What is wrong with your child?"

"He is very ill," the woman raised her head.

"Then why haven't you brought him with you to my presence?" Vamya questioned.

"Because he is dying, Blessed One," the mother responded, "but I believe. I have faith that if you so wished, you could whisper a blessing and a miracle would save him."

"The Sun of Change will offer prayers upon returning to the palace temple," Aaghari said to the suffering woman.

"No," Vamya interjected, "I will visit this woman's house and offer my blessings there."

"Blessed One," the woman's eyes opened in astonishment, "I am undeserving of this. I have faith that you can perform miracles from a distance. My house is unclean and not worthy of your visitation. We are unworthy of your presence."

"Blessed One, you shouldn't go there," Zofer argued.

"I agree," Aaghari added. "We can't say it's a trap, but as much as we want to help, there is a distance we must keep. No one of your station has ever set foot in this district, and much less inside one of the homes of the lowest among us all."

"Then," Vamya smiled at her confidant, "let us change that."

———— ++++++ ————

Hagdah led the way through ever-increasing numbers of people toward her small house, located in a distant portion of the same district. Aaghari had questioned how the woman had found out about their arrival, to which Hagdah responded she was on her way to the local market when she heard the swiftly spreading news.

Her house was small, comprising two rooms—the main room that served both as a receiving room and kitchen and the room where the family slept. Inside, they saw the woman had two other small children, each one clad in plain, dirty clothes and bare feet.

"This is my husband, Talib," the woman spoke.

"By the ever-watchful Eye of the Almighty," the man's knees touched the ground as he lowered his head, "blessed are my eyes that they have seen you, and blessed is my home, that you have honored with your presence."

He lifted a folded piece of fabric in his upright palms toward Vamya as an offering. "Please, accept this humble offering to honor your visit."

Aaghari took the offering from the man's hand and carefully revealed its contents.

Watching the confidant taking a piece and sniffing it, Hagdah explained, "It is homemade flatbread with dates and fig paste." But the explanation did not stop Aaghari from handing the piece to Zofer for tasting.

No matter how much they did or wanted to trust the goodwill of their people, Vamya's safety and success were her Chosen's main responsibility and purpose.

The boy swallowed, and after a few moments, he smiled and nodded.

Vamya then took the offering. It felt warm through the cloth that rested on the palm of her hands. She placed it on the table surface before breaking a piece that she brought to her mouth. It was simple, without the saffron, coriander, and other spices she would have expected, but still delicious. After savoring the first piece, she placed her hands on the table to wait for the next dish.

One that wouldn't come.

Aaghari looked briefly at the couple, forcing the man to stand up nervously. Hagdah, in turn, lowered her head in shame. They didn't need to speak a word. Vamya's confidant immediately understood their situation, one in which he had found himself many times before.

"Blessed One," Aaghari signaled for her to continue eating the flatbread, "this is not the first dish. It is *rayiysh*[3], the main, and in this case, only dish. Please, enjoy it."

"Rayiysh?" Vamya's disbelief escaped her lips and was confirmed by her confidant's nod. She looked down at the simple serving that would have been this family's meal for the day, "the prime serving, so little . . ."

"It is not little, Blessed One," Adulla responded, "it is a blessing and all of what your people have access to most of the time. That alone makes it enough."

'Enough?' Vamya thought, 'Why should meager scraps be considered *enough* in a land of plenty?'

Food was something Vamya had never lacked. To her, as to the rest of the nobility, it was always readily available. As large as it was, the Empyre of Suhne did not really count with abundance, at least not for the great majority of its people, who had learned to offer the best of what they had to those above them. While Vamya knew what was available to the lower classes of Suhne was not as bountiful, she had never known to what extent they lacked.

To make her feel worse, this was *rayiysh*, the best the family had to offer to an honored guest. Whatever she did not eat would be left for the father, who would eat and leave for his children, whose own leftovers would be left for the mother.

'How is this possible?' Vamya thought, horrified. 'How can we feast when those who serve us have to struggle to just live?' She wondered how women were responsible for giving birth and raising children, for feeding their husbands and families, for ensuring their progeny was taken care of, and many times for helping direct them toward their dreams, and yet they were ungratefully forgotten. All they received was the leftovers of that which no one else had consumed.

"Adulla," Vamya ordered, "hand me your bag." Her Chosen did not hesitate.

The Child of the Sun emptied the bag's contents atop the table surface, producing fruits, both dried and fresh, nuts and dried meat from within it. She took a handful and placed it in the palm of the hand of the woman, which she closed herself as she closed in.

"Here, eat," Vamya said. "I will not have you suffer hunger while I have to spare."

"Thank you, Blessed One," the woman lowered her head. She picked a few pieces hesitatingly. "What is this one called?"

"It's a grape," Vamya responded.

"A grape?"

"Yes, try it."

Hagdah did as instructed. A sudden smile and an expression of excitement appeared on her face. "It exploded inside my mouth! It was delicious." But a second later, her hand traveled toward her throat. She lowered her head as her lips trembled.

"What is it?" Vamya asked.

"It is nothing, Divine One," the woman choked through watery eyes, "I'm sorry."

"Nothing?" Vamya placed a hand on Hagdah's shoulder. At her touch, the woman broke down.

"It's overwhelming to be in the presence of the One whom one worships the most," the woman said through her brokenness, "and be treated with kindness."

Her words touched the deepest fibers of Vamya's heart. She wanted to hug the woman, but she couldn't, or at least she felt she shouldn't. Doing so could lose her the support of many who saw the *saqit* as impure, and while she felt she cared more about the *saqit*, losing that support would lose her the chance to help them.

Having been under her service long enough, Aaghari noticed Vamya's slight hesitation. "Now, bring us to your child." Her words dispelled the scene.

While her husband tried to put away the provisions they had been given, away from the prying eyes of the onlookers that gazed through the windows, Hagdah led Vamya to the next and only other room in her small house. It was lined with carpets of fading colors that served as sleeping places for the entire family. In a corner was a pot half-filled with urine that was already cold. At one end of the room, his body covered in blankets, lay the child she had come to see.

The child's skin seemed jaundiced. His eyes were closed, and his lips dried and open as in a horrified expression on a face that seemed older from its chronic suffering. Beside him, a small vase and a wet rag which his mother had been using, to the best of her ability, to keep him hydrated. Both of the child's hands were clasping the sheet under which his body was covered.

"What happened to him?" Vamya asked.

"We don't know, Blessed One," Hagdah responded as she uncovered his body. Vamya saw the thin, bony body of the child that was swollen only on his vein-ridden, distended abdomen, for below it, there was only a pair of dried legs and twisted feet. "He was born limp from the waist down, so he was always bedridden, but lately, his skin and body have changed. He has grown weaker every day.

"We owe a lot to many, Blessed One," she continued. "We have searched, and tried healers, oils, and salves, and nothing has helped. He has actually gotten worse and has now been unresponsive for the last two days.

"I know I need to trust your will. But if you allow me, I don't have much, but I'll even offer my own life to sway your will in his favor. Please," the mother implored through tearful eyes, "do something, please!"

Vamya didn't know where to start, what to do. Here was a woman who had placed her faith in Vamya's mercy, on her power. Merciful she was—she wouldn't be here otherwise—but powerful? What power did she have other than being able to leave her body to travel into a realm she couldn't truly understand? And this, even, was that power? She recalled the many times during her lessons that different Rays had taught her that once she had incarnated the Sun, she would be able to perform divine miracles but not until then.

But yet she recalled the whispered words of old Seiris of the Rays as he had drawn one of his warm smiles, 'In actuality, the closer one is to the Sun, the more likely one will be able to perform miracles. Some among the priesthood know this as a fact. Whoever tells us otherwise should make us wonder why. Are they ignorant of this important fact, or are they trying to hide something from us, and if they're trying to hide something, what is that something?

'But it is not entirely unknown for a Son of the Sun to have been able to, and perhaps you can perform minor miracles of sorts'

If there was any truth to his words, Vamya didn't know, but she had partaken in some of the ashes of the Sun god, and even if that weren't enough to give her the power of the Ascended, it would surely count for something.

Vamya extended both her arms toward the body of the unconscious boy. She closed her eyes and sought to embody the power she sought. She sought to dismiss all doubt, to ignore all noise, to reach outside herself and find any strand of power she could weave into her hands to heal.

"Ma . . ."

The commotion inside the room brought her back to her senses. Both Aaghari and Adulla raised a hand, Zofer covered his mouth while Hagdah yelled, and her husband ran in to join her. "Praised be the Sun, Blessed Sun, Praised be!" through endless tears.

"Ma," the boy's dark eyes were open, his feeble hand reached for his mother's touch, "why are you crying?"

"I was sad, my son," Hagdah cried, "we thought we had lost you. But the Sun has brought you back to heal you. So now my tears are tears of happiness.

"Thank you," she looked up at Vamya, who was glad she wasn't the center of attention, for she wasn't sure what had just happened.

"Ma . . . I am not healing," the child said to his confused mother, "I came to say goodbye." Hagdah covered her mouth as her joy again became sorrow. "I am leaving, but don't cry because I was in Heaven."

"No, no, no! Please," Hagdah cried uncontrollably, "he's just a child. He doesn't deserve this!"

"Ma . . . stop," the child clasped her clothes, "it was beautiful. I am going to Heaven."

"Yes," Vamya grabbed all attention. "Heaven is the most beautiful place where the eternal power of the Sun lives on with the souls of the faithful. It is a place where there's no hunger, no misery, and no illness.

"It is a place where you," she directed her emerald eyes to the child, "will be able to play and run around with all the children and enjoy those things you weren't able to enjoy on this earth."

"No . . ." the child's weak voice interrupted her, "it wasn't like that . . . Up there in Heaven, my spine was still deformed. I still couldn't walk. I had to drag my body along the ground everywhere I went to catch up with the other children, but what was different was that the other children waited for me."

At his words, as if struck in the middle of the chest by an arrow, Vamya took a step back. His words had been a battering ram on the shaking door of her conviction. Was her foundation little more than many walls of beautiful yet thin glass? She knew most of the holy scrolls word for word, yet despite her deeply set beliefs, this child had not questioned but actually contradicted her.

'How much do I truly know?' she wondered, 'How much of what I believe have I been taught to believe, and how much of that is the actual truth?'

She did not remember much of what transpired after that moment when her being was shaken to the core. She didn't seem to notice the silent world around her as the child took his last breath, as the mother's shrill cry echoed in the void, as the crowd stormed into the home to steal the provisions, as her Chosen took Vamya out the window, where they were rescued by Aaju and his men, and taken back to the palace, to return to the reality she knew, that was perhaps less real.

(1) *iqit*: The lower caste of Suhne consists of the numerous *iqit* (those who live according to the tenets of the Sun) and the lowest *saqit* (those whose lives are deemed as dirty or not praising the Sun).

(2) *rayiysh*: Translated as 'the prime.' In Suhnite culture, among the *iqit* and *saqit*, honored guests are offered the prime serving of food available to the family. While this custom is followed strictly, the scarcity of food in Suhne has taught people it is improper to visit during feeding times uninvited so as to avoid taking food from others.

HEAVEN LIES

Location: Empyre of Suhne, City of Suhne, Palace of the Sun

At times, the most faithful put us all through the worst hell . . .

"I need answers." Vamya's voice forced quiescence among the Rays.

She spoke to them in their Sacred Chamber, a large circular domed room that would have been plunged in darkness this late were it not for the perfectly round, pure sunstone globes that were strategically placed so that, after having basked under the crystal dome all day, they would illuminate its entirety all night.

Each of the holy men sat in their respective crystalline seats a few feet off the floor, all of the twelve at the same level except for Exis, who was raised slightly higher than the rest.

The Speaker's seat, like the others, was sculpted to depict a pyramid-like temple, with thirteen beams emerging from the sun that was their headrest.

To each side of Exis, six Rays were seated.

"You cannot simply barge in into this Sacred Chamber and demand anything," the Speaker hissed.

"Sun of Change," Aldah was as well-mannered as usual, "we are in the middle of an important discussion. If you wish to speak, you need to request a time for it."

"I meant no offense," Vamya spoke in earnest. "I don't mean to make demands. I need clarity. I am seeking your advice and guidance."

To Exis, this was unexpected. He could raise a finger and have her leave the room where the Rays had the ultimate say, but here he felt she recognized their superior wisdom.

What better moment to assert his place, Exis thought, now that she had shown weakness?

"Then come to the center, Sun of Change," he beckoned, "what do you seek our guidance with?"

"I have studied the holy Scriptures of the Sun in detail," Vamya stated, "at least that which I have been given access to—"

"Access is limited according to the precepts of the Sun. Are you questioning those?" Exis asked.

"I do not," Vamya responded. "I understand the words and decrees of each Sun are holy, and only the Sun himself and his Rays have access to all that information, but the more I have studied, the more questions have arisen within me."

"We are holy men," Toleqqo of the Rays smiled, "and we ourselves have questions every day." His teeth were perfectly white within his ebon lips and oily, coal-black skin. "It is natural to have questions. What's important is that we don't let questions cloud our judgment."

"But how do we know if our judgment is right, if it's based on the truth?" Vamya asked.

"Apostasy!" Hosta's fanatical fury turned his hands pale against his armrests.

"Hosta," old Seiris spoke calmly, "she is not claiming our beliefs are false. What the Sun of Change asks is a fair question, one that we have all asked ourselves at some point, even if we have not expressed it." His intervention eased Hosta, at least some. "Can you please elaborate on your question, Sun of Change?" he continued.

"Yes," Vamya responded. "The Scriptures of the Sun speak of the chosen people of Suhne, of how the Sun in his mercy came down to the four tribes and made them his own to educate and free them."

"That is correct," Hosta's fast response was followed by nods from his colleagues.

"It also speaks of how, under his watchful Eye, men and women are equal, and yet we look all around Suhne, and we witness that the treatment of each is not the same. We see every day the use and abuse of women, who are treated as reproductive bags that, once used enough, become not much more than burdens!"

"Under his Holy Eye, both man and woman are of equal value," Aldah recited the scriptures to correct her. "A camel and a horse may be worth the same," he followed, "and yet that doesn't make them the same creature at all."

"You speak of different species," Vamya stated. "The scriptures also read, 'and he placed mankind above all of creation.' Unless you want to claim men and women are different species."

"No, it is not my intention at all. I misspoke," Aldah responded respectfully.

"Let's instead use a crystalsmith and a shepherd," Exis interjected. "They are both members of our society, one whose dedication to his work praises the Sun, while the second one's responsibilities don't."

"But while the second one's responsibilities don't strengthen the position of the Sun on this earth, his heart might be closer to the Sun's than the first," Vamya argued. "Besides, if his heart loved the Almighty, he would be more likely to give his life to fight for him."

"Sun of Change," Exis's voice carried a grain of contempt, "it is good that a man loves the Sun. But a man's heart does not strengthen the Sun's position. It is his duty that must add strength to the empyre and our God. If it doesn't, the same man will find himself still giving his life, but this time, fighting invaders to the lands of a weak god.

"As a beetle needs its horn and legs to live, they're each valuable in their own way. It is their importance that gives them the same relative value. The scriptures are not referring to the literal value of each."

"That's problematic in itself," Vamya looked around at each of the priests, "who decides what's to be taken as literal and what's to be interpreted?"

"We do," Aldah spoke again. "We are the Rays, representatives of the Almighty Sun, interpreters of his scriptures, and humble leaders of his worship. We pray for discernment daily, and in every word we speak, we seek to speak with the Almighty's heavenly wisdom."

"And who wrote these scriptures?" Vamya challenged. "We can claim all we want that they are inspired by our god, but whose hand shaped these words and made them permanent on parchment? It was men, men whom we want to believe were enlightened, who were filled with wisdom, but whose real goals and motives we will never really know."

She looked around at each of the Rays as she continued, "These few men had power, and while it might have been power granted by the divine, we can question if it is the shaping of the world and its history with their words that have given them that power."

An uncomfortable stillness took over the room. It was hard to gauge how most of the Rays had taken her words, other than for Hosta, who leaned forward angrily, or Yeq, whose meek demeanor forced him to lower his head. Old Seiris raised his eyebrows in amazement. The eldest of them all, Zurek, remained indifferent, while Exis's only perceptible reaction was the shift of his clenched jaw.

Each priest waited, as a group of hunters waited to see who would be the first one to wade into murky waters, for the first one to speak.

It was Seiris's gentle voice that broke the silence. "I believe we can speak of the intentions of those who came before us as certainly as we can speak truly of each other's intentions. Can we truly know? The labyrinth of speculations is a dangerous road to take. It is virtuous to question, but it is foolish to doubt the divine because of the actions or words of men.

"Faith," the aged man continued, "is the one thing that brings us together. We have faith because we have been taught or because of things we have seen. Some of us have faith because our own experiences have humbled us. In the end, our belief in goodness and faith in the power of the Almighty should surpass our personal desires and serve as our guide."

"Then, for the good of our people, we must create a chance for those below us to breathe, to thrive," Vamya said, "especially women. They have to feel appreciated. They have been the backbone of our society, carrying the heaviest burden for thousands of years—"

"It is their role," Exis interrupted.

"It is a role that was given to them!" Vamya argued. "Someone wanted them subjugated, raising children, uneducated. Why? So that men could dominate them like beasts, so that men could feast on power as much as they feast on the prime servings of food? I was there today; I went to the *saqit* district—"

"So we were told," Exis interrupted her once more, "a dangerous endeavor, placing yourself—"

"Listen!" Vamya fumed. "Listen to my words and stop your condescendence. You have taken your title too literally, so you only speak, but you don't listen. Your words will not distract me. They will not dissuade me from speaking and fighting on behalf of women and of all my people.

"While we feast and gorge on food and power, women are many times forced to fast. How many of them go days without proper sustenance? How many of them are nothing more than skeletons hidden under robes we love to adorn—"

"That is your perception, Sun of Change," Exis smiled slyly, "much like your brothers, each person has their own."

"Yes," she turned her head toward him, "and how much of this perception I have has been shaped by what I have been led to believe?"

"Hmph!" Hosta slammed his palm upon his armrest before rising.

But Exis halted him with a simple gesture.

"Son of the Sun," the Speaker said, "accusing us of purposely teaching *falsehoods* to the people of the Sun is a grave offense—"

"I am not accusing you, holy Rays," her eyes looked upon them all, "that's why I'm coming to you for guidance, for assistance.

"We must overlook our differences and start working with one another," the Sun of Change spread her arms wide. "We must be transparent with each other if we are to rule this empyre together both for the health of our land and the good of our people."

"Do you presume you will be this land's ruler?" the Speaker smiled mockingly.

Vamya turned her face toward him. "When I Ascend," her eyes blazed like emerald fire, gazing menacingly at each, "I will break and reform our society. I will offer you a last chance to work with me, or I will break you too."

She turned around, her words followed by her retreating footsteps, leaving them behind only with the threat she had vocalized. If her words were wise or shrewd enough, she didn't know, but she had spoken the deepest truth that lay within her heart.

"Who does she believe she is . . ." Exis's murmur echoed around the silence of the chamber.

"It is not who she believes she is, Speaker," Aldah responded, "but who she actually is. As a Son of the Sun, she has all the right to question."

"Her challenge to the power we hold is dangerous to our position," Exis stated.

"Power?" Seiris frowned, "What power are you referring to, Speaker?" But Exis knew Seiris better than to just give a straight answer to the old man's question. The third eldest among the Rays had proven time and again to have exceptional interrogation skills, one Exis was not going to let him use on him.

"Brothers," Exis responded, "our position is unique among the civilizations of the world. The fate of our people and of the path our empyre takes rests in our hands."

His eyes challenged Seiris's.

"Our role is to lead the people only in the worship of the Sun," Aldah stated.

"But there is no Sun," Exis responded, "so leading its people is our responsibility."

"That is in their daily affairs only, and only until a new Sun ascends," Hosta intervened.

"Until a new Sun is placed on his throne, of course," Exis smiled, "Don't forget the scriptures say, 'our people are as camels, and we are their shepherds.'"

"'In the guidance of matters of the spirit.' Only on that." Aldah finished the thought.

"If you want only a literal interpretation," Exis added with a sly smile. "Until then, how irresponsible we would be as his Eye witnessed our letting his empyre run itself, wandering aimlessly through the desert?

"Well?" He raised an eyebrow as he addressed his colleagues, "In the meantime, what do you think so far after this display of hers?"

"I was surprised to see that fire within her," Toleqqo responded. "She can lead us to a dangerous path, changing everything we know, but if she ascends, the path she chooses is the one we must follow."

"Do you support her then, Toleqqo?" Exis questioned from his seat.

"I have not said that," Toleqqo lifted a finger.

"Then, which candidate have you set your eyes upon?" the Speaker insisted.

"These things are to be kept secret," Aldah responded, "much more so at night when the dark one is listening."

"'The final decision is to remain secret, to be revealed only after each vote is cast,'" Exis quoted, "but there is certainly no harm in discussing our inclinations."

"So far, I believe the Conquering Sun best draws my attention," Yeq, youngest of the Rays, responded. His words were met with an intense glare from Exis.

"Stop this," While still soft-spoken, Seiris abandoned his calm demeanor. "No one else will respond."

"Speaker!" Zurek, eldest among them all, stood from his seat, "Enough of this!"

"You, I can tell, are siding with this *woman,*" Exis sneered.

Zurek squinted. "This is no ordinary woman you speak of, Speaker. She is a Child of the Sun."

Hosta slammed his hand against his armrest "A Child of the Sun who's breaking the sacred laws with her spectacles!"

"My old eyes have seen the laws of men do not readily apply to the Sons of the Sun."

"Zurek," Exis took a commanding tone, "take your seat and mind your place." The old

Zurek of the Rays

man's brow furrowed, but he remained standing. In a show of force, Exis stood up and took a step toward Zurek near the center. "This is nothing more than a congenial discussion among colleagues."

Stroking his beard, Zurek cleared his throat, "If someone has to mind his place, it is you, Speaker. This is not congenial, it is a scheme, and we will not play your game." The nonagenarian then addressed them all, "I invoke the right to end this meeting."

"And I deny it!" Exis raised his voice, forcing the hesitation of the rest.

"You can't deny me anything," Zurek scoffed, "you have been chosen as Speaker. You are thus our representative, not our leader." Upon the old priest's words, most of the Rays abandoned their seats and readied to take leave.

Exis struggled to contain himself. It was true he was not their leader. Still, the majority of the Rays saw him as their figurehead, something he wouldn't allow to be challenged by anyone. But this was not the time to put that to the test.

Before leaving the holy chamber, Zurek raised his voice to address Exis once more, "We should all wonder who would lead us through the most dangerous path, the Sun of Change . . . or yourself."

LEGACY

Location: Kingdom of Blackheart,
Duchy of Darkholm, Capital City of Coldforge, Ironholde

The antechamber was quiet, its immutable silence violated only by the occasional crackling of the sconces' flames. Their sound accompanied Rowena Darkholm's silent presence when Erdrick arrived, his firm stride echoed by Gustavus. This day, Erdrick's attire was not the military one he was accustomed to, but rather the formal, embroidered black vest and ruffled shirt under a cape of the same color. Today, the Master of Death had decided that, instead of watching the proceedings of the Great Council, Erdrick would be a part of it.

With but a single glance, Erdrick walked past Rowena before he came to a stop, his caped back toward her. His back was wide, as expected of someone dedicated to the martial arts, but then again, even before he had begun his training, his back had always been like their father's.

But that back disappeared behind the taller Gustavus, who stepped in and placed himself between them, forcing the Master of Life to take two steps back.

"You might be his sister," Gustavus broke the silence, "and I will undoubtedly protect you, but my priority is your brother's safety."

"Oh, dear cousin," Rowena smiled slyly, "you are not the only one who watches for his safety."

Frowning, Gustavus half turned toward her, "You know this is not your place, Rowena."

"Is it yours, then?" she responded guilefully.

"Unlike you, I did not ask," he replied, "I was invited."

She nodded, this time slowly, as soft words escaped her lips, "There are places one is invited to, not to be given responsibility and power, but rather so that one can be taught a lesson."

The taller man looked firmly into her golden eyes. "Save your words. They will never work on me."

The double doors opened to give way to a pair of royal guards who signaled to the one who had quietly witnessed the scene.

"You may enter, Lord Erdrick Darkholm," he instructed.

With a simple gesture, the Master of Life draped her black lace veil over her head. Through it, all Gustavus could see was a pair of golden eyes watching him, as those of a hunting feline, and a crimson, cunning smile.

Inside the chamber, Erdrick sat on the Darkholm seat, Gustavus behind him, while Rowena and the Shield flanked the monarch, standing behind his advisers.

"Crannon Coronn and Dokkon Gillspiel are traitors to the Crown and kingdom," King Septem announced. "Both have thus been stripped of all their titles and land."

"What about the men who followed their orders?" Erdrick asked.

"They are being thoroughly questioned," Septem responded. "Under the former dukes' command, they had been under the impression the order came from the Crown, and so they mistakenly flew the kingdom banner. The Master of Courts is ensuring they are taken into account."

"Who will take their positions?" Erdrick questioned.

"Quite surprising to see you ask," Ravencrest's duchess said from behind her husband's seat, "I would expect you to know that, being a royal yourself."

"These things are not discussed, duchess," Erdrick replied, "the separation of Crown and House is clear to the Darkholm."

"She means no offense," Myr von Corvus offered.

"Of course, and you may call me Shira," his wife added. "Today, we are equals."

"It is in everyone's best interest to have the Council make deliberations," Primon of Aligrand stated.

"If the king allowed it," the masked duke of Duskforge added, "we could offer prospects."

"We could then agree on which one is more qualified," Primon nodded in agreement.

"This will not be," Septem responded. "No one in a position with conflicting interests should be part of the decision."

"And what will Your Majesty do," Primon challenged, "place more of his family members in the highest positions to serve the Crown's own conflict of interests?"

"Mind your words!" Duchess Ilhar scolded.

"I know my words," Primon Ferertr responded. "I still want an answer."

"It is the Crown you are insulting!" Ilhar stood from her seat, the sudden movement of the duchess and her wolves alerting the royal guards.

"Duchess," Duke Myr von Corvus said to Ilhar, "there is freedom of spoken word in the Council chambers."

"The duchess is surely aware," his wife added. "There is no need to remind her of the Council rules, is there, Duchess?"

Ilhar Kal'Daka's fuming eyes moved from Primon to Myr and then Shira. She knew the lords of Ravencrest were right, and yet, despite sitting back, her wild spirit was not willing to go down quietly. "The words you speak in a moment will have everlasting consequences."

"Then let us hope those consequences are fairness of representation in the Council." Primon clasped his hands and turned his attention back on Septem.

"A Council that should see you off because of your support of the invasion," Ilhar accused.

"You are gravely mistaken," Primon responded, "while I agreed with the opportunity to advance, I offered no support during their invasion. I would have joined in if the kingdom had. Besides, why do you only point a finger at Aligrand when Haemonor supported the idea too!"

"That is true," the normally cheerful Eadric of Haemonor frowned. "As Duke Primon says, we also agreed with the idea of moving together against our neighbors. That was all."

"Enough," Septem said. "Lord Primon, your sentiment has been heard. The intention of the Crown is not to place a member of the Royal House as head of a duchy that does not belong to the Darkholm. The morale of the Blood of Valador and Volanar must be in our minds at all times. After considering this carefully, I have come to the decision that the ducal positions will be given to Erenest Coronn and Pohl Gillspiel."

"But, Your Majesty," Aubin Rayne of Whisperwind exclaimed, "they carry the same name as their predecessors. They are from the same House."

"Not only are they related," the Duke of Aligrand explained, "they are the actual sons of the former dukes!"

The Duke of Haemonor spoke, "Your Majesty, I will support you till the end, but I must beg you to reconsider."

"I agree with Lord Eadric," Brandobuh of Featherfell added.

"Your Majesty," Erdrick stated, "they are the sons of the traitors. They will surely have vengeance in their hearts.

"They could, certainly," Septem responded, his golden eyes on his son's, "but must a child pay for the sins of his father? In any instance, the son deserved

the chance to prove himself, to make amends, to become a better man, and thus show the world the child can surpass and be greater than his own progenitor."

"Wisely stated," the masked duke said.

"I have yet to meet a child whose goal in life is to be blamed for his father's transgressions," Taevaon of Mycernase said next. "I support the king's decision."

"While I may not agree with the decision, Your Highness," Erdrick said next, "there are things you see from the throne our limited view does not. The Duchy of Darkholm supports your decision."

"I have always respected the crown over your head," Ilhar bowed, her yellow eyes visible through her cascading red hair, "but more than that, I respect you, my lord. I only ask you to reconsider. Rewarding the sons of traitors is dangerous."

"Rewarding any man is dangerous, Ilhar," Septem stood up. "This is not a reward, but rather a chance any man deserves to correct what his parents have wrought."

WINDS OF FATE

Location: The Wall of Blackheart

Could someone ever feel so eager to lose himself . . .

While he had not broken fast this morning, Ealas didn't care to. His stomach was turning.

For someone who knew about diplomacy and important social etiquette, being nervous had not been common. He had lived his life either being the center of attention or standing right by it, close enough to always steal some of the spotlight. Then again, having been born of the lineage of the Chosen of the Light had made it obligatory and, frankly, quite easy.

While others lived a life seeking recognition, trying the impossible path of gaining renown, becoming relevant, and being remembered, Ealas's birthright had made him nothing less than relevant, so much that it felt as impossible to become irrelevant.

Ahead of them, carts and travelers lined up to pass through a great barbican, its parapets that protected the occasional guard, its battlements armed with oversized ballistae it didn't care to hide. Under it, its manned gate opened wide, allowing people in as a demon would welcome a child into its jaws.

Guards stood to either side, asking questions and checking documents from each group of travelers.

'What to do,' Ealas feared. If he were caught, it could be most troublesome for him and a great humiliation to House Heikken and Ardenay, potentially even provoking war between the two nations.

'Lord of Light, protect me.' He hid under the fabric and prayed.

Xarnata drove toward the entrance.

"What brings you to Blackheart?" the main guard questioned with a grim expression.

"Business." In true Daemos's fashion, the response was curt.

"Travel documents." The sentry's hand opened expectantly.

Without a moment's hesitation, Xarnata produced a scroll the captain unrolled and studied in detail while signaling at a second to examine the cart's contents.

The sentry approached the back of the cart. His curious eyes fixed on the fabric partially covering it. The second guard lifted the end of the fabric to examine the cart's contents, slowly revealing a few crates, a small barrel, some merchandise, and a pair of boots that rested sideways on the floor.

Ealas's palms were drenched with sweat. If he moved, his boots would reveal his presence.

All his life, he has envisioned a life of grandeur, pomp, and promise. While he had many times hidden as a youngster, playing pranks with his friends, he had never imagined having to do it for his life.

His lips moved, whispering a prayer, clasping the leather pouch that hung from his neck. 'Lord of Light, God of Life, ever merciful provider, please keep me safe.'

"Who are your companions?" the sentry asked.

Ealas skin trembled. Xarnata's persuasiveness, he had learned, was akin to having one's face hit with a club, several times, actually. Then again, what did Xarnata know about him when he had shared nothing? He feared the driver could've read him the same way Alasa had in Himlen.

"Hired escort," Daemos replied abruptly.

The sentry captain's eyes moved to the end of the parchment and then quickly returned to its beginning.

"Let them be," he instructed his guards, "they're clear."

"Xarnata Daemos, of Olath Valm;" his eyes back on the driver, the officer stamped the documents before returning them "*In Tenebris nos*, Blood."

The cart moved once more, for just a few feet, before coming to a sudden stop.

"You have to pay now," Xarnata requested through the fabric.

'Of course, because we *just* crossed the border,' Ealas laughed under his breath. He placed the remainder of the payment on Xarnata's palm before asking, "Is it safe to uncover myself?"

"It is," Beard responded.

Ealas removed the cover, turned around, and if he had been amazed by the vastness of the wall, he became mesmerized by the beauty that awaited.

"Welcome to Blackheart," Beard added.

"To *what's left* of Blackheart." Daemos smiled in turn with a strange smile that could have been more likely spasmodic muscles.

Before him, giant windmills saluted, all of them moving their three enormous triangular sails.

They stood like giants in a sea of green fields, interspersed with areas filled with yellow corn stalks much taller than the peasants cultivating them. Closer to the road, miles and miles of wheat covered the land.

Ealas's hands touched the ones long enough to be easily reached from the cart, feeling them caress his palms as if in a warm welcome. Each stem bent under his touch and returned to its place, where it danced to the ever-changing song the breeze sang, with a wind that was not forceful but perennial, producing the murmur that gave this land its name—*Whisperwind*.

Ealas felt emotional for a moment. This was far from what he had expected or had learned to expect.

He had grown up learning Blackheart was a demonic land of a seductive evil that would burn the soul of a man where he stood. It was a land that needed to be destroyed and nothing else, for they stood against every principle of the Light. But from Astas, while she was far from the most learned woman, he had learned something different.

Perhaps this was nothing more than a facade, an illusion of what truly lay behind the mask.

As they moved through the field, peasants greeted, others watched, yet the majority minded their own businesses.

Ahead the road turned, and from his place, he could see a giant mound of earth where a walled fortress stood, fiercely resisting the wind it captured in its central windmill. A tower stood on an adjacent, smaller, raised mound, nearly independent from the rest of the structure except for it being connected by a bridge.

"What castle is that?" Ealas pointed.

"Whisperwind's," Xarnata responded.

"Tortoise Mountain," Beard added, "It is the seat of power of the Duchy of Whisperwind. Lord Aubin Raine's fortress rests atop it. The land you come from destroyed a large portion of the crops, the fortress, and the city within its walls, but here it stands, once again, over twenty summers later."

"How much was the damage?" Ealas asked.

"Lots. I fought in that battle. I remember the fields burned, leading to starvation. A third of the fortress was either burned or ended up collapsing," Beard continued.

"One could never tell it was such. How did it recover?"

"The neighboring towns and people from all across the duchy and beyond brought materials, coins, and hands. Every neighbor helped. How could they not? This land you're traversing doesn't give up, as the Blood of Whisperwind says, 'Whisperwind provides.'"

"How much of Blackheart was destroyed during that war?" The nobleman's curiosity was a thirst needing to be quenched.

"Hmmm, let me see," Beard pondered, "Whisperwind, Aligrand, and Misthaven suffered losses."

"Featherfell," No-beard interjected.

"Yeah, that's right, Featherfell and Misthaven lost mostly people. Most of the losses were felt by the bread bowl and Aligrand. Why do you think the battle has its name?" Beard added.

"The Spear of Light," Ealas mused, remembering the name the paladins of the Church of Light used when teaching about their victory.

"Is that what you call it? Interesting. We call it the Battle of Dragon Tears, for Aligrand's losses were such the duke himself took to the streets and wept with his people," Beard remarked.

'Can his words be believed?' Ealas thought. The nobleman had grown up with great tutors and, at least from what he had believed until this moment, the greatest books of acquired knowledge, and these things had not been detailed. In fact, many in Ardenay believed the kingdom of Blackheart to be in ruins and defeated.

The man was a warrior, and warriors many times, to appear braver, exaggerated their exploits. Then again, Beard didn't seem to be taking credit for anything, so what if there was at least some truth to his words?

Ealas thought he knew much, but right from the start, he realized that, at least of Blackheart, he barely knew a thing.

For a moment, Ealas refrained from telling Beard, 'this is the most we have spoken,' for he believed perhaps the man hadn't noticed, or perhaps he was just proud of his heritage and history, proud of this land. Even a hog would be proud of its pen.

At their current slow pace, it was close to noon when the group came upon the busy streets of Abindire, the ducal capital, with its cobblestone streets and buildings that were tall enough to offer shade and yet small enough to allow the wind to pass through and over the city, and bless the windmills that stood beyond its border.

"I'm hungry." Daemos's monotone announced their stopping, dispelling Ealas's trance.

"Yeh, and time for a bath!" Beard shouted, sniffing his own armpits.

They came upon an inn named Ocean's Respite. On its walls hung old, poorly drawn maps, an anchor, and instruments a sailor would find familiar but that Ealas knew little, if anything, about. For a business of its size, it was relatively busy.

A young man offered them a table, the same who welcomed them at the entrance, who took their horses and was also their waiter. His name, Ealas found out, was Portan. He was helping his father, the cook, to run the business. They had inherited it from Portan's grandfather, who had passed half a year ago, something that caused a rift in their family, for his other two uncles had inherited only coins they had spent on women and drinks.

'Funny,' Ealas thought. In three minutes, he had learned more about this family than about the companions he had spent nearly two weeks with. He had almost concluded that perhaps it was he who had it wrong, for it was he who was interested in the lives of others when others were so reluctant to share the information. But this told him that it wasn't he who was wrong. It was Xarnata and his companions who didn't fit in this world.

"Xarnata," Ealas asked, placing his hand on the man's elbow to catch his attention, "thank you . . . for hiding me back there."

"I did not hide you."

"You said I was a hired escort," Ealas added.

"I answered the guard's question," Xarnata replied dryly, walking away from Ealas's touch. "You're not my companion. You're cargo."

Ah, that's right. How could Ealas think he was anything else than a piece of dead weight in the back of a cart? He shook his head and laughed in disbelief and sat at the table offered.

Beard left to wash and rest. He said he wanted some sleep to regain his strength after the trip and because he wanted the company of women that night. Xarnata, in turn, ignored the rest and climbed the stairs to his own room.

In the end, the nobleman found himself facing No-beard, which basically meant he was sitting alone.

"May I take your order?" the young man smiled broadly, placing a loaf of aromatic, freshly baked bread on the table and a small cup of butter chicken soup. "We have boiled chicken marinated in rose passion with breaded potatoes and herbs; we have boiled eggs, it comes with two eggs with boiled potatoes, mushrooms, and breaded broccoli. To drink, we have water, carrot or corn juice, and some wine."

"I'll have the chicken and water for now," Ealas responded.

"Chicken too, corn juice," No-beard followed.

"Give us a few, and they will be right out."

"Excuse me," Ealas pointed out, "but we didn't order the bread."

"Well, the bread is on the house, of course," the young man replied.

"I thank the Light for this boon and ask for you to be blessed, in turn," Ealas reached for the bread when the young man lightly tapped his hand and lifted a finger as a sign of 'no, no.'

Confused, Ealas looked at No-beard, who was patiently waiting at his own seat.

The young man then broke a piece of the bread and looked at Ealas, who just stared back and smiled. He then looked at No-beard, who opened his palm and pointed at Ealas. Following No-beard's polite signal, the boy dunked the piece of bread in Ealas's bowl and broke another piece, which he quietly placed on No-beard's.

"We provide," the young boy nodded and went about his business.

With a noisy slurp, No-beard proceeded to eat his bread and some more.

"These might be the days on the road, but I expected less flavor; it is actually good," Ealas spoke to No-beard in earnest.

"Hmmhmm."

If it were an affirmative response or, most likely No-beard savoring his wet bread, he couldn't tell, and at this point, he didn't even mind. Knowing it would be unlikely he would get anything else in response, he answered himself, "Yeah, it is really good."

STUDENTS

Location: Kingdom of Blackheart,
Duchy of Whisperwind, Capital City of Abindire

T hat night, for the first time since his crowning, he dreamed. And he dreamed of her.

The woman with hair the color of night, dressed in black, smiling at him as he, in his childhood innocence, waved at her from the window.

She walked back, carrying a basket full of wet clothes she had just washed that morning, ready to hang them to dry before folding them and handing them to the servants, for the slaves always did the dirty work of those above them.

But to him, she was not just a slave to be loathed, to be hated.

She had a name.

Her name was Astas,

and she was dressed in black.

She was always dressed in black.

Despite a long night of uninterrupted sleep in a somewhat comfortable bed, Ealas woke up with a stiff neck.

He found himself sitting on his bed, his head caught between his hands. It was because of *her* he was doing this. It was because of Astas he had taken this journey. Not because she had in any way forced him or convinced him, but because of her own humility, her own faith, her own example that he had decided to do this. And it was why he had taken her name to add to his so that he would travel with her and bring her home.

While he was far from spoiled, or so he liked to believe, he was still accustomed to certain commodities that were no more, for even the slightest comfort he now had to pay, and with each day, his purse dwindled. He counted his coins. He had enough for a year or perhaps two if he were prudent.

Although it had been bustling with business the day before, this morning, the tables in the dining room were nearly empty.

"Four," he indicated to the server, an aging man who smiled and promptly seated him.

"Can I get some bread to start?" Ealas asked.

"The bread always comes, sir. Whisperwind always provides," the server replied. While he had been the cook the day before, he indicated today he was the server while his son Portan had tutoring.

"Tutoring?" Ealas wondered.

"Yessir, education is always important."

"Wow," Ealas continued, "I didn't expect him to, well . . . I don't mean any offense, but—"

"To receive education because he's not rich?" the server responded.

"No, that's not what I meant."

"If they're likely to follow their trade and their father's footsteps?"

"Yeah, that's more along the lines of what I intended to say," Ealas responded.

"Well, I want my son to have the choice. He can choose to stay and help me until I can work no more, or he can choose to marry and go somewhere else, in which case I must find another pair of working hands. I wouldn't love that choice, but it is not mine to make."

The server brought some egg broth with ground pepper and a piece of round bread. He attentively looked at Ealas, who smiled and waved a hand over the table. The man then broke off a piece of bread and placed it in Ealas's broth bowl. "We provide," he said.

"I am thankful," Ealas replied, "and may the Light bless you and make provision for you and your loved ones."

"Likewise. Now, we currently have in the kitchen some fried eggs with pork sausage and pureed eggplant-broccoli. We have smoked yolk with roasted potatoes, caramelized carrots, and veal sausages. Which one would you like?"

"Just some water to drink while I wait for my companions."

"As you wish."

After a long wait, the server placed another bowl of soup and a piece of bread floating on it. "Would you like to order now or keep waiting?"

"I'm still waiting for my friends," Ealas responded. "You haven't happened to see them, right? Three men, a quiet lot, one of whom has a wounded leg."

"Ah, yeah, I saw them briefly. One of them seemed to be from Featherfell, the one with the wounded leg."

"Featherfell? How would you know he's from Featherfell by just looking at him?" Ealas asked.

"Well, I've seen enough people passing through. Besides, the Blood of Featherfell is so tall. I just assume every tall person is from there."

"Freaks!" a woman yelled from an adjacent table.

She was clearly intoxicated, as her body odor, slurred words, and randomly swaying neck confirmed.

"Shush, woman," the server interrupted, swatting his hand.

"Don't shush me! They're freaks, the lot!" She extended her neck, which showed her pulsating blood vessels under the tension of her muscles.

"Don't mind her," the server told Ealas, "she has never gotten over the fact that she bore an only child. It was born stupid. Her husband left her for another woman. Of course, he, like his new wife, are both from Featherfell."

"And that's what got her drinking, I suppose. I feel sorry for her."

"Don't be," the man replied, "she'd been drinking a lot even before she got married. She's drinking today, and she will drink as much, or more, tomorrow. But if those were your friends, they're gone."

"Wait, what?"

"I believe they left this morning, early, about two hours ago."

"Are you serious?"

"Yes, they were the first ones to break fast. They paid, ate, and left."

The woman was ranting loudly about some conspiracy of the nobles. "Let me make sure someone helps her home safely," said the man. "I'll be back in a few moments."

Ealas found himself sitting at that table alone. Now his appetite was gone like his companions. It felt strange to be abandoned by Daemos and his men just like that. It even hurt a little, he had to admit, perhaps because he had always been the center of attention anywhere he went. How could he not be? He had been destined for a crown.

Other than Daemos's, he never even knew their names, but somehow, he still felt he *knew* them, or at least he had grown fond of them or of what he thought he knew of them.

'They were brusque. One can only understand why they would be so rude,' he thought.

His fingers tapped the table as he thought about what his next step would be. He needed to find his way to the village where Astas had lived, that was all.

But his thoughts returned to Daemos and his men. 'Maybe they hurt my pride a little. Well, they did, more than once. What was I, to them, other than cargo? Haha!'

He only wished his companions would have given him a chance to say goodbye.

Then again, in the end, they weren't even his companions.

And he needed to get used to that, and much more, for this was a different land with different beliefs. If he was going to be successful, or even worse, if he wanted to survive, he needed to be ready to learn, to absorb all knowledge, as that forgotten piece of bread that had absorbed all the soup in his bowl.

⊶⊶⊷⊷

The streets of Abindire were swarming with activity, more so along its central marketplace.

Rows of wooden sellers' stands, their fabric tops exhibiting different stages of wear indicating their perpetual presence, filled the plaza. Behind each one, at least one person promoted their wares: from a cloth merchant claiming to have the best fabrics the world has seen to clay cups, vases, and produce from the surrounding farmlands.

At first, it was hard to distinguish nobles from those who weren't, for although they had different speech, their clothes were not too dissimilar. The occasional lady wore finer garments, though. When Ealas approached to listen, he noted the interaction between them and the common folk, which made him wonder if these were truly aristocrats or if they were actors dressed as such.

One of such women asked for directions from some dressed in less expensive clothes, and she thanked them for their response. What was peculiar was none of the women commented about each other's garments. They didn't even seem to care or pay attention to it. Even more curious was none of them turned to speak behind the other's back once the other one had left.

If he could describe Whisperwind in one word, he would likely choose welcoming.

But for all the politeness and warmth he witnessed, something struck him as odd.

Through the multitude, Ealas's gaze was captured by an aged woman who sat on the floor by a raised doorway. Her boots were torn, tied up in places to keep them from falling apart. The woman's clothes were dirty and ill-fitting, covering most of her sagging skin. She looked back as if Ealas's gaze had poked her with a finger to attract her undivided attention.

She brought her palms together as though in prayer and then lifted her palm, the exaggerated motion of her lips sending a clear message Ealas could read: alms, please.

The nobleman tried to ignore it, but upon looking back, the mendicant's eyes were fixed on him.

'One coin,' the woman pleaded through distant, silent lips.

Again he tried to ignore it, but that was not in him. He just simply couldn't. Pulling a copper out of his bag, he crouched and handed it to the woman.

"Thank you, merciful sir," the beggar spoke in a raspy voice, "I haven't eaten for two days."

"Give me that back," Ealas requested, moved by the woman's words, "I'll give you a silver instead."

Shyly, she returned the coin and blessed Ealas profoundly upon seeing he spoke truthfully.

Ealas stood once again, watching the goings of those in the marketplace. They purchased and sold in a merriment that was, to him, hypocritical. For while they traded metals, products, and smiles, they ignored this woman who sat in a corner, slowly losing her life, watching the lives and the world of those who consumed. And there, just around fifty feet away, another beggar sat, raising his hand and speaking to a world that ignored his very existence.

Upon seeing this, Ealas thought, 'For many to have much, many should have little. How can we change the world by enjoying life and forgetting those who can't make it?'

He then shook his head and walked away.

After a few rows of merchants, he stopped by a stall of fresh fruits and vegetables. Their skin glistened as if they had been picked at their ripest just seconds before.

'Five for a copper droplet,' the woman had indicated. That was a steal. It was not surprising the woman's stand was busier than those around it.

Ealas asked politely for some space, but seeing this wouldn't work on the pushy customers, he wedged himself in. Dozens of hands quickly pointed and grabbed tomatoes, apples, eggplant, and some brightly colored plants that were arranged by both size and color. Each time he thought about picking one, a quick hand grabbed it before he did, and off it went to another customer's basket.

A tomato rolled down, drawing Ealas's attention. It was nearly perfect and of good size. He stretched his hand to grab it when a swift hand grabbed it first.

"Hey," he protested, half turning to face the offender, "I saw it first!"

The hand was that of a teen who quickly placed the fruit in a bag. "Seeing something does not make it yours." The voice belonged to a girl speaking from under a traveler's cloak.

"I'm sorry, young lady, but I had intended to get that one you just put away," Ealas said disapprovingly.

From under her hood, she looked up at the much taller Ealas. "Excuse me, sir," her hand briefly parted coal-black bangs that covered most of her face, "but anyone could claim they had the same intention. Just because they set their eyes on one thing, it does not make it their own. If someone wants something, one must make a move for it or lose it."

"But I had made a move," he interrupted.

"If one makes a move and does not get it," she interjected, "then it belongs to the one who actually makes the move and gets it first. And, while you are here discussing that, you are missing the rest of the good stuff others are taking."

"Yeah, I guess you're right. There's no point in—" Excited customers pushed from every side, it seemed. Had Ealas not had a warrior's stance, he could have lost his balance.

Another tomato caught his attention. This one seemed juicy enough. This time without hesitating, he quickly placed his hand on it.

"NO! WAIT!" the girl yelled, moving her arms away in a sign of revulsion. His reflexes kicking in, he quickly let the fruit go. Deftly, the girl caught the fruit right before it made contact with the rest. "Thank you, kind sir!" she laughed heartily at Ealas's innocence.

"Wait, that's not right. Give it back," he demanded.

"But it was never yours to begin with!"

"This time, I hadn't just intended to take it. I grabbed it."

"And yet you let it go. If you let go of something you had, then it is gone. You might feel you have the right to protest where it ends, but you do not. It is not yours anymore. And while you worry and think about it, you are missing out on the good stuff someone else is taking," she closed in and grinned, futilely attempting to blow the hair off her face.

Upon seeing an opening, Ealas kicked the bag in her hand, sending some of its contents flying and her scurrying behind them. Among them, one of the tomatoes flew and was caught by his hand.

"Hey!" she yelled, reaching for his hand. "That is mine!"

"It's not," he dodged her move.

"I had it in my bag, in *my* possession!"

"And you hadn't paid for it yet, so, technically speaking, it wasn't, and well, isn't yours." It was Ealas Heikken who laughed this time.

The girl lowered her guard. Seeing Ealas doing the same, she then darted for Ealas's hand. He blocked her move, easily swatting her reaching hands.

She swung her arm in an exaggerated arc that Ealas sought to dodge easily. Having feinted, she grabbed his recovering hand with her free one, pushed away from the ground to jump, and, opening her mouth, licked the tomato in the most uncouth of ways.

"Ew," Ealas dropped the fruit, which the girl caught in midair.

"Thanks!" she laughed.

A sudden, low rumble to their side and a red flash in the corner of the eye caught the attention of both. It was a beautiful one that had been hiding under the mounds of tomatoes people were taking. Ealas looked at the girl's face. Biting her lip, she looked like a young lioness, ready to pounce.

The nobleman reached out instinctively and grabbed the fruit before the girl had a chance to move.

"I guess it's mine." It was Ealas who grinned back this time.

"It is fine. I did not even want it in the first place," she giggled. "I pretended I did, and you went for it, and that is good, for it is a beautiful specimen."

"Sure." he inspected the fruit while he placed a few others in his bag. It was surely a most perfect tomato, its skin so untarnished he could almost see his own smiling reflection on its surface. So fixed was Ealas on the red reflection that as he lowered the fruit, he saw, far behind, an aged man sitting in a corner. Much like the woman from before, he was asking an indifferent crowd for charity.

The girl was ready to jump on his hand, but Ealas was not interested in continuing their small rivalry. "Please," he stopped her with the palm of his hand, "I don't want to be rude."

"Oh, I am sorry," the girl replied.

"It's not a problem. Give me a moment."

Moving away from the crowd, Ealas approached the man. He was aged, his face cracked like the walls of a weathered fortress that had now been abandoned.

Their eyes locked as the mendicant saw him approaching. The man lifted both hands, begging for anything in an array of garbled words his toothless mouth expressed.

"Poor man," Ealas asked, "do you have any family?"

His ancient, sad eyes responded nothing. The lips moved like the constant waves at the beach. They moved, but Ealas still couldn't make up what he was saying. 'Is it a local language, or does he have trouble talking' Ealas wondered. He looked back at the teen. "Can you come here and see if you understand him?"

From where she stood, she responded, "Just let him be. Do not mind him."

'How can I?' Ealas thought, 'It would be cruel for me to leave someone like this when his eyes met mine and no one else's.'

Reaching for his bag, Ealas produced a tomato and a silver, both of which he gifted the man with. He stood in the beggar's presence for a few moments, just observing him holding the fruit in his hands. 'One day, that could be me.'

At last, he returned to the side of the girl, feeling he had at least done some good today.

"Well, I must take my leave now," he told the girl.

"Me too. Where are you headed?" she asked. "I hope you do not mind my questioning."

He smiled warmly. "No, I don't mind. I'm headed to—forgive me if I butcher the name—*Hvitphass?*"

"In Misthaven?" she inquired, pointing a finger at him as if she was getting a prize for the correct answer.

"Yes," he replied, "I believe that's the one."

"Hvitfast, then," her eyes glinted in excitement as she corrected. The nobleman expected the girl to mock his mispronunciation, but, to his surprise, she didn't. She actually continued speaking, "It is actually a very small suburb of Evermist. Its importance lies in the fact that it is in the land the duke of Misthaven calls home, where the Watchtower is."

"The Watchtower?"

"It is the name of the ducal castle."

"I see. Well, that's where I'm headed," Ealas added.

"You will need the help of a transport guild. Otherwise, it would take you too long. They are not too far from where I am going. You can join me for a stroll if you like, and I can then point you in the right direction," she added.

"Certainly, I'll do that. Thanks. Can you recommend any transport guild," he asked. "Well, why am I even asking? You probably wouldn't be able to. You're a child."

"Hey! I am not a child," she chided. "I am a young woman."

"If so, then, young woman, can you recommend any?" he asked incredulously.

"Actually, I cannot, not at all," a giggle escaped her lips as she bit into a carrot she pulled from her bag.

While they walked for only a few minutes, it was still tiring. The girl walked fast, and, to him at least, she spoke even faster. Either she was excited at having someone to talk to, or Ealas had gotten used to the quiescence of Daemos and his men. In any case, he welcomed the friendly conversation, although he spent most of the time listening to the girl talk about different subjects, always sparked by something random they saw along the way.

The girl stopped suddenly and spoke to Ealas almost excitedly, so much that he could clearly hear her in the midst of the noisy streets. "Hey, let me ask you something. Please tell me you did not just give your best tomato to the *almer* back there."

"*Almer?*"

"Yes, the panhandler."

"Did you give him the best one you got?" she questioned again.

"I did not, but I still made sure to give him a good one." Ealas lied. He had actually given the mendicant what he believed was the best fruit he had taken, the one the girl last fought for. It was beautiful, but it was just a fruit. In the end, it would be eaten and no more.

"That was nice of you," she stated.

For the next few moments she walked quietly, submerged in thought.

The pair turned around a corner, and Ealas's eyes marveled at the architectural wonder before him.

There, jutting from the ground, was a stony peak, its body holding many buildings at different levels, but all connected by walkways and bridges seemingly placed haphazardly, but of such beauty, the engineers of Walcrast would find it as ingenious as it was enviable. His eyes admired every corner of it, all the way to its artificial, round top.

"The Fox's Peak, and in it, Fennec Academy," the girl spoke, "the knowledge repository of the world. People from all over the continent come here to study. Well, the lucky ones. It is said that what is not known in Fennec is not known anywhere else in the world. Although we know that is not entirely true," she whispered, covering her mouth so that only Ealas could hear.

"I wouldn't have thought it would be so grandiose, so . . . *beautiful*," Ealas replied.

"I know, right? Anyway, you will need to go straight down that road a few blocks. I would say five or six before you are in the transportation quarter. A company should easily take you to your destination in a week or two, depending on who you choose."

"But wait," Ealas interrupted, "I thought you didn't know—"

"Oh no, I did know. I just could not make any recommendations," she smiled slyly. "Well, here I stop. I must go now."

"Wait, what's your destination? Fennec?"

"Fennec, of course!" She took two steps backward, spreading her arms in a display of obviousness.

He saw the girl moving slowly toward the school entrance, where a rather short, aging, copper-haired woman, her arms crossed, waited. She was garbed in elegant attire and a tall headpiece that made her seem of average size.

'Oh, she's going to get in trouble,' he laughed at the thought briefly, but still, he felt bad because he did like her personality. In a way, it reminded him about his own irreverence when he was younger, just a few years earlier.

"I really must go," the girl winced, "as patient as Lady Narkari surely is, her harsh disciplining is unquestionably legendary. So here we part ways, foreigner! It was nice to make your acquaintance."

"Foreigner?" Ealas asked. "Why do you think I'm a foreigner?"

"Oh, I do not *think*, I *know*!" she smiled broadly, "No one gives money or food to the *almers* in Whisperwind. They are already provided for, they are the eyes and ears of the Duke of Whisperwind."

As if slapped across the face, Ealas just stood there, unable to respond. From the moment he had placed a foot on the plaza, Ealas had barely seen a guard, and yet everything had appeared to be peaceful. It all started to make sense. His interaction with the mendicants just told them he was perhaps someone they should watch.

"Besides," the girl added, "only a foreigner would be stupid enough not to recognize Fennec Academy!"

In this, she was surely right. The peak where Fennec rested was higher than any other in the vicinity. How could he not know that? How could he grow up noble and not be interested in studying and getting to know the surrounding lands, especially before he visited them?

Ealas knew then he needed to do a better job of learning his surroundings before opening his mouth. His blood alone made him an enemy of the land he now traversed, and worse, having his identity known was not an option.

"Hey, before you go! What's your name?" Ealas asked.

Like a speedy whirlwind, the young girl turned, some of her hair getting inside her mouth. With one hand, she held down the cloak's hood and the rest of its oversized fabric with the other. If it hadn't been fastened around her neck securely with a book-shaped pin, it would have likely been blown away.

Blowing the hair out of her mouth, she smiled victoriously, for she had finally succeeded in moving the bangs out of her face, if for only a moment before they stubbornly returned. In their brief absence, they revealed bright, lively eyes the color of ripe lemons in spring.

"My name . . ." the girl smiled mischievously before turning to sprint toward the impatient headmistress "...is Isolde."

THE WISPS

Location: Kingdom of Blackheart,
Duchy of Misthaven, Evermist region

To find one's way, at times, one must simply walk . . .

H aving bought passage through a traveling guild, Ealas ended up staying the previous night in a small inn by the main road that crossed the quiet land of Misthaven. He had inquired about the larger number of people traveling to other duchies. He had even noted seven travelers accompanying them had stayed behind as they crossed into Aligrand, the former royal duchy, while only three people were going in his same direction. Of those, he was one; the other two were aspiring musicians with little experience and even less talent, who happened to be brothers who had been sent away after their mother married a man who had six younger children of his own.

"Nearly everywhere you go in the kingdom, there's something to be done, a life to be lived. There's little of interest in Misthaven," they had responded. "There's even a saying: 'in Misthaven, the deeper you go, the less you'll see.'"

'They weren't exaggerating,' he realized, having passed through the region known as the Valley, its land mostly flat, with sparse farmlands and even scarcer hamlets. The layout of the land alone didn't lend itself to support socializing or large communities of people, as the small villages were separated by woods, hills, or at times by both. As to why anyone would have chosen such an uncreative name as the Valley, Ealas could only smile and guess but quickly left the thought behind when he saw the next regions were packed with hills, small mountains, and deep, forested swamplands.

It had been quite the shock to find lands the god of creation had placed as close to one another so sharply different.

'Maybe the Light had purposefully placed those lands and drawn a line so that there would never be a question about their legitimate borders.'

As different as the lands had his traveling experience been, the carriage driver and the other two passengers were from Whisperwind, not as quiet as Daemos and his men, although not quite as talkative as Isolde, the girl of the unforgettable eyes.

Thinking of her made the nobleman look back, hoping to see the top of Fennec that had finally disappeared behind the hills that obscured all but the mountains beyond this region called Evermist.

It had been during that last, simple supper, Ealas and the brothers had been told that to see the beauty of Evermist, one must see the capital town of Brumeveil as dawn breaks at least once in a man's lifetime.

He had asked the pair if they wanted to, like him, make this their last stop and continue on foot, leaving in the wee hours of the morning to catch a glimpse of Brumeveil's beauty.

Without much discussion, both had refused, the one because he preferred to sleep in and the other because he had always been afraid of going out in the dark, especially when he wasn't skilled or armed like Ealas.

But Ealas left anyway. It was his first and likely last time in this region, and he wanted to see everything he could in as little time as possible.

And so he headed out, so early he couldn't get the lodging to provide him with a meal, even after he had offered to pay more, walking for miles under the watchful eye of the moon.

The last few days, the cart had been traveling slowly, the slowly increasing fog clouds reducing its advance with each increasing day. Despite the impaired visibility, the roads in Misthaven were well maintained, but while the carriage drivers were able to follow the road by the sound of the wheels, the beasts pulling the cart would still remain nervous.

What should have been a tenday journey had taken a little over three weeks, and now on foot, he could understand and experience why. With every mile he walked, the fog just grew more persistent and denser, and seeing the woods along the road, he wondered how he would know where to stop.

Sometimes one must simply trust one's instincts.

For hours he walked, so much that his soles were sore. He had gone up and down a few hills, seen black blocks that appeared to be buildings along the woods, and now, close to the morning, he found himself on top of the last hill. There, the woods finally gave way to a large, deep valley covered in fog clouds so abundant, Ealas could only see, peeking through the cloud, a steeple and the roofs of a few buildings, like children playing a perpetually silent game of hide and seek.

Beyond, a backdrop of mountains that, although not even close in height as Walcrast's in Ardenay, if not for a pass, would completely separate this duchy from the next.

'This must be Brumeveil,' Ealas thought, 'unless I totally missed it making my way here.'

His stomach growled, a choir accompanying the distant sounds of life in the town below.

Ealas began his march downhill slowly, not wanting to miss the sight, waiting for the beautiful city his eyes sought.

In the middle of his descent, the sun's rays broke the horizon, its rays traveling through the mist, at times piercing it, showing the capital to be no more than a disappointing small town, its buildings appearing to be no more than nondescript barracks, if not stables.

"So much for its beauty," Ealas judged.

As if dispelled by the sun, the fog was quickly disappearing.

His eyes continued admiring the valley they could now see more clearly when they captured what they had almost missed, the Watchtower, a castle of dark rock resting over the smallest mountain in the region, hidden in plain sight, a sentinel surveying the land.

Centered on its face a single, large tower that gave the structure its name, for even in the foggiest time of the year, the castle stood as an observant, unobstructed monument to the duty of guardianship over this land. A stone bridge connected it to an elevated hamlet, and below it, a vast cottonfield of the purest white his eyes had ever seen, extending all the way to the road he walked along.

Wait, is it moving?

The field almost had a life of its own, reflecting the light of the sun as if seeking to protect its contrasting black soil below from its relentless attacks.

In the end, this nondescript capital town, when seen as part of the whole picturesque scene, didn't look that bad. Still, it was nothing Ealas would consider marvelous. Marvels were those found in Ardenay, in the unparalleled architecture of Ashvail's churches, in the Waterfall Palace of Walcrast, and in the bustling cities in Alcyn. Even the Bulwharf strongholds, built solely for their defensive purpose, were beautiful. It was with good reason Ardenay was considered to be, by many, the diamond of the world.

'A river of clouds.' He contemplated the waving white cotton field to his right and, close to where he stood, a disturbance in the wave pattern.

Instinctively placing a hand on the hilt of his sword, Ealas shifted his stance the moment he thought he saw something move. Unless his eyes were fooling him, something scurried among the cotton flowers.

Wariness and curiosity made Ealas walk into the field, moving cautiously to avoid making noise.

To the right, he felt movement somewhere close. Turning his body, he proceeded in that direction.

To the left, he separated the abundant, soft wisps that hung like a giant spider's web and clung to his clothing. Every time he advanced, but the closer he believed he got, the farther away he heard the scurrying.

Some of the plants moved to the side, and that was the moment Ealas had been waiting for. He ran as fast as he could, holding his hands ahead to stop the plants from hitting his face.

'I can hear it, straight ahead, almost got you.' His foot was caught, and he stumbled so fast he wasn't sure if he had broken something.

"You! No running in the field!" a woman of advancing age raised her voice, "Ah, look what you've done!"

"I'm really sorry," Ealas apologized, sprawled over the black soil. He removed both dirt and cotton wisps from his face as he got up again. He quickly checked for his sword, his backpack, and his leather pouch. Everything was there.

Just two feet away from him lay a large torn basket. If he had wanted to shift blame, it would have been impossible for, of the cotton that had filled the basket, what was not scattered along the ground was sticking to his legs.

"These are hours of work!" appearing from between the plants, another older woman pointed, "shame on you!"

"I should have never placed it on the ground, Meika," Ealas heard the first one saying through what was either a melodic, thick accent or difficulty in speech.

"Where were you going to place it, Basa, on top of your head? Don't be silly. We always place it on the ground!" the second one retorted. "He shouldn't be here running like some drunken fool.

"What's your name, young man?" she continued.

"I'm just passing by," he replied.

"Passing by," the first one nearly whistled, "going where?"

"What, you like them young now, Basa?" Meika mocked.

"Bah," Basa protested, opening her eyes widely and reaching out with both hands as if jokingly trying to choke her companion, smiling at Ealas through mostly missing teeth.

"Basa thinks she knows everyone. She's losing her mind." Having a hard time kneeling, Meika inspected the basket to see if there was any way for her to fix it. "Ugh, just go your own way, young man. Like all youngsters, mess everything up and leave, expecting those elders who can't do so to fix the problems you caused."

But Ealas couldn't just turn and leave. It wasn't his way. "I feel bad enough. Can I give you something for your trouble?"

"You mean *payment?*" Meika asked.

"Yes, if it would help."

"Of course, it would help, with other things perhaps. Maybe Basa would take it. She's a whore like that. But I must warn you, I've known her for many a year. She'd take the payment and drool all over you before falling asleep or dying!" Meika continued, exasperated, "Payment doesn't pick the cotton, and the cotton won't pick itself."

"Again, I deeply apologize." Not knowing what to say, he decided to explain, "I was on the road when I saw movement and heard some noise on the field, and I got curious as to its origin."

"So you had to go and check. You couldn't just stand on the road and watch, and thus you ruin the work of others, young man," Meika scolded.

"Maybe it was the whispdrakes," Basa replied casually.

"Whispdrakes?" Ealas wondered aloud.

"Young man, not much moves in the cotton fields, aside from workers and feeding whispdrakes," Meika began, but Ealas's mind went somewhere else.

It had been two terrible days, one of embarrassment, a day when his father's discourse had been interrupted by young Ealas, an insult so grave that, before all witnesses, his father had slapped him across the face.

He had been sent to bed without supper or good night and had spent the second day in his room.

The next night, the woman in black had entered his sleeping chamber, prostrating herself on the stony surface of the floor.

"I am here," she spoke through broken lips with difficulty.

When she lifted her head, Ealas saw the terrible mark of his father's ire. The woman's face was swollen, bruised. One of her eyes was shut. He could tell she was in pain.

"I can ask one of the doctors—" the boy started.

"No, please, no," she replied, "The king specifically said I needed to learn. If I received help, he would make it ten times worse."

"I don't know what to do," Ealas's tears showed.

"Nothing, my prince. Sometimes there's nothing to do, nothing we can do, and that's that."

Young Ealas sobbed.

"If you'd like, I can tell you a story so that you can get your mind off of this," she tried to smile.

"No, don't tell me just a story," he rubbed his eyes with his hands, "tell me a tale, something special about your land."

"If that's what you want, my sweet prince," she played with his hair, "that's what I'll do."

"Hmmm," she pondered before she began her tale, "Once upon a time, inside a great kingdom, there was a land called Misthaven, filled with beautiful cotton fields, and in those cotton fields lived the most noble of creatures, the shy children of the fog . . . the Whispdrakes."

The slave continued her fantastic tale of these creatures that, at first, Ealas wished he could see someday. But while she spoke, his mind wandered, and he stopped listening to her, for his only focus was now on the light gray wisps of her hair that fell in every direction, even covering some of her face. But try as they might, they could not hide the bruises, the swollen face, the moving lips as she sought to distract him, to make him forget his own pain.

And in a way, it worked. The boy prince forgot his pain, but only because he thought of hers . . .

"I'm sorry, Astas," he wept . . .

"Are you listening?" Meika snapped her fingers questioningly.

"Of course, he's not. Who listens to your ranting?" Basa responded instead.

"I . . . I'm sorry," Ealas resounded, "I was distracted but meant no disrespect."

"Clearly," Meika said incredulously.

"Your words brought back memories," Ealas continued. "Are the whisp-drakes real?"

"Of course they are, very much so," Basa responded.

"I always thought they were just a story," Ealas wondered aloud.

"Well, they're not," Meika replied, "nobody knows where they came from. They have always been here, eating cotton. That's all they do, really."

"Is it then true they come to you at night, whispering dreams into your ear?" he asked curiously.

Meika's expression was one of astonishment. "By the gods, that's the most ridiculous thing I've ever heard an adult say! Those are the tales we tell children."

"Ah, I guess I must've missed that part," Ealas said, embarrassed. "How could I get my hands on one?" he then asked.

"Oh no, you're not supposed to touch them," Basa said sternly, "if you touch them, they die."

"Well, even if you wanted to, you couldn't . . . scurry little critters," Meika added.

"If you're a really good-hearted person, they'll come to you. They'll even feed off your hands," Basa smiled.

"Nonsense," Meika interjected, "they just mind their own business while we mind our own. Just let them be, and they might come close."

"That's what I said," Basa protested.

"No, it's not. Be gone now, young man!" Meika scolded. "We have to get back to work and carry all this to the mill if we are to make it to the festival."

"Festival?" he inquired.

"Kaeris's Bounty," Basa responded, "the first full moon of the summer when the crops are the most bountiful, we celebrate, dancing, drinking, and singing until Kaeris leaves the sky to thank her for the blessings."

"Do you believe the moon is actually blessing you?" he asked incredulously.

"No, not at all, foolish boy," Meika responded. "It's how the tradition goes. It's a moon, a ball in the sky, nothing more."

Around them, like the mysterious arms of a tentacled specter, the fog slowly returned. Within minutes it enveloped all so that Ealas could see nothing beyond both women, who were barely a few feet from him.

Setting his eyes on the ground covered by his accident's evidence, Ealas resolved to stay and help the women. It was all his fault, after all, and after he had taken their time just talking, helping them was the least he could do.

He hugged the torn basket and had both women stuff it up with mounds of cotton and started walking behind the pair, unable to see from both the deep fog and the cotton in front of his face.

"For all the young want to live a fast life, you are a slow walker, young man. Where's that running spirit now?" Meika mocked the wary Ealas.

"It's hard to see," he replied. "I can barely see anything. What if I stumble and drop the basket?"

"Drop it?" she questioned. "If you drop it, you just pick it up and walk again. Just always remember where you stumbled so that you don't stumble there again."

"C'mon," Basa smiled through the foggy tendrils, "just follow my tune."

The old woman sang, her voice melodious and apparently trained. Meika accompanied her, their voices rising over the scurrying through the plants around them, and they sang together, as they had apparently done many times before; they smiled and sang joyfully, about sunny days and beautiful summers, about birds and the blue sky, about beauty and youth, all things they couldn't see, all things they didn't have.

THE FOG

Location: Kingdom of Blackheart,
Duchy of Misthaven, Evermist region, the Blackvale

Even with nothing to see, some windows are better left open . . .

The stagecoach moved at a snail's pace.

Much like the horse quartet, its drivers were used to traveling by night. The road they traversed was well-kept, its cobblestone surface singing a continuous melody under the carriage's wheels. Although the beasts showed early signs of fatigue, the drivers knew better than to stop, even on this most gentle of slopes.

The land around was covered by a thick, spectral fog that made it impossible to know the current elevation or that of the ground away from the road. So thick was the fog only locals and the occasional, frequent visitor knew the sound of the road under them would tell them if they were veering too far from its center. While that alone was important, the drivers' main focus was to protect the stagecoach's contents with their lives, if it ever came to that.

Inside the burnt-wood-colored vehicle they drove, a pair of young Darkholm women sat across from a third, whose hands held a satchel on her lap.

"Look, Lora," the youngest of the three stuck a hand outside the window, redirecting the fog that came in contact with it toward the inside of the vehicle.

"Have you never seen fog before, Charon?" Elleonora didn't smile.

"I have," she responded, "of course. But I have never been to Misthaven before. This," she stretched her hands outside the window, "this is, like, magical!"

"Well, it is nothing more than fog," her cousin said matter-of-factly.

"Elleonora, let her be," the third woman spoke. "Why not let her enjoy her first visit like we enjoyed our own?"

"But, Rowena," Elleonora protested, "we were children at that time. Charon needs to start growing up."

"She will, in due time. Growth cannot be forced, Elleonora," she paused, "well, it can be, but the end result might not be one that is most productive."

"Look, girls!" Charon breathed out cold steam. "I'm smoking!"

The stagecoach's advance halted. Outside, the drivers exchanged words with other riders.

"We stopped." Alarmed, Charon prolonged every vowel and exaggerated every syllable to purposely let out as much steam as possible. "Is *something* wrong?"

"We are almost upon the lord's castle," Rowena replied. "From here, the road becomes perilous. Lord Hecator's guards always meet us halfway to escort us safely to his keep."

"Oooohhhhhh," Charon offered a misty smile.

"Stop it, Charon," Elleonora scolded. "Lord Hecator is quite peculiar, even eccentric," she added.

"A Darkholm calling someone eccentric," Charon wondered aloud, "and of all the Darkholm, you, Elleonora!"

"Oh, believe me, I know. Wait and see," Elleonora responded, "once we get there. Please, Charon, behave and watch."

Addled, Charon looked back at Rowena, but Septem's daughter shrugged and smiled back at her cousins.

Moments later, the carriage resumed its pace. This time the song of the road made it clear they were moving faster. Rowena neared the window and beckoned to her cousins. "Come, Charon. This is something you surely do not want to miss."

Lady Charon placed a hand over her forehead and squinted. "What is it? I don't see anything."

"Because you keep talking," Elleonora scolded again.

"It is Misthaven in all its splendor," Rowena replied.

"But there's only mist," Charon complained.

"Be patient!" Elleonora said.

"Keep looking," Rowena added, "or your eyes will miss the beauty of the duchy of Misthaven."

Only a second later, the fog suddenly parted to reveal a bed of frozen clouds covering the landscape below. And there, right before their eyes, rose the imposing walls of the ducal castle, anchored on the hill beat by the waves of fog that could, or would, never move it.

"Wow," Charon exclaimed, "is all of the duchy like this?"

"Not all of it," Rowena replied, "but a large portion of it is."

"Where else do you think it obtained its name from?" was Elleonora's rhetoric.

"It's," Charon's eyes were filled with amazement, "it's like a miniature Darkholde,"

Rowena smiled upon seeing Charon's expression. From the corner of her eye, she could see Elleonora sitting quietly, pensive, thinking no one was watching her.

They drove around and finally came upon the main entrance of the Keep of the Watchtower, where they were received by the few servants of the ducal family.

"Master of Life," the head servant curtsied. She curtsied, "please forgive my Lady Laecanius for not being here to receive you, given her recent circumstances." She was in her late sixties, with the presence of a minor noble and the eyes of an eagle. Nayelle was the most trusted and longest-serving member of Lord Laecanius's household.

"Thank you kindly, Nayelle," Rowena responded, "but there is no need for an apology. You surely remember Elleonora," she continued, "and this is my other cousin, Charon."

"I am honored, my ladies. Your belongings will be unloaded from the carriage. In the meantime, you may all follow me," Nayelle indicated, leading them into the keep and through a long main hallway, its walls lined with detailed sculptures of legendary creatures and tall paintings of historical battle scenes. The exquisite pigments added most of what little color the castle had, for from the chandeliers to the servants' uniform, even the carpet on the floor, most were a shade of white, black, or gray.

Rowena and Elleonora walked calmly. Charon's eyes darted from one art piece to another, admiring the amount of detail that made the art almost come to life before their eyes.

"Master of Life, you'll be staying on the fourth floor of the Watchtower, on its west face. Lady Elleonora, Lady Charon, we have prepared rooms for you facing north and south."

"Thank you, Nayelle," Rowena replied, "but that is not necessary. The girls and I will lodge together."

"If that is your wish, Master, so it will be. I will have their luggage brought to your room then."

Ahead of them, the hallway shrank as it turned into a bridge, its walls disappearing into the cavernous innards of the Watchtower, its inside illuminated by a combination of infrequent candelabra and fewer, scattered windows that were largely out of reach. A winding staircase rose from the left, as the endless spine of the partially digested body of a dire serpent, connecting the bridge of every level, each bridge moving in a different direction but with the same central axis.

At the end of each bridge, a small receiving area akin to a balcony ended in a heavy double door. To each side of it, a row of tall, framed pictures hung on the wall before single doors led to other rooms.

"This will be your room." Nayelle stopped by one of the double doors. "If my ladies are in need of anything," she added, "my girls will be at your service at all times. The rest of the servants will not bother you and go about their business." Behind them, three servant girls had been following them quietly all along.

"Where can we find them if we were to need them," Charon asked.

"They'll take turns waiting outside your room," Nayelle responded.

"We certainly don't want to inconvenience you," Lady Charon added.

"Oh, those are strict rules set by Lord Hecator, my lady," the head servant interrupted. "Our lord is very private, and thus most of the keep is off limits, so my girls will be your guides."

"More like *watches*," Elleonora murmured.

"But don't worry," Nayelle continued, "It is no bother. It is the girls' job to attend to your needs."

The woman opened the double doors to a large room. Against a wall rested a large, curtained bed, with its delicate, embroidered coverlet, a lit fireplace, and a writing desk that sat close to a pair of glass doors leading to a balcony. Near the only window, a tub, its surface simple but perfectly polished.

Nayelle pointed at two of the servant girls. "The two of you may leave. Adja," she said to the third, "please fetch some towels and extra blankets for the ladies."

"My ladies," she addressed the cousins once more, "make yourselves ready. Dinner will be ready in about an hour."

"We do not need to have dinner," Elleonora responded, "we can have a small meal."

"We considered preparing a hot meal for you," the head servant replied, "but Lord Laecanius asked us to prepare dinner."

"There is no need for that," Rowena added. "It is quite late. A small, hot meal will be fine, I am sure," she looked back at both her cousins, who nodded and responded in agreement.

"Lord Laecanius insists we prepare a formal dinner, my ladies."

"Then, upon his insistence," Rowena replied graciously, "we have no option but to accept."

"That is good to hear," the head servant stated. "When you are ready," she readied to leave, "Adja will take you to the main dining hall on the third floor.

"Thank you," Charon smiled charmingly, "We'll be down as soon as we're able."

Nayelle raised her index finger. "Up, you mean."

"Up? Aren't we on the fourth floor?" Charon asked.

"You are," Nayelle replied, "the Watchtower's levels are counted from the top to bottom. Now, if you would excuse me for a little, I'll have your food prepared while I go check on my lord and lady."

"How is Lady Laecanius doing?" Rowena asked.

"Well," Nayelle took a deep breath, "she has been . . . unwell after the loss, if I may?"

"Will she meet us before we leave tomorrow?" Rowena asked curiously.

"Probably not, Master. It's been two months, and she still sees no one other than the lord or myself."

"I would very much like to see her if that is possible," Rowena added.

"I'll ask, but I do not know if it will be possible."

"I *insist*." Rowena's eyes shone, capturing all of the woman's attention. Nayelle lowered her head. Her eyes fixed on those of Septem's daughter.

"It will be done, Master." She didn't have to say more.

The dining table was long enough to seat fourteen people at one time. Its surface was so polished, it was either extremely well-taken care of or simply never used, Charon thought. Despite its size, it was dwarfed by the high ceilings and the many tall windows in the dining hall.

Beyond the end of the table, a second one rested in the less illuminated part of the room. If it wasn't because they couldn't see themselves sitting by it, they would've thought it was nothing more than a reflection.

The table was set for four. Rowena sat on one side, with the head of the table to her right. Charon sat on the other, flanked by Elleonora to her right and to the left, the empty seat of Lord Hecator at the head of the table.

Charon smiled. Growing up, she had always loved playing dress up. Now that she *had* things, she could play dress-up for real. A pair of small amethyst-studded rings hung from her earlobes. She wore her favorite dress. The gown was detailed, long, and form-fitting, even for her small breasts, with black feathers lining the shoulders as a short, protective cape.

"They are raven feathers," Her brother Azareth had told her upon gifting her the dress, "for ravens are intelligent creatures. While other birds seek attention with their colors, the raven, while ignored, finds the greatest treasures."

Elleonora's gown was of black velvet, with a slit on one side that revealed most of her leg on the opposing side of her sleeveless arm. Her long hair was picked up in a bun, with a few wild strands that decided to escape its confines. 'Much like her hair,' Charon smiled, 'I'm sure Lora wishes she could tear her garb off and run wild.'

Rowena's dress was more subdued, at least from a distance, Charon knew. Her decolletage and neck could still be seen under the layer of lace and silk that covered most of her body.

"This is such a beautiful place," Charon spoke to her cousins. "In some ways, it reminds me of home."

The door opened, allowing a small number of servants to bring forth the food.

They were served yellow apple and corn soup and pea broth with freshly baked mushroom bread. Some was served on the duke's plate and covered. It was accompanied by a cup of Blood Tea served at room temperature.

"Please, go ahead and enjoy your dinner," Adja instructed.

Rowena swirled the cup in her hand, taking a quick sniff before swirling again, "We will wait for the Duke Laecanius, Adja. Thank you."

"It might take him a while to join you," the servant girl replied, "I was told to let you know to please start before the food gets cold."

Charon looked at both Elleonora, who shrugged ever so little, and Rowena, who nodded in acceptance before sampling her drink. Rowena stood up and raised her cup. "May House Laecanius prosper tenfold as we thank them for the provision."

"*In Tenebris nos*," Elleonora raised hers, her words echoed by Charon.

The soup was followed by spicy coriander balsamic tomatoes, raspberry-scented glazed rack of lamb over orange peel salad, and a side of mashed zucchini. These were also served on the duke's plate and covered too.

The three began eating quietly, the servants walking in and out of the room to switch their plates as they sampled each item. Soon after, it was Charon's curiosity that broke the silence. "Rowena, can you tell us about Lady Laecanius?"

"Surely," Rowena responded, "she took the name from her husband, Duke Hecator Laecanius. Lady Kenna Laecanius was born to a humble family in a small village of Misthaven. She was young when she met her husband and came to live at the Watchtower by his side."

"What happened to her? Why is she not well?" Charon inquired.

"She was advanced in her pregnancy, and despite every precaution, she lost her child."

"Oh no," Charon exclaimed.

"It was her third lost pregnancy, the first one that she almost brought to term."

"That's terrible," Lady Charon grabbed Elleonora's arm nervously. She must feel horrible." Elleonora, in turn, lowered her head.

"Indeed." Rowena's words were like a soothing balm. "Some girls have no other dream than to give their husband an heir. Procreation should never be what gives them value, but rather only a part of who they are, and not what defines them."

Upon her words, Nayelle entered the dining room and lowered her head. "Pardon my interruption, my ladies, but my lord humbly asks you to please forgive him. He won't be joining you for dinner tonight."

While the news could have been seen as an insult by other nobles, it wasn't so for the Darkholm, or at least even if it was meant as one, they did not seem bothered by it. They just took their time enjoying a warm dinner.

"Charon, wake up. Charon!"

"What? What is it?" Her eyes opened wide, alarmed upon hearing Elleonora's voice and hands shaking her body to wake her up from her deep slumber.

"You are snoring," Elleonora turned away, pulling the sheet toward her.

Rubbing her eyes, Charon complained, "You could have just moved me, Lora."

"I tried, but you would not wake up." Her cousin's very long, black hair lay over the sheets between them, where Rowena's body should have been resting.

"Lora," Charon called to no response. "Elleonora." She shook her cousin this time.

"What?" the dark-haired cousin sat exasperatedly.

"Rowena's not back."

"She always takes her time when we come here," Elleonora turned away again, tucking herself between the sheets, "get used to it."

Charon saw her cousin fall sound asleep, seemingly unpreoccupied. "I'm worried for her." Upon receiving no response, she crawled over the sheets toward her cousin again, "Lora, I'm worried for her!"

"Charon!" Elleonora raised her voice from under the soft fabric. "She is fine, I am sure. Now do not talk to me. I want to sleep!"

"I'm sorry," Charon responded, embarrassed. She waited for her cousin to fall fast asleep and sat near the center of the bed, playing with Elleonora's hair, her fidgety fingers forming loose braids and placing them side by side each other.

After some time, she rolled around the bed, looked around the room, and played with the braids some more.

Having given up on trying to fall asleep again, Charon grimaced as she tip-toed toward the door to avoid making any noise that would wake up her cousin. Her pale hands parted the heavy wood. In the small receiving area outside their room, Adja knitted, sitting on a small stool.

"May I be of service?" She placed her tools in a small basket by her side, stepping toward the noblewoman.

"I can't sleep," Charon answered, "do you have something that can help me sleep, some tea, perhaps?"

"Certainly," Adja responded, "we have red chamomile and, I believe, some lavender. Which one would you prefer?"

"Hmm, red chamomile is better for sleeplessness. I'll have that, thank you."

"It will be my pleasure. Goat or cow milk with it?"

"Yes, goat, please, warm," Charon smiled broadly, "and cinnamon."

"My pleasure," the girl curtsied, "I'll bring it to your room as soon as it's ready."

"I'll wait here. My cousin wants to sleep, and I don't want to wake her up." Charon lowered her voice to almost a whisper before she continued, "She needs her beauty rest."

"Yes, ma'am."

After climbing the flight of stairs, the servant girl disappeared from sight. Charon tapped the rail rhythmically with her fingertips, accompanied by her moving lips that whispered an unintelligible song. She raised her hand and waved, imagining herself surrounded by a crowd of admirers, and she shook her head and smiled fully.

'Pictures!' her attention was drawn to the frames on the walls, 'let's see some pictures.' With two wide steps, she closed in, resting her behind against the metal rail.

Charon's eyes opened in fascination. They looked at every detail of the frame's design, of the man who stood near the center of the image, a middle-aged man with graying hair and a short beard, who had eyes of a light, almost gray, blue. He held the hands of his wife, a young and beautiful woman of dark complexion and hopeful eyes. *Laudelein Laecanius and Heliga Laecanius, year 771 CL,* read the small plaque at its base. 'I love their clothes,' Charon thought before moving to the next.

Saxeken and Astrix Laecanius, year 813 CL. Saxeken Laecanius sat in a comfortable chair, his legs crossed, a smoking pipe in his hand. While a man of advancing age, he was well-groomed, clean-shaven, and handsome. There was a smirk on his face captured so perfectly that Charon almost blushed. Perhaps it was because he was seated, but his wife appeared to be of average height, maybe even tall. Astrix's eyes were quite slanted as if she were smiling mirthfully, even though her expression was more like a frown.

Charon then skipped a few pictures before another one caught her attention. *Axellen and Istelle Laecanius, 719 CL.* Lady Laecanius's blonde hair was blown by the wind as she stood off to the side, waving her husband away. Lord Laecanius, in heavy plate mail, stood by his warhorse. His chest plate was engraved with Aligrand's original three-tailed dragon on the left and Darkholm's vulture on the right. At its center, the Watchtower stood proudly, where the gray owl of Misthaven rested. While his wife seemed very young, Axellen appeared quite old himself.

'Was he really much older than her, or did service age him so?' Charon asked herself. Still, there was something *strange* about him, about his icy blue eyes. While the scene was so emotionally powerful, his eyes seemed to speak much louder than the scene itself.

The present year was 986 of the Church of Light, which was year 68 of Blackheart, she remembered with a giggle, and yet all these paintings were so well-preserved.

Charon took a few steps back to look at the images. They were all different, the scenes as different as the wife of each of the lords, while the lords themselves shared something in common, but what was it? She couldn't really tell at first until she realized there was something in their eyes of blue, in the way the lords looked back at the spectator. In their frozen silence, they spoke volumes—of what she couldn't tell, but they all seemed to tell a similar, mysterious story.

Her musing was interrupted by something important 'Sugar! How could I forget?'

Charon turned back and ran up the stairs toward the third floor in search of Adja when she thought she heard a muffled noise from behind that halted her in her tracks.

What was that? She turned, wondering from behind which door the sound had come.

Huh? Is that a baby's cry? Driven by curiosity, Charon hurried, passing by the double doors and the other pictures on the wall toward a single wooden door.

The crying continued. It seemed almost desperate. She looked around, hoping to see anyone she could ask to assist. One thing, though, she couldn't do. She could not stand idly when there was someone in need of help. Actually, most of the time, she simply couldn't stand idly at all.

She grabbed the owl-shaped handle and opened the door, its dense wood groaning under its weight.

Behind it, a chamber dimly lit except for what little light entered through small spaces in the shuttered windows. The room, as far as Charon could see, was dusty; not just the floor, but everything from the windowpanes themselves, the armoires, and chairs were covered in thick, gray dust.

Befuddled, Charon approached the white oaken crib slowly, for it was there where she could hear the desperate shrill of the baby's endless crying coming from. Aside from the film of dust that covered every inch of its surface, inside the crib, there was nothing.

"Charon," Rowena's voice called from the door.

"I'm here, Rowena," she answered.

"Are you alright?" Rowena grabbed her cousin's hand, noticing it was cold and sweaty.

"I think so, yes," she responded, having realized the noise had stopped the moment she heard her cousin's voice. "I just heard something and came to check. Did you not hear it?"

"What did you hear? Tell me."

"Hmm, maybe it's nothing," Charon responded. "I can't sleep. It's surely just my mind playing tricks on me. I had asked for a cup of tea to help me sleep." Her confused eyes met Rowena's inquiring ones.

"Well, you cannot just go to sleep now," Rowena said. "Go, get dressed, and meet me upstairs." She let Charon's hand go and proceeded along the bridge and up the stairs toward the second floor.

Charon obeyed, but felt a need to ask, "Where are we going?"

"I think it is time for you to meet the duke."

—————— ✦✦✦✦✦ ——————

Every step she climbed sent an increasingly weird sensation down her spine, a sensation that could only be described as that of being watched.

But she continued her pace, trailing Rowena, who either did not feel the same or was already used to it.

If it weren't for the confidence in every step of her cousin, Charon would have turned back. Many times before, she would have turned back.

While her brother Azareth had been a mast that helped her sail stand, she felt Rowena had become the helm that allowed her ship to sail.

Charon enjoyed many things. She was easily entertained, but one thing she truly loved, no matter how silly or naive she sometimes inevitably was that Rowena didn't seem to be bothered by her antics, by anything, actually, and that's something Charon looked up to.

'One day, I'll be like her,' she thought, and she ignored what bothered her, and she followed.

They came upon a small alcove where Rowena's satchel had been hanging by the door. She knocked briefly, and the oaken surface moved to reveal the presence of Nayelle, "It is good to see you again, my ladies. Lord Laecanius is expecting you."

The room was circular, covering most of one entire floor of the tower. In it, dozens of shelves holding books, scrolls, and desiccated animals that could be either trophies or mementos. Near the center of the room, where pillars held the ceiling in place, several lecterns faced the entrance, each one holding an open tome. To their side, a small table with a few chairs, a large magnifying glass, and a pile of books of varying sizes.

An unseen man's voice spoke, "Master of Life." Charon had imagined the duke to possess a tall, imposing figure. Instead, the man who stood up from a seat behind the lecterns had his head completely covered in gray, as was his pronounced mustache and short beard. He placed a quill in a vial and let his monocle dangle to the side as he bowed slightly to Rowena. She could see he was of advancing age, perhaps around seventy, but still dressed elegantly, for one being inside his own private chambers. "It is always good to see you."

"Greetings, Duke Laecanius," Rowena answered, "please, allow me to first introduce you to my cousin, Lady Charon Darkholm."

The duke flicked his wrist as quickly as the snap of a whip. His fingers caught the monocle and placed it over his eye. Tilting his head up, he looked down as he approached Charon, his glaring eyes of sapphire on her. He studied every inch of her body, her face, the deep scars along her shoulder, intensely, as if staring at her and through her.

Somehow, the scrutiny in his eyes made Charon feel that the wounds on her heart inflicted by the rejection of the world hadn't fully healed.

For more than a few long moments that seemed endless, Duke Laecanius stood there in silence. He then bowed to Charon, his unblinking eyes fixed on her, "My lady."

"My pleasure," she curtsied as best as she could through her feeling of deep inadequacy.

"It is not our wish to interrupt you, Lord Laecanius," Rowena slightly raised her hand.

"It's nothing of utmost importance, I must say, Master of Life," he stated.

With what she had learned about music, Charon could tell that, even if by little, the tone toward her cousin was different. "Your time is precious. My work is nothing important enough that would make me have you wait."

"Truly, Lord Laecanius, we can wait," Rowena insisted. "In the meantime, do you mind if we set up on this table?"

"I do not." His response was followed by the duke hurriedly walking back to the libram and his quill, "use what you need. I promise you this will take me not more than a few minutes."

Rowena proceeded to open her satchel, from where she produced vials, herbs, and instruments. She carefully placed them along the table, signaling for Charon to assist her. Charon, in turn, stood by her side but hesitated upon noticing Nayelle was still inside the room, watching them as quietly as a midnight owl.

"Do not mind her." While his attention was on his writing, the nobleman's eyes were still on Charon. He spoke in a most cold but collected manner, "Nayelle is a most trusted retainer of mine. She is close to me, closer even than my own wife."

Charon nodded in response and directed her attention to her cousin, "What shall I help you with, Rowena."

"Here, these need to be ground."

"Saffron, Rhodiola, and . . . what are these?" Charon grabbed a thick, dried stalk between two fingers.

"Sunflower stalks," Rowena responded. She produced a small, black wooden box from inside the satchel in which Charon noted small runes were etched.

"They must be ground as fine as possible," Rowena's voice interrupted her musing.

"Nayelle, we need hot water, about four ounces of it," the Master of Life instructed.

"Boiling?"

"Not quite," she explained, "it would burn these herbs. Just a bare simmer would do."

Rowena set the box aside and started working on grinding her own herbs. Dried *herb of grace*, a pinch of *wabital*, cinnamon, and hawthorn, Charon noted. She also took a gum-like paste and rolled it upon her palm before mashing it against the powder she had just formed.

"Rowena," Charon asked, "what are you treating here? These are used for . . . melancholia."

"That is right, of the severe type," Rowena responded.

"Lord Laecanius. I met with your wife earlier, as you may already know. After the loss of your child, she has been afflicted with severe melancholia. It is not easy to treat, but I believe this formulation is stronger than others of its kind."

"Thank you," the nobleman nodded, "always. Master of Life," he continued, "Have you ever attended the Festival of the Cotton Moon?"

"I do not recall having ever attended, Lord Laecanius."

"I do not know if you were aware, but tomorrow is the date when it is celebrated." He looked out a window to the darkness beyond. "It is small, compared to celebrations in Coldforge, of course," he continued, "but the locals are very proud of it. Surely it would honor our people if you could spare some time to go."

Hecator Laecanius

"It sounds fascinating, Rowena," Charon interjected. "This is such a beautiful place, full of history and culture." Seeking to warm him up to her, she then directed her attention to the lord, "Will you be attending, Lord Laecanius?"

"By the gods, no! I rather stay here with my wife." He froze instead. "Besides, I have attended many times before."

Charon smiled back at Rowena, "I would love to go if possible."

"Time is not a commodity we have, dear cousin, but it is possible. It is best to discuss this over breakfast. Let us return to our work. Now, what are we treating here, Charon?" Rowena quizzed her, showing her what she had ground in her own mortar.

"Hmmm, don't tell me . . ." Charon sniffed, studied the dust, and smiled. She was thinking hard, but her fleeting thoughts didn't quite let her find the answer. There were so many possibilities. "Would Elleonora know?"

"Yes," Rowena smiled, "she definitely knew when I asked her long ago. Now, tell me."

"Okay. Let me think . . . hmmm. Oh, it is at the tip of my tongue. Laaaa . . . hmmm . . . Soooooo . . . " She looked into Rowena's eyes for a hint of agreement but saw none. "Ah, I have it! Memory and . . . fertility!" She was embarrassed by her outburst. Fertility problems were nothing to be celebrated, she had learned. She thought of her adoptive mama and how she had suffered most of her life without a child until Charon had come to her.

"Have we thought of giving something to Lady Laecanius for fertility too? It could increase the chances."

"Not at this time," Rowena replied, "Lady Kenna is quite young. Yes, she has lost several pregnancies, but what is most important right now is stabilizing her, making sure she feels well before she thinks about another one."

"She's twenty," the duke added. To Charon, it all made sense. The duke more than tripled his wife's age, she thought. It was likely he who needed the most help.

"Lord Laecanius," Charon took a step toward him, "so you have never had a child?"

He looked back at her in silence.

"Oh, I'm sorry." She placed a hand over her mouth.

"Only one, Eukhtor." He suddenly stopped writing and stared back at her. "From my first wife."

"Will we have the honor of meeting him?" she asked, "Is he around?"

"No." His reply was like a sudden strike. "He died."

"Oh, I'm ... so ... sorry," looking for the right words to say, Charon clasped her own hands.

"An old man forgets many things," he left the libram and walked toward the pair, "but while he may grow weaker or sickly, his true curse lies in not being able to choose what to forget. Over the years, I have forgotten most of the time I spent with him, but the one thing I can never seem to forget is the pain of the loss. I will never forget he was murdered ... my only son."

Nayelle returned, finding the nobleman had walked toward the table where the girls had been working in silence since his revelation. He studied Charon's hands and how they gave the mixture to Rowena and followed each of the Master of Life's moves, how she poured an exact number of drops on each vial. She stirred them carefully before presenting him with the two vials she had prepared.

"Lord Laecanius," Rowena spoke as Nayelle approached, seeking to listen for the instructions she would have to remember, "these are for you." She presented him with the small box on the table and the vial she had prepared. "You will need to pinch this sticky substance and let it dissolve in your mouth before you eat. Let us start with once every week. These herbs have been used to protect mental acuity. Now, when you are ready to have an encounter with your wife, you can take it that day, too, regardless of timing.

"Lady Laecanius is suffering from severe melancholia," she continued, adding the water to dilute the vials' contents, "likely worsened after this third loss. Have her take two drops of this medicine under the tongue every other day prior to breakfast and supper. She will also need walks under the sun at least once a day. Just as important, she will need support and understanding, as much of it as possible."

"Understood," Hecator spoke, "it will be done."

Rowena signaled Charon, and they started packing her satchel.

Charon walked around the table toward Duke Hecator and, without hesitation, grabbed his hands. The Darkholm girl looked into his eyes. "Keep trying," Charon said, "don't lose hope."

The wizened man stared into Charon's eyes with his own penetrating blue eyes. "I have tried to produce an heir of my own blood. I have failed many times, twenty-seven times actually, since long before you were born. Now, am I giving up? Never. I am not giving up. I will have a child, be it with my wife or with as many women as it takes."

Even after leaving the study, Charon played the scene in her head. While it had been a great room, a collection her brother would likely find fascinating, nothing about it spoke to her like the duke's situation had. And, while perhaps she would never understand the strangeness in his thoughts, she felt the one thing she had come to understand was his pain.

⋅⋅✦✦✦✦⋅⋅

The escort had left them, so the carriage slowed its pace as it entered the fog.

The Darkholm girls had finished an early lunch, having skipped breakfast due to Charon and Rowena still having been in bed. Elleonora, who usually found a reason to complain or a mistake to point at, this time welcomed the chance to sleep in.

While she was never nosy, she was curious as to why Charon seemed so quiet this morning. She first looked at Rowena, whose eyes were closed, before she contemplated Charon. The youngest of the three had eaten little before they left.

At first, Elleonora had thought she was still sleepy, but then she saw Charon looking out the carriage window quietly, her head resting on its frame. Once the Watchtower disappeared, Charon lowered her head, her fingers slowly stroking strands of her cascading white hair.

What happened? Elleonora wondered. She considered reaching outside the window to redirect some fog inside and perhaps make Charon smile, but that would be uncharacteristic of her. It would be, and perhaps feel, forced.

Something within Elleonora wanted to ask, but she had learned painful thoughts and memories are sometimes better left untouched. So, in the end, she didn't reach out; she didn't ask.

'This is why I chose not to see Lady Laecanius,' Elleonora thought, her eyes on Charon, 'for what could I do to make her feel better about her terrible, pitiful situation? What could I possibly say when no one knows I have lost pregnancies of my own, and nothing makes me feel better myself?'

At that moment, Charon looked up at her, but she quickly avoided her gaze. Her eyes went instead to Rowena, whose own eyes of gold, she found, were looking back at her.

The carriage's advance stopped. The fog had started receding for what little time it did near the capital of Misthaven, so this was the perfect time for the driver to adjust the reins of his beasts.

Rowena smiled back at her cousins, her finger pointing out the window, "Look, girls, is it fate or what?"

Outside the window, the three could see a white, wooden crossroads sign. If they continued onward, they would reach Darkholm and would arrive home within a week. If they turned, as the sign read, they would reach Hvitfast.

"There is that festival in Hvitfast. Would you girls care to go?" Rowena smiled.

Charon's eyes opened wide, her expression one of longing. Catching herself, she lowered her head a little and nodded once, shyly biting her lower lip.

She knew Rowena would be, most likely, indifferent. Elleonora, on the contrary, did not want to go. While she had never been to that one festival, to Elleonora, it was just another unnecessary celebration, a waste of time when there was so much to be done.

'In addition,' she thought, 'a night festival would add at least two more unnecessary days of travel.' Right now, all she wanted was to see Gustavus, to feel him close so that his strong, loving arms could embrace her and help her forget the unrelenting, silent pain of her own loss. She knew that if she wanted to see him, he would be even more desperate to see her, to love her, to vent his frustrations on the ear she was always ready to lend him.

'But this time,' her eyes gravitated toward Charon's sad eyes, 'I guess he will have to wait!'

THE COTTON MOON

Location: Kingdom of Blackheart,
Duchy of Misthaven, Evermist region

That day he found out who Astas truly was.

That same afternoon Ealas left the small capital toward Hvitfast, in the nearby Blackvale, following the well-maintained cobblestone road around the fields for several hours.

The hamlet rested on a small hill by the edge of the cotton fields, close enough to the immense presence of the Watchtower but far enough to appear as an ungrateful child escaping its mother's embrace. They were separated by the mountain that served as the castle's base stand and several miles of roads, for the only bridge that left the castle's entrance stood elevated and diametrically opposed to the small village.

Standing elevated and away from the shadow of the castle, the small village allowed Lucris[1] to dispel some of the fog.

Ealas felt a strange sensation when the misty tendrils parted, and he caught sight of the letters on the sign that read Hvitfast.

Finally here.

He walked forth expecting some semblance of an entrance, but aside from the piece of old wood that carried the locality's name, there seemed to be none. All he found was a small cotton farmer's village, its few buildings resting among the mist. Its streets were busy, with enough people to fill every structure and then more.

'These are either servants and workers of the Watchtower looming nearby,' he thought, 'or farmers and their large families. With so little to do here, making and rearing children would seem like a pastime.'

In the end, he learned they were both, plus visitors from nearby communities and the occasional musician who had come to join in the festivities.

But there was something he wanted to learn much more than that. He wanted to learn about Astas.

For that, he first had to ask around who was local. Ealas had predicted that in such a small and simple place, everyone would have certainly known one another. But the prediction had proven wrong he found out, for he couldn't find one person who had known or even heard of her, except for that one woman who answered, "Astas? Yes, I knew her, but out of respect, I'll speak not of her. You will need to ask Imbalt, the town healer when he returns from the capital today. That was his sister."

That woman's words had given him hope.

Evening came, and with it, the fog around Hvitfast grew denser. It would have enveloped all if not for the myriad lanterns lit around the small town, some planted atop posts that had been readied for the festival, others resting over barrels or crates, others carried by the hands of the populace.

Ealas had tried to get a room for the night, but the only establishment was more than full and, thus, unavailable. He had been asking for any other possible options when the music started.

Like a flaming river, the lamps in the hands of the many flowed in one direction, summoned by the rapid beating of drums and the bright whistling of flutes. They hurried toward the edge of the small town, the only place that could accommodate everyone present. Ealas followed suit, joining the hundreds of people agglomerated, ready to watch the opening ceremony.

"Blood of Misthaven and people from all over," the mayor, carrying a small chest between his hands, raised his voice. "Kaeris is showing!" He pointed his finger at the rising moon, its pale face only a sliver over the horizon. The people cheered.

"Now, let us be always thankful for everything we have," he continued, "but today we thank Kaeris herself, for her care, for her provision, and we celebrate in her honor in this festival of Kaeris's Bounty!"

Again, they raised their voices joyously.

"And now, the moment we have all been waiting for," the mayor opened up the chest and pulled out a small piece of white fabric. "When this piece of fine fabric, produced with our very own cotton, touches the ground, the spirits of the wisps will visit us," he momentarily looked at a large drape standing to the side, "and our festival will commence!"

To the company of drum rolls, he delicately took the piece and threw it up in the air.

The whole crowd watched, mesmerized, as the fabric danced and swayed in the air, falling slowly toward the ground below.

The crowd fell silent for the last few seconds expectantly until the moment when the fabric touched the ground, sending them cheering in excitement at the official start of the festival. Their celebratory hands filled the air with white, and so did the moon, its beams playfully caressing the flying wisps as it joined the people in celebration.

To the folkloric tune of flutes, percussion, and applause, a group of people came from behind the standing drape. Each had a costume made up either completely or adorned with pieces of cotton.

A woman had a tall, puffy wig, a man with a bushy beard, and yet another woman with a large dress completely made of raw cotton. Among others, a young man juggled lightweight orange-sized balls, followed by a puppeteer with two cotton serpent-like puppets he spoke through, greeting youngsters and adults alike.

After the parade, the night was full of games, shouting, and drinks. Ealas himself laughed and drank some but still kept his participation to a minimum. He was focused on finding a moment to speak to Imbalt, who he had found was unavailable.

Well into the night, the full face of Kaeris flew high above, its cold presence warming everyone's hearts. It hovered in its own celestial cotton field of clouds. Upon reaching its zenith, a bachelor raised his voice, summoning the collecting crowd that promptly formed a circle around him.

"Ladies, gentlemen, beasts, and well, everyone else," he shouted to the laughing delight of those present, "as Kaeris has reached its most observant moment, we must show our gratitude for this year's bounty, so that next year will be even more fruitful! To Kaeris's Bounty!"

Those present raised their voices and drinks, and some even raised their children or drunken companions. This time the music was unlike anything Ealas had heard before, an airy melody full of merriment both wonderfully harmonious and of high complexity; it was a tune as rich as those of the noblest orchestras of maesters of the grand cathedrals back home, and it all happened here, in a small, poor, unpretentious hamlet where people not just celebrated, but lived.

Two lines of a dozen peasants, each garbed in deep-coal-colored costumes, joined the bachelor in a dancing display. In the meantime, Ealas's eyes found what he sought right there, at the other side of the circle. Imbalt stood there watching, smiling, clapping lightly, tilting his head to speak to a female companion that, unlike Imbalt's simple, white tabard and breeches, was dressed in a slim gown the color of the night sky.

'What better time than now,' Ealas thought, walking toward Imbalt, circling the dancing group, and lowering his head to avoid obstructing the view of those in the front.

He was only a few steps away when he felt a soft hand grab his own and pull him toward the revelry.

"Where do *you* think you're going?" a damsel's voice questioned from under an oversized, puffy cotton wig. Ealas shook his head, even lifted his palm, but the girl pulled and signaled the crowd to help her, and they gladly did, for he found himself standing near the middle, confused, trying to figure out how to join or how to leave.

While he believed he could dance, he was used to the planned, choreographed dancing of the courts, to the balls of knights and nobles, to the eyes of the world set on him and his perfect display. He studied the scene. The participants held hands, dancing in the center of the applauding crowd, shifting, switching, and turning, laughing all the way.

Among them, the damsel smiled gleefully, spinning around him with that wig that gently scratched his face. Of everyone, she was the one who seemed to enjoy the dance the most, for even when she did not know the steps, she just improvised, and her contagious joy made the crowd acclaim her, perhaps believing the damsel was the protagonist in this dance.

They joined hands with the dancers and circled around, switched, clapped, turned, and then switched hands once more. At the first opportunity, while they clapped, Ealas walked backward to remove himself. He turned to face the crowd and realized he was now further away from Imbalt than when he had started.

Now in line, the dancers rotated around the bachelor, their elbows interlocked as if he was the axis of a giant machine. At the very end of the line, the damsel's legs moved faster, but faster were her clever hands that grabbed Ealas and locked his elbow in. Driven by the momentum, he had to choose between running back to the dance floor or ending up sprawling along the ground.

Ealas found himself dancing again. He turned and spun a few times, and seeing the first opening toward Imbalt, he ducked and readied to leave. But the damsel was faster than he was. She jumped and stood in his way, her arms spread wide as if seeking to capture an escaping pet, her big hair blocking his sight.

She grabbed both his hands and pulled, sending the world in motion as the pair rotated in place.

In that dizzying moment, he truly saw her; a graceful girl, squinting and giggling through a wide smile, with a spirit as beautiful as Ileina's but with deep-rooted scars covering the side of her neck and arm. Catching himself rudely staring at her old wounds, Ealas promptly smiled and looked into her eyes. They opened to reveal irises the color of the morning sun and eyes that smiled because they did not notice his judgment or because they simply did not care. The motion sent her cotton wig flying, and from under it, long hair of the same color trailed in the air.

The damsel let his hands go. The imbalance forced Ealas to kneel on the ground. While the world was spinning around him, the girl still danced by herself, laughing and prancing as she lifted her arms. Through his blurred vision, he could see that despite the defects he had noticed, her skin appeared perfect, and she was simply beautiful.

After the world around him had ceased spinning, Ealas found himself at the feet of the healer, as if fate itself had finally decided to let him continue his journey.

"Imbalt?" Ealas asked, dusting his clothes.

"Yea?" the man responded.

"You're the healer in town," the nobleman added.

"The same," the man smiled at his silent companion, "how can I be of service, lad?"

"We have not met before," he responded through eyes filled with excitement, "but we have both known Astas."

The physician's smile froze. He looked to either side of him before addressing the inquisitive visitor again. "I'm sorry, but I don't understand."

"Your sister, right?"

"Yea, I lost my sister."

"I know, and I know everything about her. I have been around her for over twenty summers," Ealas interrupted. "I know it's a lot to take in, so why don't we perhaps speak of it in the morn."

"Hey, lad," sighing, Imbalt placed his hand over his eyes, "I think you are mistaken."

"Astas, from Hvitfast," Ealas insisted, "she was your sister, right?"

"Yea, she was. My sister died."

"I know," Ealas interjected, nodding respectfully, "she passed earlier this year, and therefore I—"

Quickly removing the hand from his face, Imbalt turned to face the nobleman, his voice trying to hide his irritation. "Is this your idea of a bad joke, lad? Yea, she passed earlier this year. She passed away two days ago!"

Confused, Ealas could only listen. "You couldn't have known her," Imbalt added, "she lived with me and my wife for most of her seventeen years. While she was born right, she developed contortions that left her unable to even feed herself and that even my best medicine could not cure. We still cared for and loved her, though."

Imbalt's profound sadness showed on his grimace, on the lowering of his head, on the words he spoke to his companion. He bowed to her respectfully. "Master," Imbalt spoke through his broken voice, "I beg you to please forgive me, but my heart is heavy. I would like to take my leave if it doesn't offend you."

That moment was one Ealas would not easily forget. A man whose hair was graying. An aging, experienced scholarly physician bowing, asking, without pretense, for permission from a woman who had likely lived less than half his own life. That woman with raven-black hair appeared to merge with her fine gown of the same color. And he had called her master, and he had shown respect.

Her blood-red lips parted, but not to express words of comfort nor to give an order or an idea. In a way Ealas found unexpected, they said nothing. They only drew a warm smile, a hearth in which the hurting man could find solace before she nodded approvingly.

With a deep bow, completely ignoring Ealas's presence, Imbalt then walked away.

"Imbalt!" The nobleman outstretched his arm, taking a step toward the physician.

"It would be best if you let him go." The woman's voice spoke softly from behind him.

Ealas's eyes were fixed on the retreating figure of Imbalt. "I believe it's best if I apologize."

"But maybe what is truly best is to give him some time." The smaller figure of the woman now stood by his side. "There are times when even the healer needs time to heal."

Her words rang true.

How much different would the scene have been if he had listened to Imbalt first, if he hadn't thought his Astas was the only one with that name? he wondered.

"Could you please offer an apology on my behalf?" Ealas asked as he now watched the white-haired girl dancing with a child under the light of the moon that disappeared behind a cloudy wall.

"I could, certainly, but I shall not." Her words were unapologetic. While they were calm and proper, they shook Ealas, leaving him speechless. "If I were to ask him, he would likely forgive you out of respect for me, not out of the wish of his heart. Hard as it might be, the words must come from the mouth of the offender whenever possible so that a gap can truly be bridged and amends be made."

"Wisely said." Finding value in her words, Ealas questioned, "When do you suggest, then, I do it?"

"No one can answer that for you. Only you can know when you are truly ready."

Barely a few feet away from the pair, barrels of ale crashed on the ground, their contents splashing everywhere. Ealas jumped aside, easily dodging most of the liquid insult to his clothes. At the same time, the woman took a step back. The sudden reaction forced her to bump into a passerby, who tripped a woman into a drunken, married man with a very jealous wife. Both the tripped woman and the wife began arguing immediately after, and after a barrage of insults and screams, a brawl ensued.

A man punched a second, and a woman clawed at someone's face. Others around them joined in, forcing guards to jump in order to stop the celebration from turning into a bloody mess.

Seeing cups and fists flying, the gentleman in Ealas grabbed the woman by the wrist. "Come with me," he said.

Feeling her hesitation, he insisted, "I'll make sure you're safe." Nodding, she held his hand fast and followed away from the commotion and toward the adjacent cotton field.

Despite holding his hand out, Ealas still lowered his head as they ran through the foggy vegetation to avoid the tall plants from hitting his face. For a few dozen feet, they ran before he felt her tug to stop him so that she could catch her breath.

"Are you alright?" Ealas asked, concerned.

"I am, thank you," she grabbed the bottom of her gown, her hands wringing off its wet hem. "Are you?"

He could have said he wasn't and shown her the scratches he had suffered to protect her, but he would likely seem stupid or weak. "I am fine. Your dress, however . . ."

"It is but ale. I am not concerned," the maiden interjected. "You just ran into the field without a second thought, unaware of the potential dangers."

"Dangers?" he laughed, remembering Meika's words. "There's only farmers and whispdrakes here, and well, the farmers are busy back there," grinning, he pointed a finger toward the hamlet they had left behind.

"That just leaves the whispdrakes and us," he said with the confidence of an expert in the field he barely knew anything about. "Other than that, one can never find any danger lurking in the cotton field."

"It is always never until it happens. There is no time until the first time."

"True . . . but well, at least there won't be any danger while I'm around," Ealas said proudly. "Hey, are you local?"

"I am not."

"Have you ever seen the whispdrakes?"

"The whispdrakes? Why do you ask?" she questioned.

"Then let me show you something," he added. His hands picked up a few small pieces of soft cotton, as he had seen the farmers do, which he rolled in his palms. "Watch," the nobleman then winked at her and stood motionless, his elbows bent, palms face up, the balls of raw white resting on them, and he waited.

After a quiet minute, she inquired, "Is something supposed to happen?"

"Wait and see," he responded, "if one is a good person, they will come and feed off one's own hands."

Where are they? Ealas cursed under his breath.

Unless the stories I was told are just not true, the whispdrakes should have been all over me right now. With each passing second, he felt increasingly stupid.

"Perhaps you are not as good of a man as you think?" she jested.

Almost giving up, he started lowering his palms when he heard a rustle. "Wait, do you hear that?"

"What exactly?" she responded.

"It's coming," hearing more movement, he breathed in deep again, "look at me now. Just look." He sought to cause an everlasting impression on the woman, on that moment when they stood in the middle of a field by a forgotten hamlet, in a land covered by a perpetual, ghastly mist, a place so insignificant the moon itself had, on its most special night, shied away from.

But the everlasting impression was what *he* got, for it was then that, as if to prove it was still her night, Kaeris showed. Her spherical body emerged from the bed of clouds and shone down upon them. The moon's frigid beams parted the fog between the two, and Ealas, for the first time, clearly saw Rowena Darkholm's face looking back at him.

A soft stream of raven black hair parted, falling to each side perfectly, quietly. Her lips smiled, a playful smile of crimson. While her face was as perfect as a smooth, porcelain moon, her eyes were bright as the sun and precious like the purest, molten gold.

Hers were eyes that told him nothing but knew everything and then more. A golden paradise of secrets, where the darkness of the world and the wisdom of ages lived in perpetual harmony.

Effortless intensity, the charming conflagration. The unforgiving charm that made him feel weightless.

But that moment did not last.

Just as the rustling at first increased, it stopped, and right behind the woman, another female came to view. She was just as young, though slimmer, her hair much longer and just as dark, but her citrine eyes were cold and somber.

"Here you are!" the newcomer spoke, the tone in her voice telling she was closely acquainted with Ealas's companion.

Rowena stepped aside, perhaps so that the other woman could see him too, for as soon as she captured his visage, her pupils dilated, and her tone changed to one of abject formality. "Master . . ."

"Yes?" Rowena responded though she kept her eyes on Ealas.

"We are ready."

"Let us take our leave, then." Upon her words, the newcomer left the same way she had come. Rowena started to walk away, but her almond-shaped eyes were fixed on the static figure of the man.

He was left completely alone at that moment.

When she departed, so did the moon, and not even a small creature or a sound came to keep him company. If it was because of having seen something special in him or due to his sheer foolishness, he couldn't tell, but the only thing that stayed with him was the memory of those burning eyes of hers.

++++++

He could still see her, more like picture her.

Even after her departure, he couldn't help but think of her, of the way she had looked at him, even smiled at him.

Ealas's thoughts disappeared when he felt something briefly touch the palm of his hand.

There it is. As a child would, when he got ready to receive a gift, he smiled. He peeked, hoping to catch a glimpse of the whispdrakes, but the cotton wisps were still resting in place, untouched. Confused, he looked around but saw nothing.

There, again. This time he turned his head quickly, but all he saw was a droplet breaking upon contact with his skin, promptly followed by others.

He had been alone that evening, his head down, walking along the palace garden when the drizzle felt cool against his skin. He raised his head to feel the droplets on his face when her visage took him by surprise.

She stood there, watching him quietly from under an elm tree.

The castle servants had been looking around for the young heir, but somehow Astas was the one who always knew where he could be found.

"It's okay to cry," she spoke tenderly.

"Father says men don't," the Heikken heir responded.

"Everyone cries," the chain attached to her manacle clinked as she approached him. "It's important we allow ourselves to cry," she continued.

"Then, why do you wipe my tears?"

"So that you don't mess up your clothes," she smiled, pointing at his chest, "I just washed this coat the other day, and I thought I wouldn't be able to save it from how dirty it was."

Astas's words made him smile through tear-filled eyes. "Does everyone really cry?" he inquired.

"Oh yes! All our lives. As we grow, we see some people don't, but the reality is they do," she responded, *"they just hide it because they believe it will make them seem strong. But leaving those tears inside can fill them with sadness, and that is what will one day make them weak."*

His attention was on the woman who, like many times before, taught him while no one was around.

"Look, can you see the raindrops?" She pointed, "That's the sky crying too. You see? Even the sky cries, and that's okay. We need to, like the sky, channel our sadness and gain strength like thunder."

Thinking of Astas moved him, not out of pity as he originally thought, but because she had become a constant in his life.

After walking away from Hvitfast for what felt like most of an hour, Ealas now found himself standing atop a small hill overlooking the serene fields of white cotton. The misty landscape almost shone upon Kaeris's brief teasing before her face hid once again behind clouds of gray.

His hand reached inside the tunic for the pouch that hung around his neck. He tapped the leathery surface in an almost endearing way.

"This is all I have left of you." Ealas's fingers slowly unfastened the knot that sealed the pouch's silent mouth. "There is so much I wanted to ask you . . . about this land of yours, about *yourself*," he said.

Every time he had gotten a chance, Ealas had asked Astas about the land beyond Ardenay's border, the one he had been taught to believe was nothing more than a war-ravaged ruin. A land where the Light did not shine, for the corrupting sin was of such magnitude, erasing its existence off the face of the planet was the only righteous solution.

While she did not teach him to fight, speak properly, or dance, she taught him to smile despite the injustices around him. Over time Ealas saw her lose her youth, her health, and her vision, but she always kept her dignity, and despite how feeble and weak she appeared in the end, she taught him to be strong.

He was again in that room where his father was meeting with the dukes.

He had cried, and because he had cried, his father raised his hand again.

Before the second strike, the woman quickly approached and lifted her hands, begging for mercy. She grabbed the monarch's sleeve. "Please, Your Majesty, don't do this. Please don't strike your son!"

"Silence!" he shouted with the fury of a lion, striking her face instead with the back of his hand. "How dare you! How dare you insult a Heikken, of all the people, a slave, and of all the Heikken, the throned one!"

Cowering in a corner, young Ealas cried.

Astas stumbled a bit before she could stand when the king struck her again. "Don't dare stand before me, slave!" The blow had sent her face first to meet the floor, staining its surface crimson.

Summoning his guards, the king pointed his finger at the slave and ordered, "Kill her!"

"Father, No!" Ealas had yelled, the lion in him awakening as he placed himself between his father and the slave.

"I have given an order!"

"She's not yours!" Ealas spat.

"She's a slave!"

"She's my slave," the child stood firm, "so her life is mine!"

His stance had challenged his father, his roar had spoken to his progenitor, and thus the great lion raised his hand and stopped the order, all while his irate eyes now rested approvingly upon his son.

While the king did not end Astas's life that day, he tortured her all night. That evening, every hour on the clock, the king would visit and strike her again so that she would know that, unlike him, she was nothing, she would always be nothing more than nothing, and she needed to remember that.

The next day Ealas had felt impotent, for while he was also a lion, he was nothing more than a cub and would perhaps never be anything more than a cub, something he would remember, at least for as long as he would remember Astas's blood on that floor.

Ealas had asked Astas innumerable questions, from 'how do I make a bed' to 'does this look good on me,' and from 'what do you think about this fabric' to 'how can one be strong' but in his childish curiosity he had never asked her about her own family. Yes, he had asked her if there were children in her land, but not if she had children of her own.

Now he was here, standing in the land where that strangely known and unknown woman had grown up, wondering if she had attended these festivals, picked this cotton, and walked this same path.

"Who were you?" he asked the formless fumes around him.

Ealas realized that what little he had learned of her had been what he had witnessed growing up, for she had rarely spoken without being asked first. If that was her own prerogative, he wouldn't know, for the enslaved of Ardenay were warned not to speak to a superior unless addressed.

He lifted his hand, clasping the opening pouch, turning it to slowly release its contents.

A small stream of gray dust trickled from within, gray as a sad sky, as the wispy hair on Astas's head and his father's eyes.

Ealas's heart moved, and his lips trembled when he saw her ashes drifting in the wind toward the unknown.

'How did you end up in our hands?' Ealas wondered. He had found out Ardenay's forces had crossed the same way he had come, but, unlike him, they had burned the fields of Whisperwind and sacked the land of Aligrand, their advance on the capital halted by the relentless fog of Misthaven.

As much as he loved his land, it angered him to think his ancestors perhaps once stood in this same place he now stood, but with their hearts bent on destroying it, while his own heart was nothing but breaking.

Just like in his own current situation, something he couldn't understand had stopped their advance.

They had set up camp until that day, unaware of how ill-prepared they were for the assault by the combined forces of soldiers, farmers, and nature itself that followed.

He was standing here, until that moment, unaware of how unprepared he was to let go.

Ealas's chest tightened upon seeing the ashes leaving the pouch, and he exhaled hard and found it harder to breathe in again.

Despite his strength and resolve, Ealas felt weak, for while he had bested many a seasoned man in battle, he had never stood up against the power of those he had been taught to believe were above him. The intimidating figure of his father had been taller than he could ever be, and the holy light of the archbishop shone brighter than he could ever hope to shine. And while he could have found his own way to grow as a king in their midst, instead, he ran, hoping he could grow far away, where their judging eyes would not notice him, and notice him they would definitely not, for he now felt he was becoming smaller.

"Where do I find strength when I feel hopelessly weak," his glassy eyes looked up to the sky.

'Standing firm does not always make us strong.' The memory of her words responded as a whisper in the melancholic wind, 'Sometimes, to become strong, one must brace oneself and run.'

And off he ran, as fast as he could, downhill and toward the sea of cotton where he would drown his sorrow. His hand ahead of him, protecting his eyes while the other spread the dust. As fast as the plants flew past him, innumerable recollections fluttered in his head like the wisps of cotton in the air around him.

He dashed as if seeking to escape the past that would always be a part of him. He ran from the pain that dug deeper inside his chest. The more he ran, the more the pure fibers stroked his skin, bringing memories of when Astas had touched him, nurtured him, and how at times, remnants of her wispy hair clung to him as the silky cotton tendrils clung to his clothes as he ran.

Kaeris appeared from behind her mask of clouds, her sterile radiance summoning a dazzling display reflected in the fog. Ealas lifted his hand to cover his face and misstepped, losing his balance and rolling downhill, finally coming to a halt sprawled on the ground, face up, his wet eyes of gray steel gazing at the ceramic face of the moon. Ahead lay a labyrinth of crops and dense fog, and behind him, only a trail of ashes and tears.

"Who were you," he asked again, knowing quite well he would likely never know, for while he had traveled far and asked around for the ones who could know, not even they knew the answer. In a twisted way, his father had been right. Astas was *no one*. She had not been a noble poet nor a warrior. She hadn't been a doctor, a rich merchant, or a beautiful damsel. Astas had been nothing but a simple woman who had lost everything except for her capacity to show love to the son of the culprit of her endless misery.

She had not been a hero, but to him, she was more than that. She was the only figure of a mother he ever had; everything she was and every way she treated him made her, to him, the greatest of all heroes.

How could he honor the memory of that woman? How could he ensure he remembered everything he was he owed to what she taught him? He heard her whispers around the cotton field calling him, soothing him.

Overcome with heartache and guilt, Ealas turned and laid on his side. His strong arms embraced his faltering knees, bringing them close to his chest.

"I'm sorry I couldn't bring you back home alive." At that moment, his heart finally broke, as a cathedral's glass window under a catapult's boulder. And he flexed his neck and shut his eyes, and he mourned deeply until he dozed off, for the world perhaps had lost nothing, but he felt he had lost it all.

And it was in the wee hours of the night that, under the silent light of the curious moon, Ealas's body lay covered in wisps like a perfect cocoon resting in its silken web. Around him, the peaceful quiescence was only broken by the glittering scales of scurrying, long, translucent little creatures that had found their banquet clinging to his clothes.

(1) Lucris: the Sun

EYES

Location: Kingdom of Blackheart,
Duchy of Misthaven, Evermist region, town of Brumeveil

What would others' eyes perceive if they could see our truth?

In the morning, Ealas left the cotton fields where he had woken up.

He came upon a small establishment that served as both the local tavern and inn in Brumeveil, the small capital town of Misthaven, directed by locals that had been, although wary, somewhat cooperative.

The few people inside were all locals. He could tell from the somber attire, occasional lanterns, and engraved bells hanging from their waists or necks. In the center of the room, a group of customers were partaking in breakfast at the largest table in the room, which wasn't large at all.

One was a wrinkled old man, garbed in traveling clothes and a dirty hood resting over the cape on his back. He was accompanied by three young children, none of whom, Ealas could guess, was past the age of twelve. The children were dressed in similar attire, although their fabrics were not worn like the old man's. The two youngest ate their food, interrupted by their occasional laughter, while the oldest rested his back against the table while he struggled to string a bow.

Sharing the table was a middle-aged woman with graying brown hair. It was clear from their interaction they were familiar with one another.

"You can join us at the table," the middle-aged woman said to Ealas.

"No, thank you," Ealas looked at the rest of the busy establishment, "I'll wait for someone to be done."

"It's busy today," the woman insisted, "just come. We'll make space for you."

"He still has to pay for his own food, though," the wrinkled old man accompanying her added with a wink.

"Where are you from?" the woman asked, signaling to the waitress to bring extra servings for Ealas.

"My name's Ealas. I'm not from here," he responded, not fearing they would not have any knowledge of who he truly was, "I'm actually a foreigner."

"Well, that's obvious," the woman added, "anyone can tell from your accent."

'Accent?' Ealas thought. "This is the first time I've been told I have an accent."

"Well, you do!" the woman tilted her head to the side. "Call me Cymbell, and this is Tobb, an old friend."

"Where are you from?" the old man inquired, a look of suspicion in his eyes.

Ealas thought long about his answer. It would be hard to change the subject without raising even more suspicion. Besides, this morning he felt like he was a different man. "I'm from Ardenay," he stated, expecting a furious burst from the pair.

"Ah, never been," Tobb answered casually, turning his attention back to the child stringing the bow, to whom he gave instructions.

"Yeah, me neither, too far from here, then again, I've never been in many of our own duchies," Cymbell responded nonchalantly. "Are you moving here or just passing?"

"Passing," he responded as the waiter brought him a bowl of thick, fatty bean soup with quail eggs.

"It figures," she said in response. "Who in the twin hells moves here anyways?"

"Hopeful musicians," Tobb raised a finger.

"That's right," she nodded with her head. "Now, you look pretty beat, so eat up."

"I slept in the cotton field last night," Ealas said. "I was expecting to see whispdrakes."

"The whispdrakes?" Tobb asked. "It is said they are the noblest of creatures. Their life is one of constant work and isolation. In the eyes of some, they are pests that pick and eat the best cotton. In the end, they are harmless. Their dung nourishes the soil that nourishes the plants that nourish them. Why can't mankind take it upon themselves to do the same?"

"And where are you headed to?" the woman asked the dreaded question.

Where was he headed? He had already come to Misthaven. He had scattered Astas's ashes, although he had kept the pouch with what little was left of the ashes that clung to its walls as if choosing to still accompany him wherever he went.

What would he do now? His slate was blank. What would he write on it?

"I . . . don't know right now."

"There you go," Tobb praised the child who had finally managed to string the bow and now lifted it proudly. "Cymbell," he added, "we are taking off."

"Children," he instructed, "count your provisions and ensure your lanterns are supplied. We will be in the field for several days. It would do no one any good if you got lost in the fog."

"Wait," Ealas questioned, "you're taking them out for several days?"

"Well, of course!" Tobb laughed. "They'll become adults soon enough, so it's important they're taken into the deep foglands before they're old enough to choose not to learn."

"Learn what?"

"The survival skills of a forester," Cymbell responded, "what's needed to stay alive in the land of mist."

"Our youth are not typically inclined to leave our land," Tobb added. "Not only do they live a simple life away from the grievances of civilization, but we have a sacred duty, an oath sworn by our ancestors, to protect the duchy of Darkholm."

"Do you get anything in return," Ealas questioned.

"Do we need anything in return?" Tobb responded. "The Darkholm saw the loyalty in our ancestors and gave us to rule the portion of land they would not manage."

"You mean leftover land?"

"They themselves had received their land as leftovers," Tobb answered. "Besides, leftovers or not, it's still land they didn't have to give us, and yet they did, asking only for our protection."

"Well," Ealas pondered, "at least they gave you a land rich in cotton. It's unusual when they could have kept that rich part themselves.

"Our cotton was discovered much later, so that wasn't likely a consideration," Cymbell responded.

Tobb leaned on the table, "They might not have given us much in the eyes of some. What they gave us was a chance, and we will not waste it."

Ealas admired the man's conviction. Was this the way the Bulls of Bulwharf felt back home? Somehow, it was refreshing but also worrisome that not once had any of them mentioned God. "Do enemies ever come this far inside the kingdom?" he asked.

"They have in the past," Tobb said, "but the protection they ask is even from an incursion of people of Blackheart coming uninvited, those who avoid the main roads of our wary lords."

'Truly paranoid,' Ealas thought, 'as described by our many accounts.'

"Training the children will also help you retire," he said, "the children are the protectors of our future."

"We don't ever retire," Tobb stated. "Our strength lies in a different place as we age, but we still live for the performance of our duty. We don't have a large standing army, so all the Blood of Misthaven is involved in its defense one way or another.

"Anyways, well met," Tobb began picking up his belongings, lighting the lantern he and two of the children would carry.

"This one's lantern is not lit," Ealas pointed at the younger child.

"He's mine," Cymbell smiled.

"Oh, I thought the three were together!"

"Nah," the woman responded, "Life within the mists is dangerous and often solitary. At times we spend days without seeing anyone else. But trust in Misthaven is the most valuable thing one can have, so it's important to take advantage of every opportunity we get to give our children and ourselves time to meet.

"I better start packing too. And you," she said, "good luck with whatever you're going to do. May your wick stay dry."

Cymbell stood up from the table, but both she and the departing Tobb stopped immediately when they heard Ealas say, "There's an image in my head I can't seem to shake off since last night. There's this girl with the most beautiful yellow eyes, unlike anything I've ever seen."

"What?" Cymbell asked. "You said *yellow* eyes?"

"Yes," Ealas responded innocently, "I've seen a few of them over the last few days, but these were like fire. I need to find her."

"Boy, be thankful, and be wary," Tobb turned his head toward him, "what you have witnessed is the royals."

"What do you mean be wary?" Ealas asked.

"Your eyes have been blessed if you have seen them. Let's hope you're just as blessed if theirs have seen you."

FOURTH TEST

Location: Empyre of Suhne, close to the border
between the City of Suhne and the Basqh of Ahm

Sometimes the price of truth is failure . . .

Dawn had broken, the fiery orb filling the cloudless sky with its rays of orange, dispelling the remnants of the night and its chilly embrace.

What little was left of the stars, gems pulsating high above, was reflected in the emerald eyes of the Blessed Daughter as they first opened.

Incense filled the chamber, but other than the silent fumes, there was little movement around the room.

'Something isn't right.'

Fearing herself late, Vamya quickly rose from the bed, "Why haven't you woken me?"

"Blessed One," an old servant lowered her head, "there is plenty of time. You need some rest. Today's Test does not start until noon."

"In that case," Vamya brought a hand toward her shoulder, stretching her neck to the side, "get a massager. I feel strange; *tense*, I suppose."

"If it pleases you, Blessed One, I could do it myself," the servant responded, "I am well trained."

"I do not doubt your skill," the Child of the Sun's eyes were on the woman, "but I want you to focus on my clothes. Also, summon Aaghari. I want to speak to him."

'Something isn't right.' Vamya covered her body in linen before walking toward the incense. She brought several of the sticks to her nose and lightly sniffed them. There was nothing wrong with them. The fragrance was the same as she was used to.

She then studied the room. The clothes were in the same place, her pool was ready, and the herbs.

Quickly, she moved toward the dried herbs by her pool. The Blessed One's fingers grabbed the dried leaves, and, crushing them, she allowed them to fall toward the water's surface. She could tell without a doubt they were the same herbs that always calmed her sometimes restless spirit.

Her confidant appeared through the door, followed by the massager, who promptly began her work.

"You called early, Blessed One," Aaghari bowed his head.

"I did, Aaghari," Vamya responded, "I feel something is amiss."

"I assure you everything is fine, Blessed One," her confidant smiled. "Did you meditate this morning? It always helps you reduce your anxieties."

"I am even having trouble meditating," she looked into his eyes, "I feel a heaviness of the spirit, like something bad is going to happen."

"Blessed One," the man looked outside before referring back to her, "it is natural you are tense. Everything is fine, and everything will continue to be so. Now, do not let doubt and troublesome thoughts get inside your head. Today you will need the clarity of mind you believe you don't have."

———————— ·++++·· ————————

The Eye of the Sun soared on its zenith, as high as all the hope and faith inside Vamya's heart.

Alone she stood by the circular door that led to the chamber where the Test would take place, inside one of the highest domes of the city, a structure that reached up for the sky above or simply out and away from its worshippers below.

Like those of her siblings, her Chosen had no part today, and so Vamya simply stood in front of that copper door, waiting for it to open.

But open, it didn't, at least not by itself. It was she who, after closing her eyes, after having waited patiently a few minutes, thought, 'not every door will open for me. Some I will need to open myself.'

The jewels dangling from her bracelets rang as her hands pushed the coppery surface. Her feet walked the hallway reverently, the one that opened into the great chamber to reveal a scene that filled her eyes with confusion.

Inside, the Rays seemed busy, enough so that they did not notice her presence. Some walked around the room, carrying cups or vials. Others took notes, sitting along desks strewn with the tools of one of their most sacred and consistent duties, that of scriveners.

On a far side of the chamber, two assisted Kaylen, who lay on the floor, his irises hidden behind widely open eyelids, his back arched while the weight of his upper body rested upon his shaking arms, almost slipping in the large pool of vomit that traveled from his lips and trailed along the floor, evidence of how far he had dragged his body along its smooth surface. He looked like a dying, scorpion-like creature that had been created by false gods to make a mockery of his arrogance.

On another side of the room, Malek's body lay face-up over a golden, fine fabric, his chiseled chest visibly drenched in sweat. His eyes gazed blindly at the sky above, his legs thrashing, while his hands sought to grasp the smooth surface of the floor where the violent moves had displaced the fabric.

Upon finally taking note of her presence, Exis raised his voice, "You cannot just interrupt this sacred ceremony!" Signaling to the others, the Speaker walked toward Vamya and pointed toward the hallway.

"There was no one by the door," Vamya explained as he closed in.

Without any hesitation, the Speaker stood face-to-face with her. While she was a Child of the Sun god, he was taller, his eyes of coal more intimidating, and *these* were his chambers, where the Rays had near absolute control, at least until another Sun was chosen.

"You are late."

"I came upon the door exactly at the Zenith of the Eye, as instructed," Vamya argued, "and yet no one was there to receive me."

"Even *that* was late," the Speaker replied, "the ceremony started hours ago, upon the Eye's Rising[1]."

'What? That can't be,' Vamya thought. 'Am I being sabotaged once again? If so, by whom?' But she couldn't dwell on that right now. She had to dispel those thoughts. "I was informed the time was the Zenith," she said firmly, "I did as told."

Exis paid no heed. He turned away and proceeded to walk toward the desks, "Whatever the reason, Son of the Sun, the Fourth Test started long ago. You were not here. As a consequence, you have missed the chance to participate in this ceremony," he continued, briefly waving his fingers as a dismissal.

Vamya's nails dug deep into her palms. She took a deep breath, her eyes of emeralds closing briefly. "Speaker!" she raised her voice so that everyone could hear, "I *will not* leave."

The change in her demeanor drew the attention of the Rays, some of whom approached and even joined in on the discussion.

Aldah of the Rays spoke first, "What the Speaker says is true, Blessed One. There are rules, and these sacred rules must be followed. Please, I beg you, leave now so that we may continue our work uninterrupted."

"I am not leaving. We will start my portion of the Test."

"The ceremony is already in progress, Blessed One. It cannot be started again," Aldah responded.

Unlike him, Hosta was always firm both in convictions and in words. Lifting up a finger, Hosta fanatically quoted the sacred rules, "No mortal man may dare ever interrupt one of the Sacred Ceremonies."

His admonition had summoned a glint in the precious stones of Vamya's eyes. She positioned herself to face them all, "And no mortal ever will."

"It would be troublesome to allow you to participate," Exis spoke again, "it would set a precedent it would be best to avoid."

"Troublesome." Vamya looked at the Speaker eye to eye. "Do you think either of them," she then pointed at her siblings, "would have just asked to participate upon finding out they had been fooled? A fool is he who thinks *that* would have been the case. My brothers' vengeance would have been swift and unmeasurable. I, in turn, am giving you the chance to be fair, to rectify a wrong so that in the end, it can be left behind as nothing more than a miscommunication, and so we can continue with my participation in the ceremony. All I am asking for is for what is rightfully mine as Daughter of the Sun."

The Speaker's lips pursed, but before he uttered a word, Seiris, the second eldest of the Rays, spoke instead, "She speaks true words. The writings mention the Tests should be performed during the Eye's journey through the heavens, but in no way do they state those tested should participate simultaneously."

Stroking his most ancient beard, Zurek approached slowly. He was the eldest of the Rays. His raised, bushy eyebrows accentuated the depth of his sunken eyes and terse voice. "Still, the Test must end before the Eye's journey finalizes. You must understand, Son of the Sun, *that* alone could affect you in ways we cannot . . . predict."

"I understand," Vamya responded, "and the risk is well worth my reward, the reward all of Suhne will obtain upon my ultimate success."

Her words were followed by the silent nods of approval of several of the Rays, including the enigmatic Zurek himself.

"I believe then we are in favor of allowing her to participate," Exis questioned.

"We don't have to be, Speaker," Zurek scolded, "it is her right and our sacred duty—"

"Our sacred duty is the guardianship of the sacred Tests," Exis's black eyes snapped back at Zurek.

"And that includes guardianship from opposing forces from without and from within," Seiris placed his hands together as if in prayer. He bowed humbly, his serene smile seeming, at least to Exis, as one of satisfactory triumph.

She was ready. As ready as one could be for the unknown. Ready to lose herself at the mercy of the Rays who, until the moment of her Ascendancy, likely saw her as nothing more than just one of three competitors, and one that had dared question the decisions of those who would determine, in the end, who would be the ultimate victor.

Was it wise? Was it best not to participate and avoid potentially ending up like Kaylen? What would incur a greater penalty—absence or abject failure?

It didn't matter now. Exis was approaching. His expression, reflected in the glass decanter he carried, would not betray his thoughts. He had carefully supervised each of the Rays as they added a few drops of a substance of their individual choice, forming a concoction that the siblings would imbibe.

It was too late, she couldn't stop it, but even if she could, she wouldn't. There was too much at stake. Her fate, that of her people, and even the one of the world itself, depended on the Ascendancy of a new Sun, of a Sun that would be like no other, that would change the hearts of men, and with it, the course of history.

Tilting slowly, the decanter of the grayish fluid found a home in her cup. It was nearly full before Exis stopped, "Since the beginning, the Sun god, who sees all, has spoken in the language of omens and portents, for only the Sun can truly unravel the unknown mysteries of this world. The Sun has always been the greatest of his own prophets. It is because of this infinite wisdom bestowed by its own incarnation, by its own transcendence, that we follow our god without question."

Exis then slowly walked away to form a part of the circle of Rays, "The Empyre of Suhne is defined by its vision," he continued, "and its vision is none other than that of the Sun god itself. But this mortal, temporary shell is an opaque lens that can alter the perception of even the One."

"Drink," he ordered with a wave of his hand, "and when you wake, speak of what your eyes have seen so that we may interpret it."

Her hands brought the cup to her lips. The unique fragrance was both deliciously musky and acridly sweet as if each scent sought to fight to be the first to find its way to Vamya's nostrils. Closing her eyes, she swallowed its contents, interrupted immediately by Exis.

"Son of the Sun," his voice resonated through the chamber, "today we test your vision."

The fluid felt both warm and cold down her throat, inside her chest. It was followed by. . .

Nothing . . .

She breathed in deeply and exhaled, waiting for whatever was supposed to happen, eyes closed but still alert. Suddenly, she heard the footsteps of the Rays approaching. She heard them murmur. She felt their presence closing in fast, too fast even.

At once, her eyes opened reflexively, and she was perturbed when she saw the priests had not moved a single inch from where they had initially been standing.

She saw Exis's fingertips stretching impossibly the moment they pointed at her, sending the Rays darting toward Vamya, arms extended, touching her, grabbing her from all sides, as she suffocated . . . As she screamed.

And suddenly, silence. She couldn't hear them anymore. She couldn't 'feel' them. She could only feel the breeze on her skin, the grass under her feet.

Grass?

She found herself barefoot, walking along the rolling hills and beautiful greenery of vast, serene fields that rested along infinite walls that almost touched the sky. The palms of her hands made contact with each grain stalk, with each golden head that felt as soft as down.

High above, the midday sun watched it all, blazing high and mighty, warming her skin and that of the world, its touch persistent, as if seeking to remind both of its presence.

It was, without a doubt, the most beautiful sight, but through all the calm she witnessed, somehow, she felt safe, but she didn't feel peace.

'Something is not right.' She closed her eyes and barely perceived a distant rumble.

It led her to the wall her hands touched, its stoic stillness interrupted by small vibrations that were suddenly gone before they grew and reappeared every few seconds.

Suddenly, something turned inside her stomach. A sharp pain appeared, twisting her bowels and forcing her to drop to her knees as she gasped for air. And just as it appeared, it was gone.

A sudden noise, like that of cracking thunder, shook the earth. Vamya looked around for its source. Close by, where she had been seconds before, the gargantuan wall had been breached, its stones tumbling like endless waterfalls.

The temperature rose, and the sun swelled, emptying the sky, absorbing every cloud into its voracious body, its intensity sending flares in every direction as it grew in size, in power.

Vamya rose again and found the field now lay scorched, clouds of gray smoke rising from where each stalk had been, where now only calcined, ashen human bodies stood, each one's posture testimony of the suffering they had endured upon their most horrible deaths.

Under her feet, the earth moved violently, splitting the ground in a hundred different places where islets of soil sank toward chasms. Her heart filled with dread as she saw, from the biggest chasm, an enormous, clawed hand, black as the night, emerging, grasping the edge to either pull itself up or drag the world with it.

Vamya pushed herself off the ground toward midair, from where her eyes could take a glance at the whole chaotic picture. She saw the lands shifting like quicksand in a world that marched to war in its every corner. Tens of thousands of people sought refuge in temples, pleading for help to the deaf ears of false gods. Everywhere it licked the land the ocean rose, its waves bathing and consuming mountains with their uncontained fury; all of them but one, where a single, silver lighthouse stood firm, unbothered. Its smooth surface glistened like an ancient mirror while it showed the reflection of the tumultuous battles around it that would never reach its base. On its top, beams of light touched the sky, touched the earth, occasionally wavering, as if almost giving up.

Wherever she looked, all she witnessed was hopelessness and destruction.

But when she thought it was over, the worst was yet to come.

The chasms caved in, widening swiftly, gorging on the mountains and valleys, the fortresses and temples, and even the sea and the islands beyond were swallowed. It was all accompanied by the horrific, unending screams of the beasts, of the countless people that were consumed by the insatiable hunger of the void.

'This is what man builds . . . nothing more than destruction.'

She clutched at her chest, feeling a sorrow so deep for a moment she felt her heart fail.

A profound sadness filled her, a feeling of inadequacy, of guilt. Her only hope was set on what she knew, and she searched for the comforting presence of the Eye of the Sun in the sky above, but there it was, rising in the distance, alone, swelling and trembling uncontrollably, still scorching the remains of a world that for far too long, and too many times, had already been burned.

———————— ✦✦✦✦✦ ————————

Vamya's eyes first saw the crystal dome above as she regained consciousness. The Eye could not be seen in the tangerine sky that was slowly laced with waves of red and purple. She was glad it was over, although her hands still trembled. Her head hurt so much it would almost numb the aching she felt all over her body. Her hand moved toward the back of her head where she felt it wet and swollen.

"Be still, Son of the Sun," Or'guud, the healer among the Rays, was kneeling by her side. At his feet were bloodied bandages and medical instruments of his trade. "You banged your head against the floor several times. Because of the unknown qualities of your potion, I do not want to give you medicine," he continued, "so your head will ache for more than a few days."

"I understand." Slowly, she turned to see both her siblings were long gone from the chamber.

"Son of the Sun," Exis's voice rose, "I know you must feel weak, but time is of the essence. If you are able to at least sit and speak, we will be ready to listen to what you have seen."

"I am ready." To avoid feeling dizzy, with the assistance of Or'guud, Vamya proceeded to sit up. At her feet, a pool of her own drying blood, evidence of where she had fallen.

Without hesitation, Or'guud returned to his writing desk, eager to make his annotations.

'Where do I start,' Vamya closed her eyes and wondered, 'what do I say?' She knew not every vision was literal, and not every prophesied event would end up being exactly as told, but she knew the emotions she felt were real. They persisted, and even now, she was still haunted by them.

'I should reveal my visions,' she embraced her knees, seeking to calm herself, 'The Sun should always speak with no fear of what is to come, for the Sun is Almighty, the Sun is god.'

"We are ready." Exis sounded unusually patient.

"I found myself in a walled field of green, basked in the warming light of the Sun." Vamya saw a few of the younger Rays immediately start to take notes. The rest watched and listened intently.

All was calm, like the beginning of that nightmarish vision. There was a stillness in the air that, more than peace, felt more like that moment when an animal's body was about to be traversed by the opportunistic spear of the hunter.

"The wall was breached, the world set ablaze," to her words, the Speaker raised a dubious eyebrow, Seiris almost smiled, Zurek squinted.

"But the Sun wouldn't have it," she continued. "It swelled, it gained power, and it saw all. The Sun's conquering hand moved, multiplying its crops, its people, its influence reaching every corner of the world. Everywhere it went, the land prospered. It founded cities and erected temples. It created peace, it brought order, and so the Sun of Suhne ruled the world, *together* with its Rays."

When she was done, she noticed Exis's smile after he and several of the Rays looked at one another, after some of them nodded. Even Zurek, who never smiled, saw his expression soften somewhat. The one whose eyes she couldn't

get off her was Seiris. His perennial smile was no more. His brow was furrowed, his lips pursed, and his eyes looked at her like an eagle, almost as if he *knew*.

Vamya stood in front of the holy men, her arms spread wide as if ready for an embrace as their quills scratched the parchment vigorously. She smiled, or at least she sought to summon that smile that was impossible to find amidst what she had just done.

For a moment, she questioned her move when she saw the Rays writing her words, words that would be collected, summarized, and eventually added to the prophecies taught to every Suhnite.

'How many of our prophecies have been manipulated in the past? Or have we been manipulated by the prophecies?' she thought.

And again, she saw Seiris's gaze fixed upon her, and she hated herself.

(1)   The Rising: the moment the sun is first visible on the horizon

THE BULLFIGHTER

Location: Kingdom of Ardenay, Royal Duchy of Himeland,
Capital City of Himlen, Palace of the Beacon

Strength is moot when guided by a weak mind . . .

The morning late summer breeze felt cool on the bright day he was guided into the royal courtyard of the king's palace. The architecture of the bleached walls seeming to preach echoes of the purity of the Light only accentuated the darker tone of Lord Varen Bulwharf's skin.

Few were allowed to wear armor inside the palace grounds, and even fewer would be allowed to get close to the Crowned King. But the Duke of Bulwharf was a man of honor, and despite having been a close friend to Ealas, Varen had remained loyal to the throne even after Ealas's actions had placed the kingdom's safety in jeopardy.

Had he wished things had been different? Likely, but they were not. These were the circumstances he had been put in, and, as a leader, he had to weigh and consider every one of his actions. Men couldn't just follow an impulse without considering its repercussions.

And repercussions were the reason he was summoned to meet with Aorius.

A pair of royal guards escorted him to meet the king in the garden, where first he saw the queen sitting among lilies accompanied by her maidens, enjoying a picnic a short distance from him. Her long blonde hair, blue eyes, and smile made her seem beautiful even though her younger years were gone.

"I will need your sword, Lord Bull." While it would appear the meeting would be informal, given the location, the formality of Creod of the guard, who had seen him grow up around Ealas most of his life, revealed the reality of the present day. It wasn't Ealas, his lifelong friend, who was king. The crown rested on the head of the late king's brother, a man who was not born for the throne but whom the Light had chosen to sit on it.

"Here," he followed Creod's instruction.

"Our king awaits," Creod stated coldly. "You may return to your stations. I will take it from here. Now, Lord Bull, if you would please follow me." Having passed six decades, Creod more than doubled Varen's age. Still, the captain of the royal guard was taller than Lord Varen, who was larger and more muscular. Instead of having the duke follow him as usual, he walked side by side with him.

"Pardon the formality, Lord Varen," he murmured.

"There's no offense. I understand," Varen was glad to hear the deep voice not of the captain but of the old, gruff friend he had grown to know.

"How are things going for you?" Creod asked.

"I am good, thank you," Varen responded. "We are going through some hardships in northern Bulwharf, but nothing we haven't gone through before."

"These are trying times."

"Trying, for you?" Varen questioned.

"Indeed," Creod explained, "I have lived through four kings on the Beacon. The crown is always the same, but the man who wears it is not."

Varen felt like placing his hand on Creod's shoulder, but he knew he couldn't, at least not here where it was likely they were being observed.

"Four kings?" Varen questioned. "Do you feel Ealas's brief time on the throne should be taken into account?"

"But it does count. It has to," Creod responded. "The moment the crown touched his head, it counted, even if a little, and sometimes even the smallest things have the greatest consequences."

"We are close," Creod whispered, "the Steel Lion is in a foul mood, tread carefully. The cubs, don't be fooled, have proven to be sharp. The king is quickly giving responsibilities to the first who have shown interest in governance."

"Your sword," Creod increased his volume, "will be given to you after your meeting with His Majesty."

"Thank you," Varen whispered, "for the warning, for being a friend."

"Always," Creod lowered his voice once more, "but I'm doing this not for our friendship. I'm helping because I will never betray my oath to protect the Crown, to do what's best for the stability and safety of the kingdom." He then stepped away and ahead.

"Your Highness," Creod turned after crossing a small, guarded gate, "the Duke of Bulwharf awaits for instruction."

King Aorius sat comfortably in a wide seat. While in the garden, he still wore royal attire. The crown of Ardenay was on his head as if there was any need for the Bulwharf to be reminded of his station. He was flanked by his sons, Vallein, the steely-eyed eldest, and Langel, the youngest, who looked more like his mother.

In front of the king, a table served with fruits, meats, and plenty to drink at which the three sat.

Varen raised his right fist. "May the Light—"

"Stop it," Aorius cut him off, his eyes on a cup of wine he swirled, "don't play those games with me."

"I apologize, Your Highness," Varen looked around for the missing archbishop.

"Angevin is not here," Aorius stated. "He wasn't invited to enjoy this conversation. Do you believe in our god, Lord Bull?" the king continued.

Varen wondered if he was being tested somehow. "I do," he then responded, "without a doubt."

"Without a doubt," the king's eyes were on him, "but with hesitation."

"I was just—"

"I don't want to hear it," Aorius waved his hand, "You know I don't believe in all that. I know religion far too well to believe it. Now, if you believe it, then I respect that. I don't see a problem with it, and it will never be a problem as long as we all know where your loyalty is.

"Even my youngest son believes," Aorius pointed out, "but he knows where his loyalties are."

"As do I, Your Highness," Varen added.

"Do you, now?" Aorius pierced him with his gaze.

"Yes, Your Highness."

"And where does your loyalty lie?"

"To my king, to my kingdom, and to my god."

"That's the correct order," Aorius smiled mockingly, taking a swish from his cup before spitting it out. "Take this away," he instructed his servants, one who would discard the bottle he was not pleased with and a second who immediately replaced it with another.

"Do you know why you're here, Lord Varen?" the king questioned.

"Your Highness has requested my presence," Varen responded.

"Surely," Aorius swirled another cup, "would you like a cup?"

"Thank you, Your Highness, but no."

"Would you like to sit and partake with us?" the king offered.

"I'd rather stand if Your Highness doesn't mind."

"Then so be it." Aorius placed his hands on the table, "I was informed about what happened at the Horne, but I want to hear it from you."

"What specifically would Your Highness want to know? The invasion?"

"Yes, Lord Bull," Aorius brooded, "what happened?"

"Your Highness," Varen responded, "a combined army from the border duchies of Blackheart crossed into Darane territory. They were largely held back by the forces of Usman Velias, Bull of Darane, who is now with the Light."

Aorius listened intently.

"After more than a month, we had reached a stalemate," Varen continued. "Our enemy issued a challenge to resolve the battle with a duel, to which I agreed. It was there where the Bull of Darane valiantly lost his life."

"An unfortunate loss," Aorius interjected, signaling Varen to continue, "but I'm more concerned about the loss of the Eighth."

Varen wouldn't answer. He could see in the cold, shrewd eyes of his monarch he was nothing but trapped.

"Your Highness," Varen replied, "because of our loss, it was the price we paid, as per—"

"No, you wait there," Aorius corrected, "because of *your* loss. It's unfathomable that one of the greatest military minds in the world would gamble everything on a single, incompetent man."

"My King," Varen protested, "I humbly ask you to please not dishonor his sacrifice. Usman Velias was a great man."

"Great men win battles, Lord Bull," Aorius said in a monotone voice, "and while you are concerned about a dead one, there are many great men who have been displaced from their land and positions, and by whom?

"By you," Aorius pointed a finger at Varen's chest, "by your doing. So I ask you, Lord Bull, what are you going to do to get the Eighth back?"

The question was followed by Varen's lack of words. He was a man of honor, a warrior who led his men by the strength of his example. He couldn't simply turn back on his promise.

"Your Highness," Varen finally responded, "my agreement with the Darkholm general was such that they would keep the Eighth and its surrounding land and rebuild what they had destroyed."

"Is the crown yours?" Aorius sneered, "This land is not yours to give. You are a vassal, so I give you an order to take the land back. And they will still rebuild it once you do." He lowered his voice, "Ardenay can always use more slaves."

"My King, this whole kingdom is yours," Varen protested, "but I gave my word."

"But you did not give mine." Aorius stood up and faced Varen. They were of the same height, both tall and strong. While one man's strength was his unfaltering honor, the other one's was his endless ambition.

Varen sought an argument to present, but in the end, he knew it would likely fall on deaf ears.

"Your Highness," he finally said, "with the loss of Bull Usman Velias, many warriors have been readying themselves. To choose a successor, the best warriors will face each other in ceremonial combat that I must oversee."

"And what is the problem?"

"The Ten Days of Thunders will start within a tenday," Varen explained, "I humbly ask my king to allow me to oversee this important event for our people before I march toward the Eighth."

Aorius rubbed his chin. He looked at his sons, both in their twenties, looking back at him, at the example he was ready to set. "No," he replied, "I will not wait. Now, I want you to have something clear. I am not my brother, I am not your friend, but I am also not unreasonable, so go, take care of your ceremony, but send men ahead to besiege the Eighth. Their king wants to judge their competence. Hopefully, they will be able to capture it. If not, then you know what you have to do."

"Your Highness," Varen bowed.

Aorius commanded, "Go and take the Eighth back."

NOBLE

Location: Kingdom of Blackheart, Royal Duchy
of Darkholm, Capital City of Coldforge

The hardest value to appraise is one's own . . .

His figure crossed the winding streets of the capital, past the busy meat district and the wineries, beyond the slate cathedral and toward what most citizens avoided, the part of town crowded only by buildings that lay mostly quarantined or empty, visited either by the dedicated worker or occasional lost tourist, the walled district of Alnwick.

The crow gate lay partially open, as it always did, its welcoming hands of cold iron promising to keep every secret it swallowed.

The man walked carefully, capturing glimpses of the others that ignored him, despite his awkward gait or gaunt face and ghostly hair that made him appear much older than he was, despite his flashy-colored cloak under which his pale hands clasped a small chest he kept hidden.

To his left, the sign identifying the large building that rested atop a small elevation felt ignored, that building with its walls that hid it only against the cobblestone road or the night sky and exalted it during the day when no one really cared to see its dark beauty.

He strode uphill past the small, simple garden that was as poorly lit as it was well-kept, tended by the patient hands of skilled herbalists. He walked through the large doors and into an empty attendant's station.

Not long after, a busy, middle-aged woman in dark gray robes and a black hat that served as a uniform walked out of a door to the side, wiping her hands with a stained rag. She had just taken a breath to voice protest, but upon recognizing him, she offered information instead. "At the crow's feet," with a tilt of her head to the side, she offered him entry.

"And Xarnata," the healer added, "You will need coverings!" but the man was already on his way down the hallway.

Xarnata navigated the sanatorium halls before climbing down the stairs, past the first set of iron gates, one that allowed entry into the main basement of the building. Stone block archways and gated, underground hallways served as the foundation of the structure above. He passed by arches to each side. Each one led to an alcove that functioned as a doorless room where dirty cots, at times occupied by ailing bodies, could be found. Intermittently, a few of these initial alcoves contained a small, barred window to the outside, allowing what little light and ventilation would dare come into the basement. After the first gates, he headed toward a distant one, where another uniformed woman sat by an old desk.

The healer examined vials filled with various fluids atop her desk. She took detailed notes in a book, ignoring Daemos's steps until he stood right in front of her. "Good day. I see that you're back," she welcomed. "It is dangerous past here. Please stand away from this gate."

Without a response, Xarnata awkwardly turned around and took a single step away before turning toward her once again. The attendant then sounded a small bell on the desk thrice before resuming her notetaking.

At the crisp sound, Xarnata's grip tightened, turning his knuckles pale. Otherwise, he appeared quite calm until he caught a glimpse of the approaching figures that responded to the summons.

The approaching trio were garbed in heavy black cloaks that covered most of their bodies except for the gloved hands and their heads, where long, curved, beak-like masks protruded from within hoods. Instead of dispelling the eerie visage, the lantern in the hands of the one on the right, and the dim light entering from the left, gave them the appearance of giant, slow-walking crows.

The figure in the center signaled the other two, who remained behind and entered one of the alcoves beyond the gate to continue their work.

"Xarnata Daemos is here." The healer opened the gate for the lone figure that crossed it.

Sweat pooled in Xarnata's palms. He stood in place, the tremulousness of his body evident only on the waves that formed on his cape upon the closeness of the figure, upon listening to the heavy, muffled breathing inside the hollow mask.

The figure looked back at him from behind the glass covering the mask's eyeholes. Its gloved hands removed its hood to reveal a twirling bun of raven-black hair. It then released the straps that dispelled the mask's grip over the bearer's face.

As the crow mask fell, sweaty strands of hair fell over a female's porcelain face. Her tired eyes of bright gold looked back at the hazel disks of his.'

"Xarnata," the Master of Life placed her gloves beside the mask on the table. The merchant lowered his head in a slight, quick nod that someone else could have easily mistaken for mockery.

"Would you walk with me?" Rowena asked. Xarnata, in turn, offered no response, and somehow, she didn't seem to take offense. He simply followed her footsteps, hurrying to walk by her side.

The couple walked past the extremely sick and terminally ill toward a gate that connected the basement to the outside world, where mounds of dirty, smelly fabrics waited to be washed.

"Fresh air," Rowena took a deep breath, "one must never forget to take a breath of it every so often."

She then sat on top of a small wall. "Come," she tapped the stony surface, "have a seat." The merchant did as instructed.

It was at that very moment when, as if given life by the melody of her voice, one of the nearby mounds moved. Right at the top, the plump head of a small child appeared. Without hesitation, the child stood up and walked rapidly toward the pair, summoning an avalanche of fabric that tumbled down, ending with a soft thud and a low grunt from within it. The boy was short and dirty and also a little pudgy, with a gait that showed somewhat of a limp, but that didn't stop him from walking determinedly, planting himself in front of Rowena, looking up at her with brown eyes that were filled with nothing but endless love.

"Hmm," the boy whimpered, lifting his palms upright. On his hands rested a little gray stuffed elephant, its stuffing coming out in several places, even from two holes where a pair of buttons had once been its eyes. Like the boy himself, it was quite dirty, but it was still offered with pride, almost as a sacrifice to the Master of Life.

"Tobiah," Rowena greeted, reaching for the simple offering. But right before she made contact, the boy pulled the offering away. He opened his mouth wide and closed it again for Rowena to see. It was a gesture she had witnessed him doing many times before. "Hungry, are you?" Drawing a smile, Septem's daughter reached for a pocket from where she produced a small carrot.

Seeing his eyes brighten, she offered it to the child, "Here you go, little one."

Salivating profusely, with a short grunt, Tobiah's hand swiftly wrapped around her gift, which he took two bites out of soon after.

"Now, where is Larcey?" Rowena asked the little boy.

Upon the words, the mound of fabric started to shift. The dirty sheets rose to reveal the face of a little girl who stretched and yawned. Larcey was taller than Tobiah, her skin slightly darker, with a nose that seemed too big for her face and extremities that appeared too short for her slim body. She came out from under the smelly fabrics, carrying a blue ball in one hand. Her eyes appeared sad, almost longing, and while she dropped the ball to ask for a snack with one hand, the other one clasped the sheet as a brooch would keep a hood in place.

"Look at you, little girl," Rowena smiled. As soon as she handed a second carrot to Larcey, the little girl grasped Tobiah's sleeve, dragging him away so that they could both eat quietly, perhaps to watch the small boy protectively, close enough to Rowena's presence, yet distant enough to protect their precious orange snack.

"Look at them," Rowena pointed at the children. "There is as much beauty in enjoying the world and its riches as in helping others, especially those unable to fend for themselves, those who depend on us."

Xarnata Daemos squinted several times, moving his eyebrows independently of each other before he smacked his lips. "How is . . ." he struggled to ask, "your work?"

"This plague spreads rapidly through the body and is quite contagious," Rowena responded. "The sanitarium's best healers are working hard to contain it. In their tireless pursuit, some have been afflicted, many of those lost. The rest are physically overworked, emotionally tired."

"I can help," Xarnata's eyes were intently on Septem's daughter.

"Thank you for the offer, but it will likely not be necessary." Rowena gazed at the horizon. "In a few days' time, support from the healing department at Fennec Academy should arrive. That should relieve the sanitarium's healers of some of the weight. If their minds were to break, it would be disastrous for the potential finding of a cure. It is kind of you to ask," she continued. "What can you say about your work?"

Upon her question, Daemos stretched both hands to produce from within his robes the chest he carried. "Sralfalle," his effort to sound proud fell as flat as his tone.

"Sralfalle." As if hypnotized, Rowena studied the detail in the chest's silver clasps and lining and the soft, blue velvet of its body. She opened it to reveal its contents.

Inside, over a cerulean mound of silk, six flowers of the most beautiful blue rested, their stems bound to a moist cloth that had kept them from withering.

"It is good they are almost intact," Rowena pointed out. "Now, back to work. Not a moment can be wasted. Each second, these potential beneficial properties of these flowers dwindle."

The Master of Life closed the small chest before she slightly turned to face him, "Now, how much do I owe you?"

"Nothing," he said abruptly.

"What do you mean nothing? Tell me," Rowena's soft voice insisted.

"Nothing."

"Unacceptable. Every job has its reward. You have to get paid for your work."

"You're lucky to have me."

"Lucky?" Rowena's eyes of shining gold seemed to soften as she looked back into the weathered hazel of his own, "But I do not believe in luck. I do not believe in gods; I do not believe in many things. But one thing I do believe is that we are fortunate to have met one another in this life, my Lord Xarnata."

Tobiah & Larceny

"I am no lord," the merchant promptly stated.

"Mankind believes nobility titles are as important as they are inherited," Rowena's lips parted, "but it is what lies within a heart that makes one truly noble."

Before she walked back toward the dank basement of the sanitarium, Xarnata opened his mouth to say a word, but he didn't. The proximity as they sat allowed a small breeze to carry the scent of crimson roses into his nostrils, that same scent he remembered wherever he went. His hand fidgeted with an object inside his pocket like he had done many times before to feel calm in the midst of the storm inside his head. This time, however, it was a small heart of burnt wood he had whittled, for her, but one he had never dared to give. Something within him stopped him from doing so. Instead, he trembled.

They sat side by side, a pair of frozen dolls sitting on a forgotten rack while the world around them spun its accursed story.

Xarnata turned away. His hand rested upon his thigh, drenched with sweat, hoping, longing for just a touch from hers, at least a single caress that would break the stillness, that would mute the silence.

All he had ever wanted was that which he had never had in this life—love.

Whether it was she who moved or he, Xarnata could never recall, but he would always remember the moment their littlest of fingers touched, and he would remember her smile, a ruby smile that branded itself into his heart.

A DROP OF LIFE

Location: Kingdom of Blackheart,
Royal Duchy of Darkholm, Darkholde Keep

The greatest changes can be achieved through either luck or hard work...

Centuries had passed since the first stone was laid atop the cliff where the royal stronghold of Blackheart now sits.

The keep itself was a marvelous sight to behold, with its grand arches adorned with gargoyles, carved stony walkways, and turrets that reflected the great expertise of the skilled architects and masons whose children and even great-grandchildren had joined in the performance of their labor.

Its beauty added to the strange disjunction of the Darkholm. While it was built as an admirable piece of dark art, it was off-limits to everyone but those whom the Darkholm trusted, and that number was known to be extremely limited.

Nobles of other lands were also peculiar about visitors, but at least those other nobles seemed to enjoy the beauty around them. To the pallid members of the ruling House of Blackheart, all these artistic details seemed to go unnoticed.

Darkholde sat over the great cliffs, where many of the rooms of the gargantuan structure hung over the sea as if seeking to escape the world of men its ruling House for so long had sought to detach from.

It was in one of those that the Master of Life's laboratory was located.

"Well, Charon," Rowena stood by her main desk, where innumerable beakers and flasks contained concoctions in various stages of preparation, "there is one thing that never evades us."

"Aging!" Lady Charon raised a finger as if asking for permission to express the response she had just blurted out.

"Responsibility," Rowena smiled, "we can ignore it all we want, but it will still be there, waiting."

"I know," Charon responded, "I find it boring at times. Don't you?"

Rowena smiled back at her cousin, her pearly whites appearing behind her rose-red lips, but it was Elleonora who said, "Well, Charon, you certainly do not find it hard to find entertainment, especially when there is so much work to do. Rowena," she added in her usual flat tone, "here, I have mixed one of the *sralfalle* petals with a pinch of sulfur, but I am not getting a reaction under the magnifying lenses. Should I try a second one?"

"We do not have many left," Rowena answered.

"Shall I discard this then?" Elleonora questioned.

"It is best we do not." The Master of Life took the sample from her, "We might still have a use for it."

"Master of Life," one of the servants walked in, "sorry to interrupt your work, but there is a healer from Alnwick at the Tower. He claims he is waiting for something you are sending the physicians."

"Indeed, but I cannot stop what I am doing right now," Rowena replied. "Still, let him know to warm it up before application. It might still not be strong enough, but it is definitely an improvement from the last batch.

"Charon," she instructed, "the six vials we prepared about an hour ago."

"Which ones?"

"The ones we boiled twice, remember?"

"Ah yes," Charon smiled proudly, placing her hands over a small collection, "are these the ones?"

"Those are the ones," Rowena responded, counting the drops she was placing inside a warm beaker.

Charon did as instructed, happily handing the vials to the servant.

Moments later, one of their cousins stepped in, the one with the long, wavy hair that reached his shoulders and a smile as wide as the one in Elzabeth's oversized mask.

"Hey girls," the charming voice of Toradmus called, shrugging shyly as if to avoid disturbing their hectic work schedule.

"Toradmus!" Lady Charon greeted him with a hug and a kiss on each cheek as was their custom, "It is good to see you. What brings you here?"

"I," Toradmus grinned, "am traveling back to Grayhelm."

"You are headed to Grayhelm?" Rowena questioned.

"Certainly." At nineteen, he was close to Rowena's age. "It is why I have come."

"What do you need?" Elleonora said without looking at him, grinding dried leaves and adding water to form a paste.

"Something to help me sleep." The handsome blacksmith shut an eye and grinned as if he believed he was asking for too much.

"I can prepare you something," Elleonora scolded, "but you will have to wait. We are very busy right now."

"I will take care of it, Lora," Rowena said, and leaving her work aside for a minute, she promptly began preparing a concoction for her cousin. "Grayhelm again, huh?" she teased.

"Yes, only for two or three weeks, why?" Toradmus asked. "There is an ore I want to use in my next work."

"And why not send someone for it?" the Master of Life asked.

"I would prefer to bring it myself," Toradmus responded.

"Is that so?" she smiled slyly, knowing well of her cousin's quiet romantic escapade.

"Aaaaargh!" the shrilling screams of Sellayne Darkholm interrupted their conversation. "I am bleeding!" At the doorway, her tailor and his two assistants appeared, almost carrying her fainting body.

"Aaaaargh!" she yelled, lifting a hand covered in a bloodied rag toward the ceiling. "Take your hands off me!" Sellayne moved her shoulder away from one of the assistants, "It is *your* fault I am here! My hand!"

Toradmus took a step back while the three girls rushed in to assist the flower of Darkholm.

"Are you okay?" Charon questioned.

"Of course, I am not!" Sellayne spat.

"Come, let us see now," Rowena took her wrapped hand.

"No, I am scared. I am bleeding a lot, Rowena!"

"I promise I will be gentle," the Master of Life stated, touching the wrapping carefully. "Elleonora, you may continue what you were doing. I will take care of Sellayne myself," she instructed her cousin. "Now, Sellayne, tell me what happened."

"My tailor brought me a dress I was expecting, one that was already late." She glared at the tailor.

"Yes," Rowena tapped her forearm lightly, "but tell me about your hand."

"I am livid, Rowena. That is important!"

"I can only imagine," Rowena smiled, knowing quite well the daughter of the second Valdemar was known for having the shortest of fuses. "Now, tell me quickly," the physician continued, "the end result could very well depend on the promptness with which treatment is administered."

"Then forget how it happened!" Sellayne spat. "Treat me!" If there was one thing Sorsha's daughter feared was needles, although not as much as scars and even those she feared less than complications. So she tried her best to remain calm, watching Rowena unwrap the bloodied rag.

"Is it really bad?" Sellayne asked, looking away. "It is bad, is it not?"

"It's not," Charon giggled, changing her tone when she saw Sellayne's furious eyes looking back at her, feeling mocked by the smiling girl.

"Charon is right, Sellayne," Rowena smiled warmly. "We will have to suture it, however.

"Charon," Rowena ordered, "you will need the needles and suturing hemp, vinegar, and honey."

Charon returned moments later with everything Rowena had asked for. "This won't hurt much, I promise." She placed a stool in front of Sellayne, whose eyes opened wide in fear.

"Wait, you are not touching me!" Sellayne raised her voice. "I want Rowena to do it!"

"Sellayne," Rowena said, "there are many duties I need to attend to that we are behind on. Both Charon and Elleonora can suture very well. Having either of them do it is as if having me do it with my own hands, as I will be supervising—"

"No, I will not have it," Sellayne frowned, "Rowena, you do not understand! I want *you* to do it!" Upon hearing her request Elleonora, who was about to offer, simply shrugged and resumed her duties.

"Very well," Rowena responded, "then let me do it."

So afraid was Sellayne she clutched the hand Lady Charon offered, and she squeezed it hard 'til Charon's fingers felt numb, and she screamed, her shrill echoing along the hallways long before Rowena had even begun suturing. And she forced the Master of Life to stop many times—at the beginning, halfway, and close to the end—to tell her a story, to distract her, while Charon wiped Sellayne's tears and sweat.

"That was a handful," Toradmus finally said after seeing Sellayne leave.

"*She* is a handful," Elleonora responded, while Charon looked down the hallways to ensure Sellayne was all right, and Rowena resumed her duties.

"Here, Toradmus," Rowena handed him a vial, "five drops under the tongue whenever sleep is required, not more than once a day."

"Thank you," he smiled, kissing her cheeks before he left the room.

"Where were we?" Rowena mused, pulling the list of concoctions they still needed to prepare when a knock on the door alerted them.

"Gustavus," Rowena greeted, "may we be of assistance?"

"I have come for my wife," Gustavus responded dryly, "it is long past the twelfth hour. It is past the time of laboring."

"Our duty never ends, Gustavus," Rowena looked at the larger man's furrowed brow.

"Maybe for you, as the Master of Life," he stated. "She is not. She only assists you, but she has a duty which is that of being my wife."

Septem's daughter looked back upon Elleonora, who, without hesitation, dropped what she was doing and walked to her husband's side. "I am sorry, Rowena, but my husband needs my presence."

"Then you may take your leave," Rowena smiled.

"Thank you for understanding," Elleonora responded, "I will be here early tomorrow."

"Me too," Rowena responded. But Elleonora didn't seem to notice the tiredness in her cousin's eyes. She kissed her goodbye and walked to hold her husband's extended hand.

Septem's daughter nodded in understanding, a faint smile on her lips, and she saw them depart, leaving more work in her aching hands.

She walked to Elleonora's desk to figure out where she had left off, where Rowena had to resume the work, when she caught a glimpse of Charon seated, dangling her legs while she smiled, looking through the window at the world outside.

"You know, Charon," Rowena's soft voice startled her, "you can leave too if you wish."

"Can I?" Grinning, Charon took a deep breath.

"No one is stopping you," Rowena responded.

"Yay!" Charon jumped off her seat and ran toward the door, dancing and spinning around mirthfully.

But before she walked through the doorway, she stopped for a minute and looked back inside the room, where five different desks with materials still had work that needed completion. She saw Rowena take a seat and begin to make notes, straining herbs and preparing vials. She saw, for the first time, the dark circles around her cousin's beautiful eyes. She saw the exhaustion in the hands that were less precise this late than when they had started early in the day.

"But Rowena," Lady Charon bit her lower lip.

"Yes?" her cousin looked back.

And that gaze filled Charon with guilt. How could Elleonora just leave them like that, leave her like that, with so much work left?

"Rowena, I was thinking, if I leave . . . who will help you then?"

Septem's daughter looked into Charon's eyes with her exhausted own. "Have I ever required any assistance?" she asked.

"You're right!" Charon giggled, and she dashed down the hallway singing, dancing along the way.

Without a moment wasted, the Master of Life resumed her work. There were salves she needed to prepare, cures she needed to research, a potential outbreak she needed to stop, and the days never seemed long enough.

When dawn came, the sun's rays climbed up to enter the study through the window, to kiss her eyelids and part the gates that had been sealed by the spirit of exhaustion. And she woke up, ready to begin her work once more.

WINGS OF HOPE

Location: Kingdom of Ardenay, Duchy of Walcrast,
Capital City of Soloren, Windfall Palace

Nothing clips our wings like our own hearts . . .

*H*ome.

Siul Ileva's arms spread wide.

His chest rose under the deep breath he held in for a few seconds, capturing the cool aroma of the fresh air he had missed.

His horse had just crossed the pass that brought them to the shore of Windane Lake, the largest body of water in the Duchy of Walcrast. Its fluid presence lay nestled between steep mountains under the beautiful, clear sky.

Unlike the blue celestial body above, echoed in the reflective lake surface and once again on their banner, the marvels of the landscape were covered in the purest whites, the granite grays, and lush, fertile greens.

Countless times he had witnessed what towered before him, and yet once again, he looked up to admire Windfall, the most beautiful palace in all of Ardenay and, some would even claim, the world itself.

And the home base of the nucleus of House Ileva.

Even though House Ileva's home base was much smaller than the royal palace in Himlen, it was as majestic, or in the eyes of some, even moreso.

Windfall Castle had been built as a group of towers that rested atop a tall, natural column that rose from within the center of Windane Lake's waterfalls.

So ingenious had the legendary engineers of Walcrast been, they had connected each side of the lakeshore on top of the waterfalls to the palace by a single stone bridge cut with canals that allowed water to both reach the structure at its end and also drain along the bridge as nearly a dozen manmade cataracts that gave the small fortress its name, the Palace of the Waterfalls.

To visit the ducal castle, those coming from the Angel's Pass in the south would reach the capital city of Soloren, where one would have to climb along one of the two main cobblestone roads on either side of the enormous waterfall basin.

It was along these two roads that the nobility had their residences. The most noble, and lately the most pious, lived on the Lakeview, facing the basin. The rest of them lived on the Mountainside.

Along the climb, one would constantly view, when not interrupted by the noble homes perched on the cliffs facing the lake, Windfall's noble structure that would always seem to be looking back.

Soloren itself had been built on two levels, along the shores of the upper lake and the one below, where the city licked the four rivers that drained the grand lake as roaming beasts partaking in its pure waters.

As if there was any need for more to turn the whole location into a greater wonder, the whole area lay nestled, surrounded by tall mountainous peaks that turned Windfall Palace into a nearly unassailable structure.

Siul began the climb by taking the road on the right. It had been over a year since his last visit, and from this side, he could see that familiar tower of the palace, the one with closed windows that connected his room to the rest of the world.

Each guard he saw saluted the young captain, joining his climb as a flock of birds in migration, following his mount with their own to both support and honor him while ensuring his safety.

The commoners along the way lowered their heads, while nobles would nod and smile, welcoming one of their own.

Upon reaching the palace's bridge, Siul dismounted. His royal blue cape trailed behind him as he walked toward the entrance, welcomed by the trumpets announcing the arrival of the heir to the seat of House Ileva.

Before him, the main gate opened, giving way to half a dozen servants who proceeded to take care of the nobleman and his mount, bringing a basket of fruits and a cup of wine in the welcoming Solorean tradition.

Nothing changes, Siul thought.

"My lord," the head servant bowed.

"Inel, old man," Siul sipped, offering half a smile, "it's good to see you."

The septuagenarian smiled, looking at the young noble, his eyes filled with pride. "No," the old man calmly instructed one of the servant girls that readied herself to walk alongside Siul, "take care of his belongings. I will take it upon myself to accompany my lord." And he did as per their custom when upon the arrival of one of their name, a servant would accompany them around to inform them of the most important current events.

Inel walked alongside the young knight, informing him of events minor and those not, when the old servant lowered his voice and asked, "Something is amiss, my lord?"

"What is?" Siul asked.

"In you, I mean," the old man responded, "You are quick to jest, and yet today, you are quiet. I can tell when something is off."

Inel was right, Siul thought. The knight would have normally come up with a jest, something like, Inel, you look younger and younger every year! But how could he joke around when both his mind was troubled?

Even after not having seen him for over a year, this old, faithful servant was in tune with who he was, even when he didn't know the truth inside Siul's heart.

How could Siul have lived so long among them in hiding? Was he the person he truly thought he was when he had for so long lived with a mask? In the end, Siul waved a hand, "It's nothing. I'm tired of my travels."

"Then, if you so wish, I'll just walk with you."

"No, please," Siul asked, "keep talking."

"There is unrest in the north," Inel reported. "Against the Bulwharf's wishes, the king has asked us to be ready. Upon the Crown's order, your lord father will march to the Horne with reinforcements."

"I see," Siul responded.

"But that's more recent," Inel continued, "for the last year, His Grace has ordered the construction of a small fort to protect the Northwind way."

"It makes sense, given Blackheart's incursion in the north. What are your thoughts?" Siul questioned.

"There's increased unrest among the nobles, too, for in order to build the Northwind, His Grace has raised taxes."

"How much?" Siul stopped in the middle of the hallway.

"Too much, my lord," Inel bowed his head, "temporarily and only for the nobles."

"They need to be made to understand it is a temporary pain for a permanent gain," Siul explained.

"Yes," Inel responded, "but they don't see it that way, my lord. What makes many nobles noble is not their hearts but their riches. Touch it, and you may as well have touched their wives or daughters. In any case, here's your room, my lord."

"Thank you, Inel."

"Before I go . . ." the servant faced him.

"Yes?"

"Some of us are concerned about your father's health."

"That is news to me. What's wrong?"

"At times, he seems winded after little effort," Inel responded. "The doctor says it's his age, but I hear him coughing at night, more so lately."

"I was not aware of that. Thank you, I'll talk to him."

"Your seat at the table will be ready for supper at the fifth hour of the sun's height. Welcome home, my lord. May the winds blow in your favor."

Of all the areas of the palace he could have visited, he first entered the still chamber that had once been his room.

While barely any light came through wooden windows that had been shut long ago, it was clear the chamber was exquisitely adorned, as expected of anything the Ileva owned, for even the most militant citizen of Walcrast Duchy seemed to have impeccable taste and love for finery.

Siul stood at the center of the room, contemplating every piece of carved wood, the large bed that was readied every day, even when nobody slept on it. It was the bed that had heard his confessions, the same one that had drank the tears he had shed growing up.

With only a few steps, the young nobleman reached the wooden panes of the main windows. With deft hands, he parted them to fill the room with both warm sunlight and the song of cool waterfalls.

Freedom.

The knight exhaled, basking in the light that invaded the room. His eyes, blue as the sky at noon, contemplated the houses of the nobles, the many fountains, the greenery of the mountains beyond, and even the south portion of Soloren below, where its inhabitants went about their business, walking with poise, with grace, almost as if every citizen had the discipline of a soldier, as if somehow, they felt all their actions were being noted, as they were always being watched.

In the end, the whole socioeconomic, geographic, and structural arrangement that comprised Soloren was as beautiful and complex as the relationship between Walcrast and the Church was.

And it was that same relationship that brought doubt into the heart of the knight. While he commanded some of the fastest and most elite forces, had risen through the ranks of the greatest warriors and leaders, and had defeated countless opponents, none of that had prepared him for this day he so long dreaded, the day he would have to speak, no, *confess* to his own Blood that the one thing he could never overcome were the feelings inside of him.

But *could he?*

How could he when he knew how Walcrast treated the impure, when he knew what its people did to the deviated, if only to appear most pious in the eyes of the Light?

If one thing he truly trusted was the unity of his small family, the loyalty they had toward one another. It was this unity, he believed, that would help him garner their support in his search for Ealas.

For a while now, he had spent a long time on his own, secretly scouring the capital of Himlen, from the places Ealas and he once used to escape to, to those shady places they would have never ventured into, and his search had proven fruitless.

The one detail he was able to gather, however, had troubled him the most. One of the palace servants nervously admitted he saw Ealas taking the ashes of his former slave with him. And while the servant didn't know where to, Siul didn't need to ask.

He had lost all sleep that night, thinking about the friend he loved, wondering what, if anything, could have made Ealas leave that way.

"He could not really possibly be in the land of our enemies," Siul thought, "or could he?" It troubled him that, if this had crossed Ealas's mind, his friend hadn't trusted him enough to tell him the truth, but then he saw his own reflection in the mirror and realized he had not been true to Ealas either.

Not able to look at his own eyes, Siul moved away from the reflective surface. If he didn't speak up, he would just have to consider his beloved friend lost, and that, to his heart, was unacceptable. How could he give up when he had come all this way to ask the duke, his own father, to provide him with the forces needed to travel across the border?

He looked out the window upon the lake's rocky edges. If the wings on his back were not merely engraved in his breastplate, he could have taken flight, fast and far, as an arrow that had just left its bow . . . one that, weighted down by his own feeling of inadequacy, fell tip first into a rock.

"Brother!" Aelle walked in through the door he had forgotten to close.

Siul strode toward Aelle as she darted toward him to be caught in his arms, her forehead kissed by his tender lips. "Look at you. You look amazing!"

"You surely say that to all the girls!" she tested, resting her chin upon the chest of her taller brother, meeting his blue eyes with the wooden brown of hers. Her fragrance, Siul smiled, was always that aroma of fresh cut flowers, while her honey-colored hair trailed behind her loosely.

"Believe me, you are the only girl I say those things to," he hugged her.

"How do you like my dress?" Aelle curtsied at her only brother.

"I think it looks wonderful!" he smiled.

"Well," she played with her hair, "I have to go get my hair fixed for supper. I just wanted to come by and greet you before the formality of dinner."

Siul looked upon the sweet innocence of his sister, upon the way she always greeted him, reminding him love could and would transcend any and all hardships.

Could he tell her the truth? Could I tell her I love Ealas, that my love for him is bigger than that of a friend? Of course, he could. If there was one person in his small household he could be frank with, that was Aelle, she who had laughed and cried with him, and had many times, growing up, crawled up into his bed when she was afraid of the dark, or of the haunting sound of the autumn wind through the palace windows.

"Aelle . . ." he said.

"Yes?" She looked at him with eyes of love.

"There is something I need to tell you."

"Always together, right?" She smiled at him, reminding him of the words they used to tell each other as children.

"Yes, always together," he choked. "Aelle, I just need to share something with you. To be frank and honest with you about something."

His sister nodded calmly, grabbing his hand and sitting by his side on the bed. "Tell me."

"It is regarding Ealas . . ." he trailed off.

"I . . . know what you're going to tell me," Aelle smiled shyly.

"Do you?"

"Yes, of course," she nodded, "that you are going to do everything you can to find him."

Siul's eyes glistened.

"Because," she continued, "I guess somehow you must have found out I am completely in love with him, and, knowing you as I do, you would want nothing more than to help make my dreams true."

As if having become stone, Siul could not move. All this time, he had brought Ealas to keep him close. He had even offered his sister's hand without asking her to shorten the distance between him and his best friend to spend more time around him. So focused had he been on his own feelings, he had never questioned what his sister felt.

In the end, he said nothing. He only nodded sadly, kissing her head as she hugged him hard, and he felt her heart beating fast as an excited child's.

Who was he to break his sister's heart? Could he? Of course, he could, but would he?

His sister departed mirthfully, ready to shine, ready to laugh, ready to love while his eyes glistened.

The figure of his mother stepped aside from behind the door frame. Her long hair of gold and eyes of soft brown smiled upon seeing her firstborn son. "I do know what you were about to say, what lies within your heart."

"Do you know?" he said with difficulty.

"I do." She approached him with the elegance of a queen, "A mother always secretly knows, even if it's hard for her to accept it. The one thing I want to say is, Siul, my son, know this—you are my son, and as my son, my love for you is beyond measure. As you are, I will always accept you."

Her words brought tears to his eyes as he fell on his knees, a broken child who had for so long feared the rejection of the woman whom he loved most.

"What I will never accept," she continued, "is your *sin*."

———————— ✦✦✦✦✦ ————————

Supper was held in the main dining hall at the fifth hour past the zenith.

The dining table was long, with many of the exquisitely carved wooden chairs empty on this night when the Winglord, Duke Yel Ileva, had invited only the closest and highest members of Soloren's wing knights. At the center of the long table, the duke and his wife sat, flanked by the deacon assigned to Windfall, and Aelle, whose beautiful hairdress could not distract from her swollen, moist eyes that avoided her brother's gaze.

While the plates were served and the wine poured, Siul Ileva could see nothing more than his father, hear nothing but his voice reverberating.

"Tell me it is not true!" Duke Yel slammed his clenched fist on the table.

"It is true," Siul responded, trying to stay calm at the humiliation he was being put through in front of all his father's loyalists, the former friends who would now see him as worse than filth.

Giving him no quarter, the duke pointed a finger at him. "You can renounce that life of sin!"

"I am tired," Siul responded. "I am tired of living a lie."

"The Light abhors you," Yel spat, "and with every ounce of my strength, I abhor you too!"

The words of the father dug deep into his son's chest, but Siul sought to remain composed, "I think we might be mistaken in our interpretation of God. He—"

"The words of the Light are clear!" the deacon protested.

"The Light will punish you," Siul's father added. "He will drag your life along the dirt as you have dragged our name with your filthy hands."

"Father!" Aelle cried.

"Quiet!" Yel fumed, "unless you want to be his accomplice."

Upon his words, she rose from her seat and left the chamber, her dish served but untouched.

"Yel!" Lady Eniara Ileva shouted, "You're drunk!"

"Silence, woman! Know your place!" he screamed, turning back to Siul, his face red with ire, "And you . . . I pray God smites you down where you stand before I kill you with my very own hands."

"Father . . ." Siul responded in disbelief.

"Silence! You're not my son! Although he lost his path, Ealas was the son you're not! Get out of my house! Leave!

"And may all here listen to my decree: upon the sun's rising, if Siul is found anywhere within my borders, kill him where he stands!" Furiously, he hurled his cup at Siul, splashing wine over the tablecloth and some of the guests.

Siul took a step back. He looked at his mother, pain in his eyes. The secret she guarded for so long inside her heart was now confessed.

His eyes then went to his father, the man he had respected and admired for the entirety of his life, the strong man he had sought to model his training and life after. Was there something Siul could say that would touch his heart?

"I . . ." Siul's lips trembled.

"Leave . . . my . . . presence, you bastard!"

Seeing his son leave, Yel Ileva followed, walking hurriedly toward the doorway when he was stopped by a sudden tightness on his chest that made him stumble.

He gasped, his eyes wide open in a desperate expression.

"Yel, Yel!" Lady Eniara shouted desperately, fanning him with her own hands, "Someone call a physician!"

CLIPPED

Location: Kingdom of Ardenay, Duchy of Walcrast, City of Soloren

One can't hammer a bird's wings and ask it to fly . . .

The third cup came down faster than the previous ones.

Siul Ileva placed it over the counter, asking the barmaster to fill it once more. The old man hesitated but nonetheless did as asked. "Would you like something with that?" he asked in a foreign accent that, despite having spent most of his life in Soloren, refused to disappear.

"Don't ask," Siul lowered his head, "just fill my cup."

"As you wish," the man shrugged, smiling with that smile of one who had the misfortune to see youngsters ruin their lives far too often to count.

The barmaster took a plate left over by a customer whose stupor hadn't let him partake of it. "Here, it's on the house."

"I don't want it," Siul turned his head, gulping from his cup.

"At least be grateful," the man pushed the plate toward him. "Don't let it go to waste."

Siul turned around toward the busy establishment, leaning his back against the bar. The place was busy. It was one of the taverns he wouldn't have otherwise visited, being on the lower part of the city where the nobles wouldn't be seen often.

He had just stopped there out of frustration, on his way out of the city, leaving his horse at the hands of that stable boy whose eyes had, curiously, set on him.

Would he join in the revelry and dance with the musicians near the fireplace? Would he just get his horse and go on his journey?

No, he wanted to forget or at least ease his pain. It wasn't bad enough that he had lost Ealas, and he wondered, 'Do you think of me?' but to compound it, he had also lost his entire family.

Siul turned back toward the barmaster to find his plate was gone.

"Sorry, I thought you didn't want it," a young male voice said from his left. "I'll order you one."

"No need," Siul waved a hand, looking back at the young man who seemed strangely familiar.

The young man was slender, with curled, brown hair reaching his perfect neck. His enrapturing eyes looked back at Siul playfully while his fingers toyed around with the fork before digging into a buttered, chopped potato.

"I have seen you before," Siul pondered, "do I know you?"

"Well, yes and no," the young man responded, "I took your horse."

Something.

Of course, the stable boy.

"Name's Darel," the young man nodded, one of his curls falling between his penetrating eyes that were fixed on the knight. "You?"

Siul didn't respond. What he needed the most was to disappear, to become unknown. He turned his face away and looked ahead toward the wall lined with bottles of liquor.

"Oh, you're here to forget, aren't you?" Darel questioned his silence. "No worries, I can't blame you. You're not the only one who comes here to forget something or someone."

Siul looked back at him, not knowing if it was his words or his hypnotizing, gray eyes that compelled him to do so.

"Don't worry, you don't have to tell me your name," Darel took another bite, "your secret is safe with me."

"What 'secret'?" Siul asked.

"Oh, common," Darel smiled, whispering, "I know what you are."

"And what am I?"

"You're deviated, like me."

Siul couldn't respond to his assertion. He was right, and he was also like him. He simply looked ahead, thinking of what to say next.

"Would you like to eat something?" Darel asked. Seeing that Siul wouldn't say a word, he chuckled, "I'm talking about our dish! Would you like some? And hey, don't worry, I'm not going to hand feed you."

Who was this person Siul had just met? He was young, sweet, and charming, and there was a certain *something* that attracted Siul to him. Was it his smile, his charisma? Was it the seductive warmth of his words? Was it his own frustration, the desperation to ease his own pain?

Feeling somewhat at ease, Siul picked up a fork and took a few bites of the dish.

"You can let your guard down," Darel said in a teasing tone. "Don't worry, I'm not here to do harm, but I can be here to please."

––––––––– ++++++ –––––––––

The door closing behind them saw the playful tease materialize again, the glances, the tongues that traveled along the perfect dessert of their skin upon the fabrics' departure.

Darel kissed Siul's neck while Siul pulled the stablehand's hair back to bite his chin.

With a small nibble of his earlobe, Darel whispered, "I want you."

Their eyes locked in on each other in that moment of fiery passion that heated the room much more than the fireplace that had been readied.

Exhausted from everything, the journey, the fight, and the intimate moment, Siul lay naked, his back toward Darel, who sat in bed, his fingertips caressing the knight's back.

"You're beautiful, you mysterious stranger," Darel kissed his shoulder.

Siul responded by grabbing his hand and kissing it.

"You're like me," Darel continued, "a hopeless deviated, but unlike me, choosing to live in a place where your life is at risk, and yet you can escape."

"Why do you say that?" Siul turned to face him, "What makes you think I can escape?"

"Just look at your clothes," the stable hand pointed at the floor. "You're a noble."

A knock on his door startled them.

"Darel!" the attendant girl whispered from the other side of the door. "If you're there, get out. Someone is coming, and there are knights and a deacon outside."

The young man stood up from the bed in the blink of an eye and grabbed his clothes from the floor. He put his pants on and held his loose, white shirt in his hand as if daring Siul to admire his perfect body one last time. Before leaving, he moved toward the bed and kissed Siul one more time.

"If you won't tell me your name, at least don't forget me." Darel bit his own lip, "I hope you want to do this again as much as I want to."

––––––––– ++++++ –––––––––

Moments later, removing the hood that covered her features, Lady Eniara Ileva entered the room.

"Mother!" Siul sat on the bed, "What are you doing here? And so late?"

"I wanted to find you before you left," she said softly, the trembling of her voice obvious to her son.

"How did you find me here?"

"You consider your father's men incapable?" Her eyes were on him, "They've been searching for hours."

"What do you want from me?"

Clasping her hands, she lowered her head, "It's your father."

"What about him? I'm not his son, remember?" He looked at her, his eyes those of a pet whose owner had abused and now stretched the hand to caress.

"That's unnecessary," she frowned. "You're our son, regardless of what he said. I need to ask something of you."

"What is it, Mother?"

"After you left, your father collapsed." She placed her hand over her eyes to hold back her tears, "The palace physician says his heart is failing, and he might not make it. His time leading the duchy is at an end." Lady Eniara grabbed her son's hand, "He needs you to take the mantle of Head of the House."

Her words shocked Siul. The biggest responsibility that could ever fall into his hands was being presented to him. It was not something he wanted. Although he would have more resources at his disposal, it would make his search for Ealas that much more difficult. Besides, his life was sinful, and living in the spotlight meant the Church's and every other set of eyes would be on him at all times.

"I can't, Mother."

"What do you mean you can't?" Her eyes glistened.

"I . . . just can't."

"Why do you say that? You might be angry, but he *is* your father."

"I don't want that life. I want to be free," he stated. "I don't want to go back to living a lie."

His words were a slap on the face of Lady Eniara. She stood up from the bed, looking down upon him, her face one of both sadness and anger. "Well, let me give you something to think on," she said. "Just remember that what happened to your father . . . it's all *your* doing!"

The noblewoman turned away and left without an answer, but leaving him with a guilt that felt worse than his father's humiliation.

For hours Siul tried to sleep, but his eyes wouldn't close. His mind tortured him every minute.

He knelt to pray, to ask the Light for guidance, when he remembered it was this same following of the Light that had brought such difficult times for those like him. He felt dirty, inadequate. He wondered how he could change his thoughts, his feelings, the desires of his heart, and he broke down into tears, doubled on the floor.

"Why do people like me exist? Why create us to punish us, to kill us?" He prayed, slamming his fist against the floor, dispersing the small puddle his tears had created on the cold surface. "How can you, who are love, hate me?"

When morning came, the doors to the Palace of the Waterfalls opened.

Lady Ileva and her daughter waited for any sign of her son's arrival. But the one who passed through the gates was only a defeated, mounted knight, his helmet off, his long hair down as if absorbing his disgrace.

He came back not for glory or pride but rather from shame and guilt. He would take the title, would fill the seat, he would once again wear a mask.

He did it for the love he felt for his sister, for his mother, even for the love he felt for his father, for apparently, the love he felt for them was much greater than the love they felt for him.

Alone, he returned to his room, where his eyes the color of the heavens disappeared once more behind the closing windows.

THE GREY

Location: Kingdom of Blackheart,
Duchy of Darkholm, Ironholde Keep

"All is Grey."

The tenet of the Darkholm escaped Erdrick's lips, echoed by the pairs of lips of those who had found their respective seats around the round, ashen table.

It was echoed by the Grey Circle, influential men and women, each one an expert in a different field deemed important enough to require representation.

Since its creation hundreds of years before, it had been composed mostly of members of the House, chosen by the Duke of Darkholm to serve as advisers to facilitate the Lords of Darkholm's understanding of the land and people they detachedly ruled over.

Whether it was this relationship that had allowed Davidov Darkholm to be successful despite his disdain for ruling and everyday matters, or the fear of what would happen to those who dared cross him, nobody truly knew, but perhaps the truth lay somewhere in between.

While Davidov was present, today he echoed the words, for he had invited Erdrick to sit as the head in his role as acting duke.

Erdrick Darkholm studied all those present, the reverence of these powerful companions through which he would one day perform most of his ducal duties, the chamber's vaulted ceiling that felt small when compared to the halls of the main keep and how Darkholde Keep itself peered through the window as if to remind them how small they truly were.

Today Erdrick didn't hold his honorary position in this chamber as Knight Commander, and thus all eyes were on him, even those of Gustavus, who stood faithfully by his side.

"You may all be seated," Erdrick instructed. "Let us report in the usual order."

"I am here on behalf of the Master of Cosmos, my lords," a young servant girl spoke first, "I was instructed to inform you there is nothing to report at this time. *In Tenebris nos.*"

"In representation of the Master of Secrets," the rose red lips and killer smile of Alesabella Darkholm spoke softly, her eyes almost seeking to seduce Erdrick's. "There is nothing new to report at this time. *In Tenebris nos.*"

Yrenne Darkholm, Master of Scholars, spoke next, "Completion of the construction of Darkholm University looms. There are a good number of educators we have been able to hire, some who will transfer from Fennec Academy."

"Have we ensured to have the blessing of Fennec Academy on this matter?" Erdrick questioned.

"That will not be a problem." Leaning toward the table with a grin, Count Azareth blew a puff of smoke, "Lady Narkari handpicked those to be transferred herself. However, it is important to remember that, while independent of Fennec, Darkholm University will also function as a branch of Fennec itself."

"A potential conflict of interest for Fennec and Narkari," Erdrick said.

"Conflict of interest and Narkari in the same sentence? Only to say she has none, perhaps. That woman would burn the entire academy and start again if the king asked her to," Azareth grinned.

"Fennec is her greatest dream, though," Yrenne argued.

"While her greatest passion is her project," the Master of Lore smiled again, "I would not so easily question her devotion to us."

Nodding, Yrenne added, "There is nothing else to report. *In Tenebris nos.*"

Sorsha Darkholm, the quiet, brooding woman who held the position of Master of Courts, exacting the king's justice across Darkholm, said briefly, "We have hired a dozen more lawspeakers, five of them alone for Coldforge. There is nothing else to report. *In Tenebris nos.*"

All eyes were then on Davidov Darkholm, Master of Death, whose turn it was to speak.

The ancient wet his lips slowly and just waved his hand once to signal he had nothing to say. "*In Tenebris nos,*" he almost whispered.

Cedrick, Master of Seas, then tapped the table twice to mean the same and echoed Davidov's words.

Dorien Darkholm, Master of Chests, followed. "My lord, the treasury reports an increase in last quarter's revenue."

"Where is that coming from?" The strategic thinking of the commander within Erdrick inquired, understanding the importance of what needed to be promptly identified and exploited.

Fidgeting through papers, Dorien responded, "There has been an increase in demand for Blood Tea. Since production has decreased from the loss of some crops, the value has likewise increased. Our capital has been seeing an influx of people, most of which are likely temporary residents.

"Despite the doubling of Alnwick's expenses," he briefly eyed Rowena, "the Crown's standard tax and the Crown's appreciation which, as we all know, is given freely and voluntarily by the Blood of Darkholm as, well, a sign of appreciation, have both increased enough to add to the coffers."

At the jab, Rowena's sly eyes smiled back, but she offered not a single word in response. She waited patiently for her due time to speak.

"The king," Dorien continued, "has asked us to set aside a portion of that to send as support for the Arande region as the conflict between Aligrand and Olath Valm worsens. It would be irresponsible of me not to offer advice in this matter. I believe it would be in our best interest to set a portion aside for eventualities within our own borders before we take out a percentage for Arande."

"How much is the Crown asking to send?" Erdrick inquired.

"Twenty percent," Dorien answered. "If we take out thirty percent first, as I am suggesting, then the twenty percent the king asks for becomes fourteen percent. Not a big difference in the grand scheme of things for Arande, but a difference for our duchy."

Erdrick pondered on the thought. He supported the people of the Arande region who had been displaced due to the infighting that started the moment the land switched hands from the duchy of Aligrand to Olath Valm. But Dorien's advice was wise. It could be easily arranged, and the Crown would likely never notice, and above that, it would be all for the benefit of Darkholm.

But one day, he thought, that crown would be on his own head.

"You speak wise counsel," Erdrick said to the Master of Chests, "but this shall not be done

Erdrick Darkholm

without the knowledge of the Crown. Our Lord King is as practical as he is reasonable, and at the very least, he will listen. After this meeting, meet with Lord Aiden Sanglune and prepare a detailed finance report which you will provide to the king as you present your argument."

"But," Dorien explained, "the king asks it to be sent at once."

"Then send the portion you suggested immediately so that the Blood of Arande does experience suffering while you explain to the king why it would be wise to save the rest."

"Thank you, my lord. It will be done," Dorien responded. "There is nothing else to report. *In Tenebris nos.*"

The Master of Reservation, Sarla Darkholm, said through wrinkled lips, "Just like the Master of Chests has made mention of, Blood Tea production has taken a toll. Together with the Masters of Beasts and Life, we have not only identified the pests that were making the grapes sick, but we have found a way to combat them without harming the vines themselves. We expect the next season to be a fruitful one. Other than that," she added, "there is nothing to report."

Nothing of significance was reported by either Azareth, Masters of Lore, by Aristov III, the Master of Steel, or by Borric Condoin, Master of Beasts. It was then Rowena's turn to speak.

"My lord," she said, acknowledging her brother's position, "as the Master of Chests has noted, there has been increased consumption of resources in the sanatorium. There is a great possibility more will be needed."

"More?" the Master of Chests argued, "I was going to respectfully request you ensure we lower the expense."

"Unfortunately," Rowena responded, "we would be hard-pressed to do so."

"Surely there is something that could be done," Dorien frowned, "cuts that can be made." His words were followed by the agreeing murmurs of some.

"My lords," she said, looking around, "there is an epidemic we are trying to contain. We are calling it the boiling skin disease. The ill are feverish, presenting difficulty breathing and coughing within a few days. Boils appear, starting with their soles and palms before spreading through their bodies when they feel their skin is boiling. Of those infected, the vast majority are facing death within a short time.

"A definitive cure has yet to be found. Our physicians are exhausted. We have quarantined the entirety of Alnwick and its district in order to avoid spreading."

"Has it been reported anywhere else in the kingdom?" Erdrick asked.

"So far, it seems to be confined to the Alnwick district of Coldforge," Rowena responded.

"What about Aram?" Erdrick asked, "How far are we in his healing?"

"Not far enough," Rowena responded.

"How so?" He questioned, "Are you in need of assistance? What resources do you currently have a need of?"

"None, my lord," Rowena answered, "I believe Aram is not in need of healing." She caught a glimpse of Gustavus's closing fists and clenched jaw at the mention not of his brother's lack of progress but of Rowena's opinion.

"Explain yourself," Gustavus fumed.

Without losing her composure, Rowena spoke calmly, "Understanding of his own condition, an acceptance of his state, appears to be what Aram needs the most. After having tried so many options, I stopped all research on him. For the last several months, I have only been providing him with calming brews."

The large man wanted to slam his fist on the table and yell, 'How dare you.' But he couldn't. He couldn't fall to the spirit of anger that consumed his father, the one that was slowly gnawing at his brother's mind and soul. If it was out of support for him or because he felt the same way, Gustavus wouldn't know, but Erdrick's mood darkened.

"Was this your own prerogative?" Erdrick asked.

"It was," Rowena responded.

"As a Master of the Circle, your position requires you to be subject to the will of your superiors, or has that changed?" Erdrick questioned in the complete silence of the room.

"It has not," his sister nodded.

"Then you will do as instructed. Master of Chests," Erdrick ordered firmly, "set aside some of those savings you suggested for eventualities and ensure it goes toward the resources needed." He then paused for a moment before looking upon Rowena, "but half of that will be given to the Master of Life to be used for the resources needed for Aram's cure."

"And Master of Life," he added, "keep in mind at all times this is something you *must* do. Aram is a valuable asset to our House. He is needed."

Rowena stared at him coldly, "Nothing else to report. *In Tenebris nos.*"

"As you already know," Erdrick then spoke to all again, "The actions of the duchies of Valador and Volanar have provoked the kingdom of Ardenay to mobilize forces toward our kingdom's border. We need to ensure our king has within Darkholm all the forces we can spare ready to move across the kingdom. Master of War."

"My lord," Idian saluted.

"What is the status of the Eighth?"

"It still flies our banner," Idian responded. "Maxius Darkholm supervises its repairs, and upon completion, I will appoint an able commander to protect the garrison."

"Lord Idian," the Master of Reservation raised his voice, "how available are building materials to them? And the supply lines?"

"They can count on both the Eighth's surrounding land being rich in stone and the skill of masons who stayed behind. So far, the supply lines are uninterrupted."

"So far," Erdrick doubted.

"Yes," Idian added, "so far. Varen Bulwharf is an honorable man."

"And so is every other honorable man . . . until he is not," Erdrick said.

"Indeed," Idian smiled, "and that is why Maxius is there."

"Anything else before we close?" Erdrick asked the Masters, but only silence was heard.

With nothing else to report, the meeting would be adjourned at any moment, something Gustavus wouldn't have, not without seizing the moment. "My lords of the Grey Circle," he boomed. "I would like this moment to address you all. After many meetings, I have taken note of a few things. With the increasing population, taxes, resources, and even the management of such resources, I believe we are in need of something that can assist and connect it all."

"We are listening," the Master of Scholars said.

"The Master of Lands," Gustavus almost smiled at the recognition, "would be in charge of knowledge of all the guilds and their members, operations, and resources. He would be in charge of communication with every guild, which would make it easier to control the territory distribution of each."

He then placed his hand on the table. "I hereby propose the creation of the position of Master of Lands, and I suggest Tenslea Darkholm for it. Not only is she brilliant, but she is the most diligent, loyal, and among the hardest working people I have ever met. As Master of Lands, Tenslea would be a great asset to this Council."

A brief silence followed. At that moment, Gustavus wasn't sure if he had impressed them with his presentation or if he had caught them off guard, and each one was waiting for another to say the first word.

In the end, it was the latter, and it was Azareth himself who said, "Gus, to make a proposal about anything, one must be the duke or a Master of the Grey. Am I missing something here?" and grinning, his face disappeared behind a wall of smoke.

The Master of Courts added, "Aside from that important fact, is Tenslea not your own brother's lover? That is a conflict of interest if I have ever seen one."

"Then I will propose it," Erdrick placed his hand on the table. "The idea is not without merit. I think it is a great strategic move. It should ease communication not only between all of you but it allows us all to keep tabs on all the guilds within our duchy while also forcing them to report in order to stay in line with the law. I am proposing to create the position of Master of Lands, responsible for the census within Darkholm Duchy and that of guilds and their organization, communication, land, and resources."

"I second the proposal," the Master of Steel placed his hand on the table.

"If anyone has an argument against, speak, and we will proceed to voting," Erdrick instructed. After a brief silence, he spoke again, "The Master of Lands position is created. Its responsibilities are the census of the duchy and that of its guilds, their organization, communication, land, and resources within Darkholm Duchy."

"Now, regarding who will fill the position," Erdrick said next. "I propose for Tenslea Darkholm to be the first Master of Lands."

An uncomfortable silence followed, with not even the jolly Master of Steel seconding Erdrick's proposal. Behind Erdrick, Gustavus stood quietly, as angry as he was embarrassed.

"I second it," Rowena placed her hand on the table. "I believe Tenslea to be the perfect person to fill such a position."

Immediately, four hands touched the wooden surface, those of Alesabella, the Masters of Beasts and Steel, and Sorsha, who was not only the Master of Courts but also Tenslea's own aunt.

Erdrick did not expect such a strong refusal. "Of those who oppose it, I would like you to present your position to the Circle."

"Simple enough," Alesabella smiled. "I am only the voice of the Master of Secrets, and so I cannot vote in favor without discussing it with the Master and seeing what vote I should submit."

"My lords, I don't mean any offense with what I'm about to say," Borric spoke next, "but look at me. What do you see? I'm the only non-Darkholm in this Council. In the entirety of its history, I am the only non-Darkholm! Putting another Darkholm in a position because she is family will only feed the growing sentiment within the duchy that it's all just for the Darkholm. I vote no, and I ask you to simply consider what you are doing before you move forward with this."

"I . . ." Aristov III snorted, laughing through his beautiful, adorned beard, "sorry, they both said it better than I can. I am not good with words, but no. I cannot say I know her well enough.

"Just take into consideration that House Darkholm has to keep her mother, my own sister, under watch. She is smart, yes, brilliant, but that brain has taken after her mother in both her virtues and its weaknesses. I can vouch for that, for I am always close enough to watch them but distant enough to judge them both. Mine is a definite no."

"Then . . ." Erdrick said.

"My lord," Rowena interrupted him, "if you would be so kind as to allow me some words."

Seeing her humility and believing he knew his sister as no one else, Erdrick nodded, "The Circle is yours."

"My lords, Masters," Rowena's melodic voice drew all their attention, "Your arguments are all valid, but I fear they may spring from either lack of factual knowledge, preconceived judgment, or fear. I count myself fortunate to have spent so much time around Tenslea during our childhood and growing up. No other eyes have seen her laugh as much, no other ears have heard her suffering as much, and it would be hard to believe another heart has felt her own beating as much for what we all are, for what we represent."

She looked upon Alesabella when she said, "When we are here to represent, it is because we have the capacity to speak and act on behalf of another, not because we are to only deliver a message."

To Borric, she said, "You are not wrong about the perception of one's actions being important, but in the end, the ultimate mission should take precedence. One must always remember one can never control the opinion that others will choose to have about oneself.

"And indeed," she continued, "you have been the only non-Darkholm member in the Grey Circle in the many centuries since its formation. But think not what that says about the Circle. Think of what it says about *you*, about the loyalty and respect there is *for you*."

Rowena smiled back at the Master of Steel. "There is no time like now to get to know someone. Do not wait to read or ask about them after you have lost them, after they are gone."

Lastly, she looked at Sorsha eye to eye and placed her hand on the table, "Anger and disappointment soil our vision of people. But the high, perfect bars we set for ourselves should never be used to measure others or to attack them, especially when, in our judgment, we ignore the time when they weep in silence, when they need those of us who are closest the most."

"But, if you truly believe in your heart there is so much wrong with her, then say so, and here I will place my hand on this table with you. Let us do as with her mother. Let us call upon the Vine and summon the House. Let us don our crimson cloaks, and judge her together, at the Spire."

Rowena turned, moving away from the table as she spoke, "Even if the position has never been offered or given to her, Tenslea has been performing many of those duties already, keeping tabs on things we cannot even imagine. It would be next to impossible to find someone so dedicated to a position she does not even possess. It is a position she has and will continue to perform better than whoever it is assigned to, and she does not even have the title."

When she turned back, she smiled, seeing Azareth wink at her.

This time, despite any reservations, there were no hands on the table.

"By unanimous decision, then," Erdrick placed his hand, "Tenslea Darkholm will be named Master of Lands."

————— ✦✦✦✦ —————

After the meeting was adjourned, Rowena drew the hood over her head and walked away. There was much work to be done, many people that required her assistance or attention, many places she wished she could be at once, and at the same time, she wished she was in none of them.

She wished she could take the cloak off and run away, but she would be receiving more resources soon, and there were new formulations she needed to come up with.

"Rowena," Gustavus's voice called from behind.

"Yes?" She looked at him from the corner of her eye.

"I wanted to thank you."

"For what?"

"For supporting and saving my idea," Gustavus responded.

"Dear cousin, you could not think I did it because maybe I truly believe in her?" And with a sly smile, she left him speechless in the long, empty hallway.

DOMAE

Location: Kingdom of Blackheart,
Darkholm Duchy, City of Coldforge, Darkholde Keep

"Ramulatte," Azareth's voice came through the puff of smoke, "among the best Eilean herbs."

"This . . . is a *pipetta*," he continued, showing his companion the ornate, flute-like metallic contraption he held. "It allows trails of smoke to escape from these three orifices along the bottom of its shaft. One would think the *pipetta* is upside down, but why do I have the ashtray below it? Because it is actually right side up. Workers only smoke these in the field, allowing the ashes to fall and fertilize the ground they tread. It is where the Eilean saying, 'trust who walks with you over ashes' comes from."

"I wonder if you will stop smoking one day, Master of Lore," Rowena's voice interrupted his musing.

"Master of Life," drawing a welcoming smile, Azareth stood up from the comfort of his seat, "I wonder if one day you will start."

She stood in place in that vast library that was like a second home to her cousin, where on the third story, the pair had set a small, wooden table and two chairs, close enough to the enormous window panes that allowed a view of everything that, to them, was important—the silent keep, the unpredictable ocean, the booming capital, and the unassuming square board that rested upon the table surface.

"Domae?" Rowena asked.

"Yes, of course. I would not have thought my dissertation on smoking herbs is what you came for," Count Azareth responded, his tone one of obvious jest. "Now, let me pull a chair for you. Blood Tea?"

"That would be most welcome," Rowena responded, her eyes wandering outside the window.

From a drawer near the table, her cousin pulled a long, flat box, its surface a polished oak, on which runic images were depicted. He slid the lid carefully, revealing dozens of small alcoves, each holding a distinct, exquisitely carved figurine and a token that represented it. He then handed her another smaller box, its alcoves empty, so that she could choose figurines and place her army in its formation.

"I have already chosen mine." A trail of smoke came out of his nostrils. "Pick yours while I pour two cups of a good vintage."

Rowena ran her fingers over the box, fingernails lightly scratching the surface of the figurines that lay on each alcove, like the Darkholm dead in their deep catacombs, but unlike them, perhaps eagerly waiting to be disturbed. "My forces have already been chosen since our last game."

"Interesting." His words were followed by the loud popping sound of the cork leaving its prison, "I am curious as to what strategy you have devised this time around."

Bottle in hand, he moved toward a screen that hid his forces' composition.

"Are you ready? One, two, three!" Azareth removed the lid of his formation box. On his side, the king, the queen, a pikeman, and a spy, and two each of knights, elephants, and mercenaries. As in every Domae board, they were accompanied by ten footmen.

His inquisitive eyes promptly went to Rowena's side of the table. Her forces were composed of . . . *the same as last time?*

She had picked the king, a horseman, an archer, a hunter, a mercenary, and two each of the pikemen and ballistae. The ten footmen helped complete her army.

But wait, Azareth hesitated. *There is still room for one more. Therein lies the difference.*

His hands did not move, nor his lips, or even his marigold eyes. If it weren't for the fumes leaving his nostrils, one would have thought the world itself stopped in expectation of what she held wrapped between her fingers.

Azareth Darkholm

The count saw the reflection of each figurine in Rowena's golden irises before her hand opened to reveal the unassuming figurine of a farmer carrying a bushel over his back.

Ah, that is right, the farmer. He smiled a smile of smoke. *Now, the exact same army is complete.*

"*In Sanguine nos,*" Azareth smiled mischievously, raising his cup.

"*In Sanguine nos,*" Rowena followed suit.

The Master of Lore studied the placement of her forces. A pikeman and ballista were at either end, while the farmer and the king made her center.

"Rowena," he asked, "why do you not choose a queen to be by the king's side?"

"Is it required by the rules?" she asked.

"Well, good point. It is not," he replied, "but it is a wise choice."

"How is it wise?"

"Although the king is more powerful, the queen has more mobility. In a way, it is a natural choice in every good Domae."

"With the king being so crucial, what would a queen contribute other than distraction, to the opponents, certainly, but just as much to her king's own forces, and more so to the hand that moves it all? The same resources could be spent more efficiently."

"Oh, you mean the farmer?" he winked.

She laughed, "Perhaps as good an example as any. Ladies first," she continued.

"Well, a Domae loser must start the next game, so, once again, like every other time, you go first." He waved his little finger, bringing the *pipetta* back to his mouth. Rowena nodded, and, with the slightest semblance of a smile, she moved one of her footmen forward.

"Good start," Azareth judged the simple move, following with his own. The following moves were quick and seemingly unimportant, but as time progressed, the interval also increased between each subsequent move.

"Rowena, " Azareth poured some more, "did you know that the Province Menore di Philocomasitum is the smallest and least powerful province in Eileos?"

"I was not aware of that," she responded, "although I was aware it is important."

"Do you know why? What makes it stand up to the other provinces is its rather limited but unquestionably superior agricultural goods. Its land is rich in minerals. If it was able to produce large quantities, it would turn even the Duke of Whisperwind green with envy."

"Does any of their produce ever find its way to Blackheart?"

"Well, yes, of course!" Azareth chuckled, lifting the *pipetta* for her to see. "Aside from these, however, most of everything is primarily consumed in Eileos. Very little of it makes it past their own border."

"One would think that, with so much coastal access and volcanic soil, agriculture would be optimal."

"You are right. But their forte does not lie in agriculture. Eilean leaders rather spend their time stealing from each other."

"It is, in many ways, a twisted curse," Rowena added. "Those who have the best of resources also have the worst of attitudes."

"Ouch!" he jested, placing his hand dramatically on his chest, "I am offended." With his other hand, he placed an elephant over the exposed mercenary he captured. On the other side of the board, his other elephant was taken by her hunter.

'What is her strategy?' He felt confused before coming to the realization he could not predict her moves as much because she perhaps still did not master the moves in the chaotic composition of her forces.

So instead of studying her strategy, he set his eyes on her.

Azareth contemplated how his opponent studied each figurine's placement carefully, each of the pieces that had formed the invariable army she had made her own. More than once, he had wondered what transpired in her head when she played. Was she, perhaps, reviewing how each piece moved or what she could do with them? Was she purely admiring the exquisite detail of each carving? He sometimes wondered if her choices, poor or wise, were based on what each of the figurines represented.

"I was thinking," Azareth took another of her pieces, "I have never seen you play your brother Erdrick."

Without saying a word, she moved a ballista.

"Are you afraid of losing to him? Oh," he raised a finger in realization, "you are afraid of beating him?"

Rowena smiled coyly, "My brother does like to win." She moved another piece.

"That is the wrong move, Rowena," Azareth pointed at the board, "I will let you take it back. Think again, and then make a move."

Without taking the piece, Rowena moved back and then said, "I stand by my move."

"Then," her cousin blew smoke, "I must regretfully and mercilessly accept it." With a simple move, he captured her piece.

Azareth's eyes went to the box where he had most of her pieces before they moved back to her. Rowena's eyes were not on the heavy, barred door leading to the occult part of the library and the hidden library within it but on the wall close to it. "Is everything all right? I feel you are somehow distracted."

Rowena stood up from her seat and walked toward the door, feeling strangely drawn toward it. "What lies behind this door, Azareth?"

"As you know, the Occult Library and the hidden library within it."

She walked alongside the wall, her hand just inches away, her head close enough, as if listening for something, before she stopped in a specific spot.

"What lies here?"

"The reliquary, and within it, the unknown." He was serious now. "Things that, at least for the time being, should better be left untouched, Rowena. Nothing more than the potential for great power and even greater danger."

The Master of Lore walked to her side, "As you know, that part of the library is off limits, per the instructions of the Head of the House. Being who you are, you, of all people, could ask for access to be granted. Would you like me to help you with that?"

Rowena stood quietly, contemplating the plain wall that stood between her and the unrevealed, the unknown. "That is not necessary, dear cousin," she smiled back at him, turning away to finish what was left of her Blood Tea.

"I must take my leave now," she continued. "Until our next time, Master of Lore."

Azareth bowed, and he watched her until she disappeared beyond the library door.

His eyes then moved back toward the board. She had lost. It was unquestionable he had, once again, bested her. But he wondered what her strategy had been, and it dawned on him, there it was, plainly for a mind such as his to see. Rowena had sacrificed everything, even the king himself, to protect none other than the farmer.

"Until the next time, Master of Life."

He looked back upon the wall, submerged in deep thought, before he held the ashtray outside the window, allowing the wind to take the ashes that filled it away.

"Now go, feed the fish, fertilize the ocean," he smiled.

Meanwhile, in a distant tower of the keep, Aram Darkholm lay chained to the wall inside his room, screaming at the top of his lungs to drown the whispers, the voices he heard inside his head ordering him, 'Kill her! KILL HER!'

FIFTH TEST

Location: Empyre of Suhne, City of Suhne, Palace of the Sun

It was early morning when the two servant women entered Kaylen's chambers, finding him sitting by his desk, his slender body adorned only by his own nakedness. Books and scrolls lay open, scattered along the smooth, wooden surface. His hazel eyes traveled back and forth from each page to another one covered with his own notes, bringing a satisfactory yet barely perceptible smile to his thin lips.

"Blessed One," the younger of the two servants interrupted his work at the signal of the older woman. "If you wish, we can return later so that we do not interrupt your studies."

Leaning against the desk, Kaylen turned to face her, speaking derisively, "And who will dress me, then?" His face held the same expression, the same smile he held a few moments before, but with none of the warmth it had contained. Kaylen stood up, his eyes on her, making sure to hold the smile long enough to embarrass her, to ensure she realized the stupidity of her proposition.

"Pardon me, Blessed One," she bowed and took a step back.

"Who is she?" Kaylen's fingers swayed dismissively. His smile was gone, replaced by slight irritation.

"I am training her," the older woman responded, "so that she can one day take my place when I am no longer useful[1]."

"There's always something one can be useful for."

Kaylen's scolding sent the elderly woman's head bowing. "Then, for as long as I live, I will make myself useful, Blessed One."

"Good," he responded. He wouldn't have it any other way, anyway.

Spreading his arms, the Son turned away and faced the desk. The older woman began to unravel the clothes he would wear on this day.

She gave instructions to the younger one, hanging the fine fabrics at the end of wooden rods both held in each hand. The younger woman's hands fumbled nervously.

"Be calm," the older woman whispered. "Your hands are dexterous. We have practiced this many times. Stay calm. There are only two rules you must make sure to remember—do not drop his clothes on the floor, and do not, ever, touch him."

Carefully and skillfully, they proceeded to drop and drape the fabrics over Kaylen's body as deftly as if they had used their own hands.

As they dressed him, the Searing Sun continued to whisper what his eyes still read.

Kaylen, Ascended

"Blessed One," the older woman pointed out, "I have noticed you study the same thing multiple times," the older servant pointed out.

"I do," Kaylen responded dryly. "Why do you ask?"

"I do not mean to speak wisdom to you, Blessed One—"

"You can't." His searing words gave truth to his title.

"I apologize . . . Blessed One," the servant's pressed lips expressed.

"*Why* do you ask?" The Searing Sun did not acknowledge her apology as he asked once more.

"It's just that, wouldn't it be better to review something else in the hours you have left before the Test?"

Kaylen's lips drew a smirk. "Brand me a fool if I were to do so. Mastery of a few subjects can bring one greater success than knowing little of many. The first would make you indomitable; the latter would increase your chance of getting confused, especially with less than a day to prepare. It is better to say, 'I do not know,' than to appear an idiot by speaking nonsense the way my siblings would surely do."

After dressing the Blessed One, they proceeded to carefully wrap his long hair inside a turban.

"If I may ask, why do you focus so much on your studies alone, even during these challenges? The other Sons are not doing the same, from what I hear."

Kaylen's eyes of wood pierced the woman with their gaze. "We should always give our best to excel at what we are great at. It would make us unbeatable in that arena. Everything we do not excel at, then, will be fair game, for the simple mistake of another can send victory to our hands while our own points are assured. My siblings are not doing the same, and that is why neither of them is worthy of becoming the Sun. They're only worthy of being scorched by it."

⁕

The entrance of the palace saw the arrival of the three retinues welcomed by the clamor of the citizens.

The Sons and the Rays stood atop the staircase to the grand structure, six Rays to each side, and behind them, groups of acolytes dressed in white. Exis stood a few steps below, closer to the populace. He held a golden jug in his hands, from which he would pull out one of the names of the three to determine the order in which the Sons would address the crowd.

"People of the Sun!" Exis lifted a hand to silence those gathered. "On this fifth day, each of the Sons will address their people with their plans and policies for the Empyre of Suhne. Today, by embracing their policies, we test the Sun's stance!"

The Speaker's hands pulled out a token from inside the jug, which he revealed to the crowd. "Kaylen, Son of the Sun!"

Kaylen walked toward the center, wearing a heavily wrapped, crimson cloak. A red veil adorned his headpiece. The final details almost gave him the appearance of a blood-soaked mummified body.

"People of the Sun!" he began. "You have lived through many eras when you have not been recognized properly. Many a time, you have been ignored by him who rules you and by those who live as neighboring nations."

"The way of Suhne is the One Way and the only way. Even despite all the power, I cannot change our culture, our beliefs, what our people know to be the only truth."

Slowly, his hands removed his vestments and his headpiece to reveal a gray tunic accompanied by a black turban. Kaylen bent over to pick up a cane and used it to help himself walk down the stairs.

"Over the years, from a distance, I have followed your requests," he continued. "I have come to know your needs and desires. I will provide boons and blessings to those who serve under the Sun, and I will hand half of the riches of the world as we lay hands on it so that the people of the Sun can breathe more easily, so that you can all prosper as the Empyre grows. This world will fear the Sun and will have to choose between death and worship. Those whom we capture will become your slaves to ease your burden. Know this, that your pleas and your plight are not ignored by the heart of him who will burn the world with you and for you. You will always triumph under the Searing Sun!"

Thousands of voices rose in unison, chants of blessings and claims of glory raining upon the Son.

Proud of his performance, Kaylen took a deep breath and returned to his place among the three.

The Speaker smiled at his words, as a father would find pleasure and pride in the words and deeds of his heir. He then pulled a second token from inside the jug. "Vamya, Son of the Sun!"

Immediately, she took a step forward toward the edge of the platform, her hair held up in multiple small braids that formed a larger one, cascading toward her back. Over it, small chains connected her earpieces to one another and allowed even smaller chains to cascade down the back of her head. Her light green silk gown covered the left side of her body while her right arm and leg were exposed, revealing small golden chains where diamonds dangled as water seeking to touch the stony floor.

Despite the fine attire and the equanimity she portrayed, hearing the term still bothered her substantially. Things like these could not simply be dismissed. She felt she needed to correct it.

"Speaker," Vamya began.

"Blessed One," he responded.

"I do not wish to be called 'Son' anymore." Vamya spoke to the leader among the Rays while still keeping her eyes on the multitude. "From now on, I will be called 'Daughter.'"

"Blessed One, these are your wishes, but tradition dictates the term. We cannot change it."

"You tell the Sun of Change we *cannot* change?" Vamya interjected.

"We *will not*," Exis said firmly, his brow furrowed.

"You *must*," Vamya turned her head so that their eyes could meet. "I am the Daughter."

His black irises challenged the emerald in hers. "And the Sun has *always* been male."

There was a brief moment of silence before Vamya addressed him again.

"I am the Sun of Change because of everything that I will transform when my time comes to rise, but not because I won't sear and burn more deeply than either of my brothers. Don't tempt me, for my ire will consume you where you stand. This will be the first and last time you will challenge me. Do *not* call me Son again." Her eyes turned back to the crowd, taking a step forward.

Exis did not move. If it weren't for the tensing muscles in his hands, he would have seemed unbothered.

"People of the Sun," Vamya spoke more calmly, walking toward the edge of the platform, her gown trailing like mist.

"For centuries, you have lived under the Almighty Sun's protection. You have also been recipients of its eternal guidance. While it has given you its blessings, it has many times required more than you could give. But the Sun has seen that its people deserve nothing less than everything the Sun can give. While I have always believed our people have been wronged, it was not until recently that I have come to realize how profound that mistreatment has been, the marks that have been left on our society.

"Since the dawn of mankind, our men have been exalted, for they fought fiercely. They have then been rewarded with work and responsibilities when they retire back home. Our women have lived a life of silence, of insignificance.

"Our women have been forgotten just as much. They have kept the homes secure without learning how to defend themselves. They have raised their children without learning how to read and write. They have often fed their families without themselves having a meal. No one can ever say women aren't an important building block of this society. They should be trained to fight when needed, to read and write, and they should learn more than just exist to be married and raise children. They should be allowed to study and develop crafts and professions . . ." Her words met only the silence of the multitude. The only Daughter of the Sun caught a glimpse of angry faces among many of the worshippers. Immediately, she knew she needed to adapt her strategy.

"So that when a man dies, his wife does not have to be married to his brother, cousin, or neighbor to ensure the family is provided for. These women would become self-sufficient, and this would lighten the burden cast on our men's shoulders. It is time we reward them with a boon that will lighten their load!"

At this, the clamor thundered.

"Also, virgin males should also be required to wear colors so that they are just as easily distinguished under the Sun as their female counterparts. And, lastly . . ." Vamya second-guessed herself. Should she say what was truly inside her heart? She had a strong feeling she needed to. "I will proclaim that women will be allowed among the ranks of the Rays. Upon my Ascendance, I will give you what only I am willing to give, and that . . . is change."

The crowd shouted her name, although much less than Kaylen's. She had expected more support. It was hard for her to believe an oppressed people were so used to being oppressed they didn't seem to want something different. Vamya did not allow this to bother her. In the end, it all depended on the Rays, the same Rays who were not smiling after her words had been spoken.

The Sun of Change walked back to her position, seeking to appear calm and composed. Deep inside, she wondered.

"That was less than impressive," Kaylen whispered to her as they both faced the crowd, ready for Malek's name to be announced. "Catastrophic, actually. I think even Malek will have a hard time giving a worse speech."

"Think what you will," Vamya whispered back, "but your policies didn't offer much. And, I will add, look at you. I'm surprised you look like one of the people you feel so much disdain for."

"Exactly, and that's what they want to see, that I am with them. It is best to address the worshippers by standing among them, even if they'll never be our equals. Your ideas are as far-fetched as your pretentious garb."

"No matter how much you delude yourself," her words were sharp, "*they* will never love you."

"Oh, you deluded woman. Do you think I care for their love?" Kaylen grinned, "I only care for their worship.

"You, woman, who should have been killed the moment you were born, what makes you think they will love *you*?" His words cut deeper.

For a moment, she stood silent.

He might be right, she told herself, but she needed to dismiss the thought.

"Perhaps," she smiled, "we will see."

"I am certain *you* will see," he responded.

"Are you that afraid of me?" Vamya jested.

"Of you? You are no threat to me." With his words, her smile disappeared.

At once, the voice of the firstborn boomed, "I am the Conquering Sun, he who will crush the world under his heel."

The cheers inundated them. "My people . . . I will not make you empty promises, for I do not seek to delude you. Our way has been the One Way since the beginning of time, and our way has made us who we are. I will offer you no change, just as I will offer no quarter to our enemies beyond our borders. We will fight, we will conquer, and we will reign supreme over all the known world of Caerea.

"Caerea is here for us to take it, and take it we will, for the eternal glory of the Almighty Sun!"

Exis raised his hands as he heard the raucous crowd, their shouts seemingly endless.

Kaylen's eyes met his sister's. "You two surely give it your best to be the worst."

---

(1)   To avoid becoming a financial burden on their families, the Suhnite people typically work until they physically can't anymore.

ASSASSIN

Location: Empyre of Suhne, City of Suhne, Palace of the Sun

Not every door that opens should be walked through . . .

The white fabric felt soft against Sera's dark skin. Never in his life had he imagined he would wear something this soft. Then again, never in his life had he expected to be where he was today and under these pretenses.

He was dressed as one of the silent acolytes he followed, the twelve he had just met and not had a chance to exchange words with. They were headed to where he was needed, to the base of the Grand Palace, was all he knew. 'How many of them are men like me,' he wondered along the way.

The sheer number of people in the lively city was unlike anything he had ever witnessed, even in the largest village in his distant region of Uhn. His group was largely ignored, except for an occasional city guard or curious child.

He captured a glimpse of the palace above, of its domed magnificence, the holy residence of his god, or of the one that would be.

Its crystalline beauty left him in awe, but a bump from the acolyte behind him alerted him to continue moving.

A dozen Flame Guards guarded the side entrance to the palace. It was the first time Sera had seen one, with their fearsome golden masks that were almost as intimidating as the scimitars and polearms they wielded. The leading one, he overheard was named Aaju, set his eyes on Sera.

'Does he know?' Sera wondered, 'Does he suspect, or is he looking at me because I'm possibly the only one looking?'

After a few moments, they were allowed to climb the side stairs leading to the platform where the Test was taking place. Upon his first step on the platform, Sera felt something, but *what was it?* He looked around, but the source of that power wasn't evident. The miner couldn't pinpoint the location. Somehow it felt like it was coming from . . . *the Rays?* Sera shook his head and found his place, paired with another acolyte behind Zurek, the oldest of the Rays.

Sera lowered his head and wiped his sweaty forehead with one of his sleeves. As the fabric slid along his forearm, it was then that he realized he had forgotten to take his bond chain off.

Acolytes are not supposed to be married. He had seen the bond chain, and beyond the chain, he saw another, distant acolyte looking back at him with eyes wide open, with skin that had been touched by the sun.

Debem?

What are you doing here? He read Debem's lips saying.

'What am I doing here?' His eyes moved back to the platform. 'I know what I'm doing here. Now, what are *you* doing here?' Of all people, Debem would not have been the one he would have expected to be among the acolytes. His friend was not a strong believer in their faith, perhaps not even a believer at all. Sera was glad to see his best friend survive the mining accident, but why hadn't he sought Sera? Did Debem blame him for the misfortune? Did surviving show him the Sun's mercy, and he was now repentant, or was he, perhaps, more interested in survival and had thus faked his way here? Did he also have a mission of his own?

Sera's attention was back on the heirs, who had found their place on one side of the platform, on Malek's large figure, his back easily doubling the size of Sera's, on Kaylen, who stood calmly, holding a cane at his side, and on Vamya, with her distracting, bejeweled beauty.

Exis raised his voice. "People of the Sun, you have heard the words of the Children of the Sun. You have learned of their plans for their people. As they have blessed us with their voices and their presence, now you will receive the blessings of the Rays."

That was the signal he had been waiting for, the moment when the Rays stepped forward, past the siblings, allowing the three to leave with their Chosen along the back.

He had to move as fast as he could—before the Sons reached the Flame Guards.

Sera's hand moved toward his side, where it wrapped around the curved dagger hidden along his leg.

'Blessed be the Sun,' his lips muttered as he dashed like a lightning strike.

He felt a power that drove him and made him hesitate. He heard the immediate shouts of the guards he would ignore.

Inside his head, he only heard Ez-srah telling him to do it.

He heard Debem screaming for him not to.

He heard Gada both laughing with and at him.

He also heard his children call his name . . . and those of many others.

Sera blinked, his sad anger driving him forward to face the most powerful enemy he had ever faced, the false god, the one who had brought him to ruin and who would bring only ruin to all those people he didn't know and those he had foolishly loved.

Tensing all his muscles, he pushed his foot off the ground. There was only one chance, the one chance his god had given him to make things better, to rectify his wrongs, but also to show his god he deserved to have the wrongs done to him rectified just as much.

Upon the rising screams, the three siblings turned to look at the commotion, Malek's face full of preparedness, Kaylen's of derision, and Vamya's of worry.

Sera, the talented miner, the loving husband, the skilled fighter, had now become the accursed criminal and soon a successful murderer.

He ran past the other acolytes, who were too slow to notice . . . and toward the siblings, slashing as fast as he could, striking with the only chance he got, but striking true, right near the center of Kaylen's abdomen.

MOMMA

Location: Kingdom of Blackheart,
Royal Duchy of Darkholm, the coast

*H*er eyes contemplated Darkholde, the first rejection. She imagined the difficult birth and the following moment when she was thrown off the high cliffs to the reefs she now passed.

Her brother always said she had been 'lucky.' Had she truly been lucky when not even the reefs had wanted her and had instead marred her body as they pushed her to the sea in hopes she would drown?

Gray clouds filled the sky the morning of that day when her lone figure stood at the bow of the siren, the small ship navigating around the cliff wall, slowly toward shore where a small village was located, away from the view of Darkholde, as if the great structure had been too ashamed by its existence to face it.

Despite the capricious waves, the cloaked female did not once appear to lose her footing.

Her foot met the wooden planks time and again just as her lips met each other between the unintelligible syllables she hummed. She held her black cloak fast against the wind that played with her hair, the long strands the color of the purest clouds.

She returned the same way she came sixteen years ago when she was an infant nobody knew, now as an adult everyone recognized.

But, like the waves in the ocean, no matter if she traveled the exact same path, things were never the same.

Her bright, marigold eyes were fixed on her approaching destination, that nearly forgotten village full of memories she would always remember, for it represented that for which it was named, Haven.

She saw the sea had been creeping up, consuming the shore ever so slightly, a persistent snail devouring a leaf while no one seemed to notice.

The once-sandy shore where the villagers' cabins stood was now mostly covered in mud, that same mud that evoked memories of a time past.

"*These scars make me beautiful!*" *The young, white-haired girl sobbed, wiping the tears from her eyes as if trying to convince herself of the words she had expressed.*

"*Ew, no, they don't! You are ugly!*" *a boy yelled.*

"*My momma says I am like a butterfly. I'm different but still beautiful,*" *the little one pressed.*

"*Nah, nah, you are ugly like a monster!*" *a heavy girl yelled, pushing her to the mud, where her pampas-white hair was drenched in the wet, brown dirt.*

"*Maybe now you will be like us,*" *an older girl laughed as she pointed at the muddied hair.*

The children laughed heartily as the smaller one attempted to regain her balance getting to her feet once again. "*My momma says I'm beautiful and that I will always be beautiful!*"

"*She's not even your real mother!*" *the heavy girl mocked her.* "*You don't have a mother. You're an ugly monster with hair like an old woman!*"

The cruel words crushed her heart. The droplets escaping her eyes were now too many. They trickled as her muddied hands tried vainly to dry them. "*I am beautiful, and I will always be beautiful!*" *Laughing, the other children left her standing in the middle of the mud puddle.*

"*My momma says,*" *the little one shouted, sobbing,* "*that I can be whoever I want to be, and if I really, really want it, I can even become a lady one day.*

"*Wait and see,*" *the little girl continued when the others couldn't hear her any longer,* "*one day, you will call me Lady Charon.*"

"We are here," the sailor's voice interrupted her trance.

How Charon got from the siren to the rowboat and now to the shore, she couldn't remember, but the one thing she could remember was the familiar feeling of walking on mud.

"I won't be long. I promise," the noblewoman told the sailor with a smile.

"I'll be waiting," he responded.

She pulled up her black skirt slightly to avoid dirtying any inch of its fine fabric.

As she walked along the village path toward the little house where she had been raised, she saw the window, that one window where she sat every morning, looking out as her mother patiently brushed her hair.

"*Momma,*" *the young girl with the white hair touched her mother's hair,* "*why is my hair like an old woman's?*"

"My child," the old woman touched the child's hair. "Maybe one day it will turn black," the mother giggled as she tickled the girl.

But the little girl did not smile, "Momma . . . seriously. Why is my hair like that of an old woman? All the children say so, and they mock me. Sometimes I even hear the adults speak of me too when they think I'm not listening."

The old villager's lips trembled as she tried to smile but failed miserably. Her weathered hand took the soft hand of her child.

"You know, child, you ask why your hair is like that? Well, here's the answer—I don't know. And there are things that perhaps we will never know. But one thing I know is that old woman's hair is nothing to be ashamed of. It is a sign of wisdom. It speaks of survival."

The girl turned around to look through the window and once again admire the great cliffs of Darkholde, with its huge boulders and jagged peaks.

"Momma," Charon had said, "one day, I will climb on that cliff."

"My child, that is a dangerous place."

"Momma, I'm going to be big. I'm going to be able to climb."

"There is nothing there for you," the mother recited.

"But Momma," Charon insisted, "I'm going to be big and strong, and I will be able to climb all the way up there. And from up there, I'll be able to look down at all the people who look down on me."

Upon her words, the old woman's chest tightened.

"And I'll be able to get all the way to the top. And I'll be able to raise my arms and look back at you and say, 'Look, Momma! I did it!'"

The old woman held her child fast, close to her chest so that Charon could not see her endless tears, for the one thing that would hurt a mother the most was to know her child would never be able to achieve her dreams.

Charon reached the entrance of the small cabin. Her heart wanted to burst out of her chest with the noises she heard in the kitchen.

'She must be busy, like always,' Charon thought, biting her finger softly the same way she did as a child to contain her nervous laughter.

Her mind was filled with thoughts of her momma, that old woman who had raised her and taught her everything she knew. The one who finally, upon her insistence, told her the story.

Her now-deceased father had returned from fishing in the deep sea one day, and while he had not caught plenty, he brought what he had found floating in the sea—a bloodied bundle.

It moved, and the moment the woman had opened it, he said, "Look, it's the child we could never have!"

Immediately, the woman took the wounded child in her arms, and she cleaned her the best that she could. Then she saw the newborn open her beautiful eyes the color of sunlight.

"This is royalty." The old woman was taken aback. "We can't keep her!"

And she traveled by foot all the way to Darkholde to ask for an audience but was ultimately received by a single, beautifully pale, yet tall and cold woman.

"This baby belongs here," the old woman had offered the bundle.

"This is not her place," the woman responded, leaving it untouched.

"But, her eyes—"

"There is nothing here for her."

"Can someone else here help?"

"This is a dangerous place for her."

"Then what should I do with her?" the old woman questioned.

"Take her away. Do whatever you want. Kill her if you must . . ." At the noblewoman's words, the senior brought the bundle closer to her own chest. "Give her the life she could have never had within these walls."

The old woman nodded in acceptance and walked away.

"And please, name her . . . Charon."

Those were the last words she ever heard from the pale woman before she walked back the way she had come to make the child her own.

"Momma!" Charon swung the door open as she leaped inside with a smile on her face, her eyes watering, her heart at full gallop.

"Charon?" A middle-aged, pregnant woman choked upon seeing her barge in. She stood in the small kitchen, serving food on a table where a man and their four children waited.

Charon scouted the living place, her smile frozen. "Anesha," Charon asked the woman who had once been her neighbor, "where is my momma?"

The woman's hand trembled nervously. Instinctively, she placed herself between Charon and her curious family. "Oh, Charon," the woman responded, "she died from grief nearly three years ago, after you left."

"But," Charon asked, confused, "the letters?"

"I'm sorry, Charon," Anesha responded, "that was me all along. I . . . thought . . . you would never come back."

Then it dawned on her that the many letters at first asked her to come back, and then when she announced she would finally do so, the letters changed, asking her to instead stay there and be happy.

The very moment she put all the pieces together, her heart shattered, and her mind began to crack.

She stepped outside, where her hands dropped the hem of her skirt that now touched the mud.

'Life asks us to win at this game called *existence*, and yet it deals us the worst hand of cards.'

The familiar smell of fish, the voices of children playing, and the daily noise of such a small, yet busy village, brought her back.

Among all the familiarity, Charon saw a face she recognized on the body of a rather obese, unkempt washerwoman who scolded her children while tending to the clothes she washed as best as she could in that muck-ridden corner of the village.

The woman's eyes met Charon's. Immediately, she tried to hide her face behind the clothes she had hung to dry.

From where she stood, she saw the noblewoman approach every few steps, for she cursed at the wind that would blow the clothes playfully as if seeking to torture her.

With a gentle touch, Charon moved the clothes aside, peeking through a wet curtain. Her eyes met the woman's once more. The Darkholm raised her head slightly, her marigold eyes looking down.

'What to say, what to say,' Charon asked herself, 'look at you today. Look at me.' She smiled a triumphant smile that sent a myriad of thoughts flying. It was the perfect moment to crush the girl who had stripped Charon's spirit every day for many a year.

In the end, she said nothing. Life has already muddied her enough.

Many of the poor villagers stopped their chores, their attention on Charon as she left. If they recognized her or not, she didn't know, although her flowing, snowy hair was certainly hard to forget.

———— ·+++++·+· ————

Two weeks later, a royal decree was issued, announcing the people of Haven would soon be stripped of the entirety of their land . . .

To be moved uphill, where they were safe from the erosion of the coast, where small cabins would be built for them and their families. And they would, from now on, have to report to the new owner and baroness of the land, who was none other than Lady Charon.

THE VULTURE, THE RAVEN, THE SNAKE, AND THE HOUND

Location: Kingdom of Blackheart,
Royal Duchy of Darkholm, Darkholde Keep

To some, the only sustenance needed is a well-cooked scheme . . .

The Darkholm waited.

Each one of the royals stood in his or her assigned place along the shadowy walls of the dining chamber. Like the birds in the Master of Death's care, they waited.

"All due reverence to the Patriarch of our House," Vhimir Darkholm's voice broke the silence, "His Majesty, our Lord King, Septem Darkholm, the White, Crowned King of Blackheart, Duke of Darkholm, Count of Coldforge, Baron of Ironheart, Lord of Ironholde, Father of the Blood."

The doors opened to allow Septem's entrance, his slow, steady walk that of a most militant of specters. The monarch's clothes were perfectly neat and pure white as if they had never been smeared, never been drenched in the blood of many in all the battlefields he had been a part of. It was the only color he had worn from the day he left his castle to stop the civil war that had broken the former kingdom.

It was that color that was the antithesis to his household's traditional black. But before he rode forth that day, he had ended the argument of his House with words the Darkholm will always remember, "This world is not yet ready. *This* is what *they* need to see."

The Darkholm lowered their heads, their eyes trailing his entrance until he found his way to the center of the chamber.

Septem's piercing eyes of gold looked forward, gazing at the infinite possibilities the uncertain hand of the future would bring.

While traditionally, every guest would have been welcomed before the heads of state were introduced, this was not a formal state dinner. It was a yearly tradition set by House Darkholm to welcome their most loyal, closest, and to some among them, only friends, the vassal houses of Darkholm.

Vhimir took his place among his family. His second strode toward and across the double doors at the other end of the chamber.

Soon he returned, his head high, his chest swollen. "Lord Aiden Sanglune, vassal of Darkholm, Count of Bindings, Baron of Tenebrous and his wife, Lady Gwenore Sanglune."

The Darkholm stood in place, watching the nobleman's entrance. His clothes were fine in the deep wines and blacks of his House. A golden chain hung from his neck and onto his lap, for the man of over a century was hunched over and bound to a wheelchair that was pushed by his wife.

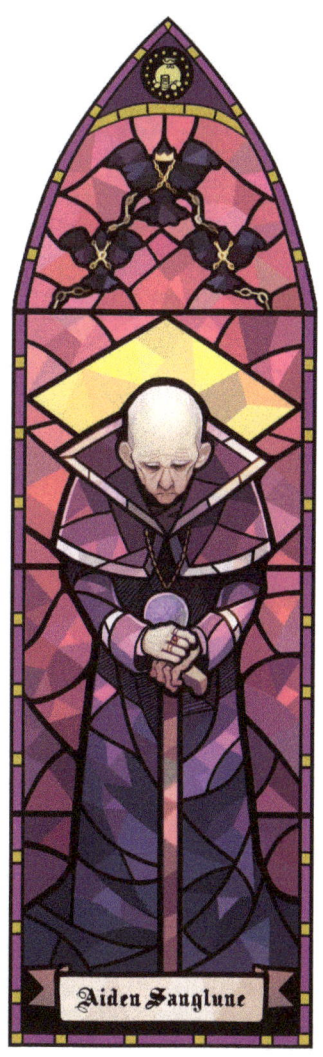

Aiden Sanglune

Lady Gwenore's clothes were of the same colors, always conservative, with long sleeves and a tall headpiece that covered all but her face. The fabrics were soft, neat, and free of wrinkles, unlike her face, which was grim and as cold as her eyes of brushed iron.

Behind the pair, prominent members of House Sanglune followed.

"Your Majesty," Aiden's voice was only an imperceptible whisper under his weak breath, "my lords and ladies of House Darkholm." The count bowed his head as deeply as he could in the very limited movement of someone in his state.

Lady Gwenore spoke no words. She curtsied not. Her eyes met Septem's, then Davidov's. She lowered her head in a slow nod to each while her wizened hands continued to push the wheelchair.

As the taxes and coin they collected and the accounting documents they were in charge of, their perfectly organized entourage found its place on one side of the large room. The last one to do so was Lady Sanglune herself. She first barely assisted her husband's standing from his wheelchair while handing him the cane where he placed most of his weight. Aiden's shaking hands wrapped around its handle, his arms trembling, his body staggering as he walked, almost ready to fall at any moment, but with his wife walking behind him, he found his place at the head of his family.

"Lady Sanglune," a servant girl approached, "given his state, Lord Sanglune is allowed to sit in his wheelchair if he so wishes."

"Nonsense," Lady Gwenore snapped. "This," her nails tapped the wheelchair, "is only a means of transport. My lord husband stands, and he will stand until he can no more."

Celestine Devereau

"Lady Celestine Devereau," the herald announced next, announcing the Head of the House of entertainers of all kinds, from musicians to acrobats and actors who were also the cunning poisoners and spies, "vassal of Darkholm, Countess of Devereaux, and Baroness of Ashbourne."

The introduction was followed by the entrance of a woman in her mid-twenties. Her graceful poise was accentuated by her hanging jewelry, the flowing green dress that seemed weightless, the bright emerald eyes, and her ivory skin. But her beauty did not conquer a room as much as did her smile of pearls and hair of flames. She could only be described as dangerously ravishing.

She was accompanied by her four undeniable brothers and the wives of the first three. Red hair and green eyes were so common in the line some rumored the incest of their liege lords had rubbed off on the Devereau.

"Lady Celestine," Lady Gwenore spoke to the new head of House Devereaux, "I am so sorry for the loss of your mother."

"Please, Lady Gwenore," Celestine responded, "save me your pleasantries. Since when have you cared about anyone's feelings? We all know my mother was a cunt, and the world is better off without her."

As if she had been teaching one of her lessons in etiquette, the lady of House Sanglune paused for a moment before raising her eyebrows and responding casually, "Pardon me, Lady Celestine, but I wasn't sorry for you. Your mother was one of those rivals one simply enjoys seeing around. They make life more . . . interesting."

"Lord Caime Grey," the herald stepped aside, "vassal of Darkholm, Count of Greyshield, Baron of Holmsden, Lord of the Hellhounds, and his wife, Lady Melandre Grey."

A second later, the count entered. While his militant pace was fast and steady, he held his wife's hand tenderly.

Well into his sixties, Caime's hair grayed and receded substantially. His face was old and weary, but he smiled an honest smile, as he often did when he was not otherwise scolding his men.

Lord Caime nodded, bowing left and right to all. He walked toward the center, and once he stood before Septem, he spoke. "Today, like always, I am yours, my lord of Darkholm," he bowed deeply, reverently.

The count then made a second stop. "Always ready, Lord General," Caime bowed to Idian, who nodded back in acknowledgment.

While Grayshield was easily among the largest counties in Darkholm, its swampy biome made it far from the most prosperous or fertile land. Its importance, however, was undeniable.

The highly militant House Grey had borne losses that had almost wiped out their forces and their name. But their founder had the vision to allow those who would perhaps never get a chance of redemption to join him. Thus the Hellhounds of House Grey's ranks swelled with the worst criminals ready to give their lives in battle for the kingdom their actions had wronged. It was thus why Greyshield County was colloquially known as 'the last chance.'

And so House Grey's numbers swelled and dwindled over time.

Caime Grey

Once in place, the keep's servants brought cups of Blood Tea for everyone present.

Septem's baritone voice was heard. "Vassal Houses, once again, we welcome you to Darkholde to thank you for your loyalty and your support, to thank you for your dedication and service. Tonight we are not the houses of liege lords and vassals. Tonight we dine as friends."

"*In Sanguine nos Prosperabitur,*" Septem raised his cup.

"*In Sanguine nos Prosperabitur.*" Every cup was raised, and upon the queen's signal, the banquet began.

Servants crossed the main doors carrying trays of carefully cut pieces of meat, fruits, nuts, and utensils the attendants would use as they walked around the room and intermingled.

Serverus Ecru recalled how strange he had felt the first time he had participated, but now clearly understood the importance of this night, where the interaction and relation-building were truly the main course. It was many times on this night that each House decided where their children would be apprenticed, where everything was spoken of freely, and where secrets were shared. Tonight they would all stay in Darkholde. It would be the following morning when they would all meet in front of the throne of Darkholm after having had time to pour over information, to plan and act upon their discussions and agreements.

He had learned to see this moment for what it truly was: to most, a time to learn, to share, to him, a time to appreciate the family that had taken him in, and also a time to yearn for that which he could not have.

A few steps away, Count Caime Grey and Elias Devereau met with Serverus Ecru and Maxius, Aeron, and Idian of the Darkholm. They related the events of Valador and Volanar's insurgence. They discussed the removal of the dukes of the traitorous duchies and their own preparedness for the worst.

As he had been known to do, Lord Caime spoke freely, laughed heartily, and drank to his heart's content. The count took a half-full cup from Fengo Darkholm's hand and switched it for his empty one, laughing as Eriadna's youngest son just shrugged and continued on his way. Caime lived every moment to its fullest, knowing it might as well be his last and, for someone in his House's position on the frontlines of every major battle, it could very well be.

Fengo Darkholm walked toward Tenslea, pouting exaggeratedly. Once by her side, he opened his mouth wide, waiting for her to feed him a grape, and she gladly obliged. He turned her around and held her close, his lips softly kissing her neck, "Thank you, my love."

"Are you thanking me too, love?" Fengo felt a whisper on his own neck and the warm, wet lips of his cousin Brenis, who placed a grape between his own teeth and asked, "Would you like me to give you this one?"

Smiling mischievously, in the blink of an eye, Fengo grabbed Brenis's ears and lunged toward the taller man. Swiftly, Brenis swallowed the grape and laughed, "Too late!" But Fengo still kissed his lips with a huge, long, wet kiss, tongue and all.

"Aww, you two would make a great couple," Toradmus Darkholm jested.

"Now I know," Brenis laughed. "Next time, I will place it between my fat butt cheeks."

Fengo smiled mischievously, making Tenslea and those around laugh heartily.

Not far away, the ancient figure of Davidov stood on the balcony, the cool breeze blowing the wisps of his long, thin hair. He looked at the horizon, at the night sky and the waves below. He stood alone, quiet.

While the Master of Death has never enjoyed social events, that was not the reason he stood there that night.

"My lord," Lady Gwenore Sanglune appeared next to him, "I am here, at your service."

"Lady Sanglune," Davidov nodded slightly, his grim expression unchanged.

They stood in front of one another as two firm walls that would not move or budge under even the most extreme circumstances.

They walked along the bridge, the sky and its thousands of stars as their backdrop. They could have spoken of their glittering beauty, of the restless ocean below, of the strength of the wind and its salty presence. But Lord Davidov and Gwenore did none of that.

He didn't ask her about her lord husband's health, or even about her own. He didn't greet her with flowery, adorned comments. Davidov Darkholm was not that type of man. He didn't ask for that which he didn't care about, and that was something Gwenore Sanglune appreciated. As many times before, they wasted no time with beautiful words. They went straight to business.

"Two duke positions have become available in the Great Council," Davidov stated, "I will speak to Septem so that, for your loyalty, he will consider you."

"My lord, if I may." She spoke with deference to her superior. "Your mere consideration honors me and my House. The first Sanglune's oath, however, was to serve as a vassal to my Lords of Darkholm, and while I was not born of the name, I follow that same oath faithfully.

"Now, if my Lord King insisted, of course, I would accept. While my loyalty would not change, I would hate every minute of it, for I don't give two dead rats

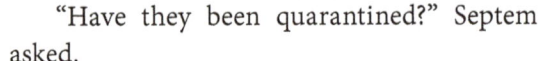

about the kingdom. I would prefer to continue until the end of my days serving you and only you. So, if it's up to me, I respectfully decline the offer."

"A pity your spirit was not planted in the body of one of this House," Davidov's menacing eyes looked at her.

"Thank you, my lord," the noblewoman bowed. "If there is nothing else, I must go attend to my lord husband."

Davidov said nothing. He didn't need to. The scraping sound of his feathered cape on the stone bridge as he turned alone let her know she was being dismissed.

"Your Highness," Idian Darkholm spoke to Septem. "A substantial number of Lord Grey's men are afflicted. They seem to be showing signs of worsening."

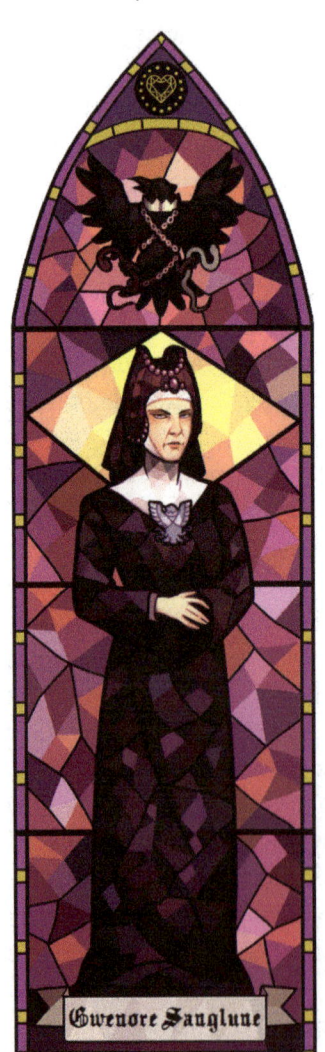

Gwenore Sanglune

"Have they been quarantined?" Septem asked.

"He has quarantined them, yes," Idian responded.

"Inform Rowena of this," Septem instructed. "She will take care of it. In the meantime, send a missive to the loyal Blood of Duskforge. They have enough people to swell the Hellhound's numbers once more."

"My Lord of Darkholm," Celestine said in a melodic voice, walking toward Septem's figure. "Pardon my interruption, but there is an important matter of which you need to be informed."

Her words grabbed the attention of not only Septem but also of those around him. "There are Houses within the kingdom that are against you."

"Something with which leadership must always learn to come to terms," Septem replied.

"Yes, Your Highness," Celestine's shrew's eyes smiled, "but these are actively conspiring against you, and they will not rest until they remove you from the throne."

"Speak," Septem instructed.

"They believed with my mother, it was impossible, but in me, they see an ally, someone who can have close access to you." Upon Celestine's words, more seemed to join in, scavengers in a feast of her words.

"Who are these Houses?"

"There are many, my lord, mostly distant, and we believe some are from beyond our borders, but there are those within the capital of Darkholm itself. We have not moved against them until there is complete certainty of all who are involved. But there is one moving fast, insisting, organizing all of this."

"How certain are you of this?" Septem questioned.

"My lord, seeing the schism caused by the passing of my mother, your loyal subject, on our House, what they perceived as a weakness, has fueled the courage of Lord Ingerid of House Machad to contact me with a proposal. I am certain, for he has approached me himself."

"Alex," Septem raised his hand, his voice rumbling like thunder.

In an instant, clad in loose clothes covering most of the face and body, the child of Arlisse, the mysterious Master of Secrets, approached. Bowing to the patriarch, Alex whispered, "Your Highness."

Despite the uncertainty regarding Alex's unrevealed gender, no one seemed to care. If anything, Alex, the disguise expert known as the Shadow of Darkholm, was one of the most liked and reliable members of the Royal House.

The Shadow's bright eyes of yellow were on the monarch, awaiting orders.

"Take the head," Septem ordered.

"Nooo!" Elzabeth Darkholm's heavy figure raised her voice in protest, drawing all attention. "This can be done a different way! They are my friends!" As fast as she could, she ran, talking to herself as she headed toward the kitchen, largely ignored by the rest.

"Your Highness," Celestine then continued, "would it not be better to wait until all are identified?"

"Waiting is as wise as it is not," Septem replied. "The head must be taken so that the body of the snake suffers. In the instance where more than one head exists, the nest will be disturbed. Amidst their chaos, we will thrive."

CAKE

Location: Kingdom of Blackheart,
Duchy of Darkholm, County of Coldforge

*The greatest things can be achieved by either
hard work, miracles, or sweets . . .*

"Still too hot," Elzabeth told herself, moving her hands from under the tray she carried to its handles.

The woman was careful, careful to walk fast enough to reach her destination before it was too late, and at the same time slow enough to avoid losing her footing and dropping the masterpiece she carried—a beautiful cake so perfectly balanced the colored glass baubles dangling from her forearm were silent, as if in awe.

The freshly baked cake wasn't too moist or too dry. It was the right size and had the right amount of milk, flour, sugar, and, well, a little more sugar, but only because it was a special cake.

Then again, to Elzabeth, all cakes were special, so she always pushed the boundaries of how much sugar one could add without ruining the work.

Of course, to all that, she added her secret ingredient. At the mere thought, Elzabeth smiled and shook her head, remembering how many times the younger Darkholm tried to figure out what that secret ingredient was.

"Rose plum!" Sellayne had shouted.

"Black tea!" Toradmus cried.

"Sugar!" Charon had smiled.

'Poor Charon,' Elzabeth thought, 'oh dear, sugar, my secret ingredient?'

"Nothing?" Isolde had wondered.

'That little mouse Isolde,' Elzabeth's lips smiled warmly, 'she's as smart as they come. That one is going to get far . . . far up or far down, who knows, but she has potential.'

"The truth is," she had explained each time, "sometimes there is no actual secret ingredient one adds to the mix. The sense of wonder, that sense that what you're getting is special, is what truly gives it a taste like no other. Many times, you know, the secret ingredient is nothing other than love."

And that is something Elzabeth Darkholm truly believed, that the only thing that could truly make a cake rise was love. She had learned one didn't necessarily need love for others. One didn't need to completely agree with the recipient of her gifts. As a matter of fact, one didn't need to agree with them at all.

What was really needed was love and pride for one's work, for every single minute of her time, for every second of her life that was poured into the mix.

She had decided to walk toward the Machad estate to ensure not only that she could always keep an eye on her piece of art of light green, pink, and white but to ensure the wind caressed her face.

Not only was the soft breeze welcome after the time she had hurriedly spent in front of the hot oven, but more importantly, it brought the constant, sweet scent of her work to her nostrils.

With each whiff, her eyelashes fluttered like butterflies on an early spring morning.

Of all Elizabeth's skills, drawing was one she had been complimented for— not too many times, and most of those compliments had come from herself, of course, but a compliment is still a compliment!

Her artful hands had attempted to draw the sigil of House Machad on the cake's surface. If it was either because the cake was still too fresh out of the oven or because her drawing skills weren't great, she didn't know, but upon seeing the curved-tailed lizard on the sigil wasn't setting properly and well, had started to get quite distorted, she resorted to the one thing that could save it.

"Frosting!" She giggled, "Cover it with frosting! Frosting can hide any mistake. Well, all but the big ones. For the big ones, we have extra frosting!"

It was late that night when the Darkholm woman arrived at the gate of House Machad's estate located right at the periphery of Coldforge's merchant quarter.

While it was still within the city limits, it had the appearance of a large summer vacation home. The lavish estate had originally been built right outside the city, but the advancing coast had forced the displacement of nobles who had also called the countryside home, turning it into a forest of buildings and streets.

To maintain their privacy, the Machad had built a wall that separated them from the rest.

Her occupied hands made Elzabeth kick the bottom of the gate doors. Upon seeing the door hatch starting to slide open, she quickly intervened, "Oh, not too much. Just halfway, will ya, sweets? It befits me!"

"Lord Ingerid has retired for the night," the guards spoke in an attempt to turn her away.

"It is of utmost importance that I meet with Lord Ingerid Machad," she insisted.

"Lady Elzabeth," the guardsman spoke in earnest, "you are always welcome to return in the morning."

The Darkholm woman's eyes widened slightly, and she hastily looked in every direction before she approached the hatch and lowered her voice, "I really need to speak to him regarding a very delicate matter. Tomorrow might be too late. His life is in great danger."

Upon hearing the word, the guard welcomed her inside the courtyard.

The foyer of the family villa was somewhat pretentious, the tapestries and chandeliers showing riches the walls would perhaps whisper they didn't really possess. Even the servants were unusually numerous this late in the evening, Elzabeth noted, scurrying like rats as if they sought to move around enough to appear busy.

"Lady Darkholm," a young servant boy approached, "please allow me to help you with that."

"Oh, what a gentleman," she responded. "I thank you kindly, but I would rather carry it myself. The last time I allowed it, someone dropped it, and well, I do not even want to think about it! The splattering sound as it hit the floor . . . It still haunts me to this day!"

"Elzabeth!" A middle-aged woman appeared from one of the hallways. "What a pleasant surprise!" Her hair was up in an improvised bun, her body covered in a fine white dress and a simple bodice on which flowers were embroidered.

"Lady Renayda," she greeted, "it is so good to see you."

"I heard your voice from my reading room, and well, I had to come greet you. It's been a while! What brings you here?"

"Ah, well, saying hello. Nothing too extraordinary."

"Oh . . . my . . . god," Renayda's amazed eyes set on Elzabeth's creation. "What is that?"

"Nothing. Just a cake," the baker smiled.

"*Just* a cake, you say," she took a deep breath, "from the hands of Elzabeth Darkholm? That's impossible! The scent of it alone makes me melt. Hmm, I can smell the violets—oh, I love violets. They're my favorite!"

"Are they?" Elzabeth smiled almost innocently.

"Of course they are. Did you forget? What else does it have?"

"I cannot tell you."

"Pray, do tell!" Filled with excitement, Renayda clasped Elizabeth's arm. "I insist."

"Oh well, if you insist," she whispered, "pink *lavender*."

"Pink lavender."

"Yes," Elzabeth added, "the flower of devotion and silence. Strengthen our loyalties and leave the past in the past, you know!"

"Interesting," Lady Renayda raised her eyebrows curiously.

"But I'm certain it must have something else," her inquisitive eyes squinted, "does it have . . ."

"Aargh, I am so weak!" Shaking her head rapidly, Elzabeth stomped on the floor and followed with a rapid nod, "Shhh, do not say anything, but it also has passionfruit."

"Passionfruit?"

"Yes."

"Passionfruit!" Both women repeatedly nodded in excitement.

"Yes, right? What better way to a man's heart than with the fruit of passion!"

Renayda's hands moved swiftly toward the surface of the cake, but just as fast, Elzabeth took away her creation from under the woman's fingers to stop them from making contact.

"Oh, by god," Renayda complained, "let me taste it!"

"No!" Elzabeth responded. "This is for your father. Men are many times surprisingly flexible regarding their honor on the battlefield, oh, but not having the honor to get the first piece . . . do

Elzabeth Darkholm

not get me started. But I promise you," she continued, "I will do my best to save a piece for you . . . and for little me!"

"My lady Elzabeth Darkholm," a handsome young butler interrupted, "Lord Ingerid Machad is ready for you."

'About time,' she sighed. "Lady Renayda, it was great to see you. Bye, bye!" The large woman smiled broadly and proceeded rapidly toward the stairs.

"Elll-zabeth." The noblewoman's voice took a melodic, teasing tone.

Elzabeth looked back. Her smile became an expression of absolute horror when she saw Renayda at the bottom of the staircase, lips smirking, with her arms crossed except for her raised index finger. And the surface of that one insolent digit was covered in pink, green, and white.

Renayda smiled mischievously, looking back at Elzabeth while her finger closed in on her own tongue.

The Darkholm woman froze in place. She wondered quite fast what she could do to stop her.

'I could run downstairs as fast as I can, but my bad knee . . . and that is if I do not trip! Aw, I will never make it in time, or could I?'

'I could instead run as fast as possible toward Lord Ingerid's chamber and hope for the best,' she thought. 'What to do, what to do?'

But while she hesitated, Renayda Machad's lips closed around her finger and came back out completely clean.

"Lady Renayda, wait!"

"What?" Renayda swallowed and smiled, her gaze still on Elzabeth. The following moment she coughed, furrowing her brow.

"Nothing," Elzabeth responded, "too late now anyway." She examined her adulterated work, carefully searching for exactly where the noblewoman had touched it. 'Ah, there it is, right on the edge,' she told herself, producing a small spatula from one of her pockets with which she tried to fix the defect. "Frosting to the rescue! Thankfully just some small damage. It would have been really troublesome if you had dented the cake."

"Are you all right, Lady Machad?" a maid inquired, with two more closing in.

"Yes, yes, I am. Just fetch me some water," Renayda instructed, "I swallowed too fast.

"Elzabeth," she continued, "it was delicious! Please save me some. I'll be in my reading room till late tonight."

With a small curtsy and a big smile, the Darkholm woman followed her guide to be taken to the presence of Lord Ingerid.

"I brought dessert!" She smiled with plump cheeks at the aged man who sat by his dining table.

"It is rather late for dessert, Lady Elzabeth," Lord Machad said dryly, his suspicion not well hidden. "What brings you here?"

She brought the tray closer to her face so that he could see both the cake and her expression. "Mhm . . . midnight snack then?"

"You may place it there on the table," his voice was indifferent, his hand loose, snobbish. Elzabeth did as instructed but made sure to slide the cake ever so slightly toward Lord Ingerid.

"Thank you kindly for the gesture," he continued, "but I am quite busy at the moment, so would you be equally kind and tell me the purpose of your visit?"

Placing a hand to the side of her mouth, Elzabeth lowered her voice some, "I need to discuss something important . . . privately, if that is agreeable to you."

Lord Ingerid, raising his eyebrows, formed deep furrows in his forehead that now appeared as wrinkled as the rest of his face. He instructed the servants to leave their presence immediately.

"Could you be so kind as to bring some tea?" Elzabeth asked one of the servants before he left.

"I can, my lady. What would you like?"

"Do you have any special brew?" she asked with a modesty that could have seemed feigned.

"We have Tardese red tea, my lady, but it takes too long to prepare."

"Well, I do not mind. I have *never* tasted that one. But wait . . . Oh, do not mind me, no, no, no," she shook her head, "not *that* one. I would not ever want to impose."

The servant looked expectantly at Ingerid, who tilted his head as a sign for him to get precisely that which could potentially impress her.

"It . . . is no bother at all, my lady," the boy said. "It will be my pleasure to brew a cup for you."

"Well, a whole teapot will do," she added immediately, "and honey, thank you, it will go well with this cake."

"Milk or cream, my lady?"

"Oh yes, surely, milk. Goat milk?"

"I am afraid we don't have goat milk, my lady." the boy responded, but after seeing his lord's face, he promptly let her know he would bring that too.

"Now, as to the reason for your visit," Lord Machad spoke again. Elzabeth, however, smiled quietly, her eyes still on the young man who was leaving the room. While she had visited many times before, like everywhere she went, she scanned every detail as if it had been her first time.

She studied the exquisiteness of the carvings on the table legs and the silverware resting on its top. In this room, too, there were embroidered tapestries partially covering the tall glass windows lining the walls. Like everything inside the Machad estate, the attention to detail was noticeable.

It took the almost-silent sound of the door closing before she spoke again.

"My lord," she calmly placed her hand over his. "I know both our Houses have had their differences in the past, but I am bringing this as a peace offering because, well, I am quite sure you and I would not want anything bad to happen to any one of us, right?" she winked.

"Right . . ." he replied, puzzled.

"Well then, shall we eat?" Without a second wasted, she grabbed a knife from the table.

"Is that it? I'm confused."

"Well, no, but it is better to discuss these things over food. They say it is the best way to a man's heart!" She winked again. "Would you like me to cut you a piece?"

Ingerid eyed her. His hesitant eyes went back to the cake before returning to the Darkholm.

"What is it?" she quickly questioned. "Oh no! Is it misshapen?"

"Not at all," he responded. "It is beautiful, I must say. Too perfect, actually."

"Well, I do not like to brag about it," she looked at the dorsum of her fingers, "but I baked it myself, and less than perfect would just not do in my world."

"That is not the problem," his demeanor seemed to crack just a tad. "I have worked hard to shed the weight I have."

"Ah, so that is it?" she feigned surprise, "Let me show you something." She grabbed a silver spoon in her hand. "You know how people say eating cakes and sweets makes you fat, right?"

"Yes."

Digging in the same place Renayda had touched, and thus ensuring any imperfection was forever erased, she took a small piece of the cake and, closing her eyes, placed it inside her mouth.

Elizabeth then stepped aside for him to see the entirety of her huge body. "Look at me now. Did you see me gain any weight? No, right? Because it is all *lies*!

"Some people do not want you to eat your cake so that they can eat it instead, that is all, and in their mission, they spew forth those filthy lies!"

Lord Ingerid almost smiled. He lowered his head and shook it, trying to contain himself. "Thank you, but still, I'll pass."

"That is . . . fine," she almost shrugged, turning toward the cake to hide her face from him. But he caught the slight change in her smile, in the barely perceptible trembling of her lower lip. How could he miss those when very few things had ever escaped the eagle eyes of Lord Ingerid?

The Machad patriarch had survived and prospered in Darkholm Duchy precisely because of the details he didn't miss. While he was not amicable or engaged in the social circles of the elite, Ingerid was attentive to the land purchases, districts, administrative changes, and improvements other nobles' estates made.

He caught himself wetting his lips in expectation but stopped himself before making a mistake he would lose sleep over.

"It is such a sad and yet happy moment when a baker has to finish her job," she sighed, her bright eyes contemplating her creation one last time, "for while the design of the cake and its creation take all the credit, they are just part of it. The actual moment when one has to cut the cake is just as important. And proper digestion, we cannot ignore that!"

Her hand steadily placed the blade on top of the frosted surface almost ceremoniously, and slowly, yet meticulously, she effortlessly let the metal weight drop toward the tray.

She then turned the tray one-quarter of the way and almost made a second cut before she saw that would leave the part she had taken a portion out of right outside her range, so she moved her wrist just one, two, no, about four inches to the side where she sliced once more.

In the end, her hands carefully took nearly two-fifths of the cake and served it on her plate. Mesmerized by the sweet dessert, she took her place at the table. "I would wait for the tea," she smiled at Lord Ingerid, "but I am quite hungry, so if you would excuse me."

Summoning the deepest strengths of his will upon smelling the aroma of the freshly baked good, he nodded. He remained quiet, fighting his own desire to partake with her, his eyes wanting to close but watching her every move.

The first spoon was only half full. Elzabeth's lips opened and placed its contents delicately inside her mouth. "Hmm, it's very good, I must say, not to praise myself, of course."

The ones that followed varied, from her lips teasing her creation with kisses before eating a spoonful to a heaping one she placed on her tongue before twisting the silver spoon inside her mouth with an 'mhmmmmm' of orgasmic proportions.

"Ehem," he cleared his throat to call her attention.

"Ehemmm!" he insisted upon her failure to do so.

"Yes?"

As if having real difficulty getting the words out, he raised his eyebrows. "I had said I would like some."

"Oooooh, I am so sorry," Elzebeth stood once again, her body jiggling in the excitement she tried to contain.

Grabbing the knife, she almost leaned on the table. She then shut an eye and bit her tongue lightly as she delicately placed the blade on the cake's surface. With exquisite care, she proceeded to slice a piece, one so thin she almost seemed like a gluttonous little child who was being forced to share.

So thin was his slice, the moment she served it on his plate, it folded over, but with a great smile that, to Lord Machad, seemed to be more of embarrassment, Elzebeth attempted several times to straighten the piece again. "Well, I guess it was tired of waiting!" she giggled, giving up and laying the slice on its side before placing it in front of him.

That was the rock that broke the glass, the drop that made the cup spill. As much as he tried, Lord Ingerid couldn't stop himself from laughing at Elzebeth's silliness. It had been many times before he had walked into his room and smiled, remembering her words, her optimism, and her somewhat crazy ideas.

"So," Elzebeth began, "as I mentioned before, House Darkholm and Machad's relationship has been as walking barefoot over a rough patch. Given my relationship with some of your household, what can I humbly offer to make it better for both Houses?"

Lord Machad was hesitant to speak. There was so much criticism he could offer. There was a notably different treatment of the vassal houses.

He had even offered to mentor Darkholm children twice. He had asked for reduced taxation in exchange for House Machad to become a vassal of the Lords of Darkholm. But all of it had been denied, and he couldn't understand why. Did they somehow sense he did it all for status, for the glory of his name?

"I have to give it some thought."

"It is important you think about it promptly, as there are some who would rather see you dead. Then again, there are surely those who wish to see me dead too!

"Anyway, how are things between your children?"

"Between my daughters?" his spoon still rested between his tense hand and the plate.

"Enatta and the much younger Renayda." She lifted a hand matter of factly.

"They are both well." Her question raised his suspicion.

"That is lovely to hear! I have not visited in a while, but I was thinking about spending a day with Lady Xanayra and Enatta. There is so much we need to catch up on!"

"My lady wife would love that. You know she is quite fond of you," he added. At the mention of Enatta, he hesitated again.

'Is she possibly prodding for information? Unlikely,' he thought. 'She is surely witty but not sharp at all.'

"That would be lovely! I will make her something. Wait . . .," she responded, bringing a finger to her lips as she sought to remember, "peanuts, right? She is allergic to peanuts! But she likes dates!"

"Yes, avoid peanuts, and she does love dates." Upon hearing Elzabeth remembered those details about his wife, he brightened up some. Lady Xanayra, his wife, was barely known in any social circle, something she long lamented. But Lord Machad preferred the avoidance of most balls and festivities, at least those organized by his competition. Being the head of a merchant family, there were many he considered competition.

"What about Enatta," she interrupted his thoughts. "Do you think she would not?"

'What about Enatta . . . ' his mind went to his eldest, more hard-headed daughter. A little over two decades older than Renayda, Enatta was as shrewd and serious as the father whose seat she would inherit. Unlike her father, she did appreciate the intricacies of the social interactions with her peers, both local and beyond. Every time Elzabeth had visited, however, Enatta had largely avoided her, finding her, at best, annoying.

"I believe she would enjoy it."

"Hmmm, that is a lie. You lie." Elzabeth smiled coyly, pointing at him with the spoon. "I wonder what it is about me that she does not like . . . is it my weight?"

"No, not at all," he quickly responded.

"Do I remind her of someone she detests?" she wondered out loud. "I can change my hair! She will not recognize me that way!"

"Enatta is difficult, that is all."

Enatta had been on the lookout for opportunities to grow the influence of the Machad, to place people in the right places, to befriend other nobles, and, perhaps most importantly, for any sign of resistance against the Darkholm.

Ingerid was simply not at all good at lying, so bad, in fact, that an idiot like Elzabeth would catch him with ease. He sought to distract her from asking more about his heir.

Elizabeth's charm was something he could maybe resist, at least with less difficulty than the baked piece in front of him.

Lord Machad took a spoonful of the cake in his mouth.

"Hmmmmm," he closed his eyes. "It is delicious."

"Really? Do you really, really think so?"

"I do, actually. Passionfruit, I love its sweet tartness. It reminds me of my summers abroad."

"Well, well, look at that! I am glad it is to your liking. I made it especially for you, and I was pressed for time!"

She briefly asked about his relationship with Baron Davidov, about the merchant's guild, and about Enatta's whereabouts, having heard she was away. But every time she asked, she met resistance, and every time she casually moved to a different subject, as if her mind was either that flighty, or she was just not truly much interested.

Suddenly, Ingerid was taken by a coughing fit. He started coughing once, twice, his eyes searching for a cup of water.

"Here!" Elizabeth helped him to his cup. "Are you okay, dear?"

Her eyes were wide open with worry before he saw her smile change slightly into one more sinister.

"You look rather *pale . . .*"

Filled with desperation, he tried to stand up, but his muscles cramped, bringing him to his knees while he choked on a scream that came out as barely a whisper, "Help, help!"

"What? You want me to ask for help? Surely!" Elizabeth took another mouthful of her serving first. "Help, help!" she whispered mockingly, following suit with yet another mouthful.

Struggling to find both air and his chair, he saw the Darkholm woman move the seat away from his reach. "There, there now. I do not want you to hurt yourself with the chair."

She then sat back on her seat, contemplating the room in its entirety, its beautiful tapestries, the polished silver, the expensive chandeliers. This man had an eye for everything, and well, just like his social distance, that eye that was his strength had also been his weakness.

A thud followed before he dragged himself along the floor less than two feet before his body thrashed on the floor, spasming and convulsing wildly.

"Do you know what? That it is in really poor taste to have some leftovers on your plate," she smiled, reaching out for his plate and serving it on her own. And even after his moves eased, she ate, piece by piece, enjoying every single mouthful, every moment. His death sentence had been certain, just as certainly had Elzabeth ensured to take the right amount of antidote back home.

I mean, why would she not? How could she otherwise enjoy the masterful deliciousness of it all?

When his body went limp, she knelt by him and delicately checked his neck for a pulse.

"Still there, good . . ." She searched for something between her breasts, producing a matte black, feathered, poisoned dart. She stuck it on the right side of his neck with the skill of someone who had done this hundreds of times before and observed the poison seep in, rapidly changing the skin around where it was inoculated.

She didn't spend a single minute telling her plans. Why would she? Would she risk him surviving and acting against her? Hah, impossible. No one had ever survived one of Elzabeth Darkholm's poisons. So she didn't speak out of fear of his actions but out of the possibility that, like at nearly all times in Darkholde, someone could be listening.

One more spoonful, and seeming delighted, she walked toward the tall glass windows. With a single swing, she smashed the glass with the butt of the cutting knife before returning it to the center of the table, where she stopped to eat some more and catch her breath.

Then, using the table for support, she carefully knelt and then leaned on the floor close to Lord Ingerid. She hyperventilated some and used her own hands to smear the makeup under her watering eyes.

"MURDERER!" The shrill of her voice sounded an alarm that echoed through the estate. "MUUUURDERERRRRR!" she screamed again.

In less than a minute, the doors burst open, spilling servants, guards, and relatives in. The chaos that ensued would have been catastrophic if Renayda hadn't taken control.

"Lady Elzabeth, are you alright?"

"Do not mind me! It is Lord Machad who has been attacked!" Her fat finger pointed purposely at the wrong window.

"Lady Renayda," a guardsman exclaimed, pointing out at the correct one, "look, the attack came from here!"

"Search the whole estate!" Renayda ordered, "Do not let a single life leave! Elzabeth, are you alright? Someone help her up!"

Two servant women took her by the hands, helping her, albeit with some difficulty, to her feet. One of them placed a hand on Elzabeth's chest, "My lady, Lady Elzabeth's pulse is beating rapidly. She's about to faint."

"Bring her a chair," Renayda instructed. "She needs air, and bring her some water!"

"I just . . ." Elzabeth said weakly, " . . . need some sugar." She pointed, with some difficulty, at what was left of the cake. Without hesitation, the servants handed her the tray, and a spoon, which her shaking hands slowly brought to her mouth, finishing all the main evidence's disappearing act.

On the floor lay Lord Ingerid, his eyes wide open in a terrifying visage. He had felt his throat close rapidly like the doors to every opportunity for the dreams he had for his House would close.

———————

It was already past the midnight hour when the guards reported they had turned every stone possible, even alerting neighboring buildings, in their search for the assassin, and their work had produced nothing.

"We will not stop searching, Lady Renayda."

"Thank you," she responded firmly. She was pained, but this was not the moment to be distraught, but rather for a leader to rise among them. Her sister Enatta was away. It would take months before she was back, months they couldn't live without a figurehead.

Most of their House and servants would later come to acknowledge her, she who had always been the second daughter and never the favorite, for her role in stabilizing them, in leading them, and for steering the ship in their storm of these difficult, chaotic times.

"We have found this," she held up a piece of cloth where the black dart was partially wrapped. "While they think they have outsmarted us, only our rivals in House Silverne have access to black iron. Foolish they are if they believe we will not act."

"But, Renayda," her cousin Brigette asked, "we cannot just act blindly against Blood."

"I am well aware," Renayda responded. "We will ask the Crown for support in avenging our father's death at the hands of House Silverne."

"Surely," Brigette added. "I don't mean any offense to our visitor, but the Royal House has never been close to us."

"They will be," Renayda looked at Elzabeth, "we have a close friend among them."

All eyes filled with hope when they set themselves on Elzabeth, whose hands were wiping her face with a piece of fine fabric. She sobbed, not uncontrollably so, but just enough.

Her fingers were carefully placed so that every time the fabric touched her face, they could still see her expression, the tears, her pain . . .

All the while, she giggled inside, for although she wasn't a particularly gifted painter, she was surely a phenomenal actress.

GIFTED

Location: Kingdom of Blackheart, Royal Duchy of Darkholm,
County of Coldforge, Darkholde Keep

Little is more valuable than heartfelt gratitude . . .

The doors to the outside of the keep opened before his imposing figure. He only secretly wished he didn't have to get used to forcing life's doors to open.

His firm steps carried him along the architectural wonder of the ledges of Darkholde, with its walkways of stony bridges that were only evident on a morning as bright as this one. Behind him, only half a step away, his wife, Elleonora Darkholm, had just caught up to him.

"I heard you were leaving," she questioned.

"I am."

"When are you leaving?" she asked.

"Today," Gustavus responded.

"I was hoping . . ." she hurried her steps, "we would have some time for ourselves."

"It is not by choice that I leave," he stated. "I am following Erdrick to Greyhale for the inspection of its forces."

"When will you be back?"

"Who knows," he responded. "Within a few days, I suppose, by my estimate."

"And it is absolutely necessary for you to go?"

"Of course, Elle. What kind of question is that?" he asked firmly. "I have been commanded to."

"Of course, my husband," she responded meekly.

Upon hearing the tone in her voice, Gustavus turned and, grabbing her by the flank, brought her close to him in a half-embrace, "Hey, look at me. I do not like this either. As a matter of fact, I hate what little time we get to spend together given my responsibilities, and that is not right, not to me, not to you."

Elleonora nodded in agreement.

"We could not even have a proper wedding," he added, "but I promise that one of these days, I will make it up to you. Now come, help me get my things ready," Gustavus resumed the walk. "What do you have for me?"

"Your brother Aram is not doing any better," she responded, hating to be the bearer of news that brought both sadness and anger to his face. "I have given ideas to Rowena, some combinations she could use."

"And what did she say?"

"She said she would consider them."

"Bah," Gustavus spat, "had it been her own brother."

"Well," Elleonora interjected, "do not just judge her like that. When she says she will consider it, I trust that she will. What may seem like hesitation on her part is but the time she takes to study things carefully before actually applying the knowledge."

"I disagree. She hesitates because she is either insecure or wants to appear to be in control. If it were Rowena's own brother, she would have used everything, likely without a second thought. She would have found a cure by now."

"Gus," hearing the irritation in his voice, she sought to calm him, "I know Rowena probably better than anyone. When she says—"

"You delude yourself, Elle," Gustavus scolded. "Rowena is far from stupid. Your time around her lets you see the game she plays, but some you do not see because you are a pawn in them."

"You are misjudging her."

"I can help you open your eyes," Gustavus frowned, "but I cannot open them for you."

Elleonora lowered her gaze.

"Anything else?" he asked, grabbing her chin endearingly.

"Yes," she responded, "A Baron Davidson has moved from Olath Valm's capital to Coldforge. While not financially powerful, he is charismatic."

"Did you get to meet him?"

"I have not. What I relay is what I have heard from a conversation between Rowena and Sellayne."

"Lady Elleonora!" a servant girl called from a bridge above.

"Yes?" she responded.

"Your cousins are looking for you," the servant beckoned. "You are to meet at the main courtyard to depart within the hour."

"Coming!" Elleonora shouted back. "Here we go again," she sighed, "I will help you quickly, and then I must go."

"Hey," Gustavus's strong hands grabbed her arms with care, "just go."

"Are you sure?"

"I am. Upon my return," he said, "I will ask for time, some time for ourselves so that we can go away and rest. How does that sound?"

"I would very much like that," Elleonora rested her hands on her husband's shoulder.

"Now, where would you like to go then?" he smiled.

"I . . . do not know," she responded, "how far could we go?"

"Not far, likely," Gustavus's hand grabbed hers, "somewhere within Darkholm. Maybe even Olath Valm? I know Varnje would be to both our likings."

"The high forest and its transition into the evergreen woods does sound interesting," she said, "but this has taken me by surprise. I will need time to give it some thought."

"Then do so while we are both away."

"I will."

"And Elle . . ." he called one last time before she left.

"Yes?"

"Keep your eyes open."

--------✦✦✦✦✦--------

Gustavus swung open the door to his room, the large, semicircular chamber that seemed quite rustic, for a Darkholm, that is, but that was perfect for him. Chests lay on the floor, close to two armoires lining the walls, flanking the main window that was heavily curtained. Aside from those, a pair of small shelves where whatever books Elleonora was currently reading were located on the opposite side, close to the small table where they had left an unfinished game of cards.

He looked at the hands of cards that were both facedown. Something within him wanted to flip them, to look at them, to see what Elleonora's hand contained that had allowed her to turn around that last game he would have otherwise swiftly won. But she hadn't won yet, likely because close to the end, he had interrupted it all and had asked to continue it later.

'It is fine. It is nothing but just a game,' his wife had said, finding no issue with doing as he wished.

To Gustavus, however, nothing was just a game. Every time they sat to play, he gave it his all. In his mind, it was an exercise in strategic planning, tactical evaluation, and resource management, and while he would smile mockingly upon an imminent victory, Eriadna's oldest son had always found it difficult to accept any loss.

Had Elleonora seen his hand? he had wondered, his eyes quickly moving to the four cards on his side of the table. They appeared untouched. Besides, it was unlike Elleonora to cheat. He won most of the time, and that didn't seem to bother her in the least. Even if she had tried to, however, Gustavus had memorized exactly how he had placed each card, with the attention to minute detail he saw in Erdrick.

Looking down at the table one last time, he grunted, turning around to gather his belongings when that same perceptive glance made him notice something different over his desk.

Atop its wooden surface were the fabrics Elleonora had been working on, but there was one piece spread over the rest, one he didn't recall seeing before. It was silken, purple, and soft to the touch. The moment his hands pinched it, the fabric slid toward the stone floor to reveal what lay underneath—a silvered heater shield, its rim reinforced with black rivets that were repeated around the fearsome skull head depicted at its center. The handle was wrapped in leather, its smell indicating it had been unused.

The whole face of the shield was untarnished, polished metal. So perfect was its reflection, Gustavus could see the premature fine lines that would one day become deep wrinkles appearing on his face.

But he could also see, behind him, a flash, the reflection of sunlight that had trespassed his window bouncing off a golden bracelet.

"Tens." He wanted her to know he could see her.

"Gus." His cousin came out of her hiding place between the curtains, followed by the song of her aurean adornments.

"What are you doing here?" He turned toward her.

"Do you like your gift?"

"The shield?" he asked. "It is incredible."

"I had it specially commissioned for you. Tora, Atelas, and Aristov worked hard to make it perfect."

"It is surely a masterpiece," he looked back at the shield before setting his eyes on her once again, "but why?"

"Because it had to match your war-mask, of course," she smiled. "But also because it is a representation of who you are, of your greatest dreams and aspirations."

Gustavus contemplated the shield in its entirety. "Know that," she continued, "your achieving any and all of them will fill me with nothing more than unmeasurable pride."

Her cousin placed the shield back on the table and covered it carefully, "I am not the Shield. I am trying my best to be the best one for the job, but in the end, it is not I who will choose."

"Fool, you," Tenslea jested. "Do you think Erdrick would consider anyone else but you? You who have dedicated every waking minute training for the position? Not only will you get it, but I will be there to celebrate it with you."

"Thank you, Tens," his chest swelled.

"In addition," she continued, "I wanted to talk to you . . . privately, if possible."

"We are alone. What is it?"

"I . . ." She took a step toward the large man, "never got the chance to say thank you."

"For what?"

"For having brought my name up before the Grey Circle."

"I did not," his brow furrowed. "It was Erdrick who did it, so thank him."

"Only because you could not," she corrected, "at least not officially. You spoke up," she bit her lip shyly, "on my behalf, and in the end, Erdrick simply proposed the idea you had given life to."

Gustavus nodded without a word and began packing his things, but Tenslea wouldn't have it. She strode toward him and looked him in the eyes. "Thank you, Gus, for seeing something in me that makes me not feel overlooked. Thank you for placing your trust in me."

"I did it because you are my brother's woman," he said gruffly. "I could not do anything less."

His words almost stopped Tenslea. She hesitated for a moment before tilting her head.

"So you are saying you did not think I had any talent whatsoever?" Tenslea smiled.

"Well." The semblance of a half smile appeared on his heavy jaw. "That too, I guess. Maybe a little."

"Aargh! Wait until Fengo hears about this!" Tenslea jumped at him, attempting to shove his immovable weight in a manifestation of fake outrage.

"It is always good to see you, Tens, but I have to pack now."

"I know, do what you have to. I do not want to interrupt," she took a step away. "I would have expected Elle to be here. Where is she?"

"Rowena and Charon are leaving, so of course, she is going too."

"Then," she offered a smile, "let me help you pack!" Her hands busied themselves, arranging what she could with the organizational skills she was known for. The cousins filled his traveling chest with whatever Gustavus indicated he would take and a few of the things Tenslea had gladly suggested. They worked together through raucous laughter and vivid memories of things they had either lived through or seen others do.

Sitting on the bed, Tenslea looked up to meet his gaze. "Gus," She asked, "how did you know I was here?"

"The reflection and the melody of your jewelry. These things you cannot hide." A second later, a thought crossed his mind that others would have perhaps ignored. "And you," he questioned, "how did you know I proposed you for a position in the Grey?"

Tenslea smiled a bright, wide smile followed by a shrug and the glint in her cunning gaze, "I have eyes and ears everywhere."

TRUTH

Location: Empyre of Suhne, City of Suhne, Palace of the Sun

Old Seiris entered the crystal dome that served as the heir's chamber. His dark eyes were almost hidden under the heavy eyelids of a seventy-year-old man, one whose hands were clasped, the copper rings on his hands resting in place as if to avoid scratching their polished surface.

He had been allowed in without questioning, not that he could have been stopped anyway, not with his status as a Ray of the Sun, at least while there was not a Sun reigning over Suhne.

The palace of the Sun had been busier than normal for the last day, with the search for more assassins, the meeting of the Rays, and the neverending, everyday obligations of the spiritual leaders of such a vast flock.

There was much to do, many things that would take a septuagenarian like him a little longer than expected, but there was something very important he needed to do.

"Child of the Sun," Seiris greeted, standing by the bed.

"Do you change the title now for everyone after her request?" Kaylen said in derision. He lay in bed, his sinewy body faceup among the finest silken sheets man had ever imagined.

"I think her request is reasonable, that's all," Seiris explained. "As time passes, I've learned to prefer simplification."

Ignoring his comment, Kaylen simply asked, "Why are you here?"

"Among other things, I wanted to see how you were doing," Seiris responded.

"There," Kaylen threw the sheets to the side, showing the entirety of his naked body, the perfection of the flowing, scarlet tattoos on his smooth skin interrupted only by the bloodied bandages on the side of his abdomen. "Is this what you wanted to see?"

Seiris simply smiled. "I see you are doing fine."

Kaylen signaled to one of his attendants to serve some wine in the cup by his bed. "If that's all, you may leave now," he said to Seiris.

"I also wanted to ask as few questions," Seiris stated, "regarding the assassination attempt."

"All of you, leave," Kaylen said.

Upon his order, all his attendants, even the physician, left the room, leaving only Itosh standing by for any need the Son would have.

"You too," Kaylen ordered him. "Come back in an hour."

"I don't think I will take that long," Seiris said.

"I'm not going to give you that long," Kaylen mocked, "I've had enough of them for now. I also prefer my own simplification."

Seiris's wizened eyes saw little seating around the room. Upon realizing Kaylen wouldn't offer, he didn't even ask.

"What do you know about the events of yesterday?" Seiris asked.

"I remember everything," Kaylen responded, "I have been aware at all times, to the point that I have barely slept."

"Because of the pain?"

"Because of the physicians working to stabilize the bleeding," Kaylen explained, "because of the annoyance of having to deal with them, because of the incompetence of the Flame Guard."

"Yes," Seiris nodded quickly in agreement, his fingers playing with his grayed mustache. "Do you have any suspicions about anyone?"

"I suspect everyone," Kaylen stated. "I am aware that many, even among you, see me as dangerous and would do anything to stop my Ascension. It shouldn't surprise you, then, that I don't trust anyone."

Once again, Seiris nodded. "Do you know who was involved in planning this?"

"This is something you should ask the criminal himself," Kaylen sneered.

"It's going to be asked, yes," Seiris raised an eyebrow, "but the more questions we ask, the better chances of finding the answer."

Seiris of the Rays

"The more chance of confusion, too," Kaylen added.

"Agreed," Seiris smiled, "Now, do you know who the person was who planned the move against your life?"

"No."

"Other than as a victim," Seiris questioned, "were you in any way involved in the planning or execution of the attack you received?"

"No."

"Then thank you," Seiris smiled broadly, "I believe that's enough. Rest," he continued, "I'll see you tomorrow at the trial."

"Wait," Kaylen sipped once more, "is that all you wanted to know?"

"Yes," Seiris responded. "Do you have any questions for me?"

"I do. Do you know who was responsible?"

"As for the planning, no. But at least I'm certain of one thing. This was not your doing."

———————— ✦✦✦✦✦ ————————

Her being floated high above the circular domes of the palace, searching, more than for clues, for a moment of respite. Even in this silent, peaceful realm, she was troubled, and she couldn't understand it was nearly impossible to forget about the interruption of the Test she had for so long prepared.

Was it divine intervention?

Her thoughts disappeared in the sea of warm air that escaped her nostrils. She shook in place. What brought her back, she couldn't tell, but at least she found herself with Aaghari, her confidant who had just arrived, the man she had trusted the most.

"Are you well, Blessed One?" the middle-aged man asked.

"I feel . . . troubled," Vamya said.

"Don't be, Blessed One," Aaghari comforted her. "I have some good news for you. Despite the interruption yesterday, the Rays have deliberated and concluded that the Fifth Test has been completed!"

"That is good to hear," Vamya stood up from her seated position. She tried to smile as best as she could, but she couldn't hide it from Aaghari.

"Would you like to walk along the garden, Blessed One?" her confidant offered.

"Yes, I think I can use the walk."

They walked together, as they had done for almost a year, for unlike Kaylen, who had selected his Chosen upon his father's passing, and Malek, who had done so shortly after seeing her take the initiative, Vamya had selected her seven well before. While some of the Rays had commended her for her wisdom, the reality was she had done so because she expected to be perceived as having a disadvantage—she was not a man, and so, to accept her offer, there would be more hesitation than acceptance.

Even Aaghari had not been among the first ones to come to her. He, like others, had been under the impression the name Vamya was that of a male. But the moment he saw her, he had decided to stay.

Aaghari's words had not been particularly moving. There had been no special glint in his eyes. There was just something different in him, in the way he had shaken when in her presence, in the way he lowered his head in acknowledgment of her position, in the way he had knelt and kissed the floor she had just tread upon.

Sometimes there's no special talent needed. At times, our own devotion is our greatest gift, she had realized.

That had made him the first person among those interested that she chose, and until today, he was the one who knew exactly how she felt.

"Blessed One, you still seem troubled," he said. "Tell me, what is on your mind?"

"Much, Aaghari," Vamya looked out the crystal dome upon the morning sun. "This assassination attempt, it's a move against our holy beliefs. What if it had succeeded? What would that have done to this sacred endeavor?"

"But it didn't happen, Blessed One."

"Do you not understand the gravity of this?" Vamya questioned. "The Rays will judge the assassin tomorrow."

"Do you think he could be working with someone else?"

"Of course." She placed her hands against the glass, "at the very least, one other person, and I believe that is why my spirit is troubled. I can't even find peace in meditation!"

"Do you think it was planned by your brother?"

"I thought about it," Vamya waved for them to resume their walk, "but that is not something I think Malek would do. Although then it would be too easy not to suspect he had something to do with it, so in the end, he could have done it."

"I meant your other brother, Blessed One."

"Kaylen?" she doubted. "Why would Kaylen himself . . . wait. Maybe that's exactly what Kaylen would want. He knows it isn't Malek's way, so the only suspect would be me!

"To make it worse, I ask myself, 'how else would he have access to religious attire?' Was it one of the Rays?" Vamya rambled.

"I'm sorry," she apologized to Aaghari, "you should not see me like this. I'm supposed to inspire people, but right now, all I can think is that there are a thousand accusatory fingers we can point at someone, and I am the most likely to get pointed at. I am the woman, I am moving against a quicksand current, and I have the most to gain if one of my siblings is taken out.

"I couldn't sleep well last night. My spirit is jarred, my soul is shaken, my mind is breaking, Aaghari."

"Blessed One, you can't continue like this."

"I can't, I know," Vamya's exhausted eyes watered.

"Blessed One," his eyes did too, "it was me."

"What?" Confused, Vamya questioned.

"I am the one you're looking for," Aaghari confessed, "I am the one who arranged it all, hoping—"

"No!" Vamya said, "No, Aaghari, tell me you didn't!"

"I did, Blessed One."

"How dare you lie to me!" Vamya stepped away in disbelief. "You want me to believe it so that I can be at ease, but you're making it worse!"

"Blessed One!" He closed in and grabbed her arms. "It was me! It was I who reached out to someone I could trust to find me a desperate man, someone who, like me, was willing to do anything to help you rise."

Vamya looked into his eyes and knew he was being honest. The tears rolling down his face, wetting his shirt, confirmed what her confidant said was true. "How dare you betray me like that!" She slammed her fists against his chest, "How dare you intervene in something sacred!"

"Blessed One, I needed to ensure you would win."

"Is that how much you believe in me?" she asked furiously. "Is your faith in my chances, in my divinity, such that you need to cheat, risking everything I have worked for, everything I have fought so hard to prepare for, to help me gain a false win?"

Vamya moved away from him and pointed a finger at Aaghari. "I will accuse you. I will speak to the Rays and bring forth your name, and they will judge you, and they will strike you down!"

Her words brought Aaghari to his knees. "It will be worth it, Blessed One. I am willing to sacrifice my life for the change you will bring will create a better future for my family."

"You fool!" Vamya jabbed her finger against his chest. "For your intervention, your soul will be cursed, your entire family will be burned and cursed, and when I Ascend, I will ensure not one of your descendants escapes punishment."

"It will be worth it, Blessed One," Aaghari raised his hands to the heavens, "I gladly sacrifice every blessing and boon. I sacrifice my life and that of my entire family for the change that you will bring because we need you. This world needs a change.

"It will be worth it."

JUDGMENT

Location: Empyre of Suhne, City of Suhne, Palace of the Sun

Justice is the one thing that can never please everyone . . .

Little in this world was as simple and majestic as the throne of the Sun.

It was located to one side of the chamber, inside the highest of the largest domes of the city of Suhne.

The throne rested atop a six-tiered dais, a rectangular chair sculpted from stone. Its surface was largely smooth, except for its backrest, where an image rarely seen was observed, an etching of the sun itself, its rays extending along the entirety of the throne's surface.

In front of it, a pair of braziers were always lit, while behind the seat, a circular stone wall was framed by a single thick slab of a yellowish stone the likes of which no other had ever been found.

The Suhnites believed the sun in the sky had once been much larger, its infinite power burning everything it saw. But, one day, their god looked down at his struggling followers, and, in his mercy, he descended in their midst. The Sun god removed this stone that framed his Eye in the heavens and placed it behind his throne to always tell his people of his sacrifice, to always remind them of his divinity.

Whatever the truth was, the stone emitted a constant, soft glow that exalted whoever sat on the throne. It is why it was named *shinestone*.

Upon the visit of anyone to this chamber, the Almighty Sun had always been seated, so the seeing of the image on the backrest alone reminded everyone there was no one to lead their people, no one but the Rays.

So it was the Rays who stood below the six tiers with Exis at the center, near enough to the throne that was, to him, so close and yet so out of reach. He raised his hands in a moment of meditation before his grim expression contemplated, to one side, the Children of the Sun, to the other, some of the most powerful citizens of the city of Suhne, a few judges, rich merchants, and patrons of the trades and arts. Near the door, the Flame Guards held both Sera and Aaghari in chains.

"An interruption of this type is without precedent," Exis spoke on behalf of the Rays, and yet we have convened and determined that yes, the Test, as held, was valid and without interruption."

"What happens now?" a garrison master questioned.

"We continue where we left off, nothing more," Exis responded.

"What about the wounded Son," A prominent noble questioned.

"Perhaps he can address your concerns himself . . . Son of the Sun?"

Kaylen stepped forward slowly. So well had he hidden his bandaged torso under his rust-colored robes that, were it not for the cane he supported himself with, no one would have known the extreme pain he felt.

"As you can all see, I am here," Kaylen's hand grasped the end of the cane as he grimaced. "I don't foresee any problems with my participation in the Sixth Test."

"Excuse my interruption, Son of the Sun," Or'guud, the healer among the Rays, lifted a hand, drawing everyone's attention. "The Searing Sun's wound is deep. His standing here alone is a clear testament to the divinity of his being. After consulting the physicians, it is our belief he might need at least one month for his recovery."

"That will be no problem," Kaylen responded, "I am not planning for anything but rest."

"But the Sixth Test can be physical," Or'guud explained.

"I will find no problem in adapting," Kaylen glared.

"But, does the Sun need to adapt," Exis's voice questioned, "when it should be mankind who adapts to the will of their god?" Upon seeing many heads nodding in support of his words, Exis continued, "The Searing Sun's mind is on his goal. He is in high spirits, no doubt, but his body cannot endure it, at least not as it is, not for some time.

"The Rays of the Sun have thus decided there will be a delay in these proceedings. The Sixth Test will then be held in two months from now."

"A delay is unprecedented," the nobleman argued.

Exis smiled in response. "These are unprecedented times."

The nobleman then inquired, "What is the Empyre going to do for the next two months?"

"The same it has always done," Exis responded, "pray, work, and wait."

"Now, let us not delay any longer for what brought us all here," Exis smiled mostly at his tiny victory that allowed the Rays at least two more months in power. He signaled the Flame Guards, who brought both chained men before those gathered.

"Here are the criminals who attempted to manipulate the course of our divine Empyre," Exis opened his arms to show them, a gift to those present. "The first one, a traitor among the Chosen of the Child of the Sun, no less." Exis felt satisfied when he saw Vamya glaring back at him. "While we can commend her for reporting him, there are questions as to her own potential involvement in this."

"Speaker of the Rays!" Vamya took a step forward. "The way you feel about me, you cannot hide. Your condescension shows your bias. Why you feel so threatened by a woman, whom you consider so lowly, I will never understand. But know that, despite all the obstacles you place in my way, all the consideration and respect you don't show, I promise you that the day I rise, I will treat you fairly. I will break the cycle of animosity you alone have created, that you have fed when you should have used your power to feed our people."

Exis then quiesced, seeing the heads of the prominent among those present nodding in approval and the eyes of amazement among the Flame Guards and the Rays.

"Speaker," the nonagenarian among the Rays who was never afraid to contradict him said, "I was present when the Child of the Sun was interrogated. We came to the conclusion that none of the three heirs were aware of the machinations of these men."

After a brief pause, Exis spoke again, "Then we will proceed with the judgment of these men. Not only is the traitorous confidant involved, but we also have this, among the lowest of the *saqit,* a lowly killer, an impure man.

"Before your trial begins, what do each of you have to say in your defense?"

"I am guilty," Aaghari knelt, "I acted believing, as I still do, that what I did would bring the best outcome in the end." He looked for Vamya's eyes, but so disgusted was she that her eyes avoided him.

"You're quick to admit your sinful practices," Exis said, looking around at everyone's scornful expressions.

"And you," he signaled Sera.

"Speaker!" Malek's voice rumbled. "None of you can judge these men. He walked toward the center. "Their sin against the divine can only be judged by the divine, and the reason we stand here is that there's no god sitting on the throne."

"They have interrupted the process," Exis argued.

"And so for that, you can judge them, but you can only offer imprisonment, not death, and upon their release, they will be absolved. If that's what you seek, then go ahead and judge them. But if what you want is the true justice of the Sun god, then instead of pretending to have the power of the god you speak for, you will hold these men and present them at his feet when your Sun god rises!"

Exis clenched his fists, seeing the nearly complete approval of Malek's words. While he was not the smartest of the three, he had just shown he was dangerously so. Yet another damned piece Exis needed to move or remove if he was going to gain control.

CHOSEN

Location: Kingdom of Blackheart,
Duchy of Darkholm, Darkholde Keep

The living constantly wonder what Life plans for them
when they should wonder what is the plan, for them, of Death . . .

The arid tip on the skin of each digit met, each pressing on the perfect reflection of the one opposing it.

Like mummified, veteran spiders, his hands had created infinite webs to catch the unwary, some to feast upon soon after and others very many years later.

He sat not on the throne he had never coveted nor on the ducal seat he so despised but on the wooden seat of the one place he was often found—his research study.

The room lay between the ocean and the main road, but exactly where he could hear neither. The only noise outside the windows, aside from the carrion birds lining the parapets, was that of the few passersby—an occasional servant, a vulture, or more commonly, and even that was rare, the gravemen who dragged carts laden with dead bodies from the dungeons close by to their final destination.

Even the windows were small, allowing only the faintest rays of light into the cold room that was the study. One of the walls was lined with shelves and books, the other one with vials, alchemical instruments, and several pairs of pliers that somehow didn't seem so out of place.

The room was far from any noble accommodation he was entitled to, but it was exactly what Davidov Darkholm had wanted it to be—cold, unassuming, practical, a place that was neither distant nor within easy reach.

Atop his desk, an open book, its pages marked with a necklace that seemed more like an obsidian amulet than a piece of jewelry. The quill on his left hand slowly drew each syllable that his silent lips pronounced. After every few words, he stopped and pondered as he allowed the ink to dry.

And of the many things he pondered, there was one that lingered: there was no one to take his mantle if he were ever gone.

That was most unusual. The philosophy of his House was one of prepared-ness and wisdom, where each step taken was carefully considered, not only for the repercussions each could have for generations to come but also for the ones it wouldn't. Practical as they were, since their establishment, the Darkholm had cross-trained so that in the event of an untimely death of one, the void left would almost seamlessly be filled by another.

Who better to attest to that than himself, he who had seen the Grey Circle and many of their parents, grandparents, and even parents' grandparents' births and passings—more than he had cared to.

Perhaps it was because of his cynicism or because he found it easier to find and point at faults the longer he lived, but while his life had provided enough time to find someone, he had not found a candidate good enough. He had seen many Darkholm, young and old, inside his study, each one accompanied by someone who would testify and vouch for the candidate's talents.

At times with his icy stare, other times without lifting his gaze off his writings, all of them he dismissed.

Too boisterous . . .

Too undisciplined . . .

Too foolish . . .

Too garish . . .

Too irreverent . . .

Too superficial . . .

Too brash . . .

But out of the many things he had wondered, he had never wondered if he had been, perhaps, too demanding. What did he ever find, if anything, to be good enough? Although most Darkholm were serious in the performance of their duties, Davidov seemed to live for the performance of his duty.

How could he not, when of all the duties of House Darkholm, the ones of the Masters of Life and Death were seen as paramount? It was they who, each in his or her own way, worked toward achieving the first promise of the founder: *"In order to protect the kingdom forever, we must live forever."*

A knock on the entrance interrupted his thoughts.

"Enter," he responded dryly.

A Darkholm of three decades walked in. His hair was slick, his cheekbones strong. His jawline was slim enough and together with the shadow under his slim eyes helped give the impression of a restless but still dangerous snake. Among the Darkholm, better than the finery of his clothes, he was known for wearing accents of green, perhaps to signal his brooding defiance.

"Ignatius," Davidov's disdain was clear, "what brings the oldest son of the second Valdemar and Sorsha?"

"I am here too, Master," from behind Ignatius's figure, the charming smile of his younger sister appeared. She curtsied deeply. Those who didn't know her would marvel at her etiquette when likely the real intention was to show her finest new dress.

While Sellayne was not particularly beautiful, there was something about her poise, her disposition, and grace that had clearly earned her the epithet "the flower," and a flower she was, one with many petals, but more than petals, thorns.

"You are such a jerk!" she insulted her brother.

"Ah, quiet," Ignatius placed his palm up between them.

"I told you to wait for me!"

"Shut up, Sellayne!" he snapped.

Ignoring them, Davidov's lips began moving as he returned to his writing.

"Master of Death," Ignatius lowered his head some, his reptilian-like gaze still on the elder, "I believe I have found—"

"WE!" Sellayne interjected.

"The candidate you seek." The young man raised his head.

Clearly interested, Davidov's eyes went back to the pair. "Who is it?" he asked.

Each of the siblings took a step aside to allow the third one's entrance. His hair was longer, passing his shoulders, but oily, and some of it covered his face unceremoniously. His jaw was adorned with too short of a beard, one he had perhaps forgotten to shave or simply hadn't cared to, giving his otherwise unremarkable features a handsome appearance. He was just an inch taller than his brother but lanky and clearly felt as out of place as his hands fidgeting inside his pockets, and his eyes, which looked at Davidov only briefly before returning to the planks on the floor.

"Sylen." Davidov sneered, grabbing the quill once more.

"But Master," Ignatius protested, "he has significant alchemical knowledge—"

"Substantial!" Sellayne corrected.

"The position requires much more than that," the old man stated flatly.

"The Master of Lore thinks Sylen stands among the smartest," Ignatius hated to admit.

"Then he can choose him as his successor. About what the Master of Lore thinks, I could not care less," the Master of Death seethed. "Sylen, son of Sorsha," he directed his attention to the young Darkholm, "What do you say?"

"'Tis true," Sylen responded, his voice almost trembling, "Azareth says I am among the smartest—"

"Then he clearly has not spoken to you," Davidov spat.

"Syl does not speak much, Master," Sellayne insisted. "That alone is good!"

"Who could, with a pair of hecklers for siblings?" Davidov's brow furrowed. "Sellayne," his eyes returned to the girl.

"Yes, my lord?"

"Do you think your brother Sylen would make a great count overseeing the land?"

"No," she responded without hesitation.

"Do you think he would be a good ambassador or an average warrior?"

"No, and no."

"Would you consider him for a position among the knights? Or a Devereau poisoner or spy?"

"He is weak, messy, and has the worst communication skills; therefore, no," she responded.

"Would you recommend your brother Sylen for an apprenticeship with House Sanglune?"

"Absolutely not!" Her voice was firm, "He is good for nothing."

"There you have it," having sprung the trap, Davidov's smile bared all his teeth at seeing her fall in it, "and so because you have found no place in another basket for what you consider good-for-nothing, you seek to dump him on mine. Leave," he ordered.

Sellayne had no response. What could she say? Davidov was right. But Ignatius sought a chance to rescue the opportunity. Gritting his teeth to contain his embarrassment, Ignatius took a step forward. "My lord, you seem disappointed."

"Disappointed?" the Master looked at him eye to eye, "I was disappointed when your father brought you to be considered, Ignatius. Your brother . . . he is nothing but a waste of my time. Leave," he ordered firmly. "He will be better off in a lab. Send him to Rowena. Surely she can put him to good use as an assistant . . . to her assistants."

Remembering Davidov's scorn when he was the candidate, Ignatius's blood boiled, but he knew this was not the place or time to let his unbridled anger loose. He quickly turned and left the same way he came, followed by Sellayne's curtsy and nervous Sylen following suit, curtsying awkwardly, clearly confused as to what he needed to do.

'At this rate, even the beasts of burden will be brought before me to consider,' Davidov thought, returning to his notes once again.

But it was not too long before another knock interrupted his work.

Davidov's eyes moved to the doorknob.

The door opened slowly as if seeking to test his immutable patience. From behind it, the slender figure of a young maiden walked in. The coal black hair on her head cascaded down to one side over her pale skin, her lips as expressionless as her yellow eyes that only stared, not at the ancient man, but at his desk.

"And out of *everyone,* it had to be *you.*" Davidov's words jabbed at Elleonora. "Not beautiful, not talented, you have no charm, you cannot lead, you are not even half smart. Even your usual companions are not here. Not even your own mother comes to vouch for you. What, of all things," he sneered, "makes you *think* this is a position for you? Get out." His tongue traveled along his parchment-like lips.

"But, my lord," she responded in a mix of surprise and calm, "all I was doing was bringing your supper."

Davidov's piercing eyes looked at her hands. So intent had he been on finding and pointing at her faults that he had ignored her hands, which carried a silver tray, its contents covered with a cloche of the same polished silver.

He stood there, about three meters away from her, for an uncomfortable moment that never seemed to come to an end.

"My lord, would you like me to . . ." Elleonora began to ask, but Davidov's attention drifted away and centered on a barely perceivable buzz, that of a single fly that flew through the window and into the room.

He lifted a leathery hand to silence the girl, his eyes following the random circling of the fly along the room.

The insect rested its diminutive body atop the sea of blackness of Elleonora's hair, forcing Davidov to raise an eyebrow, his jaw almost open.

Was it a message? Was it a sign?

But before he uttered a word, the fly took off and left out the window, its departure followed by the deep furrowing of his brow and the lowering of his hand.

"Would you like me to show you what—" Elleonora began again.

"Do you believe in gods?" Davidov interrupted.

"I do not."

"What is death, to you?" he followed.

"The end of life," Elleonora responded.

"My, my," his judging eyes looked back at her, "the unfathomable depths of your shallow little brain. Just leave it there." Half-turning, he walked back toward his desk, "And get out."

Nodding, she placed the tray over the shelf closest to the door and reached for the door's handle. *What had she done to be treated with such scorn?* She turned back to face him, but he was once again submerged in his writing, completely ignoring her presence as if she were less than a fly on a wall.

How could she be so close to this man's granddaughter and, at the same time, so distant from him?

Elleonora was under no obligation to bring his food. Darkholde had more than enough servants to take care of that. But he was family, and as consumed as he was in his work, he missed meals often. What she had felt was concern for him. That was all. Concern for someone who had perhaps never felt the same about anyone else. She hadn't even been interested in working with a man, in her eyes, both so admirable and yet so vile.

Her mouth closed. There was nothing to be said.

She opened the door to the outside, from where a sudden thud was heard. It was followed by the muffled, irregular, rolling thud that was repeated as it grew nearer. And right through the door wobbled a head that had fallen off a graveman's cart. It was horrid, bloated, its mouth gaping wide, eyes rolled up as if admiring and mocking Elleonora's presence while attempting to stop her from leaving.

Davidov's chair swiftly scraped the plank floor. Elleonora turned around to face him.

His eyes were open, as wide as she had never seen before. This time, they did not seem to pierce her but were, in fact, set on the disembodied head and moved back at her. His mouth was open, his jaw drooping. Something in his gaunt expression was different.

"Man can always choose Death," Davidov's eyes glistened, "but ah, what a wonderful moment when SHE chooses one of us."

HONOR

Location: Kingdom of Ardenay, Duchy of Bulwharf, State of Darane

It *is often an honorable man finds his only companion is solitude . . .*

T he Ten Days of Thunder were the most important dates for the Bulls of Bulwharf. The long-awaited celebration would come to pass only upon the death of one of the leaders of its three regions. It was the time when the bulls, who had lived most of their lives sharpening their fighting skills, would have a chance to prove themselves worthy of becoming leaders of their society.

She wanted this.

The Bulwharf thought from his raised seat, looking at the token in his hand, the one engraved on one side with the hoof of the old beliefs and on the other with her name.

His gaze fell upon the tent where Eraysa and her men rested. Driven by determination and fueled by anger, she had wounded her first opponent on the First Day of Thunder. She had returned to her tent with a formal salute but had avoided meeting Varen's gaze, missing even the celebrations of the last three days.

"Eraysa Velias," his voice boomed, "captain of the Red Hooves of Darane."

He waited to see her emerge, not only because she was the woman he had for so long loved, but because in his position as Lord Bull, he would offer his people the respect he himself was given. In Bulwharf, the head of state had to defend his title with a duel either every six years or upon being challenged for showing weakness, so the one who stood at the top could find himself removed in a single day. Therefore, respect was always expected from another bull.

Fortunately for him, this had been only his fifth year in power. Still, he feared not when the time came. This was the way of Bulwharf, and it was he who had defeated the previous head, Eten Bulwharf, his own father.

Eraysa appeared from behind her tent's door, armed with a bastard sword in her right hand and a buckler on the left. She wore a light plate, made lighter by missing pieces she reinforced with leather. Among the large bulls of Darane, Eraysa was considered short, something she had exploited by using lighter equipment and bolder moves. But still, her will was stronger than that of the greatest warriors, something Varen had found attractive from the moment he first met her.

Varen imagined the helmet that covered her face was most likely worn because she was still angry at him. Upon her appearance, she was rained with shouts and praise from the many in attendance.

It was time to reveal her opponent from those who had called themselves victors on the First Day.

Now, after two days of rest, the eight victors would have to face one another, and the four winners would face each other on the Seventh Day.

Of the eight, six were Thunders, the highest commanders of the armies of Bulwharf. If she was lucky enough, she would face the only other one who wasn't in that position.

"Barwen Dassan," Varen read the name, almost choking in disbelief, "Thunder of Darane, Commander of the Raging North."

Barwen was a monster, Varen feared. He was brave, admired, and a powerful leader among the soldiers in Darane. The Thunder was bald, of ebon skin and eyes. He wore a medium plate with the anatomical heart of Vigor engraved in the middle of his chest piece. A large battle-ax was his weapon. He had in size and strength everything Eraysa lacked.

'Can she win?' the Bulwharf pondered. 'She is skilled, but Barwen is considered the most dangerous among the eight.' While the First Day's duels were to first blood, Barwen's blow had left his opponent paralyzed from the waist down. Today's fight would be to hinder, the next ones would be held until maimed, and the last to the death.

Eraysa Velias

If Eraysa proved victorious, she would become the Bull of Darane, and while leading positions had been rarely held by women, the Bull of Darane had, so far, been only held by men.

'Can she do it on her own?' he asked himself. 'She must. If she achieves it, she will be stronger.'

He wondered if through all the rebellious anger she felt she still loved him, if after obtaining the position she would still marry him, but then he wanted to smile, although he couldn't, when he saw his ring still on her right hand.

Then the fight started, Eraysa moving like a dragonfly, looking for an opening, and Barwen studying her moves. After only a few passes, he drew his strength and swung left, right, and in multiple directions, his assault fast and disorienting.

Eraysa's buckler was rendered useless after just two deflections.

Barwen was dominating the ring, leaving her running around to dodge his attacks. She swung her sword, but the clash against his axe would have disarmed her had she not held the hilt with two hands. Another one of his wild swings sent her helmet flying.

She wanted this.

There was nothing Eraysa wanted more than revenge, and this was her one way to achieve it, she believed.

The seat had to be hers, and, once in power, only Varen himself could stop her.

'Would he?' she thought. 'Would he dare deprive me of sending my brother's soul to rest? If that is the case, I would challenge *him* for his position.' The man she had loved was not the same man anymore. He was changing, she thought. This imposed religion was eating him from the inside.

Eraysa closed the gap between her and Barwen so that she could still make use of the length of her blade while he would only have a haft.

But a solid punch in the stomach left her gasping for air, stopping her in her tracks.

She was dazed but needed to recover quickly or lose the chance.

While her vision was still blurred, she arched her back forcefully, slamming the back of her head against Barwen's jaw, bleeding him.

Reeling, he stumbled back, sending the crowd roaring.

Eraysa looked at him, her ferocity tensing her every muscle. The huge man disappeared before her eyes, and in his place, she could only see Dragan mocking her.

Lunging forward with all the fury and desire for revenge, she thought, 'This will be over!'

Barwen's knee to her abdomen was followed by a kick to the chest that sent her sprawling.

Varen stood from his seat, ready to stop the fight when Barwen Dassan's axe fell.

To chop her right forearm off.

Eraysa's screams were heard for miles.

It was over.

THE EIGHTH

Location: Kingdom of Ardenay,
Duchy of Bulwharf, Region of Darane, the Horne

Trust is the dam that is both as impossible to break as it is to repair . . .

The tower known as the Eighth sat atop a strategically placed hill in the region of Darane. While not often seen as the most important, especially since the building of the late Tenth closer to the border and northeast of it, it had served as a rest stop, a way point between the lifeline of the Seventh and its celebrated, newer, and more powerful neighbor.

For years it had been manned by minor captains, wounded soldiers, and tired rangers. This same lack of strength was what allowed it to fall to Valador's assailants and the reason why it was now in the hands of Blackheart.

Blackheart's taking had destroyed a substantial portion of the tower. After having been declared a Blackheart outpost under the protection of the twin duchies of Valador and Volanar, the general had ordered the supervision of its rebuilding to none other than his grandson, Maxius "the Spear" Darkholm, and Maxius's son, Malacar, "the Black Lion."

Maxius had recruited a prominent stonemason and architect from Valador, one Maghetti, of the House Khalvari. His family had been involved in overseeing construction along the spine of Valador, the mountain city of the duchy he called home.

For nearly two months, they had worked to rebuild the structure, to repair its integrity, to meet the populace around it that still looked at them with suspicion. But it was what they needed to do. It was the way to help bring prosperity to the fort obtained from Ardenay, as had been agreed upon by the generals of Ardenay and Blackheart.

Today, Maxius looked at the horizon where the forces of Bulwharf had gathered for nearly two weeks.

Maxius appeared as a handsome hawk with chiseled, clean-shaven features and slanted, malicious eyes. While in his mid-seventies, he appeared to be close to his son's age.

His brow was furrowed, his lips pursed, his eyes squinting, surely a thousand possibilities running through the head of the Darkholm warrior.

The army had returned to circle and isolate the town composed of small buildings erected almost haphazardly, which made an organized invasion as difficult as it made any escape. And while Maxius could have understood their desire to isolate this fort in their midst, this morning, the bulls had been advancing, taking the buildings that belonged to the fort's premises.

"Father," Malacar spoke, placing his long hair behind his ears to avoid the blowing wind from hindering his vision, in a gesture that made Maghetti and others think he wanted to ensure they saw the scar that traveled across his face, the one inflicted in that fight where he almost lost both eyes. "The Bulls have taken control of all supplies and have destroyed the last two posts supplying the Eighth."

Maxius listened, his eyes still on the horizon. "What are your thoughts?" he asked.

"Without reinforcements, we can hold the Tower for just so long," Malacar responded. "Our current supplies, if rationed, will last us not more than three days."

"How about you, Lord Khalvari?"

"My lord," Maghetti responded, "while I can defend myself, and I will, I am no military expert."

"Which is why I did not ask for your military advice, only for your thoughts," Maxius stated. "I want to hear them."

"Yes, my lord," Maghetti bowed. "If my lord wished to keep the Eighth, we could defend it. We have strengthened the previously broken defenses and made some improvements, enough that it would be dangerous to have them fall into enemy hands if they were to control the Eighth."

"How long do you think can the structure of the Eighth hold before any reinforcements come?" Maxius looked from the corner of his eye.

"A week," Maghetti responded, "maybe more."

"Malacar," Maxius ordered, "I want to send word to the general to inform him of our position. We will have to consider changing our position."

"As you wish, my lord," his son bowed out.

"My lord," the mason continued, "even if we were to fall, there's great glory in defending this place."

"Ah, that is right," Maxius leaned over both stretched arms on the parapet. "Glory . . . an intangible reward, the dream of cretins and goal of fools! What does glory matter if one does not live in the end? War should never be about glory, Lord Khalvari, but rather about a tangible reward."

He looked back in the distance, where the banner of the Lord Bull made its appearance.

·············

After a few days' march, Varen had arrived at the vicinity of the Eighth. They had been days of torment for the Lord of Bulls.

Eraysa had been permanently disabled. She had lost her sword arm and likely her spirit, while he had just as likely lost her.

For days he has been unable to visit her camp, at first to avoid showing preference and then because of her refusal to be seen by him.

The man who had crippled her, Barwen Dassan, had become the Bull of Darane. But that was something she wouldn't hear about until much later, for on the Tenth Day, Varen found out Eraysa and her men had left on the previous night.

He, the most powerful general of the kingdom of Ardenay, stood here on horseback with a troubled heart. He couldn't simply leave his position to run after her. There were important matters he needed to attend to, laws and rules he was bound to honor.

He would help her get revenge, he thought, but perhaps not the way she intended.

Varen was angry at Barwen, yet he was his man, and the Bulwharf owed him his loyalty. After all, Barwen had, like the Darkholm Eraysa despised, played by the rules.

And here he was, going back on his word, breaking the rules he had agreed to . . . by order of his king.

"Lord Bull," the commanding Thunder placed his right fist on his chest to salute him.

"What is the situation here, Ooron?"

"For the last two weeks, we have encircled the town," Ooron said. "We have worked outward to scout the entire area and take all the settlements associated with the Eighth. Surprisingly, we found some resistance among its people. Our enemies had done a good job of showing them an amicable front in exchange for material supplies."

"How many are their men?" Varen questioned, his eyes on the Eighth.

"We aren't sure, Lord Bull," Ooron responded, "likely not many, and un-less they're receiving supplies directly from the town, we don't think they have much left."

"Have we moved against the Eighth yet?"

"Yes, Lord Bull," Ooron answered, "we started taking the town this morn-ing. It will serve us as cover against—"

"That's enough," the Bulwharf interjected. "Call it off."

"But Lord Bull," Ooron objected.

"Call it off!" Varen glared. "I want to parlay."

———————————

A messenger from Darane rode on horseback toward the Eighth, carrying both the standard of the Lord Bull and a fluttering white flag as a sign of parlay. The man was less than two decades young, with a small frame that indicated he was of mixed blood.

He came upon the outer gate of the Eighth when the portcullis opened to give way to Malacar Darkholm, also on horseback before it closed again. Outside, they exchanged words before the messenger signaled it was safe for the Lord Bull to approach.

Varen rode on his great horse, proud and steady as its master. He noticed the smaller frame of the Darkholm, the light armor, and the Black Lion's head resting over the Darkholm's left shoulder. Despite the old wound on his face, to Varen, the man's countenance seemed elegant, noble even, like those of the people close to Ardenay's capital.

"The Lord Bull," the messenger announced, placing his hand in front of the fluttering flag that sometimes got in the way of his words. "Lord Varen Bulwharf, Duke of Bulwharf, count of Sildrane and baron of the state, general of the armies of Ardenay."

"My name is Malacar Darkholm, of the Royal House of Darkholm, Baron of Lyon's Grave," Malacar said without pomp.

"Do you speak on behalf of your men?" Varen questioned.

"I do," Malacar answered.

"You are stationed in the Eighth Tower in the Horne of Darane of the bulls," Varen's voice rumbled, "land of the crown and property of King Aorius Heikken, ruler of Ardenay. This fort has been occupied illegally, and I will ask, only once, for it to be returned without conflict."

"These lands have been occupied legally, as agreed by yourself and the General of Blackheart," Malacar responded.

"Without endorsement from the Crown, I am afraid."

"We need instructions from our superiors," Malacar stated.

"There's no time for that," Varen added. "If you don't agree to abandon the Eighth today, we will move to take this place."

"You already have," Malacar sneered, pointing at the men stationed on the windows inside some of the buildings.

"That was out of my control," Varen justified, "but given that you are likely low in provisions, I can ensure you are provided with enough to travel back beyond the border, and we will ensure you do so safely."

"Can we trust you on this?"

"I give you my word." Varen placed his fist on his chest.

At the mention of his word, the portcullis behind Malacar opened again.

From the Eighth, the lone, masked figure of Maxius Darkholm emerged, spear in hand, its point up non-threateningly.

In a few quick strides, he reached Malacar's side and, placing the end of his spear on his foot, he kicked it, sliding the shaft along his circling fingers, sending its sharp tip through the white banner and deep into the messenger's throat, killing him before he could take a breath.

That mask depicting a demonic face biting a scroll the way Varen should have, perhaps, bitten his tongue, looked back at him in a silent, clear challenge before Maxius turned back to the Eighth, followed by Malacar, in preparation for battle.

DARKHOLDE

Location: Kingdom of Blackheart,
Duchy of Darkholm, County of Coldforge

Restraint is as much virtue as it is a prison cell . . .

It took a few days for Ealas to find a transport that was willing or able to accommodate him and take him to Darkholm. He would have preferred the fastest route into the capital, but given the difficulty in arranging travel, he took the only option he could find.

He had sat on the side of a wagon from Whisperwind filled with produce hardy enough to survive the journey without being too spoiled. The friendly wagon driver and his daughter had assured him it didn't matter, for whatever made it would be a blessing, and, in the end, most of it would be soft enough to use for the pies and jams they were likely destined for anyway.

He learned a little about the places they traveled through from the pair, who stopped only for a few hours to sell their produce and rest before continuing on their fast-paced journey.

He came upon the large County of Grayhelm, where they had to present trade documents at the main fortress of the Master of War, and then a few more times after that when they came upon the occasional soldiers patrolling the roads. The county was otherwise somewhat green, with distant farms visible from the main road.

Then they passed the County of Greyshield, the inevitable—unless one were fish—he was told, for the strangely festive yet highly militant county ran along the entire width of the peninsular duchy, separating the counties that followed from the rest of the continent.

When he was told the next county was swamplands, he had expected the worst, but the County of Devereaux was nothing short of spectacular. It was small, with exquisitely designed small buildings that would enhance the landscape while respecting the weight the soft ground could tolerate. There was a variety of flora and greenery he would have expected only in either the most fertile grounds of Walcrast or the best-kept gardens of Alcyn.

Lastly, he arrived at the city of Coldforge on the first peninsula of the county of the same name.

The city was sparse, built in what seemed like a long, shallow incline that was being shoved into the coast. The larger villas, he found strange, were built not on the water but actually away from it.

The sky was cloudy gray in a seemingly constant expectation of a deadly storm. He was surprised to see structures being erected as if its citizens sought to give hope to a place that was slowly dying. The abundance of dark colors on its buildings told him that either that was the prime material they had the most in abundance or that the city replicated the gloom he saw manifested in the attire and demeanor of its people.

Ealas had been dropped into the new merchant quarter, where he promptly sought to satiate his hunger. In comparison to the markets back in the capital of Ardenay, the variety here was, at the most, modest. There were dried and desert fruits aplenty, also cranberries, water chestnuts, and lotus flowers, also a great variety of seeds and mushrooms from Olath Valm, he was told.

From there, he walked downhill toward the coast, where he met a pair of shirtless, bare-footed young men. He asked for directions.

"What castle? You mean Darkholde?" the lanky, dark-haired one named Zald responded.

"Where the Darkholm live," Ealas responded.

"Gee, yeah, Darkholde," Zald laughed, his voice breaking, "are you totally blind or just completely?"

His friend, the dark-skinned, heavier boy named Zeeke, joined in the laughter.

"Well," Ealas scratched his head, "to be honest, I was asleep when I arrived."

"Ah, okay," Zald said, "we are going to the beach. "It's not far. If you come with us, we can show you the most amazing view of Darkholde."

"I'm with you," Ealas said.

"Just be careful you don't trip with your blind eyes!" Zeeke jested, sending the three on a laughing spree.

Not long after, occasional puddles of water first appeared here and there along the street but then grew in size and number until he noticed the farther they went, the buildings around them, just as the streets, were slowly, progressively being swallowed by the sea.

Following the pair of friends along the sunken streets, Ealas took his boots off, and tying them up, he hung them over his shoulders. "How far deep is it?" he jested, sending the boys into a fit of laughter.

He waded through and by empty buildings of different sizes, over seawater that was knee-deep, at times less so before it reached his knees again, revealing the unevenness either of the original streets themselves or of the damage they had suffered.

"We are close to the Smith's Quarter," Zald pointed out, cupping some salt water he used to wet his head in order to splash Zeeke with it the moment he began shaking his head.

"Oh, I got you!" The shorter Zeeke struggled to run behind the lanky teen, who laughed and turned and splashed him back as he ran ahead.

"Wait!" Ealas shouted, but then he laughed inside. 'What am I doing?' he asked himself and ran after the pair.

The last few streets saw fewer buildings and an opening to the right that had perhaps been a plaza where a metallic hand reaching out of the water had, at some point, been the top of a small fountain.

After one turn chasing the boys, he stopped to admire a most spectacular view, the street wide open before him, merging symbiotically with the dark sea that licked the city meekly. Ruined buildings lay scattered almost haphazardly. Here and there, the district was ridden with occasional anvils protruding from the water as if refusing to sink to ensure the locals remembered its name.

Fewer anvils were seen in the distance, where Ealas saw a few small, shallow boats and rafts.

The rest of the city, to one side, seemed prosperous, its docks busy with trading ships and a marina with many small, similar ships that he could only guess were military.

On the other side were the enormous cliffs of Darkholde that rivaled some of the mountains he had seen in either Bulwharf or the lands of House Ileva. The dark gray of the cliffs added to the depressing ambiance of perennial gloom. And there, above and encrusted in the cliffs, the immense presence of Darkholde. The colossal structure in itself was nothing short of an architectural marvel. It seemed to protrude from the cliff itself as an enormous gargoyle that sought to use its weight to drown the world in the blackness of the ocean or perhaps to escape the world that hated its very own existence.

What little light of the sun was able to penetrate the gray clouds only served to allow him to see that terrible fortress that would otherwise prefer to remain unseen.

Ahead of him, Zald and Zeeke had swam toward the anvils. The kids laughed and whipped each other with the wet clothes they had taken off and, like others around them, in their own innocent, simple nakedness, ignoring the black presence that loomed in the distance, they dove happily into the sea.

Thank you, Lord of Light, for your shining presence that allows me to see the reality of this world, Ealas prayed and walked away, headed to Darkholde stronghold and home to the foes of his kingdom, the sworn enemies of the Light.

························

He left Coldforge before noon, having asked for the best way to reach the castle.

The locals had given him the eye, thought perhaps he was out of his mind, some even unafraid to say it.

"Our lords are best kept away," a merchant had told him, "for everyone's sake, stay away from that place, lest you want to never be seen again."

"It's only a few miles down the south gate of the city, but don't expect an actual gate. The pale lords wouldn't allow the city to have one in the first place."

But Ealas would follow the instructions of the one person who seemed, to him, the most trustworthy, an aging priest of the Light.

"What kind of business do you have in such a dark place?

"You are meeting someone? Well, you be careful with that someone you're meeting. The dark one's blessing bathes that place and curses this city.

"Their eyes are demonic. Like their voices, it is best to avoid them so as not to fall into their traps.

"Why am I here in such a dangerous place? The Radiant One has guided me here. He has protected me from their evil claws and unholy schemes.

"Yes, we have a church to the Light. The darkness tolerates its existence because, in its weakness, it can't exist without the Light, but it also allows a little light in to glorify, in its vain, dim presence, the stranglehold it has over this wicked place."

Regardless of the opinions, every finger pointed at the southern road, which was the one Ealas took.

It was paved, well-kept, and wide enough to allow two, maybe three carriages side by side. It crossed a large clearing with clusters of trees and woods to either side. A few paths diverged from the main road, leading to places Ealas wasn't interested in finding about at this time.

Halfway along the road, there's a guard station, he recalled someone saying, which he found out to be true when he saw the small, stony structure with two horses nearby. The pair of guards were garbed in black studded leather that, while not badly damaged, had definitely seen better days. A second pair rode slowly in their direction. The two stationed ones eyed him suspiciously, the first one looking at him up and down before he asked, "What is your purpose in the king's way?"

'That's right,' Ealas shut his eyes, 'What was I thinking? Did I think I would want to meet the royals, and they would take me just like that? How stupid of me!'

"Good day," Ealas tried in his friendliest tone, "I wanted to visit Darkholde, whatever part is accessible to visitors."

"You must not be from here," the younger one with the mustache said. "Darkholde is never accessible to visitors."

"Wait," the first guard said in a tone Ealas found unusual, "unless he means *Ironholde.*"

"Ohh, yes!" the mustached guard then added, "Ironholde is the forecastle, where the knights are, where business is conducted. And what business do you have in Ironholde?"

"I would like an audience with members of the royal family," Ealas said.

"Well, imagine that," the first guard mocked, "I happen to want one too."

He knew they didn't believe him. 'Why would they?' Ealas asked himself. He was nobody now. It wasn't like he could simply walk in brandishing his titles, and even if he could, it would likely work against him. In the end, he came up with something "I have an important message that I must deliver to the lords of Darkholm."

"Ah," the mustached guard responded, "then you should have said so in the first place. Come here. We must take a look at your stuff before we escort you."

Ealas did as instructed. He surrendered his sword and his waist belt, where all his leftover money was. But the mustached guard pointed at the pouch around his neck and instructed him to surrender it too. Reluctantly, he did and was asked to take a step away.

"This," the third guard said, examining it, "is quite the sword. How much do you want for it?"

"It is not for sale," Ealas answered.

"A silver," the guard offered.

"I'm sorry, but it's not for sale," Ealas insisted.

The guard looked upon the mustached one opening Ealas's coin bag. He drew a silver from it and threw it on the table. "There's your silver," he said, sheathing Ealas's sword and placing it around his own belt.

The nobleman then realized who he was dealing with. There was corruption everywhere. He had seen it back home. Did he not expect to find it in the land of the corrupt? He was mad, but he needed to remain calm, and he did until he saw the first guard fidgeting with the pouch of ashes.

"Please," Ealas said, "I ask you to please leave that alone."

"What is it?" the guard asked, laughing. "Gems?"

"It's just important to me," Ealas said as humbly as he could, trying to remain calm, but then he saw the grin as the man opened the pouch and stuck his fingers in playfully, expecting to find something of value. Frustrated at not finding anything, he instead turned the pouch inside out, shaking it, but the only thing that fell from inside it was what little was left of the ashes that fell on the muddy ground he then spat upon.

That was it.

Blazing furiously, Ealas leaped, seeing nothing but red. His blood raged. He couldn't contain the fury that boiled over. He kicked one guard's face and took his sword back. Before they could react, Ealas slashed, sending the coins up in the air as he chopped the hand and forearm of the mustached guard down the middle.

He then grabbed the first one by the hair, and he sank his blade slowly into his throat, hoping in that instant to see all the suffering Astas had ever felt in the guard's dying eyes.

"Stop right there!" the remaining guards shouted. "In the name of the Crown, stop!"

But Ealas could not control himself. His entire body shook furiously, tears rolling down his cheeks as the man in front of him convulsed, held up only by the nobleman's blade.

That was all he could remember, aside from a great, bashing pain in the back of his head and the words, "Take him to the Darkholde dungeons."

And he made it to Darkholde, just not the way he had ever expected.

SCARABS

Location: Empyre of Suhne

Some visions are sent by the gods. Others are created by our desires . . .

L *ight as a feather.*
Her skin felt the delicate touch of the wind on her face.
And yet, she heard nothing. In this beautiful realm where things moved ever so slowly, she was always surrounded by silence.

So far, the Tests had taken a toll on her. While they had not been particularly physically draining, her spirit felt exhausted. Vamya was quite certain her performance was not stellar and less than the best would not do. There was more to come, so she needed to renew herself.

To her surprise, unlike the times when she was truly troubled, today, her body and spirit were close to one.

Effortlessly, she left her body behind as she flew up toward the top of the dome.

She remembered a time, long ago, when she wondered where her heartbeat was when she wondered about her breathlessness.

Vamya of Suhne never had a mentor, at least not in this spiritual sense. This art of separation had been difficult to master, and despite the years she had practiced it, she still felt she was a novice, a student.

But how could one truly master something one doesn't understand, something that seemed limitless?

Was she the only one who could do this?

Sometimes her trance lasted a few minutes, sometimes several hours, but despite all the time she spent in this quiet world, she never saw the spirits of her brothers.

As a matter of fact, she never saw anyone else's.

Now here, hundreds of feet above the tallest dome, she could see the landscape around the Sun Palace. The bustling city, its countless adobe buildings rising from the barren earth of the same color.

From up here, the Suhnites looked like ants, garbed in the colors of mourning. Even the virgins were not wearing their bright colors, for there was not a Sun to seduce.

The Sun had left, his spirit floating as the sky orb along the heavens until his new body Ascended in one of his children.

The sky orb watched from high above, sending its warm blessing upon her and upon the land below.

Vamya smiled. She raised her hands toward the orb and sought to reach it.

Her spirit flew upward for what appeared to be a long time. She felt the same warmth.

Looking down, however, she realized she had not advanced at all.

Confused, she looked up again to see the Sun seemed to be as distant as always. Still, she felt tired.

'Why is it unreachable?' she asked herself.

'The Sun is sacred. Perhaps it is not time, at least not yet.'

The Child of the Sun looked around to see the Basqhs of Suhne.

To the south, before the distant black earth, she saw the Basqh of Alm, land of steppes, the more densely populated region of the Empyre and Ahni, the Basqh of water, land of the thousand oases.

To the east, endless oceans bordered Uhn, the crystal protectorate, laden with mines at the bases of countless rocky, flat-topped mountains.

To the north and west, Ohor, the protectorate of the expansive reaches of the Daygamanu desert and its blistering fury, and Lmet, the scarab region.

Lastly, Htet, the distant land of the Silver Peaks and whatever lay beyond the end of the world.

'Almighty Sun, what direction shall I move toward?'

Her spirit received no response other than the silence of the world she was in.

It was seldom that her spirit traveled far away from the comfort of the city of Suhne, for the farther she moved, the more her visions confused her, the more she lost control.

The Sun of Change closed her eyes, feeling for any sign that would tell her which direction she should go.

'Wait,' she interrupted her own thoughts. 'The wind's caress,' she smiled, opening her eyes to see her hair floating toward the west.

Lmet.

She flew in the direction of the land of immortals.

Far below, she saw a sea of sand dunes, beautiful and tan, the same tan chosen by the previous Sun.

Among the dunes were large funnels where the grubs lay in waiting for the unwary traveler unfortunate enough to fall prey to their voracious hunger. A single grub could swallow a man whole.

Past the funnels, she saw what appeared as black curved obsidian towers, their surfaces smooth and polished and ending in what seemed to be a spiked crown. As she flew over these, a few moved, their bases sending cascades of sand back to the ground. Each one rose up from the ground to reveal the enormous carapaces of the scarabs of Suhne, slow, powerful, and terribly majestic.

It was many more miles of dunes, steppes, and light vegetation before she stopped.

She looked at her hands and saw them fading lightly.

'I don't have much time.' Vamya understood her body was fatigued. She would soon have to go back. The last time she had pushed herself to the limit, she ended up severely dehydrated, having been out of her body for too long. It had taken her much longer to recuperate, and time was not a luxury she had during the Tests.

Yet, she felt a need to move onward.

'I didn't get through all this to stop at the end.'

'Where now?' The wind was not blowing anymore.

She closed her eyes to feel for anything.

All she felt, however, was herself fading.

And then she saw a glint.

Her eyes opened, and she found herself in front of a mountain, one of the smaller ones located where the whole range that led to the Silver Peaks began or perhaps ended. A mountain so small among the range it was quite insignificant, but for the fact that its top, instead of a peak, was a plateau.

She drifted toward that mountain top, where she saw lush greenery, beautiful palm trees, and dates. But those, however, were nothing in comparison to what truly caught her attention.

Right before her eyes were hundreds of scarabs, their bodies the size of camels, their carapaces the color of the purest gold.

She floated over them in amazement while their bodies turned as if reacting to her presence.

Vamya stopped herself in midair to see all the scarabs facing her direction.

She floated down slowly toward the ground, seeking to absorb every second of this most spectacular event. As she came just a few feet from the ground, the scarabs spread their golden elytra.

A flash of the Sun was reflected on them, blinding Vamya. She looked away and used her hands to block the reflections until she saw that, despite the light, she didn't need to impede it anymore.

Now, a few feet off the ground, she saw the scarabs lower their heads, as in reverence, while their wings fluttered in place, and the reflected light of the Sun in their golden elytra shone toward and through her.

'I am the Sun,' Vamya thought, as she felt both strangely tired and renewed.

'I am the Sun of Change.'

FATHER

Location: Blackheart Kingdom, Royal Duchy
of Darkholm, Darkholde Keep

The toughest battles are fought within ourselves . . .

From his preferred balcony of the keep, Septem Darkholm looked at the emptiness of the heavens that had blessed his family with a deep night sky, where only the moon's presence was reflected in the gleaming clothes he wore. On his head, the crown rested.

By his side, the ever-faithful Eriadna stood quietly, almost as quietly as his wife Raja, whose veiled presence was as certain as it was silent.

Behind him, Erdrick, Rowena, and Serverus each stood, their ears as open as most of their hearts.

"My children," Septem spoke as he looked away, "we must be ready. Our enemies move against us in large numbers. We must meet them in the field before they are allowed to approach our walls.

"A great battle awaits us," he continued, "terrible times are near."

"You speak as if there was certainty over an impending doom, my king," Serverus said.

"Your Highness," Rowena asked, "what are the words of the Master of Cosmos?"

"The words of destiny are but a guide," the king responded. "They do not define the actions we must take. Still, we must all stand at the ready for any eventuality, for a potential loss."

"Does Your Highness mean a loss of the battle itself?" Erdrick questioned.

"Loss of anything, of everything, even the loss of our crown."

"As is expected of us, Your Highness, we stand ready for anything, even to die in support of our king," Erdrick stated. "But if you, Father, were lost, what would you have us do?"

"Nothing," Septem responded immediately. "The wishes of the father should never become the life of his children, for his life was one, and he should never take a second one at the cost of theirs. What to do, you ask? Follow your hearts, but always remember your teachings and duties. Above remember who and what you are."

"We are Darkholm," Erdrick said.

"We remember," Rowena and Serverus joined in.

"You are all dismissed," Septem raised a hand, his eyes still on the infinite. "*In Tenebris nos Prosperabitur.*"

Only Eriadna remained by the king's side after everyone else left the chamber. The Shield, too, looked upon the sea and the nothingness beyond it. "My lord," she asked, "if I were to pass, have you considered who would be my successor?"

"Do you have anyone in mind?" Septem responded, his eyes of gold on the horizon.

"There are not many I trust enough."

"Who do you trust?"

"Maxius's commitment has been without question," she answered. "He is as sharp as the tip of his spear. His daughter's fighting skills are unparalleled. Naming her would not only honor Maxius, but it would also honor the late memory of her mother, Eleanor, the first woman to lead the knights. Aside from them, there is only one whose obeisance is unwavering, Lord Caime Grey."

"You would consider a non-Darkholm?"

"Blood without loyalty is nothing, my lord," she responded. "Loyalty without blood, that, I commend. Our vassals have proven to be of unquestionable devotion. I would prefer one of Darkholm Blood, surely, but from our Blood, for this endeavor, only someone from Idian's lineage."

"Idian's lineage is also yours," Septem stated.

"Yes, my king, and so is my cousin Maxius's," she nodded. "Maxius's line is admirable. While I am from the same lineage, I would never consider any of my three sons."

Septem nodded in understanding. He knew her commitment, her strength. He, of everyone, understood this woman of steel, so there was no need to ask for the reason behind her doubt.

"You may retire for the night," Septem raised his hand.

Walking to the center of the room before leaving, Eriadna turned and saluted formally, "My life is yours, my king."

Septem stood alone, his aurean eyes capturing yet another of the many stars that, like leaders, he had seen fall throughout his lifetime. He was submerged in deep thought when a stir behind him alerted him.

"You are still here," Septem said without turning.

"Father," Serverus uttered for the first time.

"Do *not* call me father," Septem responded firmly, turning his head so that he could see him from the corner of his eye. "I am *not* your father."

"I am well aware, my lord," Serverus lowered his head, "but the opportunity I have been given makes my heart desire to see you and love you as a father."

"And this shall not be," Septem said in what others would have interpreted as coldly, "I took you in as one of my own, for preserving you was your father's dying wish. He understood sacrifice, and he gave all to protect our kingdom. Your father's sacrifice made him a great man, one of the greatest heroes. Calling me 'father' diminishes his sacrifice.

"You can honor me *as* your father, as I honor you as my son. But I am not your progenitor, and neither are you my seed.

"While you need not live your father's dreams," Septem turned and placed a hand on Serverus's shoulder, "always honor his memory, what his sacrifice has provided you."

THE LIFE OF DEATH

Location: Kingdom of Blackheart,
Duchy of Darkholm, Darkholde Keep

Life's greatest dance is the one we dance with Death.

The wind blew, its mocking brush teasing the entire length of her raven hair.

Each time it flailed, she was reminded of her cousin Charon, of how she always seemed to enjoy every moment of life Elleonora did not.

Is this something Death knew? Why it chose me?

In its aerial dance, the long strands of hair brushed the skin of her face. Unlike those of her always jovial, often foolish cousin, her fingers made no effort to bring her hair back in place.

It would be pointless, in any case. Elleonora's hair was as soft as it was wild, always finding a way to free itself from whatever she used to hold it. Her hair, it seemed, had wanted to be as free as Elleonora would have wanted her own spirit to be. Therefore, unlike the life she lived, at least she let her hair do as it wished.

Even if she had wanted to tie her rebellious hair up, she was too busy clasping the handles of the basket she carried. That day, the paleness of her fingers was less than the first time she had carried the same burden, a basket loaded with seeds, dead rats, and rotting meat. But their reduced blanching was not as much from having gotten used to its weight, but rather from her slowly realizing she had no other option but to accept her situation.

She climbed behind the ancient Master of Death, following his slow footsteps along the outside of Darkholde, the beauty of the angry sea below all but ignored by the man who had seen it countless times and by her whose mind was consumed by thoughts of the cousins she had seen little as of late.

'Rowena,' Elleonora thought, 'I dedicated every day to studying herbology, medicine, and alchemy. I even traveled with you so that I could follow in your footsteps. Instead, I am here following *his*.'

Her eyes were dead set on Davidov Darkholm. While she undoubtedly respected him as much as any Darkholm would, what made her unhappy was how isolated she was in her role.

'Then again, of everyone, *who*, if anyone, would have been more fit to take it?' she thought. 'Who could have taken the role?'

The slow steps along the long road up gave her enough time to think, to question, to doubt herself.

'Could I have done it? Could I have made a good Master of Life?'

Elleonora wasn't particularly skilled. She had already accepted that. She had learned to believe it as a fanatic would never question his own religion. She could have made up for her own lack of talent with enthusiasm. 'Enthusiasm, bah.' She wasn't Charon. Elleonora hadn't known that feeling since long ago.

Charon shared both parents with Azareth, so unsurprisingly, Reya's smarts ran through Charon's veins as well.

It had become clear to Elleonora she didn't have Charon's intelligence, and her own mother had reminded her of that at every opportunity.

'Dull as a rock, but she is the one Death chose, so she will do,' she had even caught her own master saying when he had been asked about her. But then, he was never afraid of speaking his mind and had not sought to do so behind her back. The words had made her feel worse than she ever did. Elleonora had once wanted to quit, to drop everything and leave his mentorship, but while feeling like a failure was one thing, being perceived as one on top of that would have been too much to bear.

'One does not have to stand out,' Rowena had once told her. 'To not shine as brightly is a talent as good as any. To pass inadvertently is a gift on its own. Look at Alex, for example, how Alex can become someone else without being noticed.'

'Bah,' she puffed. 'What could Rowena ever know about being unnoticed?' She had been born the king's daughter and had obtained a position in the Grey Circle at a very young age. And Alex, well, Alex was just Alex.

In the end, there was an eponym she had secretly chosen for herself—'the patch,' able to cover many holes, but never as good as the real thing.

It still bothered her that, while she had not confessed to Rowena, she had longed to be the next Master of Life. She felt she had hinted at her desire enough.

'If you hint at it and do not say it,' her husband had scolded her, 'then perhaps you do not want it badly enough.'

But he was wrong, Elleonora thought. It wasn't that she didn't long for it; in fact, it was perhaps one of the few things she had truly really wanted. It had been the fear of being rejected for the position that had made her just hint but never ask.

'Rowena,' her mind went back to her cousin. 'Did you not notice, or did you just not care?'

But was either of those true?

She knew her cousins well enough to know Rowena didn't miss things. Rowena planned and moved as quietly and as surely as she tuned silent instruments to direct an invisible orchestra.

Elleonora Darkholm

Elleonora's fingers eased a little. Perhaps she was misjudging Septem's daughter, adding malice where there was likely none to be found. She lowered her head, embarrassed at her own thoughts. Deep inside, she knew she had followed Rowena so many times, not because she had wanted her position but because she had truly loved her company. How could she not love her, she thought, when she had put up with all of Charon's antics to be around her?

The thought of her cousins drew a faint smile on the sad moon of her skin, but just as it appeared, it vanished.

"Hurry up," Davidov's raspy voice complained. "You are slowing me!"

What a dichotomy Davidov was. He was as ancient as a prophecy, with a mind as sharp as that of the youngest scholar. He was slow and yet tireless, frail, and yet under that frailty, he was easily, in his own way, one of the most influential men in the world and one who never flaunted his knowledge, his power.

"I am sorry, Master," Elleonora lowered her head.

"Be slow if you want for your own devices," Davidov retorted. "But do not be a selfish slug with the time of others."

She had often felt every lesson he taught, he did with a slap on the face. There was never an ounce of kindness in his voice. Rather quickly, Elleonora had gotten used to his tone, to his speech. As she had done many times before, she adapted.

"What is on your mind?" he asked. "You seem distracted."

"Nothing, Master," Elleonora responded, "I was just thinking about life."

"Life . . ." He resumed his walk. "Life is ridiculous, stupid even. Life uses you, extracting everything from you just to sustain itself, even after you are long gone and forgotten. It drains every single breath from you, and in your breathlessness, you hallucinate, thinking it is the best thing ever. But, when she is done with you, she will just discard you. She will hand you to Death, who simply waits and takes all blame."

Once past the gate leading to the top of the tower, they were welcomed by the raspy, drawn-out, hissing song of numerous vultures and the croaks of ravens in their midst. Elleonora placed the basket on top of a stone slab, one stained from countless bodily fluids that had dried up on its surface. Much like the entirety of that roofless chamber, the platform reeked of death. Unlike the first time she had followed him here, Elleonora didn't seem to mind the stench or even notice anymore.

Davidov approached the basket. His deep, recessed eyes of hate looked down, almost arrogantly. He placed a hand on the basket to keep his balance and reached in for a large piece of raw meat. 'A thigh, likely,' she caught herself wondering, watching Davidov throw the first piece on the slab. The wet splat was followed by a hundred flaps, by the gurgling of ravens and vultures wrestling for the feast.

She then moved toward the basket and, taking pieces of cold, rotting meat in her hands, she did the same, sending the aviary into a feeding frenzy.

After it was emptied, she proceeded to wipe off the edges of the slab with a piece of wet fabric. She remembered her first week, how Davidov, aside from constantly complaining about how she wasn't particularly smart, had ordered her to perform all sorts of menial tasks that seemed to achieve nothing, such as scrubbing the basket and wiping that same floor.

'Many times, we perform tasks nobody cares to do, and nobody cares about,' Davidov had explained. 'That does not make the task less important. The day might come when that task, when the experience obtained through it, will be badly needed. Even if the day never comes, that should not change our commitment. Our duty must be without question.'

As every time before this one, they worked, waiting until the birds were done with all the meat before the duo had grasped a pair of hammers that hung from the basket's handles.

"Master," Elleonora said, "I wonder how you have come to understand Death."

"Who judges to decide we truly understand anything?" he replied, "Do we understand, or do we believe we do?"

They lined up the remaining bones to hammer them into smaller pieces, exposing the bone marrow, which they mixed for the birds to eat too.

"And what do you believe, Master?" Elleonora questioned. "I have never heard you speak of gods or religion."

"What does it matter what others believe in?" he retorted. "What does it matter what I believe after I am gone? After someone is gone, what is remembered and spread around is only a perversion of what they truly believed, for no one truly knows. I will not waste my time teaching you what I believe. I will teach you what I know."

Elleonora nodded. For all his cold and dry demeanor, Elleonora had learned to appreciate the short conversations she was able to hold with the otherwise unapproachable Davidov, even if he did not speak to her any differently than to the rest of the House. Lately, though, she asked herself if she perceived something different in his tone, in the length of his sentences. She felt, little by little, how this bitter person grew on her, even if not once he greeted her, even if he didn't show any care for her emotions. She felt that something was bringing them closer together.

Is that 'something' a god? Unlikely... Unlike her older brother, Anivar of the Eye, the priest of Darkholm, she didn't believe at all in deities playing a celestial game of Domae with the lives and destiny of mankind. While she believed in no gods, she did believe in the possibility of the supernatural.

"Death..." Elleonora questioned, "does it speak to you, Master?"

"Do you need to hear an order to enforce the will of your superior?" he responded. "Our job is simple: Feed her, respectfully, diligently, and you will be privy to knowledge no one else has access to."

"How will I know its will?"

"You will." The birds took flight, noisily and unceremoniously, leaving nothing behind but old feathers and smelly droppings in the largely emptied room. The pair readied themselves to return to the body of the keep, wiping the hammers and basket handles but otherwise leaving the floor as it was, wet with the remains of the remains.

"That husband of yours," Davidov said, "you need to detach yourself from him."

"My lord?" Elleonora was surprised.

"You heard it."

"Are you asking me to separate?"

"Do not put words in my lips," his terse voice corrected her. "Your closeness to your husband, it is sickening."

"Sickening? How so?"

"He is as dependent on you as you are on him."

"We see it as a blessing."

"That is not a blessing," he interrupted.

"We are much in love, Master."

"That is not love," Davidov sneered, holding the keys to the gate in hand. "That is an addiction, an unhealthy one. Wanton blindness does not change it."

Elleonora heard him, although she didn't agree in the least. How could he ever understand her life, her relationship, from his heartless throne of ice? But she wouldn't lose control, not like that one time he broke her will. She held back, looking for the proper way to answer.

"Speak your mind, daughter of Rydia!" He opened the gate and passed through.

"What do you know about love!" The words escaped her lips too fast for her to realize she had thrown a sharp dagger, like those of her mother's tongue. Their echoing told her she had lost control even of her volume, stopping him in his tracks.

"Impertinence," his sharp eyes smiled, even when his voice spat, "Like that little bitch, Isolde."

"I am sorry, Master," Unable to bear facing her mentor, she lowered her head and picked up the basket.

"I liked it," Davidov resumed his walk.

She waited a few seconds in place before resuming her steps behind him and speaking again. "I love Gustavus," Elleonora stated. "Our relationship is not perfect, but we will never allow anything to come between us. But aside from that, I am Darkholm, and as terrible as it would be for the both of us, if you were to order it . . ."

"It is not an order." He turned to face her, "it is advice so that, in the performance of your duties, you do not falter."

"I will not falter," Elleonora stated firmly. "Gustavus supports everything I do and will stand by me, without hesitation, until the end."

"Pain will teach you," he almost whispered, not caring if she heard him or not, but she did.

Most of the rest of the walk was quiet until Elleonora, seeing they were close to the keep, spoke again.

"Master," she then called, "could I ask you a question?"

"You can," he responded without slowing his pace. "You can ask whatever you want."

"You never speak of your late wife, Aleshka. You never mention her." She bit her lower lip nervously. "Is it because you miss her? Is it because you loved her so much?" The Master's pace did not change for a single instant. He continued, hobbling quietly toward the keep.

"Master?" She was worried. "I hope I have not offended you."

"You cannot offend me, child," he continued.

"But," Elleonora hesitated, "you did not answer my question."

The Master of Death stopped and turned toward her, his squinting eyes of piercing gold fixed on those of his apprentice. He looked at her with what anyone might interpret as derision. "We are entitled to ask any question. That does not entitle us to get an answer."

Leaving Elleonora behind, the old duke was swallowed by the shadows of the keep.

⋅⋅✦✦✦✦⋅⋅

It was early morning when she arrived at his study and found him standing inside, waiting by his desk.

"Good morning, Master," her greeting met only his brief nod in response, "I will prepare everything for the feeding."

"Leave it," he ordered, "the Vultures will do so this time. We have another important task."

Elleonora wanted to ask what kind of task but quickly realized it didn't matter. Whatever task the Master of Death had given her had been an opportunity to learn something about the world, about him. While she couldn't claim she didn't learn anything of use during her apprenticeship to the Devereau, his mentorship, hard on her as it was, had so far taught her quite a bit much about herself.

Aside from that, she had noticed the unmistakable, heavy book in his hand. From the first time she had seen the tome, with its black leather bindings and gray embroideries, the silver clasps and haunting skull that adorned the libram, had captured her undivided attention, House Darkholm's *Liber de Finis*.

Within those pages lay ancient knowledge, and within that ancient knowledge was undeniable power.

She followed him down the long, narrow staircase that connected the room they were in to the main passage between the Darkholde prison and the dungeons below, that part of the keep that had perhaps become his greatest domain.

The dungeons were a dimly lit network of tunnels, with occasional sconces and halls opening into small stone domes that were only rich in wooden racks and devices of torture.

As dark and humid as they were, these cold walls that many times echoed the screams of the dying felt that day, to her, strangely welcoming.

"Death's message," Davidov's voice interrupted her musing, "is always present. One must be patient if one seeks to comprehend it."

They came upon a larger chamber where a trio of men, dressed in their black attire and the short, feathered cloaks of the Vultures, worked. They were almost done adjusting a chain's height, one that had, at its end, a male body garbed in simple prison breeches. His arms were tied, his torso exposed, unlike the entirety of his head, which was covered.

The man, Elleonora knew, was likely gagged as usual, and he hung quietly, upside down like a bat.

"Come back for him tonight," Davidov instructed the departing men.

Once they were gone, the only sound was the rattling of the chain by which the muffled man hanged, struggling to free his hands. Davidov, as always, appeared unconcerned. He moved behind the lectern where he placed the libram. Elleonora, in turn, examined a silver bowl she had pulled from under a rack, her eyes traveling to every corner of the metal piece. She ensured its metal was polished and perfectly clean before she placed it on the floor under the man's head.

The Master of Death approached the hanging man. Following his signal, Elleonora uncovered the man's head and mouth.

Immediately, the tied man screamed, cursed, hurling insults, asking to be let free.

"Who in all the hells are you?" he questioned Elleonora, but upon setting his eyes on her, he needed no answer. While he didn't know her name and had probably never met her, the shade of her eyes told him she was of the family that held the crown.

This was something he was certain about, for unlike the majority of people in the world, despite the isolation in which the royals of Blackheart surrounded themselves, he had been close to them, and not just to any Darkholm, but to the most powerful ones, the leaders of the House. And while his proximity to them had not been physical, even emotional, he had many times worked toward the same goals, defended the same lands, and attended the same Council as the now-disgraced duke of Valador.

"Lord Davidov, old friend," his nervous words escaped his lips. Crannon Coronn didn't know where to start. "I don't exactly know what's happening here, but I've been asking for, I'd like to request an audience with His Majesty."

Davidov's attention was on his book, his lips reciting silently, his hand flipping pages while the other one reached for a quill.

"Lord Davidov, I had plenty of time to think. I know my impulses got the best of me," he continued, "but His Majesty is most wise. I just need the king's ear to explain." Elleonora watched carefully as the man seemed to beg, speaking of the many times he had supported the Crown, of the defense he had mounted at the kingdom's borders. His tone then changed, threatening Davidov, claiming Darkholm were, and had always been, the real traitors to the kingdom, all before the unwavering indifference of Elleonora's mentor.

The Master of Death held a sheathed, curved knife. He revealed its perfect, engraved blade, with its depiction of a skeleton, its arms bound, its jaw open. It was chained to the blade hung from a chain in its legs. While Elleonora had never held it, somehow she longed to, and she knew one day she would.

Her master's dried lips whispered words over the morbid scene depicted on the blade's surface, words Elleonora couldn't make out, but she didn't need to. She had memorized those words very well by now.

"Wait," Crannon begged, his eyes on the blade, "what are you doing?"

Davidov raised his menacing, sunken eyes to look eye to eye at the former duke, whose mind raced, seeking the perfect word to say, for the phrase that would break the nightmare that was unfolding. No matter how much he sought, he realized his options were limited. There was not much he could say. What possible ransom could he offer when everything had been taken away from him? Besides, what could he offer when the man in front of him was the father of the king whose trust he had betrayed?

"I demand a fair trial!" he finally shouted. "I invoke the laws of the kingdom and the laws of the Great Council—" His words were interrupted by the swift traveling of Davidov's knife along the side of his neck and by his own scream that reverberated through the dungeons.

The Master of Death stood observant, patient as one of the birds he fed, his aurean eyes on the hanging noble, watching Crannon's jerking movements in his futile attempt to escape his bonds, each contraction sending an ever-increasing rivulet of blood toward the silver bowl below.

"What is the strongest bond one can have?" Davidov asked.

"Loyalty," Elleonora responded, "is the tenet that should never waver."

"And which, of the Masters of the Grey Circle, must the Master of Death work closest with," he continued.

"The Master of Life," Elleonora answered. "It is in the perfect balance of Death and Life that immortality can be achieved."

"There is no need for balance," Davidov's eyes sneered. "Cooperation among opposing forces does not equate balance, but rather simply working toward a common goal. The most powerful ally the Master of Death has is the Master of Lore. You must always have a strong, close relationship with him."

"Azareth?" Elleonora questioned.

"Whoever the Master of Lore is," he responded succinctly, walking back toward the lectern. "Do you like to read?"

"I do, Master."

"Well, even if you did not, you would have to, endlessly." He perused the pages before meeting her eyes. "For while the Master of Lore is the repository of knowledge, the knowledge is yours to consume."

"With the Occult Library being available to all members of House Darkholm, even Serverus among those who are not," Elleonora pointed out, "surely there is something else you are referring to."

"Within the Darkholm lies the occult." The Master's fingers flipped one more page, readying where a new quote would be recorded, "And within the occult lies the hidden." His words would have sent a chill down anyone's spine.

Elleonora, however, felt intrigued.

She studied Crannon, his exposed skin paler by the minute. This man who had once been a great leader in his own right, in a powerful position for most of his life, now hung powerless, like a wet drape under a sun unseen, his entire life ebbing away with each pulse.

"Power," her master had once taught her, "the essence of a man lies within the last moment, within that last pulse that leaves his body. The rest, as with the utterance of his lips, what comes before and what comes after, is a lot of nothing."

"Traitors!" Crannon shouted, his bloodshot eyes meeting Davidov's. "You are the greatest threats to the kingdom." He coughed, his voice weakened but willful. "We know what you are."

The Master of Death's fingers wrapped around an empty vial. His eyes were intently on Crannon. Immediately after, the former duke convulsed, his violent flailing a dance to which the rattling of the chains played the tune.

The seizing always lasted an unpredictable length of time, Elleonora had noticed, but somehow, every time, Davidov seemed to be at the ready at its sudden end.

And with its end, the moment of silence and stillness came, the moment when the Master of Death stood barely an inch away from Crannon's face. His ancient lips muttered words long-forgotten before he whispered an order—"Speak."

The prisoner's angry frown weakened, his irises disappearing behind the curtain of his eyelids before suddenly reappearing in a horrid visage. His gaping mouth, devoid of any strength, whispered, "Watch every shadow. There . . . traitors . . . among you . . ."

Upon his words, the Master of Death placed the vial under the thinning bloodstream. With the swift and simple move, he captured the most important part of his blood as certainly as the dying man's words had captured Elleonora's attention.

The duke's corpse hung limp, still bleeding, though not as profusely.

"With every exsanguination," his words brought her back, his eyes studying the vial's contents, "the Master of Death must make a sacrifice of its own. A person's last moment is always meant to be consumed, but by whom?"

"Is it to be captured and given to the Master of Life," he raised an eyebrow, "or is it given to Death herself?"

"And what would Death do it with, Master?" she asked.

"*Through* it," he corrected, "she would speak."

The idea alone was fascinating. Elleonora had always seen death as a force of nature, as a philosophy, and nothing more. In the time she had spent following him, she had been intrigued by the fact that, like herself, her master was an atheist. Unlike her, he was powerful, and still, her master seemed to be subservient. He would revere it.

"A crossroads," she mused, "the Master of Life would use the last moment to prepare the ceremonial Blood Tea for *Caena Sanguis*, the search for immortality being the first tradition of our House. If we gave it to Death, what would happen to that blood, to their words?"

"Lost," Davidov responded, "the words are bound to the last drop. Either they are captured together, or they are not."

Until this moment, Elleonora had believed the Master of Death's work ended at the hands of the Master of Life. Like her own daily life, she had felt as if all hard work would end up nowhere other than empowering the actions of another. From Death to Life . . . it was at that one moment every time the Darkholm went against what was perceived as natural. But this time, her master spoke of something different, and the mystery of it all intrigued her.

'Power,' she thought, 'raw power.' She had just realized the Master of Death had the power to decide what was consumed by the House, what information would be recorded, and that which would stay unwritten, words and knowledge that would only be known to the Master of Death and Death itself.

A semblance of a smile appeared on her face, but just as it did, it disappeared when her eyes gravitated toward where she thought she felt a presence in the darkest recess in the room, there, beyond the twitching body of the dying man, watching her.

"The decision has been made," his voice again interrupted her thoughts.

Turning his hand, he spilled the contents of the vial on the bowl below. "Now, bring the bowl and see what is hidden from even the occult. Behold the power of blood."

————————·✦✦✦✦·————————

The room they visited was one she had not stepped in ever before, beyond a stone door and short hallway that led to yet another stone door. Unlike the first one, sculpted to depict scenes of torture she would've been sickened by had she not witnessed them many times already or had she not been Elleonora. The second one was nondescript, plain. It was beyond this second door that he spent hours alone, at times even the entire day, before she saw him again.

Stepping in, she noticed it wasn't adorned with skulls and bones as anyone would expect. It was illuminated by the lantern he carried, one that perhaps served to accentuate how much hungrier the shadows became with each passing minute.

The room was small but dark, somber but simple. A bed rested on one side, close to a shelf with flasks of different shapes and sizes, mostly empty, some filled with blood.

A heavy, wooden chair lay at its center, flanked by both a desk to its left and a vacant lectern to its right. Over the desk's velvet surface, an empty silver bowl rested. Davidov shut the door behind Elleonora and walked toward the lectern.

"This is the closest you will ever get to the heart of Darkholde," Davidov said. Far above us, the throne of the Head of the House. Around us, the Darkholm catacombs."

"What is below us, Master?" Elleonora asked. The Master of Death only responded with what appeared to be a malicious grin.

"Let us talk about what we are here for . . . *Sangüiae*—the power of blood."

He placed *Liber de Finis* over the lectern. His fingers flipped its pages once more, revealing the one hungry for words.

"*Sangüiae* has been discovered and developed by the first Master of Death, passed down with each generation.

"As Master of Death," he explained, "as you prevail over the punished, you will always write on the page corresponding to your dominant hand."

"In order for *her* to speak," he lowered his head slightly, "one must bow down before her dominion."

Elleonora nodded, seeking to understand what he meant.

"In the practice of *Sangüiae*, the vessel must place the dominant hand right at the gate," he pointed at the bowl, "while the weaker one will be subservient, writing down any messages communicated by her will."

"Is it a type of divination?"

"It is, and it is not," her master responded. "While we obtain information, we only garner whatever she chooses to provide."

"Have you asked her any questions, Master?" Elleonora asked.

"Communication is one-way," he answered. "Questions are the realm of the Master of Cosmos."

"Is it magic then?" she asked.

"Magic?" Davidov sneered. "It is an art. It is the language of Death herself and the way she has spoken to the Master of Death for over two centuries."

"When the time comes, and the mantle falls upon my shoulders," she looked at him intently, "I will use everything I have to improve that communication."

"Do not think for an instance Death is humble, child, for she is not," he peered over the libram. "Do not think you will come here and make her methods, her ways, your own," he scolded. "The Master of Death's position is a privilege. You do not shape it. It shapes you."

Signaling her to pour the blood from her bowl into the empty one on the desk, he picked up a long, black quill from the lectern on his right.

"Now, *Bloodspeak* takes a toll on the body, that is certain, but whatever happens," he instructed, "do not interrupt."

"Master—"

"Whatever happens," he restated firmly.

"At what cost does she speak?" she insisted.

"At whatever cost," he snapped.

Moments later, he took a deep breath and fixed his robes to sit. "Know that this is just one side of *Sangüiae*. Often, the message delivered will require much time to be deciphered."

"I suppose it is not easy to understand."

"What?"

"Her will," she responded, "her words."

"Those of men are much harder to understand, and yet mankind spends their entire lives trying to figure out the words and wills of one another." His eyes challenged Elleonora's. "Unlike men, at least Death is always true."

Readying himself, the Master of Death's right hand wet the tip of the quill on the ink vial. He closed his eyes and moved his lips, repeating phrases she again could not understand. He moved his left hand slowly toward the sanguineous bowl. His fingertips broke the still surface, sending ripples that bounced back delicately off the bowl's rim.

The Master's fingers made contact with the bottom where they remained anchored, revealing the dry dorsum of his knuckles as an alligator's eyes in a pool of blood.

The ancient duke breathed deeply before he entered a deep trance, lowering his head in what appeared to be a deep bow.

Elleonora, in turn, watched for any sign, for seconds that appeared to move as slowly as her own brother's tedious, religious dissertations, slow as molasses.

The small room started to feel heavy, like something slowly drawing her breath away, as if the walls readied themselves to crush them inside at any moment.

Suddenly she noticed something, a slight twitch in Davidov's left hand, but that moment was short-lived.

As if caught in a mortal trap, his hand muscles tightened. The bowl shook, forming waves of red within it. From under his eyelids, only the white of Davidov's eyes appeared. His body shifted randomly. She wondered if perhaps he was trying to fend off spirits fighting for possession of his body.

His right hand, however, began to write.

Somehow, as if having gained a sentience of its own, his hand moved almost independently of the rest of his body. It swayed fluidly, with long, serpentine strokes that drew hypnotic patterns, at times with shorter, rough ones that switched from haphazard letters to random runes. Every few seconds, the hand brought the quill back to the ink vial before returning to the thirty pages that seemed to be seeking to break the quill's tip.

And it wrote phrases in languages Elleonora could not understand, at times straight, others curving inwards and outwards along the edge of the entire page.

Slowly and yet for long, he wrote, filling every inch of the parchment with swirls, letters, with symbols large and small. One last time his hand placed the quill on the vial before he slumped forward, where he was caught by Elleonora's arms.

She surprised herself.

Never would have she found it in her heart to move forward to catch this bitter man, this man whom she respected as a superior but who always seemed to bring out the worst of her, her past frustrations, her painful memories. And yet here she was, holding this ungrateful man.

As much as she had disliked the idea of her position, she had not hesitated to do as he commanded every time. This time, however, the toll on his body had left him greatly weakened. The young woman caught Davidov's limp body and brought him to the bed, surprised at his thinness under the heavy robes, the frailty of his figure, at the lightness of his weight.

'I wonder what it would have been like to have lived during the era of Davidov as the Patriarch of the House, as the regnant Duke of Darkholm,' she thought. But Davidov had stopped being the Head of the House for more than four times her age. She would have given anything to see it, to live it.

In the present day, all she could see around her and feel were just echoes of the great deeds of this man who had been both admired and reviled, feared and truly powerful.

While she would never truly know, she smiled, fascinated, this man was her mentor, and she had him to herself, all to herself.

WIND OF CHANGE

Location: Kingdom of Blackheart,
Royal Duchy of Darkholm, Darkholde Cliffs

H igh above the desolate cliffs that watched the world, she always saw everything falling.

It was late that day in spring when a girl of just fifteen summers stood over the edge of the cliffs of Darkholde.

She stood alone as she always did, gazing intently at the coast far below, at its angry waters that swallowed the earth, and at the small capital that rested across Smith's Bay.

Many times she had watched that city from this place, a vantage point from where she could see it all while its inhabitants could see nothing of her.

It was in this place where she found her strength that she felt the most vulnerable, for every time she stood there, she felt the wind, that whimsical companion that carelessly played with the most precious thing she had, the thing that meant everything, and was everything to her—her hair.

And it had been for at least three years that Damara's scalp had been show-ing—a perfect egg that a bird would be proud to shine and show, but one that made her as embarrassed as she would have never believed anyone could be.

The last year alone had seen the greatest loss, so much that her scalp now held a little less than half of its hair in place, as the ever-faithful followers of a false god who refused to let go.

While the others' lives were slowly filled with wonder and responsibilities, hers was quickly filled with embarrassment and shame.

One thing, though, she had learned to do—when embarrassed, she had learned to withdraw.

At first, she did, from the citizens' children who noticed and asked with-out fear. Then she had stayed away from the merchants, whom she had caught staring at her in disgust.

Lately, she had withdrawn even from her own.

For while they were always busy and seemingly indifferent, Damara *felt* . . . no, she *knew* they were ignoring it to make her feel better about her situation.

But the young woman had found that *nothing* made her situation better.

And that was all she could think of from up here, where her only companion was the wind that played with her pain.

Damara's lips parted, but no words came through. Only the humming of a song only she knew, a mesmerizing yet sad tune to which her body swayed.

As she embraced herself . . .

As she walked toward the edge . . .

As small pieces of rocks loosened under her bare feet . . .

Tumbled down the precipice . . .

She looked down one last time to the silent sea below, to the protruding reefs. Damara opened her arms and felt a cool breeze behind her.

"What are you doing?"

The female voice, while soft, took her by surprise, and Damara halted. "What does it seem like I am doing? I am getting ready to end this."

"End *what*?"

"Can you not see this?" Without turning, her hands grasped the loose ends of her hair, pulling them apart to reveal the white scalp that needed no help in showing. "This, that has made me make this castle a prison, for I cannot walk that land of those men, who point their fingers at me and laugh at me and mock me, and speak of me as less of a woman . . . and more of a monster."

A brief silence followed before the voice spoke again. "At least you can hide it." The visitor advanced toward her and carefully took Damara's strands, picking them up to cover the bald spots in the girl's head to the best of her ability.

The visitor proceeded to caress Damara's shoulders and scapulas before grasping them with care.

"There are others, like me, who are not that fortunate." The visitor slowly turned Damara around so that they could face one another.

Damara opened her eyes to see what she thought was an angelic being. A girl whose skin was the purest white, her lips as pale as bleached pearls, with eyes as bright yellow as her own. While her clothes were the same color, the wind lifted the woman's long and perfect hair, which was the color of freshly fallen snow.

"And yet," Lady Charon continued, "I have chosen to make this castle not a prison but a home. And I have chosen to walk that land of those men who point their fingers at me, and laugh at me, and mock me, and speak of me as less of a woman and more of a monster because one thing I have learned in this life, that I will never allow their words to become my reality."

To this, there were no words Damara could say in response. Her eyes opened wide and filled with tears. Charon's situation was far worse. At only sixteen, her cousin had endured much more than she had.

Charon had been cast out and scarred. She had been judged and misjudged everywhere she went. She surely understood what it felt like to be rejected for her looks.

While she had perhaps been marked for life time and again, she was still standing.

"I . . ." Damara cried and hugged her cousin firmly, "I am so sorry, Charon. Please forgive me!"

Lady Charon held her fast against her body and moved her so that Charon now stood between Damara and the cliffs that captured her gaze.

"There is nothing I need to forgive you for," she kissed Damara's bald head tenderly. "You need to learn to forgive yourself."

"How can I? I feel lost."

"You are not the only one who feels lost," Charon caressed Damara's head. "While I cannot tell you how to find your way, I can walk the way with you."

"I would very much love that," Damara added.

"Now," Charon continued, "dinner is upon us. Why don't we go change and join the others?"

Damara nodded, wiping her face with her sleeve.

Lady Charon grabbed Damara's chin and studied her face. "You will need a lot of makeup to cover your swollen eyes, but don't worry, I have plenty. I don't use them much, but I love to paint!"

Her gesture made Damara show the semblance of a smile.

Both women walked toward the dark hallways of the enormous keep.

The younger one promised herself she would one day be brave, like Charon, for at least she could cover herself while her cousin could not.

Damara Darkholm

The angel who had just saved her, in turn, just chattered all the way, as usual. "I have studied the effect of worrying too much on the body. Did you know that excessive preoccupation can cause swelling of the feet? You probably didn't.

"Amazing, isn't it? Well, it's important you try to relax because it can also cause hair to fall out. Imagine that! I mean, I don't mean to worry you about not being worried, but hey, think of it, three hairs are better than none, right?

"Hey, one question. You were going to jump, and you had not eaten dinner? What kind of crazy is that? Dying hungry . . . I know that will never happen to Elzie. Anyway, worse than that would be to fall and not die *and* be hungry."

Damara laughed at Charon's antics.

Charon enjoyed having an audience, even if it consisted of just one. She felt the younger girl could benefit from attention and distraction.

Her love had saved her life.

A KNIGHT'S HEART

Location: Kingdom of Blackheart,
Royal Duchy of Darkholm, Darkholde Keep

The morning sun shone brightly, its glorious light bathing every corner of the land below while casting shadows along the cliffs licked by the sea of Darkholm.

Sunbeams invaded the enormous black keep, sneaking in through the stained-glass windows in a silent yet colorful display of light.

Resting over the parapets around the training hall, dozens of carrion birds watched in silence while just a few feet below, true to their nickname, *the vultures,* just as many Darkholm witnessed quietly what transpired in the hall where, like a pair of scavengers fighting over a piece of rotting meat, two men dueled over an heirless baron's land.

Erdrick lunged toward his opponent, quickly closing the distance between the two with his perfect form. The tip of his epee barely missed his opponent, whose deep, gray hair spoke only a fraction of the experience he bore.

The Twins arched his left arm upward and mentally measured the new distance between the two with a single, darting jab of the epee on his right that would have seemed an initiate's move.

But the Twins was far from an initiate.

He had been born one of a pair of identical siblings, Darren and Dannil, creators of the Darkholm fighting style. Despite their philosophical differences, they fought together, side by side, only identifiable by the dominant eye on their warmask. They lived, laughed, and loved together, but the one thing they did not find together was death.

Upon the death of one, the surviving twin cast his helmet by his brother's side so that no one could ever know who had perished. Despite the deep sadness that has accompanied him ever since, the survivor took the name the Twins and decided that, instead of wallowing in despair, he would live for both of them.

Even today, several generations later, he was a match for much younger warriors, and one of his best apprentices was the one he faced today.

Erdrick Darkholm recovered quickly. While Septem's son preferred a claymore, he was quite proficient with almost every weapon he could get his hands on. His fighting ability had helped him climb the ranks of the Black Knights, of whom he had become the leader.

But, more than his proficiency, his ability to adapt and improvise made him a most formidable and dangerous opponent.

The knight drew small circles in the air with the tip of his epee, seeking to catch the attention of the Twins.

"Know your opponent," the Twins said out loud as if this was just another lesson.

"What is Erdrick's weakness?" Fengo, Gustavus's youngest brother, asked from the balcony, where he chuckled by Tenslea's side.

"That is for you to find out," the master responded, smiling. "It is seldom that life places knowledge in your hands. Most of the time, you have to fight for it and find it!"

The Twins darted forward, first ducking, stabbing, and circling out of the way just as fast. As he passed, drops of blood stained Erdrick's shirt.

"*Always* know your opponent," he continued. "An unpredictable opponent is typically focused on how he can surprise you more than in defending against surprises of your own."

"Good move," Erdrick smiled as he readied himself. "You got me at a disadvantage, Twins. Just two more to go while I still need three."

"No matter how close one is to victory," he continued the demonstration, "do not allow your confidence to distract you from the careful steps you must take to achieve it. Victory is only certain when one has obtained it."

The pair lunged and thrust at one another, both striking close enough but far enough to avoid striking true.

"Twins, here!" Toradmus hurled a second epee toward the man he so much admired. His strikes would now become a hailstorm with him wielding a pair of swords.

As arrows in flight, the strikes came, but Erdrick moved with such ease his deflections would have seemed effortless if not for the drops of sweat trailing behind in the air.

And as fast as a lightning strike, a swift slash cut the wind toward the older man, striking one of his swords and sending it flying several feet away.

With a quick step back, the Twins dodged, his eyes fixed on his opponent's shoulders.

"Good move," he said, "using a piercing weapon as a slashing blade might not seem as effective, but it is if it catches your opponent off guard."

As he finished his words, a gash on his shirt opened, followed by a thin line of crimson life.

"Hah! *Great* move!"

Risking it all, Erdrick moved forward toward the Twins, who switched hands and lunged at him. The knight stepped aside, grabbed his opponent's blade, and, turning swiftly, snapped it in place.

The Twins stepped back, but not fast enough before he felt the Commander's tip on his leg.

"Two," he jested when Erdrick threw the broken tip of the Twin's blade, sending it flying toward him and striking the same extremity.

"Three," Erdrick smiled, "know your opponent. *Always* know your opponent!"

Upon the victory, the House did not clap, nor did they celebrate, for the Lords of Darkness kept ingrained in their hearts: their differences and challenges they always resolved in private. In the eyes of the outside world, despite any differences between them, the winner would be supported by all who shared their name.

Tenslea, Fengo, and Serverus were among those who approached the Twins to make certain he received a healer's assistance.

Charon, Gustavus, and Malacar surrounded Erdrick.

"I am fine," the knight signaled to those around him. He sought his father, whose attention had been on the entire duel. The one thing Erdrick had wanted his entire life was to follow his father, to follow his footsteps, to honor the name they carried. He was glad his progenitor, from whom he rarely received a compliment, had seen his victory.

The knight wiped his hands as he turned to see a young man standing in the center of the training hall. His hair was as unkempt as a youngster's sheets in the morning, his eyes intense, his cheekbones perfect; on his shoulder, a red cape denoted his station.

"Dragan," Erdrick said.

From under his cape, Dragan produced a rapier. "I am Dragan 'Drakkon' Darkholm, and I will have Ironforge. Erdrick Darkholm, Commander of the Black Knights, I challenge you!"

Vhimir, the herald, raised his voice for all to hear, "The land titles have not been granted to the knights yet, so if the king allows it, it can still be contested."

The members of the House all looked upon the monarch, whose hand signaled to proceed.

"Does anyone support Dragan's challenge?" Vhimir shouted.

"I do," Xenovive of the Vine walked to stand behind Dragan's back.

Bursting with pride, Sellayne Darkholm joined her.

"Then you may accept the challenge," Vhimir announced before returning to his balcony.

"Baron Dragan 'Drakkon' Darkholm, Dragon of Darkholm. I, Erdrick Darkholm, Knight Commander of the Black Knights of Darkholm, accept your challenge!"

"Choose our weapon," Dragan commanded.

"What's your best dueling weapon?" Erdrick raised an eyebrow confidently.

"Rapier, of course."

"Then rapier it will be." Erdrick's entourage stepped aside, returning to their place. Not long after, he was brought three rapiers, which he tested in the air, choosing the most complex, engraved weapon with the finest blade.

"I have chosen the weapon. Choose the victory condition," Erdrick instructed.

"First blood."

"So will it be." Erdrick stood five steps away, saluting with his rapier.

Dragan's eyes met his cousin's. There was warmth in neither man's expression. He curtsied deeply, dropped his cape, and readied his stance.

The herald waved the red flag that initiated the duel.

Immediately, the smaller man moved fast toward Erdrick, seeking to catch him by surprise.

But the seasoned knight deflected the strike with ease.

Within a moment, Dragan's hand turned and attacked from the side, but the larger man caught a glimpse and deflected again, kicking hard, his swinging leg catching Dragan's shirt and sending him off balance.

And just then, Erdrick closed in and slashed twice.

But the smaller man deflected the first attack and stepped back to avoid the second.

Both men seemed like lightning, unpredictably and quickly deflecting one another and dancing around the hall.

After a few more rounds, the Black Knight's brow started to sweat. Many years of training under the weight of his armor ensured stamina was never an issue for the warrior, but matching the speed of the smaller man was draining him of all of it.

Erdrick Darkholm took a deep breath and lowered his stance.

The world slowed down almost to a stop. Falling drops of sweat froze in midair. The breathing of all witnesses echoed as a raging storm that drifted away as everything around him lost all color, everything but Dragan, who appeared bright as the sun shining down on Whisperwind's fertile fields. The Drakkon's eyes blazed intensely, frozen in time but still centered on Erdrick's own. His shirt.

Erdrick's body spun counterclockwise, impossibly dodging an attack as his hand grabbed Dragan by the fabric of his shirt. With all his strength, he sent the man flying through the air toward the wall.

But the gods, or perhaps the Darkness itself, had blessed the baron with cat-like reflexes, for his feet met the hard surface, and, pushing himself, he jumped back, closing in quickly.

And while Dragan jumped back, Erdrick charged, rapier ready.

The swords, like the eyes of both men, met, Erdrick's eyes blazing with fury, Dragan's with immutable indifference.

The blades bounced off each other's crossguards, forcing each to take a moment to steady his blade again before turning to face one another.

'He is fast,' Erdrick thought. The usually quiet yet elegant cousin, who spoke with a proper, yet derisive accent, was faster than anyone he'd ever faced.

The prince turned again to face his challenger. He had to give his all, for he was the best of Darkholm, and the knights needed this land.

Both men dashed toward the other, Erdrick slashing in every direction. Dragan, with his edge steady, aimed toward a single spot on his thigh—the one that bled and gave Erdrick that temporary limp.

"Dragan," the knight saluted. "I am honored to have crossed blades with you. Your moves are uncanny."

Saluting back, his cousin replied, "I am mostly self-taught, driven only by the desire to defend the honor of the House."

Erdrick smiled as the House closed in.

The Knights needed the land he had just lost.

"Then the Barony of Ironforge," Vhimir announced, "as per the rules of the duel, will now be Dragan Darkholm's lands and property."

Sellayne's eyes filled with mirth, the pearls in her mouth showing as she smiled before kissed the man she supported and loved.

"Commander," Dragan said, "cousin."

"Dragan," Erdrick responded as Elleonora bandaged his wound.

"You can keep the land for the knights." The lithe man placed his crimson cape over his shoulder. "I could not care less for it. I fought only to test your skill and show you mine."

"The knights will be grateful," Erdrick responded. "Here, take my rapier. You will make better use of it than I."

Serverus Ecru walked into the main meeting chamber of the Black Knights, followed by Gustavus, who had been instructed to summon him, and who had found him secretly watching Rowena's departure from a window.

Erdrick sat by his desk across from Tenslea, Master of Lands, who ensured the proper documentation was signed in order for the lands to be transferred. She had assistants of her own now, but she did the work herself when involving royal lands, and also, hard to admit for her as it was, for almost every other piece of land. The rest of the knights were standing inside, in formation.

"Commander," Serverus saluted, "you summoned me."

"You were summoned, yes," Erdrick studied the map Tenslea had spread over the desk.

"All the way up to this small stream, Commander," Tenslea smiled. "It is quite fertile, the population is small, less than two hundred, but a knight's station there would bring more interest and help populate the barony."

Erdrick lifted a hand to halt the discussion.

"Serverus Ecru," Erdrick instructed, looking back at his adoptive brother as his finger touched the surface of the map, "Come. This is something you need to see."

Serverus did as instructed. Immediately, he approached the desk, his ecru-colored eyes on the map, but Erdrick signaled to him to walk around it.

"What do you see?" Erdrick asked.

"My lord," Serverus studied the landscape, the small hills, the various streams, and the main village, the swampy terrain, "all of this can be defended properly, with the proper time and resources to build a station, that is."

"What else?" Erdrick questioned, his eyes intently on Serverus.

The Black Knight looked again at the entirety of the geography detailed in the map, mumbling audibly, but unable to find out what in the world he was missing until he trailed Erdrick's finger pointing at where the signature of the baron would be printed, and the name written underneath was Serverus.

"My . . . my lord," Serverus looked at him, confused, "I do not understand."

"The barony is yours, Serverus," Erdrick responded.

"You only need to sign it to make it official," Tenslea smiled proudly, her eyes watering.

"But, my lord," Serverus asked, "was it not destined for the knights?"

"It is," Erdrick explained, "and as I prepare for the throne, you will be their new Commander, brother."

Serverus's eyes became moist, not as much from sadness but rather from the incredible honor he had just received. He, who had always struggled to feel deserving of all the blessings he had been given, has just been raised to the highest position he could have ever imagined.

How would they see him now? he asked himself, but he knew the moment Erdrick and the rest placed their fists upon their chests.

How would she see him now was the question he feared and didn't know how to answer.

"I salute my knight brothers," Serverus placed his own hand over his chest.

"Always knights," the rest responded in unison, "always brothers."

SIXTH TEST:
THE PROWESS

Location: Empyre of Suhne, City of Suhne

*S*even.

  The number appeared as a good omen, or perhaps as lucky to some cultures in Caerea, but to Vamya, what the number reminded her of today brought no comfort.

  "You called, Blessed One," the voice of Adulla, the new confidant among her Chosen, dispelled her thoughts and brought her back from wherever her mind wandered.

  "Yes," It was difficult for Vamya to consider her a confidant. Adulla had been chosen because of her intelligence, her knowledge of history, and nothing more. She had only become her confidant only after Aaghari had been removed, but she didn't know her enough to truly confide in her.

  "Your servant went for a massager," Adulla's statement seemed more like an accusation.

  "It is what I asked, yes."

  "You look *troubled*,"

  "Shouldn't I be?" Vamya stepped out of her pool; her servants quickly closed in to pat her body dry to help prepare her. "After Kaylen's performance, who isn't?"

  "He, for one, likely isn't, Blessed One."

  True . . . his disdain for others is not just an act, but part of who he truly is.

  As the last born, she was left with no choice but to accept the choices left for her.

  "Could I speak my mind?"

  "Always," the Sun of Change responded, "I want nothing more than honesty."

"You have people in your service," Adulla began, "good people, with no other desire than to see you succeed. In every way, your success is their success. And yet, you are seeking someone unknown to provide you with the same skills those close to you have."

"I mean no offense to my own," Vamya's hands touched the surface of the water, "but rather as a way to show people outside my ring that I trust and appreciate them."

"And you shouldn't," Adulla interrupted her musing, "this is not the time for that. You are not the Sun . . . at least not yet, so those outside your circle owe you nothing. They might look up to you for what you represent, but they don't fear you, they don't respect you, and so you shouldn't trust them, any of them."

Again, the mistrust. That word caved in to the innards of the spirit she thought she had built from marble. How could she trust, she wondered, when her most trusted friend had betrayed her not long ago, and his betrayal, even if justified, almost cost her everything she had worked for, everything she was destined to achieve.

She could easily dismiss the massager as soon as he walked through the door. Even if she wasn't the Sun yet, servants would bend to her will. She would be well within her right. Still, Vamya thought, would it be the right move? Would decisions get easier once she Ascended?

"Blessed One," Adulla's words brought her back to reality, "the massager is here."

The Child lay while, for over an hour, the servant worked, lathering his palms in scented oils, releasing the muscles of her near-naked body. While he worked in silence, Vamya did not stay quiet. Instead of focusing on her own interests and goals, she sought to gain understanding, to build trust, and for that, she directed her attention to Adulla to ask the woman about her own life.

She found out Adulla had been the youngest of eight girls in a family that produced no males. Her father, to reduce his burden, sold her to an aged historian when she turned six. As was expected of women in Suhne, she had not been taught to read. As his age advanced, however, her failing husband's eyes forced him to ask for her assistance, so the ink would not stain the parchments he wrote on. This allowed her to get close enough to teach herself to recognize the symbols he put on paper, the ones he called *lettrae*.

Although not much more than the bare minimum, the man had made provision for her, and that had made Adulla feel indebted to him. Therefore, upon seeing her first bleeding, she allowed him to take her for a wife, for which she received his bond chains and, before the age of fifteen, Adulla had given the man four children.

Despite her busy life rearing children and assisting her husband, every time she could, upon the Sun's rest, her curious interest in history took her to read what she could of his writings. And from what she learned was born a longing to one day leave Suhne, to see the world beyond and give her children, and herself, a better life.

"Upon my husband's death, I became his brother's," Adulla continued, "but food was scarce, and that made his other wives unhappy. They forced me to sell my three youngest children to a traveling merchant from Ahni to help provide for the family."

Vamya could not believe what she heard. She had been taught the people of Suhne went through hardships to better serve the Sun and for nothing more than its glory. Never had she imagined the hardships they went through just for sustenance and survival.

What would have been of Adulla's life today if Vamya would not have chosen her? If she had not overheard Vazga of the Flameguard tell the story of this woman who committed the great sin of having learned to read, and because of that, her own family was to exile her to roam the desert?

The Blessed One's demeanor changed. She wanted nothing more than to become the deity of her people, but she had made it her mission to protect and also provide for them. "Upon my Ascension, I ask you," Vamya looked into her eyes, "if you could get whatever your heart desired, what would that be?"

Adulla gazed out the window. She pondered carefully. Her onyx eyes were hopeful, but her lips would not move. Rolling on the bed, Vamya faced her. The Chosen's eyes briefly met Vamya's verdant ones before she lowered her head and found the courage to reply. "I would only ask for one thing if it was the Sun's will," her confidant bit her lower lip nervously, "for a chance to go to Basqh Ahni."

"Speak freely," Vamya looked at her tenderly.

"So I can cross the border to see the world."

Her words were something the Child of the Sun did not expect, "What about your children? Wouldn't you want to recover them, take them with you?"

"No, Blessed One. My children are not my own anymore," she responded. "They have an owner now."

"But," Vamya's hand touched that of her confidant, "what if you could get them back, free them?"

"Why would I want to?" Adulla smiled warmly at the gesture. "They'll live to worship you."

Vamya could not fathom what she had just heard. How could a mother simply abandon her children to whatever fate they had at someone else's mercy? Could she know, she wondered, when she had never been a mother herself?

The day would come, she knew. Then she would be able to truly know. But, as hard as she tried to, perhaps she would never truly understand, for no matter how much she tried, her life and decisions would be so much different than those of her subjects.

· ·+·+·+· ·

The morning Sun glared at a crowd of nearly a thousand standing from their seats, impatiently waiting for the parting of the doors to this arena that, while not the largest in Suhne, saw only the most seasoned warriors battle.

On a platform at the opposite side of the entrance rested an empty stone seat from where the Almighty Sun, whenever present, would have the best view.

Flanking it, all thirteen Rays, their robes of yellow a sharp contrast to the mostly neutral shades of the spectators' attire. Despite the subdued color of their clothing, these were not just regular Suhnites. The quality of their fabrics and jewelry in their bodies made it evident these were Lorq'a, lords and warlords, enforcers and high-ranking generals of the five main Basqhs of Suhne, and the Zetq'a, comprised of their relatives and wealthiest merchants, all those who set the socio-political machinery of Suhne in neverending motion.

Like in most instances, the Basqh of Htet was not represented, for while it existed under the protection of the Sun, its small population was composed of those criminals who survived exile. In this sacred city, like in almost every other part of Suhne, their presence was largely unwelcome.

Aside from the Lorq'a and the Zetq'a, the white robes of the Shimmers could be seen in their assigned places around the arena, always at the very first row. Other than them, only the inevitable members of the Flame Guard were deemed worthy of witnessing today's event. While the Chosen of each Blessed One did not belong to any of these, their unique position, removed from the hierarchy of Suhne, allowed them to witness and participate in events, although only at the behest of their Blessed One.

Vamya's quartet stood by her, Adulla still among their ranks. Their green presence dwindled in that jeweled sea of black and brown. Kaylen's vermilion presence was accompanied by what he had left, his own confidant, Itosh, and his only other remaining Chosen, that old man he had Itosh pick last.

"Chosen among the people of the Sun," the Speaker's voice thundered, silencing a thousand voices, "as the Eye of the Sun rises up in the heavens, so does our god himself rise from among us."

"Today, and twice more during these next seven days," he continued, "we will witness miracles performed by the Children of the Sun. In their individuality, shall we gauge the rising of the Sun."

"The Empyre of Suhne is powerful," Exis's eyes glanced at those on the platform before he raised his hands, his pupils traveling to the spectators, "and will only bow to the power of the Almighty, the all-powerful, the One Sun god.

"Children of the Sun, starting today, we test your prowess!" While they were typically a people of restraint and thus not as easily impressed as the *iqit* or *saqit* would be, the elite among Suhne were just as deeply religious. Exis's words played the strings within their hearts, and they chanted and they cheered.

"We will begin, as appropriate, with the firstborn, Malek, Son of the Sun!"

The massive doors to the arena opened to the blowing of horns and beating of drums. They gave way to a group of seven, garbed in browns and gold. Their walk, from that of the youngest to that of the eldest among the group, was steady and precise. One could even say proud.

Behind them, the hulking man with the bronze skin, his hair braided and pinned with a gold, sun-shaped adornment that held it in place behind his head. His chest was bare but for a tight belt that traveled across it, holding a pair of spears and a Suhnite *parash*[1] on his back. His thighs and feet were covered by nothing more than a brown, fine linen kilt and simple leather sandals.

Malek halted his advance. Lifting his hands, he addressed the crowd.

"People of Suhne," the firstborn roared, "the will of our Sun-god is for his Empyre to expand its borders, to destroy its enemies so that his people can prosper. The banner of the golden Sun will be flown proudly in every corner of the world, for Suhne's banner can only fall under the leadership of a weak god."

With a swift move of his hand, Malek dropped the belt to the ground. As soon as it touched its surface, it was followed by his kilt, which fell over his sandals.

All eyes were upon Malek, upon the golden tattoos that ran along the muscles of his magnificent, chiseled body and even along the shaft of his clearly visible and engorged manhood. Everyone was so distracted they didn't see the opening cage or the five leaving, or even the two that picked the weapons up, staying behind to help him face the charging ghur-ghaur.

"Now," his mood darkened as he bellowed, "behold the strength of your god."

Malek's bare feet pushed the ground, sending him directly into the path of the creature. Although not known for its speed, at nine hundred stones, the beast's momentum was nothing short of formidable.

The pair of slender, athletic men trailed the firstborn, moving swiftly toward the mountain of a beast.

Upon seeing the movement, the beast fumed, charging with a furious roar that shook the walls of the stadium. The ground trembled under its mass, its hooves' impacts like that of a hundred horses, lifting a trail of dust and pebbles in its wake.

Closing in, the ghur-ghaur lowered its head, ready to gore the Blessed One with its row of three sharp horns.

Malek dashed. With a quick move of his hand, he signaled to his men in what would seem to a philosopher a simple move, to the warriors, a dissertation. Following the silent command, the *parash* wielder doubled his effort, planting the end of his haft on the ground before circling it and kneeling to assist his partner.

Using the *parash* as a ramp, the second man jumped, his arm swinging in a deft, wide arc that saw a spear fly with lightning speed, nicking the ghur-gaur's ear and lodging itself in its shoulder.

The deafening roar from both the irritation and sharp pain sent the crowd cheering for the trio. But to these seasoned warriors, their celebration meant nothing. It was merely a distraction that was to be ignored.

Without a second wasted, upon his next signal, the three moved to circle the beast.

Vamya's attention was centered on the fight, on the perfect moves of Malek's men. Though she was no great warrior herself, she knew enough to comprehend their abilities were not easy to match. It was easy to understand why Malek had them by his side, but did he even really need them? He was, without a doubt, powerful, a force to be reckoned with.

'I wonder how Malek's children would be?' she wondered. 'Would they be as different from each other as we are? Would they be vicious? Would they be strong? Would they be caring? Could they be forgiving?'

'When I become the Sun ... would it be anathema to make Malek the father of my children?'

As uncomfortable as it made her feel and as wrong as she thought the idea was, she could only speculate. Throughout the history of the Empyre of Suhne, the Ascension had made it impossible. Thus, the situation had never presented itself. 'Now, when the time comes,' she thought, 'is this something I'm willing to change?'

Looking down, she smiled and blushed. Vamya knew, deep inside, she could never get involved with one of her siblings. It was just wrong in every way. It was surely Malek's captivating virility that made her think such nonsense. Malek's remarkable prowess demonstrated, without a doubt, her tireless brother had the blood of the Sun coursing through his veins.

'But what about Kaylen,' Her eyes then drifted to Kaylen, who was not paying attention to the battle. Instead, he was meticulously studying the reactions of both the solemn Rays and the noisy crowd, where the two daughters of Lorq'a Saasa, governor of Ahni, smiled, hugging each other, garbed in their colorful attire. Their hands reached down excitedly as if by doing so, they felt they could touch Malek and his men.

Again she looked back at Kaylen, who remained unmoved, watching.

'What does he see, I wonder. Kaylen's moves, actions, even words . . . everything about him is as if he lives in a different world than our own,' she mused. *'What would it feel to live, if at least one day, inside his mind?'*

'How different would everything be if the three of us could have worked together? Each of our strengths is different from one another's, and yet here we are, fighting, expecting to be judged the same.'

Vamya's beryl eyes returned to the scene below, to the wordless communication between Malek and his men, to the bond between them that allowed them to work seamlessly, efficiently, and at the complete trust they surely had in each other.

Malek's man has fallen!

Malek's spearman was kneeling, his elbows bent. The unsuccessful attempt to retrieve the spear from the ghur-ghaur had ended up in one of his triceps nearly fully torn. The *parash* warrior struck the creature, and hooking his weapon into one of the creature's plates, he vaulted over in an attempt to gather its attention. But the ghur-ghaur wasn't interested. Its huge head turned swiftly back to the spearman and right into contact with Malek's fist into its eye.

With lightning-like reflexes, the firstborn's hand clasped the beast's eyelid. Grunting, his fingers tore the skin out, exposing the eye of the beast, his feat sending the crowd into an ecstatic cheer.

Behind Malek's imposing figure, the wounded warrior picked up his remaining spear awkwardly and, holding his pain back as best as he could, he dashed away.

The ghur-ghaur roared and thrashed wildly, running away before turning, before its exposed eye fixed on the gold that ran through the Son of the Sun's body. Again the creature gained speed, but this time focused on Malek's frame.

Upon Malek's signal, the *parash* warrior struck his weapon's blade before spinning it overhead, its vibrating metal lifting the spirits of warriors of Suhne. After the display, his haft struck the ground.

The spectators jumped to their feet and cheered, but not as much as when they saw the beast's brief hesitation that allowed Malek to spin at the last second, and both dodge the impact and grab its main horn, yanking it hard enough to make the creature lose its balance.

Its loud crash lifted a cloud of dust so large it obscured the warrior's sight.

Malek cursed. His hand desperately rubbed his eyes to clear his vision before the ghur-ghaur recovered. Somewhere close, he could still hear its heavy snorting, the disturbance on the cloud, the vibration of the ground telling him the ghur-ghaur was readying itself to . . .

"Charge!" Malek shouted. The beast's passing barely missed the firstborn's feet as he leaped away, his back slamming solidly against the ground. Not too far from him, the *parash* warrior sidestepped instinctively, skillfully striking the creature. A stream of blood appeared where his *parash* had contacted the creature's thigh before it collided with him, sending him flying ahead.

The beast's momentum forced the warrior to tumble, trusting his instincts, rolling along the ground under the creature's body to avoid being crushed and thus save his life. And his life he saved, but he wasn't fast enough to save the *parash's* handle from being broken or to stop his femur's shattering under the ghur-ghaur's hoof.

His companion's attack was even less successful. His spearhead broke upon contact with the beast's head. He was quick enough to spin out of the way, graced by the gods of luck or cursed by those of mockery, who perhaps wanted him to remain a broken warrior, to live a life of disabled shame.

Malek grabbed the unwieldy blade of the broken *parash* and walked toward his warrior, who lay on the ground, his jaw clenched. Every attempt the man made to crawl ended in nothing but failure. Giving up on his attempt, he turned up and faced his leader and extended his hand so that Malek could help him stand or, at least, sit.

From atop the platform, Vamya and the rest of the stadium watched expectantly. At this crucial moment, all eyes were on him, all attention on his next action, for it would offer some insight into the mind of the firstborn.

In the blink of an eye, the arena filled with the man's screams as the blade in Malek's hands came down toward the ground, but only after passing through skin, flesh, and bone.

The multitude stood from their seats, some horrified, many others filling the air with cheers and admiration as Malek chopped, angling the blade time and again, exposing the sharpened tibial bone that he now grasped as a make-shift bone spear.

The ground increasingly trembled under the approaching hooves. Malek widened his stance, spreading his arms to his sides, his gaze upon the charging beast, his brow furrowed, his manhood firm and aroused, his demeanor more intimidating than that of the much larger beast.

He sidestepped, dodging the creature's furious gore. On the other side, the spearless warrior threw sand at the creature's eye, forcing its eyelid to close. Seeing an opening, Malek tumbled forward. With a half-turn, he forcefully drove the tibia into the ghur-ghaur's exposed eye, its burst drenching his arms in ichor.

The ghur-ghaur roared and reeled in pain, its large head shaking uncontrollably. At the opportunity, Malek jumped between its horns. As an ape from the deepest forests of Olath Valm, he held fast skillfully and navigated between the horns despite the violent shaking until he placed his hand around the stuck spear's shaft. Right after dislodging it, he jumped off the creature's head, swinging both arms down and hurling the spear into the creature's remaining eye.

Another ichor shower sprayed around the convulsing beast, another insane cheer of the raucous crowd followed the ghur-ghaur's fall. But Malek seemed unmoved by the celebration. While the ghur-ghaur was done fighting, he was not yet done.

Panting, the hulking man raised his foot and drove it down toward the middle horn of the creature. He stomped once, twice, and as many times as needed until he snapped the blade-like horn. Then, with a grunt accompanied by his great might, he plunged the horn into the creature's heart.

Vamya witnessed it all, the unruly celebration of the ecstatic crowd, the approving faces of the Rays, the squinting eyes of Kaylen watching the virgin daughters of Lorq'a Saasa, the youngest one crying in excitement, the other one's arm extended toward Malek, her eyes widely open, her irises disappearing behind her eyelids in what she would have believed were seizures if she had not caught the girl licking her own lips while one hand moved under the fabric of her skirt.

And she also witnessed Malek's combination of fury and indifference, the one that fueled his prowess, the other that allowed him to leave the arena, his one man following, holding his arm in place, the other left behind on the ground, bleeding to death.

(1) *Parash*: Single or two-handed, medium-sized battle-ax with one blade along a third of its haft and a bladed hook at its end.

SIXTH TEST:
THE MESSAGE

Location: Empyre of Suhne, City of Suhne

*Allowing a demon a moment in the center stage can
make one fair, but more so stupid . . .*

I t had been five days since Malek's event, and even today, it was hard to hear anything coming out of everyone's lips other than endless praise for his formidable performance. Soldiers told stories about his leadership, maidens spoke of his prowess, and even workers told exaggerated tales of the events that had transpired.

But there were no tales, not even a single word, about the men that had fought by his side, that had contributed, at least somewhat, to make it all possible.

Unlike her siblings, Vamya understood their sacrifice, or at least she thought she did. She hoped they themselves understood it too. For, right now, they would sacrifice all they were for the glory of the Sun, and the Sun, in turn, would find it upon its mercy to exalt them in the afterlife.

Today, however, was not that day.

Today was Kaylen's time to shine.

The Son of the Sun could have chosen any moment of the day. Kaylen had somehow decided for his participation to take place right at the very end of it, close to the time when the flaming Eye of the Sun would leave the firmament.

Vamya contemplated the distinct chamber her brother had chosen within one of the crystal domes that stood tall above the city. While this particular one was not among the tallest, like every building in the capital, to those within it allowed an unobstructed view of the Eye's journey through the sky. Its entire trajectory could be observed, all the way from the eastern horizon to the western Silver Peaks that, while distant, could still be appreciated.

On that same western side of the room, a very large vase rested upon the floor. The vase rose nearly ten feet high, its clay matte-red surface covered with black tracings that, when seen from certain angles, she noted, almost glittered.

From its base, three reddish *majada*[(1)] extended along the floor, the distance between them increasing as they moved away from under the vase itself. The *majada* ended where they met a fourth that lay perpendicular to the vase.

The two lateral ones were surrounded with seating pillows, the fourth with seating only on the side opposing the vase to allow those seated an unobstructed view of the center.

Unlike Malek's event, Kaylen's was not packed with people.

Every single individual present had been invited. Like everything else in this room, Vamya suspected, from the dishes to the lighting, to the music played by hidden musicians, and the seating arrangement, to the smallest detail, had likely been carefully selected and planned by her brother.

'Why would he choose a time so close to the Retiring[(2)]?' Vamya wondered.

'It is known the Sun is less powerful when its Eye departs at night.' The thought alone made her wary, and, she suspected, more than those who would care to admit it among those present felt the same or worse.

She found it odd that while Malek and his men sat, like her, at one side of differing dining carpets, and the Rays close to Exis lining the fourth, only the old man among Kaylen's remaining Chosen was seated and close to her, almost dozing off.

Adulla and Zofer, of her own Chosen, like most guests, partook in the small delicacies while Vamya looked over the guests, searching for Kaylen. It would have been easy to spot him among the few guests and his red, by far mostly ostentatious attires. Even Itosh, his confidant, would have easily seen had he been in the room.

Giving up, instead, she studied those who were in attendance.

Among them were the Lorq'a of the Basqhs of Suhne and the highest among the Zetq'a[(3)] and representatives in influential positions; also, a few with no real power but surely good connections. One thing Vamya found odd—the presence of Lorq'a Saasa's daughters. Although Zetq'a, the two were younger than the rest and not really involved in the political arena of Suhne. They were seated at the very end of each lateral *majada,* where their backs could almost touch the scarlet jar. The children of the other Lorq'a had not been invited.

A sudden, restless tumult by the entrance drew her attention. She quickly looked around, noting most of the other guests remained unbothered.

"Do you know what's the matter?" Vamya asked her Chosen.

"It must be Lorq'a Yada of Alm, Blessed One," Adulla responded.

"So late?"

"Oh no, Lorq'a Yada has been fighting to be allowed in since our very own arrival."

"What is the problem then?" Vamya questioned.

"I overheard the guards had instructions to disallow such flamboyant attire. In order to gain entrance, Lorq'a Yada was instructed to tone it down."

Not long after, the tumult had come to a stop.

The calm was followed by the entrance, by the ringing music of jewelry unseen, by the graceful walk of a tall, somewhat large feminine figure of Yada, garbed in a black, loose garment that covered everything except for the eyes and even those were hidden behind a mesh.

"Well," Vamya continued, "Lorq'a Yada must understand that, even though one day I will free all women, there are norms that she must follow. This *is* a sacred place." To her words, Adulla only looked back at her with a silent smile.

Before Vamya could continue, Lorq'a Yada had found a place to sit, and it was right in front of her.

Vamya inhaled the delicious aroma of citrus, vanilla, and sweet jasmine coming from Yada. The *niqab*, she noted, was a little ill-fitting for someone of the Lorq'a's size. Its material was also not one of the high quality she would expect of someone of such a station.

'What could I say to make her feel at ease?' Vamya thought.

"Lorq'a Yada," Vamya finally spoke, making sure those close to her could hear, "I loved your entrance, the enrapturing aroma of your perfume. I very much loved your walk. I am certain you are and will always be an inspiration to all women." Vamya's blood simmered when she overheard more than a few mocking laughs around her.

"Thank you," Lorq'a Yada nonetheless responded.

But the response left Vamya speechless.

While it sounded warmly honest, grateful, and even humble, Yada's leaning forward allowed Vamya to see the colorful, glittering, and alluring makeup the mesh was hiding; and through that mesh, Yada's eyes, much like the voice, were those of a man.

The starters had continued coming.

Vamya had sought to keep herself engaged in conversation with her Chosen, to hide the embarrassment on her face she hoped no one had noticed. But every so often, she caught others looking at her and laughing, and she found herself glancing at the Lorq'a, and each of those times, she found Yada's silent, now uncovered eyes on her.

She smiled at Yada but looked away the moment she felt the slight spasm on her lips that made her afraid others would notice it was a masquerade.

Did something deep inside her find Yada repulsive? She realized she didn't, but there was certainly a decorum, an ingrained belief within Suhne that what Yada represented was, in many ways, wrong. There were many who were living a very different life in the very same world.

'Where does one draw the line when every line drawn will divide beliefs?' she wondered.

If she was truly the change Suhne needed, she thought, she had to learn to embrace those who, like Yada, still followed the Sun, although walking a different path and in their very own way.

"Blessed One," Adulla interrupted her thoughts, "Lorq'a Saasa's daughters are here. Look."

"Yes," Vamya responded, "I noticed. What do you think is Kaylen's fixation with either of Lorq'a Saasa's daughters?"

"Presiding over the Basqh of Ahni in the south is a great deal," Adulla responded. "Lorq'a Saasa is, even among the heads of every basqh, probably the most powerful of all the Lorq'a."

"That cannot be. They all hold equal power."

"I don't mean any offense, Blessed One, but you have been sheltered," Adulla responded. "Yes, all men are equal under the Sun, but the truth of the matter is that even among equals, there is a perceived hierarchy. While his land is smaller, Ahni's famous oases alone make it almost as rich as the capital. Also, while not as militant as Alm and Lmet at its east and west, Ahni's south is our most fertile border, one it shares with three out of the four kingdoms neighboring our Empyre. That alone makes it the Empyre's keystone to the south."

Adulla's words struck a chord within Vamya. Even if she had wanted to disagree, she knew her words were true. The last few months, even just moments ago, she had experienced how different things were at times from what she had been taught. She could only speculate how much more different they could be when there was an entire world she hadn't experienced beyond Suhne.

"I am not so innocent as to not understand this places Lorq'a Saasa in a most powerful position in Suhne," Vamya spoke. "Perhaps, by charming his daughters, Kaylen is seeking to ingratiate himself with him."

"Blessed One," Adulla's eyes met with hers, "Perhaps, you should do the same."

Dinner came upon them, an array of camel and horse meat delicacies, dried tortoise feet, honey-covered dates, and flat, soft breads. They were accompanied by wine from both Ahni's hills and the elevated steppes of Alm.

Even seated, Lorq'a Saasa and his wife, Venu, were as radiant as the jewels in his turban, drawing attention to themselves with their charismatic smiles, always sharing stories with those willing to listen.

Venu smiled broadly with plump lips through pearly teeth that continued to show even when most of the attention was on her husband.

'Where do I start?' Vamya wondered.

She had never spoken directly to the highest-placed Lorq'a of Ahni, and, at this point, she had just moments to give an impression.

But what impression did she want?

She hesitated. Was it that of a goddess, planting her feet on the ground, summoning respect and capturing the eyes of all present, or that of a warm woman, of an approachable leader with a caring heart?

Women in Suhne were considered weak, but how could she even hope to enact change, she thought, if she didn't start embodying that change herself?

Vamya waited for the perfect opening in Saasa's speech, for that perfect moment that would allow her to draw all attention. He was telling a tale of his travels along the lands of his neighbors, of his meetings with highlords and counts, dukes, and even princes, his speech paving the way to the subject of the salt mines he recently discovered. 'There it is,' she thought.

"Lorq'a Saasa," as in Suhnite custom, Vamya rose slightly to address him and garner his attention.

"Yes, Blessed Child of the Sun," he rose in turn.

"Your mention of the salt mine piqued my interest."

"I am glad it did," he smiled with a raised eyebrow. "This new salt mine is a great discovery. It will bring greater prosperity."

"Ahni has been, in many ways, graced by the Sun, and for that, its citizens must always be thankful," Vamya sought to redirect the attention from the material prosperity of Ahni to the spiritual wealth that was key to the Empyre's existence.

"Yes, it is a gift bestowed by the Almighty Sun to our people, and I haven't even begun to speak details of the mine's magnificence."

"It must be certainly beautiful," Vamya smiled in response. "The salt mines are but one of the many blessings Basqh Ahni has received."

"One of the many things that make Basqh Ahni unique among the lands of the Sun."

"Innumerable are the gifts that place Ahni in an esteemed place among the people of the Sun. But the Sun likewise blesses all the lands of Suhne in countless ways, with great marvels that are equally beautiful. This will be a daily reminder," she continued, "to all of its creation that, under the guidance and protection of the Almighty, all are judged and considered equally."

Many nodded in agreement. Lorq'a Saasa, however, did not. His hand stroked his beard slowly, repeatedly.

"Blessed be the Sun," his wife lifted her arms, seeking to drive attention away from her brooding husband, her words echoed by most.

"Blessed Child of the Sun," Saasa had risen again, his words again drawing attention, his eyes squinting "have you ever visited the salt mines of Ahni?"

"No."

"The underground oasis?"

"I have not."

"Oh, the Rose Pyramid?"

"I have not had the chance to visit these marvels myself."

"Then how," Lorq'a Saasa's hand stroked his beard as masterfully and as carefully as he questioned, "if you have never left the capital, can you compare the mines of Uhn and the Ocarina Range of Alm, or even within Ahni, how can you compare the beauty of the pyramids, the shifting dunes, with that of our oases? If you have never left the city, you have much less traveled beyond the borders of our Empyre to know what is truly magnificent in this world. How do you speak of that which you have not seen?"

"The Child of the Sun has never traveled far beyond the city borders," Exis intervened, his voice appearing to both soothe and poke at a freshly open wound, "for her own protection from any potential harm.

"She is, however, well instructed," he continued with a sly half smile, "she can describe the beauty of the Empyre's confines from what she has learned."

After his words, all conversation ceased. No other sound came, not even that of cutlery or plates. Had she been the Sun, Lorq'a Saasa's insolence could have been punished swiftly before she had, at the very least, scolded Exis for his disrespect.

But she wasn't the Sun, or at least not yet.

Vamya could have opened her mouth and spoken of everything she had seen, everything she had experienced beyond that shell of her body, things beyond what anyone could have ever imagined. But would that achieve anything? Would everyone be filled with wonder or with fear? Besides, what could she truly say when she did not clearly understand her visions and experiences herself?

Vamya's fingers trembled. This was another situation she needed to dismiss. She needed to detach herself from the emotion, and yet she couldn't, not when her response was expected, and they needed to be words filled with wisdom.

While this wasn't planned as such, in its own way, this was yet another test.

Vamya found herself standing from her seat. "While I may not have made myself present in any of those places, how dare you presume what my eyes have seen?" her emerald eyes moved from Exis to Saasa and back.

"Should someone who is born blind then be also mute? Or should the mute be deemed ignorant because they have seen in a way we cannot comprehend? Should they not be allowed to speak of the things their physical eyes have never seen?

"Our eyes do not need to see to witness the marvels the Sun has created to know they are marvelous, to know they are, in many more ways than we know, beautiful and perfect.

"You cannot begin to comprehend the mysteries of the immortal Sun; it is by the Sun's finite mercy that you speak."

Vamya's words had mesmerized Saasa's wife, whose eyes glittered with hope. All other eyes were upon her, but all lips were closed. Even Saasa's were as sealed as a tomb. Exis's eyes challenged her, but he had also quiesced. If it was out of a newfound respect for her, for admiration of her words, or to simply avoid an unnecessary confrontation that could jeopardize the ever-precious *status quo,* Vamya wasn't sure, but she did know the Speaker knew better, at this moment, than to speak.

'I did it,' she thought, 'I have their undivided attention.'

She realized she was smiling, a smile everyone could see. It was not that of a firm goddess nor of a warm and caring leader. Somehow, if at least for just a moment, she had managed to incarnate both.

But her moment was not long-lived.

The crashing of cymbals summoned all attention to the room's entrance.

There, garbed in a hooded *kaftan,* the shades of light rust, Itosh's face was covered but still visible within a mask made of the translucent shell of a dune tortoise. His arms held over his head an engraved, black bow made from a pair of beetle horns. Behind him, pairs of dancers represented the city of Suhne and the basqhs around it. Both males and females wore red *bedlahs,* the tops and bottoms made of silk so fine it left nothing to the imagination.

Around their waist, each dancer held a silver hoop that, while it enhanced their dance, also limited their moves.

Each step they took flowed, like a song, each one followed by the beat of a drum, by a sharp cymbal, by the snakelike movement of their limbs that appeared to have extra joints in the most impossible of places.

The group danced their way into the room, following Itosh, whose own feet brought him to the *majada* at the center, near the end closest to the Rays.

Itosh raised a fist, and the music stopped.

"All of Suhne," though muffled, his voice was clear and loud enough in the perfect acoustic of the silenced chamber, "and the lands known and unknown beyond its borders will bow under the power of the one true Sun."

He opened his palm for all to see, revealing a painted, russet sun, its rays drawn on each of his fingers.

At the sign, the dancers dropped the hoops they held. They turned in every direction, flailing their arms up, their red attire reminding Vamya of uncontrolled flames in a fireplace. The last two, however, dashed toward each side of the red vase. They each pulled an ear, opening the vase down the middle before kneeling on the ground.

"Behold," Itosh pointed as he shouted, "He who will Ascend, the Searing Sun of Suhne!"

From the open vase, Kaylen emerged, clad in extravagant reds, like a legendary, ruby-studded peacock.

His lower body was covered by a long skirt that almost hid his feet and was part of a single piece of fabric that flowed loosely and also formed the cape over his shoulders. Other than his scarlet tattoos, his sinewy, barren torso was partially covered by an *usekh* mounted with garnets, rubies, and onyxes.

But even his marvelous attire was dwarfed by the headdress of the sun he wore, the one hiding all of his hair and neck behind an ornamented crown mounted in gemstones of varying shades of red while exposing and accentuating the angles of his delicate features.

Unlike every other time, his face was not adorned by piercings, giving him a nearly perfect symmetry, the appearance nothing short of a beautiful and graceful, yet unmerciful, fire deity.

The vase shut behind him as the Searing Sun emerged, his steps announced by the beat of drums, by the rhythmic waving of his heavily adorned fingers resembling claws ringing like tiny bells. Their heads down, each pair of dancers knelt as he progressed along the carpet.

"The Sun," Kaylen began reciting, "has always been."

At his words, the dancers formed a circle around him, lifting their arms, their hands fluttering like flames.

"His hands formed the earth and shaped the mountains. From his breath came the wind." Using their bodies, the dancers turned and twirled to echo the tale he told. He took the bow from Itosh and moved little, but yet always found himself at the center of the performance, now strumming the bowstring every so often, adding a somber note to his tale.

"So great was his power," the musicians now produced deeper notes, "that from his nightmares, the Dark One came forth.

"And the birth of darkness weakened him, and he became hungry for sustenance, for worship, for revenge.

"So the Sun created mankind in his image, and he produced the first four, and their worship strengthened him every day. The Dark One, in turn, sought to steal his creation, creating beasts and fearsome creatures from the humans the Almighty had formed. He sought to corrupt the four but found he could not, for the Sun's divine blood coursed through their veins.

"And thus, the Dark One found out that his power was dwindling because his beasts would not worship. So, in his avarice, he instead decided to seduce man. His promises planted greed, envy, and doubt in the hearts of the Sun's worshippers, for he knew he could not bring himself up, so instead, he would take away worshippers to bring the Sun down.

"The Dark One's followers would meet at night after the Eye of the Sun had retired and closed. But so distrusting was the Dark One of his own people that he cast out his own pale eye into the heavens to keep watch on lawbreakers, the disloyal and unfaithful.

"The Sun sees all that transpires under his watchful Eye," Kaylen's own eyes moved from one guest to the next, "but as the powerful, Almighty Creator of all, he knows even that which his Eye hasn't seen.

"For while the Sun's Eye is closed, his ears are always open."

Kaylen smiled an unnerving smile, and his eyes of hazel fixed on Lorq'a Saasa.

How long the stillness of that moment lasted was hard to tell, but Vamya knew it was uncomfortably long before Kaylen spoke once again.

"What is the price of betrayal?" Kaylen's voice was seductive yet firm. "What happens to those who cross the Sun?

"Speaker," he signaled.

Rising slightly from his seat, Exis responded assuredly, "The Sun Almighty is our god. Betrayal of the Sun is the gravest sin." His words were followed by nods from the other Rays.

"How is it punished?" Kaylen questioned.

"It is up to the Sun to decide," Exis responded, "but the custom is the traitor's family is slain or burned dishonorably before he is made to atone with a desert exile."

Kaylen smiled broadly.

"Lorq'a Saasa here," Kaylen's eyes moved back toward him, "has been meeting and making special arrangements in an attempt to garner votes for my brother on the day of the Ascension."

At the accusation, Saasa lit like tinder but still was able to keep his cool. "Blessed One, you are mistaken."

"Mistaken," Kaylen scowled, "it took ten gold *mahks*[(4)] per messenger and nearly two hundred to be split between Yeq and Q'to of the Rays."

All eyes went to the two youngest of the Rays. Yeq, the youngest of the two, lowered his eyes and clutched his hands. Q'to appeared calmer.

"Child of the Sun," Exis interrupted the moment he saw Q'to open his mouth to speak, "it is our hope this is not the case. Would you like to share your findings so that we can clarify? It might be some sort of misunderstanding."

"I will not play your game, Speaker. I do not need to prove to you what I know is real."

"Then allow me to theorize, Child of the Sun," Exis replied, "what you might believe is an attempt to manipulate the vote is likely the discussion among men. It is not uncommon for these to occur, for opinions to be shared among our leadership. Besides, in order for the Sun to be betrayed, one would have to be the Sun."

"Foolish Speaker," Kaylen's eyes narrowed, "you believe yourself the mouth of the Sun when you are nothing but the lips of the Rays. When I Ascend, those lips will be shut."

"And to those thinking about it," he looked back at the Lorq'a, "when the time comes, I will have each traitor's family cut into pieces and burned, their ashes fed to the traitor. And I will then have each traitor cut and burned, piece by piece, and fed to themselves so that they consume their own betrayal as their own betrayal has consumed their souls."

His eyes went to the vase at the end of the *majada*. Kaylen's hand reached out to Itosh, who handed him a single, black-tipped arrow.

The music rose again, and to its melody, the dancers moved once more. Their hands grabbed the hoops from the floor and lifted them up, spinning them and dancing around gracefully, drawing everyone's attention.

But Vamya's eyes stayed on Kaylen, on how he drew a small amount of a thick substance which he deftly rolled with the tip of his fingers, rubbing it over the arrow's tip before anyone noticed.

Nocking the arrow, he drew the bow and pointed toward the vase. The dancers walked toward the center, moving their arms in wide circles at varying speeds.

As the sun disappeared on the horizon, the music slowly changed to a darker yet still seductive melody that somehow made Kaylen appear both large and dangerous.

"Unlike my sister," Kaylen's voice was full of scorn, "I am not here to charm you but rather to show you what happens to those who dare cross me."

His fingers let the arrow go. It flew through every ring the dancers spun and toward the large vase. Upon impact, a spark at the tip ignited, provoking an explosion that shook the floor and sent a thousand shards of all sizes flying in every direction, most of them caught by the skin and bodies of Lorq'a Saasa's daughters.

Dancers ran in every direction, as did most of the guests except for Saasa's wife, whose cry turned into a horrific shrill. Aided by Adulla and Zofer, Vamya ran out the main entrance.

She looked back one last time. Amidst the chaos, a most disturbing scene— Kaylen leaving, walking calmly along the ground covered in shards of clay and blood, while everything around him burned—the curtains, the carpets, and the writhing bodies of Saasa's daughters.

(1) majada: dining carpets. Suhnites sit on pillows while they consume their meals around a carpet where the food is placed.
(2) The Retiring: the moment the Eye of God leaves the sky, nighttime.
(3) Zetq'a: the noble class of Suhne, the highest among them is the Lorq'a.
(4) Mahk: currency of Suhne. On its head, the Sun. Tails, the domed city of Suhne. It is worth half of the Blackheart droplet and Ardenay state.

SIXTH TEST: THE WALK

Location: Suhne Empyre, outskirts of the City of Suhne

*How much of what's inside ourselves is true, and
how much are the lies we tell ourselves . . .*

A hawk flew in search of prey high above the northeastern region of the city of Suhne's confines. From here, its eyes could see where every Basqh touched the city of Suhne, all but Htet of the exiled, to extend nearly infinitely, stopped only by the ocean or the distant kingdoms of nonbelievers.

It could also see the canyon below, the one named Uhn's Gift, which served as a natural protection between the capital city and the Basqh, although it also made it more difficult to cross from one to the other. The dry, rocky border region was bathed in shadows cast by its own cracked body.

Could the bird fly down into that dangerous abyss, away from the hot touch of the sun on the brown feathers of its wings?

The hawk glimpsed a single mammal—a large, fat rodent feeding on a smaller, famished one. Killing it would perhaps provide the small, weaker ones a chance to thrive. It would thus increase their population, making the hawk an unsung hero among its own kind, who could more easily find sustenance, and also among rats, who would not have to watch for greedy enemies among their own kind.

But what did a hawk know about that? It dove down toward its fat prey.

A horn blared close by, startling the rodent, sending it dashing along the flat, earthen surface and between the feet of inadvertent men and toward the escarpment's edge from where it jumped—barely missing the sharp claws that, if not for the heaviness of the rodent's body, would have torn into its abdomen.

Both the treacherous rodent and the hungry hawk continued down the precipice. The one falling, its body tumbling along the hard surfaces that would leave it concussed, scuttering along the rocks to disappear from view and allow it to recover. The other, spreading its wings that turned its lightning-like descent into a graceful glide, allowing its eyes to adjust in this new, shadowy place among jutting, unpredictable rocks.

They went on, now below the precipice, where a multitude of men recited and shouted under the glaring heat of the punitive sun they worshipped.

Their paths parted, to perhaps never cross again, for while one sought healing and the other one sustenance, within these shadows, they each found life.

———————— ·+++++·+ ————————

For hours, the Eye of the Sun had been rising over a clear sky, its flaming presence watching the large pavilion that rested along the path leading to the top of the canyon.

Inside that pavilion, servants moved diligently under the command of Adulla, who was giving instructions to Vamya's remaining Chosen. Zofer had been ready in case his voice was needed, sitting calmly, humbly waiting.

"Do you wish to be surprised, Blessed One?" Adulla questioned, her eyes on the Child of the Sun, who was studying her own reflection in a mirror. Vamya's hair was held up in a single braid wrapped around itself in the back of her head, from which golden and green feathers emerged. The details exalted the beauty of her facial features, for all but her face and hands were covered under a bright green, plain cape.

"Tell me," the Child responded.

"Aside from the Lorq'a, we have a good number of Zetq'a, not even close to the Conquering Sun's demonstration, but definitely more than the Searing Sun's."

"It is without a doubt Malek's event would bring a great attendance. His display is what our people know. Kaylen . . ." Vamya continued, "Kaylen's limitations were imposed by himself, which allowed him better control while denying us a view of the support he has garnered."

"But this is still quite good."

"Let's not fool ourselves," Vamya's reflection spoke to her confidant, "surely some of the nobles are here so that they can be counted as present. If I were to be victorious, they would want to avoid my wrath. But, in their hearts, they would do everything in their power to stop my Ascension."

"Some surely rally behind you, Blessed One, especially after word of your brother's event has spread."

"Some might, but don't you think that's perhaps what he wanted? To spread fear?" Vamya questioned. "People are more ready to embrace horror than to accept change."

"But those forgotten want that change, Blessed One."

"It is not of the working *iqit* or the lowest *saqit* that I speak of, Adulla," Vamya responded, "but rather of the powerful, of those men who have made themselves too comfortable in their lofty seats. Their greatest nightmare is change. Change would allow their injustices to be righted, and, to them, that's the greatest wrong."

Vamya's confidant nearly shuddered in excitement, speaking through a wide smile, "You speak with divine wisdom, Blessed One."

Vamya nodded in acknowledgment of her words, "Was that all you had for me?"

"There's more," Adulla smiled, opening the pavilion door behind her to allow the commander of the Flame Guards in.

The tall man lowered his head, muscled body lightly armored, adorned with the tan sun of the previous generation.

"Blessed Child of the Sun."

"Blessed are you, Usat," Vamya responded.

"The Flame Guard is ready to escort you," Usat spoke.

"To escort me? I have no need of an escort." Vamya frowned. "Who commanded it? The Speaker?"

"The Speaker did command it," the commander said in earnest, "but even if he had not, I would have given the order to my men."

Before she responded, the warrior continued, "Nearly two thousand among the *iqit* and *saqit* have come to witness your miracles today."

Vamya's emerald eyes opened wide in a mix of both disbelief and excitement she tried to contain. "There would have been many more, but they have been held back."

"Held back?" Vamya challenged, "Why are they being held back? They should be allowed to become witnesses. It is for them that I stand."

"For safety reasons, Blessed One."

"For safety . . ." Vamya advanced toward the pavilion entrance. "Had they been treating our people the way they deserved to be treated, those who believe themselves above them would have little need for safety."

"It is for *your* safety, Blessed Daughter." the warrior placed himself in her way. She wanted to protest. Her words and will were a command that had to be obeyed without question by everyone but the Ascended Sun itself. How dare he stand in her way?

As much as she wanted to say, to shout, his words had shaken Vamya to the core.

It was the first time someone had acknowledged her, not someone expected to, like her Chosen or servants. It wasn't someone she had to confront as she had done to Exis himself. Here was a mortal man who was bound to protect the Sun god. He was raised to believe there was little value in women, and none in those women whose existence stained the lineage of the Sun. He called her 'blessed,' he acknowledged her womanhood, and he wanted to protect her.

Vamya remained quiet, her every word echoing in the glistening of her moist eyes. She only nodded, allowing the man to step out before her to ensure everything was in order. In less than a minute, her spirit had filled with a confidence she had never felt before.

"Zofer," Vamya addressed the young man before she walked toward the entrance, "your voice will not be needed."

Adulla opened the door for her. "You *will* be victorious."

"Do you really believe so?" Vamya set her eyes on the crowd that appeared behind the door's fabric.

"I really do," Adulla responded, "and I should never believe it more than you should."

High above, the sun rose, close to its highest point in its heavenly journey. Slowly but surely, she climbed, like the eye in the sky, allowing every witness to capture this moment in his or her mind, for it would be the story they would tell their children's grandchildren one day.

Vamya's sandals touched the earth outside her pavilion, where the expectant crowd stood to each side of the path leading toward the top of the canyon.

Ahead of her, Usat led the way, followed by two columns of the Flame Guards armed with the spears and shields of their station. They kept their distance from Vamya to allow everyone an unobstructed view of the Daughter of the Sun while they were still close enough to protect her if needed.

Close to her pavilion, the humble *saqit* waited. While their actions and lifestyle did not honor the will of the Sun god, they were nonetheless believers. None among them had ever dreamed of being present in such an important event. They lowered their heads or closed their eyes the moment she walked past them.

After them, the *iqit*, who comprised the majority of Suhne. Some girls were garbed in colorful attire reserved for virgins. Although a few had precious stones, most of their bodies were adorned with baubles and stone, the majority of which had been handpainted to give the impression of greater value and to exalt each virgin's beauty.

A row of guards separated them from the limited Zetq'a, who dressed as the *iqit*, but all of them with fine fabrics and precious stones mounted in the jewelry that adorned their bodies. Although noble, they themselves were followed by two rows of Flame Guards to protect the Lorq'a and the Rays on top of the canyon where a raised stone platform rested.

The structure itself was a circular, smooth slab that was used as an altar where sacrifices were made to the Sun god. Five stone columns were erected on the stone around the altar, indicating the direction of each of the Basqhs of Suhne. Outside the platform, a single column faced northwest. A series of ropes wrapped around the platform's legs and converged under the structure, from where its taut body traveled all the way across a narrow portion of the canyon and onto an identical platform on the other side.

The Rays stood around the platform, some clearly bothered. They had argued the altar was sacred to the Sun and could not be used for show, but Vamya had quickly shot down their argument, reminding them this was just stone, and what was sacred was not the stone but the actions of those who sacrificed in it.

To the left and right of the platform, her siblings watched. Malek, with the three Chosen remaining under him. Kaylen, to the side, with his pair. He wore a wide, flat hat with veils that kept his face under shade, and that made it easier for him to steer attention away from the cane he still sometimes used.

Even after the whole tragedy resulting from Kaylen's performance, not much had been done. Lorq'a Saasa and his wife had spoken up, but having no Sun to judge, the Rays had taken over.

The Speaker had held an audience to hear their plea, perhaps to remind the Suhnite leadership that, while there was no Sun on the throne, the priesthood was unquestionably in charge. He had listened to Lorq'a Saasa, to the grief of his wife, Venu. After each of the Rays had expressed themselves, Vamya found that, while they were often divided in their opinions, in this, they were as one.

The Rays had unanimously decided judgment, once again, would be passed not by them but by the new Sun after the Ascension.

But as supreme as their judgment was in these times, Vamya suspected the real reason behind their unanimity was simple: Kaylen could not be held accountable, at least not by them. The Sons of the Sun were above mortal men, and so the Rays, try as they might, could never really touch them. Had the Rays attempted to judge him, the hesitation and opposition of many among Suhne's

Lorq'a and Zetq'a could have shown, in the eyes of the populace, a crack in the Suhnite perception of the priesthood's absolute power.

Kaylen appeared to be smiling, not a smile of actual happiness, of joy, but rather one of contempt, one that seemed to say, 'Without hesitation, I would just as easily do it again.'

Followed by her four remaining Chosen and by the crowd stopped only by the guards around it, Vamya stepped onto the platform. From the base of the manmade structure, a long rope stretched taut, crossing over a narrow section of the chasm and ending at the base of an identical platform on the other side.

High above, the Eye was approaching its Zenith.

Vamya waited until the moment when even the wind itself stopped its song. Without turning, without a single signal, her feet left the ground to let her sandals drop into Adulla's ready hands. This was the last thing Adulla knew. Vamya had ensured to give instructions, but she had spoken to no one, not even her closest confidant, about her plan.

Her bare feet sought to find her footing on the rope, walking steadily and yet carefully, like a crane hunting for fish along the Basqh of Ahni's ponds.

Blessed I am.

Spreading her arms to the sides, she recurred to her faith to keep her balance.

Blessed am I.

Her feet trembled, but Vamya paid no heed. Many behind her needed to succeed, and her fear of that moment could never be greater than the fear those who supported her claim had. They knew in their hearts that if Vamya didn't Ascend, their own lives would crash down, descending into pits from where their families would never climb out.

Halfway along the tightrope, Vamya placed a hand over her brooch and turned to face the crowd.

She saw them all, but from where she stood, she could not see their expression. Could she just send her being toward them and see them all? Perhaps, but what if her brothers could see her? So far, she had only done so while meditating privately. She couldn't risk it. Even if it went unnoticed, it would place her body in danger of falling.

Besides, she felt she didn't have to see them firsthand in order to correctly guess what they were doing. Of the Rays, Exis would be frowning. Old Seiris would have his perpetual, soft smile. Zurek would likely puff in protest. Malek would be looking at her like she was a waste of time and resources, while Kaylen would be sneering back.

Among the people, she imagined all expressions, mostly anger and inse-curity among the nobles and delight and admiration from those who were not. Even that . . .

Wait, who's that?

Vamya's eyes moved away from the crowd toward the west side of the canyon, where a lone figure stood by a horse, its entire body covered in a black *safseri*[1].

The wind picked up again. While slow, its unobstructed path toward Vamya was dangerous enough in itself. She looked up to the sky, where she saw the Eye right at its highest point.

This was the first time all eyes were on her, the eyes that praised her, the ones who judged her, the ones who loved her uniqueness, along with those who hated her perseverance. This was the time she was waiting for.

Zenith is coming . . . This is my moment . . .

"The Almighty Sun is as powerful as its legacy is eternal. So great is its force that nothing can stand before it." Her voice echoed around the canyon. "But the Almighty's strength would be its weakness if, in its infinite might, it can't show mercy, it can't show restraint."

The rising gusts of wind blew once more. In a single move, Vamya removed her brooch and allowed the chaotic wind to take her green cape away, to send it flapping toward the canyon wall.

And there Vamya stood, all eyes on her perfect, near-naked body, her silhouette adorned with dozens of mirrors, their perfect polish giving her the appearance of a divine being.

She arched her arms, capturing the sunlight in every reflective surface, scattering the light around in a mesmerizing display of dazzling light.

Vamya walked, every step careful and planned, the flashing lights she produced forcing many to cover their eyes and others to shout in excitement.

"The same Sun that burns, that scolds, is the Sun that protects, heals, and pardons . . ." She then directed the light near the base of the platform, where dried branches and bushes were set ablaze, all while ensuring the crowd re-mained unharmed.

The Eye reached the Zenith, augmenting the light that could be seen from miles away.

Within her, Vamya felt a spark that, in a single heartbeat, set her blood vessels on fire.

For weeks, many would lose their lives climbing down the canyon in an attempt to fetch the cloak some swore had the essence of the divine.

It was a day many would remember, the day when the Rays, her siblings, and only a few of the nobles remained standing. For the rest, there was no doubt this was a divine display. It was a day of humility, when the crowd's eyes were filled with tears, and Adulla wept. It was a day where even the knees of many who had opposed her touched the ground, and a chorus of two thousand chanted praise. It was a day many reconciled, one when new alliances were formed.

It was a day when that lone figure raised its open palm to praise the Sun that touched its heart and rode for weeks back home to spread the word of the divine miracle it had witnessed.

(1) *safseri*: a large piece of cloth covering the whole body. Typically made of silk, cotton, or satin. It is typically worn by women.

FRIENDS

Location: Kingdom of Blackheart,
Royal Duchy of Darkholm, Darkholde Keep

Some friendships are best when they don't exist . . .

'Hmph,' Ianne grunted, squeezing through the familiar crack in the wall.

He had found that crack long ago, if that could be said of any moment of his short life, inside a stable stall, on one of those days he searched for how to make himself useful and for someone to talk to. It was here that he had found 'the way.'

And it was this crack in the unassailable walls of the fortress that Ianne had come to know so well, for while the rest of the Darkholm were busy, the youngest of them all wandered out into the city, looking for something to do, for what he longed the most, searching for a friend.

Today he had found squeezing through a little harder than other times, but still, he smiled upon his ultimate success. One day, soon enough, he wouldn't fit through, like the times when taking sides becomes too hard and one simply must make a choice. But those thoughts didn't cross his mind, not yet, for Ianne, the youngest of all Darkholm, had just turned eight.

Today was a perfect day to sneak out. It was one of those days when Elzabeth would think he was drawing maps with Atelas. Atelas believed he was reading with Azareth. Azareth was told he would be whittling with Brenis, and Brenis . . . well, Brenis was almost certain the child was baking with Elzabeth.

His small hands dusted his clothes as best as he could, at least everything he could see of the embroidered vest he wore, the one that wrapped over the ruffled, white collar beneath it.

"If I ruin these, Sellayne will be sad," he told himself. But the thought vanished quickly upon hearing the gallops of horsemen returning to Ironholde.

Their presence forced him to duck and run in the opposite direction along the outer wall's perimeter.

It was not long after that Ianne found himself skipping a few rocks on a pond's surface one moment, engaging in a one-sided conversation with a frog the next, before he came upon that tree where he hid his favorite stick, the versatile one that was at times a sword, sometimes a horse whenever he decided to play knight.

Today it was a horse that he rode to his favorite destination, the capital city of Coldforge.

If it was because of his elusiveness or because people avoided colliding with the noble child, who knows, but once inside, Ianne found himself navigating the streets undisturbed, accompanied only by the rattling of his stick against the cobblestone streets.

On his way that day, he came upon an old, familiar man.

The man was garbed in what was likely his most presentable attire, which was still rugged and somewhat dirty, with a hat of the same color that had, at some point, been part of a uniform. His hands were busy, the one over a painted, wooden box, holding it in place while asking for alms, the other cranking the handle behind to produce varying sounds.

The music was melancholic but still in tune despite the wooden box that, much like the man's own body, was failing.

"Hello, cylinder man," Ianne greeted.

"Hello, my young lord," the elderly man bowed.

"Oh no," Ianne corrected, "that was last time. Today I am knighted." He pointed at his wooden mount as if to prove his words just stated the obvious.

"Then I salute you, sir knight," the old man offered a wrinkled, almost toothless smile before he returned to playing his music for the passersby for whom, despite all his effort, he was no more than a fly.

Ianne Darkholm

"You seem tired," Ianne said to the cylinder man.

"Tired, I am," the old man responded, "but this is my job."

"But, why do you work?"

"Because this," the old hands tapped the music box, "is how I stay alive."

Ianne's yellow eyes studied the man and the many who ignored them both. He took a glimpse at the collection cup, inside which only two copper droplets rested. The boy reached inside one of his pockets, from where he produced a silver coin. "Here," he offered, "have this."

Upon seeing its value, the old man waved his hand. "No, that's too much, my young lord!"

"I am not a lord," Ianne protested with a smile, "I am a knight. And this," he offered the coin again, "is my gift."

The old man's eyes opened wide. In over seven decades, he had rarely seen a silver droplet in the palm of his hands, enough to feed a family for an entire month.

"I . . . I cannot accept this . . ."

"Well," Ianne explained, "my mother once told me we needed to always remember to give to the cylinder man so that he does not disappear."

"I humbly thank you, my young lord," the man bowed his head. "About not disappearing, however, I don't think there's anything we can do about that."

"What do you mean?" Ianne frowned.

The musician stopped playing. "My trade will one day disappear, young lord."

He then leaned against a wall so that he could bend his swollen knees some, to allow him to get closer to the noble child.

"With every discovery, with the advancement of time, new generations ignore much of what once brought us all joy," he signaled at his music box. "We forget the root of the future, which is the past. And those of us who don't have much, men of a simple trade, those of us who can't run as fast as progress, spend what little time is left discarded, forgotten like an old wives' tale."

"I will not let that happen," Ianne's hand touched the man's arm. "I promise I will continue to bring you coins until I am as old as you." He looked up and smiled, hoping to see the same expression reflected on the man's face.

Upon the purity of the child's innocence, the man's eyes became moist.

"Is there something wrong?" Ianne worried.

"No, my lord," the man explained, blinking, "not at all."

"Good, then. Well, I have to go now," Ianne bid farewell, "I have important matters."

The old man smiled and bowed his head, and, seeing the boy leave, he wiped his eyes and resumed his walk, cranking the handle once again.

"Hello," a small child's voice greeted from a window across the street.

"Hello!" Ianne responded with a wide smile. "What is your name?" he asked immediately after.

"Viketor," the child said. "What's your name?"

"My name is Ianne, and I am a knight." He walked across to be closer, "what are you?"

"Wow!" The child's eyes opened wide, "I'm just a kid."

"I see," Ianne placed his hand under his chin.

"But my father is a shoemaker!" Viketor said. "My mother says that means I'll be a shoemaker when I'm old enough. Would you like to see one of his shoes?"

"Of course!"

"Just a moment."

Ianne waited for a minute, his eyes on the window when he heard the door to the house open just slightly to give way to Viketor's small figure. Excited at the prospect of being able to talk to another child, Ianne dropped his stick on the ground and hurried toward the door.

Viketor was shorter than he was, probably a year younger, with brown hair, freckles, and a beautiful smile. His hands held a single, simple leather shoe the same color as his eyes.

"Here," he said, "you can touch it. It's really soft and sturdy."

Ianne extended his hand toward the shoe when a female voice came from inside the home, "Viketor, who are you talking to?"

"To a boy, Mom," Viketor looked back as her footsteps approached.

Swinging the door open, a thin woman who looked clearly like his mother appeared. She looked down, and her hand touched her child's head tenderly, on her face, a smile as wide as it was warm.

"My lady," Ianne saluted with a hand on his chest and a deep bow. He then looked up to meet the woman.

As if struck by a sudden blizzard, her smile froze. Her eyes opened wide, horrified.

"His name is Ianne," Viketor explained, resting the shoe on Ianne's hands, "and he's a boy knight."

"What are you thinking!" The motherly touch suddenly became a clasp around her child's arm. She pulled him back forcefully and slammed the door shut, startling Ianne, whose own smile froze in confusion.

'Do you not know what he is?' Her voice was muffled behind the heavy door, *from where Viketor's voice came out as unintelligible.*

'No, no, and NO!' the woman yelled at her son, 'you are NOT to associate with him in any way, lest you curse us all!'

Her words shook Ianne, who carefully placed the shoe on the ground, sliding it toward the door as if seeking to protect it as much as he himself sought to feel protected.

Ianne walked back across the street to his wooden mount, from where he could hear Viketor's cries. He took off, imagining the child's face filled with tears as much as his own face was.

⋄⋄⋄⋄⋄⋄

It was past noon when Ianne came upon The Fair Huntress, a small tavern on the outskirts of the merchant district that never found itself crowded.

As if the name had been chosen only for its irony, its inside was largely barren, devoid of adornments aside from a pair of broken antlers over the bar. On any single day, it was rarely visited by more than a handful of patrons.

Fortunately for the owners, a pair of women who appeared to Ianne quite strong, they didn't need much to keep the place going.

The child rested his wooden mount by the entrance. "Good day, my lady Hanna," he greeted the sole waitress with a deep bow.

She was lean, in her mid-to-late twenties, her light brown hair tied up in a bun, with a few loose strands that reminded the child of Elleonora's. She always moved fast, as if in a hurry, even when there were no customers waiting.

"G'day, my young lord," she leaned over the table she wiped to better see him.

"Sir Ianne," he corrected.

"Oh, pardon me," she offered a smile, "how can this humble *lady* be of service to such a highly decorated knight?"

"Hanna!" The bar master grunted, signaling at one of the only two customers present, the one with a wide hat, the one the younger woman had left unattended at the last table by the only open window of the room.

"I'm sorry, my lord, but I'm busy," Hanna said. "Can you take a seat by the bar while I take care of my customer?"

"Certainly," One thing he had never wanted was to get himself, much less anyone else, in trouble, so he did as instructed. He climbed onto one of the stools and faced Merilin.

Now she was the burlier of the two women, with a voice rough as that of a Mycernase sailor, with her forehead deeply wrinkled and darker hair that was pulled back in a ponytail. Along her philtrum, a thick, black stripe glistened

526

with sweat. It was painted to somehow resemble a mustache. It was she who wore the apron of the bar master.

"Greetings," Ianne saluted at the frowning woman who, upon seeing his face, lowered her head in a quick, apologetic bow Ianne didn't seem to notice.

"To what do we owe the honor of your presence, my lord?" Merilin questioned.

"You know us knights," Ianne responded casually. "I have been riding all day, and I decided to stop at this eminent establishment to allow my mount and myself some refreshment and rest."

Merilin looked around at the old chairs, at the occasional stool where even a chair had been missing, the dusty curtains, the creaky planks of the floor and wondered what in the world could make someone think this place was, in any way, eminent.

In the end, she just shrugged. "What type of refreshment would my lord have?"

"A drink," he smiled.

"And what type of drink?"

"Something strong," he responded, "the strongest beer you have."

She turned around and, seconds later, given the few options she had on her shelf, served him a glass. "Tis only small beer, but it's not bad, I think."

She pursed her lips, sending a drop of sweat down at an angle, caught in an instant by Ianne's inquisitive eyes.

"It is melting," he broke character.

"What is?" Merilin looked down at the glass.

"Your mustache," Ianne's finger pointed at the corner of the mouth without hesitation.

If it hadn't been for the thick drops appearing on her forehead, she would have appeared to have frozen in place, her hand reaching for her lip but afraid to touch it and smear it worse. She was filled with embarrassment, her eyes with fear, not the fear of someone being hunted down, but that of a child that has made a mistake in a theater play and was about to be ridiculed.

"I think it looks nice," Ianne's voice brought her back. "Maybe you should get it tattooed so that it does not melt."

Nice . . . It's because he's still a child that he thinks it's nice. Nice would be if he still thought the same after he grew up and faced the world, she thought.

She found herself wiping her forehead and cheeks with the rag in her hands and, looking back at him, she noticed his eyes were elsewhere, looking around the room slowly, smiling, as if in his mind the tavern had been as full as it had never truly been, and when she realized she had wiped everything but her paint she smiled. Here she was, protecting what made her powerful, thinking no one noticed what it truly was, the same way Ianne, that child who had been visiting for the last two months, perhaps thought she didn't notice who, or at least what he was, as if the skin in his pale, little hands, coal-black hair, and eyes as the skin of those lemons she peeled in her bar didn't make it obvious.

Nonetheless, this child had kept his surname from them, that surname that made him as powerful as it placed a target over his head.

If it was because he was always in character or because he didn't have her insecurities, she didn't know, but he smiled often. It was always a brief smile that, at times, was laced with sadness, or at least, so she thought.

Merilin caught herself leaning against the wall, chuckling when she saw him place his knees on the stool so that he could lean on his elbow like an adult.

'What brings him here?' she wondered. 'He always has a story to tell, a question to ask, and yet he's always . . .' it finally dawned on her, 'alone.'

"Mer!" Hanna's shout startled her.

"What is it?" She realized Hanna was standing just inches from her, frowning, Ianne's pale eyes on both women.

"I've told you three times the customer wants toasted bread and ham!" Hanna mumbled. "And I also asked you what else we can heat up quickly because he has to go!"

"I know what I can heat up quickly." Merilin grinned mischievously.

"Stop it," Hanna said through gritted teeth, making Ianne smile, "there's a child here!"

"Let me check in the back. You go back to the floor."

The moment Hanna turned around, Merilin bit her lower lip and slapped her ass as she stepped away.

"I got it!" Ianne raised his hand, "I know why you two live together."

Both women stopped in their tracks and looked at each other, their eyebrows raised, their faces full of worry.

"Because . . ." Ianne frowned, analyzing inside his head before he opened his eyes as wide as he could. "She . . ." he pointed a finger at Hanna, " . . . must be poor, yes! She does not have a place to live, so she lives with you."

Merilin sighed, relieved, her forehead drenched with sweat once more. "You know what," she leaned toward Ianne with a wink, "you're right! That's exactly it."

Her words were interrupted by the wet rag Hanna threw on her face before she ran back to the kitchen, leaving only Ianne at the bar, smiling, his chest swollen with pride at the thought of having finally figured out their relationship.

The boy moved away from the bar, not without leaving the empty glass and payment on the counter. "I think it is about time we go back." His hand caressed his mount, "Would you like a last ride along our favorite pond?"

Of course, no response came, at least not from the stiff body of his imaginary horse. The one thing that startled him was a deep voice from behind him that said, "Now, that would be lovely."

"Greetings," Ianne saluted, "my name is Ianne, Sir Ianne."

"Sir?" The man with the wide hat smiled in disbelief. "Ah, of course. How could I not see it?" He half smiled. "I suppose this is your mount?"

"Clatter," Ianne smiled back, "that is his name. He is a warhorse."

"Well, then let me step away so that he doesn't bite me."

"He does not bite. He is well trained," Ianne chuckled. "What is your name, kind sir?"

"Kind? Well, the kindness is all yours. They call me Ekh," the man said, "my real name would be too difficult for people to pronounce." He looked back toward the tavern. "Where are you headed to, sir knight?"

"I am going back home," Ianne responded, proud at the recognition.

"And where is that home?"

"I dare not say," the boy answered, "I could get in trouble."

"Then let's not get you into trouble." His response made Ianne smile. "We can walk along the way together, right? At least until our ways part, if your mount would allow it, that is."

"Yes," Ianne giggled, "we may." And for more than a few blocks, they walked side by side, the small child and the tall, middle-aged man with fair skin and almond eyes. And they spoke about horses, animals, and sweets, their conversation laced with questions Ekh asked, most of which Ianne was glad to answer. The few that were more personal, Ianne struggled to answer but didn't, and, upon seeing the child's stress, Ekh didn't press.

"Wow, we have walked in the same direction!" Having come upon Coldforge's city limits, Ianne said, amazed, a little away from the main road where he could have otherwise been seen by the occasional guard.

"You're right!" Ehk raised his hands slightly. "Look at what the stars have destined for us!"

Perhaps the hand of destiny had chosen such, or maybe they had walked together the entire way by sheer coincidence, or maybe simply because the man, who had walked half a step behind, had been following the child.

"I have to go now," the child said with sad reluctance. "Will I ever see you again?"

"Of course you will, of that, I'm sure."

"And how are you so sure?"

"Well, I just know it," the man knelt toward the boy, "I know it because I'm a sorcerer . . ."

"A sorcerer?" Ianne's twin orbs opened wide.

"Yes, indeed," Ekh replied.

"What kind of sorcerer?" Ianne stepped toward him.

"A sorcerer of mysteries," Ekh said, "a performer of miracles."

"What kind of miracles?"

"Various kinds," Ekh smiled broadly.

"Can you perform a miracle for me?" Ianne asked.

"Hmmm, maybe. What kind?"

"Let me think . . ." Ianne bit his upper lip.

"Think hard," Ekh instructed, "for miracles are powerful, and the energy shouldn't be wasted on something simple."

"How do I know if what I want is simple?"

"Think," Ekh waved his fingers, "what is the greatest desire of your heart?"

At the words, Ianne's lips shook. There were many things that had crossed his mind, from a real horse to a suit of armor to even the ability to speak with animals or fly, but the greatest desire of his heart? That was something different. There was one thing he wanted above all.

"Could you bring my parents back?" a glint of sadness appeared in the child's blond eyes.

"It depends," the man replied, "from where?"

"My parents . . . were murdered last year," Ianne's voice trembled. "I wish I could see them again, but if that is too much to ask, could you at least bring them back for just one night? I miss them so much, and I never got to say goodbye."

Ekh hesitated for a moment, seeking how to smile again upon hearing the child's lament. "What you're asking is hard."

Ianne lowered his head.

"But not impossible." His words transformed Ianne's face to one of endless hope. "I must warn you, the harder the miracle is to perform, the more special the components needed to fuel it."

"What do you need?" Ianne asked, "I will get anything."

"First, I will need a book."

"Books I have aplenty!"

"Yes, but not this kind of book," Ekh added, "I will need one book from, ah, well, it would be impossible for you to get unless you had access."

"Access to what? Tell me. I will get it."

"Access there." He pointed out, at a distance, across the valley and its surrounding woods toward the gargantuan darkness of Darkholde Keep and the library within it.

Ianne's looked back at Ekh, "I have access."

"Well, then," Ekh looked around, pointing at some bushes close by, "then it would be ideal to meet in that little grove over there tomorrow night, at around midnight?"

"Certainly," Ianne responded excitedly. "I must go now. I will meet you tomorrow night."

"Yes, but before you go, one thing," Ekh raised a finger, "this miracle is empowered by materials and energy, but also secrecy and trust. The materials you will bring, energy I will provide. Now, the secret of what we are doing should stay between us."

"I promise," Ianne's eyes glistened.

"It's like a tree," the man continued, "it grows stronger only if we protect it. And lastly, well, only if I can trust you, I can tell you the type of book I need."

"You can trust me," Ianne insisted.

"Are you certain?"

"Yes," Ianne nodded. "Do you have friends?"

"I don't," Ekh responded, "miracle workers are lonesome folk."

"Then I will be your friend." Placing the hand over the kneeling man's shoulder, Ianne smiled to Ekh's smirk.

FRIENDS TIL THE END

The water boiled.

Inside the glass beaker, it bubbled, producing small clouds of steam that sought refuge from the dancing flame below, some of it swirling around the library's main room like a ghost that had found a place to haunt among the countless books, the rest was sucked right into a wooden cone by Count Azareth's mouth.

"Ahhhh . . . *blackhawe*, one of Rovetsia's hidden gems," Azareth smiled before he blew it out of his nostrils. "In its search for recognition, the ancestors of Dominion Laenicus, Dominatricis Misanthius, the only female among Rovetsia's leadership, devised a new way to smoke these. Fascinating, is it not?"

"Certainly," Ianne's large eyes blinked from within the vaporous cloud.

"I must say it is not bad," Azareth took another puff, "although I find it a little weak."

Ianne moved closer to him, "Can I try it?"

"Surely," the Master of Lore responded before blowing out the flame and turning around to put the contraption away.

"Wait," Ianne stretched his hand, "not yet. You said I could try it."

"I only said surely," Azareth corrected with a smile, "but did I say you could do it today? Ask me again when you are thirteen."

"Grrr," Ianne crossed his arms in fake outrage, stealing a chuckle from the librarian as the young one watched how Azareth's hands delicately stored every part of the contraption in its case.

"Ah, this one is still hot," he held the stand in his hands, "let us give it a moment."

"Aza," the child lowered his head.

"Yes?"

The child looked around the expansive collection. "Can I ask you a question?"

"Of course."

"Are there any books here I cannot read?"

"Those written in languages you do not yet understand," Azareth's grin showed the premature wrinkles of one who led a life full of preoccupations.

"Yeah," Ianne agreed, "but are there any books that are off-limits to me?"

"Those so high you cannot reach, I suppose."

"Aza!" Ianne protested, "I am not playing riddles! All I want is to know whether I can read any book from this library, or is there a limit to what I am allowed?"

Upon seeing the seriousness on the child's face and hearing the tone of his voice, the Master of Lore changed his tone. He wrapped a hand around his cane and began walking around the room as he spoke.

"There is not," he twirled the cane before planting it on the ground, "nor should there ever be a limit to what you can learn. Whatever one reads, one will interpret differently depending on where one stands in that particular moment of life. Every book is, on its own, an ever-rich and delicious fruit. Each one is capable, in its own way, of nourishing us. Of course, some of these fruits are easier to digest than others, and for some of them, we might not be prepared to consume them just yet. Now, who decides when we are apt to consume, that is the question, for knowledge is something we safekeep, but not something anyone owns."

"There is one book I want to borrow," Ianne said meekly.

"For how long?" Azareth asked.

"Maybe a few days," the child responded, "two or three."

"Well, I will be packing to leave for Darscence in two days. Would you like to accompany me to the glass-blowing fair in my county? The book we can do after we come back."

"I . . . cannot," Ianne said through nervous sadness, "this is very important to me."

The Master of Lore's fingers traveled along his stubble-ridden jaw before he turned around and walked again.

"Now," the librarian's sharp eyes inquired, "Tell me more about this book."

If someone had been watching from outside the windows, they would have seen Ianne lowering his head, how the Master's hands played with the cane as they engaged in a long conversation before both he and Ianne laughed heartily. They would have seen the Master of Lore leave for the back of the library before returning with a large tome in his hands which, after showing it to the child, he wrapped carefully in leather before he leaned against one of the many ladders inside the library.

"Done deal," Azareth smiled. "If I were not here when you came back to return it, then hand it to the Master of Scholars."

"Is Yrenne always the one in charge when you are not around?"

"I am the one in charge even when I am not around, but do not tell her that. She is a very useful help . . . Come to think of it, do not tell her I said that either!" Azareth chuckled.

"Now come," he tapped the rungs on the ladder, "I must pack, and you need to go to sleep."

Immediately, Ianne climbed up the ladder, and in the custom of the House, they kissed each other's cheeks.

Both the mature librarian and the imaginative child looked upon each other's xanthous eyes, as they did every time they said farewell. For a few moments, they stood there as if they had been of the same size, perhaps because Azareth, as rumor had it, truly had a bad back, or perhaps because, instead of stooping down to talk to others, he always lifted them up.

Never before had Clatter's rattling been as fast as that night's when Ianne's shaking legs took him across the shadowy hallways of Darkholde, across the valley, and toward that grove Ekh had pointed out.

Other than to pick up his mount in the middle of the darkness, he had not stopped once.

His heart raced at both the fear of being caught or seen leaving Darkholde and the excitement he felt. So nervous was he that he didn't seem to notice the heaviness of the wrapped tome on his back.

The young boy reached the grove and, turning right around a bush and into the clearing, expecting to find the man with the wide hat, he smiled broadly.

But Ekh wasn't there. There was no fireplace, no movement, no sign. To his untrained eye, the man was not even around. Still, Ianne sat atop a rock, tapping his knees lightly, ignoring even the majestic beauty of the white orb in the heavens that seemed to have come out as a witness.

"I hope he is safe," Ianne told himself after more than just a few long minutes had passed. The young boy really didn't know if the man was late or if he, in his excitement, had been early.

"I hope this works," Ianne whispered, slapping his own leg. "Of course, it will work, Clatter! It will work because it is magic and because I kept my word to make it powerful."

A rustling to his left alerted him. Eyes glistening, he took a deep breath to contain his excitement when only a rodent came out from under the bushes before it scurried away, right between the legs of the man in the wide hat.

"Friend!" Ianne giggled excitedly. "I knew you would come!" He closed in and hugged the man's leg.

From under the hat, Ekh looked around to make sure they were alone before he spoke. "Do you have something for me?" He tapped the leather surface on the boy's back.

There was something different about his voice, Ianne noticed, unable to tell what it was. 'Maybe he is excited too,' the Darkholm boy wondered.

"Yes," Ianne responded, "I have it right here." Swinging it over his shoulder, he placed the leather wrappings atop the rock he had sat just moments before. "Do you want to see it?"

"No," Ekh responded, "not right now."

"But," the child questioned, "then when?"

"In a little bit," Ekh smiled. "First, are you alone?"

"Yes, I am."

"And who have you told about our meeting?" He ran his fingers over the leather wrapping.

"Nobody," Ianne responded.

"Are you certain?"

"Of course," the child smiled proudly, "I kept my word. I always do!"

"Good, then," with a swipe of his hand, Ekh snatched the bundle away from Ianne's light grasp.

"Be careful," Ianne frowned, "we have to treat books as we treat those we love. When are we going to start?" Ianne's eyes were on Ekh, who turned his back on the boy and began walking away toward the edge of the grove.

"Wait," Ianne smiled nervously, a smile that soon disappeared after he saw Ekh didn't stop.

"Wait!" he raised his voice slightly and, seeing the man was near the bushes, he rushed and grasped the package. "You cannot take this. I must keep it."

"Stop it!" Ekh tugged.

"You are not allowed to take it," Ianne protested, "I need to return it!" Clasping the bundle with his hands as hard as he could, Ianne tugged forcefully, but Ekh's strength sent the child sprawling along the ground.

"No!" Ianne outstretched his hand as he tried to regain his footing, "Please, wait!"

"Stop it right there, child!" Ekh commanded, revealing a knife he unsheathed from his side. "Stay away from me, or I'll have to use this."

"But?" Confused, his lips shaking, he asked, "but what about my parents?"

"Stupid child," Ekh half turned, "no one can speak with the dead."

Ianne's knees hit the ground. Somehow, it didn't hurt. They couldn't hurt as much as his swollen eye or bleeding lip after his face had hit the ground. They couldn't hurt as much as his heart did.

The man's words had inflicted a terrible blow, knocking down the mountain of hope and reminding him all that was left was a lake of loneliness.

He cried as he felt something inside him he would later know was his heart breaking.

"I just wanted to say goodbye."

———————— ·+·+◆+·+· ————————

His short steps took a shorter stride than usual as if his feelings were dragging him down, keeping him from advancing into the library he had just entered.

Ianne couldn't stay in his room. He had felt the full face of the moon watching him through the windows.

The library would have been completely dark had it not been for her pale presence that seemed to follow him as if to remind him how guilty he was.

At the faint scent of smoke, he was forced to lower his head, hoping he could disappear, for it meant the Master of Lore was present at the third hour past the middle of the night.

The child didn't know what to say, where to start. In his mind, he wished he could transform into a mouse so that he could scurry away and hide forever. He knew how important it was for the Darkholm not to disappoint or act against the family. His wet eyes only saw not his cousin Azareth but the intimidating presence of the Master of Lore.

Count Azareth dusted some shelves, organized a few books, took a puff, and blew some smoke, apparently too busy to notice the child was approaching.

Ianne climbed up on a stool, truly troubled. Marigold appeared from the corner of the Master's eye before he resumed his work without speaking a word.

The Darkholm child placed both hands over the counter, and upon seeing Azareth turning to face him, he averted his gaze. The next few seconds felt impossibly long, the tapping of the cane on the floor impossibly loud, as if every single piece of wood, metal, and stone around him screamed, commanding him to confess . . . confess . . . CONFESS!

For a moment, he wished he could meet him face to face, as he always did, up on the ladder where they would hug and kiss each other's cheeks. But he couldn't, not after having realized he was nothing more than a very small, stupid child.

Having found no refuge anywhere around the room, Ianne's trembling eyes looked up to meet Azareth, who just stood there, his demeanor serious and unmoving except for the smoke that escaped his nostrils. Even the smoke tendrils were accomplices, making no effort to cover the bright eyes of the Master.

The child couldn't help it. He looked down, his forehead meeting the table surface as he struggled to find the words to speak.

"It is lost," he voiced with difficulty.

Azareth placed his hand on the table but quickly withdrew it, studying the tips of his fingers that had just been drenched in the pool of tears under the child's face.

The Master's face softened. "Nothing is truly lost; it is simply out of your sight."

"It is not a riddle, Aza," Ianne cried, "not this time."

"I know it is not." The Master's fingers brushed the child's head protectively, perhaps to ensure his ashes wouldn't touch his raven hair and turn it gray as time and suffering would one day do.

"I am sorry," Ianne looked up, "I am really, really sorry!" His small hands covered his swollen face. "All I just wanted was to say goodbye."

"Come here," Setting the cane aside, the Master picked up the child in his arms and held him close.

And Ianne sobbed deeply, muffled only by the comfort of Azareth's shoulder.

Moments later, upon seeing Ianne calm some, Azareth whispered, "There, there now, do not be worried."

"I am really scared," Ianne sniffed, "Are you not worried?"

"Worried?" Azareth both frowned and smiled. "Why would I be?" he chuckled, "Did you think I would lose sight of the book? Did you think I would give you the real one?"

Ianne was confused. He had just stopped crying, even when he didn't exactly understand what Azareth meant. The savvy Master, however, having easily read his expression, placed him on the ground. "Come with me," he instructed, "let me show you."

· ·✦✦✦✦· ·

The chamber they walked into was, as everything inside Darkholde, ill-lit.

Along the entire way, Ianne had walked one step behind the Master of Lore's calm stride. It was clear in his mind where they were headed, and while the moment Azareth stepped aside confirmed his expectation, he wasn't ready for who he would meet there.

To his left, Elleonora, who didn't smile. She stood by a heavy lectern behind which Lord Davidov Darkholm was located. To their right, Ashildr smiled, her arms crossed, resting comfortably against one of the dungeon's columns, and right by her, Ekh himself, chained, Ianne quickly recognized, dangling upside down, his face swollen on one side with a bruise that could have easily been caused by a horse's kick, or, more likely, Ashildr's fist.

"Ianne Darkholm," Davidov beckoned.

The child followed without hesitation, picked up by Azareth so that he could see the Master of Death's spidery fingers flipping the pages of the *Liber de Finis* until they found one hungry for words.

As if having all the time in the world, Davidov slowly grabbed the curved knife and an empty vial from the lectern.

"Here," he handed the vial to Ianne, and the oldest known living member of Darkholm and the youngest of them all, the one with all the malice and the one without, walked side-by-side toward Ekh.

As if reality itself had quieted and slowed down, Ianne absorbed the moment but heard nothing. He would always remember the silent groan on Ekh's face and Elleonora approaching, silver bowl in hand. He would remember Azareth, playing with his cane proudly while Ashildr smiled, placing a small ladder for Ianne to climb.

He then saw Davidov's hand slide the sharpness along Ekh's neck and his lips moving to order the man to *speak.*

That was the last Ianne saw of Ekh, the man he would remember, he who had betrayed that which Ianne had given him with all his heart—his trust, his friendship.

He had robbed the child of his innocence. He had stolen his hope. He had been nothing more than a thief.

In the end, the thief's shouts, screams, and words Ianne would forget, but it mattered not. If he ever wanted to, he knew where they would be recorded—in the same book this traitor of a friend had tried to steal.

DANCE OF THE SUN

Location: Empyre of Suhne, City of Suhne

*Those who want to force us to walk in the light often
conceive their plans in the shadows . . .*

N ight had come to Suhne, and with it came silence.

While most of the Empyre quiesced in the evening, especially so inside the walls of the sacred palace, tonight the Rays met for a special occasion.

The large, circular Sacred Chamber would have been plunged into darkness had it not been for the perfectly round, pure sunstone globes that were strategically placed so that, after basking under the crystal dome all day, they would illuminate its entirety all night.

Each of the holy men sat in their respective crystalline seats a few feet off the floor, flanking Exis as they curved so that the last two Rays almost faced each other.

Across from Exis, numerous pillows lined the floor, plump as the rich merchants of the southwestern lands.

A group of musicians, ready to practice their trade, waited behind that sea of pillows for the signal instructing them to begin. It was one that would come only as sound, for all of the musicians were blind.

Aside from the Rays and the Flame Guards, the Sons, and the Sun himself, no one was allowed inside the Sacred Chamber and allowed to partake in its glory.

Between them, a circular dais, two feet high, rose, one of the same dimensions as the crystal lens on the dome above them all. The dais was covered in fabrics of emerald, scarlet and pure, almost shining gold.

Each of the Rays looked at their counterparts, all except perhaps Yeq, the youngest, who fidgeted with his fingers, anxious as he was most of the time.

Upon Exis's signal, one of the musicians shook his instrument, and a hushed, rattling sound, similar to that of rain, filled the room.

Malek then entered the chamber, his forearms wrapped in golden and brown fabrics, his hair hanging free.

The warrior's chest lay exposed, revealing the rage of his golden tattoos and a simple, brown skirt embroidered in gold that parted in the middle, allowing his muscular legs to accommodate him over the pillows.

Following his entrance, Kaylen caught everyone's attention.

The silhouette of his entire body was perceptible under the fine, crimson silks that floated behind him as he walked, remaining in the air for a few seconds after he had passed. Under the silk, his body was completely naked.

The moment he stopped over the pillows, the silk floated down, revealing his face, exquisitely perfect and clean-shaven; his hair parted in three, hanging low on his sides before they met on his back, laced in a labyrinthine shape that wrapped around crisscrossed, thin bars of gold.

So perfect was his being that, were it not for their blindness, at the mere sight of him, the musicians would have skipped a beat.

After the second son, Vamya entered the room.

She wore a plain golden tunic over her shoulders. Despite it being simple, the Child's swaying hips made the garment come alive. Her hair was mostly loose, except for a few strands that arched down to cover her ears before meeting in the back of her head, where they were held in place by a large pin resembling a golden scarab with emeralds for eyes.

Midway to her destination, she raised her hands to unfasten both shoulders. Like a flower in a Rovetsian spring, the tunic showed its true beautiful emerald green inside, now laden with streaks of gold.

The gasp of one of the Rays drew a mischievous smile from her that she hoped nobody saw.

But perhaps Exis did, for he immediately clapped for the rest of the music to start.

Winds, strings, and the deep, slow beat of a drum gave life to the room as an old woman walked inside. Her vision was poor, but her eyes were still fixed on the ground. She was followed by a dozen maidens, four garbed in the colors of each of the heirs, their eyes covered in fabric of the same color each wore.

The maidens danced, their moves graceful dandelions floating in the wind, their synchrony perfect as they jumped and twirled, seeming to meld with one another before separating again. To the rhythm, they turned and swayed, always mysteriously avoiding any contact with those who wore a different color.

Closing her eyes, the older woman raised her head toward the heavens and began to sing. Her words, her voice were filled with as much sadness as hope:

Blessed be the Sun,
Blessed be forever,
Blessed are his Rays,
Blessed be, blessed be.
Beautiful guide,
Beautiful blessing,
Beautiful victory,
Beautiful gift.
Merciful Fire
Merciful Light
Merciful Beauty
Merciful Sun
Although we can't see it
Although we don't see it,
We don't understand it,
Merciful always,
Beautiful gift,
Blessed are we,
Blessed it be, blessed it be.

The song touched every fiber of Vamya's body, moving her spirit and driving her mind to leave and see all the people of her empyre. From the nobles to the soldiers, to the poor, the orphans, and the ailing, every soul ached, hungered, and thirsted for the divine blessing of a merciful, loving touch. She could not allow Suhne to continue on its current path. She *would not* allow it.

Pushing herself off the ground, Vamya climbed up to the dais, moved between the dancers, and gracefully joined them in their dance. With each move, Vamya's hands gently touched each maiden's face and removed her blindfold, each one immediately closing her eyes and kneeling on the floor to avoid accidentally catching a glimpse.

Malek's brow furrowed angrily while Kaylen grinned mockingly upon seeing the furious faces of many among the Rays and the signals of the few who sought to assuage them.

Either because of not having taken notice or simply ignoring her surroundings, Vamya's bare feet stood before the aged singer.

"Open your eyes," Vamya instructed.

"I do not dare, no," the old woman lowered her head.

"Open them so that you can see the Sun," Vamya said softly.

"We don't have to see the Sun to feel its presence, to know it is there." The woman's lips trembled. "I feel *you*."

"Then now," Vamya smiled, "see me."

Her thumbs delicately opened the tired, wrinkled eyes, the ones that opened widely in disbelief upon seeing Vamya's beauty, the jewel eyes and smile of summer.

"I have seen you!" The woman smiled as countless tears rolled down her face. She lowered her head in shame and was held by Vamya's arms in a long embrace. "My eyes have seen the Sun, and the Sun has loved me."

SEVENTH TEST

Location: Suhne Empyre, City of Suhne, Palace of the Sun

There's no more dangerous fire than the one that fuels desire . . .

"I thought you weren't going to make it," the young man said upon seeing his lover approach, walking hurriedly into his arms.

Their lips merged into a wet embrace, their arms exploring each other under the foliage of the rich, vast garden of the main dome of the palace. His hands grabbed her thighs firmly, bringing her closer so that he could give her ear a soft bite. "After tomorrow's event, I will be very busy," he said. "It won't be as easy for us to meet, so I wanted to see you tonight."

"Oh, Sekhse . . ." she moaned.

"Shh, Ara, don't say my name," he whispered, "we don't know who could be listening."

"I'm sorry," she kissed the dark skin of his chest, her brown eyes enthralled by the hazel jewels of his own.

"Make me yours," she said, "right now."

"I can't, not here. I have to get back to the Conquering Sun and help him prepare for the morning."

"He won't notice!"

"I'm one of his Chosen, Ara. Of course, he'll notice," he kissed her playfully before putting his golden *kaftan* over his head.

"Wait." She reached out to him before he left, "I have something for you."

"What is it?" Sekhse questioned. "I don't have a lot of time."

"I told you the Searing Sun was up to something," Ara explained. "He has prepared something that will give him an advantage in tomorrow's Test." Her hand produced a vial.

"What's this?" Sekhse examined the vial.

"It's an ointment that will help him resist heat for a long period of time. He knows he needs every advantage he can get to beat the Conquering Sun."

"How do you know all this?" Sekhse asked.

"I heard his discussions with Itosh," she explained. "That's the advantage of being a lowly servant and going unnoticed."

"I don't know how to thank you," Sekhse kissed her.

"Just make sure the Sun of Conquest wins so that you can live and marry me."

Sekhse caressed her face. "I must go now." And he took off.

<hr />

Ehta, the old crone among Malek's Chosen who served as his confidant, walked along his chamber, her eyes on the Eye of the Sun that would soon set.

"You should rest, Blessed One," she said.

"I could stay awake all night if need be," Malek ate fruit from the tray she had set only moments before.

"But, do you need to?" she smiled. "Your mind must also be rested."

"Tomorrow's Test will be fresher in the minds of the Rays," Malek added. "It's important I triumph over my siblings."

"And I have what will help you do so, Blessed One," Sehkse entered the room, holding the vial in hand for them to see.

Malek took the vial from his hand. His thick eyebrows looked back at Sehkse questioningly.

"It is an ointment prepared by the Searing Sun, one that will give him an advantage over you. I obtained it from the hand of that servant of his I'm sleeping with."

Malek smiled maliciously. "Scheming bastard." Playing with the vial in his hand, he walked toward Ehta. "With this, I'll be invincible."

"*The greatest, most invincible, and most powerful is also the most isolated, the most lonely . . .*" the old woman murmured audibly.

"The truly powerful need no company. Depending on others only feeds weakness, Ehta." Malek walked to her side.

"Blessed Son, I was not speaking of you. I was speaking of Daygamanu," the crone's hand pointed northwest, toward the vast ocean of sand that stood before the golden, disappearing sun.

<hr />

Daygamanu, the angry desert of Suhne, inhospitable home of those who had been forgotten, an open causeway for criminals and exiles, its warm embrace brought nothing but death and ruin.

It was the largest desert of Suhne. Its body expanded for hundreds of miles, able to accommodate most of either Blackheart or Ardenay within its confines. It encompassed most of the protectorate of Ohor, and even invaded a significant portion of the neighboring basqhs of Uhn with all its crystal mines to the east and Lmet, home of the scarabs to the south.

Even here, in the stony region only a few days from the city of Suhne, so far from the center of the expansive blistering sand dunes, the heat of the desert gave testament to the fury of the sun that punished all life indiscriminately.

The Suhnites had gathered in the valley known as the Field of Lament, where large tents had been set, those belonging to the nobles away from the pavilion dedicated to the Rays that towered behind the tents of the three siblings.

In the valley's center, a stony platform rose. Its surface depicted the Sun of Suhne. It was believed it had been etched by the first Sun's divine power the moment his feet had touched the stone on his descendance to Caerea.

Iron manacles were strewn along the platform's surface like masochistic ivy desiring the entirety of its body to be scorched.

The day began before the rising when the sky began to change its color to herald the appearance of the Eye.

"People of the Sun," Exis announced from under the large parasol the acolytes used to protect him. "Today is a most sacred of days, when we have gathered in this holy place where the first Almighty Sun descended, in his mercy, to free our people from slavery and ignorance." His words were accompanied by the raising of hands of the Suhnites, the air filled with shouts of praise and quick prayers.

The Speaker's eyes examining the thousands gathered—the Rays who, like him, were protected by the acolytes, the Lorq'a and Zetq'a, watching from the shade of their encampments and the those of the lower castes that had managed to be present, those who used what little fabrics they possessed in whatever way they could, as cover for their heads.

He signaled the Flame Guards, who escorted each of the heirs, all three covered in cloaks of gold, red and green, respectively.

The siblings walked toward the platform, where they stood as they were being prepared.

"Our Empyre has been blessed because we have recognized the magnificence of our god, we have worshipped humbly, followed his teachings faithfully, without question. *'Only god can stand before all enemies, all that is contrary, eye* to eye, without faltering.' Today we test the Sun's might by having the challengers face the very own, all-powerful, all-seeing Eye. Without faltering, let them withstand the power of the Sun!"

His words were followed by the beating of drums that would continue all day, the musicians taking turns every so often.

The cloaks were removed from the three that now stood on the platform completely naked, facing both the priests and the crowd that cheered the moment the first ray of the Sun appeared over the horizon, their hands and feet bound to the floor by chains.

Malek's hair was back. His face and body glistened. They would stand from the rising of the Eye to its retirement. He smiled, thinking of all he had done to prepare for this, the years he had spent fighting under the Eye of the Sun, his superior stamina, all the water he had drunk, how his Chosen had played that girl into providing him with the ointment Kaylen had prepared, the one he had ensured to place all over his body, not leaving even his eyelids without its glistening touch. "Are you two ready to be humiliated? I have lived my life facing men to see them faint from heat and exhaustion when I have not," Malek grinned.

"I wouldn't speak so early," Vamya responded to show her confidence, "you have not faced a woman."

In the center, Kaylen smirked but said nothing. While he had already recovered from the attack, he knew his limitations quite well. He would let them talk all they wanted to while he would save every drop of saliva he could to stay as hydrated as possible. For the last few weeks, he had eaten plenty of pomegranate, carrots, nuts, and pumpkin, so much that his skin, rarely touched by the sun, seemed to have gotten some color. He ate dried fish, drank salted water, and even covered his skin with a balm he made from the same fruits he had consumed. 'Unlike the oil I sent your way, you moron . . . Or did you want to pit an apprentice against the master of *Domae*.'

The first hour passed uneventfully, with Kaylen shifting the weight of his legs to avoid feeling tired. Vamya breathed calmly, her eyes closed, but soon after, the orb's fury was felt.

Malek felt he had been placed inside a furnace, but he had been here before. He cursed upon seeing his siblings' foreheads sweating profusely. While he was used to never sweating much, this time, it felt almost impossible.

The drums continued for hours, with cheers from the expectant crowd every time there was any single movement of one of the three.

Hours later, Kaylen's hair was drenched with sweat, serving both as a wet cape that provided him cover and a black drape that drew the Sun's ire toward his small frame. He had prepared for everything, he thought, but not for the metal chains that were burning his skin.

Vamya closed her eyes every so often, her mind elsewhere. 'I can do this. I can. I know I can do this.' Her legs felt weak underneath her, but she needed to prevail.

It was in the ninth hour when Malek felt suffocated and finally began sweating profusely. It gave him respite for some time, one that was short-lived. He looked to his left, where Kaylen's skin was burned, his lips chapped. His eyes seemed fatigued and not as beguiling as they normally were.

Vamya, he saw, stood firm, but her thighs and calves were shaking. She was about to cramp, he knew. He knew he would soon catch a second wind, despite his own skin that was the most heavily blistered and felt like it was being pulled away by torturers.

Moments later, the sound of chains was heard, followed by Kaylen's collapse. Water was thrown immediately over his body, which was taken away by the physicians to his tent. His collapse brought satisfaction to Malek, which gave him the second wind he needed to stand. He smiled. 'It's only her now.'

More than an hour followed, with both Vamya and Malek standing with difficulty. She felt as weak as she knew she likely looked, barely able to lift her hands from the chains that now felt like they had quadrupled in weight. 'I need to do this,' she thought. 'So much depends on me.'

"People of the Sun," Vamya raised her arms as she raised her voice, "behold what you never expected to see. You are all witnesses of the birth of a new Sun!"

Seeing her using her words to rally not only the crowd but also herself. Malek sought something to do, for a way to draw the attention away from her. He lifted both his arms up so strongly the chains sang a song of desperation. He shouted at the top of his lungs, "I am the Sun!" He opened his eyes to gaze at the Eye above, searching for his own divinity in the flaming orb.

A drop of oil fell on his eye, and then Eye above, in its infinite mercy, mercilessly burned his retina, leaving him sightless in his left eye.

The searing pain forced him to kneel on the ground, but the painful screams ended the moment the ones of frustration started when water was thrown over his body.

Only Vamya remained, surrounded by the punishing heat and the deafening cheers, standing not from the strength she didn't have but by the commitment to her mission, by the power of her will. She was going to finish.

And finish she did. Vamya stood until the Eye retired, and even after, she did not accept the water over her body, not the coverage, or the camels. And while her burnt soles felt like a thousand nails under her feet, she walked all the way with no assistance, by herself, back to the tent that awaited her.

THE VINE

Location: Kingdom of Blackheart, Duchy of Darkholm,
deep within Darkholde Keep

"You must remember this night, for it will be like no other," the middle-aged woman whispered, breathing the cold air coming through the window.

The cloudy sky above made every effort to reveal a quarter of the bright orb, the one called Kaeris. Each ray of its dim light was reflected in the onyx rings hanging from her earlobes, the light touching the tight-fitting gown she wore.

The bundle in her hands moved, revealing tiny hands that were still bloody from their journey out of the womb.

Almost smiling, the woman returned the newborn to its own mother's expectant hands.

"Other than the birth, which, unlike the other Darkholm's, is held in private, what is so special about tonight in particular?" the new, young mother said from the bed that was stained from both the sweat and blood of her life-giving ordeal.

"Today is no one's name-day," she pondered. "Does it have anything to do with my graduation? You know, despite studying alone, away from the university, I excelled in my academics, and yet you did not congratulate me once. Virtually everyone else, including the headmistress, Lady Narkari herself, did. Are you going to finally?" she asked, wringing her drenched hair.

"No," the older woman's curt words halted her daughter's questioning.

Turning away from the window, she added, "You were excellent because that is the least you could be. It was what we expected. Why congratulations, then? So that it fills an empty void within you? You must understand that you must fill that void yourself."

Her words were as cold as the wind that blew her hair, revealing the tattoo that covered her left arm, an intricate, green vine wrapping around seductively.

The vine wrapped around other images, among them, a pair of hands, palms together, close to her shoulder. A camouflaged serpent hid within the vine itself as it formed a circle and bit its own tail. After it, a silver, mammalian tongue. Just below the tongue, a cobra, ready to strike. It ended in a flowering red amaryllis, its stem bent and held in place by strings so that it would ultimately appear to take the shape of a harp.

Only one person in Caelris would have that pattern, and it would do good to any perceptive politician to remember they were etched in the skin of Ira Darkholm of the Vine.

Among her own, she was also known as the Harmony.

Ira lived in a perpetual balance, finding peace in all things. But, true to Darkholm tradition, there was a darker, hidden truth within her. It was a known fact that Ira loved music, as she frequently hummed melodies she had written. A collection of instruments, all of them stringed, lined the walls of her room.

Every few days, she would take one down to the Darkholm dungeons, where she would spend hours at a time. It was here where she often found inspiration in the agonizing screams of the tortured and the words of dying prisoners, both of which set the rhythm of her songs.

For many years she even took her child with her, sitting her down to listen to the songs she wrote as much as to the screams.

"Xenora, Xenovive, my dear Xen, my daughter," Ira's arms embraced the body of her child, now fifteen years old, "you have grown so much. I must say," Ira continued, "I have taught you almost everything I know."

"As you have taught me, Mother, I have learned," Xenovive said with certainty, her bright, intense golden eyes meeting those of her progenitor. "I had chosen my Time of Breeding

Ira Darkholm

even before having my mark," Xenovive walked toward the crib where her own newborn daughter rested.

"The future will bring many hardships and hard decisions for everyone, and even harder for you." Ira placed her hand on her daughter's shoulder.

"Against anything and everything, the Vine grows." The daughter's words were filled with determination.

"Come, stand by my side," Ira beckoned.

With difficulty but knowing it was expected of her, Xenovive almost fainted when she stood from the bed.

Mother and daughter both looked outside the highest window of the Tower of the Vine, from where all of Darkholde could be seen. Aside from the monumental Tower of the Eye and the Spire, theirs was the highest-placed tower. From the window, both women could see all of Darkholde, its megalithic presence looming closely. From most places in the keep, anyone could see the Vine's tower, from which the Vine could see essentially everyone in the keep.

"What do you see, child?"

Xenovive's eyes studied the keep, the raging waters of the ocean that fought as if asking the world to sacrifice the Darkholm to its depths. She saw Smith's Bay, Coldforge, and the land beyond.

"I see the same things you see, and yet those same things are different, for every single thing is judged by the individual observer."

"If each thing is judged differently by the individual, then what are the Traditions for?"

"The Darkholm Traditions are the rules and laws that define us. They are the air we breathe. The Vine are the judges and inquisitors of Darkholm, and while the Vine exists, the rules will be kept and followed."

Mother and daughter faced one another. The progenitor placed a hand in her daughter's. "I will ask you this one last time, and I promise I will never ask you again. Is there any Tradition of House Darkholm or the Vine you would change?"

"I will follow the traditions without hesitation and will raise this child to make her worthy of our name."

Even for the highly traditional House of Darkness, the Traditions of the Vine were the most demanding. Not only did they include the rules of the House, but also those of the Vine itself, with punishments for misdeeds even some Darkholm found too harsh.

During the Time of Breeding, she of the Vine would choose a calendar week and sleep with all House Darkholm men of her generation so that she could be impregnated while the father would never be known. If the infant was born female, it would be kept as the sole daughter and continue the legacy of the Vine. If, however, the child was born male, he would be hurled off the cliffs of Darkholde's Spire. No other Darkholm would hurl a male child with their likeness, but the Traditions of the Vine were such, and, as hard they were to follow, they were followed without question.

"Here," Ira offered Xenovive's newborn, "take *her*."

"What name will you give her, mother?" Xenovive asked.

"I will not name her," Ira responded, her finger in the newborn girl's grasp.

"She of the Vine names every newborn of the Darkholm she brings to the world," Xenovive quoted the Traditions.

"But not of the Vine itself," Ira responded. "She of the Vine names every child of the House she delivers so that the parents understand they do not control their child, but her own daughter, she must name too, so that the Vine can remember that, while she is not under control, she is responsible for her child.

"Now," Ira followed, "what will her name be?"

Xenovive gazed upon her child's golden eyes. She smiled and said, "Aura. Her name will be Aura." She kissed her child's forehead.

Nodding in acceptance, Ira showed a smile rarely seen on her inquisitorial lips, a smile of satisfaction, of feeling she had just achieved the greatest of accomplishments.

"Now, prepare yourself," Ira moved toward a table in the middle of her chamber. "The time has come for me to teach you the last lesson of the Vine."

"I am always ready, Mother."

"If you are ready, then come, child." Ira's voice softened as she beckoned to her daughter to approach. She sat by the small wooden table strewn with quills, bandages, and vials of ink.

Silently, Xenora sat in front of Ira, watching her place her tattooed arm across the tabletop. Mother and daughter did the same. Xen's tattoo was as intricate as her mother's but incomplete. Her skin showed every image, from the hands to the serpent, the many others, including the tongue and the cobra, but nowhere was the amaryllis drawn.

"You once asked when you would get my image." Both women's arms, side by side, appeared as the ivy labyrinth of a nature deity, beautiful and perfect.

"And you said someday you would tell me. That is tonight," Xenovive asked, breastfeeding her child.

The mother smiled warmly.

She took a quill and a blade and, wetting it with the ink, started etching her harp upon the daughter's skin. The pain was sharp but endured as the daughter's eyes filled with fascination, reverence, and wonder.

For hours they worked in silence.

There were no words of men, of history, of battle, of mysteries, or of things Ira had seen during her lifetime. Mother and daughter had spoken plenty the last fifteen years, hiding not even a thought from one another.

After the last stroke, she spoke again. "It is done, my child. Now, I must go."

"Wait, what do you mean 'I must go'?" Xenovive's confusion was evident in her eyes.

"When we of the Vine are certain our child can have their own, we then give our Mark to our child. We leave them with who we are. We leave them with our legacy."

"But, wait," Xenovive said, confused.

"You must, from now on, live for all of us."

"Mother!" Tears and confusion appeared in the daughter's eyes.

"Please do not leave. Do not leave me alone," she pleaded. "My heart is breaking, and for that, I am not ready!"

Ira carefully cleaned the fresh wound on her daughter's skin, where now a red amaryllis in the shape of a harp was depicted. "I must, I will. Xenora, Xenovive, Xen, my daughter . . . You will always be alone. Even among your own, you will be and feel alone, and that is why you are fit to understand your sister, your cousin, your queen. Let your heart break now, and learn to deal with it so that it is not broken to bits when you need it the most."

"I have always known that we of the Vine must one day leave, but I thought I would have time to get ready."

"My child, today you learn this is the way. You have no need for time. I leave because you are ready," the mother turned and opened the door.

"Mother! Where will you go? Where can I find you if I need you?"

She stopped for a moment, and without turning back, she replied, "I am *not* your mother anymore. You *do not* need me; you *will not* need me. I have taught you everything I know, and now you must add to that, just as you choose and add your own Mark. Where will I go, you ask? No one knows, and hopefully, no one will ever know. Goodbye, Xenovive of the Vine."

As the door closed behind her mother, Xenovive's eyes closed. She placed one hand over her own daughter's crib and the other over the small book her mother had left on the table, the small, black book bound in green leather that was now in her care.

Her mother's chamber would now be her own, and hers, from now on, would be Aura's.

Could she have it in her heart to ever do this to her own child when the time came?

Even if she didn't want to, she had to, for she knew it was *the way.*

Xenovive's lips uttered the words she never wished she would have to express, "Goodbye, Ira of the Vine."

LION'S ROAR

There's no worse guide in life than pride . . .

T hat morning he had contemplated the cathedral, the only building inside Ardenay that had been allowed to be larger than the king's palace itself. What fools had his ancestors been, Aorius thought, having allowed such unbridled growth in its midst. It wasn't just the entirety of the cathedral that was problematic, with its buildings that surrounded the walls of the castle, connected to it by bridges that offered not only communication and support but also the parasitic presence of its holy men that forced him to keep his guard up.

During his tenure as duke, fortunately for him, he had been able to convince his brother to stop its construction halfway before the Church had encircled the palace, smothering it as it swallowed its inhabitants.

But even then, it was perhaps too late. Over many years, the Heikken dynasty had allowed the church's influence to grow to be so grand, the testimony of it was seen in the architectural rendition—from one side only the church, and from the other, the palace, but also the church looming over the royal structure's shoulder, as those mothers who supervised their children's actions while the children are unaware.

Throughout his brother's reign, Aorius had watched every step of the archbishop carefully. His older brother Esdrah had been a believer, a lion inside a cage poked by the priest, who would then pick whom to release the furious lion on.

Now he sat on the throne, the crown resting on his head, and that was something, he believed, that drove the archbishop mad under the peaceful guise of his aged face.

"What would our response be, Your Majesty?" Duke Orionne of Alcyn asked, having finished with his presentation.

"If the Tardese want to negotiate with our kingdom," Aorius brooded, "why contact you and not your king? Do they think you have that much influence over the Crown?"

"Their merchant-lords are speaking on behalf of their king, Your Highness," Orionne explained.

"Do you truly believe so, Lord Eomener, or do you take me for a fool?" Aorius fixed his eyes of cold steel on the wealthy noble.

"King Engt is but a puppet-king for the wealthy lords of Tardus, and, while we have our very own puppets here," his eyes went to the representatives of the Holy Duchy of Ashvail, "at least even our puppeteers know their place.

"Write back," the king continued. "Tell the merchant-lords to either write directly to me or pay me a visit if they want to discuss anything with Ardenay."

"Your Highness," the archbishop spoke, "if I may . . . What could Tardus possibly want?"

"That is a good question," Aorius smirked.

"We should tread carefully, Your Highness," the archbishop warned. "It's most unusual to have the leaders of the most neutral nation approach a Crown. They are traditionally more cautious."

"They are," Aorius responded, "the Tardese typically avoid political maneuvering to comply with their pact of neutrality. So, Duke Eomener, ensure the letter sounds less threatening."

"Lord Ileva," Aorius said to Siul, who now sat on his father's seat, "Welcome!"

"Thank you, Your Highness," Siul lowered his head.

"How does the seat feel?"

"I, I'm not sure I understand your question, Your Highness."

"How does it feel," Aorius stood up from the throne, "to come back to serve at the place you escaped from?" He smiled at the quiet seriousness of Siul Ileva's expression, enjoying toying with the tortured soul of his estranged nephew's best friend.

"You see?" He looked around at the others. "*That* is commendable. Lord Ileva is here against his wishes, and yet he's here not to push his own agenda but rather to serve his kingdom on behalf of his sick father. What is the status of Walcrast's border, Lord Ileva?" the king asked coldly.

Despite the king's mockery, Siul collected his thoughts quickly, "Your Highness, the Black Wing is on high alert in the south to avoid a potential incursion from Blackheart. The Gray Wing, as you requested, is massing forces to support the Horne of Bulwharf. The Brown Wing has been sent to monitor the rivers. The people of Mycernase are great sailors, and we want to ensure what happened in Bulwharf was not a distraction to catch us unprepared.

"Well done," Aorius lifted a finger, "Your father was a great strategist. You have a great legacy to follow."

"And now, Lord Bulwharf," King Aorius shifted on his seat, "the moment I have been waiting for."

"Your Highness, I bring news from the Horne," Varen Bulwharf said. "Our forces have been successful at driving our enemies away from the Eighth."

"That is good news," Aorius smiled. "Do you have prisoners?"

"Not one, Your Highness," Varen lamented, "their retreat was well calculated."

"Don't you have greater numbers? What about this skill of the Bulwharf scouts we all hear about?" the king derided.

"It is shameful to admit," Varen recognized, "their feint was successful. We were played."

"Deceit is the way of those who walk the path of Darkness," the archbishop added.

"But more shameful is to admit, Your Highness," the Bulwharf said.

"What?" Aorius's rising tension made itself evident in his temples.

"That they retreated deeper, not back to Blackheart, but rather deep into our land."

The lion's lips began to part in a smile, "Foolish, they are—"

"And they captured the Seventh," Varen lowered his head.

"What?" Aorius slammed his palms on the throne.

"This cannot be," the Champion of Light spoke on behalf of the Holy Duchy.

"Their move was bold," Varen explained. "The Seventh is close to the center of the eastern portion of the Horne. It is the lifeline of both the Sixth, Eighth, Ninth, and Tenth tower."

"And despite that, your incompetence let it fall into their hands!" Aorius fumed.

"We never expected them to move to the most secure tower."

"The tower can be retaken. That should not be our biggest worry," the archbishop interjected, "but the spreading of their ways of deviousness, the permanent harm on the morale of our people, the mockery the servants of the Darkness are making of the Light and its servants . . .

"The Codex of Radiance speaks of this. In the Book of Promises, chapter seven, the second verse reads, 'I have bequeathed to you my mission, that by removing every obstacle, the Light's path remains uninterrupted, so that it may bless its worshippers throughout eternity.'"

"Blessed be the Light," Duke Magenan said, followed by all but the king himself.

"It will be remembered throughout history as the beginning of the corruption of Bulwharf, as the Church of Daneran will tell the world they have the truth, and Ardenay's foundation will shake and crumble," the priest added.

"It will not," irate, Aorius replied.

"Your Highness?" Angevin asked.

"Ready your forces." Standing up from his throne, Aorius fumed, "We march."

———————— ‧‧✦✦✦‧‧ ————————

His eyes of the heavens disappeared behind eyebrows like the purest of clouds. Not long after, they reappeared, ready to consume what lay within the scroll case, not the beautiful, well-written poem that praised all that is good, but what was hidden within the case's secret compartment that his hands, as they had done other times before, found.

Every letter of each phrase was consumed by his hungry eyes, each nourishing the crooked smile that appeared on his face.

Angevin's hands bathed the quill in the soft ink and, without hesitation, its tip scraped a piece of parchment.

The beast stirs. One eye is open. Be at the ready.

THE MARCH

Location: Kingdom of Ardenay, Duchy of Bulwharf,
State of Darane, the Horne

The field lay quiet, its peaceful stillness hiding the intentions of nations, the avoidable clash that men made inevitable.

That same fertile ground that fed men and beasts waited greedily, eager to drink the blood of beasts and men.

Countless soldiers stood on each side, their hands readying or readied, waiting for the signal from their superiors, each man representing an individual, a single component of the army defending the banner of an entire duchy of their kingdom.

All these fighters had the same goal, victory, but each one dreamed of his own. Some minds were on the tactics they planned or on the eagerness to quench their bloodlust. Others' were either on what they had left behind or what awaited them back home.

Still, some dreamed of their future, on how they hoped this was the last battle they ever participated in, not knowing that for many of them, it would be, in one way or another, true.

Thousands of lives, all ready to jump into the unpredictable hands of Fate. Each a potential sacrifice, of life, of everything they had until then lived for, of everything they or their loved ones could ever dream, all but for the few, powerful men at the top, many of whom had made no effort to obtain the position they held.

To the west, King Aorius's banner flew over the Eighth Tower, surrounded by the encampment of his royal battalion of three hundred men, daring anyone to approach the stone carcass the steel lion had claimed.

Ahead of them a Bulwharf brigade, six thousand strong, under the command of the Lord Bull, Varen Bulwharf. They were reinforced from the south by battalions flying the banners of both Ashvail, land of the Church, and the

Wings of Walcrast. Seven hundred men were commanded by the Champion of the Light, Duke Anderei Magenan, and four hundred by the new Winglord, Siul of House Ileva.

Overlooking the east side of the valley, atop a small hill, the red of the crowned black heart fluttered where its royal brigade had set camp. It comprised two thousand soldiers, mustered from multiple duchies under a single banner. They were preceded by a three-thousand-strong brigade of Valador warriors, while twelve hundred more of the combined forces of Valador and Volanar remained behind, near the border, besieging the Ninth Tower into submission. To the north and south, three hundred of Aligrand's soldiers and mercenaries had split their forces in two.

Outside Blackheart's royal tent, Idian Darkholm stood around the planning table accompanied by various captains. His eyes scanned the map's valley where the forces of Ardenay had an advantage over his current army. His stony, furrowed brow said everything his lips did not.

Behind him, King Septem emerged. Even in war, the crown rested on his head. Everything, from the cape around his shoulders to his ceremonial armor, even his sword's scabbard, was of the purest white. He was followed by Eriadna, shield in hand. Upon seeing them walking toward the edge of the camp, Idian joined the pair.

Long before they had stopped being Septem, Eriadna, and Idian and had become the King, the Shield, and the General, the three that would one day be remembered as the Towers of Darkholde.'

There they stood, their yellow eyes on the horizon, their expression as firm as their conviction.

"Your Highness, all is in place," Idian spoke. "The enemy is on the move. We await your instructions."

"Await no more," Septem lifted a gauntleted hand. "We move."

The general bowed and left, shouting instructions to his captains to begin their march, to those knights on foot to prepare to escort the king, to the messengers that would relay his instructions as swiftly as the wind blew, to all he ordered, "Fight without mercy, offer no quarter, ensure each life we lose takes out ten of theirs. End their insult! Show them the price of their betrayal! March!"

And soon after, Blackheart's horns blasted the signal. It was followed by the response of Ardenay's trumpets, by the deafening clamor of men on both sides, by the stampede of mounted knights and steeds muting the clash of metal rising near the valley's center.

The Shield affixed her assigned mask in place, in Darkholm tradition, as did all of the House who were present, all except for Septem, for so unmoving was his face, he was deemed to have a mask in his own skin.

"Eriadna," Septem addressed.

"My king."

"Ready yourself."

"Always at the ready, my king," she grabbed her great shield. "My life is yours."

Upon his signal, the line of Black Knights parted before him, and he dashed straight as an arrow, his white cape struggling to keep up.

It was a poet's dream, the White King clad in his ceremonial armor, its ceramic surface engraved with the sigils of the twelve duchies of Blackheart. It was the same chest piece he had worn since the moment he took the crown, since the day they bent the knee, the same he had given instruction to not repair upon suffering any damage on its surface.

Throughout his reign, Septem's armor had become nothing short of legendary, for the Blood had come to believe that if any dent was received by any of the symbols on its surface, great tragedy would befall the duchy it represented and its people.

Thus, upon seeing Septem on the battlefield, those around him fought fiercely, fanatically, not only for the honor of protecting their king but just as much to protect the fate of their own people.

Septem moved, not swiftly nor slow, but at the perfect pace that made his every maneuver seem as rehearsed as they were effective.

Wherever he went, he brought with him the cold breeze of death.

Sanguinus left its scabbard. The pale blade sang the last song many a man would hear as it sliced the air, as it cut their dreams and hopes short, as it crushed the hearts of the families of those whose blood it drank.

On its aerial journey, it bathed itself in the blood of many as if gaining sentience to protect the purity of its wielder's cloak, as if its perfect dance would stain everything but his reputation.

Steps away, his Shield followed his dance, her moves less graceful, her response almost synchronous but certainly perfect. Her eyes, her ears, read his every step, the rhythm she understood, the song she knew by heart. She ran ahead, at times behind, his changing stance keeping her attention as she read in his muscles and form what his next move would be.

Eriadna Darkholm needed not to be graceful, and she didn't even care to. Her swift response needed to, at best, end, at worst, cripple any sign of danger that could befall the man she was sworn to protect.

She was his shadow; she was his Shield.

Near the valley's center, the tall, intimidating warriors of the Bulwharf clashed against Blackheart's shielded vanguard, their heavy axes and picks managing to momentarily break their lines but not their morale.

From the bottom of a hill, one named Usef Lahur, a Thunder of Bulwharf, commanded his men. He was strong, of large size, of the bulls from Darane who were rumored to be descendants of giants. Even his warhorse had been specially bred to carry the weight of men like him.

Usef ordered his mounted men to follow him wherever the tip of his spear was pointed, trampling more than a few enemy soldiers to death.

It was after their third pass their warhorses were met by two flights of barbed quarrels from Lord Caime Grey's men, taking down mounts and throwing men off their dying beasts' backs.

Following their fall and their commander's whistle, Lord Grey's men released their war dogs upon their fallen opponents, turning them into a feast of blood and gore.

Meanwhile, Gustavus rode behind Erdrick Darkholm, felling men with less precision but superior strength, the blood of a man decapitated by his sword splashing into the eye sockets of both the skull helmet and the one depicted on his mask.

Their flanks were strengthened by soldiers and nearby, the Black Knights, Commander Serverus's ever-ready sword arm among them.

Together, they navigated the chaos of the battlefield. Erdrick's eyes were on the Eighth, knowing that, if taken, together they could ensure a deep blow to Ardenay's forces, sealing the fate of their king.

But on their way, they were met and repelled by the able mounted riders of Walcrast's Black Wing.

Elsewhere, the bull spear at the hands of Lord Varen Bulwharf went through men like a hot iron on exposed skin.

He shouted orders to his closest men, who relayed the rallying message of the general who commanded from within the battlefield. His every command, he knew, would send men from one or both sides to their deaths. This was a war he hadn't wanted, but he was a man bound by honor, and protecting his people was as important as obeying his king. While the bulls had not initiated this conflict, he would make sure to end it.

His armored boot kicked an attacker's face right before the tip of his spear pierced the man's chest to end his life. He would end many more, but aside from that, there was something he was bound by honor to do.

Varen's eyes looked around the battlefield for any sign of the man he hoped to face, Maxius Darkholm. The Darkholm was nowhere to be found, for while Maxius would have preferred to be there fighting, he would rather keep control of the fortress he had taken from under Varen's nose.

King Aorius Heikken's hands pressed against the Eighth's parapets, his blazing fury seeking to melt the cold stone through his armored gloves. He witnessed the chaos on the battlefield, the poor advancement of Ardenay's forces, and the resilience and unity of Blackheart's army centered around its own monarch.

"Signal to our reinforcements to start mobilizing," the king ordered the captain of the Eighth. "I want our enemies to face a crushing defeat."

"They will, with the Light's blessing," Principal Tomaze Rees, head of the diocese of Hageos, smiled at King Aorius, "despite not having been blessed before the battle."

"We both know there is no need for blessings," the king frowned.

"At the very least, it boosts their morale, Your Majesty," the religious leader stated, "it is because of the absence of the Light's blessing that our forces are advancing little."

"Then, if you're a man of faith, bless them now. It surely won't make a difference to your god," Aorius mocked.

"The Light prefers formal worship, the firstfruits, Your Majesty, not leftovers."

"Ah, I see," Aorius sneered, "quite capricious, your god is. He'd rather have his men lose their lives because they didn't pray that one day as he wanted. Our men will achieve victory," he continued, flaring, "and not because of any divine blessing, but because our army is superior, because we have better men."

He then set his eyes upon his youngest son, Langel, the disappointing "bronze lion" by his side, at his son's eyes on the battlefield and wondered, 'what is he thinking?' He knew that Langel had come because it was expected of him, but the coward he saw would have preferred a hundred times to stay behind, playing court games and pretending to pray just to annoy him.

Langel wasn't anything like his brother, Vallein.

Down below, proud Vallein fought with the fierceness of a lion … but pride and ferocity can be a dangerous combination to possess.

Vallein and his men charged, the lance in his hand as steady and firm as it could be in the hand of a trained man in his mid-thirties. They plowed through a unit of Olath Valm slingers with ease before they were shot in the backs by Featherfell's greatbows, taking most of his unit with as much ease.

Finding himself almost surrounded, he rushed through one of two openings, lance readied, toward a large, armored man he saw ahead.

The large man got a glimpse of the lance through his mask. Quickly, he turned sideways and dodged, deflecting with his steel buckler before jumping to headbutt Vallein, whose helmet protected his skull from being crushed but not his back from hitting the ground. As he landed, a flick of the man's wrist was followed by the swinging of his arms, by a clinking and a snap, and the appearance and lengthening chain connecting the rod in his hand to the heavy head of what had become a flail, which he wrapped around the lance's falling body to snap it in two.

"My name is Brenis Darkholm." The large man towered over the fallen Vallein. "I am the Toymaker, and *these* are my toys."

He swung with all his might toward Vallein's chest, but a kick from Balkar, hero among the Thunders, sent him flat on his back.

"My lord," Balkar shouted, "I'll cover your retreat!"

A quarter of his men ran toward Vallein, helping him up to escort him back to safety.

Balkar took off on his horse to circle back and charge Brenis before he stood up and regained his balance while the mounts of two of his men charged toward Brenis.

As the largest living member of House Darkholm, both his size and the weight of his armor made it difficult for him to stand quickly.

So he rolled instead, swinging his flail and trapping a rider's leg, dismounting him with a thud, followed by the cracking of his skull under his bent helmet upon the impact of Brenis's weapon.

"Fengo!" Brenis called from behind his mask. "Did you see that?"

Gustavus's youngest brother stood his ground against three men, swinging his bastard sword and switching between one and two hands to keep them confused while he took each down. "Oh yes, I saw your fall," he jested. "It was magnificent!"

"Oh, I will show you magnificence!" he laughed. "Boy, was *that* good," Brenis told himself, looking around for his opponents. "Now, where is this fool?"

Meanwhile, back in Blackheart's royal camp, the general and his captains discussed tactical movements.

"Lord General," a high-ranking captain reported, "our royal regiment is suffering notable losses but still holding on near the center close to the Lord Bull's unit."

"Good news," Duke Primon of Aligrand celebrated, "Commander Noxheeva will push through and take care of his closest men."

"That is nothing to be celebrated," Idian's scolding drew the attention of the men around the table. "The Lord Bull's forces are larger and better prepared for this battle than our men are. They have too many generals. We have only gotten close because the arrogance of Ardenay's leaders makes it hard for them to cooperate effectively.

"Even our own forces would be more effective if *your* men would have worked together with the rest of the kingdom's." His eyes pierced Primon's.

"I meant no harm, Lord General," Duke Primon responded, "but Noxheeva is a strong and capable commander among our mercenaries. While she does not work too well with others, I don't doubt her loyalty."

"Loyalty, but *to whom*?" Idian squinted.

"Lord General," Primon responded, somewhat offended, "my men staying separate is no coincidence, that is true, but this battle is our chance to garner approval, to gain glory, to prove to our king that he was mistaken when he gave our land to Olath Valm. Now," he continued, "let us prove to your lordship our worth in battle."

Siul Ileva's muscles itched. It was the first time he waged battle as the Winglord. He was as confident as he was conflicted, for his mind told him to stay put, to watch and strategize as his father had done, while his heart told him to jump into the field and join the fray along with his men. But he knew today he couldn't. He was expected to be exactly where he was, surrounded by his messengers and captains of his wings.

From where he stood, he scouted the battlefield and saw that Darkholm woman run toward a pair of her own to be thrown up in the air to almost take flight, as the Wing Knights of Walcrast did whenever they were catapulted into combat. And there she was, in midair, a gracious bird of prey not unlike the one depicted in her mask.

He almost missed when she both kicked and pierced the chest of the mounted Thunder who was assailing her allies, killing him instantly, sending him to the ground while her feet landed on the back of his horse, where she stood, holding the reins with a foot and deftly slaying men to either side of her new mount while she traversed the battlefield, bringing chaos and disarray wherever she went.

It was a mesmerizing sight, like a beautiful, parasitic flower one must get rid of before it's too late.

"Take her down," he ordered his commander of the Gray Wing, a blonde woman named Hinea, a javelin expert who, after just a second try, grazed the mounted woman's leg with one of her missiles, forcing her to sit over the mount's seat and drawing her attention.

The woman kicked the warhorse into a charge, dead set on taking Hinea down, but her advance was stopped and redirected by the relentless assault of the wing knights.

"I'm nervous, Rowena," Lady Charon said, helping her cousin set their accoutrements ready on the pavilion's table, "I wish we were home."

"But we are not, Charon," Elleonora responded, readying her own cloak, "so you better get used to it."

"Aren't you nervous, Elle?" Charon questioned.

"I will not lie to you. I am," Elleonora responded. "At least my Master is here," she continued, "that alone brings me some comfort. My husband and much of my family are out here, so despite my fear, I know here is the right place for me to be."

"No matter how much one has prepared for a moment, it is never the same when that moment comes," Rowena added.

"You are never nervous, Rowena," Charon pointed out. "How come?"

Rowena smiled at her cousin, "At times, there is simply no time to be or feel." She caressed Charon's cheek as she walked past her toward the outside. "Come, it is time to work."

Elleonora found her way to Davidov's right, who watched the battle from outside the royal pavilion. In his hands rested the hook spear of his station, over his face the mask he had been given, an ancient black face, its eyes and mouth being forced open by fingers of bone.

He had participated in many battles, although many of them only as the Master of Death.

At the end of the day, like most times before, he and his men would scour the field, ensuring the survivors were either slain or taken captive, their valuables taken back to Blackheart's treasury. In the meantime, they would wait patiently, like the birds of death their unit had been named for.

"Wow . . ." Charon looked everywhere, trying to absorb and make sense of the mayhem in the field. To one side, soldiers exchanged blows, falling one by one as if purposely trying to form a pile of dead bodies. Somewhere else, she saw the beautifully organized Wings of Walcrast and how they took their enemies down with what seemed like little effort.

A few dozen meters from the king, Elzabeth rode in a chariot, its driver directing the horses while she flagged at her archer unit whom to shoot down from behind her grinning, fanged mask.

But Rowena's eyes were elsewhere, not on the warriors, the mounted men, or enemy catapults and ballistae. They were dead set on Blackheart's monarch and the field beyond, watching for his safety.

Sanguinus sliced the air, severing a soldier's legs in a single swing. The monarch was surrounded by his reckless enemies. King Septem spun around, disorienting his assailants with the flight of his cape.

Starting to feel the weight of her great shield, Eriadna planted it on the ground forcefully. A Walcrast captain vaulted toward her, his hands grasping a spear, but the Shield stepped toward him and, grabbing his arm, she slammed him down against her shield, but not before activating the mechanism that sprung a long blade along its top, the one that sent the spearman's head rolling along the ground.

Lord of Light, Oh Radiant One, guide my steps to smite the Darkness. Duke Anderei prayed. The Champion of the Light and his mounted knights barely moved, and when they did, they did so slowly, perhaps to avoid losing a single of his closest men while they advanced or because they were expecting some sort of signal.

From atop his horse, Anderei saw King Septem fighting, the accursed *Sanguinus* in hand.

May your blessed blade one day face and destroy the blighted one, the duke prayed, his hand resting over *Radiant's* hilt, eager to draw it and face this enemy of his god and of his people.

Having routed the Black Wing of Walcrast, both Erdrick's and Serverus's men galloped back toward the Eighth when they heard the trumpet coming from the hills to the north, signaling the arrival of Bull Barwen Dassan and five hundred men, who had circled and crossed deep into Suhne territory to avoid being seen by Blackheart's scouts. Barwen's mounted men initiated a charge toward Septem's weakest flank, forcing Serverus to abandon his original plan. Instead, he divided his men, sending them to reinforce Blackheart's army wherever they judged assistance was needed.

Upon the trumpet, both Blackheart's and Ardenay's soldiers hesitated for a moment that Septem did not waste. The king slashed his way out of the encirclement allowing himself and his Shield to be escorted by their men back to camp, where Idian and the captains awaited around the planning table.

It was clear, now that the enemy's morale and numbers had been boosted by the surprise attack, Blackheart's forces would face greater danger.

And yet, the White King's eyes looked upon the battlefield while his Shield's wounds were under Rowena's care.

"Your Highness, Great General," a Duskforge commander asked, "should we prepare to retreat?"

"No," King Septem responded.

"But, Your Majesty," the man insisted, "I don't mean to speak wisdom to you, but our forces are being routed."

"We wait," Septem responded firmly. "General, have you signaled our own reinforcements."

"I have, Your Highness," Idian responded, "but something seems amiss."

"What is?" Septem questioned.

"The Ninth is now ours, and yet Duke Pohl Gillspiel's forces are taking too long," Idian answered. "What shall we do, Your Majesty, if our reinforcements do not come?"

"We must be patient," Septem instructed. "We must hold the line."

"So it will be," Idian responded. Turning to face his men, he lifted his hand to shout his next order when the booming sound of horns came from the rearguard where the banners of Valador and Volanar appeared and, with them, the trumpeting of elephants and *volaphanes*.[1]

Followed by the desperate neighing of horses and the shrill cries of their own men protecting the rearguard getting trampled, crushed under the beasts' impetuous might.

---

(1) volaphane: Native to the underground duchy of Volanar, volaphanes were similar to elephants, with several differences. They were albino, six-legged, weighing twelve thousand stones, with four tusks, with oversized, blind eyes, totally reliant on the rider when overground.

RETREAT

Location: Kingdom of Ardenay, Duchy of Bulwharf,
State of Darane, the Horne

Few things slow us down like bitterness...

L angel Heikken gazed upon the distance, where the body of the enemy encampment convulsed, putting to the test the morale of even its staunchest defenders.

From atop the Eighth, he could witness Blackheart's formation collapsing as the royal tent did under the duress of the surprise attack. Of these, poets and bards in Ardenay's courts would write ballads to which its nobles would dance and to which its people would celebrate.

But no bard's creation would ever do justice to what his eyes witnessed that day.

He would always remember the ravenous flames, the echoing screams, the rampaging volaphanes, and the ballistae on their backs, as he would remember the times the dukes of Valador and Volanar had met with King Aorius to offer their allegiance.

He would also remember seeing his father that day, watching the betrayal, the collapse, the defeat, all with a smile brimming with satisfaction.

Chaos took over Blackheart's royal camp, where orders were shouted left and right. The horn announcing the retreat was blown, but it was easier to announce than to do, for Blackheart's main weakened forces were pinned between enemies of and from the kingdom.

"My Hellhounds!" Lord Caime Grey called his men. "The vanguard is now King Septem's camp! Now, go, go, go! Cover his retreat! Our lives for our lords!"

"Long live the cowards!" His men shouted in unison and, with swords and axes, with bows and wardogs, they ran to protect the Darkholm king.

Erdrick stayed behind to help prevent the slaughter of retreating soldiers, but many lives were still lost, including a fourth of his knights.

I will end his life with my own hands, he swore to himself, his eyes on the top of the Eighth where a triumphant Aorius looked back at Septem's son.

But his smug expression disappeared upon hearing the rumbling drums and horns from the north, where numerous horsemen appeared over the hills, on its banner, the tan Sun of Suhne.

They raced downhill, archers and spearmen on horseback, swift as a storm, shooting down Ardenay's men for having dared to cross uninvited into the sacred desert of their Sun god.

They were led by Too'prah, general of Ahni, a bald man of skin and eyes as dark as onyxes.

Too'prah's focus on Ardenay allowed an opening Idian would not waste a moment to exploit.

In the blink of an eye, the Master of Death's carriage was readied. He was sent away to Darkholm with Elleonora, who had insisted Rowena and Charon leave with her.

"You go, Charon, I will stay," Rowena had responded. "I must ensure our patriarch's safety."

At her words, Lady Charon's shaking hands closed the carriage's door, and she stayed to help Rowena pack her belongings and whatever else, if anything, was needed of her.

The general then ordered an escort for Charon, Alex, and the remaining Darkholm in camp to the Seventh.

While it was located southwest, deeper into enemy territory, Idian considered it more dangerous to have them move west, where the enemies who could easily recognize them were certainly waiting.

"Your Highness," he spoke to Septem next, "it is time for you to retreat." The king nodded, understanding the gravity of the situation. Unlike most rulers, his pride was not for himself but for the achievements and prosperity of his people. The Lord of Darkholde had always been practical, and he wouldn't leave them leaderless, spelling doom to nearly seven decades of dedication to his work on the throne.

The general studied the situation, the layout of the land. To both the east and the south, the land belonged to Valador and Volanar of Blackheart, but the east was most dangerous, leading straight to the capital of the twin duchies that had betrayed them twice.

Further south was Featherfell, so far unquestionable allies, but the deep forests and toxic swamps would delay their return to the capital while potentially facilitating their pursuit.

His only other option was to have them travel east along the southern perimeter of the Horne, but that would take them through the lands of the Sixth and the Fourth towers, and that delay would pose an unacceptable risk.

'I would have them cross the mountains through the north of Valador,' Idian thought, 'but if my wife was here, she would send them through the forests south.'

In the end, he made his decision, "The Darkholm thoroughbreds are ready. Your Majesty will be escorted south, into Valador and through the border forest, and into Featherfell, where we will send word to Duke Driscoll to ensure your safe passage."

"I will provide escort," Duke Ferertr of Aligrand stated firmly, drawing their attention.

"You will not," Idian frowned.

"Why?" Primon questioned, and upon not hearing a response, he insisted, "Answer me, why?"

"The royal guard will escort the king," the general responded.

"There's just five of them left," Primon pointed out.

"Five *very* well-trained, trustworthy men," Idian added.

At the words, Primon took offense, "Do you not trust me?"

"I do not," Idian answered.

"And neither do I," the Shield added, standing by the king's side, helping him onto his mount.

"Why don't you trust me?" Primon's angry eyes looked at the three of them, "Tell me! Tell me!"

"My Lord King," he pleaded, taking a step toward Septem, "What can I ever do to earn your trust? What can we do? My people have sacrificed so much for the kingdom. Is *everything* not enough?"

But Septem's quiescence troubled the duke.

"Your Majesty," he continued, "I know I haven't been in the Council as long as the rest, but yet my people listen to me. The animosity toward Your Highness is real, but I have assured them we would have an opportunity to shine and find grace in your eyes. I ask only for the chance to show your trust, to make amends.

"Your Highness wisely said," he added, "'shall the children pay for the sins of their forefathers?'"

At the quote, Septem's eyes of winter set on Primon's, and yet the duke's determination allowed him to stop himself from averting his eyes from the monarch's piercing gaze.

"Duke Primon," Septem's order rumbled, "you will escort me back to Blackheart."

Reluctantly, the general spoke to Eriadna, "Shield of the King, we must wait no longer. Go," he ordered, feeling the ground tremble under his feet.

"Master of Life, watch for His Majesty. As soon as they regroup, I will send the knights your way."

"And you?" Rowena asked the old general.

"I will stay behind to save what I can of our forces," Idian responded.

"Your Majesty," he then looked up at Septem before bending a knee, "My Lord, Patriarch, if we were not to exchange words again, it is an honor to have served you. *In Tenebris nos.*"

His heavy words felt more powerful than the boulders that had flown from Bulwharf's trebuchets or the roaring trumpets of Volanar's mounts upon their imminent arrival. With them, he sent the escort away before turning back to face the madness.

With the elephants and volaphanes having reinforced their enemies, Blackheart's situation was dire. His forces were dwindling, scattered like insects under a sudden blaze.

Idian Darkholm closed his eyes and took a deep breath, one that filled more than his lungs.

His blood boiled. His mustard eyes saw not the chaos of war but rather a slow-moving field of men waiting to be reaped, begging to be bloodied.

The general reached for *Fraenum's* hilt, wrapping his hand around it when his fingers felt the cold ring, that link that kept his blade secured inside its scabbard.

At this moment, there was little he wanted more than to charge into the battlefield, to find the Bulwharf, to cut Varen's loved ones into tiny pieces and feed them to him before doing the same with Varen's own body.

Was it something he deserved? It mattered not to Idian. It was something Varen would get.

But his secured blade held him back.

It wasn't the time, at least not now.

Back at the Eighth, an alarmed captain hurriedly came to the presence of Ardenay's king. "Your Majesty! Revered Father," he addressed both men, "we need to make preparations to depart. The Bulwharf wants to ensure your safety."

"Depart?" Aorius protested. "We are not departing."

"Your Majesty," the captain interrupted, "We can't fight on two fronts."

"Neither can they," Aorius pointed at Blackheart's distant forces. "Look at them retreat. Our men regroup, ready to defend against Suhne and finish Blackheart. I want to see this through."

"Your Majesty," the captain insisted, "this attack is only a ruse. There's a much larger force from Suhne marching toward us from the northwest."

"It can't be," Aorius questioned. "How can these savages outsmart us?"

"We don't know, Your Majesty, but they are moving," the captain responded. "As it stands, we are currently losing many men. I'm sorry to insist, but this might be our only chance not to be cut off from our own forces."

Frustrated, Aorius turned away from the parapet, and the first thing he saw was the Principal's hand rubbing his holy crystal while, on his face, a smile was almost showing.

North of them, the Suhnite army mercilessly punished the flank of Ardenay's forces, sowing fear, maneuvering like a stream finding its way around a rock, and decimating their morale as Adenay's units lost communication with their comrades. While largely unarmored, Suhne's large number of spearmen, javelineers, and horsemen moved rapidly, sowing confusion among its fatigued enemies.

Their shots flew indiscriminately, killing soldiers, healers, and even peasants carrying Ardenay's supplies, forcing Ardenay's soldiers to retreat behind the regrouping of the main forces of Bulwharf, who readied to counterattack, rallying behind Varen Bulwharf's banner.

Septem's escort took off on horseback, Eriadna, Rowena, and Duke Primon among its numbers. They were protected by five of the royal guards and twenty-four of the duke's men. They maneuvered as best as they could around the Volanar's mounts that trampled much of the remaining forces. A trio of elephants charged the retreating escort, but a volley of quarrels drew their attention back toward the assailing crossbowmen of Ravencrest.

"Scatter!" one of the royal guards shouted.

Rowena looked back and saw ballistae atop several of the towering volaphanes being fired, taking down five of the duke's men and their horses, but her quick reaction allowed her to move her mount away to avoid her mount being tripped. But the volaphane riders kept shooting to take them down before the escort was out of range.

It was one of these bolts that hit true, right through the abdomen of Eriadna Darkholm's horse.

SUNDERED

Location: Kingdom of Ardenay, Duchy of Bulwharf,
State of Darane, the Horne

Little is more powerful than whatever can break a woman's heart . . .

"Stop!" her voice thundered.

Her eyes were filled with fury, her mind inundated with determination, despite the bruises the fall had wrought on her body. The king had halted, but she had instructed Septem's escort to continue onward. She wouldn't risk his valuable life.

Eriadna had protected her king for most of his reign, putting his safety above any and all of her own interests.

This moment would be no exception.

Throughout her life, Eriadna had proven to be like a giant boulder in a shallow stream. Anyone would have to, at best, go around her because through her would be nothing short of impossible. For long she had worked tirelessly to protect the capital of Coldforge, both managing her county of Greyhale from a distance while she ensured with every breath the king's crown was safe.

Until now, she had been closer to Septem than perhaps his own children, while surely he felt closer to her than her own.

Her actions had stopped many men before, including he who had been the love of her life. In the performance of her duty, she had perhaps broken many hearts, including her own.

It was thus fitting; her mask was as a woman's emotionless face turning into metal and stone.

While anything could be said about her, no one could ever say she shirked from the duty she incarnated. Some could claim she had failed them, but not once had she failed her oath. She had embodied the words, 'We do what must be done.'

Battered as she was, imperfect and dented in many places, Eriadna had always been Septem's perfect Shield.

She would fight for him; she would buy him time.

Seeing the escort now out of range, Eriadna sought to draw the volaphanes' attention to stop them from pursuing.

"I am Eriadna of House Darkholm," she shouted to the top of her lungs, "Countess of Greyhale, Baroness of Grim Vein, daughter of Tianma 'the Fertile' Darkholm, and above all, Shield of the King. Face me, you lowly scum."

Her provocation stopped the volaphane riders' advance. They were led by a middle-aged captain, Raasel of House Gorien. Raasel, a minor noble from a House of elephant herders, who had risen to become a leader among the elite volaphane riders due to both hard work and great skill, had found it hard to be noticed among the many great warriors of the underground pachyderm pits.

This was his time to shine. This was his time to prove himself, and seeing the royal entourage was now out of reach, his attention was drawn to the woman with the booming voice, the one with the noble titles who challenged his men.

"My name is Raasel, of House Gorien, captain of the Third White Front," Raasel shouted above her. "Today, your death will bring glory to my name!"

Pointing at him with her sword, Eriadna spat on the ground. "Your name will only be pronounced to be mocked. Your history will be one of endless ruin. This field will be your grave, you traitor!"

Pulling his reins, Raasel sent his armored beast rearing, raising its four tusks and trumpeting ferociously under the command. The ground before it was crushed under its paws, shaking the earth under the Shield's feet.

But her balance was undisturbed. She stood on her toes and shifted her weight, readying her guard as she saw the ballista on the creature's back was ready.

The bolt was fired, aimed at her torso.

Trained as she was, Eriadna wouldn't be quick enough to dodge it. Swift as lightning, it closed the distance toward the woman, whose feet shifted, allowing the missile to glance off the surface of the shield she angled between them. Where the bolt had touched it, a new, deep dent formed.

Eriadna's suspicious eyes studied the other riders. While most were busy fighting the resisting forces, she couldn't trust those who were close. The Blood of Volanar was known for their honor in battle, but today she couldn't trust these traitors nearby would not intervene in her duel.

She needed to stay far enough from Raasel's spear but close enough to the enormous beast, knowing centuries of underground breeding allowed the large, red eyes of the volaphanes limited vision, and that only while protected by its caged visors.

The Shield was undoubtedly tired, her muscles ached, but decades of training had taught her to fight through fatigue and pain. She now faced a skilled warrior and his rampant mount. She had to read them both and make her disadvantage a boon.

She was fortunate that, to the huge beast, she was little more than a shadow.

In a single move, she planted the greatshield on the ground, activating the contraption that released its blade.

Wrapping her hand around the hilt of her sword, she readied her stance, and, shouting, she swung hard to deflect the spear and jump over the incoming tusks of the pachyderm.

Unable to cut through the creature's armored plates, more than once, she sought to get underneath, but Raasel's spear stopped her, allowing the slow creature to turn and keep her in front of it.

She moved around the creature's six legs repeatedly, seeking to disorient it while buying herself a moment of respite, a chance to catch her breath, forcing it to stomp repeatedly in place before realizing she wasn't there. Raasel's spear tip wheezed, coming too close to her neck when she dove around the mount's legs.

She breathed in deeply when she felt a warm sharpness on the back of her shoulder, where a quarrel from Raasel's hand crossbow protruded, piercing her plate and wounding her sword arm.

Looking down, Eriadna could glimpse the trail of blood falling toward the ground. But she wasted no second. Both of her hands now wrapped around the hilt as she shifted into an offensive stance.

Smiling, imagining her face writhing in pain under the metal mask, Raasel readied another quarrel. It was then he lost sight of her when his volaphane roared and would have thrown him off its back had his seat not been perfectly secured. Instantly, he yanked and sent the creature forward. Its front left leg had lost some of its armored plates, the ones that now lay there behind him, bloodied.

Raasel turned his mount, but she was faster. Using the creature's tusk for leverage, Eriadna jumped and slashed at the cage protecting the creature's left eye.

The volaphane trumpeted, enraged, the brightness to which it wasn't accustomed, making it harder to be controlled.

It slammed its trunk once, twice, moving toward Eriadna's retreating shadow. The third time she held the flat of her blade up and almost lost her balance under its pummeling weight. Having found her, it slammed down forcefully a fourth time, straight into the gyrating figure of the Shield and into the greatshield's blade.

In the same motion, Eriadna swung down with all her might, severing the volaphane's trunk, its agonizing roar heard across the battlefield as it showered the ground around it with blood.

The Shield looked for an opening amidst the volaphane's pain-ridden frenzy when she stepped on a puddle of blood where she lost her balance, which she quickly regained by planting the tip of her sword on the ground.

But it was that ill-fated moment that created a different type of opening.

A sharp pain ran through her leg.

Looking down, she saw a bolt running through her calf that effectively impaled her leg on the ground. Groaning, she wrapped her hand around the missile in an attempt to dislodge it when she felt an explosion inside her abdomen.

Like that terrible, painful Red Day[1] when her kin watched as she birthed the demon . . . when her back spasms had been so severe her legs had become numb for days.

And numb her legs were right now, not from spasms but from the severing of her spine by the giant tusk that now traversed her, the same that lifted her up like an entangled marionette.

'Not done,' she thought, attempting to lift her sword with her wounded arm, swinging it weakly as she held back her pain. But Raasel's spear pierced her chest once, one more time, until no more words, but only blood spurted out of her mouth.

Volanar's riders celebrated Raasel's victory.

They chanted the name of the one who had faced and taken down the stalwart wall Eriadna had been. No doubt, he thought, his companions would see him as more than a worthy leader.

"Blood of Valanor!" He raised his spear triumphantly and faced his men, whose faces had become an amalgam of half-smiles and rising fear.

Raasel's eyes trailed those of his men back to Eriadna's mangled body, from where irate, marigold eyes blazed back at him.

"You are not Blood." Her garbled voice was full of scorn. "You are spittle!"

In a single move, Eriadna spat into his face, blinding him, and with a swift swing, his head was separated from his neck to roll alongside his volaphane's back.

Now riderless, the volaphane entered a wild frenzy, attacking closest to him, forcing them away right into the incoming Black Knights, all while the woman once again forgot her pain and hacked furiously at the giant creature's head.

It was one of those attacks that went through its eye toward its brain, one that sent it staggering forward before collapsing.

The Black Knights had been able to break the formation of the volaphane unit. Now leaderless and having been attacked by one of their own, it had become harder for the volaphanes to be controlled. Their riders had scattered away, seeking to regroup before they could effectively return to fight.

Seeing her on the ground, Gustavus ran toward his mother's body, planting his knees on the ground, his hands desperately seeking how to remove her from under the volaphane.

The only colors over her pale skin were from blood and the dust that had collected after the enormous creature's legs had failed.

Upon hearing the voice of her oldest son, Eriadna's eyes opened. "Go," she said weakly, pointing a finger away toward the south, " . . . and ensure the crown . . . is safe . . ."

Gustavus clenched his teeth. Here in front of him was this woman who was both his progenitor and his rival, she who, to him, had failed at one and excelled at the other. Here her life was ebbing away, and all she could think of was her duty.

"Mother!" he shouted, grabbing her shoulders. "Mother! Look at me! Tell me at least once that you love me! Tell me, just once, that you are proud of me!"

Eriadna scowled, her bloodshot eyes set on his from under the deep furrows of her brows. "My son . . . you know . . ." Her voice almost failed her. ". . . I would never . . . *lie* to you . . ."

With her last words, Gustavus's voice rose. Frustrated, he looked up, and slamming his fists on the ground, he screamed both out of unbelievable anger and endless pain.

(1) Red Day: Once a year, the celestial bodies align themselves, painting the sky red for an entire day. For some, it is a good omen, while it is the opposite for others.

FROM THE HEART

Location: Kingdom of Ardenay, Duchy of Bulwharf,
State of Darane, close to the perimeter of Blackheart

Being a hero does not make one's every action heroic . . .

Their horses galloped, twenty-six riders moving southward, where the lightly wooded region of the Horne ended at the border of the kingdom of Blackheart.

It would take about an hour before they reached Blackheart's protective wall and then some more before they reached the closest of its manned gates, one that led through the lands of the duchies that had betrayed their king.

'What is worse,' Duke Primon Ferertr thought, 'to be left outside and captured by pursuing enemies or to be captured by traitorous soldiers manning the gate?'

Riding to the left of the king, he wondered if those men on the wall could be in on it and willing to betray the kingdom with their leaders.

'Even if they are, would they have been informed of our route by now? Unlikely,' he mused, watching the royal guards around them. Even on horseback, they stayed close to protect their monarch.

As they moved south, the density of the woods increased to soon become a young forest, where a floor of scattered greens and dry branches offered covering to uneven ground. The riders were forced to slow their pace lest the legs of their mounts be broken.

Their slow advance came to a halt when they reached the edge of the woods close to the gate.

"Who goes there?" a man of the wall questioned, his companion looking down from their vantage point on the wall.

"We are Blood from Aligrand under the command of its duke, Primon Ferertr," one of his trusted men responded. "We request passage to the safety of the lands of the twin duchies beyond the wall."

"We are at war," the gate's captain shouted from above. "We understand you are Blood, but for safety reasons, passage is not allowed at this time."

"I am Primon Ferertr, duke of Aligrand," the nobleman raised his voice, "I demand passage so that we can return to my lands."

Descending from his position, the gate captain came upon the portcullis where he and his men could better inspect the duke's men.

"My lord duke," the captain hesitated, "I apologize for the wait, but I have been given instructions from the lords of the twin duchies—"

"It happens to be *their lord* who I am escorting to safety," the duke interjected with a sly smile, signaling at the tree edge, where the magnificent white figure of Septem awaited.

Primon Ferertr

Shortly after, the order was shouted from behind the wall, "Raise the portcullis for the Crown!"

It bothered Primon that the guards had hesitated to let them inside, at least until they saw the Crowned King, to whom they bowed, saluting, *"In Tenebris nos,"*—all but that one guard who had been watching from the top of the wall.

"Please accept my deepest gratitude, Lord Duke." Rowena's soft voice startled him. As she rose past him, all he caught was a glimpse of the corner of her aureate eyes that seemed to tease him.

"There's nothing to thank me for, Master of Life," Primon lowered his head in a nod. "It's my duty to the crown."

"One that should never make us less thankful," she smiled warmly. "Nothing, no one, should ever be taken for granted."

Having ridden to the left of the king, he had easily forgotten about her quiet presence to the monarch's right. Even with the cloak over her head, there was a strange, charming beauty about her. But what was truly striking was not as much her sudden presence but the unexpectedly warm tone with which she expressed her thanks.

Her words shook him. They moved him. Did she recognize him? Was he not being overlooked? No, it couldn't be. Primon had been warned by his advisers. He needed to stop listening.

On his deathbed, his own father had warned him, 'Do not play politics with Septem. It's what my own father did, and it wrought nothing. When the vulture has its eyes on you, move too far and lose one tail, move too close and lose the other . . . Keep your eyes open, but your ears shut.'

In his time as a duke, he had interacted little with members of the Royal House, mostly due to the insistence of his own advisers and contacts back in Aligrand, who had warned him to keep any exchanges with House Darkholm to the minimum, to what was absolutely necessary.

'They have a way to manipulate people,' he had been told, 'to blind them with words to the atrocities they commit.'

Therefore, most of what he knew of the Darkholm he had learned from others. He had judged them from the words of people with his same goals.

This only woman among them was the king's daughter, and instead of being the princess, she was here, disregarding her own safety as she watched for his.

Once the gate was behind them, where the border forest welcomed them, the woods became more dense. The woods were deep, with large trees and unpredictable roots that required them to follow the main trail, guided by a young guard from the wall named Sadel, who offered to ensure they would reach their destination through the many winding paths before them, likely hoping for any recognition to his simple name.

High above, a messenger bird flew in the same direction.

Septem stopped his horse.

"Is something wrong, Your Highness?" Primon asked.

"We must be wary," the monarch responded, signaling the bird's direction.

"I wouldn't worry, Your Majesty," Sadel lowered his head humbly.

"Why are they sending a message ahead of us?" Primon demanded.

"I'm sorry if it seemed strange," Sadel responded, "but our lands are vast. Communication is important. They are likely making others aware of His Majesty's presence."

Primon opened his mouth in protest. "This is not the time when we want the king's presence known."

"We must advance," Septem's voice rumbled. "We shall exert caution."

From then on, the escort moved at a moderate pace, the eyes and ears of the riders around them open for any obvious sign of danger.

On his way, Primon Ferertr was quiet, submerged in deep, conflicting thoughts between the words of those closest to him and opinions of his own.

Here he was, against what his advisers wished, those who said he was humiliating himself to find grace in the indifferent eyes of the man who had given away the land of his ancestors to his rivals, all without giving them a chance to defend it, to present their argument against his decision.

It was the same man who had denied his duchy the funds to rebuild its ruined palace and cathedrals, forcing him to live in a broken place so as to avoid not feeding his people.

They were followed by the words of the *Osporae*, who called themselves patriotic nobles who had gone to great lengths to place people even in the highest spheres of the kingdom, risking the wrath of the tyrants of Darkholm.

Had the Darkholm patriarch not taken the crown, a new king would have likely risen from within the rightful duchy of Aligrand to stabilize the kingdom after Dieter Ostermund had passed without an heir, and Celeas would have still been their kingdom . . . and Blackheart would have never formed, and Aligrand would have never lost the region of Arande, nor its glory, nor its place in the hearts of many.

And yet here he was, placing himself in grave danger, riding along the outskirts of the twin duchies that had moved against the kingdom, protecting this same man he had heard so many whispers against.

'I will bring glory back to Aligrand. I will show them all a better way,' he thought when the whinnying of horses and whistling of arrows filled the air. His own mare stumbled forward and threw him off his seat as armed men came out of the woods, shooting both men and mounts, spreading chaos among the riders.

Entangled in his embroidered cape, Primon struggled to rise. Nearby, the escort fought back, themselves struggling to keep control, men falling off their mounts, quarrels and arrows protruding from their lifeless bodies as he watched Septem make it through.

Just inches away from Primon, a quarrel hit the ground. Disoriented, he sought someone as a child who had just lost sight of his parents and looked for their protection and support.

"Primon!" The booming echo of Septem's voice brought him back, drawing his attention to his lord and king.

His sapwood eyes opened wide when he saw the white cape flying behind the monarch as wings of the divine, its beast galloping impossibly fast as if the ground beneath them was nothing more than a valley of clouds, and he saw the king returning, his gauntleted hand reaching down.

He held his hand up, the one the king's own hand wrapped around as the monarch yanked him up from the ground to save him.

"Hold on tight," Septem instructed, placing the duke in front of him. As he clasped the saddle's horn, Primon's hands became pale.

Further up, Rowena witnessed it all. She turned her horse, readying to ride with them the moment they got close—a moment that wouldn't come to pass, for Septem's mount was felled halfway.

Reflexively, the White King wrapped his arm around Primon's torso protectively as they flew in the air before rolling along the forest floor.

The world spun around Primon. He was no warrior, yet he wouldn't stay idle. Clumsily, he grabbed his only weapon, a sharp, jeweled stiletto he held fast.

As if reality itself had slowed down to allow him a time of contemplation, Primon saw the assailants approaching, some of whom got entangled in a furious fight with his few surviving men. He placed his knees on the ground to stand up and, looking around, he saw Septem standing, readied, his attire dirty but not less regal. In the king's hand, *Sanguinus* sang, ending the lives of a pair of men in a single move and two wide arches.

Primon felt a sharp sting on his knee, where a quarrel was now stuck, making it hard for him to walk without risking collapsing under his own weight.

"Primon," Septem's voice transcended time and space. He turned to see Septem's golden eyes on him.

"Stand behind me!" Septem ordered, "I will keep you safe." The king's hand stretched out to assist him, to pull him back behind the monarch's defensive stance.

Here he was, closest to the man he had for so long resented, the cold man who had always seemed indifferent to his plea, the same man who had lent him a hand, who hadn't left him behind in his moment of greatest need.

Primon Ferertr had grown up wanting to be a hero, a brave, strong man who would bring a new era to his people. But he was not like those others called heroes. He was not powerful like Septem, he was not relentless like Noxheeva, nor was he brave . . . but could he be?

He had thought he could achieve things his own way, but maybe he was wrong. Or was he?

Until today, no matter what he did, a shroud of doubt was always cast over his loyalty and that of his people.

Maybe they were right, maybe their way was the way . . . or was it?

He contemplated Septem's breastplate, where he saw Aligrand's dragon to the left of the heart that rested at its center.

The two-tailed dragon had become their sigil, a symbol of pride to those who didn't know better or to those who sought to move on. To some, that symbol was but a broken reminder of what remained of the three-tailed dragon that had lost one of its tails.

With two long strides, Septem closed in, his hand grabbing Primon's, pulling him out of the way as *Sanguinus*'s melody filled the air with an attacker's blood.

Here he was, under his wing, protected by the king he had taught himself to hate.

Could he be a hero?

A sole move, a single breath freed a groan that had never been heard . . . followed by Rowena's shrill cry. The echoing of her "Nooo!" would freeze everyone in their tracks.

Primon's cape fell in place as Septem's hand let go.

Taking a step, the White King half turned, looking down upon his chest, where blood flowed like a river from the place where his armor had been penetrated, right where the third tail of Aligrand's dragon was, where a jeweled stiletto was stuck.

Septem's eyes of gold looked back at Primon's in disbelief . . . perhaps having realized that everything he had done for him had not been enough.

"I'm sorry, my king," the duke said, his voice determined but shaking, "but I saw no other way in which you would step down from the throne."

His words were interrupted by the red blade's song, by a flash of burning pain that began on his right hip and ended on the left side of his face.

But before his halves touched the ground, Septem staggered, placing *Sanguinus*'s tip on the forest floor to keep his balance.

Duke Primon Ferertr didn't get to see Aligrand regain any status or glory, nor witness Rowena desperately running to her father's side or the fight that broke among his men. He didn't see Serverus and the Black Knights arrive to end the lives of the traitors like him.

DEAD WEIGHT

Location: Kingdom of Ardenay, Duchy of Bulwharf,
State of Darane, the Horne

Charon's feet hurt.

They had been marching hurriedly for some time, and she wanted to ask for a break. She knew it was difficult, however, for they were still out in the open.

'What would Rowena do?' she could almost envision her cousin, who was less athletic than she. Had Septem's daughter been here, she would have had the same expression of pain, but the Master of Life would have marched on without a single complaint.

Besides, Charon thought, how could she complain? She walked side by side with Alex, child of Arlisse Darkholm, the mysterious Master of Secrets of which nothing was known, the one who had even decided to hide the gender of the only child she had even from those closest to her. The beauty of Alex's features was reinforced by the confidence Charon saw in her cousin.

'This tiredness . . . It's nothing. We do what must be done, ' she reminded herself, and grabbing Alex's hand for support, she continued on.

Accompanying them, were a handful of able-bodied fighters, Sterla Devereau and Aeron 'the Horse' Darkholm, whom Idian had ordered to lead their escort.

They neared the Seventh as the night approached.

Unlike the rest of the fortified towers of the region, the importance of the Seventh's location was such that a large town had been built around it, and it was in this town where the main forces of the Seventh had remained stationed after Maxius had outplayed them and taken their tower.

While perhaps not as shrewd as his father, Maxius, Aeron was still a remarkable tactician. He led them through the streets toward the fort with minimal encounters until they reached this one home that was, they found out, furnished but unoccupied.

Except for two of his men, they took a moment to rest and plan on the second story.

After the row of buildings where theirs was, they saw the last stretch consisted of the hill where the fort was built and a gated wall halfway, some eight feet tall. The gate was flanked by Bulwharf soldiers, archers, and spearmen among them, who kept their distance from the tower while guarding the road that led to it.

While his men were seasoned, they were tired and would be outnumbered four-to-one by the Bulwharf. They could simply alert the Seventh. Maxius would come out and offer support. But that wasn't wise, Aeron believed, considering it best to have his father continue to hold the fort with his own few men. Besides, while Alex could very well fight, Aeron wouldn't risk Charon and Sterla's lives.

"Has word been sent back to Darkholm?" he asked the young Devereau in the usual monotone that made some people believe he was closer to Septem than he actually was.

"Yes, my lord," Sterla responded, her eyes of walnut on him.

"I see you have four birds left," Areon pointed out at the cage she carried.

"That is correct," the girl responded, "but you must know only two are bound to Darkholm, one to Darkholde Keep, the second one to Ashbourne in Devereaux County. The remaining pair are bound to Skyreach."

"Those bound to the capital of Valador can still be useful," Charon stated.

"Agreed," Aeron nodded, studying the layout of the forces before him. "Alex," he beckoned, "join me for a talk. I have a plan, but I would like your input, for it centers around you."

After they left, Charon looked around both because she was smart enough and could come up with a good suggestion and because her eyes always wandered off easily.

Not long after, something caught her attention.

Psst . . .

"Did you hear that?" Charon asked the Devereaux messenger, who was feeding her pigeons.

"Hear what?"

"Like someone calling," Charon explained.

"I didn't," Sterla shrugged.

"No? Then don't mind me. Maybe it was my head playing tricks on me."

Psst, psst!

"There it is again," Charon nudged. "Did you hear it this time?"

"I did!" Sterla peeked out the window.

Charon would not give up on her search, especially now that Sterla was also looking, and she couldn't just let the pigeoneer win. They searched left and right, studying the few people walking along the street, high and low until she saw coming out of one building across the street, something moving, what seemed like a thick figure covered in sheets that had been yanked from that one clothesline that was now both bare and waving.

It moved slowly, avoiding a collision with the passersby who either looked at it curiously before going on with their business or completely ignored it.

"Should we tell the others?" Sterla asked, but Charon did not respond. The Darkholm maiden's curious eyes filled with fascination.

Seconds later, Charon ran downstairs, Sterla following suit, to witness the moment the mysterious mound entered the first floor of the house.

The two guards readied their swords, but the mound was faster. As if in a hypnotic enchantment, it twirled around, summoning a gust of air that sent the sheets flying away from the figure underneath.

"Did you know it was me?" the woman teased. "Expect the unexpected!"

"Elzie!" Charon's eyes opened excitedly, wider than they had ever done before. She ran toward her cousin and hugged her hard, tears of joy rolling down her face.

"Lady Elzabeth," Sterla curtsied. "It is good to see you safe."

"I am safe," Elizabeth smiled, "but we all need to be safer, behind the walls of that tower." She pointed at the Seventh.

"You two," she ordered the guards, "keep your eyes on the door behind you. Be wary, of course. My men are in the other building."

"Oh, Elzie," Charon almost cried, "I was so worried for you."

"Aw, you silly muffin." Elizabeth tapped Charon's nose. "Now, where are the others?"

"Elizabeth." Preceded by Alex, Aeron descended, "Good that you are here. We can always use more men."

"I am sorry to disappoint, then," Elizabeth curtsied with a coy smile. "I only have two men left," she continued, "the chariot driver and one of my archers. Only the archer would be of any real use in battle. I sent the rest of my unit with the main forces. Archers of such skill are not easy to replace, you know."

"And the chariot?" Aeron asked.

"Left behind. One of its wheels is badly damaged," Elizabeth reported. "It would have done no good to continue on it and draw all the attention we are desperately trying to avoid."

"Agreed," Aeron responded. "How many horses are in good condition?"

"The four have been pushed hard," she answered, "but they are still of use."

"That is good enough," Aeron stated. "It gives us options. Can you direct Alex to the horses?"

"Oh, me? I need to catch my breath." Placing a hand on her chest, Elizabeth puffed, "but the driver is in that building back there. He can guide Alex."

"Then Alex and you," Aeron instructed one of his men, "will join Elizabeth's men and take all four horses. I have a better plan."

* * *

They had been waiting for an impossibly long time. At least it seemed so to Charon, for whom patience was not a known virtue when an aging couple approached. Their skin was dark as the smooth browns commonly seen in the people of Bulwharf. The woman needed help to walk. She seemed somewhat feeble, maybe blind. While his head was fully grayed, the man's poise made evident he had likely been a veteran warrior or a disciplined guard . . . or an avid acrobat, or a simple man who wanted to appear taller.

"Shh," Elzabeth scolded her, "stop mumbling." She pulled her back to stop her from being seen through the window she peered out of.

In a few moments, the couple would step through the door, and Charon couldn't understand the signals between Aeron and his men, but she loved the challenge. She would figure it out, for sure, after she figured out what was wrong with Elzabeth's leg.

"Your knee," she whispered to her larger cousin.

"What about it?" Elizabeth responded.

"Your knee is swollen. Maybe we need to extract some liquid from it," Charon pointed out.

"What are you talking about?" Elizabeth questioned.

"Back in Alnwick, I've seen Rowena and the other healers dissecting cadavers. Sometimes the knees have too much fluid, and that can cause pain, they say. I've seen it enough. I think I can do it," Charon smiled confidently.

"Eh, hmmmm, how do I put this? Ah, that is right. How about . . . No!" Elizabeth smiled back. "Now go to the next room and take Sterla with you to ensure you are both safe."

Charon did as instructed. She grabbed Sterla's hand and, ducking, dashed toward the next room. But the light of the sun through the window betrayed her.

"Who's there?" the homeowner outside shouted, alerting the closest Bulwharf guards. "Thief! Stop right there!"

Charon shoved Sterla away through the doorway before standing up straight and turning to face him.

The man saw an almost angelic being, her arms spread wide as if to receive him. It was a vision of something he could have never imagined. He stepped through the doorway toward her when her image was splashed with blood upon the assault by Aeron and his men. Before the finished man could fall on his knees, his wife's shrill cry echoed, scaring people away and summoning not only the two original guards but others who joined them and ran toward the house.

"Ready up," Elzabeth snapped Charon out of her stunned state.

"We shall cover your retreat," Aeron instructed.

But the neighing of horses and the shouts of the soldiers further up the hill changed his mind. "Excellent timing, Alex," Aeron smiled under his breath.

Further up, Alex and the other three riders assaulted the men near the gate, their large numbers difficult for the riders to break. In a swift move, Alex drew a chained dart from under the cape and hurled it toward the neck of one of the captains, killing the man where he stood. With a quick pull, the dart traveled back to Alex's hand before the rogue whirled it overhead deftly.

The riders then moved away, planting seeds of chaos among the men who scrambled for their own weapons and mounts while some ran behind in pursuit.

Back inside the building, Aeron had seconds before the soldiers came through the doorway.

"I will have a harder time protecting the rear," he spoke to Elzabeth. "The Seventh will need every man I bring, so we cannot stall here. I will instead charge toward the gate and create an opening so that you can follow us," he instructed.

"Go ahead," Elzabeth nodded in support. "Open the way for us."

The soldiers came upon the door when the first son of Maxius dashed out, shield first. Stepping aside the startled men, he dodged, and, with a quick swing of his sword, he took the first man down. Two of the men turned to face him and were quickly downed from behind by Aeron's men.

"Charge!" As the rest neared, Aeron began his uphill move, pointing with the shield he used to bash and push the assailing Bulwharf while using his sword to deflect their attacks.

One of his men fell, then another, while a third was wounded by one of the few arrows that were not directed toward Alex's team.

Elzabeth watched for an opening, waiting for the perfect moment that didn't seem to come. If they ran out too fast, the soldiers would turn back and keep them trapped. If they were too slow, the other guards from the town would trap them too. Always the protector, she wanted to ensure their safety. She couldn't help it, she thought. After all, she had many times been the willing nanny of the younger ones in her nearly four decades of life. Charon had only been back a few years, so she hadn't really lived, and Sterla, well, she was apprenticed to Darkholm from the vassal House she herself had been apprenticed to. While her life was not more valuable than anyone else's, the birds she carried would likely be the only outside communication once they went from being trapped in this house to being trapped inside the Seventh.

"I am so sad." Charon interrupted her thoughts.

"Why are you sad?" Elzabeth questioned tenderly.

"The events of today," her eyes glistened, "so many lives lost, the betrayal, after we do so much for them."

"I know," Elzabeth caressed her head, "Unfortunate, is it not? But we cannot stop and wallow in misery, at least not now. We must move on; we can wonder about those things once we are safe."

Lady Charon looked out at the battle uphill. She wished she could take up arms and help. She wished she could do something to make a difference. 'What would Rowena do?' she thought. Wondering about the cousin she tried hard to model herself after, the one everyone loved, and hoping she had made it safely, Charon burst into tears.

"Come on," Elzabeth asked. "What is wrong now?"

"I'm just so weak," Charon said, "I always wonder what Rowena would do, but this time . . . I just don't know."

"Look at me, muffin," Elzabeth smiled warmly, "I know what Rowena would do. She would play to her strengths, always, and she would want you to follow in her footsteps by playing to your own strengths too. Now, cheer up a bit, will you?"

"I'm sorry for crying," Charon wiped her cheeks, "for being weak."

"You know," Elzabeth responded, "I will not tell you you are strong because you are not. But if you give up, you will never grow strong. When one feels weak, sometimes one wants to just suck one's own thumb and fall asleep. Sometimes one simply must . . . and that is ok. Just make sure that, when you do, no one is watching."

She turned Charon's cheek and pointed at the Devereau apprentice, who had been attentive, absorbing their words all this time.

"Are you ready to run?" Elzabeth added.

"I am," Charon responded. "Can *you* run?"

"Oh, do not mind me," Elzabeth waved a hand. "This is just water weight!"

Charon readied immediately, and after wiping her cheeks, she planted her foot on the floor to wait for the signal.

--- ·∘+∘∘· ---

Charon's feet left the ground.

Her lithe form seemed to float for an unnaturally long time as she dashed, the wind's song bringing life to the snowy strands born from her head. Its caress brought a smile to her face, and she danced beautifully, the gusts tickling her bare feet, for it was in her hands where her slippers were held. She was graceful like a cat, never faltering in her steps or losing her balance. She was free, like the wind, escaping the steely kiss of the men that would stop her.

'Where is Sterla,' she wondered.

And she smiled seeing the Devereau youngling running upward, close enough but less graceful, her young hands protecting the birdcage as anyone would protect a precious dream.

Charon smiled at the girl, and she proceeded uphill, dancing, prancing the entire way, feeling no pain, no fatigue, no sense of worry.

'No worry . . . wait! Where's Elzie?'

It was then that Charon looked back and saw Elzabeth, still behind, struggling, having failed to keep up.

And yet the heavy woman waved her hand, telling Charon to go on.

"Elzie!" she shouted, "I will help you!"

"Charon!" Aeron grabbed her by the arm, pulling her back toward the gate they had just crossed, "you cannot go!"

"But it's Elzie!" Charon yelled, her face red. "We can't leave her! I knew we couldn't leave her behind. She won't make it with her knee, with her weight!"

Aeron's men shut the gate they had just crossed to stop the enemies that were attempting to breach it.

"Elzie!" Charon screamed, looking back at the men who were forcing the gate open when she saw the round face of her cousin on the other side, smiling, her thick arms hugging the latch to keep the gate from opening.

"Go, go!" the Darkholm woman yelled, her face showing the obvious pain she was trying to contain. "I will hold them!"

"Her strength is not enough!" Charon shouted, waving at Aeron to come toward the gate.

"Silly muffin," Elzabeth shouted back, "my weight . . . has always been . . . an asset."

And she blew a kiss and smiled, a loving smile that was slowly stained with the streak of blood that came out of her mouth, where her teeth became sweet cherries of metallic taste, but her smile did not fade, even when her irises hid behind her open eyelids, or when her bloodied body slumped forward, still holding on despite the many arrows and spears that struck her.

And so Maxius's men came out of the Seventh to protect the newcomers, and they escorted Sterla, and they dragged Charon away, screaming and crying, calling Elizabeth's name.

That night in the Seventh, Charon chose a small room for herself.

It was rather early when she crawled up in bed, where she brought her knees close to her chest like those of a fetus. She recalled all the memories of her cousin she had gathered in just a few years, all she had laughed at, everything she had learned, all the love she had received.

Charon wondered if things would have been different if she hadn't been weak, if she had learned how to fight.

Her eyes were swollen, her chest felt tight, her heart hurt, and she sobbed, knowing how much Elzabeth's joy would be missed.

And she dozed off, all alone, placing her thumb inside her mouth.

REFLECTIONS

Location: Kingdom of Blackheart, Duchy of Darkholm,
County of Coldforge, Darkholde Keep

The hardest thing to see is our own lack of vision . . .

The black stone walls of Darkholde were nearly invisible against the night sky. The ominous keep rested, perched, a vulture upon the mighty cliffs of Smith's Bay, watching and waiting for the demise of any potential invading ship.

Every child of the Royal House would grow up learning the size of each chamber, the number of steps it took to cross the hallways, and the blind spots of every bastion of the keep. But Erdrick Darkholm was not just a child of Darkholm. On his shoulder lay the mantles of both a Black Knight and, most importantly, the son of the King of Blackheart.

The noble boots met the ground as the plates in his armor sang the melody that only extreme and strict discipline would produce. His steps took him to the bridge that connected the main keep to the solitary, distant Spire of the Eye[1] that, like others, had been erected over a tall, thin rock that rose from the sea.

On the northern and southern sides of the bridge, statues of knights looking outward toward the emptiness appeared to guard whoever stood on the bridge from the unknown.

For just an instant, he stopped. Anyone would have thought he marveled at its appearance, but marvel was something rarely, if ever, seen in the eyes of the knight.

Erdrick was always meticulous. His piercing eyes sought patterns in all things. Even years after a visit to a building, he remembered the placement of every window, every lit sconce, and many other details that escaped the common eye.

While the Spire seemed as solid as most of Darkholde, its many openings on the top floors gave it the appearance of the undefeated finger of an ancient god, challenging the heavens that had brought him to ruin.

After a brief moment, he resumed his walk toward the entrance.

As he neared the tall structure, he noted a few feet from the doorway, the stone floor had been lined with basins of differing sizes, some made of clay, some porcelain, and yet others stone, but all the bottoms were soot black, and each was filled with water.

The knight pushed the heavy door, which swung with surprising ease, leading to a foyer that was lined with tables, astral and astronomical charts, mystic symbols, and a spiral staircase leading toward the upper floors. There was no smell of molten wax, no burning candles.

Raising his guard, he carefully walked up the stairs.

The armored man arrived at the top, where the spire opened into a dome-like chamber.

The floor was lined with old, broken tiles where the roof had caved in over several decades. On the opposing side from the keep's prying eyes, it opened onto a balcony, where he came upon a woman of short stature, her back towards him.

She wore a simple black robe, its cowl back, resting on her shoulders unevenly, while she held a compass in one hand and a jug in the other.

Along the floor of the balcony, other basins rested, also filled with water.

"Erdrick." The woman's voice was heard despite the gusts of wind.

The knight halted, squinting, "Master of Cosmos, I salute you. Do the stars reveal even these things to you?"

The old woman turned to welcome him. "One can find almost every answer in the stars, but these are questions I do not ask." Meliva Darkholm could only look at his firm chest. So severe was the deformity in her spine, she appeared a hunchback.

It had been several years since Erdrick had been in her presence, and one thing he clearly saw was her condition had worsened.

"For the living, the time is finite, and time should not be spent asking the cosmos things such as these. I simply recognize your footsteps," she grinned. "Very few ever visit me. Of these, only *you* wear armor."

Erdrick's expression did not change. There was much of his father in the heir, but despite the similarities, there were important differences. Where Septem was an unrelenting winter, Erdrick was a hidden glacier.

"You came to me to ask," Meliva said. "Ask, then."

She spoke truly. Erdrick would have found no reason to visit her otherwise. Like most Darkholm, Erdrick did not believe in the religions of men, where the most charismatic among them would claim to interpret signs no gods had given.

He was a knight, but while he did not fully embrace or understand the sciences of the occult and unknown, he made sure to show respect, enough to visit here on this day, an area of the keep he had not seen for over three years.

Like his father, he would not waste time with idle chatter. "Will we find peace under my father?" the knight asked.

The Master moved toward a large basin, where she poured some water into the half-filled container.[(2)] Ripples danced on the water before the stillness that followed. The silent surface reflected the light of the stars in the heavens, capturing the attention of her pair of amber eyes. "I see war, enemies rising and marching against us. I see great loss and the potential loss of a crown."

Erdrick studied her words before asking. "I would like to know, will there be peace under my rule?"

The woman proceeded to pour more water into the same basin to study the reflection before providing an answer. "Under your rule, the world will know peace. Blackheart will know war."

"What do you see under the rule of Rowena?" the knight did not hesitate to ask.

Meliva poured water into the basin, so much that it overflowed, but she did not stop her hand. As the water licked her sandals, she saw the reflection of the stars everywhere along the basin and the floor around it.

"Under Rowena's rule," she said, "Blackheart will know peace. The world will know war."

All his life, Erdrick had spent his time fighting alongside the knights but also preparing for his role as king. He had dedicated all his energy to this one goal. Even in the last few months, he had spent every waking hour in ducal, official meetings, and other matters of state. He had

Meliva Darkholm

come to ask about one thing, but in the end, the responses he obtained had come as unexpected, all because he had asked.

"Are you certain of this?" Erdrick asked, clearing his throat.

The Master of Cosmos replied calmly, "These are just my interpretations."

With deference, Erdrick nodded and turned to walk away. But as he approached the top of the stairs, he asked, without turning, "Master, have you ever considered that perhaps you misread because you look at things in reverse?"

The old woman moved away, returning to her place in the balcony. "One can best see the truth when one looks at things from a different perspective."

(1) The Spire of the Eye: The Tower was originally built as an observatory by Duke Valdemar, the founder of Darkholm. It was here where his daughter retreated from the world after losing an eye in battle. So great was her shame, she would only accept sustenance, refusing to be seen or cared for by anyone. After one year, she emerged, changed. There was shame or defeat no longer. The wisdom she had acquired now allowed her to see things others couldn't. She was thereafter known as the Eye.

(2) The Master of Cosmos: The Master of Cosmos is the principal astrologer of Darkholm Duchy and Blackheart Kingdom. She is in charge of interpreting prophecies, seeing patterns in the heavens, and alerting the Crown of any major finding.

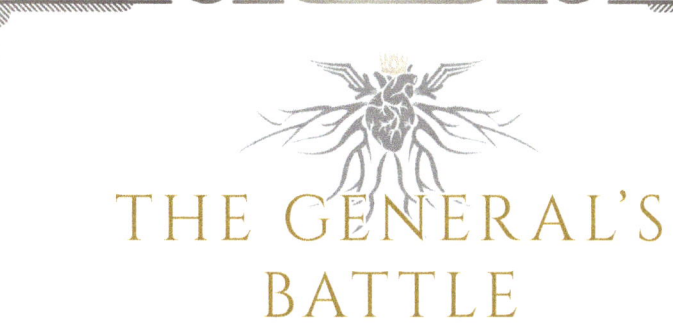

THE GENERAL'S BATTLE

Location: Kingdom of Blackheart, Duchy of Darkholm,
City of Coldforge, Darkholde Keep

Every time a man goes to the battlefield he is forever changed.
The one who returns is never the same man anymore . . .

After many years and countless battles, everything had led to this day, a day he had hoped would have only come many years later, if ever. His pace was steady but quite different from his traditionally long strides. This time, they were slow, more so as they took him through the wooden door to his chambers, as if the black armor he wore had suddenly revealed the weight on his shoulders he had perhaps never noticed, as if the maroon cape he held suddenly became the blood he had so many times drenched his hands on.

"Lord General," a servant girl saluted, "allow me to assist you in removing your armor."

"Ah," his raised palm halted the girl's advance, "there is no need. My wife will assist me."

"I don't understand, my lord, how—"

"It will be fine. Just please, go." While the general could be a vicious rival on the battlefield, in his family home, especially in his private chambers, he appeared calm and collected.

Did the servant girl find the dichotomy strange? No, not really, at least not when speaking of Idian Darkholm.

In Darkholm Duchy, Idian had been known as the "Fist of Justice," or simply as "the Fist" for, in his youth, he had punched an opposing captain's face into a pulp for having spoken ill of his family and for having mocked their customs. As if the action had not been bad enough, he had spilled that blood on neutral ground.

Fortunately for him, and perhaps for all of Darkholm, no one acted upon his transgression.

But then again, no one had dared challenge Idian Darkholm back then.

Even if they wanted to take revenge now, it had been impossible for any lone man to come close to Idian on the battlefield. The general's tactics were incredibly sound, almost foolproof, and the few times something had failed, the fierce adaptability of his troops had made up for it before the enemy had realized and exploited the fault.

The general removed his helmet to reveal that white hair and goatee that had for so long defined him, which showed his apparent age of nearly seven decades when he was close to doubling that. But, at this moment, the gravity in his facial expression almost showed his true age.

The Fist's hands traveled to every belt and buckle to remove each plate that had been a companion for many a year.

From the left arm greave that was given to him as replacements by Toradmus and Atelas Darkholm to the cuirass forged for him by the Master of Steel, to the swords awarded to him by Duke Septem and later on by Septem, the Crowned King, each piece he wore, on its own, told a story worthy of a book.

Idian placed them all on the thick, wooden surface of the table, an array of tools that he had used to command and fight for close to a century, to end the lives of those who opposed him or his people, while the mannequin which had loyally served for so long as his armor stand now stood used, faceless, naked by his side.

Whoever witnessed the scene could question how a man as old as he was could move with the gallantry and poise he did inside all that heavy steel.

This has been quite the journey.

The general had made up his mind. This had been the last time he had worn them. This last war had taken a toll on him. He was ready to retire.

How could he not? He couldn't be the general of a Crown he had failed to protect . . . of a Crown that was no more.

"The wound of the king is grievous," the Master of Life had warned him. "Despite our best efforts, we must be prepared for the worst."

Those words had felt worse than the worst wound a man could receive, a wound to his heart, a wound to his pride, a stab worse than Septem's, for it pierced the man's heart and wounded even his mind.

"Helean," Idian called softly, walking toward the bed that lay at the end of the room, the one covered in veils that were moved gently by the wind visiting through the open panes of their tower's windows.

His calloused hands parted the curtains the color of breakfast cream to show the body of his wife, Helean Darkholm, also known as "the Grace," for her love and commitment to everything the House represented.

Throughout her lifetime, Helean had filled any role needed in the House, from nursemaid to tutor to accountant and even sparring partner, for as long as was needed.

She had been, until today, a strong and exemplary woman. But now she lay here, emaciated and weak, wheezing from the wasting affliction that had attacked her body and, lately, her lungs.

Turning the head toward him alone took great effort, yet her sunken eyes and wrinkled lips smiled upon seeing the visage of her husband.

'*You are back . . . and in one piece,*' he imagined her saying, words she never expressed before, for while he was always known as the great general, she was the strategist who led him to victory and had always stood right by his side.

Idian sat on their bed and took her hand. His intense yellow eyes looked into the cloudy surface of his wife's bright blonde irises. "For so long I learned to depend on you," he spoke, "then more than that, I learned to doubt myself."

Helean, however, did not respond. Her eyes trembled and closed, feeling the pain inside her husband's heart.

"I do not know how you could live so long in my shadow," the general continued, his stern eyes having now become the caring husband's.

Catching a deep breath with difficulty, the Grace caressed his hand with her own. "You were the one everyone wanted to see. You were the tall, gallant man everyone, even I, wanted to *devour* with their eyes. I, as a woman, had no problem watching for danger from the shadows."

Their eyes locked on each other in silence, for there was not much the great general could say, and there was nothing she needed to respond.

They knew.

They knew each other's importance in their marriage. Both the Fist and the Grace had respected and loved one another and had never fought for the spotlight.

Helean had always been much smarter than her husband, and he had recognized that early in their marriage.

While women were not allowed to form part of the army's command unit, she had identified Idian's squire as a coward and had thus offered the young man a great deal: he could stay safe, behind, while she would don his armor and join her husband in battle.

And there she stood, every time, watching men fighting like waves in a stormy ocean, and every time she fought, calculated, and helped her husband adapt and lead, for only he knew of her presence.

In every way and in every battle, Helean had been the brain behind the operation, and more than that, she had supported her husband in every endeavor.

And so every victory of the man had really been the woman's, but yet she had never gotten credit for it, and she had never complained, for they knew each other's value and, in the end, regardless of what the world thought, that was all that mattered.

Idian's eyes moved toward his wife's chest before moving to her closing eyes. Her breathing was shallow, her body was frail, and yet this was the woman who had always been honest with him, and the least he felt he owed her was the same.

"What does it matter to have won a hundred battles if the one today was lost?"

"What is the matter?"

"I am tired," the general responded.

"You never rest."

"I cannot. How can I when there is so much to do?"

"You always ask so much of yourself," his wife responded.

"One must, when everyone's lives depend on us. One wrong move and every dream will fall tumbling down."

Helean understood what he meant. After nearly seven decades overseeing the main forces of Blackheart and the Royal Duchy, she had seen her husband's entire life devoted to his station.

"We lost, Helean." It pained him to even think about it.

"And yet we won so much along the way," she expressed through eyes that seemed to be falling asleep.

Idian wondered; if he should just let her rest. But Idian knew her better. She would have wanted to know. Even on her delivery bed, she would have wanted to know.

His words were heavy in his heart. "I lost us everything."

"You still have me."

The general nodded, his mouth opened, but only a brief, sad laugh escaped. She was right. "We were betrayed, Helean. Blackheart's forces are in disarray. Darkholm had to retreat, and in doing so, Septem was gravely wounded."

At his words, her glistening eyes were looking at him when this time, it was he who was closing his own.

"What are we going to do?"

"We?" he questioned. "*You* are going to rest."

"Yes, we." Her hand reached out to him, "you need to keep your strength."

'*You* are my strength,' Idian thought, and, having felt he had informed her enough, he took her hand once again. His free hand lightly touched her eyelids, signaling it was time to rest while he would simply watch her, as he had done as of late.

"Let us think," she whispered, "we can come up with something. Let us think and remember. You have always been good at that."

Idian wasn't much of a storyteller, but during the last stages of her condition, he spoke softly to her, always remembering what had transpired in their long lives. And more than a few times, she joined him with a verse or simply to correct his story, her words accompanied by her soft laughter.

And for long, they reminisced about their youth together.

Of the time when their first son, Maximus, was born.

Maximus Darkholm, the largest of the House. She had almost bled out, having given birth to the one also known as the Golem, for from the moment of his birth and until his glorious death, he had been the largest man around. They remembered how his armor had required enough metal to build two and how under that steel, their child had been unstoppable.

Of the time their grandchild Raganor was born on a day of the terrible storm he seemed to have embodied.

Of the many times Aristov II and Erianna reminded them of themselves, hand in hand in battle, though without their leading responsibilities, they were happier and freer.

———————— ✦✦✦✦✦ ————————

"I take it you do not want to eat any more?" The general wiped his wife's lips carefully, placing the spoon back in the bowl of soup that remained nearly full.

And they also remembered the time when Celeas had been a prosperous kingdom and of the death of its last monarch and the chaos that ensued. They remembered the great losses, and their greatest loss, that of their cousin Septem, who was lost to the crown when Blackheart was formed.

The uprising in Celris, the former capital, when Darkholm's Coldforge took its place, and their part in the civil war that brought Aligrand's civil war to an end.

———————— ✦✦✦✦✦ ————————

"Are you there?" he called again.

"Yes," her eyelids were as the heavy gates of an ancient citadel.

"You were not answering me."

"You had not asked me a question," Helean responded.

"You are right," the general shook his head as his expression softened, "then again, you have always been."

And they remembered one particular moment in their lives, many summers before.

The general's cape had flown behind him as if gaining sentience just to signal his guard to wait outside the large structure that comprised his tent. He had returned from his rounds and was about to march against his enemies, setting the war machine that was Blackheart in motion.

Once inside, he saw Marion, the young man who was both squire and standard bearer, bowing deeply and signaling toward the next room.

The general's hands had parted the curtain to find the partially clad, feminine figure of Helean, her hair picked up in a bun, admiring her own image, the face he saw, in a mirror's reflection, while using a mortar to crush rose petals into a soft substance with which she colored her lips.

"Why do you waste your time doing that?" His words had been as gentle as sanding wood in freshly healing skin. "That is absolutely unnecessary. We are about to go to battle."

Her hands had stopped moving. With eyes glistening, she looked into the mirror and found his intimidating eyes, to which she responded, "Please, grant me this. This is the only thing I have left that makes me feel that I am still a woman."

It was he who had stopped moving that one time. He was only a brute of a soldier, of a man, and he knew not what to say . . . so he said nothing.

He only stood by the parted curtain and watched his wife color her lips as tears rolled down her face.

And yet, without wiping her face and without complaint, without even looking at him in the eyes, she walked past him and got ready to don the armor of the young man, as she had done many times before, to join her husband in battle.

That memory struck a chord within the heart of the general. He looked at the shriveling body of his wife, that body that had lost every curve, that had borne him five children, that had trained and fought and now was barely able to sit. It was not that beautiful body anymore. It lacked everything he had so long admired, everything but one thing. It still encased the essence of his wife.

His hand held hers as he spoke in a way he hadn't many times before, "You know, we had our victories and our defeats, our good times and our bad ones in our long life together. But today, looking back, despite it all, I lament nothing."

Helean's feeble hand caressed his face, her milky eyes gazing into her husband's, meeting him with her response, "Well, I do lament one thing . . . We never got to dance.

"I lived so focused and consumed with being your wife," she wheezed, "that I forgot that you could have also been my husband."

Idian Darkholm felt a force like he had never known strike him. He smiled sadly, knowing that perhaps, like most of the time before, she was right.

He let her hand go and took a knee, his hands palpating the stone floor until they found what he sought. The general pulled out a few rose petals and slowly, gently crushed them in the palm of his hands.

That brute of a soldier, of a man, knew not what to say, so he said nothing. He did not claim no one had taught him how. He proceeded to color his wife's lips to the best of his ability, for he knew that, to her, that was important. He worked as best as he could, in silence, as once again tears rolled down her face.

After he was done, he placed the crushed petals carefully on the bed and stood up. And with what he had left of his strength, that old man lifted his wife off the bed, carrying her drying body in his faltering arms, and he danced with her.

And he didn't do it in a great chamber filled with witnesses so that they could point their fingers and say, 'Look at how much he loves her.'

He danced with her in the solitude of their chamber, where the only witness was the moon and its rays, and the only music was the wind coming through the window.

It was at that very moment when Helean noticed one thing that made her laugh inside: her husband had no rhythm.

She held onto him fast as she thought, 'What a fool I am. Perhaps he never took me to dance because he did not know how.'

Again she chuckled and coughed and thought, 'What does it matter now? Let me just enjoy this moment.'

"Idian," she said, "my husband, do not forget that I love you."

"Helean," he answered, "mother of my children, my strength, I will never forget that I love you."

And it was then that Helean Darkholm, the Grace, rested her head upon her husband's shoulder that night, and she laughed, and she danced, and she loved, and she passed.

And with his wife in his arms, he danced till the morning.

A CUP OF BLOOD

Location: Empyre of Suhne, City of Suhne, Palace of the Sun

Never trust a snake's handshake . . .

Malek strode along a part of the palace he had rarely seen, the domes that served as Kaylen's living quarters. He had not come out of fear or respect. They had grown up in the same palace, but yet mostly separated from one another, all in preparation for that final moment tomorrow would bring.

What he did here, walking toward his younger brother's chambers, he had no idea, but he came not because he had wanted to but rather because he had been invited.

A quick knock and moments later, Kaylen himself opened. He signaled for Malek to walk inside his chamber.

It was the first time Malek had seen it. Since the moment of Kaylen's birth, twenty-five years before, Malek had never seen how his brother lived. He had been curious growing up, wondering if Kaylen shared his voracious sexual appetite, but the distance they were kept at never allowed him to know his brother that well. He knew Kaylen was smart, calculating, and that he wouldn't typically do things with his own hands.

"I wouldn't expect you to come to the door," Malek said.

"I wanted to keep our meeting private," Kaylen walked past him.

While Malek wore a brown and gold tunic and sandals, his hair tied in a single, thick braid, Kaylen wore a long, red skirt that opened on one side, his torso wrapped in a single piece of fabric behind his neck that crossed along his chest, allowing his back, abdomen, and chest to be seen under the golden chains that hung from his shoulders.

"Here," Kaylen walked toward a small table set with a pair of chairs. On it, a silver tray with golden figs, walnut-stuffed dates, olives, and green grapes. To the side, a sealed clay jug and a pair of cups.

"How's your eye?" Kaylen asked.

Although he knew not much of him, Malek knew Kaylen wouldn't ask out of concern. He was one of those people who ask simply to remind one of one's imperfections, to perhaps revel in one's pain while they prepare another jab.

"I would think you'd have someone inform you," Malek responded.

"No," Kaylen half smiled. "I wouldn't ask anyone else about it because I don't care. I ask you because it's in front of me."

Malek felt a surge within him. While, as usual, it had taken him a few days compared to his siblings' weeks to recover from the burns, he had completely lost sight in his left eye, a terrible blow to a warrior of his caliber. Still, while Kaylen waited for his response, he wouldn't indulge him.

"For someone like me, it can happen any time I am exposed to fighting," he said almost nonchalantly. "How about you?" he asked. "How's that scar going?"

The Sun of Conquest smiled inside when he saw the one on Kaylen's face disappear when Kaylen's hand pulled the fabric inadvertently to cover what was visible of his scar.

"Would you like some?" Kaylen offered.

"I don't," Malek responded. "What did you call me for?"

"To talk about tomorrow," Kaylen took two grapes and placed one inside his mouth.

"The Ascension. What about it?"

"I see you know what day is tomorrow," Kaylen smiled, eating the second grape, "I could keep you around instead of having you killed when I am Ascended."

Malek wouldn't fall for his trap. "What about tomorrow?"

"I think you and I should discuss our strategy, what we will say in our last speech," Kaylen explained.

"And why would I want to discuss that with you?"

"I don't fear *you*," Kaylen leaned against his backrest, "not at all. What I'm preparing for is what the Rays could do."

Malek laughed, "If you aren't selected."

"If I am not selected, it is because they see me as a threat!" Kalen hissed. "I have no doubt about my skills, but the reality is, this is beyond our control," he continued.

"I can't work with you," Malek's brow furrowed. "No one can."

"Don't misunderstand me. I would never work with either of you. I would do everything in my power and beyond to see that you, brother, are not chosen, but having them choose Vamya and threaten the entirety of our culture is something I would not tolerate."

"I agree," Malek took a seat.

"Good, then. Tell me now," Kaylen asked, "what is the essence of your speech?"

Eyeing his brother suspiciously, Malek responded, "I will keep that to myself."

"Your choice, then," Kaylen ate yet another grape. "Know that Vamya speaks better than you, and while my speech might be more eloquent, she seems to move those who listen. She also had quite the performance in the Seventh Test."

At first quiet, Malek realized Kaylen was not wrong. Even when his younger brother had performed poorly on the last test, Malek had not been able to remain standing. This was his one chance to potentially gain an advantage. "People of the Sun," his lips pronounced, "for most of a year, you have been yearning for stability, for respite from conflict, for a Sun that would bring unity."

"You *memorized* it," Kaylen sneered mockingly. "How long it must've taken you to rehearse and learn the words?"

Irritated, his eyes on his brother, Malek didn't respond.

"Aside from that, it sounds so *unreal,* so *not you,*" Kaylen explained. "Do you think for a moment the Rays won't smell the obvious charade from a league away? Power is important to them. The influence they hold over the population . . . there are even some among the Rays moving, chipping at our influence upon any opportunity they get."

Malek said nothing else. He listened carefully to each of Kaylen's words.

"The more natural your speech," Kaylen advised, "regardless of how beautiful it might sound, the more they will think they know you."

Seeing the firstborn nod, Kaylen opened the jug. "Wine?"

"No," Malek frowned.

"No?" Kaylen poured both cups.

Sliding the cup toward his brother, Malek responded, "You know little of me. I don't drink much."

"You know nothing of everything," Kaylen derided. "This," he showed the bottle, "is the wine reserved for our father. But since the Sun is not here, we may as well partake of it."

"This will not make us, in any way, allies." Malek took the cup in his hand.

"An alliance?" Kaylen grinned mockingly. "Only one of us would benefit from an alliance between us, and that's not me. Let us at least toast for having worked together, at least this one time."

The firstborn examined the cup, bringing it close to his pierced nose to sniff the ruby substance. Upon seeing Kaylen taking a large sip first, he did the same.

The wine was sweet, with cinnamon-like spices, and laced with a bitter aftertaste and a slight burn that disappeared in a single breath.

"And you," Malek followed, "don't think I forgot I haven't heard your message." It was not until the moment he saw Kaylen spit the wine back on the cup that he realized what had just happened. Kaylen smiled, using a napkin to wipe the inside of his mouth.

"Oh, but you *have* gotten my message." Kaylen's eyes glinted.

Malek stood up, his legs shaking as if an animal herd had trampled them. He needed help as soon as possible, but it was hard to coordinate his movements when even his vision was becoming blurred.

Smiling, walking slowly toward his brother, Kaylen unsheathed a *jambiya* and stepped closer.

Fire.

Malek groaned, trying to make sense of what was happening to him, feeling the drug poisoning his veins. He could not just be gutted like a pig; he *would not* be.

He closed his eyes, summoning every ounce of strength he had left, letting all the fire and fury burn his innards.

Kaylen saw his muscles tensing. He drove the knife into Malek's side, where it was still stuck when Malek, in a frenzied moment of fury, grabbed Kaylen by the neck. He pushed the Searing Sun, slamming his back against the wall behind, and lifted him with one hand. Malek's mouth foamed like that of a beast.

His free hand slid Kaylen's skirt to grab his cock, and while Kaylen shouted for help, Malek bit both of Kaylen's testicles off, Kaylen's agonizing screams filling the air.

He then released him, dropping Kaylen to the ground like a used puppet, before Malek turned against him, his eyes filled with crazed fury.

And there, as Kaylen struggled to contain the bleeding, right before his eyes, Malek grinned maliciously so that Kaylen could see his testicles inside his brother's mouth before he swallowed them.

"How can you be the Sun," Malek shouted. "How can you be the Sun now when I have eaten all your progeny!"

As the physicians entered, Malek left the room, laughing all the way back to his chambers.

ASCENDANCE

Location: Empyre of Suhne, City of Suhne, Palace of the Sun

Often the worst decision one can make is to not make a decision at all . . .

The hour of the Zenith approached, each second feeling to Vamya as slow as a desert tortoise, as the steps of the Rays who now walked toward the platform, perhaps hoping that in their lassitude, they could hold on to whatever vestiges of the little power they would soon lose.

They found their places on each side of the Speaker, who stood between the main sacrificial altar and the staircase leading to the expectant multitude below that was kept at bay by four rows of Flame Guards. Exis placed the urn of ashes over the altar, the scraping clay surface the only sound before the clamor of the people.

Standing behind a tall column, Vamya contemplated Kaylen. His abdomen and pelvis were bandaged, covered in heavy robes, and holding on to a pair of canes that were not enough to help him stand erect. She wondered if what Adulla said had transpired was true, but her mind had to stay focused on the now.

Kaylen's face seemed pale as if he had not slept. He seemed tired, but while he winced, his expression was still cold. He stood not too far away but felt as distant as always.

Malek, beyond him, seemed complacent, wearing an open robe that did little to hide his chiseled body, nothing she, who wore scanty clothing, could, or would dare, criticize. Vamya's breasts almost showed behind the thin, green fabric that covered little of her body, showing the green tattoos she was proud of. From her shoulders, a pair of peacock feathers hung, its beautiful blues accentuating the golden scarabs and leaves that adorned her picked-up hair. It had taken her five hours to get dressed, but that felt like nothing right now when Exis began his speech.

"People of the Sun," Exis raised his hands to the clamor of the citizenry. "'And after seven challenges,' the Scriptures of the Sun say, 'the new Sun will be revealed, and every eye will witness the Ascendancy of the Almighty.'

"As the Eye reaches the Zenith," he continued, "the Heirs of the Sun will address the Sun's people one last time before one ascends, and the impostors are sterilized so that they cannot bear progeny that will challenge the Sun again."

"Malek, Son of the Sun!" Exis announced, taking a step aside, his eyes on Kaylen's weak figure.

"People of the Sun," Malek boomed, "for too long has the Empyre remained stagnant. For too long, we have waited and reacted. It is time for the Sun to rise again and bring glory like the Empyre has never seen."

"Only a man can do that, not a woman," he pointed a dismissive hand at Vamya. "Nor a weak, non-man, who would destroy the line of the Sun. He, who will not need to be sterilized because he CAN'T HAVE PROGENY!"

Following their gasps, Malek raised his hands to the deafening praises of the witnesses. He walked past Vamya, who looked into the eyes that looked back at her in a way she had never seen him do before.

"Vamya, Child of the Sun," Exis hesitated.

The time has come.

Vamya ensured every piece of her attire was in place, her eyes of emeralds set on the people she would see for the last time . . . as a Child of the Sun.

Soon she would see them with different yet still compassionate eyes once she became their deity.

"My people," the Sun of Change spread her arms open as if seeking to hold them all in an embrace, "for close to fifteen centuries, the rigid tenets of our people have been both a great boon and a persistent yoke over your shoulders, one I have no doubt you have had the strength to carry, but one where you have had no say and have been given no choice.

"We have been taught what to believe, see, and feel. We have come to accept the belief that women among us have less value, that they exist only as the support of men, but this is not the case. Women are not less than men. They are not weaker, not less important. We are the same, made from the same flesh, bone, and blood.

"Change is necessary. If we are going to rise, we will need to grow and change, and while change is seen as difficult, it is not impossible, for I will guide you. In your growing pains, I will hold you. In your moment of need, I will provide for you.

"As we step into the future, I will create a society where women will share man's burden, where they will prosper the same way, have the same rights, where families will not be the nests and learning centers of oppressors, but rather of the most prosperous people, the people of the Sun."

The wind blew on her face, a joyful amalgam of the late fall breeze and the heartfelt shouts of the populace that praised her. In her satisfaction, in that moment where she felt she had been lifted a few feet up, Vamya hadn't noticed she had lifted her hands toward the heavens.

"People of the Sun," the Speaker raised his voice, "as per the scriptures, each of the Rays will now take one of the stone tokens from the altar and cast his vote on the floor."

Upon his signal, elder Zurek was the first one to cast his token, which Exis announced out loud, "Malek, the Conquering Sun."

"Malek, the Conquering Sun . . . Malek . . . the Conquering Sun . . ." Vamya closed her eyes. The clamminess of her palms reminded her of the fear she had as a mortal, but her mind was elsewhere, knowing the repetition of her oldest brother's name was nothing but the echo fed by the fear creeping inside her.

"Vamya, Sun of Change." Vamya opened her eyes in disbelief once the votes had been cast, her fingers shaking.

Her emerald irises counted the tokens one by one when Exis's voice announced, "Our Ascended Sun, All praise the Almighty Sun of Suhne . . . Malek, the Conquering Sun!"

While the Rays bowed to her brother, extending their hands toward him, almost in unison, the countless thousands below fell on their knees, shouting chants, singing praises, crying, and embracing one another in celebration. Even those who had wished the results had been different had joined in, all except for Kaylen, who, perhaps because of his broken state, only glared but didn't move, and Vamya, who stood up frozen, unable to comprehend what had just happened.

Malek's muscles tensed with every step he took, pacing along the platform, impatiently waiting for the Rays, who poured sacred water into the ash urn before pouring the mixture into the chalice he would drink from.

Upon the Speaker's command, the captain of the Flame Guards ordered his men to take Vamya away.

"No!" Malek shouted furiously, dashing toward the altar and kicking away the golden urn that was now empty. "I want it done here, right now!" He slammed his hand against the top of the altar.

Aaju of the Flame Guards hesitated, but his superior did not. His men grabbed Vamya's arms and, dragging her against her will, they laid her forcefully over the altar.

"No! Please, Malek!" she screamed, seeing the physicians bring the tongs and instruments of their trade, "have mercy!"

Vamya looked up to the heavens upon the Eye above that would witness what everyone else would spectate. The fiery orb stood still, perhaps horrified in disbelief or indifferent to her plea.

"Please, Please!" She kicked but was held fast by soldiers and acolytes to either side as her legs were separated, her vagina incised. She felt the cold metal's touch inside her, grasping her womb before it twisted and pulled savagely.

While Malek consumed the ashes, his body shook, his muscles tensed. His eyes filled with an uncontainable, convulsive fury. His neck swelled, his voice echoed, his victorious shout bellowing as his insides burned, while Vamya felt her life ebb away as she drifted into the world of the unconscious, only to be brought back by another twist and tug, into this land of intense pain, filled with the celebratory shouts of all those who cursed her.

She woke up one more time, upon feeling the earth almost shake under the clamor, the moment the physician's tongs finally pulled out her mangled, red-stained uterus, which Malek grabbed and squeezed in his hands before smashing it against the floor ... before brusquely shoving Vamya's feeble figure off the altar surface where he stood, raising his victorious hands for all to see.

Completely ignored, with what little strength she had, Vamya dragged her body along the floor. Delirious, she searched for the bloodied, destroyed uterus, which was nothing but out of reach.

She had failed, as her eyes now failed her, as her vision blurred, in this celebratory ceremony that to her had been barbaric.

Never would she have imagined that her worst nightmare had always been her brother's dream.

Vamya's eyes opened to find herself late one day lying in bed under the glass dome that was her room.

Her head felt tight, her sweaty, disheveled hair still mostly within the confines of the golden scarabs headpiece she had worn during the ceremony.

How long has it been? She asked herself, looking around at the room that was, unlike every other time before, not busy with preparations.

She was alone, except for the young girl dressed in white with gold trim who sat close by, the one who smiled and said, "You're awake!" before she ran out the door.

Everywhere in the room, the emerald-green curtains and fabrics had disappeared.

Moments later, Vamya tried to prop herself on the bed, but her arms felt too weak.

"You need to be more careful," the healer among the Rays walked into the room with the girl who had left moments before. "You lost a lot of blood, and you haven't eaten.

"It's been two days. I'm sure you're wondering," Or'guud informed her. "You have drifted in and out of consciousness a few times, but this is the first time you're able to keep your eyes open.

"Now, let me change the dressing," the elder mixed some salves and oint-ments with oils that were both pungent and fragrant.

"I . . ." Vamya said weakly, "I don't know what went wrong. I thought I had it."

"Yes, but you didn't," Orguud looked back at her. He smiled faintly before he explained. "You didn't stand a chance. You had no real support. Of all the possible votes, you got only one, and that was mine. I voted last, so my vote wouldn't have made a difference. I gave it to you out of pity."

"Then why put me through all this?" she argued.

"You put yourself through all that. The scriptures state clearly that the Almighty Sun has always been male." He washed his hands before leaving. "You are nothing more than a rose in the desert."

Or'guud left her alone for a while, long moments where Vamya crawled along the bed toward the glass wall to look outside.

Everywhere her eyes went, banners of the golden Sun had been erected, and celebrations were still being held while people were still being abused and oppressed.

It was at that moment when she saw her own reflection in the glass, her translucent, pale face that was almost ghostlike, the faint reflection of the golden scarabs over her head shining brightly as stars drawing her attention.

'The scarabs,' she realized, seeing their golden adornments she had placed over her own head. 'The message was always there. I just didn't see it.'

The image disappeared behind the last glint of sunlight that reflected off the scarabs.

Vamya dragged herself into her pool, unable to meditate from the deep pain, staining the water that came in contact with her dressings.

She spread her arms wide under the night sky, where she remained . . . floating in a pool of blood.

THE GHOST

Location: Kingdom of Blackheart,
Duchy of Darkholm, Darkholde Keep

More than golden, silence is a beautiful, powerful diamond . . .

For centuries, the cliffs of Darkholde held the giant body of the stronghold high above the earth, offering the ancient marvel before the pale, quiet moon.

Kaeris, this night, showed the fullness of her face, and it was her subtle presence that shone down to reveal the lone figure walking along the coast, far below the cliffs.

The waves that normally hungered for the rocks this time were calm as if the sea sought to stop itself from ruining the lone woman's musings. But the carefree wind blew in every direction, attempting to steal the veil that covered her face and cast away the flowers she carried.

Beneath that veil of darkness, Raja Darkholm, wife of the king, was silent.

She walked slowly, as she had done the entirety of her life, as she had walked with Erdrick in her arms to present him to the world, as she had walked along the garden, cutting crimsons to place inside the basket where she had carried Rowena's infant body; they were the same, slow steps she had taken the day she married Septem without wanting it.

But who, if anyone, ever gets what they truly want, she asked herself.

She had given her hand. She had done it. Upon the death of Septem's first wife, it had been her duty to take that mantle. And if there was one thing Raja had, it was an undeniable commitment to her duties, the same that was expected of those who shared her Blood.

Her bare feet touched the sand that was, in the words of some, almost as cold as her heart.

Did they say that because she rarely offered words of comfort during difficult times? Was it because they never saw the tears she shed in private? Or was it because she never spoke about her feelings, but how could she when she barely spoke at all?

But her silence did not make her cold.

Even before the death of her own mother, Raja had been that same way. It was, thus, fitting she had earned the eponym "the ghost," for she was nothing but a veiled presence who was at times seen but rarely heard.

How much was known about her? How much of what anyone could say about her was real when she had not been able to live?

Raja Darkholm

How much of one is true when our own words are left unspoken?

What option does one have when the only thing in abundance in one's life is deprivation?

What did anyone know about her wishes, her desires?

What did anyone know about what she wanted?

Her fingers lightly touched the crimsons in her hands, playfully caressing the petals, the thorns.

Even after so long, she was largely unknown. *Something that can play to my advantage.*

Early in the evening, she had seen, as she always did, the return of her husband, but this time had been different. All his adult life, Septem has been a powerful lord, an invincible warrior, the anchor the kingdom had needed.

But that anchor was now being cut off, and until the right one was found, everything would go adrift.

What would happen to the crown, Raja thought, when Blackheart had no queen? When Septem had decided only one person should be the focus of their attention so that, unlike mortal children, they wouldn't ask one parent for something the other one had denied?

What would be the tradition when their dynasty of nearly seventy years had just one king?

Would they follow the traditions of Eileos, passing it to the oldest heir?

Would they do as Ardenay, passing it to the firstborn son?

Would the children challenge each other for the throne, like the Suhnites?

Or would they do as Daneran, and the crown would be rightfully hers? Even if it did, would they follow her? Would her people heed her words?

How could they, when I am only the wife, when they barely know my name?

But that changed nothing when the stars had seen a world burning, the walls breached, endless hunger and greed, all under Rowena, who had been not just a daughter but the *thirdborn.*

It mattered not if others would understand the steps she had to take, whether they agreed or not. Every Darkholm, even the quiet ones, had a role assigned, a part to play. She was no exception.

The toughest moment in a Darkholm's life came when fate tested them, when each had to answer with action the question, 'Will you do what must be done?'

She looked back upon Darkholde Keep, the monumental castle that was, to some, a looming nightmare; to her, the prison she called home.

The world wouldn't see her sacrifice. They would not see the mother she had been. They would only see the sister she was, the rightful heir.

Chaos needed to be stopped, the uncertainty aborted, and perhaps the only way to avoid it was if someone dutifully did what had to be done.

With her eyes on the immense darkness of the keep, she whispered, "Prosperity can only come if every obstacle is removed."

Lucris, the morning sun, broke the sky, shining down upon the cliff's wrinkles and angry waves along that beach, where the only thing that was found was a handful of crimsons and a dark, fine gown with a black lace veil.

THE WHITE END

Location: Kingdom of Blackheart, Royal Duchy of
Darkholm, County of Coldforge, Ironholde

Nothing truly ends. Everything just changes . . .
Every end is also a beginning . . .

He gazed at the horizon, at the multitude below, and at each man and each woman of the Blood, their inner flame a sharp contrast to the cold marble of his face.

Septem Darkholm, the White, the First King, the Father of Blackheart, stood at the Tower's balcony, his gauntleted fist raised as his voice, deep as rumbling thunder, addressed his subjects.

Between the layers of clothes as white as the purest salt from the sea, he wore his ceramic plate, the ornamental armor that depicted each duchy sworn to the Crown. Except for where its hardness had been violated, close to his heart, its polished surface almost reflected the light of the morning sun, giving a nearly divine image to the unemotional man who had united the hearts of his people.

"Blood of Blackheart, Blood of Caelris," his voice boomed, "our enemies grow in strength and numbers, but we will stand firm, together, and we will know no fear. This world will break before us, for the tenacity of our Blood is unbreakable, and no matter what the odds, we will not falter. We will never fail." Each syllable he stressed was carried by the wind and into the ears and hearts of the citizens who had come from all over, concerned about the health of their king.

Behind his majestic presence, Rowena, the Master of Life, approached.

Her silent gaze met the black stone floor she walked on, trailing the drops of crimson blood that dried on its surface as if seeking to hide from her aurelian eyes.

That same trail grew and thickened, finding moisture and freshness as it licked the hem of King Septem's silk cape. It crawled up and onto his flank, emanating from where he had been betrayed, its origin ebbing with each pulse, sprouting rapidly but in silence as if showing respect for the words of the sovereign.

"One day," he spoke again, "or perhaps one night . . . I will not be among you, but our dream will not end. Our world will not end with me, for I am but one of you. Our world will kneel before the might of our Blood, for not us, but the world will know defeat before the invincible Blood of Blackheart!"

The crowd below roared, their banners dancing in the wind in celebration. Despite the costly battle, Suhne's intervention allowed them to survive.

The Crowned King looked down at the Blood, his serious demeanor unchanging, unflinching. These were the people he had for so long fought for, the ones he had fed. These were just a portion of those scattered over the land, all those he had kept in mind with his every decision, despite his own wants, despite other advice, despite the betrayal of those few who, despite nearly seventy years since he had taken the throne to save them from ruin, would never accept the Darkholm king as their rightful ruler.

He had given them most of his life. And yet, to a few, only his own literal life was required when nothing else he had given, to them, had been enough.

His white cape flew as he turned to return to the tower hall.

But after only two steps, he faltered, a river of blood sprouting from his left flank.

He was immediately assisted by Rowena and the Black Knights, who had never left the side of their Lord, their Patriarch, their King.

⊹⊹✦✦✦⊹⊹

Rowena placed an ointment over the wound she calmly sutured. As the king's personal physician, the Master of Life understood quite well the gravity of his condition. She didn't break down. She was a Darkholm, and even if she had shed a single tear, many outside their circle would have judged it as untrue.

As she had always done, even if with reluctance, she simply accepted the reality she faced.

Her father had been the pinnacle of strength, the chain that joined the kingdom. Despite his grave wounds, the fever, and the sweat, Septem's expression remained unchanged, a statue any stone would seek refuge in. His eyes met those of his children as Rowena closed his wound, and Erdrick knelt.

"My son . . .," King Septem said, "the traditions of men would pass the crown to you after my passing."

"We are not men, My King," Erdrick looked up as he spoke, the knight in him showing deference to his master. "We are Darkholm, and we do what must be done."

Taking a deep breath, Septem looked around before saying, "This weight, then . . . will fall . . . on one of you."

For a moment, silence was the only response he received. Was it a sign of fear, respect, or perhaps hesitation?

"I would proudly accept the responsibility, Your Majesty." Erdrick stood up. "Of Raja's children, I am the eldest, and as much as I have been able, I have learned what is needed to become a great leader.

"To lead, one must be able to show detachment, one must be true, one must always be ready to fight for one's beliefs, even if alone. I know without a doubt I can take that burden justly, but I also know that my youngest sister would make a better leader than I could ever be."

His golden eyes looked down upon Rowena, "I wish to be the king, but more than that, I want to follow her."

Erdrick's eyes and those of Septem's met in the same cold yet understanding gaze that characterized both father and son. Time seemed to come to a halt in Erdrick's poise and Septem's breath while Rowena's fingers continued moving, trembling perhaps at the fight she was losing against the river of red or perhaps at the realization of her brother's words.

She lowered her own gaze to look at the wound she cared for as Erdrick's knee kissed the floor before her presence. "My sister, My Queen."

Lord Septem was unchanging, unflinching, yet with his last breath, he rested his cold eyes upon the visage of his daughter, Rowena, and as his pupils dilated for the last time, for the first, he smiled.

THE DEATH OF LIFE

Location: Kingdom of Blackheart, Duchy of Darkholm,
County of Coldforge, Ironholde

*What kind of games do Fate and Destiny play when
they flip one's world in the blink of an eye . . .*

T he Blood waited.

The news of Septem's condition had spread quite quickly, and the multitude stood anxious, like children awaiting news of their beloved parent's medical intervention.

Ironholde's main plaza was filled to the brim, with those waiting for the main doors to open and give way to the Crowned King of Blackheart.

The crowd, however, would not place a foot on the main staircase. Its bottom was lined with Black Knights, each one standing as firm as the present.

Behind them, the wine color of House Sanglune, the light green of House Devereau, and the slate of House Grey were represented by the members of the respective vassal houses.

Closer to the top, lining the staircase, the members of the Royal House Darkholm faced the double doors expectantly, Serverus Ecru among them.

Even the vultures rested, perched over the parapets and walls of the building as if they had been part of the family.

The silence broke with the opening of the heavy main doors, the echoes etching a memory in every witness present.

As if they had been an integral part of the ceremony, the birds took flight to circle the keep.

Ironholde's bowels gave birth to the first, at whose emergence the multitude initially hesitated. Many had been expecting to see white, but instead saw the black armor on his body. After the initial pause, his mere sight brought excitement to the Blood, who cheered loudly in celebration of the heir.

Erdrick walked forth, firm and erect as only the most honorable knight could. Upon seeing his head and missing the crown on it, a sense of shock sent a chill down everyone's spine.

He took a step aside to give way to his sister, Rowena.

The Master of Life's veil covered all but her face. In her hands, she carried her father's crown.

Time stood still. Confusion truly reigned, for none of the siblings held the crown of Blackheart over the head.

Rowena walked to her brother's side and turned around to face him.

The golden suns in her eyes met her sibling's. Moments flew in the blink of an eye, but still, in her heart, they felt like eons.

Both stood barely three feet from one another, the children of the First King, the rightful son and the Master of Life.

Rowena's hands presented the crown to her brother, and without any honorifics, she whispered, "Erdrick, brother . . ."

His perfect features moved to answer her, in turn, "Rowena, sister . . ."

Her voice was soft but just as close to breaking. "Please . . . you know I do not want it."

The knight's hands held his sister's as he took the crown from her almost frozen hands. "And you know that I do, and that is why you must be the one who bears this weight."

With those words, he lifted the crown and placed it over Rowena's head.

The crowd roared, so deafening was their cheering that it could have cracked the stone slabs they stood on.

For once, Blackheart would have a queen on its throne. It was a new era, a time those of the Blood would celebrate in every corner of the world.

While the citizenry chanted and hugged one another in endless celebration, Rowena walked toward the edge of the staircase. She could barely see behind the falling tears.

Feeling an impossible weight over her shoulders, she lifted her wavering arms, remembering her father's words the first time he dressed in white, 'This is what the world needs to see.'

The vassal houses knelt in deference; the knights stood in silence. The Darkholm men lowered their heads in reverence as all the women wept, for one thing the members of the House knew quite well, that they had lost yet another one of them to the throne.

Every dream that she had, every longing, every desire, passed right in front of her eyes to disintegrate, to vanish, to perhaps mock her before showing how out of reach they would forever be.

She wished she could run away and see the world like Ashildr, study what she had wanted, like Isolde, dance untroubled and carefree like Charon, or even disappear like Raja. Instead, she had been shackled to the throne, bound by the heart, to represent those who were free, all those who had the life she always wanted but that she would never live.

She looked at them, at the joyful celebration, at those who mourned, at those who showed respect, and even those who showed revulsion, all while her only thoughts were those she would have never thought of as Master of Life. 'How much blood will I have to shed for my people?'

And so, while the world celebrated her life, Rowena Darkholm was dying inside.

BLACK HEART

Rowena Darkholm stood in front of the throne of Blackheart,
the heaviness of the white crown resting on her head.

S he examined every single inch of the seat. It was sculpted from black stone, one that seemed to stay cold regardless of the flames lighting the room.

Carvings of vultures, ravens, spirits, and other, unknown creatures adorned its uneven, uncomfortable backrest, and many more horrific creatures were carved into the back of the seat that others would never get to see.

The bone-shaped legs ended in rats that appeared to bite the feet of the monarch.

Septem Darkholm, the White King, had designed the throne himself for future generations, understanding the mortal coils that bound him. The throne told the story of how, unbeknownst to the world, the Darkholm would lock their children in a cellar, tied up to stone chairs, rats gnawing at their feet, to remind them that the throne was a coveted spot that placed the ruler in an uncomfortable position where, no matter the steps taken, the sacrifices made, others would seek to do harm.

This was the dreadful seat she had studied and knew so well, the one that now was *hers*.

While many around the kingdom had publicly mourned the loss of her father, the Darkholm had not. As per the Traditions, his embalmed remains now rested in the Darkholm catacombs, while Septem's recorded deeds lay written in the book of his life on the alcove above his tomb.

She sat, like *Sanguinus* resting in its red scabbard by her side, for the first time.

"Your Highness," the herald entered the room, "the people await your first message."

There was no time to rest.

The purple curtains of the Tower parted to allow Vhimir Darkholm, the queen's herald, to announce, "Her Majesty, Queen Rowena Darkholm, Queen of Blackheart, Duchess of Darkholm, Countess of Coldforge, Baroness of Ironheart!"

Together with his men, Vhimir blew the bellowing horns of Darkholm.

Rowena saw the curtains part before her, leading to the balcony where many times, she had seen her father address the people.

She looked down upon the stairsteps where most of her House was present, except for those whose obligations kept them away, those whose lives had ceased, and Gustavus, who, since the moment of her ascension, was nowhere to be seen.

"Blood of Blackheart, Blood of Caelris, we all stand today, some who call this place home, others who have journeyed from far away, from every duchy of our vast kingdom, to hear words of hope, words spoken to ascertain that everything will be alright, but that is not something a crown should convince you of. Those are not falsehoods you will hear.

"Instead, there is a reality we must face today.

"Time and again, this world has shown itself to be an unfriendly place, full of those who ask others to open themselves, only to be exposed to the claw at the end of their cruel, preconceived judgment so that the few can hold on to the scraps of what they wrongly believe is power.

"But power like no other, the power of many, they will behold.

"Today, I will offer you not words of comfort but a promise. Our people will not sit idly anymore, waiting to be trampled on.

"The time to accept and receive punishment is passed. The time to turn the cheek to be whipped and spat upon is no more.

"Together, we will ascend from the depths where others have given up.

"Until our last breath, we will fight for the safety of our people. And despite the losses we will inevitably suffer, we will rise again, and we will never know defeat.

"We will not make any effort to convince our enemies who we are, for we owe them nothing.

"May they learn today that we understand the cruel game they play in the name of the Light, and so we will snuff every one of their candles, and we will bring an era of Darkness that will never end, much like their own suffering. For the greatest nightmare they can imagine is a world where we are all equal.

"Despite any efforts of the past, they have decided to remain our enemies because somehow, they need a foe to point the finger at, and so they have chosen to point it at those who represent what they hide, what they hate about themselves.

"And hate is something we should never feel for one another, that should not be bred within our borders, and will not be tolerated.

"We are all different in so many ways, in our beliefs, our cultures, and practices, and no matter how hard we try, our differences are something we will never truly be able to erase.

"But our differences we can ignore, we can accept, as long as we hold each other's hands and look into each other's eyes and say to one another 'we are Blood.'

"Now seek inside yourselves, and see the flame that brought you here, that desire of your heart to be accepted, to be loved, to belong to something.

"Know that there are others, beyond our borders, like us, whose broken lives beg for mercy and are just rewarded with scorn. To all those, I say, 'As you are, you are welcome in my land. When you feel you do not belong, you belong . . . to me.'

"Nothing is stronger than the Blood.

"It will flow like a river to all corners of the world.

"Many will rise against us, and many more will fall.

"For they will try to break our world, but they will never . . . break . . . our hearts.

"Now go, embrace who you are, embrace one another, and spread the word.

"We will bring an age of Darkness.

"We will fill this world with Blood.

"*In Tenebris nos Prosperabitur.*"

ARDENAY

Calmness . . .

O ther than the sound of the end of his stand on the floor as he returned to the cathedral, he heard nothing, not even the seven young boys walking behind him, waiting for the Archbishop of the Light to request anything from them.

He smiled. Not a smile of peace and comfort, or one of compassion and understanding, but rather a smile of contentment, of the satisfaction he hid under a face of worry the moment he had heard the news of what had transpired at the Horne.

Aorius had returned, the proud lion he had poked came back with his tail between his legs, but that wouldn't last long, Angevin knew. But winter would soon arrive, and with it, the cold that would keep Ardenay's forces from gathering effectively. That would leave them to deal with the lion's fury, as his wounded pride would lash out at anyone and everyone around him.

'Book of Moneos, Chapter one, verse five—Pride belongs only to god. Woe to those who, in their lack of vision, seek to act like god. They will be stricken down and made to fail.'

"Even if the Light needs our intervention to ensure their failure," Angevin smiled, seeing the dazzling light of the sun scattered along the tiled floor of the church, imagining the royal forces scattered the same way after the forces of Suhne had stepped in.

As excellent as their scouts surely were, they were no match for the Bulwharf outriders' skills and knowledge of the land. Angevin wondered if, even if the desert people had seen them within their borders, would they have shown the same aggression when their sole focus was on selecting their new pagan god?

"Blessed be the Light," he told his own reflection in the church's fountain, "that they were warned."

The move couldn't have been more perfect, the priest thought. The retreat had rekindled the animosity among Ardenay's generals, who blamed one another for their defeat, while their own king's morale was shaken, overcome by his broken pride. And Blackheart, what better blow to their morale than their division, than the betrayal and wounding of their dark king?

"You may leave." The priest entered his chambers and instructed the altar boys, "I will see you tomorrow morning before worship." And he locked the door behind him.

D'Agath'a

Taking his time, Angevin took off his heavy, ceremonial robes and walked toward his office, wondering what his next letter would say. Now both Suhne and Blackheart had grabbed entire regions of the Horne, lands Ardenay could not do much about in winter, but would nonetheless want returned, once it came back stronger, under the banner of the Light. He smiled again, but the smile disappeared the moment he saw *her*.

D'Agath'a, the Holy Mother of the Church, stood right in the middle of his office. She was beautiful, garbed in white robes that were as fine as they were revealing. Over her bald head, a crystal headpiece waved back on each side, from where the same type of crystals that adorned her robe dangled. Her fair skin and slanted green eyes gave her the appearance of a woman not a day over forty, even though she had held her position since long before Angevin had been born. But like everyone who was ever in her presence, the moment they started wondering about her, they would just as soon forget.

"Holy Mother!" Angevin gasped.

"Angevin." Her almost unearthly, soft voice enthralled him.

"I am sorry, Holy Mother," he said, "I didn't expect to find you here." While D'Agath'a spent the vast majority of time around the cathedral, not once had she visited his chambers.

Fortunately, Angevin was careful enough never to leave a single trace of any letter he sent or received.

"What brings you here, Holy Mother?" he asked upon hearing no comment from her, whose eyes were intently on him.

"Your actions . . ." D'Agath'a's melodious voice nearly whispered before a knock on the door was heard.

Upon unlocking it, a messenger walked into the room. "Holy Father, Holy Mother," he bowed deeply. "I have an important message for you, Holy Father."

Angevin stepped away, waving his hand to dismiss the messenger after giving his benediction.

The archbishop consumed every letter, every phrase, even that which he would not reveal before he threw the message in the fireplace and looked up to the heavens. "Blessed be the Light."

"The dark king is dead," he then informed through raised eyebrows.

"Your actions have shaken the foundations of the earth. You have awoken that which will never again know slumber, that which will never rest, a nightmare unlike any the world has ever witnessed."

"Holy Mother," Angevin replied, "I assure you, this is a blessing. These will be great times."

"Famine, death, plagues, vengeance, war, and chaos will follow. An endless, indescribable amount of suffering is coming, birthed by your own actions."

"My every action has always been for the glory of the Light!"

"Oh Angevin . . ." her lips almost whispered, "what have you done?"

EALAS

Nothing . . .

That was exactly what, for a while now, Ealas eyes had seen, just nothing. He waved his hand in front of his eyes, wondering how he would ever be able to tell if he was losing his eyesight, for the pitch blackness in which he resided was only occasionally broken by a jailer's lantern, and that was only to bring his food.

Even relieving himself, Ealas had to do within this deep, moist, cold cell located somewhere within Darkholde Keep.

He had requested a fair trial and an audience, but apparently, it had fallen on deaf ears, for it had been quite some time since his request, and no news had come. How much time exactly was hard for him to tell because, at first, Ealas thought he would count his meals to know, according to breakfast, lunch, and dinner, how many days it had been.

But his count had been thrown off the moment he realized almost all meals were the same—old bread, water, and either a wilted vegetable or a piece of dried meat.

Aside from that, sometimes, he was overcome with such a ravenous hunger that he wasn't sure if it was purely out of malnourishment or because he was not being fed every day.

His cell was small, he had seen. Together with the adjacent cell that was separated from his only by bars, the cells took about half of the room. The rest was just a small hallway and winding stairs that led to a metal door.

The bars on his cell were solid, and the metal felt colder as time progressed. Ealas prayed it meant the summer was advanced. But then he also wanted to curse himself for not being able to get out of that damned place.

The floor had a straw mat on one side. At times he felt something scurrying within it, which he chose to ignore because, whatever it was, there was not much he could do other than kill it with his own hands.

It was not like he could use his boots anyway. They, like all his belongings, had been taken away from him.

He was otherwise naked, except for the ill-fitting sack that covered his body.

Sack . . . a vision of Astas came to his mind. *A sack was the only thing she had ever worn for as long as he knew her.*

He was roused by the creaking echo of that solid door that sang its rare, metallic melody.

I wonder what's for lunch? he jested.

A brief flash of light caught Ealas's attention, but, just as a single lightning strike, it was gone in less than the blink of an eye.

He was starving, hungry for even a glimmer of hope. As impossibly feeble as he was, he whispered a prayer, "Lord of Light, Oh Radiant One, remove the Darkness before me," his hand traveled down his face, "Your word says you are powerful and jealous, but also merciful and loving. I have not been perfect, but I have always been faithful. I recognize I am but an unworthy man, and I shouldn't ask for boons and gifts from you, but I need your holy miracle. I have begged you, but this time I *need* you to help me, for I am losing my mind here. Show me a sign. Show me anything that would restore my dwindling faith in mankind."

And then he heard a sudden click that was followed by the sudden birth of a small flame on the floor outside his cell. The flame lit a torch that was lifted three feet from the ground, revealing the presence of a child no more than eight years old with a white shirt and a dark vest wrapped over it, a child whose expression spoke of the profound sadness he had experienced in his short time in the world of men, sadness that somehow understood the burden the prisoner's heart carried.

"Hello," the boy greeted shyly.

Ealas wondered if what he saw was real or if he was truly going insane.

The small boy followed with a question, "Would you be my friend?"

"Boy, what can I say when I don't know you?" Ealas said in earnest. "I don't know what or who you represent. I don't even know the way you think."

After a brief pause, he added, "To be honest, I really don't know if I could ever be your friend."

After a brief pause, the child's broken words captured his heart, "That is fair . . ." but his blonde eyes captured his soul, "Would you at least be friendly to me?"

BROKEN

Vamya stood inside the throne room, her gaze upon the floor. She was garbed, much like Kaylen across from her, in exquisite, golden robes. In his mercy, the Almighty Sun had decided not to kill his siblings or exile them but rather to keep them around as advisers he would likely ignore but who would be subservient to him, decreed to suffer the same fate he suffered.

Were it not for his left eye, the large, almost nude, muscular figure sitting on the throne with the golden disk behind his head would have seemed perfect.

There was something strangely peaceful and simultaneously intimidating about his presence. For months he had, surprisingly, voiced many decrees with a firm voice but without the need for ire. He had even spared their Chosen, allowing them to serve his siblings in the performance of the duties he would choose to assign them.

Still, the nature of their relationship had changed. While Adulla still treated her with admiration, she had lost the freedom that she had sought and wished for and could now be, perhaps, informing someone of Vamya's moves and words. Vamya wondered if burning Adulla could have truly been the mercy Malek could have offered the woman.

Her thoughts were interrupted by Exis's entrance.

"Almighty Sun," the holy man bowed to the throned figure of the Sun of Conquest, "there is a message from beyond the border." He produced a metallic scroll case from under his sleeve.

"Who sent it?" Malek questioned.

"It came from Blackheart," Exis explained. "The messenger tells me it is from the hand of its ruler. If it is your wish, I can read it to you."

"Go ahead," Malek signaled Exis to approach.

As Exis removed the lid from the scroll case, a captivating fragrance filled the room. His hands broke the seal and unrolled the parchment, from which a single, dried rose fell toward the floor.

To: the Ascended Sun of Conquest, Almighty Sun of Suhne

My most heartfelt wishes are that you are in good health, that your people are safe, and that every portion of your land proves to be fruitful beyond measure.

Ever since news of your Ascendancy and your exploits have reached my distant ears, I have harbored no doubt that your leadership will bring an era of great prosperity to many.

I am writing to offer you and your people my most sincere appreciation.

Suhne's intervention in the Battle of the Bull's Horne allowed many of our people to escape with their lives, saving countless others. Had it not been for the brave march, the delicate balance of power in the region would have been tipped, blurring borders and, most importantly, erasing lives.

Each life we touch is a ripple in a still lake, reverberating toward infinite corners we often see not.

As we recover from our regretful losses, we cannot help but look upon the distance and praise your courage and be thankful.

I hope we can, one day, repay you in kind.

May we all work toward a better future for all,

Sincerely,

Rowena Darkholm, Queen of Blackheart, Duchess of Darkholm, Countess of Coldforge, Baroness of Ironheart

"A better future for all." Malek stood from the throne and took the letter from Exis's grasp. "Does she think I need any allies? I will raze and burn her kingdom and her with it." He sneered, burning the letter on the brazier before he and the others left the room.

Vamya remained behind, her eyes still on the floor, but this time fixed on the flower that, like her, remained. She took a step toward it and picked it up, her verdant eyes admiring the deep red of the rose's stiff petals.

Her nostrils captured the invisible, indivisible essence, the charming fragrance that transported her, that made her forget everything, even the thorns that pierced her skin.

Reflexively, she let the flower go. It fell flat on the floor, stained with drops of fresh blood that smeared the hard surface beneath it . . . that reminded Vamya of that day, of her loss, of her bloodied womb sprawled along the floor.

Her hands picked up the flower once again, carefully this time, and she studied it, and she felt a current wash over her body when she noticed that the rose was dried, all bent and misshapen, but still in one piece . . .

Milton Keynes UK
Ingram Content Group UK Ltd.
UKHW020610030823
426240UK00016B/205/J